THE WITHERED

AMY MILES

A PERMUTED PRESS BOOK

ISBN: 978-1-68261-108-1
ISBN (eBook): 978-1-68261-109-8

The Withered
Wither (Book One), Resurrect (Book Two), and Affliction (Book Three)
© 2016 by Amy Miles
All Rights Reserved

Permuted Press, LLC
permutedpress.com

Published in the United States of America

WITHER

BOOK ONE

ONE

The lights flicker overhead.

I stare up at them, listening to the intermittent hum of the dying fluorescent bulbs. The dim lighting provided by the backup generator casts an eerie glow on the room. Shadows multiply in the corners. My head twitches at every sound, sure that I hear someone creeping down the hall.

A chill has fallen on the room. The fever that arrived earlier this morning has left me flushed and weakened. I didn't tell the nurses. Part of me didn't want to bother them. Another feared that they might throw me out onto the streets like the rest of *them.*

Condensation from my breath hangs before my mouth and a slight tremor has begun in my lips. My fingers cramp as I tighten my grip on the pistol in my lap and try to ignore the aches in my legs.

The gun, though small and easily managed, feels foreign in my grasp. It's not mine. I took it off a man on the street early this morning. He had four rounds in his pocket and several lay scattered around his body in the gutter. A single hole in his right temple and the splatter of crimson on the brick behind told me that it wasn't stealing. Not really.

Halos of light dot the window before me, fires set long before the sun fell behind a blanket of heavy cloud. Intermittent gunfire to the east sounds muffled through the panes of glass. That is the direction I saw the men coming from.

Dark shapes converged on the frozen hospital lawn less than half an hour ago. Twenty of them in total. Some appeared slighter in stature. Others, large enough to wrestle with a grizzly. All seemed focused on the fortified front doors of the building.

It was only a matter of time before the survivors came for us.

Unease settles heavily in the pit of my stomach as I glance toward my mother lying in the bed beside me. No expression. No movement, apart from the slow rise of her chest. Her lips hold a tint of blue, but that is nothing unusual.

I draw my legs up into the chair, crossing them before me. *What are they waiting for?* They must have found a way inside by now.

The scraping of chairs and the rapid staccato of voices from down the hall faded away a few minutes ago. I watched from the door of my mother's room as those few remaining nurses and doctors emptied the waiting room in an attempt to barricade the doors. It won't last long, but maybe someone can get away.

I should have left the city when the turmoil first began. The news anchors tried to spin their pretty little lies about how the military had everything under control, but all you have to do is look out a window to know that things are falling apart faster than anyone could have predicted. Anarchy rules the streets.

Little more than a week ago, the world sank right into hell. I just stood by and watched it. What else could I do?

People started disappearing. Tanks and armored military trucks rumbled through the streets at all hours of the night. Quarantines were established and martial law was enforced for a time.

I could have escaped before the rioting really began, before the gangs formed and innocent blood painted the streets of St. Louis. It would have been easy to slip by unnoticed, clinging to the shadows. One person can hide well enough. But I didn't leave; I stayed...because of her.

I remember the last words my mother ever said to me: "I love you." But it didn't matter. Those words could never be enough to wipe away years of bitterness and resentment, to heal neglected wounds left to fester, to right a thousand wrongs. Too little. Too late.

A part of me will always wish that I could have said *I love you* back to her just that once and actually meant it. That my final words were not spoken with animosity. We never had that sort of relationship, though. Never hugged. Never flopped down on the couch just to chat. We were cohabitants in an empty home, and even then I hardly ever saw her. Not until the accident that left her devoid of speech, thought, or any other basic human activity.

I don't really know why I came each day to visit or even why I stayed. It's certainly not out of loyalty. Maybe some twisted part of me just wanted her to wake up so I could get some closure. Maybe I'm just that messed up. Or maybe I was scared. Scared of being truly alone for the first time in my life.

A loud crash from beyond the door wrenches me from my thoughts. My messy curls tumble from their ponytail as I whip around. Several more crashes follow in rapid succession, each one making me jump.

"We need to turn out the lights," a nurse says from down the hall.

"No." Another speaks up. Her words pinch with fear. "They already know we're here."

The sound of shoes pounding against the floor reaches me as someone hurries past my room. I hear the stairwell door burst open.

"Wait! What about the patients?" A lengthy pause, interspersed with loud bangs against the double glass doors that have sealed us in, makes my pulse race. I cling to my gun as I wait for the answer.

"It's too late for them."

I close my eyes and a single tear curls down my cheek. *I don't want to die. Not like this.*

A scream echoes down the darkened corridor as a rain of glass pings against the tile floor. My palms feel sweaty. I draw the gun into my chest and lift prayers heavenward, though I find myself unsure of how any god could allow such horrors to happen.

Pushing up from my chair, I cast a glance back at my prostrate mother and then slowly draw open the door to her private room. Through the narrow crack, I spy men scrambling to climb over a pile of chairs, tables, and couches stacked chest high at the far end of the hall. Their clothing is wrinkled and smeared with dirt. Their beards and hair, unkempt.

Blood slickens the floor as the men rise to their feet among the shards. The large glass doors behind them stand open with a gaping hole smashed through. A chained padlock swings uselessly near the floor.

I shudder as the men survey the hall. Dark circles shadow their eyes. Their gaze is wide, crazed. I know that look. The look of desperation.

My heart hammers against my ribs as two men break off from the pack and leap onto a middle-aged nurse fleeing into a patient's room. Her scream is shrill as she slams against the wall. Fragments of drywall fall to the ground as the unconscious nurse slumps toward the floor.

The men begin tearing at her. I'm paralyzed with fright as I watch them raise bloodied hands to their lips. They lick their fingers, ingesting the warm, sticky fluid. Its bright red stains their beards.

They have gone mad!

Closing the door, I lean against it and cover my ears as new screams replace the nurse's. A fog settles over my mind, combating the adrenaline pumping through my veins. I shake my head, fighting to remain focused.

Sweat clings to my brow and upper lip. My head feels light and airy as I scold myself. *Keep it together!*

Two doctors remained behind to care for the patients too ill to evacuate or those left behind by family members too afraid to enter the city to collect them. Four nurses stayed as well, though I'm sure more than one has fled.

The screams grow louder. I hear grunting down the hall as men try to break through a door. The wood creaks and groans, finally giving way.

"Grab the supplies," a man yells. The sound of hurried footsteps quickly follows. By pressing my ear against the door, I can tell they are getting closer.

Doors bang open and patients' rasping pleas echo in my ears. A tremor works its way through me as I scan the room. My mother lies on the bed before me in a catatonic state. The bathroom is to my left, but it's too small to hide in. The window to my mother's right is made of thick glass. Even if I could break through it, I would never survive the five-story fall.

I rush toward a supply cabinet and tear open the doors, rummaging through bandages, cleaning supplies and bedding. The handful of bullets I scavenged this morning won't last long. I will need a backup weapon if I have any chance of surviving the night.

Nothing! I bite my lower lip as I realize there is nothing of use. Not a scalpel. Not a pair of scissors. Not even a needle.

The lights flicker again overhead and then fade for the last time, plunging the room into darkness. I clasp my hands over my mouth to suppress my scream as something large slams into the door of the room. I hold my breath and wait for someone to enter, but the door remains closed. I clutch my gun to my chest.

Think, Avery! I pound my fist against my head. *I can't shoot them all.*

My lips quake as I sink down the wall, covering my ears to muffle the horrific clamor of death that fill the once peaceful ward. The sounds of butchering diminish, but the hammering of my heart in my ears only increases.

Another loud bang against the door sends me scuttling on my hands and feet toward my mother's bed. The steady droning hiss of her breathing machine catches my attention. The battery pack must have kicked in when the generator failed. They will hear it!

It is inevitable. This hospital wing is easy pickings.

The fifth floor is for long term care patients like my mother. Some are recovering from strokes or heart attacks. Others, like my mother, are trapped in a coma with a slim chance of ever waking again. None will put up much of a fight.

I should have left when I had the chance.

"Check that one," a man commands. It sounds as if he's only a couple of feet from my door. I stifle a squeal and dive head-first under my mother's bed. The mechanics of the lift tear at my sweater. I suck in and squeeze. Sharp metal jabs at my back, nicking my flesh.

"You been in here yet?"

My breath catches at the nearness of a feminine voice. *Please don't come in here. There's nothing for you.*

"What are you waiting for? Check it out!" the man yells back.

The back of my jeans rips as I thrust my leg under the bed just before the door swings open, spilling the dim glow of a dying flashlight through the entrance of the room. The feet that approach are small, definitely those of a woman. She walks with a hint of a limp as she approaches the bed.

I bury my face in my arms, focusing on small half breaths. *They will see me. They'll know I'm here!*

"I found another live one!" she shouts. I can tell by the way her soles screech on the tile that she calls over her shoulder.

I stare through thick strands of ginger hair as two people arrive in the doorway. The sounds of screaming have died off, replaced by an eerie silence.

"She one of them?" The work boots on the right pause as they reach the end of the bed.

I don't want to die, shuffles on repeat like a skipping song in my mind. I reaffirm my grip on the gun, pointing it at the feet before me, but I don't pull the trigger. Not yet. I wait for a good shot.

"Does it matter? She's still breathing," the woman responds.

"Ignorant cow!" A wad of phlegm lands on the floor near her feet. "You put any of *their* blood in you and you're as good as gone too. Ain't you learned nothin' yet?"

The woman pauses less than six inches from my head. The tips of her shoes tread on the hem of my sweater. "Fine. Then who's gonna check her?"

A gravelly laugh from the doorway sends chills down my spine. "Why do you think I sent you in here?"

"Aw, come on Rhett. You know I had to check the last one. I still have nightmares over that. I swear that thing looked at me!"

The man at the end of the bed steps forward. I hear garbled cries as the woman's heels lift off the floor. "You know the rules. Bring back the goods or don't come back. If I tell 'em you ain't done your part, whatcha think they're gonna do to ya? Hmm?"

I hold my breath as she drops to the ground and stumbles back a few paces. I imagine her rubbing her throat as she takes several rasping breaths. "Haven't we got enough yet?"

I long to reach out and draw my sweater back, but I dare not move. Even in the dim glow of the flashlight, they might see my hand.

"No." The clipped response from the doorway sends my heart plummeting into my stomach. "There ain't never gonna be enough."

Enough of what? What is it they want?

"Get it done," Rhett commands and turns. "And don't ya forget that tubing when you're done."

The door swings closed, leaving me trapped with the remaining man and the shaken woman.

"I can't do it, Pete. I don't have it in me tonight." There are a few seconds of silence then a grunt of displeasure. "If you don't do it, it'll be both our hides on the line. You heard what Rhett said. I'm not sleeping outside camp again. No way. The streets are no place to be after dark," the woman says, inching backward.

The waver in her voice doesn't surprise me. I've seen what's on those streets. Murderers, rapists, and things far worse...the Withered Ones are out there.

"I know how you like it," she lowers her voice as she coaxes him. Sounds to me like she's done this before. "That feeling of power you get. I've seen it in your eyes."

I hear the sound of scratching from above and wonder if this man has a beard as well. "Yup."

"So you'll do it for me?" The man approaches the bed. His silence unnerves me. Why doesn't he answer? "Take her out, Pete."

For as long as I live, I will remember those words and the sounds that follow. Pete moves faster than I could have imagined. He plants his feet and lunges forward. I hear a deep thud, followed by tearing.

I cover my mouth and clamp my eyes closed as the man growls overhead, pounding his fists. Bile rises in my throat as a sharp metallic scent fills the air. Tears roll involuntarily down my cheeks. *I'm sorry!*

There is nothing I can do to stop my mother's brutal slaughter. We may not have seen eye to eye, but no one deserves this.

Pete shakes out his hands at his sides, sending blood splattering against his pant leg and floor. Moist warmth flicks against my arm and I bite down hard enough on my lip to draw blood of my own.

My silent scream is guttural, soul shaking at the sound of splintering bone. It echoes off the walls, ringing in my ears. I feel faint as I imagine Pete snapping my mother as easily as a child cracking a dried twig.

I wait for the blood to begin pouring down from the bed above, but it never comes. The man and woman fall still on either side of me. I hear the sound of pattering, like water against a bathroom sink.

What is happening? What are they doing to her?

Though a tremor seizes me, I clamp down and force myself not to move, terrified of making a sound. Of being discovered. Of listening to my mother's heinous death.

Do something!

Summoning a courage that I don't feel, I kick out at my mother's IV pole. It crashes to the ground, making the skittish woman jump back. Her flashlight clatters to the ground. "What was that?"

"Ain't nothin' but you, woman."

One glance at the far wall reveals my illuminated shadow. *Shit!*

I grab the man by the ankle and yank with all my might. He cries out as his footing shifts and he topples to the ground. A waterfall of blood rains against the white tile floor and splatters my face. I gag at the feel of its warmth trailing down the ridge of my nose. I crawl out from under the opposite side of the bed, spitting my mother's blood to the side as I head for the woman.

The walls look like a scene from a horror movie. Blood splatters trail down the once cheerful yellow walls. The floor is slick as I rise. The back of my sweater dampens with blood as I press back against the bed.

My hand shakes as I lift my pistol. The woman glances toward the door, her frizzy auburn hair a sweaty web around her forehead. I tighten my grip on the trigger and aim, noticing a split second before I pull the trigger that there is an angry rash on her left cheek that trails into the neckline of her coat.

The shot is deafening. My hand recoils and I almost lose my grip on the gun. The woman's eyes widen with disbelief as she slides down the wall, clutching the crimson stain blooming along her abdomen.

A swell of pride floods through me but is lost as I am slammed from behind. I watch the tile rise up to meet me in slow motion as a crushing weight settles over me. I turn my head, narrowly avoiding crushing my skull against the floor. My gun clatters out of my hand as my breath is stolen away. Dark spots encroach the perimeter of my vision as pain nestles into my ribs.

The man's breath is hot and rancid, puffing against my ear. His long, beefy fingers curl around my arm, pinning me to the floor. "Get Rhett," he yells toward the woman. "This one's coming with us."

I listen to her moan behind me but don't hear any footsteps of retreat. My cheek smashes into the cold porcelain, grinding bone and flesh. I kick and flail, useless against his weight.

"Get off me!" I screech, trying to claw free, but the blood coating his arms makes it impossible to get a firm grip.

Panic floods through me as I'm reminded that I'm not some super badass chick with ninja skills. I'm just a girl from the wrong side of the tracks who wishes she could be.

"I'm gonna cut you nice and slow," he breathes into my face. The scent of cheap alcohol on his breath is nauseating. From the corner of my eye, I notice black spots dotting his lips. "Gonna make you beg as I gut you."

I fall still, terrified of the glee I hear in his voice.

The sound of gunfire from down the hall startles both of us. I take my one shot and slam my head back, grateful to hear a sickening crunch. His grip eases slightly.

"Bitch!"

An elbow to his side and a swift kick once I wriggle forward leaves the man enraged. He cups his nose as blood pours from it, trailing into his matted beard. My nails crack and splinter as I claw along the slick floor, fighting to dig into the grout lines for leverage.

The door stands open wide before me. The wounded girl must have escaped. A blood trail leads into the hall, illuminated by the fallen flashlight. I look around in search of my gun, but it is lost to shadow. Clambering to my feet, I use the sheets on my mother's bed to rise.

My stomach falls away when I find my feet and discover the horror this man bestowed on her. Blood no longer pumps through the wide gash in her neck. It pools in the dip of her collarbone. Streams of crimson trail down what little is left of her arm to soak into the sheets. Her chest is concave, shredded as if by a rabid animal instead of a human. Much of her flesh lies in ribbons. The muscles in her neck have been flayef open by a knife. Her eyes are open, unseeing but looking right at me.

"Oh, God!" I press my hand to her neck. The warmth of her blood between my fingers and the reality of her brutal end makes the room spin.

One thought slowly surfaces as Pete lumbers to his feet behind me. *He has a knife.*

Looking back over my shoulder in the fading light, I see him wavering on his feet, searching the floor. A glint of silver near his feet makes my heart stop. *Please don't see it.*

He raises his gaze toward me as he grabs his nose and realigns it. A look of unadulterated fury stares back at me and I realize he won't need the knife to hurt me.

I leap to the side a second before he strikes, pushing off from the wall and spinning just out of reach. My cheek smacks into the supply cabinet when I misjudge my escape. I steady myself and fling open the doors, desperately tossing the contents at the man as he turns on me.

Pete bats them away and closes the gap between us. I bring a bedpan down over his head when he takes a swipe at me, but it doesn't faze him. "Got you, girlie!"

His hand wraps around my arms as I try to run and yanks me toward him. I shriek and rake my hands down his arms, feeling his flesh curl under my nails. His arm snakes around my neck, choking off my air.

Gunfire pings against tile and metal in the hall but my attacker is lost to the disturbance. I hear screams in the distance as I fight against his grip, kicking and landing punches that seem useless. *I'm going to die! Oh, God, please don't let this happen!*

My screams become strangled gasps as he shoves me to the ground. His legs wind around my waist, stilling my fight. He slams my temple against the floor and stars light up the room. Blood trails down from my eyebrow, stinging my eyes. I feel the impact again and again but am helpless to stop him.

"Pretty girl gonna die," he crows in my ear as he reaches over my head. My eyes bulge as the cold steel of his blade pressed to my cheek. His free hand squeezes my throat.

The light in the room fades and lethargy seeps through my body as oxygen is withheld. My hands fall to my sides. I can feel myself slipping away.

"Please." I stretch out my hand for help as a pair of boots pauses in the doorway and turns toward me.

A gunshot at close range makes my ears ring. The grip on my neck releases. Warm matter sprays my face. A foul sludge slips between my lips as I fight for breath. The approach of footsteps sounds like the march of a giant in my wounded ear drums.

Large hands roll me onto my side, pushed away from my motionless attacker. I claw at the floor as my lungs expand, gasping in air. A distorted voice calls to me, but I can't make out the muffled words. The only thing I can think of as I stare bleary eyed up at my savior is that their face looks wrong, elongated, and grotesque. Then the darkness takes me.

TWO

A fever consumed me sometime during the night. Frequent delirium makes me hear voices that do not exist. They come and go. Sometimes they are nothing more than a whisper. A part of me almost wishes they are real. Then I wouldn't feel so blasted insane!

Nausea impairs my every thought as I roll my head to the side to vomit. I hear it splatter against the floor, but I don't open my eyes. The retching will only grow worse if I do.

There is nothing left in me now. What little food I scavenged from the hospital vending machine is long gone. My stomach twists in knots spoiled with acid. Every inch of my body aches, though it is not the pain that makes me ill, but the scent of rot that hovers around me.

I feel as if a steel wool pad scratches against my throat when I swallow between heaves. Warm blood seeps from newly opened wounds along my eyebrow and hairline. With each retch, pain lances through my eye.

"Easy," a voice soothes. Large hands wrap around my arm, supporting me until my stomach empties.

I'm delirious again. Now there's a body to go with the voice. I spit and wipe at my mouth, disgusted by the foul aftertaste, then fall back against the sweaty cushion beneath my head.

Pressing my stomach, I will the cramping to ease. Slowly it does, though I have no real sense of the passage of time. Only misery and darkness. No light brightens the back of my eyelids. No sound reaches me as I slip in and out of a restless sleep.

Some time later, a damp cloth is pressed against my temple and I lean into the coolness. My fever has begun to ease. The aches are not nearly so pronounced. The relief I feel subsides when the cloth is removed. I hear splashing water and covet the refreshing chill until the cloth returns a moment later, only to find a sense of clarity beginning to return. I become aware of my surroundings. The scent of musk and disuse. Sounds of gunfire in the distance. Muffled shouting. The tremor that rises from the floor with each explosion in the distance.

When I hear the steady inhale and exhale of breath nearby, I tense. Fingers press against the inner flesh of my wrist and I bolt upright, suddenly convinced of the fact that I am truly not alone.

"Stop." The grip on my wrist tightens as I buck against the stranger. "I'm not going to hurt you."

"Get off me! Someone help me!"

Bright light flares beside me, shining up to the ceiling. I blink several times to adjust to the light as the man grabs my chin and forces me to come eye to eye with him.

"I'm not going to hurt you," he repeats with emphasis, his gaze never wavering from mine.

My hair falls in sweaty clumps over my face but fails to hide the man before me. His face is angular and his jaw strong. His dark eyes are narrowed with concern. A heavy growth of stubble lines his face, revealing a hint of sandy blond amongst the darker brown of his facial hair. He doesn't look much older than me. Maybe twenty-two or twenty-three, at the most.

His grip eases on my arm, but he does not pull away. I can tell he is waiting, but for what, I'm not sure. Maybe for me to freak out and start wailing like a banshee in fright, or to attack and attempt to flee. As the room begins to spin around me, I realize I'm in no condition to do either.

"How are you feeling now?"

I ignore his question. "Where am I?"

"You're safe."

"Is anywhere safe now?" I croak, rubbing at my throat. The flesh is tender, bruised. I wince, remembering the hands that sought to end my life only a short time ago.

"This place is, for now." I watch his eyes shift, rising to survey the damage I did to my eyebrow. Judging by the burning sting, I have reopened several new wounds. "Are you done fighting me?"

I can tell that he knows I'm barely staying upright. I am weak, far too weak.

"Don't really have much choice," I grumble. My shoulders ache as I hold myself aloft on the edge of a futon, sitting only two feet above a small, matted shag rug that may have once been a neon green. Now it is splattered with drying remnants of my earlier bouts with nausea. Heat floods my cheeks as I look away.

"I tried to clean you up the best I could. You had me worried for a while. I didn't think your fever was going to break."

At the mention of my fever, a chill sprints down my spine. Am I infected too? Am I going to turn into one of the Withered?

Determined not to think about it, I notice for the first time that he is dressed in fatigues. There is a Marine Corps emblem on his chest. "Are you a soldier?"

"Yes, ma'am. Stationed out of MCRD PI. " I stare up at him. That term means nothing to me. "It's a Marine base located in Parris Island, South Carolina. A recruitment training facility."

"South Carolina?" I rub my forehead. My headache is getting worse and my head feels too heavy for my neck to support, but I fight against my weariness. I try to focus, to keep him talking until I can determine his motives. "How did you end up here in St. Louis?"

His expression darkens. "We were reassigned a couple weeks back."

He says nothing more, but he doesn't have to. Everyone knows the government screwed up. This man and countless others were sent in to clean up its mess. What the government actually did was cause a shit storm that no one was prepared for.

"How bad is it out there?" I turned off the TV long before the rioting took out the power plants. I didn't want to know. Didn't want to hear their version of the truth. The problem is no one really knows what the truth is anymore. Guesses, opinions, and speculation are all there is now. I guess in the end it doesn't really matter.

He looks away from me. His Adam's apple bobs once and then again before he speaks. "It's not good. We've lost New York, Chicago, LA and countless other cities."

"To *them?*"

"The Withered Ones?" I nod, not liking the way the term rolls off his tongue with hardly any emotion. "No. They are the least of our worries."

I'm not sure I agree with that.

I always prided myself in being prepared for anything. Self-defense classes at the Y and a few street brawls have helped me to survive on my own, but nothing could have prepared me for this. The term "zombie apocalypse" has been thrown around. It's sure as heck not like what I was expecting!

I spent hours at the hospital window watching the Withered Ones shuffling along the streets, waiting for the gruesome deaths to begin, but they never did. They show no signs of hunger, or anger or fear, but I stay clear of them. I keep waiting for this to all be some sick joke, and one of them will finally decide I look tasty and take a chunk out of my arm.

Glancing toward the window, I strain to hear the moans on the street below. They are out there. The Withered Ones, or Moaners, as some people like to call them now. A fitting name, I guess.

"You thought I was becoming one of *them*, didn't you?" I ask after a moment of silence. "Of course you did," I answer for him to fill his continued silence.

How could he not? Fever is the first symptom. Anxiety. Unexplained pain. Rashes. Delirium. Sudden lowering of temperature to abnormal levels. Tremors. Loss of memory and a dozen other symptoms that pop up randomly. The end result is always the same...an all-consuming nothingness left in this disease's wake.

I saw it at the hospital. Watched the woman in the room across the hall from my mother slip into an eerie void. She was among the first, the doctors said.

I don't know what they did with her. She just disappeared from the ward. Maybe the military disposed of her. Maybe the doctors did. After more people started turning, I stopped asking questions.

He slowly nods and lowers his gaze so that his face is shielded by the brim of his camouflage hat. "Then why did you stay?"

"I had to know for sure. Turns out it looks like you just have a common flu bug, mixed with a heavy dose of shock."

What would he have done with me if my fever hadn't broken? Would he have left me here, locked in this tiny apartment to slowly starve to death? To beat endlessly against the door in a futile attempt to escape?

"Would you have put a bullet between my eyes?" I ask. He clears his throat and turns his face away. His posture grows rigid and I have my answer. "Nice to know."

I look at the room around me and notice black garbage bags duct-taped over the windows. Peering around the flashlight beam beside him, I spy used candles on the tabletop, their wicks long since spent. The furniture in the studio apartment is a hodgepodge of garage sale finds. Nothing matches. Nothing smells good.

Glancing at the ceiling, I discover that all of the air vents are covered. Torn drapes are shoved into cracks around the window sills. "You think it's in the air, don't you?"

When he glances back at me, I notice something akin to appreciation in his gaze. "We don't really know what caused the mutations."

"You don't know or you don't want to say?"

His gaze narrows. "I don't know."

I nod slowly. "Someone does."

"Perhaps."

"Still. Better to be safe than sorry, huh?" I spy an upturned gas mask on the floor and realize the distorted face I saw before passing out was this mask, not a person's face. I wonder why he has it. I've seen a few people darting around the streets with clothes tied around their faces. Maybe the military knows something they don't deem important enough to share with the general public?

Growing up on the streets, I've learned a thing or two about reading people. You have to when you don't have anyone to watch your back. I can't get a firm read on this guy. He stays near enough to express concern for my well-being, but not so close that it alarms me. He is cautious in how he moves, always slow and deliberate when he shifts, and always watching me.

Trying to appear as if I have a choice in the matter, I lower myself onto my elbows. The trembling in my arms eases minimally. It is only a matter of time before I'm forced to lie down completely.

I glance at the array of pill bottles, wet cloths and cleaning supplies accumulated on the floor nearby. "I guess this means you don't intend to hurt me."

I watch his face for any hint of deceit but see none as he shakes his head. "No, ma'am. That's not my way."

He backs farther away but remains in a crouch not far from my feet.

"What's your name?" I ask. Reaching near to the point of exhaustion, I push up on the cushion and struggle into a fully seated position. I feel better upright, more in control, though the tilt of the room reminds me that I'm far from well.

"Cable."

I wait for him to continue, but he doesn't. Instead, he falls silent. "You got a last name to go with that?"

"Cable is just fine, ma'am."

"I'm no 'ma'am.'" I brush the hair back out of my face. My cheeks still feel warm and my skin is sensitive to the touch. "You can call me Avery."

When he cracks a small smile, his closed-off expression softens. "I knew an Avery once. Had a mean streak to go with that flaming hair of hers."

The wistful tone in his voice makes me wonder. "She steal your heart?"

He laughs, lowering his head as the memory grips him. "Nope, but she managed to swindle me out of a few days' worth of lunch money, though."

"You got taken by a girl?"

It's hard to imagine a man of his build being fooled by a girl, no matter his age. "Nah. She was a pretty little thing. I practically offered it up to her."

I cross my legs before me, enduring a moment of lightheadedness. I clamp my fingers around my knees and focus on breathing until it passes. When I open my eyes I see that he's watching me again. "How long have I been here?"

"Four days."

"Four days!" My voice cracks with surprise as I jerk upright. "How did I...what did you...what the heck?"

Cable pushes back into a seated position, drawing his legs inward to balance on his tailbone. Reaching over, he grabs a wet cloth from a bowl sitting beneath a cluttered end table and hands it to me. I press it to my forehead, grateful for the refreshing coolness. "That guy back at the hospital messed you up pretty bad. You were in a lot of pain when I first brought you here so I gave you something to help you rest. You needed it.

"I wasn't sure I was going to be able to carry you out of there." He pauses to swallow as his gaze grows unfocused. His lip curls with disgust. "I've seen my fair share of death in the past, but never anything like that. That was twisted stuff."

I curl inward, crossing my arms over my stomach in a protective huddle at the memory of my mother lying in a pool of blood, open and exposed like a carcass left on the side of a road. Nothing can erase that memory from me. Nor the sounds, smells, or fear that I experienced trapped beneath her bed.

I won't miss my mother. Not in the normal sense of the word, at least. She was familiar, even if she wasn't always wanted. Still, she deserved better. "The blood wasn't all mine."

He nods and takes the cloth as I offer it back to him. He dips it several times in the water and then hangs it over the side. "I figured that out once I got you back here and cleaned you up."

I run my hand down my bare arms and grow still. I was wearing a sweater at the hospital.

Glancing down at my chest I see that I'm wearing a black tank top that is two sizes too big. My breath catches as I lift the blanket spread across my lap and discover that my legs are bare. "You undressed me!"

He points to his right and I follow the direction of his finger. There, hanging on a makeshift drying line are my sweater and jeans; torn and soiled but far less bloody than they should be. "You went into shock. I had to get you warm."

"So you thought *removing* my clothes was the best option?" Heat races up through my neck and settles into my cheeks as I splutter.

His expression is impossible to decipher, but I would bet money that there's a hint of humor buried within his dark eyes before he looks away. "You were wounded and covered in blood. I had to know the extent of your injuries. I'm sorry if this has caused you some discomfort."

"Discomfort?" I run my hands through my hair, wincing at the ratty tangles. On a good day, my thick curls are hard to manage. I can only imagine how terrible I look now. "My mother was torn apart while I laid beneath her, listening. I was attacked and bludgeoned nearly to death only to wake to find some complete stranger has been groping me in my sleep. What's to be uncomfortable about?"

He uncrosses his legs, only to cross them once more before pressing back his shoulders and then raising his chin to meet me face to face. No hiding. No backing away. "I told you, that isn't my way."

Tucking the blanket under my arms, I tap my finger against my leg, trying to get a read on him. Nothing about his posture screams guilt. No flush in his cheeks. He doesn't look away as if embarrassed by his actions. In fact, he seems rather confident that he did the right thing, despite my accusing glare.

"All right. Let's say you are legit." I concede for the moment. "That you only want to help me. Tell me what happened at the hospital? Why were you there?"

There is a clank of metal and I notice dog tags hanging from his neck as he stretches out his long legs before him. A ridge of muscles appears in his thighs as he flexes. "The hospital was overrun. My team and I did what we could to neutralize the threat."

"Your team?"

He nods. "I had nine men under my command. We were on patrol in the area when we saw the lights go out. It didn't feel right, so we decided to check it out. Once we saw the front doors busted open, we knew it was a raid."

Despite a headache trying to drill a hole through the back of my head, his words bring clarity as I focus on this new information. I always did like trying to solve puzzles.

"Do you know why they were murdering people?" He grasps his dog tags and slides them back and forth across the chain, stalling. "Cable?"

He looks up as I use his name for the first time. His jaw flinches, but he quickly averts his gaze. Even from his profile, I mark the pinch of his with disgust. "They were on a blood run."

"A blood run?" I lean my head back against the cushion. The muscles in my neck ache from remaining upright for so long. I need at least another's day of rest to recover. "What's that supposed to mean?"

He leans toward me, his lips slightly parted before he speaks. "How much do you know about what's been going on?"

I shrug halfheartedly. "I'm not really the news-watching kind of girl."

"But you know about the deaths?"

"Duh." I rub my forehead, wishing I could search the apartment for a bottle of pain meds. This headache is a real bitch. "That one was kinda hard to miss."

I don't know many of the details, only what the news anchors told us before the stations went down. What started out as a few bizarre deaths up north led to a country-wide outbreak.

Death swept across our land like a biblical plague. Entire families wiped out in mere days. The body counts rose faster than could be controlled. Mounds of decaying bodies were tossed in landfills, mass graves set alight to prevent the spread of the disease. Hospitals were overrun. All the while I stayed close to my mother's room. I knew she wouldn't get sick, not with being stuck in a clean room for risk of contracting a normal infection, but what about me? I figured the best place to be was smack dab in the hospital if I started to feel sick.

The government gave us hope a month ago when they released the MONE vaccine. Our cure for an unnamed enemy. Our redemption.

They were wrong.

The injection that was meant to bring us salvation brought us a living hell. The death count may have slowed, but the human mutations began within days of the drug's release. The government scrambled to figure out what went wrong with the vaccines, but it was too late. Whatever this new pathogen was, it spread quickly through the populace.

The Withered Ones were born. People not alive, but not entirely dead either. They walk the streets, unblinking and unaware. The only sound they make is a rasping moan and shuffling footsteps. A zombie, for all intents and purposes, but nothing like we anticipated. I think I could have handled the flesh-eaters a bit better.

That was the beginning of the end.

Desperation and the remaining scum of the earth rule the streets now. It was inevitable that gangs would form, prisons would empty, and evil would assume control, but the true fear runs much deeper. In the early hours of the night, you are left to wonder: *Am I next?*

I suppose that is another reason why I didn't run when things got bad. Where can I hide when our deadliest enemy may already be inside me?

"We think the vaccines triggered some sort of chemical response in those already infected with the pathogen," Cable informs me. His voice is lower now. His grave tone makes me want to hug myself and crawl back under the blankets and ignore everything outside this apartment. I tried to do that at the hospital, but the world came knocking. "I'm not sure anyone left alive really knows how it spread or even why. It hit so fast that there was no way to contain it once it spread."

"But someone must know the true source. I mean, they have a slew of symptoms to pick from, right?"

Cable scratches the back of his neck. "That's the problem. None of the symptoms are completely the same. Some seem pretty constant, like a fever, but it's different for each person. Half the time it's impossible to know if they've just come down with a cold. By then, it's too late."

He rubs his hands along his arm, scrunching up the black fabric. He stares beyond me, his expression as blank as those *things* shuffling along the streets below. "There were rumors at my base. People were suspicious of government involvement. Terms like population control and terrorism were thrown around. Other people thought it might have been some crazy Middle Eastern dictator that found a way to use chemical warfare on our food supply. Others thought maybe there was a mole in the CDC that tampered with the MONE drug results."

I'd be lying if I didn't admit that I'd had similar thoughts over the past couple of weeks. I wouldn't put it past the government to be somehow involved. Plausible deniability and all that crap.

"But the Moaners started showing up after we were given the vaccine," I chime in. "Shouldn't that mean that was the cause of the mutations?"

He turns his hands upward and shrugs, shaking his head. "Could be, or maybe it was just bad luck. The CDC was working on this mystery, last I heard, but that was over a week ago. It's been mostly radio silence since then. My guess is they ran out of time."

"Or manpower," I mutter, shoving my hair back from my eyes. It clings to my cheeks, plastered to my neck.

"That too." Lifting his hat, Cable rubs his hair. It's sandy blond, like the highlights along his chin, and short, probably at one time was spiked, but has since been matted down. "About a week ago I heard static on our comm channel. Nothing unusual, especially now, but a faint message came through that I'm not sure I was supposed to hear."

My hand falls away from my forehead. "What was it?"

"The message said 'blood is the key.' That's when the riots really began and we were called in. My guess is someone else was listening in on that same message."

I rest my head back against the futon cushion. "It's not like that message was much to go on. How could someone take those four words and create such chaos?"

"What other source of hope did they have to cling to?"

"Hope?" I snort. "How does 'blood is the key' bring hope to those lunatics out there?"

"It doesn't, but if they want people to follow them they have to pretend that it does."

"So the leaders of these gangs tell people there's something in the blood that can save them and their brainless minions will do whatever it takes to get it?"

"Pretty much. That's why they hit the hospital."

I frown, thinking back to the odd sounds I heard at the hospital. "Was my attacker trying to collect my mother's blood as some sort of cure? If so, there's no way gutting her would have worked. I'm no doctor, but I'm pretty sure mixing the wrong blood is a bad thing, not to mention how easily it could be contaminated when collected incorrectly."

"Desperation drives people to crazy things, including what happened to your mother. I don't know what they are doing with the blood, only that they are rounding up survivors for it."

I heard the screams on the street, knew innocent people were being hurt, but I never dreamed they were being rounded up like animals. The idea sickens me, but a sudden idea makes me mouth fall open. "They're making their own blood bank," I whisper.

"It would seem so." Cable's hands drop to his sides, his fingers uncurling against the floor. Color flees from his fingers under the pressure. "They are systematically taking out quadrants of the town at a rate faster than we can keep up. We are low on men. Half of the guys I came here with have turned, others were mowed down. A few are missing and presumed dead."

His jaw clenches. "Before anyone really knew what was happening, they hit every gun, pawn, and redneck shop they could find to stock up. They raided grocery stores for food and blew up a shopping center after they depleted its resources. Then the bastards built walls around themselves. They are shut up tight near the center of town. I lost several good men trying to breach their wall."

"How could they build walls so quickly? It's only been a couple of weeks."

An explosion rattles the window. Cable glances toward the window, his expression grim. "Like that. They blew up entire city blocks, downed buildings all around them. They have snipers on the rooftops. We try to get near them and they pick us off."

Wrapping my arms around me, I feel a shiver ripple along my spine. "Why not just drive a tank in here and blow them all to hell? Don't you have jets or something with bombs?"

"Sure." He shoves his hat back on his head. "We could do that, and risk murdering hundreds, if not thousands, of innocent men and women in the process."

I notice that he doesn't mention anything about children and figure he's trying to gloss over that fact. I appreciate that side step. I've never been one of those people who liked seeing kids get killed in movies. It's just sick.

Lowering my head, I fight to ignore the growing ache in my neck. My muscles are taut. My stomach churns as I sink a little lower. I'm tired, more so than I ever remember being. My mother used to brag to her friends that I was the healthiest kid she ever met. I can count the times I had a cold as a child on one hand. The flu hit me once every couple of years. I guess I've hit my quota for a while.

"I used to watch movies about the apocalypse," I say, placing a hand on my stomach. Even though it is empty, I fear another bout of dry heaves may be in my near future. "Thought it was kinda cool, ya know? Even with all of the death and destruction, I always saw it as a rebirth, but this isn't life. It's not even surviving."

I fall silent, thinking over the enormity of what has been lost and it's only beginning. Things will get worse. They always do.

For the first time since waking, I become aware of the chill on the air. Cable's long sleeves are pulled low over his wrists. His pants are tucked into his boots.

"It's cold." He starts forward in response to my statement, as if with the intent of tucking in my blanket but I jerk back and he instantly falls still. "I meant it's cold in general. Not that I'm cold."

He sinks back to the floor. "They took out this section's power station last night. I don't know what they are thinking. Blow that thing up and the rest of city goes off the grid, including them."

I bite my lower lip, thinking over what he'd said about them stocking up. If anyone in this city is prepared to wait out this apocalypse it's them. "Maybe that's the point."

"What is?"

"If I wanted to take control of a city, I'd go after the essentials first: water, food, fuel and weapons. They've already done that. Now if they send people running scared, they have free reign over anything people need to survive. It's the dead of winter. When the survivors begin to starve, or the next ice storm blows through, people will be forced to come to them or die."

Cable tilts his head to the side and I spy the hint of a tattoo rising from the back of his collar. "Makes sense, only I don't think there will be any dealing. Those gangs are out for blood. You can't negotiate with madness."

"Don't I know it." I rub the back of my neck to ease the pain. Multiple sites along my body ache. It's hard to tell what pain is from my recent beating or from the fever. "Did you lose any of your men at the hospital?"

"A few."

Silence hangs between us for a time, thick and impregnable. I should say that I'm sorry. Most decent humans would, right?

"Did you kill that guy that attacked me?"

His gaze hardens before he nods.

"Good."

"Good?" He brings his knees up into his chest and links his hands in front of his laced combat boots. Splatters of dried blood cling to the soles. "You think killing a man is a good thing?"

I shrug, trying to appear indifferent as I tighten my grip on my waist, desperate to ignore the tremble in my fingers. "He would have killed me."

"I reckon he would have. Still doesn't make it right, though."

His answer floors me. Glancing toward the door, I see his gun propped against the wall. I don't know what kind it is, but it's big and mean looking. A heck of a lot scarier than that pistol I lost. "Why do you carry one of those if you don't intend to use it?"

Glancing toward his weapon, Cable frowns and looks back at me. "Why do you carry a gun when you have no clue how you use it?"

My mouth drops open. "How do you—"

"I had to put the girl down that you shot. You missed her heart by a good half a foot. The bullet went through the top of her stomach. She was suffering when I found her." He clenches his fists and looks up at me. "My guess is that you got off a lucky shot."

"So?" I bristle at the accusation in his voice. "At least I defended myself."

"Yes, ma'am. You did, but that isn't good enough."

"I told you, I'm not a 'ma'am,' so cut that crap." I slant my body away from him and cross my arms over my chest. "I survived. That's all that matters now."

"No." Cable pushes up from the floor in one smooth motion. When I look up at him I'm shocked by the deep slump of his shoulders. His expression is slack, his eyes dull. "This world isn't lost until we give up on it, and I'm not about to do that."

I cling to the blanket, feeling exposed and wearied by this stranger's whiplash morals. I should feel more gratitude for his risking his life to rescue me, but I don't. Not right now.

Instead, I decide to divert his attention. "Where is this place?"

"East side of town. Not far from the river." He walks to a window and peels back the curtain of black plastic. Hail pings against the window. An icy mixture streams down the glass panes like tears, cleaning away the filth. "It's not my place. I had a friend who crashed here from time to time."

"Had?"

He lets the plastic fall back into place then turns to look at me. This time, it's a hard, piercing look. "Yeah. Had."

I fall silent as he glances toward the empty armchair across from me and quickly looks away. I can tell he's upset. We have all lost someone. None of us are immune to mourning, though I'll admit I'm better off than most. There's no one in my life that I care enough about to shed a tear for.

"You'll be safe here," He says after a moment, visibly shaking himself. "You need to rest up a bit before you're ready to move."

"Move?" I ask, feeling a little stupid for acting like a parrot repeating everything he says, but my head still feels too light. Too unsettled. The quiver in my fingers has yet to fade and my stomach doesn't seem ready to settle anytime soon. I glance down the hall and pray that I can make it to the toilet in time if I have to.

"We can't stay here. The gangs are on the move, trying to expand their territory. My orders were to secure the quadrant near the hospital and return to base. It's only a matter of time before this area is lost."

I drop my legs over the side and tuck the blanket around me. The dark blue fabric of the futon is faded and tatty, the stuffing beginning to migrate toward the floor as I shift. "What about your team, squadron, or whatever you call it? Don't you have others like you that you're supposed to be with? Some commanding officer to report to?"

I get the distinct feeling that he has no desire to speak of such things as he begins to collect his gear. I consider pressing him, almost eager to do so as payback for him getting an eyeful of me while I was passed out, but I let it go.

Pursing my lips, I push up from the futon and rise unsteadily. I almost think that I've managed to pull it off until I topple backward, my head slamming into the cushion. Cable is by my side before I am able to recover.

"I can do it myself," I growl and shove off his hand. "I don't need you."

He backs away but doesn't go far. This annoys me. "What's with you, anyways? You one of those guys with some stupid hero complex? Is that why you joined the military?"

I glimpse a hint of a smile, but it fades just as fast as it appears and I realize that this guy is tough, but not as tough as he wants me to believe.

"I'm from the south, where people still have manners."

"And you're implying that I don't?"

He shrugs. "A thank you for saving your life would be the normal response."

"I said thank you." At least, I'm pretty sure I did at some point.

"Did you?" The corners of his mouth twitch. "It must have gotten lost in all of that self-righteous independence crap you've been spewing since you woke."

My mouth hangs open in disbelief. Is this guy for real? Now he's going to lecture me on being a feminist? I start to whip out a comeback, but he turns his back on me and heads for the door. "Where are you going?"

He pauses at the door to don a jacket. I spy the name *Blackwell* stitched into his chest and wonder if it's his name or if he grabbed the coat from another soldier. Reaching into his pocket he draws out a pistol.

"Hey! That's my gun!"

"Not until you learn to use it." He chambers a round and tucks the gun into his waistband. "I'm going for supplies and to see if any of my men made it out. Stay here and stay down. If you're quiet, they won't know you're here. If you get into any trouble, just barricade the door and wait for me to get back. I won't be longer than an hour or two."

He grabs a gas mask from the table beside him and pulls it down over his head. He places the hood over his head and slips into gloves, concealing nearly every inch of bare skin. It's not the cold that he hides from, but from the invisible killer he thinks is out there.

When he opens the door, I consider asking exactly who *they* are, but I don't. I consider lying back down to rest while he is gone, hoping that he will bring water to still the unease in my stomach, but I don't. I even consider barricading the door like he said and hiding in the corner until he returns, but I don't.

I don't do anything that I should.

Later...I will regret that decision.

THREE

I grew up in a sleepy town in northern Kentucky, not too far from the Illinois border. One stoplight. One mom and pop grocery store that still had small glass jars of candy near the register. Old tree-lined streets with a tire swing dangling in nearly every backyard. White picket fences straight out of the *Leave It To Beaver* era. Everyone knew my name. I could trust people back then.

I miss that place. Especially right now.

Looking out from behind the black trash bag covering the grimy window of Cable's fourth-floor hideout, all I hear is chaos in the night. I can almost smell the fear and smoke fumes filtering in through the glass and try to prepare myself to enter a world where people have run amok. I guess in a way, I don't blame them, not after what Cable told me.

I never wanted to come to St. Louis. Of course, I never wanted my dad to bail on us either, but as my mom used to say, "Shit happens to the best and worst of us." My older brother, Connor, made out better than I did. Not long after we moved here he took off to be a groupie for some stupid rock band touring the east coast and I haven't seen him since. He never even knew about mom's accident. Never wasted a single minute at her bedside.

Bastard!

With a pained grunt, I force myself to focus as I slip on a navy blue hoodie I scavenged from the bottom of the closet. It smells of stale man sweat. I pinch my nose and second guess myself for the twentieth time since I stumbled off the futon. Is it really safer out there on the streets than in here? Cable did save my life. That's gotta count for something, right?

I shake my head and wince at the throbbing in my neck. It coils down into my shoulder and makes my fingers tingle. I've always done best on my own. I'm not about to start needing people now.

Discovering a pair of jeans on the floor, I slip them on. They are loose at the waist, tight around my hips and nearly three inches too long. I sink onto the bed to roll large cuffs then pad across the hall to the bathroom.

After relieving my swollen bladder, I lean against the sink. Judging by the ring of yellow staining the porcelain bowl and the thick coating of limescale residue on the faucet, this apartment definitely used to belong to a single guy. A very disgusting guy.

I glance at my reflection in the mirror. The skin around my right eye is puffy and angry looking, the bruising dark and extensive. I have several small bandages patching my chin and cheek, hiding some of my freckles. Dark ginger hair lies in tangles about my face, the fringe around my forehead still matted from fever sweats. My lower lip is a deep shade of purple and split down the middle. My hazel eyes are lifeless, dull. Dried blood trails the curve of my cheek. I knew I looked bad, but I had no idea it was *this* bad!

"Maybe I'll look roughed up enough that no one will want to mess with me when I leave." Wishful thinking, but it's all I've got.

After digging through the contents of the medicine cabinet, I down a couple pain pills then stuff the bottle in my pocket. I grab some stomach pills for good measure then turn away from my image and limp back across the living room, feeling a sense of urgency to escape before Cable returns. He would try to stop me. I can't let that happen. Gun or no gun, I'm not waiting around.

I feel out of place in a strange man's clothes as I grab a plastic bag to stuff my jeans in. My sweater is still too damp to defend against the frigid night air. My red Chucks bear a hint of moisture, but they will have to do. Even with Cable's scrubbing, blood still stains the white soles.

I pass by a stack of plates piled haphazardly with molding food on a small two-seater table and chair setup in front of a lifeless TV. Stacks of credit card bills teeter on the edge, unopened and long forgotten. I tread as lightly as possible on the wooden floor as I press my ear to the front door. The peeling paint scratches my cheek as I listen for sounds. I hear nothing beyond my own labored breathing.

Brushing my hair back out of my eyes, I take a deep breath and draw the hood up over my head. "You can do this. Hit the stairs and don't look back. Don't slow down. Just move."

I glance back at the gas mask lying on the floor. Indecision hits me. What if Cable is right to be cautious? What if I can get sick just by breathing?

My pulse dances in my throat as I make my decision and turn away from the mask. I unbolt the lock and grasp the knob, slowly opening the door to peer out. The hinges squeak loudly. A gust of frosty wind seizes me from the right and I realize the window at the end of the hall is blown out.

Gathering my courage, I release the door and hobble for the stairs. The door slams behind me with enough force to vibrate the banister beneath my palm. I wind down a stairwell that has an overwhelming stench of mold and body odor. It seems to leach from the walls.

In the flickering of light entering through the window before me, I notice that the wallpaper to my left is yellowed and peeling. At one time, it appears to have been a pale pink, but it's hard to tell under the water stains that trail from the walls above. The floor is old wood, knotted and gouged over the years.

"And I thought my place was rough," I mutter under my breath as I pause on the bottom floor, breathing hard. I stifle a cry and duck low as a car alarm bursts to life. Headlights spill through the windows then disappear again, leaving me in near darkness.

Leaning forward, I wipe the window with my sleeve and peer out. Flames pour through a shop down the street. Maybe at one time it was a small pharmacy or liquor store. The fire rises high into the night, flickering against towering brick and wood sided buildings. In the light I spy four men jumping and shouting, glass bottles illuminated in their hands.

I'm trapped.

Despite the cold flowing under the wide crack at the bottom of the door, a bead of sweat trails down my brow. My head feels weightless as I pause to focus on my breathing. It won't do me any good to step out there if I'm just going to pass out.

I glance to my right and spy several cars weaving down the streets. There is debris in their way, making the path treacherous in the dark. The men celebrating down the road turn to inspect the new arrivals.

Shouts are quickly followed by gunfire. I watch in horror as a man slams his elbow into the rear window and drags a woman out by her hair, kicking and screaming. Seizing my chance, I decide to make a run for it, ignoring the shrieks of fear. The instant I open the front door I am assailed by the scent of garbage left out to rot. Cat urine is nearly as potent. I press my sleeve to my mouth and take a shallow breath as I keep to the shadows and move away from the fight, wishing that I could plug my ears against the screams and laughter.

My hoodie catches on the brick as I weave around overturned garbage bins and discarded bicycles. Suitcases spill from forgotten vehicles, their engines dead and cold. Car doors stand open like empty tombs as I pass. Apartment windows remain dark, blinds pulled and curtains were drawn. I wonder if anyone has remained in this part of the town.

Gunfire up ahead makes me eat pavement. It chews at the skin of my palms and knees, but I choke down my cry. That was close.

At the ping of bullets hitting metal and brick, I belly crawl toward an abandoned car. Crouching in the space of an opened passenger side door, I peek into the back seat to make sure nothing is going to leap out at me. A vacant child's car seat sits behind the driver's seat. It's pink material is splattered with flaking blood. I shiver and draw my gaze away, checking under the car to be sure I'm safe.

Screams spill out into the night, shrill and filled with terror. A man's bellow cuts off suddenly. An eerie silence follows. I clutch the seat belt for support, feeling the fibers dig into my bloody palms as I frantically look all around. Which direction did that come from?

The narrow streets and tall buildings make it nearly impossible to determine the location of the screams. A loud explosion comes at me like a rolling echo and rumbles in my chest as a fireball rises into the sky from two or three blocks away.

I trip over my laces as I get to my feet, using the car to steady me. Staggering back toward the edge of the building, I slip down the darkened alley. The sound of my shoes slapping the ground is covered by more gunfire. This time, it sounds closer.

Headlights pass by, zipping erratically. A crunch of metal is followed by a steady honk of the horn. They will hear the sound. They will come.

I know who *they* are now. Cable tried to warn me about the rioters, but I didn't listen. He said they were in another part of town, over by the hospital. That's at least ten miles to the west by my best guess. Have they moved into this area so quickly? Has the entire city already been lost?

I look around to get my bearings. I'm not overly familiar with this part of the city. I lived farther west, toward the outskirts of town. I used to take the Metro each morning to see my mother and return long after dark. That was before the Moaners arrived.

Reaching the end of the alley, I hug the wall and peer around. This street is not as well lit, and that scares me. Shadows mean plenty of hiding places for things lurking in the dark.

As I step forward, glass crunches beneath my sneakers. I look up to see that the streetlight overhead has been knocked out. My hands seek purchase on the building for support as I gulp in air. Darkness encroaches along the edge of my vision.

"Don't pass out. Don't pass out." I chant to myself for a minute until the dizziness passes. I clutch my stomach with my free hand and double over, desperate not to be sick. Grabbing the stomach meds, I fight with the plastic cap then toss back a couple of pills without looking at the dosage. I hold my breath and count. After a minute, I feel better and rise.

As I push off the wall, my fingers sink into a hole. I turn and trace the indentation. Six more span a two-foot radius. Bullet holes.

I search the fire-lit street behind me. My mind imagines all sorts of foul things crawling toward me in the dark. Evil men with lurid thoughts. Faceless people endlessly walking the streets. I listen for the telltale moan of the Withered Ones but hear nothing.

I look to the darkened windows all around and wonder who lived in these homes. Did they make it out alive? Did they become Moaners?

The florist at the end of my street back home was among the first to go missing in my neighborhood. She used to set up her wares each afternoon and sell to the businessmen as they returned to their wives or rushed to rendezvous with a weekend lover. Next, it was the mailman. An entire week went by without a single delivery. At first, I thought it was a little odd. Then it became downright worrying. The post office never bothered to send anyone else. I haven't seen either of them in two weeks. I'd like to say that I believe they caught wind of the coming panic and skipped town, but I can't.

The kids that used to hang out on my street corner, playing chicken with taxis or dodging in and out of stores in small groups, vanished not long after. Poof. Gone.

Ten days ago, during those hours in the night when I was halfway between sleep and dreamsville, I heard shouting and the rumbling of engines. Men on loudspeakers directed soldiers who scurried out of open bed trucks and Humvees. They broke down doors and ransacked homes. I curled my pillow around my head and hummed as loud as I could to cover the shouting till the sun rose. When I awoke, silence had fallen over my street.

That was the last night I slept in my house alone. After that, I stayed at the hospital.

The sound of glass crunching underfoot behind me makes me freeze. I strain to listen, praying that I'm mistaken. Maybe it was a cat. Judging by the smell, there are plenty of those still around.

Another crunch. And another. The shuffling gait makes my pulse thump in my ears. I hear heavy breathing now, a rasping that sounds like wind funneling through a moist cloth.

"Oh, God, no!"

If it were daytime, I would easily be able to see vacant, glassy eyes. Pallid skin. Oily, unkempt hair falling over her face. It is a her. I can sense that. Maybe it's her body odor that alerts me, or the small catch in her breathing.

The thing walking toward me doesn't move fast, doesn't show any sign of hesitation at the sound of nearby gunfire. It just keeps coming.

I back toward the light, terrified of being seen, but there is no way I'm staying in this alley with her. At the exit, I pause and glance around. I'll be exposed when I step out, but it's a risk I have to take.

I take three steps backward and hit something cold and solid. A scream erupts from my throat as I turn to see a man standing behind me. His cheek-length blond hair is matted with filth. A deep gash has peeled back the skin over his right eye. Flesh is torn from his jaw, revealing six teeth buried in his gums. There is no recognition of pain. No attempt to stunt the blood seeping down his face. He does not look *at* me, but beyond me.

His right foot is turned inward. He steps toward me and I panic. I trip over the gutter and land hard on my backside. Still he comes. Unseeing.

I have never been so close to one of them. Judging by the foul scent clinging to his clothes, he turned a while back. Perhaps as much as two weeks ago, when people first started disappearing.

Over my shoulder, I see the woman behind me. She can't be more than five steps away now. The stench of feces emanating from these two makes my eyes water.

Scrambling to my feet, I ignore the pain in my palms and knees as I narrowly miss the man's step. He jerks as his broken foot lands unevenly in the storm drain. His hoarse moan grows deeper as he twitches, trying to yank his foot free. I cower against the wall, watching in wide-eyed disbelief as the woman emerges from the alley and walks straight into the man.

Turning to the side, my stomach heaves in response to the sickening snap of bone. The woman barrels over him. Together they fall toward the street, the man's foot now attached only by a stretched bit of skin.

I can't look. I hear the sounds of their struggle, but I can't bear to see it.

A hand falls over my mouth and I rear back. "Don't make a sound."

I buck against the stranger's grasp, but he holds me tight, pressed against the length of his body. He is taller than me and much broader. His hand across my mouth muffles my screams.

He pulls me backward down the street, forcing me to stumble to keep up. After dragging me a full city block, he pauses at an intersection. I can feel his torso shifting to look behind. "We're almost there."

I fight against him, digging in my heels to slow us down, but he doesn't relent. His grip on my mouth shifts so that I'm incapable of biting him. His arms tighten across my shoulders, leaving me with little option to fight back.

In the distance, the Withered Ones continue to struggle against each other in the street. They don't stand up. They don't roll off each other. Instead, they lay, one on top of the other and flail, like a fallen infant.

"In here."

The grip on my mouth falls away and the hand across my chest releases me. In the split second that I consider screaming for help, I am thrust into a darkened doorway and fall into blackness.

FOUR

Pain ripples through my palms and knees when I hit the floor. Dust rises up around me, choking out the clean air. I pound on my chest and roll onto my side.

"You'll get used to it," a masculine voice says from behind me. The metallic ring of the lock sliding into place feels foreboding as he steps around me. "Follow me."

"I'm not going anywhere with you," I wheeze, gripped with a dizziness that leaves me temporarily immobile. My arms quiver as I try to push off the ground, but they give out on me.

"That's not the right answer, missy." An arm wraps around my waist and hauls me to my feet. I beat against his grip, but my escape into the streets has left me weakened. The man chuckles and hoists me easily into his arms, ignoring my pathetic rebuff.

I feel suffocated in his embrace, though I'm not sure if the blinding heat is coming from him or me. I stare blurry-eyed at a row of tall grimy windows as we pass. The light is a stark contrast to the darkness surrounding us. I stop counting after we pass the tenth window and realize somehow I have made my way down toward the river where the old warehouses stand.

The sound of my captor's footsteps echo around me as we burrow deep into the building. It feels hollow, enormous in size. Hulking shadows fill the room. The man weaves effortlessly around them as if he has the eyes of a nocturnal feline or a really great memory. I'd bank on the latter.

My head bounces against his chest as he ascends a set of stairs. My eyes droop with heaviness. "You are safe," are the final words that I hear as my body betrays me and my eyes fall closed.

From time to time, I think I hear whispers in the dark. Voices hushed and muffled, but I can't place them. My forehead feels damp, cooler than the rest of my body. I try to turn my head but am held still.

"Don't move. Not yet."

"Who are you?" I taste blood as I swallow. My lower lip splits down the middle and I almost welcome the blood over the lingering cottonmouth taste.

"A friend."

"Yeah? I had a guy tell me that earlier today. Didn't believe him either." My lungs feel on fire as I turn toward a light glowing bright a few feet away. As my nostrils flare, I detect the scent of gas.

A delicate hand presses against my cheek. "You've been ill for several days. It's lucky that Alex found you when he did."

"He didn't find me," I grunt, shoving the girl's hand away from my face. I try to peer through the light to match a face with her voice but it is too brilliant and my eyes are sensitive. "He kidnapped me."

I spy a pursing of her lips just beneath the glow of lamplight. Water splashes nearby as she wrings the cloth out that was on my forehead. "He wouldn't do that. Alex is a decent man."

"Sure. Any girl would be lucky to be snatched off the street by a complete stranger." My side feels unnaturally tight. I place a hand there and feel bandages wrapping my bruised ribs. Thoughts of another healer strike me as I try to steady my breathing. *Cable.*

I'm not well, but I'm a far sight better than I was when he found me. I guess I have that to be thankful for. "Where am I?"

"Our Haven. At least, that's what I like to call it." I can almost see the girl smile as she turns away. The wistfulness in her tone surprises me, though. She sounds young, naïve. "Alex went to fetch you another blanket. I think your fever is starting to break finally. You should have heard Sal and Devon getting into it with Alex over you."

"Why?" I cough and wince as I grip my side.

The girl grabs the gas lantern and moves it away. I blink several times to clear away the lingering effects and finally spy the girl beside me. She is young, perhaps no older than sixteen or seventeen. Her eyes seem kind. I noticed that her fingers are slender as she presses the back of her palm to my forehead.

I raise a hand to push her away and realize the tip of my finger is sore. "I don't remember hurting myself," I mutter as I inspect the slit.

The girl's lips purse as she looks away from me. Her hair falls in greasy white-blonde strands over her face, hiding light dots of freckles along her nose, a much smaller patch than my own. I notice that she sits sideways beside me and roll my head to see a swollen belly pressing against her tight shirt.

"You're pregnant."

She laughs and nods. "And you're observant."

I smirk at her whiplash response. I roll my head away to look up at the ceiling, noticing uneven ceiling tiles held aloft by silver strips. I must be in some sort of office. Surely the ceiling of a factory would be far more vast and littered with exposed piping or sheets of metal roofing. Rain pings off of it from the space beyond the closed door to my right. One glance at it tells me that the door is locked. Figures.

The room I lie in is small, not much larger than the studio apartment I shared with my mother. A couch lines the far wall. Something lumpy and decidedly human in shape is curled up on the cushion. Soft snores rise and fall from the shape.

A darkened window looks out of the room. I can just make out a hint of light and remember being lifted up a flight of metal steps. I've been brought to a room that overlooks the factory below. The fluorescent lights overhead are dead. The only heat in the room comes from a small metal canister with plumes of smoke rising from within.

"Is this your home?" I shift, trying to roll onto my side, but the girl holds me down. She places a pillow beneath my head and lowers a cup of water to my lips. I drink greedily. The cold fluid spills over my lips and down my chin, but I don't care. I feel as if it's the first drink I've had in weeks.

"For now. Alex and Devon have been talking about moving across the river, away from the city. I overheard them talking about the dangers if we stay, but they never say anything openly to me. They all think I'm too young."

Her lips tug into a pout. I start to speak, but a door across the room opens and a man steps through. Even though it was dark when the stranger snatched me off the street, I recognize him from right before I passed out.

"Well," his smile is oddly genuine for a kidnapper, "look who's decided to rejoin the land of the living."

A woman follows behind him. She turns just this side of the door and closes it. "She's awake?"

Her voice sounds clipped and breathy. I shield my eyes from the lantern light to make her out. She stands off to the man's side, her arms wrapped tightly around her ample bosom. Wavy hair sits on top of her head in a bun, curling at her temples. Large red-rimmed glasses sit askew on her nose, magnifying the crow's feet around her aged eyes.

"Finally." The girl offers me a small smile, grabs her cloth and bowl and rises unsteadily to her feet. My captor rushes forward and grabs her arm.

"I'm fine," she reassures him with a smile. He steadies her a moment longer then releases her arm. When she walks toward a cherry wood desk, I notice that she waddles.

The older woman squints at me from behind her bottle cap lenses. "I still don't like it. It's not safe to invite strangers." The woman's chiding voice is one of those nasal tones that remind you of nails on a chalkboard, but a smidgen less annoying. Only just.

"Invite?" My snort turns into a hacking cough that leaves me with a splitting pain in my side. I grimace and hold my bruised ribs. "You're off your rocker if you think I want to be here, lady."

"Lady?" She bristles and adjusts her glasses upon her nose. A chain dangles down from either earpiece. I wouldn't be the least bit surprised to spy a hearing aid or two as well. "My name is Victoria, and I'll thank you kindly if you will address me as such from now on."

My captor dips down before me and smiles. "Don't mind Vicky. She's a prickly one, even on a good day." He offers me his hand in formal greeting, but I don't accept. Finally, he lets it drop. "The name's Alex Thornton. Pilot extraordinaire... well, at least, I was until all of this crap hit the fan!"

I stare at him. He stares back, appearing unfazed by my obvious lack of caring. "Why did you bring me here?"

"You're sick." I turn to look at the pregnant girl as she lowers herself onto a chair against the wall. As she sinks back, I can't help but notice she looks as if she's about to pop.

"So?"

She refocuses on her stomach. "So you needed help. We all need a little help at times."

"I didn't ask for help. I'm just fine on my own." I press on the ground in an attempt to rise. My arms quake and give out on me a second time, spilling me back onto the thin mattress I'm laid out on.

"You were saying?" Alex helps me rise to a seated position against the wall. He presses the back of his hand against my forehead and his smile fades away. "She's still a bit feverish."

"It's better than it was, though," the girl speaks up. At a vicious glare from Victoria, she draws inward and falls silent. I stare at her. No girl this timid will survive in this fallen world. She needs someone to protect her from people far worse than the likes of this old bat.

"I told you time and again that she shouldn't be here." A cold voice calls from the couch. I glance over to spy a man in his mid-forties emerging from the blankets. His hair is receded at the temples and splattered with gray. "She's turning into one of *them*."

Victoria paces back and forth in a stunted line. Two steps left, then shuffles back again. She fumbles with her hands before her, almost like she longs for knitting needles to busy her hands. "I knew this was bad," she moans and pats at the wild strands falling from her poorly constructed bun. "Bad, bad, bad."

"Quiet," Alex commands. He places his hand upon my chest and I smack at him. He ignores me as he presses against my side, splaying his fingers over my bandaged ribs. When he lowers his head to press it against my breast, I whack him hard enough to get his attention.

"I am not one of them."

Alex shrugs and draws back, leaving me in peace. "I think she's right."

"How can you be sure?" the surly man over his shoulder presses. I don't like the look of him. He seems shifty. A real loser that would give me the creeps any day of the week. I glower back at him as he gives me a once over. "Then again, she could be good for something."

"She's not coughing," Alex interrupts as I ball my fists against my lap. "No phlegm in her throat. I don't see any rash or blisters, and she's obviously aware enough to be preparing to smash your nose in, Sal. And for good reason." He turns to look at me. "We aren't like that."

"Sure you're not." I scowl as Sal rolls his eyes. "You're just a bunch of good Christian men looking out for an old lady and a teenage girl. Nothing wrong with that."

Color seeps from Alex's face. His gaze narrows, but he says nothing in response to my biting remark.

"The signs could be hidden," Victoria speaks up as I start to slide to my right. I notice she has inched closer, her fretting mounting with each step. She reminds me of a squirrel, pulsing her bushy tail to show her nervousness. Her beady little eyes don't help her case any.

I push against the floor and right myself fully. "If you think I'm going to sit here and let you people strip search me, you're nuts! Toss me back out on the street if you want. That's where I'd rather be anyway."

"It's too late for that." I turn to see a man enter the room from the door Alex and Victoria emerged from a few moments before. I try to see beyond him, to make a mental map of my location. When the opportune moment strikes, I am out of here and I need to make sure I run in the right direction.

At best guess, I would say the new guy is probably hanging out around his mid-thirties. His skin is dark as night and the top of his head gives evidence to recent hair growth on what I assume was once a shaved scalp. Two rolls of fat appear along the back of his head when he sinks down beside Alex to look at me. "Too much risk now that you know where we are."

"You're worried that I'm going to tell...who, exactly? My best friends out there blowing shit up?" I laugh and shake my head. "I've got no one left to tell, dude."

The young pregnant girl in the corner finds my gaze. "Don't you have anyone out there worried about you?"

"Do you?" I counter.

She looks stricken, and for a moment, I almost feel sorry for my jab, but the moment passes as she turns inward again. I meet the new guy's direct gaze. "Look, I didn't ask to come here. Your boy over there dragged me down the street against my will. All I'm trying to do is get a ride out of here."

"A ride to where?"

I turn to look at Alex. I can almost picture him as a pilot, sitting behind the controls of some jumbo plane, jetting off to Hong Kong or Australia. He has the look and the swagger. Albeit probably a lot less pronounced now. I bet he even rocked the aviators every chance he got. "Anywhere but here."

Alex shakes his head and pushes up to his feet. He runs his hands through his hair and blows out a deep sigh. "There's nothing out there anymore. Trust me, I've seen it."

"You don't know that. There will always be pockets of survivors."

"That's a kid talking for you." The man before me laughs. The whites of his eyes seem brilliant against his dark skin. "This isn't a movie, girl. This is real life, and contrary to what you might like to think, this shit is real. People are dying beyond these walls. Some in ways I don't even want to speak about. You hit the road in your condition and you won't last the night."

"And I will here?"

He smiles. "There's a better chance of it."

"Wow." I turn my head to spit to the side. Blood tints the glob of saliva that lands a few inches from Alex's shoe. "That's really reassuring."

The man rises and walks away, heading toward the door. With his hand upon the handle, he turns back. "You're gonna have to grow up fast, kid. This world is no place for fairy dust and happy thoughts."

When the door closes behind him I bark out a laugh. Alex glances down at me. "Sorry," I smother my laugh as I rely on the wall to hold me upright. "I just think it's funny that he totally referenced Peter Pan when he was trying to be all macho."

There is a twinkle in Alex's eye. "Devon has his moments. They are few and far between, mind you. You just gotta learn how to roll with his moods."

"Is that what you do?"

He grins and dips low, grabbing my arm to help me stand. I follow his lead, only because I don't have the energy left to fight. "All I can promise you for tonight is a place to sleep and a little food in your belly. Tomorrow everyone will decide if you can stay."

"And if I don't want to?"

He eases me down onto a thin sheet-less mattress spread out on the floor not too far from the pregnant girl. She casts a furtive glance in my direction but says nothing as I lay my head back. Alex bends low over me. His hair looks wind-tousled and I wonder if he's been outside again. Maybe to round up his next victim. "You sure you don't have someone out there looking for you, missy?"

I start to speak, to give him a definitive *mind you own business* response but I pause. Cable is out there. Will he come looking for me? Has he already given up and skipped town with his team?

Alex chuckles. "I thought so. A pretty girl like you must have someone that still cares."

I roll my head to the side to watch him walk away, knowing that my hesitation just gave him the upper hand: knowledge.

Annoyed with myself, I roll onto my side and stare at the wall. I hear footsteps from time to time, whispers in a distant space. At one point I'm sure I hear a cry of pain, but it vanishes the instant it arrives.

Victoria's mutterings drive me up the wall, but no one else seems to pay her any mind. They must be used to it. After an hour, I begin to wonder if she's a little bit off. Maybe her dementia is legit or maybe she's starting to change.

At some point, I doze off, despite my efforts to remain alert. I don't trust Devon or Sal. I'm still on the fence about Alex and Victoria. The only one who seems halfway normal is the teenage girl nearby, but she isn't saying anything. Doesn't make a sound. Her silence is a bit unnerving since she was so chatty before. Maybe I really did hurt her feelings.

Remorse floods in as I watch her smooth her hand over her belly. Her smile is filled with expectant love and it makes me ache for that connection. I don't think my mother ever looked at me like that.

"I had a kid once," I say to the ceiling. Startled, she turns to look at me. When she doesn't say anything, I breathe out a sigh and roll onto my side to meet her expectant gaze. "The guy was a real loser, but for a while, he made me feel special. Took me to a movie. Bought me ice cream. Won this ridiculously large teddy bear when the fair came to town. Small stuff that no other guy had done for me before. Guess you could say I fell pretty hard. Stupid really, but it happened."

She shifts to cross her legs before her, draping a blanket over her to ward off the chill on the air. The fire has died down with no one to tend to it. Sal fell back asleep a while ago on the couch, ignoring his fire tending duties. His snores were a welcome change only so that I didn't have to listen to Victoria's rambling.

"His name was Tommy Wainright. Had a mop of the blondest hair you've ever seen and more freckles than a spotted owl." I smile at the moment. "My little boy had his coloring, but he had my eyes and nose."

The girl leans forward and props her elbows on her knees. "What happened to him?"

My smile falters and I glance down at the floor, wondering why I allowed myself to open that door again after so many years. "Found a better home and never looked back."

Her eyes widen. "You gave him up?"

I snort and shake my head, curling my knees in toward my chest. My back curves, allowing me to hug myself into a ball. The stretch in my muscles feels good now that my fever broke. "I didn't give anything up. My mother stepped in and took him from me."

"How could she do that?"

Anger, set on a low simmering these past few years, begins to bubble up within me. "I was fourteen. An unwed and unfit mother. My own mother said she wouldn't lift a finger to take care of someone else's offspring. Can you believe that? She couldn't even call him a child."

My back teeth grind. I take three slow breaths, as familiar as they are necessary. A trick I've learned over the years of living with my mother. "I only got to hold him for a moment," I glance over at her and smile, "but it was the best moment of my life."

She looks sad as she places a protective hand over her belly. "Did you ever look for him?"

"No. I never did. I couldn't. What sort of mother doesn't fight for her child?" The words catch in my throat as I shake my head. "Maybe I was too young. Maybe I would have done a crap job of taking care of him, but I deserved the chance to find out. I deserved a mother who would, at least, have a little faith in me."

She lowers her head. Her eyes cast downward, her lips purse. I can tell that I've made her sad.

"You never told me your name." I draw her back.

"Oh! How silly of me. I'm Evangeline." Her smile pushes aside her sorrow. This sweet girl's sympathy touches me and I'm reminded of the girl I once was before life became a battleground. Maybe she and I share more in common than I first thought. A snap judgment has gone awry. "My friends called me Eva for short."

"Nice name. I'm Avery." My returning smile is tentative but genuine enough. I wish that I could offer more. She seems like a nice girl, but nice girls always end up getting hurt. For her sake, I hope I'm not the one who does it. "When are you due?"

"I don't really know anymore. I've lost count of the days."

"Are you excited?"

She falls silent for several moments, long enough to make me think that she will refuse to answer, but finally she responds. "I've always wanted a boy. Ever since I was a little girl and the neighborhood girls would torment me. They would dip my hair in honey and laugh when the bees would come for me. Boys aren't cruel like girls are..." she trails off and places her hand over her swollen belly button, "but I know they will come take him away from me."

"Who will come?" I push upright and draw my legs under me. I have no way of knowing what time it is or even if it is still night. I feel stronger than I did before, but not by much.

"The soldiers."

I blink, sure that I've heard her wrong. "Why would soldiers take your baby?"

"Experiments, of course. Haven't you heard what's going on?"

Brushing my hair back out of my face, I press my hand to my neck. Still warm but not as bad. "No," I shake my head, feeling the ache that's settled deep into my neck muscles. What I wouldn't do for a good dose of pain meds right about now, I looked for my pill bottle when I awoke earlier, but they were gone. No doubt Alex confiscated them after I arrived. "I've been out of the loop."

The soiled layers of her skirt brush against the floor as she moves toward me. She glances over at Victoria and waits until the older woman's snores begin again. Between the old bat's whistle snores and Sal's foghorn, there's no way I'll get any more sleep tonight.

When Eva is within a couple feet of me, she pauses and tucks her skirt under her legs to seal out the cold rising from the concrete. Even at this height, the cold feels inescapable. "I had a younger sister before I ended up here. Her name was Claire. Sweetest little face you ever saw." Her smile wanes. She clasps her hands in her lap. Strands of hair fall about her face, concealing her from sight. I get the feeling that's exactly what she needs at the moment.

"Mom and dad never planned to have a second child. They called it a miracle, but I think it was an accident. I never really minded that Claire was doted on. I guess a part of me was excited about the idea of my son having someone close to his age."

Tears swim in her eyes as she looks up. She wipes them away and offers me a sad, pained smile. "Before all of this, I used to go pick her up from daycare. I wasn't able to go to school anymore because of my pregnancy, so I offered to be on babysitting duty."

She falls silent for a moment. New tears trail down her cheeks, but she doesn't brush these away. "About two weeks ago I went to pick her up and she was gone."

"Gone?"

Pale, thin fingers fumble at the neckline of her dress. I watch as she grasps a thin chain and draws out a small golden cross. She holds it between her fingers and closes her eyes. "I could see blood seeping out from under the front door of the daycare. It stained the concrete of the first step. I didn't know what to do. I was scared but couldn't just walk away. I pounded on the door for a while, but there was no answer."

She pauses and stares at her upturned hands as if the blood was still on them. "Finally, someone heard me yelling. A neighbor from down the street, I think. He broke the window and unlocked the door."

Her voice catches. "Mrs. Spurneky, the owner, fell out onto my feet when we opened the door. Her throat had been slit from one side to the other. I still remember her eyes..."

I take a deep breath as I fight not to picture my own mother's death. To remember the fear and the sounds. "Then what happened?"

Her fingers quake as she continues. "We found three other bodies. All women I knew as teachers from my sister's class. Each one had a look of shock on their face. Gun shots to the forehead and chest. That neighbor rushed out of there so fast you'd have thought there was a gunman on his tail. I told myself that he was going for help, but no one ever came. He just bailed on me.

"I searched the entire building and couldn't find a single child. I'd guess there were over thirty that went there every day. All gone."

"If no one was there, then how did you know it was soldiers that took your sister?" I ask.

Watery eyes rise to meet mine. Her lower lip trembles. "I found one of their radios. Must have been left behind. I turned it on, but all I heard was static. When I found my way back outside, I noticed a footprint in the edge of the blood trail. I'm sure it was a combat boot."

When she falls silent this time I let it sink in. I don't want to speak anymore. I don't want to hear any more tales of how messed up our world has become. How could a grown man run away and leave a helpless pregnant girl all alone? How could soldiers break into a preschool and steal children? And for what purpose?

"Did that happen around here?"

"No." She wipes at her nose. "I'm from Ohio. After we lost Claire and things started to get weird, my mom sent me to visit my Aunt Edith."

"Did you find her?"

Evangeline shakes her head. "I was on Alex's plane when we were rerouted here. When the stewardesses took off and left me alone, Alex found me. He took me in, kept me safe."

I nod, finally understanding why she is determined to see Alex as a good man. "Well, it looks like he's done right by you so far."

She offers me a tiny smile. "I should probably get some rest."

"Yeah." I lie down as she crawls back to her bed. It seems like the easier option for her rather than standing. I listen as she settles down. It only takes a few moments before her breathing grows slow and steady.

I glance toward the door, the only exit that I've discovered since arriving. Maybe I could pick the lock without anyone hearing, and maybe I could sneak out onto the street and find my bearings, but not yet. As desperate as I am to leave, I also have to be smart about it. The only reason Alex got the better of me was because I was weak and vulnerable from illness. I won't make that same mistake again.

FIVE

I miss the sun. Miss its warmth and false cheer. I miss how it chases away the shadows and almost makes me forget all of the darkness around me.

For three days, I have been stuck here. Three long, endless days without any hint from the outside world.

Despite my prolonged captivity, my relationship with Evangeline has bloomed, far more than I should have allowed. Her laughter is soft, her humor sweet and innocent. For a girl who has obviously had a rough go of things recently, her sunny disposition seems like a precious trait. One that I could probably use a bit more of, if I were honest with myself.

As the days passed, I found myself protecting her from Victoria's barbs. Eva would always brush it off, claiming that Victoria didn't really mean it, but I know better. I've met women like her. Women who get their jollies by lording over younger women, pointing out their faults with the express purpose of making themselves feel lofty, still important.

During one of my chats with Eva over a lukewarm pot of bland-tasting soup, I discovered that old Vicky is a retired high school science teacher. My initial impression of her was spot on. She is rude, harsh and a no-nonsense sort of person whose greatest weakness is having no clue that no one wants her around. I still haven't figured out how she fits into the group...or even how the group was formed to begin with.

Salvador Jenkins has been unofficially dubbed "Sleazy Sal" in my books. One of those guys you know is trying to work out a situation to benefit themselves. Eva told me he used to be a used car salesman. I wonder why that doesn't surprise me.

I watch Sal like a hawk when he comes near Eva. I don't like the way he watches her as she moves. It's not an entirely lustful gaze, but it's certainly an inappropriate one for a girl her age and in her condition.

Devon is a prick. No way around that fact. He rubbed me the wrong way my first day here and has been grating my nerves ever since. Whenever Alex is around, he manages to tone down Devon's strong personality, but if I stick around long enough, we are gonna clash hard.

Alex is a wild card. One that I'm still trying to decipher.

Other than Evangeline, I suppose I trust Alex most. Though he's a bit cocky, he seems decent enough. He cares for Eva. I've watched how he tries to help her whenever he can, bearing her burden of chores without complaint.

A soft moan draws me out of my musings. I turn to look at Eva, rising to go to her side, but she motions me back. "I'm fine. Really."

That's the third time she's said those exact words in the last thirty minutes. Each time she does, it doesn't help to convince me. The signs of her progressing labor increase. The pains started nearly three hours ago, but she told no one. Only bit her lip and forced a smile. She may be sweet, but that girl's got iron in her, too.

I admire her. In spite of her silent throes of agony, she remains a hard worker. Eva sits quietly in the corner of the office, peeling carrots with a glorified butter knife. Victoria sits nearby, plunging her fingernails into a potato to dig out the eyes that have begun to grow. I'm not really sure where the provisions came from, especially ones that are moderately fresh. Alex must have gone on another supply run.

I've learned not to ask questions that I have no hope of getting an answer to. That doesn't mean I'm unobservant, though. I watch and wait, learning my companions' intentions.

None of the members are related. None seems to have known each other prior to the week before and yet here they are. Every time I try to speak to Eva about it she goes tight-lipped, and I'm beginning to wonder if she wasn't the only stray Alex picked up at the airport.

Their accents don't seem to fit with the Midwest. Alex's lack of any discernible accent makes sense, I guess, because he's a pilot. I'd peg him as a California guy, myself. Eva has a bit of a northern clip to her words that would match up fairly well with her Ohio lineage, but I'd bet tonight's dinner that one of her parents was from Boston. Only Devon Meeder, the Peter Pan quoting guy, sounds Midwestern. He fits right in.

It's my guess that he's the one who brought everyone here to this factory. He seems to have an understanding of the area. The real question is why he chooses to linger when he should be running. My gut tells me there is something here in the city that calls to him. I'd love to find out what that something is.

Glancing over at Eva, I watch as her fingers curl into her palms. Her breathing hitches, her eyes close as she presses back into the wall. I capture Alex's knowing gaze. He says nothing, though he is just as aware of her condition as I am. Why else would he have joined in with the peeling party? That's girls' work, according to Sal.

Casting a cautious glance at the closed door to my left, I hear voices on the other side. Devon and Sal are within. In the three days since I have been here, I have hardly glimpsed into that room. They are hiding something. Of that I am sure.

There was never any official vote for me to join the group. No welcome party or hugs all around. I stayed, biding my time. Sooner or later, the men will have to leave. When they do, I've already decided that I'm getting Eva out of here. Victoria is on her own for all I care!

With each day, I grow stronger. My ribs ache less. My fever has been gone for three days and my stamina returns. If it comes down to a fight, I stand a good chance against Sal and Victoria. Devon, though obviously a once-polished businessman, looks like he's spent his fair share of time on the streets. He has the swagger and the large gold nugget bling on his fingers to prove it. The one kicker is Alex. I'm just not sure which way he would sway.

Sooner or later, the group will be forced to move on. The food supply must be running thin. The last of the vegetables at Victoria's feet have begun to wilt. Clean water has grown scarce. We've taken to melting some of the icicles that formed overnight in a pot near the corner.

Burst water pipes have left the drinking water in danger of contamination. I'm not nearly thirsty enough to risk it, but I'd be happy to let Sal test it for me.

A hiss of breath returns my attention to Eva. I tense, poised to rush to her side, but she offers me a pained smile, shaking her head again. I ease back and count the seconds in my head. Her contractions are only five minutes apart now.

"Aren't you done yet, girl?"

I glance up to see Victoria hovering over Eva like a mother hen, too dense to see what is right in front of her thick lenses. "You'd think we had plenty of gas to spare for cooking," she clucks, jutting her chin toward the gas lantern sputtering near her feet. A small pot of water struggles to boil.

I rise to go to Eva's side, but Alex beats me to it. "Ease off, Vicky. She's not feeling well."

Victoria pushes her glasses back up her nose and shoves aside the frizzy strands of hair falling into her eyes. Her stern gaze narrows on Eva's quivering lip. "Is she sick? Did that blasted girl give her something?"

"I've got a name, you know?" I toss my peeled onion into the sack at my feet and rise.

Alex raises a hand to motion that I remain back. I begrudgingly stay put, but not without shooting the old bat a lethal glare first. "Why don't I finish up for you, Eva, huh? You need to get some rest."

"Yes." She nods and hands him the bunch of carrots. As he takes it from her grasp I realize blood stains her palms, her nail beds painted crimson. I grit my teeth at the evidence of her torment. She is young, scared, and practically alone, and I won't stand by and watch Victoria poking and prodding her.

"Coddling won't fix a lazy child." Victoria tsks and stirs the soup. "Back in my day—"

"Shut her up, Alex, or I will!" I wrap my arm around Eva, helping her make her way across the room, past Victoria's pot of murky water soup. A chicken-based stock, or so Alex claims. It doesn't smell like any chicken I've ever had before.

Eva's steps are slow and cautious. I glance back at Alex over my shoulder. His posture is rigid, his elbows digging into his thighs as he leans over and steeples his hands before his mouth, whispering to Victoria. He'd better be putting her in her place.

Soon everyone will know that Eva's in labor. Then the screaming will start. I need to know if Alex is with me on this.

What will happen if he's not? Will Devon gag Eva and force her to endure her child's birth in silence? He is already wound tighter than a spring. He paces every time he enters the room like an animal, wild and caged. His own inner demons have begun to eat at him. Sooner or later, he will snap. I don't want Eva anywhere near him when that happens.

"Won't be long now," I whisper in her ear as I ease her to the floor. I gave her my thin mattress during the night to try to help ease the ache in her back. It didn't help much, but it's all I could do.

"We should tell Devon," Eva says, her head lolling to the side. I mop her brow with the back of my hand. Sweat clings to her rosy cheeks. Her eyes are glossy, her lips pale.

"No." I shake my head. "Let Alex take care of him while I look after you."

A ghost of a smile touches her lips as she closes her eyes. "I'm glad you're here."

My throat clenches as she closes her eyes. I clasp her hand in mine, allowing her to rest for the remaining two minutes she has left before the pain builds once more.

All too soon, her breath hitches and her fingers clamp down on my hand. I ride through the pain with her, drawing inward to ignore the loss of circulation. I vow, no matter what, I will stay by her side as my mother never did for me.

"That's it," I whisper as her grip slowly loosens. A breath of pain slips past her lips as her body relaxes once more.

"Laziness, that's what it is." I look up to see Victoria pacing nearby. Her hands flutter before her, as they have been prone to do of late. Her gaze seems unfocused, her recent bout of insomnia starting to take its toll on her.

"Do you ever shut up?" The woman just never stops.

"Nothing wrong with stating a fact, dear," she responds with a syrupy sweet tone that makes me want to throttle her. "The truth never hurt anyone."

"It will when I rearrange your face," I mutter under my breath, eliciting a soft chuckle from Eva. I wink at her and then watch as Alex frowns and crosses to exit through the door. I wait to hear the telltale click of the lock, but it doesn't come. His preoccupation was the first mistake I've seen him make.

"I'll be right back." I pat Eva's hand and rise, heading straight after him.

"Wait!" Victoria shouts, bustling up behind me. "Where are you going?"

"In there."

"You can't! You're not permitted." Her hand feels cold and wet when it lands upon my arm. The gas burner isn't wasted on scrubbing water for the vegetables.

"Don't touch me." I shove her off and place my hand on the doorknob to open it but jump back when Devon appears in the doorway, his broad frame filling the space.

"What's going on out here?" His gaze falls on me, standing less than a palm's width from his chest. "Well?"

I step back, not the least bit intimidated by him, but his limited bathing opportunities have left him with a funky smell. "Eva is going to need supplies. It's time."

His jaw tightens as he looks beyond me to see Eva curled up in the corner. A soft moan escapes her and another wave of pain has begun to build. "No. We can't risk it. Sal said he saw men on the streets below. Those gangs have moved into the area. If they find out we are here, we're all done for."

From the corner of my eye, I see Victoria nodding in agreement. His callous words leave a bitter tang in my mouth as I step forward once more. "Eva is about to have a baby and that means things are going to get pretty nasty around here. Blood. Slime. And God knows what else is going to be coming. I don't have a clue how to deliver a baby, and I'm betting you don't either. The least we can do is to find some clean towels, boil more water, scavenge blankets, diapers, food, and, heck, even a doctor if we can find one."

Devon's eyes narrow. "Those are all luxuries that we can no longer afford."

"Luxuries?" My anger tips dangerously close to the edge. My pulse pounds in my ears as I rise up to meet him as close to eye level as my shorter height allows. "That baby and Eva may die without them."

When his shoulders begin to rise into a shrug I snap. I slam my fist into his jaw hard enough to crack my knuckle. Pain radiates through my hand.

"You bitch!" He staggers back, his shoulder taking the brunt of the doorframe.

His livid glare doesn't still my anger as I jab him in the chest. "Have you no empathy? No emotion? How can you call yourself any better than the beasts that walk these streets if you feel nothing for that poor girl? A girl who you're supposed to protect!"

"There's no need to overreact—" Victoria says, but cuts off when I turn to glare at her.

"Overreact? You're too blind to even notice that she's been in labor for hours! All you care about are your stupid potatoes." I'm sure that my shouts can be heard to the far reaches of the building, but I don't care. Maybe someone with some common sense might hear me and come to our aid.

I round on Sal as he steps into the doorway behind Devon. His frame is smaller, his shoulders not nearly so broad or strong. He stands a couple of inches taller than me, and in the gap, I see that he is not alone. Alex follows my gaze as I shift past him to the two people sitting on the floor off to the side.

"Who the hell is that?" I storm forward, brushing Sal aside.

Sal recovers and shoves the paunch of his stomach into me, forcing me to back away. Alex quickly steps up behind him and together they walk me backward so they can close the door. "None of your concern."

"There is a man and woman in there. I saw them." Their faces were pale, their eyes wide with terror. They looked filthy, hair matted and clothes several days worn. I glimpsed enough in that brief moment to know that they are not here by choice.

Devon tugs on his shirt, visibly pulling himself together. His shoulders square as he pushes back off from the wall. Alex gives him a brief nod and I see his countenance change. Gone are the laugh lines I've come to know when Alex tells stories of distant places to Eva late at night. Gone is the friendly smile. He is all business now.

I cross my arms over my chest and scowl, standing my ground. Victoria begins her staccato pacing and I have to force myself not to scream at her. "I want to know what is going on in that room."

Devon exchanges a loaded glance with Alex, who nods and approaches, taking the lead. "Those people in there are no one. Just a couple of stragglers we picked up a couple days before you came. They were sick so we kept them separated. That's all."

"They didn't look sick. They looked terrified," I counter.

"Looks can be deceiving," Devon says in a deep baritone voice. I watch his muscles flex as he crosses his arms over his chest to match my combative stance. He's a heck of a lot more imposing in this position. I was right to not underestimate him.

That's when I notice a dot of blood on the inner flesh of the crook of his arm for the first time. It is barely noticeable against his dark skin, but the shine of moisture catches in the light.

"Oh, God." I step back, sickened as the truth sinks in. "You're no better than those people on the streets!"

Alex holds up his hands as I begin to back away. The bruising scattered along his forearm is suddenly a stark contrast from the pale flesh of his inner arm. "Now hold on just a minute. It's not what you think."

"No?" Hysteria rises in my voice. "You gonna stand there and tell me that you're not stealing blood from them? That you haven't created your own mini blood bank? How did you even know to do that? Was it Eva's radio? Were you spying on the military?"

Devon stiffens as Victoria's head snaps around. "You never told me that's why those people were in there."

"Oh, come off it, Victoria." I yank at my hair, feeling as if madness is only a step ahead of me. "Are you really that dense? Did you not hear their screams or did you just not want to?"

She steps back, her face blanching at my attack. Her hand flutters at her throat before she turns and sinks onto a chair, beginning to rock slowly.

"You all act like you have a freakin' clue what is happening out there, but the truth is, you don't. None of us do."

"Isn't that the point?" I turn to look at Alex. "We don't know how this thing spreads. We don't know how to stop it or protect ourselves against it. So we do what we can with the little knowledge we possess."

"That message was cryptic. You don't even know what or if blood has anything to do with a cure or prevention. The message was cut off before they could say why or even how it could be used. How can you allow yourselves to jump to such extremes without the facts to back it up?"

"Because we want to live," Sal says without emotion.

"And what about them?" I point to the closed door. "Don't they have that same right?" I retreat as Devon and Sal approach, shifting backward until my spine is pressed against the door on the opposite side of the room. The one door that leads to the stairs and the factory beyond. The one Victoria came through only a short while ago with her bucket of vegetables. *Please let it still be unlocked. That rotten woman has a terrible memory.*

As Devon and Victoria's voices begin to rise in a dance of angry accusations, I grip the door handle and test it. I nearly cry in relief when it gives way.

"Enough!" Alex's shout echoes off the walls. Eva moans and curls in on herself. My grip on the door wavers at the sound of her pain. *I can't just leave her with these people.*

"Now that I have your attention," Alex says, smoothing his hair back from his face, "I think it's time we all had a chat about reality."

He motions for me to move away from the door and sit down. The urge to throw open the door and bolt is so strong I nearly give in, but another moan rises from Eva. Her back arches and I know that I have no choice. I can't turn my back on her. If I do, she's as good as dead.

I sink down beside her, placing a hand on her arm. The muscles in her neck cord, her teeth gritted against the pain. Her screams build deep within in her throat. It's only a matter of time before she lets go.

"I realize this may come as a bit of a shock to you," Alex begins, waiting for me to turn and look at him, "but bad things happen to good people, including those two in that room. Reality tells us that not everyone is going to survive. I, for one, am not willing to just roll over and die. Are you?"

He stares at me long and hard, but I fight to show no emotion beyond the flaring of my nostrils in repressed anger. Devon nods in agreement when Alex glances at him, and for the first time, I realize that I was mistaken. Devon isn't the one in charge. Alex is.

When the pilot turns to look at Victoria I almost feel sorry for the ashen woman. She looks faint and trembly. I can almost see the moral dilemma waging in her eyes, but she cowers under Alex's stern gaze and nods.

"What we do is for the good of the group. You all need food and water. A safe place to sleep. How can we provide that for you if we become infected? If Eva needs blood and we can't give it to her, then what? We just let her die because we didn't prepare?"

Bile rises in my throat at the sound of Alex's justification. "You think that makes it okay?"

"Yes." I flinch as Devon closes the gap between us. His button down dress shirt is soiled and the pocket torn away. His pants are filthy, as if he has been rolling in the mud. I can't help but wonder what he's been up to behind that closed door. "You know those gangs are stealing blood. Why? Because it's the only way to survive. If that's what it takes, then so be it. I can sleep at night knowing that I did what it took."

"We aren't stealing their blood, Avery," Alex says in a softer tone. "We're borrowing it."

"Borrow?" I snort and shake my head. "How exactly are you planning on giving back to those people?"

"By allowing them to live."

The cold insensitivity of his statement sends chills down my spine. "And Eva? What if she has complications beyond her need for blood? Will you just let her die for the betterment of everyone?"

Alex's Adam's apple bobs as Devon looks to him with indecision. "She is part of the group."

"So are they." I point toward the closed door.

"No. They are outsiders."

I am rocked by Alex's blatant callousness. Maybe I didn't know him as well as I thought. I rise to my feet. "So am I."

"Not anymore."

"Why not?" I press, stepping forward. "Isn't that why you brought me here? To use me as a blood donor, too?"

His hesitation doesn't go unnoticed by everyone in the room. Even Eva has rolled onto her side to listen as she pants between contractions. I want to go to her, to ease her fears, but this needs to be dealt with.

"I'm right, aren't I? You grabbed me off the street in the hopes that I could be a match for someone here." I whirl around, looking each person in the eye. "Well, who is it then? I must be a match otherwise, I wouldn't be here right now."

Alex averts his gaze. Devon remains stony faced. Victoria looks bewildered. A look of hurt betrayal tints her grimace. She may be an idiot but at least, of this crime, she's innocent.

"You're a universal donor," Sal speaks up from the back of the room where he lounges against the wall.

"I see." Lifting my finger, I run my thumb over the healing slit that I noticed when I first woke. "You tested my blood while I was unconscious. Clever. I'll give you that much."

"It's not like that—" Alex starts but falters under my damning glare.

"Oh, no." I shake my head, my hands quaking at my sides. My pulse beats like a bass drum in my ears as I turn on him. "It's *exactly* like that."

Devon bears his teeth as he towers over me. I don't back down. Alex pushes Devon aside with far more ease than I would have liked and steps between us. "Yes, you're useful, dammit, but that's not why I kept you."

"Then why?" I press into his face, forcing him to look at me as he spins his lies. Although I'm several inches shorter than him, he reacts instantly to the animalistic growl that bursts from my throat as he tries to grab my hand. I whip my hand away and crack it across his cheek hard enough to make my palm sting.

A vein pulses down his forehead as he steps back. A red patch grows along his cheek. I wait for the return hit, preparing myself for the pain, but he doesn't move. Doesn't speak. After a moment of tense silence, his hardened gaze softens and the lines along his forehead disappear. His shoulders sag as his head dips low. "Because you remind me of someone. Someone I once cared very much for," he whispers.

Devon glances over at him. His displeasure is clearly written in the tensing of his stance. He starts to speak when a terrible howl from behind me makes my heart plummet into my stomach. I whip around to find Eva curled tightly into a ball, her mouth gaped open as tears spill from her eyes.

"What's wrong with her?" Victoria shouts, covering her ears against Eva's shrieks.

Glancing down at the mattress, my throat clenches at the sight of a small trickle of blood seeping out from beneath the folds of her dress. "Oh, God! She's hemorrhaging."

"What do we do, Avery?"

I cast an incredulous look at Alex. "Why the hell are you asking me? I don't have a clue!"

Eva's screams mount as she thrashes, curling inward then arching back. Her stomach heaved and sweat begins to dampen her hair.

"But you've done this before. Eva told me about your kid."

I press my palm to my forehead, trying to think around Eva's screams. "I was in a hospital with people who knew what the hell they were doing!"

From the corner of my eye, I see Devon backing away. Sal slouches against the far wall, looking indifferent to the scene before him.

"Victoria?" The older woman glances at me as I shout her name to be heard. "You're the group know-it-all. What do we do?"

She presses a hand to her hair, patting it as if lost in thought. She looks down at Eva but says nothing. Does nothing. She just shakes her head and clams up.

"God!" I yell and rush toward Eva's side. "You are all useless!"

I grab my blanket and roll it up beneath Eva's head. Her eyes clench tight, lost to the pain. "Someone get me something for her to bite on so she doesn't sever her own tongue."

Alex is the only one to react. He rushes toward a stack of boxes and begins digging, tossing packing peanuts and bits of tape over the side. Victoria watches from a distance as I brush Eva's hair back from her face. She is pale. Blood has begun to slowly stain through the front of her dress.

"That's a lot of blood," Alex says as he drops beside me. He hands over a long thick wooden stick and I realize it's a snapped broom handle.

"Something's wrong." I gently pry open Eva's mouth between screams and place the handle between her teeth. "Bite down on this. It will help."

Her head moves, but I'm not sure she's coherent. Grabbing the end of her skirts, I begin tearing them, casting them aside. Blood coats my hands as I ease her legs apart. My stomach lurches at the sight, but I force myself to remain focused. Devon backs away, his head shaking rapidly as he fumbles back over a stack of crates that fall far too close to Eva's head for comfort.

"Leave," I shout, pointing a bloody finger back toward the room with the cowering couple. Devon rises and rushes on the door.

"Do you have any needles?" I ask Alex. "Tubing? Something to start an IV so I can transfer blood to her?"

Alex shakes his head. "Nothing. Someone tripped over the one line we had left and snapped the needle. Sal's doing, I'd say. That's why I went in there to check. I knew Eva might need it sooner or later. We've been collecting blood in bowls and trying to cover them with pieces of cardboard, but even that's useless now."

My hands clench against Eva's knees as I bite my tongue at their stupidity. They aren't even preserving the blood they are stealing!

Eva moans and rocks to the side, her knees trapping my hand. A steady trickle escapes between her legs. "Someone throw me a towel."

From the corner of my eye, I glimpse Sal a moment before the door closes behind him. Victoria begins her frantic pacing, right past a small stack of clean cloths. I watch her, waiting for her to hand them to me, but she doesn't. The squeaking of her shoes drives me over the edge.

"Get out!" She jumps at my scream, her eyes wide behind her red-rimmed glasses. "If you aren't going to help then get the hell out of here so I can think."

Victoria sniffs indignantly, hesitates as if she might actually consider helping, then hurries toward the door.

"Coward," Alex mutters under his breath beside me.

As I scoot closer blood soaks into my pant legs, warm and sticky. "She's a science teacher. She must know how to stop this bleeding. She's dissected animals, for pete's sake!"

"She's scared."

"I don't give a shit, Alex. Go in there and force her to focus. Eva's life depends on it."

I wipe my hands on my shirt and prepare to try to search for the baby's head but pause when I feel him staring at me. "What?"

"How are we going to do this?"

I've been asking myself that same thing over and over since I first noticed Eva's contractions. "I don't know, but we are going to. Somehow. I won't let her die."

SIX

Exhaustion weighs down on me as I fight to keep Eva with us. My knees bruise from kneeling on the floor. The sound of her screams makes my ears ring. The worst part is not knowing if it's from labor pains or something worse, something internal. My hands tremble as I sink back, pressing my bloodied hands against my thigh as I use my arm to wipe my brow.

I'm worried about how much blood she has lost. Eva is barely conscious and she hasn't begun to push yet.

The hairs on Alex's arms are matted with blood. The shirt in his hand pressed against Eva to slow the bleeding has begun to soak through. We ran out of towels fifteen minutes ago and began using clothes. Alex gave the shirt off his own back to help. It's not sterile, but if we don't do something she's going to bleed out and it won't matter.

"She's not going to make it, is she?" Alex says beside me. It is not really a question and we both know it. Without help, Eva will not last much longer.

The towel I wipe my hands with is soaked through and just as sticky as my hands. Victoria finally got her head out of her backside and managed to scrounge up some minor supplies from the warehouse. A small first aid kit, a couple moving pads that are stained with oil, a mop bucket to hold water to clean our hands in and some unused mop heads to soak up some of the mess on the floor.

As Alex pulls his shirt away, I spread Eva's legs and cry out. The crown of the baby's head is within sight. At least, I think that's what it is. The idea of grasping this tiny life makes me nauseous, but I'm the only chance Eva's baby has. But what happens after that? What if we can't stop the bleeding? How do we care for the baby if Eva dies? What if... I have a million of those questions going through my mind right now.

Pushing back off my knees, I rise. Eva's head has rolled to the side. She stares blankly at the wall. "I'm going for help."

"No." Alex struggles to rise. His own legs must be suffering from the same pain that mine are.

"She's going to die. We both know it, Alex. You have to let me try to find help."

He shakes his head. "Sal could go. Or Devon. I can't let you be the one to go. I have no clue what I'm doing here."

I reach out and grab his arm, digging my cracked nails into his flesh just enough to get his rising panic to subside. "You told me earlier that Eva is part of your group. That she is yours to take care of. I'm asking that you let me help you do that."

He glances back down at Evangeline. "We both know Sal and Devon don't care about her like we do. If you want her to make it you have to let me go."

I realize, staring at him now, just how deep the extent of his feelings of responsibility for her goes. He has proven that he is willing to do whatever it takes to protect his own, even stealing blood from an outsider. Now I need to lean heavily on that need if Eva has any chance.

"She's only sixteen, Alex. Can you really live with yourself if she dies on your watch?"

He closes his eyes and shakes his head. "What if something happens to you? What if someone follows you?"

I bite on my lower lip as I look around for a solution that will placate him. *So close.*

And then I remember Eva's story. "Do you still have the radio Eva brought with her?"

"Sure." He motions toward the closed door. "We've been monitoring the military's movements with it."

"Okay. If anything happens to me, if I don't come back, I will find a way to contact you. Keep it with you, no matter what." The moment his shoulders sag in reluctant defeat, I race for the door, shoving Victoria aside. I barely have time to feel vindicated when I hear her topple to the floor as I race down the metal stairs and through the vast warehouse.

The first time I came through this darkened maze I had no real idea of how large the factory was. Shadows rise up before me just seconds before I slam into a piece of machinery and bounce off. Battered and bruised, but fueled by a new round of screaming from behind me, I rush past the endless row of windows in search of a door.

Years of disuse and grime smudge the glass, affording only a dim light to see by. The sun looks to be on the rise and I'm desperate to feel its warmth on my skin again.

The blustery cold steals my breath away as I throw open the door. The wind tugs the handle from my hands and it bangs loudly against the brick wall. I squint against the brilliant dawn, shielding my face until my eyes have a chance to adjust. I don't recognize any of my surroundings. In the distance, I can see the arch gleaming like glass against the brightening sky. A bank of storm clouds moves off to the East leaving the city in temporary sunlight.

Without thinking, I sprint down the road, weaving around potholes and abandoned cars. Graffiti decorates the brick walls around me. Some of the roofs have caved in, charred and left to ruin by the fires. Bullet holes scatter the streets, in car doors, through glass windows and mailboxes.

I skirt the opposite sidewalk to avoid a burst fire hydrant that gushes water high into the air. A Jeep is jacked up on the hydrant, its alarm blaring and lights flashing. There is no one inside, but I spy a puddle of blood beneath the open door as I jog past.

Before all of this happened, I would never have walked down these streets, even in broad daylight. Every city has its places that you don't go alone. This was one of them. The other lies across the river, my path of escape should I ever make it out of here.

I hold the stitch in my side, counting the slaps of my blood stained shoes against the pavement as I run in spite of the pain in my ribs. I grow warm beneath my scavenged hoodie and pull it over my head, tying it around my waist. The cold air feels amazing against my exposed skin, cooling the heat trapped within the black tank that I wear beneath.

After several minutes, the arch begins to rise into the sky and I discern shops dotted along the street, interspersed with offices and entrances to condos. I race around a corner and come up short.

Less than a block away, people mill about. The stench wafts my way and I'm forced to double over, clutching my nose and mouth. The scent of rotting flesh, urine, and feces hit me like a wrecking ball. Death lives here.

I rise to my full height and then up onto my toes as I spy a familiar sign. Nearly thirty Withered Ones stand between me and a pharmacy on the corner two blocks away. It is small but should have something that I can use to help Eva.

Glancing down the street, I look for a way around the Moaners, but the path is blocked by a pileup of cars. It's either go straight through, or add a few extra blocks to my journey. Time is not on my side.

"You've got this," I whisper to myself as their raspy moans echo down the alley toward me. "Nothing to it."

I walk cautiously forward, watching those closest to me. A girl wearing a Washington University sweatshirt slams into a wall ten feet in front of me. She stumbles back and slams again, repeating the action with maddening persistence. The flesh of her forehead clings to the trail of blood she has left on the wall. Her shattered nose gushes, the bone, and cartilage concaved into her face. The bones of her right cheek splinter, poking through her flesh.

Clutching my stomach, I step past her and try to ignore the squelching sounds each time she hits the wall. I come upon a man of Asian descent wearing a business suit. Shattered metal-framed glasses slide down his nose as he bounces off the trunk of a car and veers into my path. I swallow my scream as I duck to miss his flailing arm. The scent of gasoline is strong on him as he passes.

I clutch my head with trembling hands as I remain crouched. Three more shuffle past me. One has a huge gouge out of her leg. Teeth marks have torn through muscle and scored bone and I wonder if a dog got a hold of her. As soon as my immediate path is clear, I rise and come face to face with three men less than eight steps before me. Their eyes are vacant, unseeing. The one on the right is missing an ear. A gaping wound oozes with blood, trailing down his neck and soiling his white suit coat. The nails on his right hand have been torn away, leaving flies to swarm the fleshy beds of his fingers.

The second man's cheeks are shredded. Between strips of flesh, broken teeth jut upright like shark's teeth. His neck looks like ground meat. The stench surrounding him nearly debilitates me. My eyes water as I raise my shirt to cover my mouth and nose, only sucking in tiny, necessary breaths.

The third man is covered in muck, his hair and every inch of his body is coated in bits of old garbage, soot, and refuse. His clothes are torn and bloodied. He walks with a pronounced limp, but he appears to have fared better than most.

The three Withered Ones seem to keep pace with each other walking side by side, though they show no conscious thought in doing so. I duck beneath the raised arm of the limping man on the right only to find myself face to face with another small group.

My throat clenches as I realize I've burrowed into the heart of death central. "Just breathe and keep moving," I whisper to myself as I crawl forward on my hands and knees. I stifle my cries as I bounce between legs. Their fingers claw through my hair, tugging me back as they continue on their mindless walk. My shoulders grow slick with gore. I pause and flick a patch of skin off my shoulder and shake out my hair. Bits of fingernails fall from my matted curls.

"Oh, shit." I allow only small gulps of breath as I fight to still my rising panic. The air tastes foul on my tongue.

"Almost through," I try to reassure myself as the legs before me begin to dwindle.

I cry out as a piece of glass on the street slices my palm. I falter to the right, slam into the leg of a man, and buckle under the weight of him falling on top of me. I scream and flail, writhing to be free in spite of the shattered glass beneath me.

Blood splatters my face and enters my mouth as I beat against the man. He doesn't fight back, doesn't yell or show any sign of pain from my attack. His arms and legs continue to move as if he were still walking.

Slowly, I crawl out from under him and drag myself up onto the curb and press back against the wall. I stare at the Moaner, horrified to find most of his left side has been torn away.

I roll to my side and hurl as bits of what looks like ground beef slide off my sleeve. I wrench my hand away. As I empty my stomach onto the sidewalk, I realize that the scent is actually an improvement.

Wiping my mouth clean, I'm forced to gasp for breath and my stomach instantly begins to churn anew. I long for a fresh country breeze instead of this vile, stench-ridden street. I beat at my arm, removing any signs of that man from me before I pull my legs into my chest.

My fingers tremble as I hold myself, watching the Moaners walking side by side. I bury my head in my arms and count slowly to 100. I listen to their stunted steps until they move on, like a herd without direction.

Slowly the air begins to clear and I raise my head. I wipe tears from my face and glance toward the pharmacy. It's only a block away. Determined to save Eva, I force myself to my feet and scan the surrounding streets, peering around the corner for any sign of more Withered Ones. I spot two females at the end of the block to my right and four more to my left, but the path directly to the pharmacy is clear.

"Eva needs me." I gather what few shreds of courage I have left and sprint toward the glass doors of the shop. I slip several times in dark puddles and pray that it isn't urine. Less than a minute later I hit the front door and bounce off, my footing unsteady in the collection of glass on the doorstep.

I peer into the darkened shop and feel the hairs on the back of my neck rise. There is a moan from within.

I turn and press back against the wall, swearing under my breath. "Really? Does someone have me on their 'let's fuck with Avery' radar today? Scenes like this in horror movies never turn out well."

The sun has risen over the top of the nearest building, the heat helping to ward off some of the biting cold. The wind whips mercilessly down the city streets, chilling me as it seeps through my bloodied clothes. "At least it's not nighttime," I mutter to myself, though walking into a pitch black building makes this fact pretty much irrelevant.

Glass crunches beneath my shoes as I duck and slip through the empty-framed front doors. The open sign jangles against the door as I reach for a shopping basket to carry my items in. I freeze and wait for the metallic clanking to cease, holding my breath. I hear nothing, but the knowledge that I'm not alone makes me cautious. There is, at least, one of them in here. Most likely more.

After moving only a few feet into the store, the amount of visible light diminishes drastically. I rise onto my toes, squinting against the dark in an attempt to see the aisle signs. "I don't even know what I'm looking for," I mutter under my breath.

The shelves are ransacked, much of their contents either stolen or left scattered on the floor. I force myself to tiptoe past the shampoo and conditioner aisle though I would dearly love to grab a few bottles for later. I pass a row of sunscreen, cold medicines, canes, and those little round pillows people sit on after surgeries. When I hit the vitamin aisle I stare long and hard into the shadows to make sure nothing is moving before darting down to find prenatal vitamins. I snatch boxes of gauze, tape, hydrogen peroxide, and pads to help with the clean-up.

I snag a box of gloves and am heading to find baby formula when I hear it. Sluggish footsteps. I press back against the shelf and listen, trying to drown out the sound of my racing heart as I try to decide where the steps are coming from.

My head whips around at the sound of a loud crash, followed by the cascade of cans falling. It must have hit a display. Crouching low, I inch toward the back of the aisle and peer out. The light spilling in from the windows on the far side is blinding, making it hard to see anything in the shadows. Something hits my foot and I clamp my hand over my mouth to still my cries.

I hear thrashing and more cans spiraling across the floor. I reach down and grab the can at my feet and hold it upright. "Of course, it would be baby formula!"

If Eva is too weak to push without help during the delivery, there's no way she will be strong enough to feed her baby. I don't have a choice. Tucking the shopping basket beneath my arm, I creep forward in the dark, collecting any can I find in my path. I reach for one final can, praying that I have collected enough when a hand seizes mine.

It is unnaturally cold, the skin loose and sagging. I scream and buck as fingers curl around my wrist, locking down. The rasping moan grows louder and I feel myself being tugged forward.

"Get off of me!" I beat the hand, scratching and clawing, yanking with all my might. That's when I smell it: a new scent of sweat over the scent of death.

I hear a footstep behind me a second before a bag is pulled over my head and I'm yanked to my feet. The gruesome grasp releases me. I hear a gunshot nearby as something sharp stabs into my upper arm and my protests grow weak.

"No." My head swims and my eyes flutter closed. "Eva needs me..."

My wrists are pinched together in cuffs as I am hauled to my feet. I see dots of light through the dark hood but trip over my basket and nearly face plant when my legs don't react as fast as I need them to.

"Easy with this one. We need her unharmed."

I turn my head at the voice. "Who are you?" My question goes unanswered. Strong hands grip my arms as I'm lifted off the ground and carried out of the shop. I hear the rumble of a large engine, feel the heat from it as I'm placed on my feet, held aloft by the men beside me. Their grip on my arms is tight, though I can barely keep my head upright as I sag against them.

"Why are you doing this to me?" My words slur as my head falls backward. The muscles in my neck pull taut.

The sound of clanking metal chains sounds distorted in my ears. A tailgate squeals as it lowers before me and I'm hauled inside. Darkness rushes in as my head hits the metal floor, the pain insufficient to keep me lucid, and I lose consciousness.

SEVEN

My head hurts. Not like a small sinus headache. More like someone using a buzz saw to separate the two hemispheres of my brain.

My body feels weird, heavy, and lethargic. Shooting pains rise along my neck. As I try to lift my head, I realize that my wrists and ankles are bound. I am seated upright, my chest and thighs strapped down tight enough to cut off circulation. A blindfold covers my vision, pressing tightly against my closed eyelids.

Dripping, as maddening as it is constant, sounds around me. There is a high pitched beeping coming from somewhere behind my head.

"Hello?" My voice cracks and I clear my throat to try again. "Is anyone there?"

I hear breathing in the dark. Slow and steady. Rhythmic. It scares me. Almost like a prank call gone too far.

"I can hear you." I hate that my voice trembles.

Nothing. No response. I call until my throat is raw, but no one answers my pleas.

Slowly, my other senses begin to kick back in. I become aware of the beat of my pulse in my neck and realize that it pulses in time with the beeping from behind my head. It must be some sort of heart monitor.

I smell nothing. Literally nothing. It is as if the space has been sanitized and then stripped of all recognizable scent. A clean room. My lips part and I breathe deep, hoping to taste something on the air, but even this test fails me.

I am alone in the dark. No. Not alone. Just ignored.

"Let me out of here!" I scream. I listen as my cry echoes around me. I twist against my restraints but manage only to burn my skin.

"Hello?" I listen again, focusing on the echo. I'm in a large room. That much I do know. The sound does not bounce back at me, but diminishes as it travels away. I turn my head this way and that, attempting other calls. At best I can tell there is a wall to my left, not far away. Nothing before me or to my right.

"Think, Avery. Just focus on what you know."

I'm in a shitful of trouble, that's what I know! My panic begins to rise and I struggle to squash it down.

I freeze at the sound of grinding gears. The sound is distant. I let my head roll back to my shoulder as a door bangs open. Heavy footfalls head my way. Several people approach, but they don't seem the least bit concerned about being heard.

"Where's the new one?" A man asks.

"At the end. She's been...resisting."

A disgruntled *harrumph* greets me less than a minute before I sense movement in front of me. I wish that I could open my eyes, sneak a glimpse of my captors. Instead, I rely heavily on my other senses.

I note the ticking of a watch. Smell the scent of cologne attempting to mask the alcohol. I feel a cold breeze on my arm and wonder if the door they entered through was left open.

"Is she awake?"

I keep my breathing slow and steady. A hand presses against my neck and I force myself not to react. The man steps back. "Her vitals are steady. It is possible that the sedation has begun to wear off again."

Again? I don't remember waking up here before.

"How much have you managed to collect?" The gravelly voice belongs to a seasoned man, perhaps in his fifties or later. His words are clipped, no-nonsense. This is a man who is obviously used to giving orders and having them instantly obeyed.

"We have removed two pints so far, but I'm still waiting for the test results to come back." A meek voice speaks up. I hear the rustling of papers and imagine him to have a clipboard in hand, sifting through my charts.

"Not good enough, doctor. I want triple that."

"But sir—"

"No excuses. We are running low. Our soldiers' lives depend on it."

I have to fight not to react to that. I remember giving blood when I was a bit younger at a mobile Red Cross unit that stopped at a church just down the street from me. To be honest, I went for the food afterward, not for some noble notion that I was helping people. I was hungry. My mother had been on one of her drinking binges again and the only things in the fridge were baking soda and butter.

That day they took one pint of my blood and it was enough to leave me woozy for a while. I didn't like that feeling. In the end, I decided the food wasn't worth it.

Now this guy wants to take half of my blood and call it a day? Oh, hell no!

"I have rights," I croak, lifting my head.

"Rights?" Thick fingers paw at the blindfold over my face, tearing stands of hair from my scalp. The blindfold slides down around my neck and I'm forced to blink several times before my eyes adjust to the brilliant light overhead.

It is a medical light, round and domed, like what you see on TV. My mom used to have a thing for watching reruns of *ER*. As I look around, I see several machines that look vaguely familiar.

"And what rights do you think you still have?"

I turn my head to the right and glare at a stern looking man. His temples are flecked with white against his cropped graying head of hair. Lines mar his face, streaking his forehead. His eyes are dark and cold, demanding.

A green uniform encases the man, tailored to perfection right down to his shiny black shoes. A colorful array of medals dangles from his chest. He must be high-ranking to be decorated like this. Perhaps a general or commander of some sort.

"I'm an American citizen. You have no right to detain me."

His throaty laugh grates against my frayed nerves. Beside him, three soldiers snicker behind their hands. A doctor, with a three-quarter length white lab coat, shifts uncomfortably. He wears a matching uniform beneath his coat.

As I look beyond him, I see a darkened room that stretches out before me. The ceiling is metal and domed. It looks like an aircraft hangar that's been converted into some mad scientist's lab.

I am in a long row of chairs, each with its own light, heart monitors and a web of tubing. Men and women sit in the chairs, motionless and unconscious.

I turn to glare at the man, knowing he is in charge. "This is wrong."

"No." The humor in his eyes vanishes instantly as he steps forward. His arms cross behind his back and he leans over me. "What is wrong is that my men are dying out there trying to save your sorry ass. Trained soldiers, good men fighting for freedom, are being cut down by the scum that think they own this city now."

"I'm not one of them!"

He rises back up and appraises me coolly. "You're right. You're part of the cure now." He turns on his heel and starts away.

"Wait!" The man pauses but does not turn. I grit my teeth, blowing out a breath before I speak. "I had a friend in the city. She was in danger, needed my help. I have to get back to her."

The general doesn't respond, doesn't make a sound as he resumes his march away from me, leaving me helpless and hopeless. I lower my head as tears sting my eyes.

"I'm sorry," a voice whispers beside me after the resounding echo of the door slamming fades away. I lift my head to see the doctor is the only one who remains. "About your friend, I mean."

"Then help me escape."

He shakes his head. I notice his hands are small for a man. His stature not nearly as imposing as the others. This man has most likely never seen a day of real battle, certainly not hand to hand combat. He is a doctor. A man who might still have a conscience.

"She was only a girl, a teen who went into labor," I press, praying that I can reach his humanity. "She started bleeding. We tried to stop it, but she just got weaker..."

He closes his eyes. His head lowers as he shakes his head.

"Please," I beg without apology. "I have to help her."

When he raises his head, I see evidence of his compassion in the curve of his lips but then he turns aside. His fingers work the buttons of the machine beside me and I watch the IV drip increase. Another increases the flow of blood trailing from my arm. As the doctor silently works, checking my feeding tube and monitoring the output of the catheter snaking out from beneath my hospital gown, I begin to feel weakness anew.

Finally, he stops and turns to look at me. My head presses heavily against the headrest. His lips purse and he shakes his head. "I'm truly sorry. I'm sure you cared for your friend, but she was probably dead long before you were even captured."

He turns and starts away, my file tucked under the crook of his arm. "He's going to kill me."

The doctor pauses. "No. I won't let that happen."

My eyes slip closed as the sound of his footsteps retreats. Tears stream down my cheeks as I mourn the loss of the only friend I've truly had in a long time. Eva wanted nothing from me. She extended friendship for the sole purpose of being nice. That is rare in my life.

I have no way to monitor time as the hours pass. Lethargy comes and goes. The doctor returns twice to readjust the machines. Neither time does he truly look at me. Not like before.

The silence seeks to drive me crazy. I call out from time to time, knowing that no one can hear my hoarse cries over the steady droning of mechanical beeps filling the air. None of the other captives move or wake. Why have I not been sedated again like them?

My vision grows fuzzy, my eyes ache from peering into the dark in search of an escape route. For all intents and purposes, there are no walls to this room. None that I can see or hope to reach.

Just as I'm about to drift off again, I hear a sliding footstep against the floor. A burst of adrenaline shoots through me, waking my senses as I wait for another shuffle or the moan that I fear might come. Surely they have Moaners here as well. The commander said he is losing men. That can't only mean to bullets.

"Hello?" I call out and wait, straining to hear. Another sound. Followed by cautious footsteps. I can see movement in the shadows beyond the borders of my light. They move with stealth, far too fluid for a Moaner. "Who's there?"

"Shit," a husky voice breathes out. A pair of boots enters the ring of light first, followed by a lean waist, broad torso and strong jaw. I lift my gaze and blink rapidly, sure that I'm dreaming.

"Cable?"

He pauses at the foot of my chair, his gaze flitting over me. He looks intense, perplexed and rigid. "I thought you got out."

I bark out a laugh and my head falls to my right shoulder. He rushes forward and helps me lift it again. My chest rises and falls with exertion. "Not all that different than last time, huh?"

His expression tightens in light of my attempt at humor. He glances back over his shoulder. "I have to get you out of here."

He starts to reach for the straps holding my arms down and then hesitates. He glances all around. "Why are you here?"

"I got lost looking for the bathroom," I croak, rolling my eyes. "Why do you think?"

"No," He says in a hushed voice as he peers back over his shoulder again. "I mean here, in *this* room."

My attempt at a shrug comes off as more of a slump. "They didn't exactly give me the grand tour when I arrived."

Cable's gaze narrows in on a chart hanging next to my IV pole. He steps carefully around my feet and grabs the papers, flipping through. I roll my head to the side to watch him. The effort is exhausting.

I wouldn't have thought it possible but his expression darkens further. "You're a candidate."

"For what?"

When he looks up, I can tell that whatever it is, I really don't want to volunteer. He places the chart back down and steps to my side. "Getting you out of here won't be easy. We'll need help. My men won't be back from their patrol until tomorrow. We will have to wait until then."

"I can't wait that long." Panic pinches my voice, making me sound like a terrified mouse. "That creepy general guy wants to take all of my blood."

Cable's head snaps up. "What?"

"I heard them saying they wanted to take more. A lot more."

He wipes his hand over his mouth as he blinks rapidly. "But that doesn't make any sense. You're a universal donor. They should let you rest so you can generate more blood, not steal it all and risk killing you!"

I close my eyes, feeling a heavy pounding in my head. "Maybe you need to admit the fact that your boss isn't such a good guy."

I sound sleepy. I feel sleepy. I surface only when Cable presses his palm against my cheek. He leans in close. "I won't let them hurt you. I promise."

EIGHT

They came for me in the middle of the night. I heard their heavy march first, followed by the shouted commands to prep me. I remember my arms feeling like lead when they finally removed my restraints. My arms fell over the sides of the chair, like useless limbs, but still I couldn't resist. My legs were no better. I had no energy, no will to fight back, even as I was placed on a stretcher and taken from the room.

I have only a blurry memory of a biting cold hitting my exposed skin as I was carried from the hangar. The whirling sound of helicopter rotors filled my mind as we passed by and entered another building, this one white and exceedingly sterile-looking.

Hands jostled me as I was placed on a soft surface. A mask was placed over my face though there was no need for medication to knock me out. I was barely lucid as it was.

Now I am awake. I feel stronger, though only slightly. My surroundings have changed. I sit propped up against a white wall on a small cot in the corner of an empty room. There is no other furniture save for a porcelain toilet in the corner. A large pane of glass lies on the wall before me. I'm being watched. I can feel it.

A new team of doctors monitors me now. None of them speak to me. None of them look at me, beyond a general perusal of my physical condition. They are cold, callous.

With my knees tucked into my chest, I stare at the tube feeding into my wrist. They no longer take blood from me. Now they seem to be giving it.

My hospital gown is gone, replaced by long white pants and white cotton top, the sleeves drawn up to allow access for the IV. My hair has been washed and falls in waves about my shoulders, frizzy from air drying. My skin smells of lightly scented soap, clean and blood free. The remnants of my wounds have been cleaned and bandaged. I've been sterilized, too.

My questions fall on deaf ears. The one-way glass is my only connection to the outside world and a reflection of the only thing I have left to depend on: myself.

I have not seen Cable in what feels like days and know nothing of his whereabouts. A part of me hopes that he is trying to find a way to fulfill his vow. To save me from this cage. Another part of me believes that I will never see real daylight again.

During the endless hours I've spent beneath these brilliant fluorescent lights, I've begun to question Cable's intentions. I knew he worked for the government, even suspected them of being corrupt after speaking with Eva about the missing children, but is it really a coincidence that he stumbled across me in the blood bank? How did he gain clearance for what was obviously a secured room? He is a familiar face, someone that I might be inclined to trust. Has he been swayed to betray me?

"How are you feeling this evening?" a voice calls through a speaker near the door.

I turn and look at the silver box, then lower my head again. I do not recognize the voice. It is feminine. The first I have heard since arriving in this godforsaken place.

"I expect you to have questions." The clank of a lock captures my attention, as does her thick, foreign accent. I place my feet on the floor and curl my fingers around the cot's frame as the door slides open. Just beyond her in the hall, I see two soldiers with guns at the ready.

A tall brunette enters, her heels clicking against the tile floor. Her hair is piled in delicate curls around her face. Her eyes bear a hint of eye shadow. The overwhelming scent of her floral perfume makes me wipe my nose as the door closes behind her.

I scan her button-down dress shirt, the white a near perfect match to the walls behind her. A tight, navy blue, knee length skirt hugs the curve of her hips. Four-inch heels carry her toward me. As I stare at her, I can't shake the feeling that I've seen her before.

She pauses a few feet away and clasps her hands before her. Up close I notice a thick sheen of foundation pasted onto her skin. "You have nothing to fear from me."

"Why do I think *that's* a lie?"

She ignores my sarcastic remark and motions to the end of the bed. "May I?"

"It's your bed. I'm just visiting."

The bed creaks under her weight. She curls her legs back under, crossed at the ankle, as she shifts to look at me. "We are not your enemy, Avery. I realize that all of this might seem a bit extreme, but it's for your own good."

"Really?" I turn my torso to look at her. "Cause I'm pretty sure kidnapping an innocent person, stealing her blood, and then performing experiments on her is still all sorts of fucked up, even in this new world."

The corners of her lips twitch, almost hinting at a genuine smile. Her hands lay one over the other in her lap. I notice that her nail polish is cracked, the glossy tips recently colored over. Upon closer inspection I realize that my first impression of her Barbie doll exterior was wrong, though I'd give her points for trying to pull off the look.

"Rough day?"

She blinks. "Excuse me?"

"You have bruises on your arm. Kinda look like mine." I raise my forearm to show her a nearly identical set of marks, bearing evidence to the manhandling I received when I was brought here. "My mom used to date some pretty nasty guys. Always had a knack for finding the beaters. I know a thing or two about cover-ups and yours is pretty decent."

The woman's gaze darts toward the glass then falls to the floor. She clears her throat and straightens her spine. "You are a very special girl, Avery. We have no intention of harming you."

"Not exactly feeling the warm fuzzies right now." I draw my legs up into my chest and cradle myself. The surface of the cot is hardly what I would call comfortable, but after weeks spent camping out on the hard floor beside my mother's bed or sleeping next to Eva in that warehouse, it feels like a five-star hotel.

She nods. "I imagine all of this must be hard to understand. My name is Natalia and I've been commissioned as your liaison, your go-between."

"Between who, exactly? Me and the US government? Russia?" Her gaze narrows. "You're not American. The crappy accent was a dead giveaway."

She glances toward the window again and stares for a moment. I follow her gaze, knowing there is no way she can see through that glass. After a minute of silence passes, she lowers her head.

"Twenty minutes," she murmurs under her breath and rises.

I stare after her as she moves swiftly toward the door. She slams her palm against the metal twice. The door opens an inch. "I'm finished with her."

A tall, heavily armed soldier sweeps his gaze past her to me as he opens the door. I smile and wiggle my fingers at him in mock greeting. His scowl deepens as he allows her to pass then slams the door.

What just happened? I lie down on the cot, rolling to my side so that I'm facing the wall only a few inches from my face. It would not surprise me if there were cameras that can see me from every angle in this room, but I feel better knowing that the faceless men behind the glass window can't see.

Twenty minutes. What is that supposed to mean? She'll be back in twenty minutes? Something terrible is going to happen? Maybe it's another experiment.

I clasp my hands and tuck them under my head, wincing at the tug of the IV in my arm, and I force myself to rest. A mock rest, one with the sole intent of appearing to sleep, but my mind dashes through countless scenarios. The more I try to puzzle through Natalia's conversation and the change in her demeanor, the more frustrated I become.

Minutes tick past slowly. I count the seconds in my mind, wondering just how many were lost or miscounted during my mental rants. Surely it is nearly time, yet no one has come for me. I hear nothing beyond the walls of my cage. The painted concrete block is soundproofed, probably so no one has to listen to my screams.

I roll onto my back and stare unblinking up at the ceiling, unwilling to feign sleep any longer. *Idiot. She was just trying to get a reaction from me. Another stupid mind game.*

Rubbing my hands over my face, I rise to the edge of the bed and cradle my head in my hands. My elbows dig into my thighs as I release a deep breath. *When am I going to stop falling for this shit?*

I hear something. Raising my head, I glance around. A tremor works up through the floor into the soles of my bare feet. I start to rise but pause as I see a vibration in the glass window. Cocking my head to the side, I watch the mirrored surface appear to ripple.

The blast catches me off guard. I throw up my hands to shield my face as thousands of shards explode. Small nicks appear on my arms, slicing through the thin fabric of my clothes. Lines of crimson begin to appear along my body as I slowly uncurl to see a darkened hole where the glass once was.

A man stands there, waiting. "Cable?"

Placing his hands against the window frame, he launches himself through. Glass shatters beneath his boots as he rushes to my side. He offers me an apologetic grimace before ripping the IV from my arm, disconnecting me from the monitors. They beep loudly just before he kicks the cart over. As he reaches out to cup my face, I realize his palms are wrapped in fabric. "Can you walk?"

"Not exactly." I glance at the sea of glass all around. Cable follows my gaze to my bare feet and instantly sweeps me into his arms.

"Be ready to run. Keep your head down. Stay close behind me."

He hoists me through the window and into what looks like some sort of operating room. An array of scalpels, needles, and monitors stand before me. A bin of tubing wrapped in protective sealed bags hangs along the wall. A heart monitor's green flat line trails silently across the screen at the head of the bed. Three clipboards with charts, printed cardiograms and who knows what else lies on the table to my right. I fall still at the sight of the name on the top of the page: Avery Whitlock.

"Oh, God!" Flashes of memory seize me as I stare up at the darkened dome light. "I remember."

I step back into Cable, stopped by the breadth of his chest. "Don't think about it. Just move."

"They know my name," I call after him as he rushes to the door. As he tugs it open to look out, I hear the blaring of sirens for the first time. "How do they know my name?"

"I told them." His response is flat, unemotional.

I close the gap between us and seize his arm. He glances back at me with mounting agitation. "I only ever told you my *first* name."

His gaze softens as he places his hand over mine. "Do you really think they wouldn't know everything about you by now?"

His words leave me cold as he ducks his head back into the hall. I curl my toes against the frigid tiles, wishing for a pair of warm fuzzy socks. Heck, I'd take a pair of flip-flops at this point!

"Follow me."

I do, as if on autopilot. We clamber over two fallen soldiers that once guarded my door, pausing for Cable to check their weapons. "Why aren't you taking the big ones?" I ask as he tucks a small pistol in his back waistband.

"Too bulky."

Motioning for me to follow, one gun held at the ready, I weave around corners, down halls and past countless doors that all look the same to me. I don't know how he doesn't get lost. Cable marches forward, his posture tense yet confident.

Explosions rock the building. The lights flicker overhead. "What's happening?"

I duck low as another explosion hits farther down the hall. A wall collapses in and we are forced to backtrack.

"Cable?" I struggle to breathe as I jog. What little energy I gained from my time spent prisoner in my white room is rapidly fading.

"You want the long version or the synopsis?"

He grabs me by the arm and I slam into his chest. His arms curl around me, his body a shield against a collapsing ceiling less than ten feet in front of us. When the dust settles he draws back up. "I think short!"

Brick and drywall dust his hair gray, but it doesn't dampen his smile. "It's an old fashioned mutiny!"

"Mutiny?" The word is torn from my lips as he tugs me toward a door. He slams through it and pulls me into a hall almost identical to the last, but this one is decorated in beige tones. Bodies dot this hall, but none appear to be moving. The hallway lights flicker overhead, some damaged by the shootout. A spray of bullet holes lead past us and around the corner, but I hear nothing in that direction.

Cable releases my hand and sprints ahead, pausing at an intersection and for the first time, he looks lost. I spy a red glowing exit sign to my right. "Over there!"

He turns back and shakes his head. "We aren't going out there."

The desire to turn tail and race for that door is nearly unbearable. Exit means freedom. I watch as Cable turns a corner up ahead and bite down on my lower lip.

Can I really trust him? Should I?

"Avery," he hisses down the hall toward me. I look up to see his head poking around the corner. "This way."

I hesitate a second longer before making my decision. "Shit."

My bare feet slap against the cold floor as I rush to catch up. I'm only distantly aware of the fact that my side no longer aches. My ribs are bound tightly, but the bruising must have begun to heal. *How long have I been here?*

Cable waits for me at the end of a dark hall. "Watch your step," he calls out just before I spy a pile of glass from the light overhead.

"Where is everyone?"

"This building was on strict lockdown from all non-essential personnel. Only the doctors and scientists come here at night to check on patients. Once the battle began, they took off. They're not here to fight but to research. Most of them have never seen a day of combat."

"Lucky them," I mutter. Another explosion rocks the building. A crack forms in the wall beside me and I rush ahead, not wanting to stick around for the next blast. "Friends of yours?"

"Something like that." He takes my hand and raises his foot, booting the door before him open. Darkness and a frigid cold reside on the other side.

"Where are we?"

"Shh." His fingers tighten around mine as he leads me into the room. He pauses a few feet in. There is a clattering of metal then silence as he pulls me forward. The echo of the door closing behind me feels out of place as he leads me through the dark. I hear shouting now. Gunfire covers the sound of sirens in the distance.

The floor feels like ice beneath my feet. A chill rises up through my legs and it doesn't take long for my teeth to begin to chatter. I hear an odd click and sense movement before me.

"Here. Grab hold." Cable places my hand on something cold and metal. I stiffen as his hands slide down my waist and he hoists me up. "Buckle up."

It is only when I feel the material of the seat and jerk at the sound of the door closing behind me that I fully realize that I'm in a vehicle. I wait in the dark as Cable feels his way around the front of the car and hauls himself into the driver's seat.

"How can you see?"

When the headlights flick on I find myself staring at the contraption on Cable's head. They look like a set of binoculars, but not nearly the same. "Night vision," he grins and tosses them into the floorboard.

The throaty growl of the engine vibrates in my chest. Cable taps the steering wheel, peering out into the light.

"What are we waiting for?"

He doesn't respond and instead watches the dark intently. I wrap my arms around myself, rubbing to keep warm. A couple minutes pass before a rectangle of light appears in the far corner of the room. Two dark shapes slip inside before darkness prevails once more.

"Who is that?"

A moment later the back door opens and I see a familiar face rise into the vehicle. "No way! I'm not going anywhere with her!"

Natalia's eyes widen as she looks between me and Cable. He grits his teeth before meeting my glare. "She helped save your life. She's coming too."

"She experimented on me!"

"No." I turn fully in the seat to look at her. "I had nothing to do with that. I told you the truth. I was merely a liaison."

"I remember you."

"Of course, you do," Cable says, hiking his thumb over his shoulder for her to get in. "She watched over you during your recovery."

I refuse to look away as Natalia buckles her seat belt. I don't care what he says. I can smell a rat when I see one and she is all kinds of rotten.

Another man climbs in after her. He has baby smooth cheeks, clear blue eyes, and a grin as broad as his shoulders. He holds out his hand to me. "Eric Phelan. Heard a lot about you."

"Sit down and shut up," Cable growls as he shoves the vehicle into gear. I'm thrown back as he slams on the accelerator. Eric cries out as he tumbles to the floor, flailing to grab hold of the seat.

"Are you insane? You couldn't give him another minute to strap in?" I press my hands to the dashboard as the tires squeal and we barrel toward a wall.

Glancing at the green glow of the clock on the dashboard, he shakes his head. "Not unless you want to stick around for the barbecue."

I brace myself as we crash headlong through the hangar doors. They crumble away, peeled back like the lid of a sardine can. My head ricochets off the headrest. The Humvee rattles and shakes as Cable fights for control of his wild skid.

A huge dark shape looms ahead of us. "Look out!"

Cable swerves to miss the dangling propellers of a copter, only to take out a collection of gasoline barrels. They spiral across the tarmac, spilling fuel.

"Haul ass, Cable!" Eric's hands grip the seat behind me. His face looks pale as he leans between us, shouting out directions. I grab onto the door and hold on. Natalia buries her head in her arms. A scream escapes her lips from time to time.

As we race between two hangars, my head whips around at the sight of a large yellow vehicle. "A school bus?" I turn on Cable. "So it's true? The military really was stealing kids?"

"Now is not the time," Cable says through gritted teeth. He spins the wheel and I'm thrown against the door.

I watch as he glances frequently from the road to the clock and pray that whatever is supposed to happen hurries up. Soldiers pour from the buildings. A heavy gunfight rages all around. I don't know how on earth they know who is good and who is bad when they are all wearing the same uniform!

Lights on the guard towers sweep the grounds, zeroing in on us. A twenty foot high concrete wall looms before us, filling the windshield. I glance at Cable, noting the lack of color in his knuckles as he grips the steering wheel and guns the accelerator. "Cable?"

"Wait for it. Wait for it!" From the corner of my eye I see something large emerging from the shadows. I spy the long barrel as it swivels and takes aim.

Boom.

The windows rattle as a fireball erupts before us. Smoke and dust roll over the window. Debris rains from above, denting the roof of the Humvee. Natalia wails as we burst through the wall and into the night. Our headlights illuminate trees and an overgrown path as we bounce and skid to a halt.

"You have a tank?" I gasp, clutching my chest.

"Sure do." Eric lets out a whoop as another blast echoes from behind us. I imagine the tank must be securing our departure.

Cable breathes hard as he reaches out for me. "You okay?"

"Pretty sure I just wet myself, but yeah. I'm good."

Eric laughs and pounds Cable on the arm. "Nice moves, dude. You were right. You are the better driver."

"I'll collect on that bet later."

I tense at the hard line in Cable's voice. As the last of the smoke clears, I see a bright light lock onto to us from above. I lean forward to see a chopper in the air.

"Stand down." A voice calls over a loudspeaker. "Turn your engine off and evacuate the vehicle. We have been authorized to use force if you resist."

Natalia huddles low in her seat. Her hair is a disheveled mess. Her pristine clothes rumpled and dark with sweat. The sound of her whimpering fills the vehicle.

"What do we do?" I turn to find Cable glancing back at Eric.

The baby-faced soldier pulls up his sleeve to reveal a watch and shakes his head. "We gotta delay."

"Is this thing bulletproof?" I ask, staring at the large manned gun above.

"Not like you'd hope it would be."

"What's that supposed to mean?" I grab onto the door as he spins the wheel, gunning the gas as he steers the vehicle off the road. Bullets ping against the hull. Several deep dents appear in the side. Natalia screams, but I ignore her as I try to keep my eye on the chopper.

"It means we are armored, but only to a point. Keep your head down!" he shouts back as he spins the wheel again.

The spotting light is blinding from above as the chopper banks to pursue us. Cable cuts the headlights and drives under low hanging branches of a large maple tree. The tires skids to a stop, the engine settles into a deep rumble. The patch of trees won't give us cover for long. "You seriously think they can't see us here?" I gawk.

Cable ignores my comment and keeps his eye trained to the broken light overhead. Bits of bark tumble down as another round of gunfire strikes the tree. A loud ping of gunfire behind me makes me cower against the door. I hear a cry of pain and look back. Natalia clutches her shoulder.

"Shit." Eric reaches over and presses his hand to her arm. "She's hit, Cable."

"We all will be soon if we don't get out of here." Cable puts the car in reverse and sneaks between two trees. "Eric?"

"One minute!"

I spot other vehicles barreling toward us from the outside of the wall. Their headlights bounce as they hit deep ruts. The chopper overhead circles once more. Dust bursts up from the ground as I watch the trail of bullets approaching from directly ahead of us.

"Now?"

I turn to see Eric staring intently as his watch. His lips part and mime counting. Three. Two. One.

The sky behind us erupts with fire. The ground rumbles as half of the base goes up in flames. The outer wall crumbles and collapses. I watch out my side window as the pursuing vehicles swerve to miss the falling debris. A large chunk of the wall smashes into the hood of the front car. Its back end flies up into the air. The second car brakes too late and slams headlong into the underside of the lead vehicle. Both erupt in flames. I watch in horror as flaming bodies thrust themselves out of the vehicle and writhe on the ground.

"Oh, God!" I grasp my stomach as I turn away. I wanted to escape, but not like this. Those men were probably just following orders.

The chopper veers off. Cable punches the accelerator and guns for the forest in sheer darkness, lit only by the scattered light of the moon peering behind clouds overhead. My head rocks from side to side as we navigate the uneven terrain. The ride is rough, but I feel safer than I have in weeks.

"Get us out of here," Eric says, pointing away from the path before us. "No main roads. We have to find somewhere to lie low."

"What about that chopper? Won't more come back around for us?" I glance over my shoulder, but the skies seem clear apart from the huge plume of smoke from the fire.

Eric grins. "Nah. We just blew up all of their big shiny toys. It'll take them a few minutes to regroup."

I turn forward as Cable re-engages the headlights. "Now what?"

Cable takes his eyes off the road only for a moment to look at me. "We run and don't look back."

NINE

I stare at the black radio handset in my hand, listening to the static. I have tried every channel, even ones I know the military would be scanning, but I had no choice. I gave Alex my promise that I would find a way to reach them, no matter what.

"This is Avery calling for Alex. Do you read me?"

Static fills the cab of the Humvee. I call again several times, switching the stations. "I promised I would call you. I'm sorry I couldn't get back to you. I was...I was delayed, but I'm waiting for you now," I say, leaning my head against the window. I feel stiff and cold from sitting so long.

"If you hear this message, please leave the city. We are located thirty miles east of your last position. We have to leave soon." I release the button and press my hand to my lips to still their trembling. The cold is brutal today.

"Alex...come find me."

The door to the barn opens and I raise my hand to shield my eyes from the light. I spy Cable's elongated mask first as he slips into the dark, leaving the door open to the outside.

"You've been out here all day. Any luck?" Cable swings himself up into the driver's seat beside me and removes his gas mask only once secured inside. His face is clean, his hair freshly washed. A shadow of stubble darkens his square jaw. He looks refreshed despite spending a night tossing and turning in his sleep. I heard him cry out in the dark. Nightmares from the past plague him. I wonder what it is that he dreams of.

"It's been three days and I'm no closer to finding them than I was."

Cable nods, lowering his head. I sigh, resigned to trying again later. I turn off the ignition and hand him the keys.

"You know we can't stay much longer." He fiddles the keys between his fingers. "Sooner or later someone is going to hear that message and figure out where we are."

"I know." I flex my fingers then clasp them before me, wishing for the hundredth time that I had a pair of gloves. The abandoned farmhouse we crashed in the night we escaped from the military base smelled of old people and mothballs, but it had basic supplies. Sweaters that were a bit too snug on the men. Floral blouses that I would rather die than wear, but Natalia didn't seem to care. Come to think of it, she hasn't cared about much since we arrived.

At first, I thought it was some sort of post-traumatic stress. Cable said that it's possible. People handle death and climactic situations differently. Eric has stayed by her side since we arrived. He leaves her unattended only long enough to pop open a can of soup and returns to spoon-feed her.

Cable and I searched the attic and found trunks of old clothes, photo albums, and keepsakes, but no trace of winter outerwear. I tucked all of the floral shirts aside for Natalia and grabbed a fluffy sweater. It's way too big on me and has a tendency to billow in the wind, but as long as I keep my white shirt tucked into my pants, it works fairly well.

Shoes are one area that I lucked out in. I guess me and the grandma who lived here share a size 8. I found a pair of brand new tennis shoes hidden in the back of a downstairs closet and enough hand-knitted wool socks to keep my feet toasty for a long time.

Cable thinks the old folks probably left when the world went down the crapper. There are tire tracks in the yard. The barn doors were left wide open. Even some of the cabinets were emptied. I hope he's right.

"Do you think maybe you should let it go?" Cable asks after several moments of silence.

"I can't." I stare out the grimy windshield. The sun is bright today, breaking through the cloud cover for the first time in what feels like months. I long to feel it on my face, but it's too dangerous to go out during the day. We are still too close to the military base. From time to time we hear the choppers as they work in a grid, searching. Eric seems to think they have bigger problems than hunting for us, but I have my doubts.

It's the way Natalia looks at me when she thinks I don't see. Piercing. Searching.

I've yet to find out exactly what it is that she did for the military. Whatever her relationship was with them, there is one thing that is certain: Eric is far too fond of her. I suspect that's the reason Cable let her hitch a ride out, not because of anything to do with me.

"I have to know," I whisper, turning away from the sunlight that ends just at the edge of the barn we are parked inside. "Eva needed me and I left her. I can't do that again."

Cable taps his fingers against the steering wheel, deep in thought. He does that a lot. At first, it was a bit off-putting, making me wonder what secrets he might be trying to worm his way around revealing. The more time I spend with him, I realize it's just his way. He's a thinker.

"You know their chances of survival are slim. That entire section of the city was overrun two days after I found you. If they didn't get out before that then they are lost."

I close my eyes and press my forehead against the window. The cold glass bites my skin, but I ignore it. I told Cable all about Eva, about the group and my promise. He has actively supported my decision to remain behind, until now. I know we can't wait anymore, but I can't willingly leave either. I just don't know how to make him understand.

"Eva couldn't have been moved," he whispers, running his finger along the curve of the mask.

"I know." Exhaustion and remorse fall over me. I have so many things to be thankful for. Shelter. Food. Protection. People. Why isn't that enough? Why can't I adapt to this new world of loss and pain, to let go of the things that would seek to hold me back? "I knew better than to let myself care."

I stiffen as Cable grasps my hand. Lifting my head, I turn to look at him as tears that I've been resisting escape down my cheeks. "You're human. It's in our nature."

"So is murder, theft, and a million other atrocities. Is that in me too, Cable? Am I going to become someone I don't even recognize just to avoid becoming like them?"

I point out the window and he turns to look at a Moaner shuffling through the yard. Several more follow behind, some leaving a path of entrails in their wake.

"I don't know," he answers with brutal honesty. His gaze is conflicted as he turns to look at me. He tries to offer me a reassuring smile, but it falls flat. "I hope not."

I pull my hand away from him, tucking it into my side. "I thought you were like those other soldiers."

Closing my eyes, I refuse to see the look of pain that mars his face. Cable is a good guy, I understand that now, but being a good guy doesn't mean I can trust him.

He shifts in his seat. I hear him hit the pedals as he turns to face me. "I guess I deserve that. If roles were reversed, I'd have a ton of questions too."

I open my eyes to see that he is leaning toward me. The planes of his face are hard, but in a good way. The new stubble enhances his good looks. In this confined space I realize just how aware I have become of him over the past few days.

"I saw the bus..."

He swallows hard. Turning away, he places his hands on the steering wheel and sighs. "I don't have all of the answers. I'm sure that surprises you." He smirks but I'm in no mood. "Look, I heard rumors but never saw any kids myself. They weren't where I slept, ate, or worked, so if they were there, they were buried deep."

My breath hitches as the memory of the base exploding floods back in. My hands begin to tremble as I press them to my stomach. "Did we kill them?"

"What?" He twists toward me. "No. Of course not!"

"How do you know? They could have been forgotten in the firefight. The tank could have misfired and crushed them. They could have—"

"Stop." He grasps my hands and squeezes. "Worrying about this will only make you sick. It's best to think positive and trust that they got out."

I stare down at his hands, clasped around mine and I'm desperate to believe him. To soak up an ounce of his optimism, but I can't do it. "Eva told me that her little sister was taken by the military."

Cable nods. "Natalia worked with a few kids at a different base somewhere up north. Said it was all routine tests. Nothing weird that she could tell."

"Do you trust her?"

"Natalia?" He shrugs and releases my hands, sinking back into the seat. He draws his leg up and rests it against the wheel. "I don't really know her. Eric vouched for her so that's good enough for me."

"Really? It's that easy for you?" I cross my arms over my chest to ward off the cold. "I think we both know that I've got every reason to have trust issues right now. You seem to care about keeping me safe. Eric seems decent too. If you want me to play nice with Natalia I'm going to need more than just a friendly handshake that she's good."

"Like what?" I can tell he is hedging and that makes me all the more suspicious.

"How did she have clearance to come speak to me? What does she know about what they did to me? Why did she aid us in escaping? Who beat her?"

Cable leans back away from me and turns his gaze outward. When he reaches up to stroke his throat, grimacing at the windshield, I turn to see a woman stumble less than ten feet from the hood of the Humvee. Half of her arm has been torn off. The bone protrudes from the rotting flesh. White maggots crawl over the open wound. My stomach churns but I force myself not to look away. To truly see the horrors that have consumed this world.

"Eric says that Natalia is complicated."

I return my attention to Cable as the woman disappears around the edge of the barn. "That's not good enough."

"Well, for now, it's going to have to be——" he turns his head at a raised cry and leaps from the vehicle, pulling his mask into place as he goes. I'm right on his heels as we sprint toward the house.

"This isn't over," I call to him as we hit the porch.

"Kinda figured you'd say that." He takes the stairs two steps at a time. I'm winded by the time I reach the second floor, but he's hardly broken a sweat. "What is it? What's wrong?"

Eric appears in the doorway, his face a mask of sorrow. His chin trembled as he steps aside. I can tell by the swelling around his eyes that he's been crying. "Her fever is gone."

I pause in the doorway as the two men go to her bedside, not wanting to intrude. Cable sinks down beside Natalia and takes her hand in his. He presses his free hand to her brow. "She's freezing."

"I know." Eric tosses his towel aside and brushes past me. I watch him leave, his shoulders sagging and his steps heavy as he descends to the lower floor.

When I turn back I see Cable's head bowed low. Four blankets lay draped over Natalia. Dark shadows line her eyes. Her cheeks are sunken as if she's been without food for weeks instead of only a day.

"I didn't take you for a praying man."

"Never used to be." He places her hand beside her and then lifts her bandage. The bullet that entered through her shoulder in our mad dash to evade the chopper was a clean hit. Eric and Cable have been diligent to keep it clean, but the fever began within a day of our arrival here.

Her skin is unnaturally pale. Her veins prominent against her frail arms. When he opens her mouth, I see that her tongue is coated with a thick substance. He opens her eyes and they stare back at him with no reaction. She looks as if she's begun to wither right before our eyes.

My breath catches as I close my eyes. "Of course," I murmur and lean against the doorframe. "She's turning, isn't she?"

Cable clears his throat but doesn't answer. He doesn't need to.

I sigh, rub my forehead and look at him. "I'm sorry. I've never seen it happen before. Not this close, at least. Last time it was in the hospital and they kept the woman secluded for the most part."

"Well," he turns his face up to look at me. Cable looks exhausted. Lines carve deeply into his face. His hair hangs limply against his forehead. He shakes his head slowly and I'm touched by the sorrow that he feels for a woman he barely knew. "You're about to get a front row seat."

He continues to look at Natalia, seeming to be willing her lungs to continue to expand, her brain to continue to function. He reaches to his side and retrieves a knife. It isn't long or particularly nasty looking, but it looks sharp as he withdraws it from a black leather sheath.

"What are you doing?" I call out as he grips Natalia's arm and presses the blade to her flesh.

"Testing."

With a flick of his wrist, a thin but deep wound appears on the back of her forearm. No scream. No flinch. No sign of pain. He hangs his head and the knife goes limp in his hand. I enter the room and kneel down beside him, tucking the blade away.

"It's not your fault."

He wipes at his nose and shoves the blade into his pocket. "I'm just sick of losing good people."

I know the feeling. Even though I may not have anyone else in my life, I've grown to care about a couple of people and I don't want to see them get hurt. "You hungry? I was thinking of making soup for dinner."

"Nah." He shifts on the edge of the bed. "I'll stay for a little longer."

Feeling like a bit of an outsider, I rise and close the door behind me, heading downstairs. I find Eric sitting on the hideous pink couch, staring out the window. He doesn't notice me until I sink down beside him.

"Hey, Avery." He offers me a forced smile and brushes his hands through his hair. He looks terrible. A splotchy beard has consumed the thin growth of stubble he arrived with. Eric hasn't slept, hasn't taken the time to eat. His vigil at Natalia's bedside was constant. "How are you doing?"

I release a breathy laugh and shake my head, resting it in the palm of my hand as I lean on my knee and stare at him. "Shouldn't I be the one asking you that?"

He slumps back into the couch and grabs a pillow, hugging it to his chest. His black hair falls in waves over his forehead and not for the first time I wonder why he was never told he had to shave his head like the rest of the soldiers. His style just seems too...messy.

"She knew it was coming. Started developing the symptoms a few days back but didn't want to say anything. She knew the consequences if she did."

I purse my lips. "So that's why she was caked in makeup."

He nods and fiddles with a stray thread that has come loose from his jacket. "I told her to do it. Thought it could give her a few more days before someone found out. The doctors should have noticed right away, but they were preoccupied."

"With what?" He glances over at me and I grimace. "With me?"

"You caused quite a stir back there."

"But why?" I lower my leg and turn to face him. "What made me so different than all those other people? Is it my blood?"

Eric tilts his head side to side. "Not so much your blood, but your plasma."

"And to those of us who aren't doctors in the room that means what exactly?"

"All right," he twists his torso to face me. From this angle, he looks even worse. Deep bags hang under dull eyes. He is pasty and thin. Thinking back, I'm not sure I've seen him eat more than a spoonful of soup since we arrived. "You've heard about universal donors, right?"

"Sure. Some people have a blood type that can be transfused into anyone."

"Exactly." He holds up his fingers, gesturing with surprising animation. "The number of people who have this sort of blood is right around 40%, give or take a few thousand."

"So I'm one of those?"

"Nope." He ducks his head in low and speaks in a hushed tone as if someone might overhear. "You're even better."

He reaches out and grasps my wrist, turning it over. I watch as he brushes his thumb over the bluish veins in my wrist. "You, Avery, have something very rare. A blood type that allows you to be a universal plasma donor. Only about 1% of people have that, and since we've lost a considerable number of those people recently, you've become even more valuable."

"But why?" I draw my hand back from him. I trace my finger down the curve of a vein, lost in thought.

"Because the government thinks your plasma could be used for a cure."

I turn to see Cable hit the bottom step. He wipes his knife across his pant leg before meeting our gaze. A wide patch of blood stains his right side. Small splatters dot his face. Eric tenses beside me. He wavers in place but remains upright. I reach out and grasp his hand as he closes his eyes. A guttural groan rises from his throat, but he doesn't say anything.

Cable claps his friend on the shoulder, squeezing tight. I watch Eric fight back the tears, battle his grief. I don't know what to say, what to do, so I just sit and wait. Slowly, Eric regains his composure. He takes deep breaths, his fingers clenching tightly against his knees. Finally, he nods and Cable releases him.

"Plasma is a pretty amazing thing," Eric says with a pinched voice.

"Eric," I whisper, shaking my head. "You don't have to..."

"Yeah, I do." He wipes his nose with his sleeve then the tears from his face and raises his chin as he continues. "Easily put, it's a life-saving resource that we are sorely in need of now."

Cable sinks back onto the floor before us. Over his shoulder, I see that the sun has begun its descent. The night will soon fall and we will be forced to barricade ourselves in again. Last night, a chopper came too close for comfort to our camp. I overheard Cable and Eric talking this morning about the likelihood that tonight's search would expand to include our farm. Chances are we may have lingered one day too long.

Eric stares out the window, emotion seeping from his face as he comes to the same conclusion I just did. It's too late to bury Natalia. We will have to wait until morning.

"How do you two know so much?" I ask, trying to pull him back.

Both look toward the ceiling and I mentally kick myself for not thinking. Eric returns his gaze to me. "She was trying to help, Avery. She wasn't like the general, driven by a need for results. She saw the person as well as the problem. I wish you'd had the chance to get to know her. I think you would have liked her."

I'm not sure what to say, how to respond. It is true that I didn't know Natalia. It's also true that I didn't want to, not after she became connected to those experiments. In my mind, she was guilty by association.

A muscle running the length of Eric's neck tightens as he clenches his jaw.

"I'm very sorry for your loss."

He nods but doesn't speak. His fists clench in his lap. Cable leans forward and plunges his hands into his hair and an uncomfortable silence hangs between us as twilight falls over the farmhouse. The door to the barn was left wide open. One of us will have to go and secure it before the choppers come. Looking at Cable and Eric, I decide it will be me.

"We can't stay here any longer," Cable says, staring first at Eric, then at me. He winces before he speaks, knowing that his words will be salt in our open wounds. "The past will only slow us down."

A gargled sound erupts from Eric. He surges to his feet. "Sorry," he mutters as he staggers toward the bathroom. I collapse back into the sofa as I hear him retching.

"Was that really the best time to bring that up? And what's with you not cleaning your knife before you came downstairs? Are you trying to give him a mental breakdown?"

Cable's jaw clenches with each accusation. This is a hard death to accept for both of them, but this...it just seems callous. So unlike him.

"Natalia is gone. Your friends aren't answering. I can't risk all of our lives for what ifs, Avery. It's my job to protect you."

"No." I push to the edge of the couch. "It's my job to protect me. And where will we go?" I ask before he can contradict me. "Which road will lead us somewhere safe? You still wear your mask, for goodness sake! What if we head north and the air is contaminated there? Or west and the food has gone bad? What if we hug the coast and realize the seas are poisoned too?"

"I don't know," he shouts, rising abruptly to his feet and begins to pace. His voice is thick with emotion when he speaks. "I don't have the answers. I just know that we can't stay here. It's too dangerous."

"We can't leave her," Eric whispers from where he leans heavily in the doorway. He wipes his mouth and spits to the side.

My heart goes out to him. The strong man that sat beside me looks lost and broken. Cable sighs as he turns toward his friend. "Natalia would have ordered you to go."

At his words, a pained smile stretches along Eric's face. "And I would have ignored her like I always did."

I rub my hand over my face, weary and tired of saying goodbye to people, even the ones I may not have liked. "One more day," I whisper. "Give us one more day to give Natalia a proper burial. If I can't reach Alex by tomorrow night, then I'll leave with you."

Cable leans forward, his hand covering his mouth as he surveys me. His gaze is intense, but I meet it all the same. Finally, he nods. "Okay. One more day."

TEN

Sweat beads along my brow. I duck and swing. Pain bites into my knuckles, splitting the skin, but I swing again, and again. I spin and weave, thrusting my fist up. It connects with the grain bag with a deep, gratifying thud.

"I think you got it." I spin around to find Cable standing behind me, leaning lazily against the barn door. "What'd it do to tick you off?"

"Nothing." It feels good to sweat, to move without having to cushion my ribs. For the first time in weeks, I almost feel whole again. "I just needed to let off a little steam."

Cable tucks his hands deep into his pockets. "The funeral was pretty rough, huh?"

I nod. "It was my first."

"Really?" He straightens slightly at that. "You never lost a grandparent or neighbor?"

"Nope."

"What about a goldfish? Tell me you, at least, flushed one of those."

I laugh and look over at him through strings of hair. I found a bit of yarn to tie back my mass of curls, but several chunks have fallen free. "I'm pretty sure Goldie doesn't count."

"Goldie, huh? And I pegged you for an unconventional sort of girl."

"Sorry to disappoint." I place my hands back on the grain sack and prepare to begin again. After a moment, I turn and find him still staring at me. "I usually vent in private, if you don't mind."

His expression is obscured behind his mask, but I'd wager he's grinning.

"Why do you still wear that thing, anyways?" I wipe my brow clean with the bottom of my shirt. The chill morning air nips at my stomach as I let the material fall back into place. I switched out my sweater for a frilly floral shirt when I woke, in respect of Natalia's final moments. The instant it was over, I chucked that shirt in the trash and traded it for a men's long sleeve cotton V-neck shirt that is two sizes too large. I knotted the material at the base of my back and rolled the sleeves.

Cable watches me for a moment as I turn my back on the bag and plant my hands on my hips. My knuckles sting where the skin has split. I can't help but feel smug as Cable slowly removes the gas mask. "Habit, I guess."

"Still think this crap is in the air?"

His broad shoulders rise and fall in a shrug. He uncrosses his legs and walks toward me, leaving the sun at his back. I spy large patches of shadow moving across the field beyond. The clouds have begun to move back in. I can feel a change on the air but keep my fears to myself. The last thing I want is to be caught in a winter storm while on the run, but I gave my word. One day and I would leave and never look back.

"I reckon it won't make much difference now." He tosses the mask aside.

"Why's that?"

Cable hikes his leg and sinks down onto a square bale of hay. The whole barn smells of it. That, and spilled oil from the relic of a tractor in the far corner. He kicks out his leg, his boot slamming back into the hay. He rubs his hands together, losing himself to that inner world that nothing can penetrate, then grabs my pistol and begins methodically cleaning it.

I sigh and turn back to the feed bag. My grunts are the only sound in the barn for several minutes. I duck and weave as if matching wits with an opponent. I'm sure Cable knows that I'm faking most of the moves. A soldier with any decent training would see right through my bravado, but I can't just sit around and wait. I need to prepare. If what Cable and Eric said yesterday is true, my life is in danger from far more than this contamination. What started out as a need to vent has become something like borderline desperation.

Glancing over at Cable, I consider asking him to teach me how to use that pistol, but we have very few weapons as it is and far fewer bullets. I notice that he's laid the gun in his lap and is busy scratching at his palm. I squint to look closer, wondering if he's picked up a splinter while hunting for supplies, but when he sees me staring he shoves his hands in his pockets. "I'm sorry about Natalia."

"Me too."

"I uh..." I rub my hand along the back of my neck. "I just want you to know that I support your decision to move on. It will be good for Eric to say goodbye but not linger."

Cable looks around the barn, leaning back to look up into the rafters overhead. Tools hang from rusting chains: hoes, shovels, pitch forks, and something that looks like a handheld tiller for a garden. "She genuinely cared about people," he finally says when he returns his gaze to me. "Eric most of all. I think they could have made it, you know? A decent couple."

I sink down into a crouch and wait for him to continue. For once he might actually be in a talking mood. "Eric knew her from before all of this. I guess he was kind of sweet on her back then but she never really had time for stuff like that. Her work was her life. By the time Eric figured that out, it didn't matter anymore."

Grabbing a handful of hay, he shoves a long strand between his teeth, as if he's always done it. There is a weird familiarity about the action, making me wonder what Cable was like in a previous life, before the mutations, before the Marines. I can't recall if he ever told me where he was from. Only that he was from the South.

"Why did she help me?"

Cable leans back, crossing his arms over his chest as he rests his weight against the wall. The weathered wood holds firm, despite the knots and evidence of termite damage near the floor. "She was a scientist. One of the best, according to Eric. She spent her life devoted to helping people, to discovering cures to unspeakable horrors. You were a piece to a larger puzzle, but she knew if you remained there you wouldn't be able to help the world."

"Help the world?" I scoff, rolling my eyes. I sink down onto the ground, tucking my legs before me. I dust my hands off on my pant legs, leaving dirty hand prints behind. "I'm just one person."

Cable's expression tightens as he leans forward. "For all we know this whole thing started with a single person, a single virus, a single mutated gene. Why would you think one person couldn't fix it all?"

Blowing my hair out of my eyes, I shrug. "Because I'm no hero."

"How do you know?"

I avert my gaze, focusing intently on the bald tractor tire sitting beside him instead of his piercing gaze. "I just do."

"Hmm."

I listen to his steady inhale and exhale, wishing that he would leave. He makes me uncomfortable at times. Usually, when he's trying to get some deep message across to me. It's not that he lectures me, but it's pretty darn close to it.

"You don't know me," I whisper, turning my cheek to press it against my knee. My muscles ache from training. My head feels light and airy. I've pushed myself farther than I should have. I'm still recovering, but I will go crazy if I do nothing but wait and pray for a miracle.

My pleas on the radio have gone unanswered all day. Last night, not long after the moon hit its highest peak in the sky, we heard the choppers fly over. Their light shining in through the windows would have woken me if the noise hadn't. We'd planned for that, made sure we hide in interior rooms just in case. They couldn't have seen us from the air, but that won't stop them from checking all the same. The question is: how many other homes do they have to search before ours?

"You're a good person, Avery."

"What is good? Helping an old lady across the street? Giving a kid a balloon just to see them smile? Handing out money to a homeless person who is hungry?"

I raise my head. "None of those things matter anymore, Cable. There is no good left in this world. Only greed. Only murder and evil and nothingness."

"You're wrong." He slides off the hay bale and scoots toward me. He never breaks eye contact with me as he draws near. I can smell the scent of sweat on him, see the sheen on his skin. He spent most of the morning helping Eric try to hotwire the old Ford truck in the yard. A hose sits near the front of the Humvee that was used to siphon gas in the hopes that it will work in that old clunker. He also worked to stash our supplies in bags for us to carry out of here if we had to leave on foot. Planned tirelessly on securing the house, wiping all evidence of our presence except the Humvee. Not much we can do about that.

He has hardly stopped long enough to close his eyes for a few minutes since we arrived here. He's done the work of five people. I could never fault him for not caring about our protection. No. I'd almost fault him for caring too much. I know where that path leads and I wouldn't want that for him.

Cable motions with his hand between us. "You and me, we're still good. We give a shit." He points toward my chest. "I've watched you these past few days and have witnessed your desperation each time you switch on that radio. You risk your own life each day we remain here, and for what?" He ducks his head to meet me in the eye. "For a friend."

I wrap my arms around myself and rock slowly. "She's probably gone."

"Yeah," he nods in agreement. "She just might be, but you never give up hope."

"I should never have let myself care. I've spent my whole life keeping people at arm's length. It was safer that way."

"That's a hard way to live."

I shrug. "It's how I survived."

"And that?" He turns to look at the grain bag. "You learn that along the way too?"

"Maybe."

He stares down at my hands, no doubt noting the bruised and cut skin. "I could teach you to shoot."

"No." I shake my head, knowing that I'd only waste precious ammunition. Maybe if we come across a pawn shop or gun cache somewhere then I'd be willing to learn. "That's your thing."

"So, what? You think you're going to pummel them to death?"

I smirk, laughing at his grim expression. "I've learned a thing or two living on the streets."

His mood shifts as he rubs his jaw, his nails grazing another day's addition of growth. "Killing someone, even in self-defense, isn't easy, Avery. Don't fool yourself into thinking that it is."

Cable's words fall heavily over me, stealing away the smile that teetered on my lips. "Have you done it?"

His nod is slow and forced. He refuses to meet my gaze. "Seventeen. That's my count so far."

"Before or after the world fell apart?"

His adam's apple bobs. "Fourteen after."

I blow out a breath and lean back. "And the other three?"

He shakes his head. "They were a mission. Nothing more."

"As easy as that, huh?"

Cable falls still. "I didn't say that."

"No, you didn't, but you're sure as heck trying to make it sound like that."

"What do you want me to say? That ending a life gets easier each time you do it? Well, I hate to tell you, but it doesn't. Each time is just as fucked up as the last."

I lean forward and wait for him to re-engage with me. "You killed twice for me. I know that cost you something."

A vein pulses down the center of his forehead as he struggles to control his emotions. Guilt? Shame? Fear? I can't tell. Probably a mixture of all of those.

"You did what you had to do. There's no fault in that."

He drills his gaze right into me and for a split second, I recoil. "There is always fault in death. Especially when it's face to face. Those final moments haunt you forever."

I reach out and place my hand on his forearm. He looks down at it. "That's what makes us different than those people out there."

He follows the direction of my arm as I point to a small cluster of Withered Ones emerging from the dense tree line. The wooden fence proves too tricky to maneuver for the two on the far left side of the group. The others walk on, leaving their companions behind to repeatedly march into the fence.

"They aren't people," he says.

I purse my lips, hesitating before I speak. "Maybe they still are."

"What do you mean?"

I jerk my head toward them. "What do you see?"

He clears his throat and pulls his hand out from under mine. The warmth of his skin lingers only a moment. I rub my palm against my leg to remove the feeling of his touch. "Six Moaners out for a stroll."

"They aren't strolling, Cable." I wait for him to tear his gaze away from the Moaners to face me again. "They are walking, in the same direction, at the same speed."

He slowly turns back toward the doorway. I lean forward, near enough to see the pulse thrumming against his neck. "They are in step with each other."

His breath hitches as he finally sees exactly what I have seen for the past several days. "That's not possible," he mutters under his breath.

"And yet it is happening."

His brow furrows as he turns to look at me. His eyes widen as his nose brushes against my cheek. I quickly sit back. His gaze searches mine, but I turn away, tucking my hair behind my ear. Clearing his throat, he repositions himself, placing space between us. "I never noticed before."

"I did." I trail my fingers through the dirt. The barn floor is a mixture of dust, old fallen leaves and stray bits of hay. Beneath is a layer of hard dirt. "I think one of them grabbed me."

Cable's head whips up. "What?"

I chew on my lower lip, digging my nails deeper into the ground. "Before I was taken by those soldiers, I was in this pharmacy looking for supplies. I heard it when I entered. It was dark, pretty much impossible to see. To be honest, after the herd I passed through in the street I'm amazed I went in there at all."

A smirk tugs at his handsome features and I know he's about to toss out some crap about me being stronger than I think I am, so I rush ahead. "It grabbed me by the wrist. I could feel how cold its skin was, like a tepid bath on a hot summer day. It felt...wrong. The skin was loose, kinda floppy I guess."

"What happened?"

"A bag came down over my head and the next thing I knew I was being tossed in the back of a truck. Woke up in that blood bank a while later."

I stare at dust motes floating through the air instead of him. I feel him watching me, weighing my words. "I know it sounds crazy. Trust me, I've wondered if I'm losing it so many times, but I know what happened."

"I believe you."

"Do you?" I lower my gaze toward him. He stares back with an unwavering gaze.

"Yes. I do."

"Why?"

"Because you said it."

I laugh, shaking my head and the moment of tension passes. "Are you always so trusting?"

"Pretty much."

"Must be a southern thing."

"No. I just prefer to think good of people."

"That could get you killed one of these days."

Cable smirks and pushes himself up from the ground. "Well, then let's hope today is not that day."

He offers me a hand. I brush my hand over the ground to cover my doodling and pause. "Wait a second."

Rising to my knees, I place my palm against the dirt and sweep my hand wide across the ground. Cable crouches down beside me. I trace my hand along a deep groove in the dirt, hardly unusual to find in a working barn, but something about it feels too straight, too perfect.

"Look!"

Leaning low, I blow against the dirt and reveal a distinctive wood grain beneath the layer of dirt. Cable begins to follow my lead and a couple minutes later we uncover a trap door. "Well, how about that."

I loop my finger through a small hole cut into the wood, but Cable places a hand on my arm to stop me. "Maybe we shouldn't."

"Shouldn't what? It's not like we would be trespassing any more than we already have."

"I know, I just think—" he cuts off as the sputtering of static bursts from the open door of the Humvee. I scramble to my feet and race for the radio.

"Hello? Is anyone there?" I lean in close, fighting to hear the garbled voice, distorted and faint. "Please repeat. I can't understand you."

"This...Alex...coming...you..."

"It's them," I call back over my shoulder to Cable, only to find him right behind me.

"I heard. Let's see if we can clean it up a bit. Go grab Eric. He's better at this than I am."

I toss Cable the handset and tear out of the barn. My shirt billows around me as I race across the lawn, grabbing hold of the porch post to swing myself up the steps. "Eric!"

The screen door screeches and slams behind me as I search the bottom floor. I move swiftly up the stairs and check the bedroom we shared the night before. The bathroom is empty, as are the spare rooms. I fight to still my breathing as I turn toward the only door left closed.

"Oh, Eric." I reach out to push open the master bedroom door. The morning light filters in through the white eyelet curtains, graying with dust. The pale rose colored rocker that sits beneath the window is empty. The pictures of a smiling man and woman standing proudly on their front porch stare back at me. White hair and big smiles contained within a frame boasting the "best grandparents in the world."

The bloody bed covers dangle on the floor. The pillows bear evidence of two heads, a dent on either side of the bed. I step toward the partially closed bathroom door and hold my breath as I listen to the steady drip of water. The door squeaks on its hinges as it slowly opens. Grimy white tiles offset the pink soaker tub and vanity. Wilted flowers droop from a glass vase residing on the double window beside the bathtub. Droplets fall from the tap into the bath, collecting into a tiny stream as they trail down into the drain.

Spinning around, I look into the linen closet and behind two sliding doors to reveal an old side by side washer and dryer that has a manual dial.

Eric isn't here.

"Avery?"

I turn at the sound of my name and head for the door. I pause in the doorway, casting one last glance at the room. "Cable?"

"Downstairs."

My feet feel like lead as I descend. I should have paid attention to Eric's mood shift. I should have spoken to him, expressed my sympathy. I knew he was hurting, mourning in his own silent way. I assumed with the way he poured himself into fixing up that truck that he needed to get away...

I hang my head. "He's gone," I whisper, realizing that he probably slipped away while I was beating up the grain bag when my grunts masked the hum of the engine starting. We should have seen this coming. Cable helped him get it ready. We gave him the perfect opportunity and he took it, leaving us behind.

"He took the truck," I say as I slowly descend the stairs. Cable nods, placing his hands on my arms as I stop on the final step.

"I know. It's what he would have wanted."

I sink down onto the step, feeling numb, cold. "Why would he just leave us like this? He took our supplies and our only transportation."

Sinking down into a crouch before me, he shakes his head. "He couldn't let go."

I wipe at my eyes, realizing that my emotions have betrayed me. It angers me that I'm crying, that I'm feeling weak when I should be strong. I swallow hard. "He was a fool."

"Why? Because he loved her?"

"Because he let her drag him down."

I rise and try to push past him, but Cable stops me, grasping my arm. "Don't shut down. Not now."

"Why not? What good has caring ever done for me?"

His grip loosens, his hand slides down my arm to take my hand in his. I stare at it, knowing that I should pull away, but I don't. "Because your friends are coming."

ELEVEN

I watch Cable shove cans of food and packages of homemade dried jerky into a spare pack, digging deep into the back of the cabinets for food we never thought we would need. He rushes through the kitchen, opening and slamming cabinet doors in search of more supplies. Spare canning jars, filled with water from the well out back, line the counter. He moves with purpose and speed. This worries me.

"Do you need any help?" He hasn't spoken in nearly three hours. Not since he told me my friends were coming. He doesn't seem all that happy about the idea. "I could help, you know?"

Cable looks back over his shoulder at me, as if realizing for the first time that I'm still here. "I need you outside. Keep watch on the west. That's where they should be coming from."

Something about the way he says *they* makes me wonder if he actually means Alex's group. I close the gap between us and grab onto his arm, noticing how the early evening light filtering in through the kitchen window has begun to wane. Twilight will be upon us within the hour. We need to be gone by then.

"Stop." He resists and I tighten my grip. "Stop, Cable."

"There's no time for that," he grumbles, pulling away. He ducks low and searches under the sink. He grabs a box of matches, shaking it to see if it is full then stretches to reach a half empty pack of batteries that look as if they may have begun to corrode. "We have to be ready to leave the moment they arrive."

"Why? What aren't you telling me?" He goes still, the backpack falling slack at his side.

"Look, I know you're upset about Eric. I want to go look for him too, but you're wasting energy. He's probably halfway to the Illinois and Kentucky border by now. When Alex gets here, we can all help fill the extra packs. Who knows, maybe they have their own supply stash."

He rubs his hand across the top of his head, mussing his hair as he grimaces down at the floor. "It's not Eric that I'm worried about. He can take care of himself better than most people."

I duck down beside him, our knees nearly touching. "Then what is it?"

He swallows hard and focuses on his hands after briefly meeting my gaze. "I think your friends are being followed."

"By who?" My grip tightens on my knees as I balance beside him.

"I'm not sure. I've been worried for days that someone will have heard your messages. Worried that if the military did trace the call that they would bide their time. They could have busted in here at any time if they wanted to."

"But why would they wait?" Cable stares hard at me and slowly his meaning sinks in. I blow out a breath and sink back onto the floor. "More people. More blood."

He nods, looking as sickened as I feel.

"So what do we do? We can't just leave them for bait."

"I know." He grabs a rag from under the sink and wipes his brow. Despite the chilled air in the house, sweat beads along his forehead. His cheeks hold a faint flush. "I've been trying to figure it out. To find a way to minimize the damage if there is a showdown."

"You don't have to do this on your own, Cable. I know I'm not a soldier, but I've been through a lot in my life. I've learned a thing or two about taking care of myself when I need to."

"I can't risk that. If it comes down to it, we're going to have to fight."

I glance toward the barn through the kitchen window. The doors are closed, concealing the Humvee within. It won't do us any good now that we siphoned the gas and switched it over to the truck that Eric stole. That was our solution, our way to hide out in plain sight. Now we are stuck.

I don't blame Eric for his decision. Not really. I guess, if I stopped to think about it, I might have done the same thing in his position if I were consumed with grief.

Shaking my head, I know that's not true either. I couldn't just leave someone behind like that, no matter how much someone's death affected me. "Fine. So we fight."

"It's not that easy, Avery. If the military is on their tail, then they will come heavily armed and with far more men than we could take out."

"So what do you want to do? Leave?"

This question places a heavy burden on him. Cable is a good guy—almost too good. He places the weight of the world on his shoulders and no one is strong enough to carry that.

"No. We don't know for sure that anyone is following them, but I'd rather be cautious."

"Agreed." I nod. "What do you need me to do?"

"Hide." He slowly rises to his feet and turns his back on me. I hear him resume shifting through things on the counter.

"No way!" I push up from my knees. "I'm not going to just go bury myself in some dark hole while you take all of the risks."

He sighs as he turns to face me. "I was afraid you were going to say that."

My eyes widen in shock at the flash of silver he swings down in an arch toward my head. Pain splinters at my temple and I crash to the ground.

When I wake, my head feels as if it's been smashed in a trash compactor. My nose feels slightly ajar. Dried flakes of blood mat my hair to my temple. My eye is tender and slightly swollen.

"Why is it always my head?" I groan as I roll to my side.

A moist cloth falls away from my face. Small chunks of ice patter against the ground beside me. Pressing my palm to the side of my face, I feel a chill. "A jerk and a gentleman at the same time," I grumble as I slowly rise.

The throbbing in my head increases as I sit up. The air feels cold and thick, making it feel as if I can't catch my breath. I push back slowly and cry out as I hit a wall. My fingers search about me in the dark. Splinters of wood burrow into my fingertips as I trace along the wall. I ignore the pain and slowly work my way around the small space.

From above, a rectangle of light can just be seen. The light darkens. I raise my face toward the ceiling and cough as dirt rains down. My fingers guide me along a set of wooden steps that lead up. I can feel cold seeping through the space beyond the steps and hurry to sink into the dark hole behind. Earth presses against my shoulder. I lean my head against it to ease the pounding as shouts reach me for the first time.

Overhead, I hear the grinding wheels of the barn doors sliding open. My pulse thumps in my chest as I listen.

The voices above are muffled. I strain to hear what they are saying, to determine if they are familiar to me. *What if it's Alex and he doesn't know we are here? What if they haven't been followed and they think we've left them? What if Cable is hurt and can't tell them where I am?*

Indecision keeps me stalled in place. I want to see, to find my former group to make sure Eva is safe, but something holds me back. In the distance, I hear the ping of gunfire and shiver.

"Shit." The person standing overhead shifts away and the light reappears. I crane my neck to see, listening to the return fire.

Cable was right! They were being followed!

Chaos erupts around the farm. Gunfire fills the air. I hear screams of pain drowned out by the roar of engines. The scent of smoke slowly begins to filter into my nose. I press my sleeve to my face, taking only shallow breaths.

I can't see, repeats through my mind as panic begins to overwhelm me. The dark is thick and suffocating. *It's a big room with windows. Lots of doors. A high ceiling.*

I used to do this when I was a child when fear of small spaces would seize me. My mother never locked me up. She may have been a crap mother, but she wasn't cruel in that way. No, my captivity was self-inflicted. I would hide to be alone, to escape the crushing fist of one of the jerks she brought home with her after work. Some of them weren't too bad. Others...it was better to be afraid of the dark than be within their reach.

I duck at the sound of a loud thud overhead. I hear footsteps, slow and controlled. Something heavy is rolled over, dragged a few feet.

"No. Please!"

A close range gunshot covers my scream as I cower back. Something wet slaps my forehead. I reach up and touch the warm liquid. It is thicker than water. Blood.

Holding my stomach, I double over and try to block out the sounds of a struggle overhead. Grunting. Swearing. The repetitive thuds of blows landed.

Please don't be Cable!

More shouts rise in the distance. I raise my head and listen, realizing that the rapid gunfire has lessened. Have we been overrun? Have they called a ceasefire to hunt for me? It was all over far too soon to have been the military, but who else could have attacked? Maybe survivors from a nearby town looking for supplies?

I hear the snapping of bone above and hold my breath. There is a long, pained groan and then silence. The victor stumbles back and the wooden trap door creaks underfoot. The person halts. The thrumming of my pulse against my neck intensifies as the seconds pass. Then I hear it. The sweeping of a shoe against the ground. Someone above me searches for the edge of the door.

As the creaking of the wood comes again, I dart from my hiding place, rising to my full height, arms stretched out before me as I head toward where I think the far wall is. My fingers clash with rubber tipped handles, the metallic clanking of tools sounds loud and echoey in the small space. I know the person above heard.

I grab wildly at a handle and yank, but it doesn't budge. Raising my foot, I press back against the wall, tugging with all my might. *Release, dammit!*

The wall emits a loud wooden groan a second before the tool releases and I'm thrown to the ground.

"Hey!" I freeze at the shout overhead. "There's someone down here!"

I press back into my hole just as the trap door is yanked open. Unnatural light spills into the hole. I cover my eyes until I adjust to the sudden brilliance. Heavy steps descend into the dark. The earth crumbles against my shoulder as I flatten against the wall.

"Hello?"

I hold my breath, clinging to the tool with sweat-slick hands. The dual handles feel heavy in my grip. I run my finger along the wooden handle and down the long length of the metal head and realize I grabbed a pair of pruning shears. The metal feels gritty, worn. Most likely so rusty I won't even be able to open them. *I have the shittiest luck ever,* I silently bemoan.

The man reaches the final step and pauses. I watch from beneath the stairs as he ducks down and surveys the room. He raises his hand to try to peer around the light spilling over his back. "I know you're down here. I'm not going to hurt you."

I reaffirm my grip. Beads of sweat drip from my brow and land on my nose. Despite the cold, heat flashes through my body, setting me on edge.

"It's safe to come out," the man calls again.

I raise my sheers and poise the curved metal end through the stairs, aiming for his upper thigh. Soon he will move and I'll lose my chance.

I allow myself a brief inhale and hold it, wishing that time could slow so I would have more time to think, to plan, but it doesn't. It speeds up. The muscles in my arm constrict and I draw back my arm to strike.

A shout from overhead startles me. The shears slam against the wooden step as I recoil. A shadow hurtles down from above. "Get away from her!"

I crawl out of my hiding place at the sound of his voice. When I rise, I find Cable on top of the man, pummeling him with his fists. I feel paralyzed as I watch the muscles in his back constrict with each swing. The scream of pain snaps me out of it. "Cable!"

His arm pauses, cocked back as he turns to look at me. His face is flushed and glistens with sweat. His hand is bloodied, his face covered in scratches and dirt. His hair is matted with blood, but I can't tell if it's his own. "You...okay?" he grunts.

The man beneath him groans. His leg shifts, bending at the knee before it falls still against the ground.

"I'm fine." I look down at the man's torso. Though it rises and falls with breath, I can tell he's badly wounded. "I could have taken him."

Cable wipes at his face, managing to smear the blood rather than clean it away. "I know. The thing is, I didn't want you to need to."

"Still trying to save the world, huh?" The erratic beating in my chest slowly abates as he stares at me. An odd flush rises along my neck under his intense gaze. It feels intimate.

He nods and a small twitch tugs at the corner of his lips. "Yes, ma'am. One pretty gal at a time."

A telltale blush betrays the impact his statement has on me before I turn away, dipping low to retrieve my shears. Cable looks down at my weapon. "Haven't seen that one used before."

I shrug. "I improvised."

"That's good." Cable grunts as the man beneath him begins to stir. "Why don't you go on up? There's someone waiting to speak to you."

I look toward the light as hope flared in my chest. *Eva!*

I set my shears down, propping them against the wall and rush for the stairs. I'm nearly topside when I hear a grunt of pain and turn to see Cable crashing to the ground. The man kicks out at him as soon as he falls.

"No!"

"Stay there," Cable grunts as the man throws himself on top.

The two men roll side over side, their legs entangled as they disappear into shadow. I peer into the dark, ducked low, desperate to see. "I can help."

"No." Cable's voice sounds strangled. My legs go weak at his howl of pain. Standing there, knowing that he is in trouble, that I could help, is maddening, but there is little room down there. If I were to go back down I might take away any advantage Cable may have of getting the upper hand, so I obey.

Another cry of pain brings them back into view. Two pairs of feet kick out. A low punch strikes at someone's kidneys.

"No!" My heart stops in my chest at the plea. A piercing cry cuts off and silence falls over the space. One set of legs collapses to the side. Only the sound of heavy panting can be heard.

"Cable?" My call is too soft to be heard so I try again. I watch the survivor roll away, knees bent, chest heaving with exertion. I close my eyes at the sound of vomiting. The scent wafts toward me, turning my stomach.

"Cable? Dammit, speak to me!" I grip the edge of the trapdoor as my mind flies through escape scenarios. If the other guy won, I'm in a world of hurt!

"I'm here," comes a hoarse response.

My shoes clatter against the wooden steps as I rush down and find him curled onto his side and pull him toward me. My grip falters on his arm as my hands become slick with blood. "You're hurt."

"Not...mine," he rasps, clutching his ribs. I spy his glock lying on the ground beside him.

"I don't remember hearing a gunshot."

He coughs and rolls, grimacing. "Out of ammo. Took out a few of the raiders outside."

"And my pistol?"

"Gone. I used everything."

Cold dread washes over me as I look to the light above. I don't blame Cable for using what little ammo we still had to protect us. It was the right call. I'm just worried about what happens once we hit the road without any bullets.

As I lower my gaze, I notice the dark pool growing beside him. I tug Cable away, disturbed by the idea of it touching him. He grunts in pain as I fight to prop him against the wall.

I turn to look at the other guy. Now that my shadow no longer conceals him, I spy the set of shears plunged deep into the man's chest. "Oh, God!"

Cable grips my arm, keeping me from moving forward. "Don't."

"He could still be alive."

"Avery..."

The waver in his voice breaks through my growing need to see, to check that we are safe. I hear his grief and stop resisting. Cable killed a man in cold blood. I can't begin to imagine what must be going on inside his head.

"He's not wearing a uniform," I whisper, staring at the pair of white tennis shoes lying in the light. I turn to look at Cable. "He's not military."

Cable shakes his head. "It wasn't them."

My voice catches in my throat. I yank out of his grasp and dive toward Cable's attacker. His face is buried in shadow but when I reach his side I see his dark skin and the gold nugget ring on his finger.

I close my eyes and collapse back onto the floor. My breathing catches as I recognize the ring. "You killed Devon."

Cable coughs, his feet digging into the ground as he fights to stand. I turn away from Devon and throw my arm around Cable's waist to help him rise. "Couldn't see," he rasps.

"Shh," I whisper, easing him toward the steps. His limp is pronounced, making it hard for me to help from my shorter height. He is much heavier than he looks. "It was an accident."

His grip on my shoulder tenses and I pause. "I thought he was trying to attack you."

I don't tell him that Devon tried to coax me out, claiming that I would be safe if I did so. I also don't tell him how close I came to taking Devon out myself. "It was dark. There was no way you could have known."

Cable hisses as I squeeze his side to help him up the steps. "I should have known. Should have stopped. I just sort of lost it…"

"No," I grunt as we take each step at a time. He is hurting. His steps move with exaggerated caution. "It was my fault. I should have recognized his voice. Should have come out sooner."

He pauses, forcing me to halt. I look up to find him glaring down at me. "You are not to blame. It was my job to protect you, not the other way around."

I ease Cable down onto a stack of wooden crates. They were filled with sand and carrots when we first arrived, making me think that the old folks who used to live here probably had intentions of turning that trap door space into a food cellar. Maybe that's why there were so many empty wooden shelves down there.

"I told you earlier that I'm not your job." I step back and cross my arms over my chest, watching as he clutches his stomach. Blood seeps from his nose. His eye has already begun to swell. His lip is split. Who knows what other injuries lie beneath his shirt. "You don't have to always come to my rescue."

A slow breath whistles between his teeth before he responds. "Maybe I want to."

I start to speak, to tell him that I'm just fine on my own, but I hesitate. If Cable hadn't come to my rescue, it would have been me with blood on my hands, with remorse that could never be removed. I would be tainted. A killer. Devon was innocent. I may not have liked the guy, but down in that dark room, I would have done whatever it took to survive. If Cable hadn't come for me, I would be the murderer.

I look toward the barn door and realize the light flooding in comes from the remains of four large vehicles. I raise my hand to shield myself from the firelight and spy bodies prostrate on the ground. Smoke filters past the door. An orange glow flickers off to the left as well.

"You set the house on fire?"

Cable slowly nods. "It was a distraction."

"That's why you were so anxious to gather the supplies."

He nods again, wincing as he coughs.

I sigh and sink down beside him. "I forgive you for knocking me out."

"Really?" His eyebrows arch in surprise. "Figured you'd hold onto that grudge for quite some time."

"Don't you think for a second that I didn't consider doing just that." I grin and place my hand on his knee. "I know you did all of this for me."

His gaze falters and he looks away. "You're the only person I've got left."

"Well," I smile and pat his leg. "I guess that makes us family."

Even as I say, family, I recognize that the word doesn't fit. Not for us. Not now. I have begun to care for Cable and that scares me. In more ways than I care to think about.

TWELVE

I walk in silence, listening to the fire spit and crackle behind us. The woods are illuminated by the flames, both directly behind us and farther into the distance. I remain by Cable's side, his arm around my shoulder, allowing me to assist him.

The pack on my back is heavy, filled with hammers, chisels, a small ax, and a pretty wicked looking mallet, but it is not nearly as heavy as my heart. Eva was not with Alex's group when I emerged with Cable from the barn.

I spotted Alex first. He worked with Sal to toss unfamiliar bodies into the flames. The two-story farm house was ablaze, sending a plume of smoke into the night air that would easily be seen for miles around. Victoria puttered about, randomly kicking at the deceased. I'm not exactly sure what her point in doing that was, but the old bat wasn't exactly all there the last time I saw her. She seems worse off now.

When Alex looked up and saw me under Cable's arm, a sad smile lit his face, but it quickly vanished when I told him Devon had fallen. I didn't say how or why. Cable noticed but didn't say anything.

It didn't take long for the barn to catch fire. In the flickering flames, I could see some of the Withered Ones in their moaning march across the fields. I knew they wouldn't make it with the flames setting bits of hay in the yard alight, but there was no point in trying to stop them. They would probably continue marching until the flames finally consumed them. A part of me felt that was a better fate than their endless, mindless walk.

Now, Alex leads the way through the dark woods. He has two packs on his back. As does Sal. Victoria refused to take more than one, garnering her another livid glare from me. When I first met her, this might have bothered her, but now...she seems different. Like the last cog on her gears finally popped off.

None of us speak as we head into the woods. The forest feels safe, and I, for one, want to stay clear of people for a good long while. We have supplies enough to last us a few days and some crude tools that can be used as weapons if it comes to it. We will make it. The question is...for how long?

It's not just the military we have to watch out for, or the gangs tearing apart St. Louis brick by brick. Now it's the survivors in small towns that we will meet. Those people desperate enough to put a gun to our head when they want something.

And what about the virus? We are no closer to discovering how it ticks. Hiking through the forest isn't about to help that situation either, but none of us are ready to face another slaughter. Ours or anyone else's.

From time to time I look toward the other fire well off in the distance, wondering who started it and if there were any survivors. Is it a coincidence that both fires started around the same time? Did the same men who follow Alex's group follow another?

The moon rises high overhead. A bitter cold descends, but we don't stop. Moving keeps us warm. Cable shelters me from much of the brutal wind. He must be suffering. His coat was lost to the battle. He has only a thin long-sleeve shirt to protect him from the winds now.

"Wait up!"

Alex pauses and circles around to me. Cable's teeth chatter. "We can't stop."

"Cable is freezing. Do you have anything to spare?" Eric took all of our supplies, including the last of the clothes we'd scavenged.

I look to Alex and follow his gaze as he turns to look at Sal. The sleazy creep crosses his arms over his shoulder and shakes his head. Anger simmers low in my belly, but Cable's weight holds me back. "Alex?"

"Let me see." He swings his pack off his shoulder and kneels. The sound of the zipper is loud in my ears. The woods are quiet tonight. Far too quiet to be normal. It is unnerving.

I watch as he shifts cans and used bottles half empty with water. He removes a worn cloth that is stained pink. When he looks up at me there is a pain in his eyes. I look away, biting my lip to keep back the tears. I want to ask about Eva, to hear what happened at the end, but I'm afraid of hearing it. I want to believe that she survived, that she lived to hold her baby, but I don't believe it anymore. Not really.

"It's all I've got." Alex holds out a small blanket. It is threadbare and tattered on the edges but large enough that it could shield Cable's back and arm.

"Thank you." As I take the blanket from Alex I realize that his hands are shaking. He meets my gaze briefly before quickly turning back to his pack. The weight of Eva's loss sits heavily on his shoulders. There is anger, too. At himself? At me for leaving them behind? I honestly don't know, and I don't have the stomach to ask. Not yet.

Alex zips his backpack and slings it over his right shoulder. The second pack is larger and heavier, weighing down his left side, forcing him to walk unevenly. He returns to Sal and Victoria's side while I see to Cable.

"Your friends seem intense." Cable's teeth chatter so hard I fear he will bite his tongue.

I set my pack on the ground and shake out the blanket. "They aren't my friends. They just sort of took me in."

As I wrap the blanket around him, I notice how close we are. I can feel the warmth of his chest against mine as I rise onto my tiptoes to tie a knot around his shoulder. It won't do much to warm him, but it should, at least, be a buffer against the winds. I sink back to my flat feet. Cable grasps my wrist as I start to turn away. "Sometimes we don't get to choose our friends. Especially not now."

I glance back toward Alex's group. It is smaller now. Devon is gone, as are Eva and the two people they had locked away. Seven becomes three. How many more will be lost in the coming days?

"I know." I look down at his grasp on my wrist, remembering when we first met, how sure I was that his intentions weren't entirely pure. He has proven to me time and time again to be honorable. I don't think I could have found a better friend. I've surely never had one so good before, except Eva.

"You miss the girl, don't you?" He whispers as I ease into my pack and place his arm over my shoulder. Alex helps Victoria back to her feet and moves out. Cable and I remain a couple dozen paces back and a visible divide develops within our group.

"I just wish I knew what happened to Eva." Although Cable gently tried to pry information from me over the past few days about what happened to me between the time I left the apartment and arrived at the military hangar, I wasn't overly forthcoming with details. All except for my need to see Eva again. The rest was better left unsaid.

"Why don't you ask them?"

I shrug and feel the burn in my shoulder muscles. Helping Cable was never a question, but it is taxing. I don't know how I will be able to keep up with Alex's faster pace. He marches as if the Devil himself is on our heels. The trouble is...he just might be. "Sometimes not knowing hurts less."

"Are you so sure you want to assume the worst?"

I look up at him and notice the sheen on his forehead in the moonlight. "Are you feeling okay?"

"You mean apart from the knife in my side and the wrecking ball that slammed into my head earlier? Yeah. I'm good."

"No." I slow down, noticing how labored his breathing is. "You're sweating."

"We're walking."

"It's freezing out here."

"Is it?" He frowns and looks around us at the darkened woods. The fires have fallen behind us. The barren maple trees and towering pines spread ever before us. The terrain is uneven, dangerously inviting for a twisted ankle.

I stop completely and force him to halt. I press him back against a tree and roll my shoulder once I'm free of his weight. He doubles over, clutching his side as he breathes deep, looking as if we've just finished a long distance sprint rather than hiked for an hour.

"Something's wrong."

He shakes his head, his head bowed. "I'm fine."

"Liar."

His shoulder shakes with a deep throaty chuckle, but he sucks in a breath as the pain hits. His arms quiver. "You're barely on your feet, Cable."

"I'm fine."

"Are you always this stubborn?" I plant my hands on my hips and wait for him to look at me. When he does, I see a glint of humor in his eye.

"Not so fun when it's being directed back at you, huh?"

"Alex!" I cup my hands and call out to the woods. I can no longer see them or hear their heavy-footed traipsing. It's a good thing we aren't trying to be quiet; otherwise, we'd be a dead giveaway. "Alex!"

A moment later I see the swinging flash of a dim light heading toward us. I wait, using one hand pressed against Cable's hunched shoulders to keep him upright. Alex comes around the side of a tree, a frown deeply etched onto his face.

He starts to speak but takes one look at Cable and closes his mouth again. "He's hurt."

"We all are." A burn rides along Alex's cheek and down his neck. The skin looks angry. It needs to be cleaned, but he refused. Apparently Cable and I aren't the only stubborn martyrs in the group.

"He's worse. We need to stop for a bit."

"Can't do it." He shakes his head and reaffirms his grip on the two packs. His gaze travels beyond me, back in the direction we came from. Fear pinches his handsome features, making them distorted and ugly.

I help ease Cable to the ground when I feel his legs begin to buckle then rise and stare down Alex. "I'm really getting tired of being treated like a pathetic, helpless little child. I can handle it, so you might as well spill whatever little secret you two have been keeping from me."

Alex and Cable exchange a glance. Alex shrugs, but it is Cable who responds. "The military base was sacked."

That I didn't expect. "What do you mean sacked? How? By who?"

"The gangs spilled over the river, took out most of East St. Louis a day ago. Guess they decided they'd like to expand their horizons without any threat to oppose them so they sacked the base. Weird thing is, it looks like someone else beat them to it."

Cable gives me a warning glance so I remain quiet about our escape from the base. Alex sinks down into a crouch and I follow if only to keep at eye level with him. If I start thinking about how sore I am then I'll be inclined to give up completely. "Things fell apart real fast after you left...after Eva..." Alex looks away. His Adam's apple bobs and he wipes his hands over his face.

I bite down on my lower lip and squeeze my hands into balled fists, savoring the pain my nails inflict on the tender flesh of my palms. Alex grabs a stick and hurls it toward a tree, seeming less than satisfied by the tiny smack of wood, probably hoping for it to snap in half.

"They broke down the door less than an hour after you left. Devon and Sal nearly got caught trying to get Victoria out. Stupid, really. She moved as slow as molasses and couldn't keep her trap quiet when she was told to." He heaves a weighted sigh and sinks all the way to the ground. His hands splay over the cold earth, sifting decaying leaves. "I stayed with Eva till the end. I owed it to her."

"Did she...did she feel any pain?" My voice cracks. Cable reaches out for my hand and twines his fingers through mine. I'm grateful for his presence.

"Pain?" Alex's gaze grows distant as he slowly shakes his head. "No. Those last few minutes I spent at her side she didn't feel much of anything. She lost consciousness within minutes after you left. I didn't know what to do, how to help."

"I'm sorry," I whisper, drawing my knees up into my chest. A tree root presses against my tailbone, but I ignore it. "I wanted to come back..."

"No." He crosses his hands over his knees and I see dirt buried deep under his nails. "It's good you got out."

"She didn't." Alex turns to look at Cable. "She was captured."

"By who?"

I close my eyes and try not to remember the feel of the bag over my head, the fear of waking without senses, confined as a prisoner. I hear Cable giving Alex the rundown, but I tune them out. As I think over all that has happened, a new thought hits me and I break into the guy's conversation.

"You never said Eva died."

Alex blinks. "Well, no. That's because she didn't."

My fingers uncurl as I scoot toward him. "Where is she? Who took her?"

Alex frowns. "The military. I thought you knew that."

A blanket of cold falls over me. "Why her?"

"They wanted her baby," Cable says in an emotionless tone that seems out of place for him. All this time, he has fought for what is good and right. Why this time would he not seem to care?

"Why?"

Alex rises, dusting his hands off on his pants. "I need to catch up with the others. We haven't put nearly enough distance between us and those gangs, and I, for one, don't want them coming down on us in our sleep."

"Cable isn't ready to move yet." I protest, knowing exactly why Alex chose this moment to interrupt. What happened to Eva doesn't sit well with him. How can it?

Grunting with effort, Cable presses back against the tree and rises. I follow suit. His grimace releases when he is fully upright and he nods at Alex. "We'll be behind you."

"I'll try not to get too far ahead. If we get separated, just head toward the sun."

"That's hours away from rising," I say, noting that the moon still hangs far too high overhead.

"Devon told me about a town not too far from here. There's a railroad that runs right into the heart of it. Keep the tracks on your right and you will find us. We'll set up camp and wait for your arrival."

"And if we don't make it?" I ask.

Cable steps forward and settles his arm around my shoulder. "He'll move out when he has to. That's the way things are now. You take care of your own."

I watch as Alex gives my friend an appraising glance. "You found yourself a good guy, Avery. Take care of him."

"I will." Though I have zero intention of going it on our own. Despite having grown up as a loner all my life, the past few days have taught me a very important lesson: I need people, even if I don't always want them.

THIRTEEN

I don't really know how Cable and I made it through the night. His limp as we neared the deserted town was so bad I felt as if I would stumble with each step he took. My back ached and my heart thumped, pain shooting behind my eye. When we spied a candle in the window of a brick and white-sided church I prayed that it was Alex and not some stranger looking to steal supplies.

It took me less than a minute to sink into oblivion after we were inside. I welcomed it. Victoria's mumbling and Sal's snoring were not enough to wake me as the sun rose and fell once more on the land. When I finally roused the following morning, I felt rested but plagued with a penetrating ache that could not be ignored.

"Filthy stinkin' weasel," Victoria says as she putters past. I sweep my gaze behind her to see the remnants of a haughty sneer on Sal's face.

"What's that all about?" I ask, rolling to my side. The wooden pew was hardly a suitable bed. The sweater I used as a pillow has left my neck in a crook. I rub at the sore muscles, hoping that Cable has improved enough to not need me as a crutch today.

Alex thrusts his knife toward Sal, the tip dripping with juices from an apple he just sliced open. My stomach growls at the sight. They must have come through one of the orchards not far from the base. "Victoria thought she could outsmart Sal. Bet him her food ration that he couldn't solve one of her riddles. Guess ole' Sal ain't as dumb as he looks after all."

"That's terrible. She must be hungry."

He shrugs and pops another piece in his mouth before passing me a slice. The flesh is softer than I would like but still tastes sweet. "A bet is a bet. She'd have made him pay up if she'd won."

I draw my legs under me and reposition my sweater to cover my lap. The scent of mothballs has begun to fade, at least.

The air in the church holds a strong chill and I stifle a shiver. "What'd he stand to lose?"

"His hair."

I blink, sure that I've heard him wrong. "His...his hair?"

Alex nods and wipes his knife on his pants. "She says it's not fitting for a man his age, and with his state of hair decline, to be wearing a mullet."

I clasp my hand over my mouth to stave off my snort, but it's not enough. Giggles erupt from my lips and Alex's grin broadens. It feels weird to laugh again. Haven't had much reason to recently. "Even though I'd hate to live with her gloating, I almost wish she'd won," Alex says.

"Me too." I raise my hands overhead and stretch, feeling each muscle pull taut. It's going to be a long day.

As I lower my hands, I see Alex glancing at me from the corner of my eye. I blush and wrap my arms over myself, feeling self-conscious in my skin-tight white shirt. If I'd had a better option, I would have left any memory of my time spent at that military base firmly seated in the hottest part of the fire, but clothing is limited now. I can't waste needlessly.

Turning to don my sweater, I find Cable's spot empty. I hadn't realized he was awake. "Where's Cable?"

Alex shrugs and pops the final bit of fruit in his mouth. "Said he needed some air."

"In his condition?" I frown and hurry to lace up my sneakers. My white pants are stained and dingy, more brown than anything now. Rubbing my fingers along my pants, I feel the dirt embedded in the fibers. I feel gross, but I'll have to wait for a wash.

Slipping out of the church, I sneak down the front steps and look around. Cable is nowhere to be seen. I creep out to the road and use an abandoned car to shield my body. The road splits in three directions. Cable could be down any of them.

"Cable," I call, cupping my hands over my mouth. I duck down and wait to see if there is a response. Being out in broad daylight bothers me. Despite the frigid cold that keeps us company at night, I feel safer.

A noise from the street to my right captures my attention. I call his name as I head in that direction. The noise sounds like someone kicking a can, but I follow it. Three blocks to the south I discover four Withered Ones on the road. They stumble forward together, with only a couple of feet separating them. One tumbles over a mailbox while the others continue on, oblivious to their loss.

I creep up toward a cottage style home with blue shutters and a peeling white wooden fence. Remnants of flowers lie buried and lifeless beneath the window sill as I peer into the house. No sign of movement.

A loud crash sends me ducking low. I look all around for the sound. Slowly, I rise, planting my hands on my hips as I chuckle. There, scampering through the gutter, is a small raccoon with its head stuck in a can. It runs straight ahead and bashes into the curb before scurrying off in another direction.

"Scared of a household pest. Wow, this is a new low, even for you." I turn to head back toward the church and freeze. A block down on my right I see Cable, perched atop the hood of a truck. He is bent over his knees, his head buried in his crossed arm. I run full out toward him, terrified of how exposed he is.

"Cable," I hiss, waving my arms to get his attention as he looks up. His face is ashen, his chin trembling. His eyes are watery, but he doesn't try to cover his tears. I stop beside him and place a hand on his leg. "What? What is it?"

"I found it."

I glance all around. He has nothing in his hands. Nothing sitting beside him on the hood, and that's when I see it. The faded red paint on the hood of an old beat up Ford truck, more rust than metal now. "Cable," I whisper as he slides off. I wrap my arms around his waist and hold him as he cries into my shoulder.

Now that I'm close, I detect bullet holes in the hood. The windshield is a mass of spider webs. Blood stains the driver's side. The door hangs open, but no one is inside.

"I'm so sorry."

Cable releases a shaky breath as he pulls away. "I checked inside. Eric and all of the supplies are gone."

Why did he have to go for this walk? Why couldn't he have just stayed in bed a little longer and left this town with the thought that Eric made it to wherever he was headed? That he would find peace and happiness?

I glance at the neighborhood around us. Middle-class homes. Manicured lawns. Basketball hoops standing at the end of long driveways. Even a birdbath or two decorating the lawns. Not the sort of area you would have expected a drive by in days past.

"We should get back."

He nods and turns to follow, though I can tell he is reluctant to leave. Losing Eric the first time was hard. This is far worse. I can only hope that his end came fast.

As we walk back toward the church, I cast furtive glances toward Cable. He is sullen. I don't want to push him, so I remain quiet as we walk side by side down the street. I keep an eye on each intersection, each window curtain but nothing moves apart from the random Moaner.

"How are you feeling?" I ask as the church appears one street ahead.

"Well enough." His response is flat.

Movement on the church steps captures my attention. I wave toward Alex, signaling our return. I pick up the pace as he waves back and heads inside.

"I don't like the way he looks at you."

I glance back at where Alex stood a moment before. The porch is empty now. "He's harmless."

"You so sure about that?"

"Yes."

Cable turns slowly to look at me. The change in subject seems to have woken him up a bit. "Not all guys have good intentions all the time, Avery."

I bristle and pull to a stop. "Are you jealous?"

"No." He shakes his head and brushes his foot along the street. He tucks his hands deep into his pockets. I can tell by the way he holds his arms close to his sides that he's still hurting. "I just see things."

"Well, so do I, and I think you're jealous."

I wait for his reaction, knowing without a doubt that there will be one, but what I see surprises me. No humor. No laughter. No crinkling of laugh lines around his eyes. Instead, he grows all the more serious.

"What's wrong?" I whisper and reach out to grab onto his arm.

Though he speaks to me, he does not look away from the vacant porch. "It's been bugging me all night. Probably why I went for a walk this morning. Always did think better outside."

I wait for him to make his point. My patience is on a thin rope today. Must not have slept as well as I originally thought. Or my mad dash through town in search of him has left me frazzled. "Those men that followed Alex's group onto our farm didn't seem like they were giving chase."

I fall still. "You're saying you think they followed closely behind Alex?"

He slowly looks over at me and the anger I see darkening his gaze chills me far more than the blustery winds the night before. "I'm saying I think Alex led them to us."

I start to speak, to deny that Alex would do such a thing, but I stop myself. How well do I really know Alex? Devon? Who was calling the shots when they came to us?

"Just be careful," he whispers next to my ear. "Keep your eyes open. We don't really know who we can trust."

I turn to look at him and realize that our lips are scant inches apart. I breathe him in, savoring the distinctly masculine scent that surrounds him. I lick my lips and pull back slightly, unnerved. "And I can trust you?"

The hard lines of his face soften as he reaches out and cups my cheek. His palm feels rough but warm against my skin. "With your life."

I stare into his dark eyes, lost in the moment. A long time ago I trusted a guy. That had been a big mistake, one I swore I would never repeat.

A throat clears nearby and I look up to find Alex staring down at us, his hands planted on the church railing. His shoes are laced, his jacket buttoned, and both packs rest on his back. "It's time to move out."

I glance up at the sun and frown. "It's daylight."

"Yes. It will help us get our bearings. Sal and Victoria are preparing to leave. Figured I'd give you a few extra minutes to gather your things."

"Thanks." I watch as he walks away and sigh. "Here we go again."

I start to climb the steps, but Cable tugs at my arm. "Remember what I said."

I do. And I will also remember everything that was left unsaid between us.

When we reach the edge of town without further incident, I breathe a sigh of relief. The hours pass by just as slowly as the night before, but we don't stop when dusk falls. We keep walking, trying to stay ahead of whoever it is that might decide to come looking for us. That list seems to be getting a bit too long for my liking.

Alex and his group remain well ahead of us. From time to time, I spy their flickering lights. Cable and I move slowly, carefully picking our footing in the moonlight. Cable warned me against using flashlights. They are too easily seen from a distance, and who knows when we might be in desperate need of light in the days to come?

Hours turn into days. They all feel the same, look the same. The cold is constant, so much that at times I almost forget what being warm felt like. For several days, we stick to the forest, pitching rustic campsites made with blankets and spare clothing for bedding. We huddle around small campfires at sundown, squashing them out before night hits and the light could be seen from a distance. We sleep back to back, Victoria and I in the middle, Cable behind me and Alex and Sal behind Victoria.

The nights are long as we shiver together in silence. It feels wrong to rest when we should continue moving, but exhaustion weighs heavily on all of us. Victoria begins to show signs of struggle as the terrain becomes more unstable. My ankles are a constant ache as flat farmland gives way to hills and rock.

We spot stray Moaners from time to time. One of them was stuck in the mud of a river bank, sunk up to its knees. It clawed at the air in its relentless attempt to move forward. We found another caught in a hunter's trap. The metal claws buried so deeply in the bone of its leg that it could not get free.

The Withered Ones don't bother us, well...not any more than can be expected. I awoke to one trampling through camp in the early morning hours two days ago. It tripped over Victoria as she slept, sending her into a full blown panic attack as the rotting woman flailed atop her. We got a late start that morning. It took hours for Victoria to calm down.

Just outside a small town, we found a landfill and spent a few hours digging through trash. Never in my life would I have imagined that I would do such a thing. At least, not to this degree. As Alex and Sal sorted through a small pile of things I would consider to be questionably useful, I hunted down Cable, only to find him caking his body with mud. He said it was for the bugs. Even in the dead of winter, the darn things seem to find a way of getting you.

Yesterday, we found an old shack to sleep in. It stank of animal feces and urine. We kicked most of the nests out of the corners before we bedded down. I slept with my sweater tied around my nose to help with the smell, but I slept better than I had in nearly a week. I was semi-warm.

This morning, I woke to find Cable feeling better than I'd seen him in days. Color has returned to his face. The flush in his cheeks has begun to fade. After a meager breakfast of cold beans out of a can, we all crowd around Alex's map. We are still heading south, but not nearly fast enough. Even if we manage to avoid military or gang detection, the elements might take us in the end.

The terrain continues to change. The gentle rises become hills with high enough cliffs that you could do some real damage if you fell. We skirt along hiking trails, realizing that we have entered a state park. We pass picnic benches and small wooden buildings hosting the first toilets we've seen in days. I won't deny that I teared up a bit when I saw real toilet paper and made sure to stuff a few extra in my pack for safe keeping.

The march through the night is hard. Although the hills block some of the winds, around a bend, it funnels it straight at us. I huddle behind Cable, grateful for his height and the breadth of his chest. From time to time, he reaches back to hold my hand in the dark. Though his fingers are cold, his grip is reassuring.

Just before dawn, we spot an old graffitied rail car on the far outskirts of a small town. Alex and I help ease Cable inside and close the door behind us. We spend the whole day in the box, warm and snug. As night falls, I can feel Alex's reluctance to leave. No one would look for us here. We are out of the way, off the main roads.

Leaving Cable to his rest, I sneak over to Alex's side. "You look lost."

He stuffs his fists into his pack, trying to shift the contents around to find a more comfortable position. "I've got a map."

"That's not what I'm talking about."

"I know." He stares up at the ceiling. Small cracks in the roof allow moonlight to filter in from above, creating trails on the floor. "Sal is acting a bit off."

"More than usual?"

He nods and rolls his head to the side to stare at the snoring man. "He's been complaining more than usual today. Small things. Like how his teeth ache or he can't stand being too close to the fire because it's too strong a smell. He's irritable."

I frown and look over at his slumped figure. "That's nothing new."

"But it is." I turn to look at Alex, peering through the dark to see him. "Normally, he's just ticked about the cold, about being hungry or that his feet hurt. Now..." he sighs. "I don't know. Maybe I'm just being hypersensitive about everything."

"No." I rub my hands together to warm them. With the sun hiding for the night the cold has returned and what warmth the day brought has been stolen away. "That's good. We need to be."

He rolls onto his side and looks past me. Victoria's muttering rises and falls, even in sleep. She is speaking to someone, her mom by the sounds of it. She keeps talking about a puzzle but it makes little sense. "How's your friend?"

"He's mending. Too stubborn to stop long enough to properly heal."

"Have you looked him over to make sure he doesn't have any internal bleeding? Looks like that other guy roughed him up pretty good."

I swallow down my guilt. Alex still doesn't know that Devon was the man who left Cable in this condition and I have no intention of ever revealing that, especially not if it could put Cable's life in danger. "I haven't had time."

Alex snorts.

"What?"

"Nothing." He crosses his legs out before him and places his hands behind his head.

"Tell me."

"What's there to tell? It's obvious you like the guy."

"I don't...no. We're friends."

He whistles low and soft. "If I had a dollar for every time I heard a girl say that."

"It's true."

"Sure it is. You tell yourself whatever it is that you need to get through the day, but I believe what I see."

I cross my arms over my chest, annoyed by his insinuation. "You're wrong."

"Could be." He rolls onto his side, placing his back facing me. "Guess you're the only one who would know."

As the silence falls around us, I return to Cable's side. His breathing is steady. His eyes shift back and forth, evidence of a deep, restful sleep. I lie down beside him and press my back against him for warmth. Cable stirs and shifts his arm. His hand falls along my upper thigh and I lie perfectly still. After that, sleep takes half the night to find me.

When I wake, I discover I'm the last to rise. Cable and Alex stand beside the open train car door, looking out in the direction of the town. My stomach clenches as I see them motion toward it. I don't trust towns. Not anymore. We've done just fine staying clear of them, but our supplies won't last long. Sal is a bigger guy and eats more than his fair share. The rest of us try to compensate, but we can only do that so long. Cable needs proper nourishment to finish healing.

I groan as I force myself to rise. My back aches and the muscles in my neck are stiff. I stretch out my arms overhead and then attempt to touch my toes.

"Sure must be nice to be so limber."

I raise back up and find Sal openly staring at me, or rather straight down the drooping neckline of my shirt. "You're an ass."

"Never claimed not to be." He chucks me a stale crust of bread and moves away. I grab it off the ground and dust it off, irritated that life has become a subsistence of such meager rations.

"He bothering you?" I look up to see Cable towering over me. His fingers loop over the bottom of his camo pants pockets, his stance portraying a casualness that I know he doesn't feel. The planes of his face are too hard. His eyes narrowed and piercing.

"I've handled worse than the likes of him."

Cable emits a throaty grunt. "I'd like to handle him a bit myself."

I laugh and stretch out my hand. "Help me up, will you?"

The muscles in his arms flex as he easily pulls me up. "You must be feeling better," I muse, standing awkwardly with my hand in his. I know I should step back, to draw my hand away and gather my pack, but I don't. I spent all night thinking about him, wondering if Alex was right. Am I starting to like Cable too much? Is it noticeable to everyone except me?

"I am, thanks to you. You'd have made quite the nurse, you know?"

I finally pull away, making sure to shove that hand deep into my pocket so he can't see how it trembles slightly. I brush my hair back from my face and tuck it behind my ear. "I never really liked blood, or math, science, or even school for that matter."

He leans in and bumps me with his shoulder. "Then it will be our little secret."

I watch as he walks away. *Should I have secrets with him?* I frown at the thought, knowing that I am heading for trouble. I need to space myself from him or risk giving him the wrong impression. Even though I like Cable, I can't afford to feel anything more than general friendship for him. Not in the world we live in now. Too many people are lost. Too many go to an early grave. It's best to not let yourself care. That's how you survive.

I turn and scowl at Sal, who appraises me openly again. "What are you looking at?"

"The only show worth watching in this shithole. I think you'll find I'm not the only one entertained."

I follow his gaze and find Alex and Victoria standing near the back end of the train car. Both watch me and then swiftly look away. I sigh and grab my pack off the ground. "I'm going for a walk."

"Need some company?" Sal calls.

"Not from a worm like you!"

As I leap down through the door, I hear his laughter. It sounds wheezy in his chest.

I tug hard on the straps of my pack and march away, head lowered against the winds. I need to be alone, to set my thoughts straight. Ever since this crap started I've been forced to be around people and I don't like it. My mother always used to harp on at me about how unhealthy it was to be a loner. She never really got that it's what I like, what I thrive off of. Not everyone can be a people person.

With no conscious decision, I head for the backside of the town, hugging the woods for cover as I scope it out. Alex and Cable were planning to do the same, but if I can save them the trip while working through my frustrations, it's a win-win in my eyes.

As I near the first building, I duck low, my back pressed against the vinyl siding. Somewhere up ahead, a screen door slams shut, only to be caught up by the wind and slammed again. The foundation of this home seems a bit off-kilter, as if the whole right side has begun to sink into the dirt. The neighborhood looks a bit rough around the edges. Not really the most ideal place to live, but I guess someone had to do it.

Craning my head, I peer through the window. The interior is dark. Sheets hang over the windows to block out the sunlight, or other things. Tables are overturned. A recliner sits upended. I turn to look back in toward the house and scream, rearing back from the window.

A hand clamps down over my mouth and I buck against the strong grip. "Easy," a voice calls in my ear. "It's just me."

Growling in frustration, I shove Cable's hand away. "I wanted to be alone."

"And I wanted to make sure you didn't do anything stupid." He raises his eyebrows and jerks his head toward the house.

Point taken.

I rub my hands down the front of my pants, trying to ease the quaking in my fingers. "What made you scream like that?"

"Be my guest." I point to the window and step back, leaning against the wall. I watch him, waiting for the same horror that I experienced, but his expression hardly changes. "Really? Nothing?"

Cable pulls away from the window. "I've seen suicides before."

"That woman's face is wallpapered to the drywall. Her brain is coating the window. How you can be so blasé about it?"

He shrugs. "Maybe because it was her choice?"

"Her...her choice?" My voice shakes as I stare at him with open incredulity. "How is that a choice? She shoved a gun in her mouth and pulled the trigger. That's not a choice. That's the epitome of cowardice."

He shakes his head. "You didn't see, did you?"

"See what?" I look toward the window.

"The baby."

My breath catches as I rush forward and peer in again. This time, cradled in the woman's lap, I spy the child. Its face is pale, its eyes open and unseeing. Its mouth opens and closes, its arms pawing at the air.

I sink back and feel Cable standing behind me, offering me help to remain upright. "She knew..."

His grip tightens on my arms. "Imagine what that must be like, to know that your child is going to become the thing that has everyone terrified and there is nothing you can do to stop it. Could you live with that? With knowing that you couldn't save your own child?"

A penetrating cold sinks into my soul at the thought. "It's always the people you love most that hurt you deepest."

Cable slowly turns me around. "It doesn't have to be that way."

"But it is. It always has been. Why should things change? Especially now?" Warm tears seep from the corners of my eyes, trailing down my cheeks. I didn't mean to cry, don't want to, but staring up into Cable's knowing gaze I feel exposed.

"You shouldn't be here, Cable."

"Why not?" He asks. His grip loosens against my arms as his hands trail down to take my hands in his. I hate that I crave his touch, that I find myself needing it.

"Because I don't need you."

His smile nearly breaks me completely as he steps closer. "I thought you would have figured it out by now."

"Figured what out?"

He leans in so close that I'm sure he means to kiss me, but he pulls up just shy of my lips. He stares intently into my eyes before his face shifts away, his breath trails along my cheek as he pauses beside my ear. "I'm more stubborn than you. I'm willing to wait as long as it takes for you to realize that you may not need me, but you *do* want me."

FOURTEEN

S parks flicker. The hum of electricity is lost over the roar of an engine.
"Yes!" I cheer.

Cable emerges from the driver's side of a beat-up pickup that may have at one time been considered a sports model, judging by the attempt at a spoiler on the rear tailgate. He leans over the wheel and taps the fuel gauge. "It won't get us far, but it's something."

I rest my head back on the bench seat beside him and grin. "A day without walking is bliss. I'll take it!"

Cable grins at me and closes the door. He twists his torso gingerly and puts the seatbelt on. He starts to put the truck in gear when he senses me looking at him. "What?"

"Nothing," I smirk. "It's just that I didn't take you for the seat belt wearing kind of guy."

A broad smile crosses his lips. "Well, when you've got precious cargo on board, you tend to take every precaution."

I look away, knowing that he can see the flames licking at my cheeks. My fair skin does little to hide it.

"We won't all fit in the cab," he says, as if nothing were amiss with his previous statement. "I'll take the back with Sal for a while. We can trade off later."

"Why you? You're still trying to heal. I can sit back there just as easily."

He glances at me from the corner of his eye but says nothing. He doesn't have to. I already know what he's thinking.

"We've got some supplies. A couple blankets and enough water to last us for a while. If we load the food and water near the back, I can huddle against the cab to block most of the wind."

"Are you always this logical?" he asks as the truck jerks into gear and begins rolling forward. We are on the far end of town. By now Alex, Victoria, and Sal should have cleaned out the houses nearest the train car. After finding that baby, I couldn't bring myself to search the houses, so I stuck to the shops.

The pharmacy offered some supplies. Antibiotics. Pain meds. Fresh bandages to wrap Cable's bruised ribs, though they seem to be improving greatly with each day that passes. My nasty bandages were used as kindling two nights ago when the cold became too much to bear. In the final store, I found ointment to heal the blisters on Alex's face.

"Only when I want to get my own way."

He laughs and reaches out to turn on the radio. I don't know if he does it out of habit or if he's searching for something, but when only static bounces back at us, he turns the knob and falls silent.

I stare out the window at the faceless homes, at the drawn curtains and doors left open and forgotten. Christmas lights nailed to rooftops flap in the wind, nearly three months overdue. The cheer of the holiday season gone forever.

We weave around abandoned cars and Withered Ones wandering the streets. I watch them as I pass, realizing that in the past week I have nearly grown immune to their presence. The scent of decay isn't quite so strong anymore. The sight of torn limbs and maggots feasting on rotting flesh doesn't turn my stomach now. I never dreamed that I would become immune to it all, but I guess it becomes a matter of perspective.

Watching their endless walk brings two emotions now: sadness and wariness. Though I know no one else shares my ideas, I can't shake the feeling that something isn't right with them.

"Do you even see them anymore?" I ask, without turning away from the window.

"I'm swerving around them if that's what you mean."

"No." I press my nose against the glass as Cable slows the truck. We inch through a herd of Moaners. Several bump repeatedly against the hood. Cable slows to a near halt in an attempt to let them veer off in a new direction. When they don't, he pushes the accelerator. The truck rises and falls over the crushed bodies and we continue on our way. "I mean, as people. Or former people, I guess. Are they just things to you now?"

Cable is silent long enough to draw my gaze back toward him. His fingers grip the steering wheel as we are forced to slow again. We went nearly all morning without seeing a Withered One and now they flock to the one street we need to be on to get us back to our group.

Putting the truck in park, Cable sighs and drops his hands from the wheel as we wait for them to pass. "I can't think of them as things."

"Why not?" I draw one leg up onto the seat and turn to face him. I note that the deep bruising along his cheek and temple has faded into an ugly yellow now. The cut on his lip has begun to heal nicely. He no longer holds his side when he breathes.

"My brother is out there," He speaks to the windshield instead of me. His gaze is fixated on the grotesque faces before us. I try to ignore the strips of flesh being torn from the passing bodies by the sharp edge of the broken side mirrors, or hear the raspy moans that make goosebumps rise on my arms.

"You never spoke of a brother before."

"Lenny and I never really got along too well. I guess that comes with the territory, though. Half-brothers tend to butt heads a lot."

"Sounds like you care about him, though."

"He's family, even if my scumbag dad decided to mess around. I don't hold that against him."

I pick at a scab on my arm where thorn bushes tore at my skin a few days ago. By the time we figured out we'd marched straight into a massive briar patch, there was no choice but to keep going. "My dad ran out on us when I was younger. I remember hurrying home each day after school and waiting on the front step of our porch for him to come back. He never did, of course. My mother moved us to St. Louis not long after. Never really forgave her for that. I was sure one day my dad would walk up that path for me and wonder where I'd gone. When I got older I figured out the truth."

"What was that?" Cable flicks on the windshield wipers and I grimace at the smear of blood as he tries to clean away the carnage left behind.

"That sometimes no matter how hard you try, things don't work out. People leave for their own reasons. You just gotta suck it up and move on. Put them in the past so they can't hurt you anymore."

Cable looks over at me. The path before us is clear if blurred by the red haze predominate on the windshield now. "Sounds like that didn't work out too well for you."

I blow out a weighted breath. "I'm still working on it."

The truck begins a slow roll forward. Cable ducks his chin to see through a clear patch. "You can't keep the whole world out, you know?"

"I can try."

"Sure." He yanks a bit of the fabric off the torn seat cover and leans out the window to wipe the glass before him. It helps a little, but we'll have to do a better job before we hit the road. "Just make sure you don't include me in that, huh?"

I turn away so he doesn't see the tiny smile that betrays me. My eyes widen and I grip his arm. "Cable!"

The truck jerks as he slams his foot on the brake. He follows my gaze in silence. There, standing between two houses is a Moaner. Most of his face has been torn away. His shirt is ragged, his scalp bald apart from a few stray tufts of hair.

"Are you seeing this?" I ask, unable to tear myself away from the man. His eyes are a milky blue. He stands with an unblinking stare into the distance.

"He's not moving," Cable whispers. His voice sounds hoarse.

I turn to look at him. "I've never seen one do that before."

"Me either." I can tell by the color leaching from his face that he's freaked out, but trying hard not to show it. "Let's get back. The others will be waiting for us."

I nod in agreement, but the truck is already moving at a faster pace than before. It only takes us five minutes to maneuver around the debris in the road and arrive back at the train car. Victoria paces near the steps, her hands tucked around her waist. Her lips move rapidly and I realize that she's slipped into another muttering phase. She's been doing that a lot more lately. She's taking to speaking with her deceased mother a lot, sometimes about trivial things like the cold or how hungry she is. At other times, it seems as if she's trying to puzzle through the outbreak. It's scary that some of her mutterings are beginning to make sense.

Alex looks up as we roll to a stop near the overgrown track. Sal sits with one leg dangling from the car, appearing unconcerned and indifferent to our arrival.

"You're late." Alex opens my side of the truck and helps me out. I feel a bit unsteady on my feet, still shaken by the Withered Ones.

"Got trapped by a herd in town." The driver's side door squeals as Cable shoves it closed.

Alex glances back toward town. A deep frown settles onto his handsome features. "It's been a while since we saw any of those."

"Well," I grunt as I toss a cloth grocery bag full of bottled water into the truck bed, "we found one."

"But all together?" Alex hefts two large black grocery sacks of clothes, towels, and medical supplies into the back. "I know you two told me you'd seen it before, but I was kinda hoping you were just yanking my chain."

"There's something else." Cable grabs a cardboard box from beside Alex. I'm relieved to see it filled with boxed foods and canned goods. The homes must not have been completely emptied.

Alex pauses. He looks between us, but I let Cable tell him about the Withered man that we saw. Alex reacts similarly to how we did. Visible disbelief that is quickly followed by a deep-seated fear that begins to spread with alarming speed. He looks hollow, his face haggard.

"What do you think it means?" He asks as he shoves the tailgate closed. The supplies won't last long, but we should be good for a week, maybe more if we are lucky. That means we can head back into the woods where we can be safe.

"It means we need to stop sleeping where we are exposed," Cable responds.

"The Moaners have never been a threat before." Alex glances back at Sal and Victoria, keeping his voice low enough that it doesn't carry.

Cable looks to me. "Avery noticed they are starting to alter their behaviors. Small things, but still enough to be concerned about. I'd rather play it safe. If we can't find a house or abandoned building to crash in, we need to find a way to make this truck more secure. Just in case."

Alex glances at the cab. "It's too small."

"Then we find a cover." I turn to look back into town, knowing that I really don't want to go back in. I'm spooked and not afraid to admit that. "Maybe at the next town, we can find a truck cover, plywood, or something to give us some shelter."

"Agreed." Alex wipes his brow. His cheeks are flushed. I wonder how many houses they had to search through to find what few supplies they brought back. Or how much help Sal and Victoria actually were. "Do we tell them?"

"No." Cable rests his arms over the side of the truck. He looks tired. He hasn't been sleeping well. At first, I thought it was nightmares but now I've begun to wonder if his time clock is all out of sorts. "There's no sense worrying them."

He looks to me and I nod in agreement, though not for the same reasons. I don't think Victoria could handle the stress and Sal...the less he knows, the better.

Within ten minutes, we are prepped and ready to leave. After a heated debate of who would be sitting in the truck bed with me, Alex finally wins and Cable takes the wheel with Victoria pressed in next to him and Sal on the far right. I huddle into my blankets as we turn onto a dirt road leading away from the town.

I don't know its name or anything about the people who once lived here, but I do know that I hope to never see it again.

Alex remains unusually quiet over the next few hours. We huddle close for warmth. With a blanket beneath us, and one wrapped around us, we savor the trapped body heat but little can protect us from the winds that bite at our cheeks. It's slow going even on the back roads. Weaving around abandoned cars and backtracking to avoid major pileups takes up precious daylight.

The sun beats down on us from overhead, warming the top of my head. I lift my face to the light, enjoying this rare time of travel during the day.

"I'm worried about Sal." Alex breaks the silence, glancing back over his shoulder.

"More than earlier?"

He nods and tucks the blanket high under his chin. "I noticed something this morning. Something I've seen before."

I shift and knock knees with him. I start to apologize but realize he's too lost in thought to care. "There are spots on his mouth. At first I thought they were blood, maybe he bit his lip in his sleep or something, but there are more. The idiot chews with his mouth wide open so I noticed a few more on his gums."

"Maybe it was just food. I saw him tucking into a candy bar before we left." The fact that he never bothered to share with the rest of us angered me but didn't surprise me. He's not the sharing type. Sal is one of those guys who is in it for himself and holds no pretense otherwise.

"No." Alex glances over his shoulder at Sal. I follow his gaze and frown. There is a red patch of skin just below his left ear. It seems to be trailing up into his hair. As I follow the trail I see a large patch peeking out near his ample bald spot near the crown of his scalp.

"You think he's turning, don't you?"

Alex scrunches up his face then wipes his nose on the blanket. "Maybe not, but I've seen the signs before."

"In who?"

"My co-pilot, right before we were grounded in St. Louis. At first, I thought it was just stress. We'd done two long hauls back to back and that was against regulation. We were bone tired. Anyone would be. I was almost relieved when they grounded us."

"But it wasn't because of your work schedule, was it?"

He shakes his head. His teeth clatter together and he shrinks farther under the blanket. "Charles lost his wife and son while we were in the air. He never even knew they were sick. That was the excuse the airline gave us when we landed, but I could see it was more than that. There were soldiers everywhere toting guns big enough to take down a jumbo jet. We were put in some sort of quarantine. Never saw him again."

"What happened to him?"

He shrugs. His wind burned cheeks look dry and near cracking. I duck my head under the blanket and feel around in my pack, searching for the ointment. I'd forgotten that I had it.

"Here," I hold out the bottle to him. "It might help."

Alex offers me a smile and dabs the clear medicine on his cheeks then slathers it over his burns. His sigh of relief is audible over the winds. "Thanks."

"Must hurt like a bitch."

He laughs. "I'm tougher than I look."

"A survivor."

He nods. "I've learned to do what has to be done."

As a new silence hangs in the air between us, broken only by the chattering of teeth, I can't help but wonder if that goes so far as to betraying us back at the farm. Though Alex has shown no signs of wanting to harm us, I know that the doubts Cable put in my mind about him will linger for quite some time.

FiFTEEN

We moved steadily south over the next four days, but our progress was stunted by a blown head gasket on the truck, leaving us stranded on the side of the road less than thirty miles from town on that first day. We continued by foot, moving parallel to the highway to stay on course. On the fifth day, we were hit by the mother of all winter storms, driving us back into the shelter of the forest. It crashed over us like a tidal wave, spilling arctic air from the north. By our best guess, we have traveled nearly eighty miles from St. Louis, but it is not nearly far enough to outrun winter.

By the time we stumbled across a hunting cabin deep in the forest, we were all nearly frozen through. Cable and Alex remained alert for the first two days as the storm raged, but I found myself able to relax for the first time in quite some time.

The Moaners seem to have vanished again, leaving us in peace. Maybe they don't like the cold either. If that's true, I may change directions and head to Canada!

Though I have not seen a Moaner in nearly three days, they haunt my dreams, chasing me with gnashing teeth and rabid eyes. Anger. Desperation. Condemnation. None of those emotions make any sense but waking in the early hours before dawn, each one feels real to me.

The winds that battered the cabin have fallen still, the loud howling diminished to its normal gale. The icicles dangling from the pitched roof drip onto the wooden porch, making it a dangerous skating rink at night. The ice has receded greatly beneath the heat of the sun, the first time we've spied its presence in days. It is a welcome sight, if for no other reason than to bring a bit of cheer once more.

The cabin is cozy, snug and warm. Whoever built it meant for it to be a vacation home, not some shanty used only for fishing or deer season. It is well insulated and stocked with enough wood to last us weeks. The cupboards were bare when we arrived, but we have made do, spreading our remaining rations thin.

The A-frame shelter isn't large, but it fits the five of us well enough. A king sized bed is housed in the loft, accessible by a leaning wooden ladder. Another bedroom sits off the small kitchen. Two twin beds fill the small space, with a single dresser between. A gas lantern sits on the empty table top.

Cable and I took the bed in the loft, seeing as how we have become used to watching over each other. Cable remains a gentleman, wrapping himself in a separate blanket before huddling up behind me for warmth. Victoria and Alex claim the twin beds while Sal sleeps on a pull-out sofa, though he prefers the recliner more. I suspect he remains out there to rummage through our things in the middle of the night. I try to listen for his movements in the dark, but the inviting comfort of the bed draws me into a deep, restful slumber.

Our time spent here has not been bad. In fact, it has almost felt like a little slice of home. After rising this morning, and seeing to the more basic human needs, I resumed my usual spot by the window, lounging the day away. I read a book this afternoon. It wasn't very good. Some stupid hunting how-to novel, but it passed the time well enough. I may have even learned a thing or two about setting traps.

It feels weird to not be walking, to not be fighting to survive. I could get used to that.

Now I sit in the corner of the cabin in an oversized rocking chair and watch the people in my group. Victoria buzzes like a contented little bee. The clacking of knitting needles can be heard over the crackling of the fire in the stone hearth. I don't think I've ever seen her so happy. The stash of yarn and needles she discovered in the upstairs loft was all it took to bring her out of her weird depression.

"Look at her," I whisper to Cable who sits on the floor beside my knee. I rock slowly, enjoying the warmth of the nearby fire. "She looks so happy."

"She is."

"It's just yarn."

Cable turns his head to look up at me. "It's familiar, something from the past. Maybe it will do her some good"

I try not to speak to Victoria. She and I have had our differences in the past, but her most recent decline into crazy land has left her as my least favorite conversation partner.

Alex sits perched upon an old wooden barstool across the room, his gaze focused on the back of Sal's head. When he first mentioned his concerns in the back of the truck I thought he might be overacting, but even I've begun to see changes in his personality.

Increased irritability. Spreading rash along his neck. A facial tic under his right eye. He scratches in his sleep, muttering and moaning loud enough to wake all of us. In the light of day, I see a change in his eyes.

Cable follows the direction of my gaze and frowns. He drops the corner of the rug that he was fiddling with and turns, speaking from the corner of his mouth. "I don't want you near him when I'm not around."

"Done."

His eyebrow rises. "Really? No argument? No 'I can take care of myself' crap?"

I laugh and resume my rocking. "The guy's a bona fide creep. I'll happily place him in your charge."

"Huh." He sinks back against the wall. "Well, I never thought that would happen."

"Disappointed?"

"I gotta admit, I am a little."

I smirk and rise from the chair. "I need some air."

Cable glances toward the window. "It's going to be dark soon. Not sure that's wise."

"This is the point where you realize I don't care." I grab a towel off the back of a chair beside the fire. Several pair of socks and shirts hang nearby. "I'm just going for a wash."

Alex looks up. "You'll freeze."

"Well," I pause with my hand on the door and glare pointedly at Sal, "maybe, this time, I can get a bit of privacy and I won't be gone long."

I didn't intend to slam the door behind me, but the wind rips it from my hand. I shiver and rub my hands along my arms. Maybe this wasn't the best idea.

No. I need to go. To be alone for the first time in a few days.

Cable has been after me to join him for a sunrise walk since the storm broke. He claims that it's well worth losing sleep over. I still have my doubts, and zero intention of taking him up on the offer. I try to tell myself it's because I don't want to risk spending time alone with him, but, this time, it's a bunch of bunk. I just really love to sleep!

Alex and Cable scouted out a nearby river with a pool of water mostly enclosed by rock walls and steep cliff faces. The water is sure to be freezing, but much of the winds should be blocked.

Cable was kind enough to drag pails of water up to the cabin for Victoria and me to bathe yesterday. For all of its quaint charm, this cabin was built rustic. The bathroom was just that...for bathing. No indoor plumbing. Only a large claw foot tub and a wash basin. And no lock, so Sal was happy to discover as I was in the middle of disrobing for a wash last night. I vowed that I'd rather be dirty than let him see me naked again.

After days of lying on dirty floors and tramping through mud, muck, and deer shit, I'm desperate to feel clean. To wash the gnarls and dirt from my hair. What I wouldn't give for a bar of soap! The last of it was used on our clothes just this afternoon.

I know we will have to move on now that the storm has passed, but I'm none too eager to go hunting around another town. The last one left a bad taste in my mouth.

Following the path in the fading light, I tread lightly, careful not to step on the few remaining patches of ice. Leaves crunch beneath my shoes. The night approaches and with it comes a flurry of activity as the forest wakes around me. It won't be long before dusk is lost to me. I need to be back before the final drops of light fade from the sky.

Picking up the pace, I clutch my towel and hurry down the path. It has been well used, though not recently by the looks of it. Much of the grass is matted down, but stray bits have begun to poke back through the trodden path.

Up ahead, I see a glint of water. I place my hand against a tree and hoist myself over the final obstacle, a downed log whose innards have long since rotted away.

Placing my towel over the tree, I quickly pull my shirt over my head. A shiver ripples along my skin.

"Why does it have to be winter?" I grumble and hop around, removing my socks and shoes. The instant I am completely bare I race for the water.

The water splashes high against my thigh as I rush into the stream to hip height. The recent storm has made it feel more like a river as it overflows its banks. My teeth begin to chatter within seconds. I scoop handfuls of water and rub it against my sensitive flesh. The frigid water is invigorating and my shivering helps to keep me warm.

A crack of a branch nearby drops me to my knees. I scan the woods before me, listening for any unusual sounds in the night. An owl hoots from the treetops. The wind rustles the leaves along the ground. Naked tree branches clack together overhead. I feel as if I'm being watched.

My lower half burns from the cold water, but I dare not rise. I can sense a presence. The question is...are they alive or withered? An enemy or a friend?

Several minutes pass without a sound. My teeth chatter as I wrap my arms about myself. I have to get out or risk hypothermia, but not before I know who or what I'm dealing with.

"Sal? If that's you out there I swear I'll tie you to a tree and leave your sorry ass behind for scaring me!"

Silence.

I begin to quake and know I don't have a choice. I'm about to turn toward my towel when I see movement about a hundred yards ahead of me. A flash of green against the dark trees and then it's gone. Its gait was halting but fast.

Shit!

Turning on my heel, I prepare to dash toward my towel and come up short. There, standing just behind the tree, is Cable. His eyes are wide as they trail over my body in the fading light. A flush rises above the stubble lining his jaw.

Standing perfectly still, I feel exposed, bare to his sight.

"I uh...God, I'm sorry. I didn't mean to..." He averts his gaze when I attempt to cover myself with my hands. "I mean I intended to come find you, but I didn't think you'd be like that. Shit," he wipes his hands over his face as if trying to mentally remove the image of me from his mind.

"Did you see it?"

His hands fall away, instantly alert. His gaze floats beyond me. "See what?"

"The Moaner."

He closes the distance between himself and the edge of the water, motioning for me to hurry to his side. My feet feel like blocks of ice as I trudge through the water toward him. "It's gone now," I say through chattering teeth.

"How can you be sure?" He risks a glance down at me and then jerks back up when he looks a bit too low.

"I saw it leave."

"Leave?" His brow furrows. "You make it sound like it came, stayed for a while, and left again."

"That's exactly what I'm saying." I wrap my arms over my chest and cross my legs.

"That's not possible, Avery. They don't just watch people. They don't feel anything, do anything beyond walk forward."

"I know what I saw."

He rubs his neck, slowly shaking his head. "You must have been mistaken. It's too dark to really see anyway. Maybe it was a deer or coyote?"

"I know what I saw," I repeat. It bothers me that he doesn't believe me, but I guess if our roles were reversed I'd have a hard time believing it too. "Can I have my towel now?"

He jerks around and snatches it off the log. As if realizing that he can't just toss it toward me, he hesitates. Despite the ache in my lower legs from the freezing water and the fact that I've just been caught out in all my glory, I close the gap between us. He raises his gaze for a moment then lowers it again, the towel dangling from his outstretched hand.

"I'm cold."

"No kidding." He shakes the towel at me. I take it from his grasp and he wrenches his hand back.

Wrapping the cloth around me, I wring excess water from my hair. "You act like you've never seen a naked girl before."

He swallows hard, then raises his head to meet my gaze. "None that didn't give me previous consent."

I laugh and step toward him. "I forgot. You're not like that, are you?"

A muscle along his jaw flinches. "No."

"Well, then I guess it goes without saying that I'd appreciate you not telling the others about our...encounter."

I grab my clothes and hold them to me, wondering if I'm really going to have to ask him to turn away. His blush deepens as my intent finally sinks in. He spins on his heel. Rushing to dry myself and slip into my clothes, I hop about behind him.

He cocks his head to listen and I hear his deep throaty chuckle.

"You try putting jeans on when you're wet," I snap.

He turns away but not before I notice his shoulders rising and falling with laughter. He props his arm against his side and angles toward me. "Use me."

"Well," I pause and look him over, "isn't that a fun proposal?"

He whirls around, his gaze wide and unblinking.

"I'm not decent yet!"

"Sorry!" Heat stains his neck as I grab onto him and sort out my pants. With my hair still dripping, I shove my shirt over my head and nestle into the warm fibers.

I kneel down and conceal my feet in socks and shoes before standing. Though I am fully dressed, I still feel exposed. Tucking my hair behind my ear, I hesitate, no longer sure of what to say.

"I guess you're wondering why I followed you..." he begins. His voice wavers and he falls silent. I almost feel sympathy for his embarrassment. Almost.

Of course, that crossed my mind a time of two. Cable has proven himself to be a gentleman. I can't imagine he came for a peep show like Sal, but then why else would be have come so close? I wasn't exactly being quiet as I splashed about.

"I was worried about you." He casts a surly glance toward the woods. "I guess I had a reason to be."

A trembling begins in my fingers that I'm not entirely sure has anything to do with the cold. What I told Cable was the truth. No human walks with the same style of stunted steps as the Withered Ones. As impossible as it may be, I know one of them was watching me. I just have no way to prove it. "I'm glad you're here."

"Really?" He seems slightly taken aback by my admission.

"Okay, well maybe not in this exact situation, but you know what I mean."

A smile slowly spreads along his lips. "Do I detect a hint of need in your voice?"

"Ha. Did you hit your head on the way out here?"

Cable grins. "That would make you feel better, wouldn't it?"

"Little bit."

Water drips from my hair as we walk. I wring it again. Droplets patter on the leaves underfoot. The back of my shirt has begun to soak through. "Cable?"

"Yeah?" He turns back to look at me. I sympathize with his desire to get back to the cabin. These woods have lost their feeling of seclusion for me now.

"I think that Moaner came from around here."

He stuffs his hands in his pockets as he pauses. I can't help but wonder if he's got his knife hidden there. It wouldn't surprise me. "Okay, let's say that you are right. That somehow one of those things had the capability of thought and reason. What makes you think it's from around here?"

"Because he was wearing a camouflage jacket, just like the one I found inside the cabin for you."

"This area is bound to have a lot of hunters. There are rednecks everywhere! It might not mean anything."

"Or it could. We should warn Alex, either way."

Tugging the towel from my shoulder, I bend over and wrap it around my head. Cable's stern expression cracks when I rise back up and twirl it around my head. "Not a word," I growl and begin tromping back through the woods.

Cable follows close behind but not so close that I feel as if he's invading my personal space. *Ha. It's kinda hard not to when the guy just saw me naked!*

I glance back over my shoulder. Cable has grown quiet, introspective, during the five-minute hike back. I wonder what he's thinking about. Surely it can't be me. At least, I hope seeing me naked wouldn't put that sort of sour expression on his face.

Why the heck do I care what he thinks about seeing me naked? It was a mistake. One I'm not about to repeat any time soon!

As the light from the cabin finally comes into view I pause and turn, placing my hand on his chest to stop him. He stares at my hand. Through the thin layers of his shirt, I can feel the thumping of his heart, feel the heat trapped within. "Look, before we go back in there I just want to thank you for coming after me. I don't blame you for seeing me naked. I mean, it happens, right?"

"Sure." He shifts his weight to his right foot and looks away. "Though that's not quite how I imagined it happening."

My lips part in surprise. Did he just say he imagined seeing me naked?

I clear my throat and try to gather my frantic thoughts. Raising my hand from his chest, I place it against his cheek until he looks back to me. "You're the only friend I've got now, Cable. I don't want things to be weird between us."

But I know they will just by the look in his eye. Cable wants me and I'm starting to think that the feeling is far more mutual than I would like to admit.

SIXTEEN

I listen to the steady rise and fall of breathing coming from the lower floor. The door to Alex and Victoria's room is partially open, per her request. Alex humors the old lady, simply so he won't have to hear her ranting about how it's not safe to sleep near strange men, apparently even at her age. Sal is sacked out in the recliner, no doubt drooling on himself again.

There's no way to tell time, but I feel as if I've lain awake most of the night. The heat of Cable's back presses against mine but for once, it feels suffocating instead of inviting. Every time I inch away from him I feel the emptiness and sink back.

I'm messed up. That's the only explanation. I punch at my pillow in frustration that only comes from hours of staring blankly at the ceiling. When I do, Cable stirs. I hold perfectly still as he rolls over and presses up against me. His arm winds around my waist.

My lungs go through a temporary paralysis as he pulls me closer to him. I am hyper aware of every part of his body that brushes against me as he shifts: the feel of his hand curling around my hip, the weight of his arm along my side and the gentle breath against my neck that makes me shiver.

His legs curl in around behind mine, molding perfectly to me. I suck in only tiny breaths, terrified of waking him, of shifting enough to bring him out of his dream. His fingers tense against my hip and I bite my lip, trying desperately not to think about how good it feels to be touched. It's been a long time since I let anyone get close like this.

Sure, there were guys along the way, but I hardly remember their faces. They were needs that were met, nothing more. Cable is different, no matter how much I wish he weren't.

Would it really be so wrong to encourage him? Just once?

I press back into him and close my eyes, imagining what it would be like for his arms to wrap around me, to hold me. The feel of his hands on my bare skin, his lips trailing down my neck. My pulse jumps at the thought of feeling him above me, moving together in unison.

A warm tingle begins in my abdomen and grows, expanding outward as my thoughts turn to things best left to the dark. My fingers curl around the covers as I bite my lower lip. My breath catches as I imagine the feel of his hands on my breasts, kneading, and teasing.

I turn my head and rock my hips back into him. I pause, waiting for a reaction. My skin is warm, sensitive to each breath that washes over my bare shoulder. My tank top suddenly feels restrictive and I long to be free. To let the cold night air soothe the fire raging within.

Cable breathes heavily behind me as I grind my hips against him. He stirs in his sleep, his fingers curling against my hip. A breathy groan escapes from between his lips and I nearly lose it.

There's no going back now. Not now that I'm consumed with need.

I reach back and grasp his hand, slowly drawing it over my hip and down between my legs. I press his fingers against me and turn my head to stifle a moan into my pillow.

The muscles in his forearm go rigid and I know he's awake. He angles his hips away from my ass, obviously aware of how tightly he was pressed against me. "Avery, what are you doing?"

"I can't sleep," I whisper, rolling my face so that his mouth is beside my ear.

"I can see that."

"Am I bothering you?" I bite on my lower lip and he hesitates. His fingers flinch against me and a shiver trickles down my spine.

"I wouldn't call it bothering." I clench my legs around his hand and his breath grows haggard. "Stop."

"Why?"

"Because I'm trying to be a nice guy right now and you're making me forget my reasons for doing that!"

I smile into the dark. "Maybe I don't want you to be a nice guy right now."

He goes completely still behind me. "Avery, I don't think this is such a good—"

"No." I release his hand from between my legs and push away so that I can roll over and face him. I place a finger against his lips to silence him when he starts to speak. "Hear me out."

I wait for him to protest, to pull away and try to stop me again, but he doesn't. Maybe I've affected him more than I thought.

"I get that you care for me and you know me well enough to know that I don't let people in. Not people that I could feel for. I've lost a lot of people in my life and I've dealt with it, but sometimes I just need to be held. Not because it means something or that I'm looking for some deep bullshit connection, but because it's what I need. Just one night of not caring, of not worrying about how long I have to fight to survive in this godforsaken world. One night to feel something other than this blasted cold or endless hunger. I need this."

The darkness is so complete that I can't see his expression, read the fear or doubt in his eyes. I know it's there. He's always trying to find ways to protect me, even from himself, I'd imagine, if the situation called for it. Cable wants me. I saw it plainly etched into his face earlier tonight and felt the evidence pressed against my backside only a moment ago, but there is another emotion that I saw lingering in his gaze, and *that* something needs to stay buried tonight.

I push on his shoulder until he sinks onto his back. I rise beside him and extend my leg over his waist, my movements slow and cautious. His skin feels blistering hot as I settle down on him. His abdominal muscles are taut, his arms rigid on either side of my legs as I run my hands over the hard contours of his chest to hold his shoulders I wait for him to push me away, to tell me no, but he doesn't.

"Say something." I lean down and whisper into his ear. The dry strands of my hair tickle his chest.

He doesn't move. Doesn't speak. I can practically hear the battle raging in his mind and start to pull away, knowing that his honorable side will win out, but he stops me with two little words.

"One night," he vows as he reaches up and cups the back of my neck, crushing his lips against mine. My fingers curl around his shoulders as I press into him. My mess of curls spills around his face.

His hand rises from my neck and winds through my hair, holding me in place. His free hand squeezes my thigh, his fingers achingly close to where I long most to be touched. Cable's kiss is long and deep, breaking apart only when he's forced to gasp for breath. His chest heaves as I hover over him. I smile as he lifts his head to stroke my bruised lips with the tip of his tongue.

I love his scent. The taste of his lips. I don't pull away as he claims my mouth once more. I wind my hands down from his neck, tracing the muscles that flex as he pushes upright and settles me firmly around his lap.

I explore freely, savoring the rise and fall of the muscles lining his arms and across his defined chest and abdomen as his tongue explores mine. His skin pimples beneath my touch as I trail my fingers down to the path of hair leading beneath me.

I can feel him pressing urgently against me and bite my lip as he thrusts his hips. I shake my head, breaking the kiss, wanting to lengthen the moment yet desperate for release. I grind back against him and enjoy each flinch and groan that he makes.

"Shit, Avery" He rolls his head to the side as I dip my hand down between my legs and grab hold of him. "You're going to be the death of me."

I lean down and nibble on his lower lip. "At least you will enjoy it."

"More than you know." He wraps his arms around me, sealing me into his embrace. He is scorching against my chilled skin.

I've always known Cable was strong, but observing it before and feeling it now are two very different experiences. I melt against his touch as his hand rises to my waist, pushing my hips to create friction. My hips grind against him until I'm desperate for more. I break off the kiss and grasp the hem of my shirt, tugging it over my head.

"I can't see you," he growls, his fingers digging into my side.

Curling my back, I lean down and nip at his ear. My breasts graze along his chest and he arches up into me. The sensation of his bare skin against my swollen nipples wrenches a moan from my lips as I rock. "You saw me earlier."

"It's not the same." His hands move restlessly along my bare back, tugging, and pushing.

Grasping his hands, I place them on my chest, filling his palms. I lean into him, resting my head atop his as he begins kneading my breasts. "Then memorize me with your hands."

My skin aches with sensitivity as his thumbs swirl around my tender flesh, pinching and tugging me into oblivion. My breath catches as he lowers his head and sucks my nipple into his mouth. My hips buck as I hold his head, begging him not to stop.

A groan rises from deep in his chest as I push back into him, grinding then pulling away. A flush grips me as I roll off him and rise from the bed, shedding the last of my clothes in a rush. I can't wait any longer.

The bedsprings squeak and I smile, knowing that he's in no mood to linger either.

Kneeling on the bed, I prepare to straddle him again but he grasps my arms and rolls on top of me, pinning me down. The scent of his skin is heady as I bite at his neck, my nails raking down his back. His growl echoes in my ear as he spreads my leg with his knee and buries himself inside me. I wrap my arms possessively around him.

The bed squeaks and groans as Cable finds a rhythm that leaves me breathless and wanting. I rock with him, whispering in his ear, urging him on. He follows every command, every plea for him to speed up or slow down. He draws himself back, taking me to the edge of frustration then slams hard, stealing my breath away.

Raising my hands overhead, I grip the wooden bars of the bed and bury my face in my arm. Small whimpers escape my throat, fueling his thrusts. Sweat clings to my body as I wrap my legs around him, arching upward so that he sinks deep.

"Look at me," he demands.

I roll my head and stare up at him, startled to realize that I can make out the contours of his face. I release my grip on the bed and wrap my arms around his neck, drawing him close. "I see you."

The headboard beats against the wall with increasing speed. I buck my hips up into him, increasing the friction between us. His head arches back and the muscles along his neck pull taut as he thrusts one final time. Goosebumps rise along his skin. His arms strain with exertion before he collapses, nestling his head against my cheek.

I hold him, feeling a tingling warmth spreading through my body. His chest rises and falls rapidly. He gulps in a breath, wrapping his arms around me.

"Thank you," I whisper as his breathing slows.

He raises his head. His skin is clammy, sensitive to the touch as I glide my fingers over his arms. He flinches as I reach his side and trail down to his waist. "For what?"

I smile and brush the matted hair back from his forehead. "For giving me what I need."

He reaches up and cups my cheek. His gaze still holds the haze of passion, but there is a deeper emotion hovering just below the surface. I know that I should turn away, ignore that I see it, but he won't let me look away as he smiles. "Who said we're done?"

I arch my eyebrows as he untangles himself from my arms and crawls backward, his tongue trailing between my breasts and over my abdomen. He pauses as he comes to rest between my legs and presses a kiss against my inner thigh. As he nestles closer, I close my eyes and lose myself to the moment.

When I wake some time later the sun seems wrong, too bright and hidden from the windows before me. I groan and rub my eyes, feeling sore and exhausted.

"You know, if you're going to have sex the least you can do is scream louder so I can enjoy it too." I bolt upright. Cable's hand falls away from my bare breast and I struggle to yank the tangled sheets out from under him to cover myself in front of Sal.

"Do you mind?"

"Not at all." He leans against the banister and stares openly.

"Cable," I hiss and smack him on the arm. He rouses and my stomach tightens at how good the tousled look is on him first thing in the morning.

"What?" He grabs the pillow and tries to tug it over his eyes.

"I need your help."

Cable tenses at the tone in my voice. He emerges to find Sal grinning down at us. His tanned skin darkens as he moves toward the edge of the bed. I quickly tuck the sheet around me. Cable doesn't seem to need it at the moment. "You have three seconds to get your ass back down that ladder before I toss you over that railing."

"Fine." Sal raises his hands in mock surrender, pausing long enough to try to get another good look at me. "I just thought you might like to know we're leaving."

"Leaving?" I tuck the sheet around my legs for good measure. "Who the hell decided that?"

Sal shoots me a wink. "Wouldn't you like to know? I'd be willing to let you in on that delicious little secret if you lower that sheet just another smidgen."

Cable growls and surges to his feet. Sal's eyes open wide, but he quickly sinks into a knowing smirk, tsking as he shakes his head. "I expected more from you, Avery. Any girl should have been screaming with that guy in bed with you."

Grabbing the front of his shirt, Cable shoves Sal back. His heels come off the floor and for a moment I'm convinced he intends to follow through on his threat.

"Cable!" His arms flex. I try not to notice the curve of his backside as he turns to look at me. The tattoo that I spied ages ago peeking through his shirt trails down from shoulder to waist. A waterfall of ink in the shape of a rugged looking cross spans the breadth of his back. The sight of it surprises me. I never took Cable as a religious man. "He's not worth it."

"Aw. Sticks and stones, love." Sal blows me a kiss. "When you get tired of him, you know where to find me."

With a vicious growl, Cable shoves him off the balcony. I watch as Sal's arms pinwheel and listen as his scream is cut off with a loud whump.

"What did you do?" I yank the bed sheet off and hurry to the ladder. Alex peers questionably up at us from beneath the loft and I cower behind Cable for cover.

Alex's hair is damp, his face ruddy from a recent washing. It must be later than I realized for him to have time to bring water back from the stream and boil it.

"He's fine." Cable turns and walks away. His fists clench at his sides. It's obvious just how hard it is for him to get himself under control.

Sal shouts as he fights to right himself, his fall broken by the couch. I meet Alex's gaze before I return to Cable's side. I place my hand on his arm and he flinches.

"Sorry," I whisper and draw back. I turn away from him to find my clothes, but he pulls me back. He wraps his arms around me, my back pressed to his chest as he rests his head on top of mine.

"I don't want to pull away from you. Not like this. I'd planned for something a little less drama-based."

I close my eyes, knowing this moment would come. I just didn't have time to prepare myself for this awkward moment when lovers become friends once more. "You don't have to. At least not too far."

He presses his lips to the back of my head and releases me. I walk away from him, attempting to put the events of the night behind me, but some things are harder to forget. Cable touched me in ways no man ever has, deeper, more intimate. Not in the physical realm, but emotional. I told myself in the early hours of the morning as he slept beside me that nothing would change. I wish I still believed that.

SEVENTEEN

I scowl at Sal as I hit the bottom rung of the ladder after dressing in silence with my back turned to Cable. My footsteps sound unnaturally loud in the quiet cabin as I pass by him to face off with Alex.

"You saw what he did?"

Alex nods and stirs his spoon around the lip of his metal coffee mug. It's filled with only hot water, but I've discovered over the past few days since being here that in his mind, it's almost like having the real thing. "Saw what Cable did, too."

He doesn't say an accusing word about Sal's untimely fall from the loft, or the events that led up to them. I can tell by the deep blush riding high on Victoria's cheeks behind him that my tryst with Cable before dawn didn't go unnoticed by anyone in the house.

"So that's it? Just brush it off like it's not the creepiest thing in the world to have a guy watching you while you sleep?"

"While you are naked, you mean?" As he turns his gaze away and takes a sip I notice that the tips of his ears are red with embarrassment, or anger. I can't really decide which.

"That's...that's really not the issue at this point," I stammer and wrap my arms around my waist.

"The pre-dawn wake-up moans say otherwise," Sal quips.

"Go fuck yourself," I snarl, turning to glare at him.

"All right," Alex sets his mug down. "That's enough, you two. We all have to live under the same roof. Obviously, we are going to have to make some...adjustments to make it all work."

My fingers dig into my sides as I shake my head, letting my hair shield me from Alex's gaze. The need to retreat, to rush out into the woods and hyperventilate over this morbid embarrassment is unbearable. "There's no need," I mutter. "It won't happen again."

Alex grabs my arm and draws me back as I try to move away from him. "What happened, happened. I've got no say in that. I just want you to be careful."

"I am."

"Are you?" In the late morning light I notice that the blond hairs along his chin, jaw and cheeks have begun to fill into a beard now. I can't say that it seems all that fitting for the fly boy airline pilot, but he seems more down to earth now. More likable. I think this new life, as crazy as it sounds, suits him better.

"Cable and I have an understanding." I stare down at his hand on my arm until he releases me and steps back.

"Those have a way of being forgotten. I should know. I was the king of one night stands that ended badly."

"Who said it was a one night stand?" I challenge.

Victoria stares hard at the counter before her. There's no food left to eat, but I'd bet she'd rather bury her face in that hunting book I found yesterday than be stuck standing here in the middle of our discussion. "I know your type, Avery. You don't settle down."

"Maybe I do. Maybe I don't. That's none of your business either, now is it?"

"Not normally." He shakes his head. "But it becomes my business when other people are involved."

I glare over my shoulder at Sal. He wiggles his fingers at me and blows another kiss. Anger simmers low in my belly, but I don't show it. I don't want to add fuel to Alex's fire. "Cable and I have nothing to do with any of you."

"You're wrong." I turn back to look at Alex, surprised by the tension in his voice. "When were you going to tell me you two were followed last night?"

"Followed?" I glance toward Victoria, noting that her head has raised up a bit. "Followed by who?"

"I was hoping you could tell us. What I do know is that there were four sets of prints out there this morning when I woke. Yours, Cable's, mine and another guy. Sal pissed in the corner when he woke up so it wasn't him, and Vicky here has tiny feet. So that leaves a stranger stomping up to our doorstep while we slept. I don't know about you, but I'm not too keen on that idea."

I push back against the counter, needing the pressure of it to keep me grounded. "I saw a Moaner in the woods last night."

"So?" I blink, surprised to hear Victoria speak. It's been so long since she joined in an actual conversation I'd almost begun to wonder if she was really present at all.

"So it followed me. Or at least, it watched me from a distance."

Sal snorts and pulls the lever of the recliner. He pushes it out to its full length, laying back and crossing his hands under his head. Even from this distance, I regard the rash that has grown down his arm. His eyes look hazier than normal. "Little Moaner got you scared? I'd have thought a tough girl like you could take one on."

I start to snap back at him, but a voice calling from above stops me. "Avery's right. There was someone in the woods last night and they didn't just pass through. They stopped and watched. That tells me that whoever it was took a bit too much interest in us for my liking." Cable's boots clunk as he leaps down the final three steps of the ladder.

His pack is slung on his back. His hat is firmly in place, tugged low enough that I can't quite make out the direction of his gaze, but I feel like it's firmly focused on me.

"What was it watching?" Alex tugs at his sleeves. The chill on the air is more prevalent this morning. Only wisps of smoke coil up from the fire now. I guess there was no need to keep it going since Alex decided to ship out.

"Me bathing." My cheeks flush red as I hop up onto the counter. The Formica is old and peeling away from the wall. Not the most stable seat in the room but it's the nearest. If I'm walking all day I might as well get the last few ounces of rest in that I can.

"Wait a second." Alex holds up his hands. He takes turns between staring in disbelief toward Cable and accusingly at me. "You're telling me that you think some Moaner stopped for a peep show last night, then followed you back here?"

"Almost impossible to believe, right Avery?" Sal chortles.

Cable adjusts his pack, buckling it around his waist to even the weight. Without food, the pack caves in at the top. His boots are laced high to support his ankles on the hike. I can tell by the way he's standing that he's wrapped his ribs up nice and tight, though he didn't seem too concerned with them last night.

"Avery?"

"That's what I saw, Alex."

"Cable?"

He only shrugs in response to Alex's question. I can tell by the hard set of his jaw that it's taking every ounce of restraint he possesses not to go and throttle Sal.

Alex scoffs, shaking his head. "Fine. If you two don't want to tell me the truth, that's fine. Grab your shit. I'm done with this place."

"Alex, we're not—"

"Save it." He glares openly at me. I'm taken back by his hostility. "If there's one thing I can't stand, it's liars. I should know. I'm one of the worst, but this...this is different."

I look to Cable for support, but he shakes his head and turns his back. I sigh and leap down from the counter, resigned to face a really long day.

We hike through the afternoon, pausing only for small sips of water we discover seeping through the sediment at the base of a large set of stone steps naturally carved into the rock. It tastes earthy but clean. A path winds through the large boulders, making our passage easier, but we veer away when the trail begins to head back toward our previous direction.

South—it is the only direction that matters at the moment. I never really asked Cable or Alex why this was the decision. East or west seem just as good a candidate as any. I'd veto north in a heartbeat unless that whole bit about Moaners hating cold turned out to be true.

Sal marches at the head of the pack, his mouth running faster than his feet. He rambles about nothing and everything, all at the top of his voice. I've seen Alex trying to talk to him, but Sal shoves him away and continues on.

I exchange worried glances with Cable but say nothing. I know he is thinking the same thing I am: if there are any survivors in the area, Sal will bring them down on top of us.

The sun beats relentlessly from overhead. Beads of sweat trickle along my spine beneath the thick layers of clothes and the bulk of my pack. I had hoped once all of the food was gone that it would be an easier load to bear, but the lack of nourishment only makes the trek that much harder.

Cable remains behind me, drawing near only when we reach a steep slope. His presence is both welcoming and unnerving at the same time. Each time he grasps my arm to ease me down another boulder, a tingle begins beneath his fingers and I'm instantly swept back into the memory of sleeping in his arms.

I know he feels it too. It's obvious in the way he releases me the second he knows I'm safe, snatching his hand back as if I've burned him. He helps Victoria from time to time as well. I guess he's trying to prove that it's not favoritism or some crap like that.

"Hey, Avery." I look up to see Sal twirling atop a wet boulder. The spray of a larger waterfall has left the rock face dark and slick. "Wanna dance?"

"Alex," I shout out in warning. Though he's hardly spoken a word to me since this morning, he rushes forward to intercept Sal.

"Hey, buddy. Why don't you come down from there before you get hurt?"

Sal's face scrunches up. Spittle seeps from the corner of his lips as he shakes his head. I pause several feet below, watching Alex carefully pick his way up to meet Sal.

"What's he got that I ain't got, anyways?" Sal yells and spins once more. His footing is precarious. "Sure, he's kinda good looking, got arms the size of a tree, but I've got experience that he can't compete with. That's gotta count for something, right?"

"Sal," Alex raises his arms. He's two rocks below Sal and not nearly close enough to avoid disaster. "I think I've got a candy bar in my pack. I'll share it with you if you come down quietly."

He seems to contemplate it for a moment, brushing his hand along the length of what little hair he has left. Victoria was right to try to get him to chop it off. That greasy mullet is repulsive.

"Listen to him, Sal," I call out.

His gaze shifts to look at me. "Not till you promise me that dance, sweetheart."

Alex jerks as Sal's foot slips, but the fool merely laughs and spins on one foot. His heavy paunch seems to balance him as he leans forward and creates the image of a fat, hairy ballerina.

"Cable?" I say. He stands beside me, his hands tucked deep into his pockets and once again I wonder if he has a weapon concealed there.

"I know. There's nothing we can do about it."

I stare hard at him. "Yes, there is."

I ease past Victoria and approach the base of the rocks. Even from here I can feel the frigid spray of the water. A small rainbow hovers in the air before me, the mists illuminated in the dappled sunlight. Clouds have begun to move in. There is a change on the air and I pray that we find shelter before the next storm. They seem to come so fast these days.

"One dance, Sal, but you have to promise to keep your hands above the waist."

"That's where all of the good stuff is anyway." He spins to face me, a wide triumphant smile lighting his face. "I knew I could convince you. You're a smart girl. You just need the right leverage—"

His cry startles birds from the trees. His arms flail and the crazed look in his eye shifts as the realization that he's going to fall sinks in a moment too late. Alex reaches out for him, grappling to catch onto his foot as he teeters. "Sal!"

His boot slips off the rock and he plummets backward. Cable outstrips me as I race to climb the rocks.

"Oh, poor, poor Sal." I turn to see Victoria wringing her hands before her. "All he ever wanted was to be loved."

"Stay back," Cable warns as he inches his way around a boulder overhead. The ledge is small, barely wide enough to hold the toe of his boot. Alex approaches from above, both converging on Sal's last location.

A part of me knows that I should ignore his warning and go to Sal's aid. Another part, the more callous realist, wonders: what's the point? He is turning. Everyone knows it. It's only a matter of time before he becomes one of *them*.

Cable disappears from sight. The top of his back disappears behind the rock. Alex plants his hands and feet between the two rock faces and shimmies down. Several minutes pass without any sound.

"Is this when the screaming starts?"

I turn, surprised to find Victoria has managed the initial climb up to me. She looks lost and frail. Her face is drawn. Dark circles line beneath her eyes. I smile and motion for her to join me, sucking in my pride as I place my hand around her shoulder. She leans her head on me and I'm choked by the overwhelming scent of perfume. Where on earth did she uncover that crap?

"They'll be fine. We all will be."

"You always did know how to make me feel better."

I frown and pull away from her. "Vicky, are you feeling okay?"

Her brow furrows and her gaze drifts far off. "Stop fretting over me, mom. You know I hate that."

Mom? I stare at her a moment longer and am shocked when I see her stick her thumb into her mouth. *She's regressing. Isn't that one of the symptoms too?*

I press my palm to my head, trying to think. I remember before the news reporters went off the air that there was a long list of symptoms to watch out for. So many of them mirrored the common cold or flu that it left everyone sure they were next. Was this one of them?

"It will all be fine." I squeeze her shoulders and lead her toward a rock a safe distance away. "Why don't you rest here for a bit while I go help the guys?"

"You'll come back, right? You promised." Her mouth puckers as she shakes her head. "You promised you'd come back, but you never did. I waited for you..."

Shaken by her words and how closely they hit home with my own father, I step back and hurry away. That is all kinds of messed up right there!

"Cable?" I shout. At this point, it won't really matter if anyone hears us. Either they will help or we'll fight. I doubt things could get much worse. "Cable?"

"We're here." The grunt comes from my right and I lean around the rock and see Alex and Cable struggling toward me. Sal hangs limply between them, unconscious. Blood trails down from his head. His skin appears ashen.

I hurry forward. "Is he dead?"

"Probably should be." Alex winces as he stumbles under Sal's weight. Of the entire group, Sal's got the largest frame. Big boned, as he tried to call it. That gut is all beer and Twinkies, if you ask me.

They lower him to the ground a few feet ahead of me. Leaves and dirt stick to his scalp wound as his head rolls to the side. There is an ugly cut along his hairline. The rest of him looks miraculously unharmed. I'd have expected at least a broken bone or two.

"Found him wedged between two rocks. Lucky bastard can't even kill himself right." Alex wipes at his nose. The end is pink, as are the tips of his fingers. He presses on his lower back and arches to stretch out his muscles.

"He's an idiot."

Alex nods in agreement of Cable's assessment. "In more ways than one." He turns to look at me and his expression changes. "Thanks for at least trying to help. I know you didn't want to."

"It was the right thing to do. He would have given away our location."

"Yeah, probably so." Alex turns and surveys the woods. The dark gray rock face behind us rises nearly fifty feet overhead. It curls around us in both directions. It's not a terrible spot to be in, but I would have liked to find real shelter for the night. "I guess we set up camp here."

Cable drops his pack. He sinks down low and digs through the contents to find several slightly dented plastic bottles. He holds them out to me. "Might as well fill these up while we can."

"What are you going to do?"

He points back toward the path we left less than half an hour before. "I'm going to follow that and see if we can find shelter. Judging by the look of those clouds we are in for a rough night."

"I'll come with you." Alex splashes water on his face, rubbing it through his hair. He cups his mouth under the trickle of water and drinks deep before rejoining us.

"You're leaving me with them?" The prospect of staying being with a highly perverted man and an old woman suffering from a bought of crazy mommy issues doesn't sound the least bit appealing.

"We'll be back before sundown." Alex takes an empty bottle from my hand and tosses another to Cable. "Fill up before we leave."

He splashes through the water, heading away from us. Cable stands beside me, unmoving, but I can tell he wants to be nearby. "We won't go far."

"I know." The flat tone in my voice affects Cable. He stiffens and thumbs the edge of the bottle cap in his hand.

"I wouldn't go unless I felt I had to."

"It's fine. I don't need a babysitter."

"Avery—" he reaches out for me, but I pull back.

"Just go. I'm fine."

He sighs and taps the bottle against his leg. "Why is it when you say you're fine, I get the feeling you mean the other thing?"

A small smile tugs at my lips, but I don't turn to let him see it. I know he doesn't want to leave me behind, but he does, because he should. It's times like this I hate being a woman. I'm not a caretaker or a nurse, but people keep trying to make me into both.

EIGHTEEN

The sun hangs heavy in the western sky. Its fading rays offer little light or warmth to the darkening woods. Victoria rocks back and forth on the ground beside me. Her mutterings are incoherent, grating on my nerves.

Sal sits with his back against a tree, his hands and feet bound by strips of the towel that I tore apart while he was still unconscious. I don't trust him. He is too erratic. Too unstable. Too...Sal.

I know it's the transformation progressing that causes his overbearing personality to explode. Though I've only ever seen it happen once before with Natalia, she hadn't reacted anything like this. That's the frustrating thing. There's no easy way to pin down the symptoms because they seem different for each person.

"Must be nice to have three guys hot for you," Sal says, spitting to the side. Blood tints the saliva, darkening the rocky path nearby. "Bet you love making us squirm. Though I guess Cable can stop squirming now, can't he? You already gave it up to him. Guess I'll just have to wait in line and you'll eventually get around to me after you mess with Alex's head a bit first."

"Fuck you." I hurl a stick out into the woods, wishing that I could smash his nose in. I should have gagged him, but I didn't want to get close enough for him to bite me. He's infected and I won't take the risk of any of his bodily fluids touching me.

His raspy laugh sounds moist and clogged. A sudden intake of breath followed by intense coughing makes me turn back toward him. His face grows red. If his hands were free I'm sure he'd be beating on his chest, but he isn't free. I sit and watch his struggle, his face shifting through pale pinks to dark purple. His lips begin to take on a blue tint though I guess it could be a trick of the light.

Sal's eyes begin to bulge. A vein pulses down his forehead.

"No, no, no!" Victoria rocks faster, clutching her hands to her ears. There is a steady tremor in her fingers.

Sighing, I rise and approach him. He looks at me, unseeing. I crouch before him and hesitate. It would be easy to let him go out like this, suffering like he deserves. I could do it. Just let him choke to death, but as I glance back at Victoria I know it would unhinge her completely.

"Ain't that a bitch." I ball my hand into a fist and beat on his back. He splutters, gasping for breath. Three more pounds on his back and a glob of mucus bursts from his throat. I turn my face away, sickened by the sight and potent smell. "Don't say I never did anything for you."

I push off on his shoulder and return to my spot, actively ignoring him as he slowly recovers. The wheezing is new. I only wish I knew how many more symptoms he had to go through before the end.

"What the hell is going on here?"

I look up to see Alex appear around the bend in the path. His light blond hair picks up the final rays of twilight. Cable marches behind him, his taller frame lost to the shadows. Alex drops what looks like a large rolled garbage bag and rushes to Sal's side. He places two fingers against his neck.

"His heart rate is all over the place." He turns to glare at me. "What did you do to him?"

"Nothing."

"Liar, liar, liar," Victoria mutters. "Kill, kill, kill."

Alex's gaze hardens. "Did you try to kill him?"

Cable steps between us as I start forward. He raises his arms out to keep me at bay. "I'm sure Avery didn't do anything to harm Sal."

"Oh yeah?" Alex doesn't seem to buy it for a second and my anger multiples. Why the heck would he take the word of a crazy woman over me? "How do you figure that?"

Cable turns to look at me over his shoulder and smiles. "Because if she wanted him dead...he would be."

I nod in silent agreement, thankful that he understands just how close I came to letting it happen. Alex doesn't need to know that, though.

"He started choking. I whacked him on the back a few times and he recovered. No big deal." I shrug and push Cable's arms down. I don't need to him to protect me from Alex. He's not the one I'm worried about.

Alex's hands are planted on his hips. He stares down at the mess between Sal's feet then up at Sal. I detect by the way he shifts that he's looking for some sign of bruising around his neck, probably finger impressions to prove my guilt. When he finds none he closes his eyes and sighs. "Why is he tied up?"

"I don't trust him," I say simply. I would have thought that much would be obvious.

"Did he try to hurt you?" I turn and offer Cable a smile before shaking my head no. "Good, 'cause if he did..." he lets that statement fall away.

Alex runs his hands through his hair. Stray bits of twigs fall from the matted strands. There are wide tears in his shirt and for the first time, I notice just how disheveled both he and Cable look. I narrow my gaze on a cut along Cable's arm and reach for it.

"What the hell happened to you two?"

"We found supplies," Cable replies, but I feel like there should be more to that statement.

"What, did you steal them from an angry bear?" I roll his arm over and see more cuts, some of them deep. Blood trails down his arm in jagged vines. He doesn't hiss when I press my finger near the wound, but there is a tightening of pain around his eyes.

"Alex?" I turn on him, knowing Cable will try to keep the truth from me.

"We ran into some survivors. They had what we needed." His indifferent shrug doesn't fool me. He refuses to meet my gaze as he pushes past and kneels beside the garbage bag roll that he dropped upon first arriving. I follow after him, shaking Cable's grip off.

"You stole this stuff?" He nods and begins untying three rope knots that hold the bag in place. "And the survivors?"

Alex's hands fall still. His shoulders curl inward, his head bows low. "They won't be needing this anymore."

I whirl around and stare at Cable. His hand is pressed tightly to his pocket. I close the gap between us in three long strides and yank his arm away. He cries out but doesn't stop me as I shove my hand deep into his pocket. The interior is moist.

Something cold touches my fingers. I draw my hand out and open my palm. Two weapons lie in my hand: a bloodied hunting knife and a coiled bit of wire.

"Oh, God," I drop the weapons and step back. Blood stains my hand. Innocent blood. "You killed them?"

"What?" Alex whirls around. "No, of course, we didn't. They had turned into Withered Ones."

I glance at Cable. His expression is unreadable. "So why is there blood on these?"

Alex points to the pack on Cable's back. "That's from dinner."

Several hours later, I sit beside the small fire, watching the dancing light flicker against the trees. The smoke billows up, lost to the gray expanse of clouds overhead. Breath hangs before my lips as I warm my hands. The air has turned bitterly cold.

Cable uses his knife to slice off a charred piece of wild hog. The tusks bear signs of blood from where Cable and Alex tried to subdue the animal.

Cable hasn't said much to me since my earlier accusation. He helped me set up the six-person tent in silence. It's obvious from the confidence he exuded during set up that he spent many of his summers camping. I was all thumbs trying to get the darn poles to stay up.

The tent is bright yellow, hardly what I would call good camouflage, but beggars can't be choosers. It will keep the wind off us tonight. I'm thankful for that.

Alex emerges from the tent. He looks exhausted as he wipes his hands over his face. "Vicky is sleeping. She's pretty messed up about what happened."

"And Sal?" I cast a furtive glance toward the zippered door. My protests that he should remain tied up fell on deaf ears as Alex takes Sal into the tent.

"He's passed out from fever."

Cable meets my gaze then drops it again. "He shouldn't be in there with us tonight."

Alex groans as he sinks down onto a rock and takes the offered piece of meat from Cable. Juice runs down his lips and into his beard. He wipes his arms across his mouth to clean it away. "I thought we'd been over this. He's part of the group. We care for our own, even when he's not the most likable guy."

"He's dangerous." Cable tosses a bit of fat and skin onto the fire, watching it burn.

"He's in no condition to hurt anyone."

"You're wrong." Both men turn and look at me. I keep my gaze focused on the deep blue flames. "Sal knows he's turning. I saw it in his eyes earlier when he was choking. He's no fool, Alex. He remembers why you kept me in the group."

Cable lowers the leg of meat he has been working on carving with his knife and turns to stare at me. "What's that supposed to mean?"

I meet his gaze head on. "They knew about my blood. That's why they kept me around. I was supposed to help Eva."

The bone snaps in Cable's hand as he rounds on Alex. "Is that true?"

Alex swallows a large piece of meat. "It was...at first. But things changed."

"What things?" Cable's voice is low and deadly. I don't know if Alex notices the way Cable's grip tightens on his knife, but I do.

"The point is," I break in, "that Sal thinks my blood can heal him, or, at least, prolong his fate."

Cable's hand moves back toward his lap, a visible sign of relaxing, but it's just for show. If Alex makes one wrong move, Cable will attack. I can't let that happen. Though I don't agree with some of the shots Alex has called recently, there is strength in numbers.

"But your blood can't heal him." Cable takes another bite and slowly chews it. "You're not a universal donor and you're sure as heck not a cure."

Alex's back straightens as he looks toward me. "But I thought—"

"No." Cable tosses the meatless bone onto the fire and wipes his hands on his pants. "If her blood were mixed with his, he'd still die. Probably in a worse way than he already is."

"We tested her blood. Victoria said she was a universal donor."

"She wasn't completely wrong." I set my portion of meat down, my stomach no longer happy with the offering. I relay the details of my time spent in the company of the military, what we'd discovered. As I speak, I watch Alex visibly pale and wonder if he had held out hope that someday I could save his life too.

Maybe he didn't bring those men back to the farm to capture us after all. Maybe it really was a coincidence. Maybe Alex had different intentions all along.

One glance at Cable reveals that I'm not the only one thinking it.

"So what do we do? Leave him here? Let him change?" Alex rubs absently at his arms. "Victoria would never allow it. She's a tough girl in her own right. She wouldn't leave him before."

"Then he'd probably kill her and risk mixing their blood," Cable says, staring blankly into the fire.

"There's only one choice," I whisper. My stomach twists at the thought. I don't think I could do it. Not in cold blood. If only, I'd let Sal suffocate when it would have been by natural causes.

Cable remains silent. Alex's mouth slackens. His eyebrows rise in disbelief as he stares between us. "You're talking about murder."

"No." Cable presses his knees together then rises. He stares down at Alex. "That's survival."

He turns and walks away, heading into the forest. I wonder if I should go after him, but I can't leave Alex. Not until I can make him see reason.

"He's not well, Alex. You know that. It's only a matter of time before he turns."

"So then let him turn!" His nostrils flare as he kicks out his foot. A bit of dirt snuffs out the flames on the edge of the fire pit.

I draw in a breath and hold it for a moment until I'm sure I can control my frustration. "If he turns, he will be in that tent with us, or on a hiking path, or God knows where else. Do you really think Victoria can handle seeing that? She's already in some sort of shock over what happened back in St. Louis."

Slipping off my rock, I kneel beside him and place a hand on his knee. I've never intentionally touched Alex before. He swallows as his gaze settles on my hand. "Sal is part of the group. I know that, but how long will he continue to be Sal? You saw his desperation. We all did. Can you really live with yourself if he kills me or Vicky in our sleep? Can you live with yourself if you wait too long?"

Alex's skin becomes ghostly pale. His hands tremble. He sucks his lower lip between his teeth. "I never wanted people to look to me for answers."

I sink down beside him and wait as he blows out several deep breaths. His gaze grows distant, lost to the past. "I thought Devon would be a good leader. He seemed strong willed, level headed, but then he took in that man and wife. Locked them away and said it was for our own good. For Eva's."

He rubs at his chest as his eyebrows pinch in a grimace of long claimed regret. "I tried to tell myself that it was the right thing to do. To protect our group, but you were right. We were no different than those men who roamed the streets. We became the one thing we hated the most."

Reaching up, I place my hand on his forearm. His skin feels cold to the touch, despite the fire before us. "You did what you had to do to survive."

He nods slowly. "And that's what we have to do again."

He turns his gaze away from the fire to look at me. I see a haggard man, wearied and burdened by the impossible choices laid out before him. I feel the same way. I just hide it a bit better. "I can't do it."

I'd struggle to follow through with it as well. Sal and I may have an intense dislike of each other, but at the moment, he's still alive, still human. Could I really look into his eyes and know that I'm the last thing he would see?

"I'll do it." I look up to see Cable has returned. The wire from his pocket is wound tightly around his hands. His feet are firmly planted, his chin held high. He has the look of a man who's set aside all emotion to get a task done, no matter how horrifying it may be.

"Cable..."

He shakes his head and I fall silent. "I won't let you have blood on your hands. We've made it this far without that."

"Someday, I will have to kill."

He nods slowly. "But not today."

Alex buries his head in his hands. "I can't believe we're even talking about this. It's so...so sick."

"It's reality," I whisper, hugging my arms about myself. Has the world really sunk to this low? That innocent people are sacrificed for the greater good. I guess that happened before all of this. Kids died by the thousands each day from starvation or lack of water. Homeless died on the streets from the cold. Wars were started for financial gain.

The world hasn't become more twisted. It's just simpler, in some insane way. You fight. You survive. Nothing else matters now.

"Not tonight." Alex says, slowly raising his head. "Vicky is in there with him right now. If we are going to do it, it has to be when she's not around."

I look to Cable and note the tension in his jaw. His grip on the wire doesn't loosen. His stance doesn't ease.

"I'll take the first watch. Make sure things stay quiet. Cable can take the second watch, and Avery, the final. If we make it through the night then we can deal with it tomorrow."

"And if not?" I question.

Alex opens and closes his mouth. He doesn't have the answers. None of us do.

NINETEEN

Sleep eludes me for several hours. I listen to Cable and Alex talking by the fire, focusing on the rise and fall of their tone in an attempt to will myself to sleep. Victoria rests beside me. Her frizzy hair is plastered to the side of her face, her glasses askew on her nose. Sal snores on her other side, loud and as obnoxious as usual. I should have put myself between them, to ensure Victoria's safety, but I couldn't bring myself to be near him.

The night is cold and endless. The hours trudge by as if time no longer holds any meaning. I'd like to kick old Father Time in the crotch to get him motivated again. That would show the bastard I mean business.

I lie motionless when Alex returns some time later from his shift and crashes down beside me. I don't shift away when he presses his back against mine. Instead, I wait until his breathing grows deep and steady before I inch away.

Through the tent wall, I watch Cable's shadow, lit by the dwindling flames. A spark flares as he leans forward and tosses another log on the fire. I'm worried about him. He needs to sleep.

More than that, I'm worried about his mental state. Offering to kill someone must mess with your head, even if you've killed before. Cable told me once that you never forget, and you never forgive. I don't want Sal's blood on his hands any more than I want it on my own.

Alex shifts in his sleep and elbows me in the ribs. I grunt in pain but have nowhere to go. A shadow falls over me and I look up to see Cable standing by the door. "I'm fine," I whisper. "Just Alex taking up too much room."

"Well, shove him back over."

I smirk as he turns and heads back to the fire, giving Alex a jab in the side for good measure. He snorts in his sleep and rolls away. Tucking my arm under my head, I roll to get comfortable and freeze.

In the flickering of the firelight, two eyes stare back at me. Mangled hair and a full beard make Sal look even fiercer than I remembered. His lip is curled into a feral snarl. The bruise along the side of his face looks angry and puffy.

"Cab—" my scream cuts off as Sal launches himself at me. His hands grip my throat as he sprawls over Victoria. The woman wakes and wails like a banshee beside me, beating against Sal's side. He doesn't seem fazed by her attack. His eyes remain locked onto me.

His grip on my throat is unnaturally strong. His fingers dig into my flesh. My lips part, sucking in air that has nowhere to go.

Victoria's screams sound garbled in my ears. I claw at Sal's hands, tearing skin back from his forearms, but he doesn't relent. Pure, unadulterated rage stares me in the eye and I'm terrified his face will be the last thing I see.

"Get off her!"

Sal's face distorts as a fist slams into his cheek. Blood and spittle splash my face and the grip on my neck decreases but doesn't disappear completely. I gasp for breath, taking small sips of air into my burning lungs. Heat flames in my face as blood pumps loudly in my ears.

"Alex, get him off her!"

I'm only vaguely aware of someone clawing at me. Sal's face reappears. I spot the maniacal gaze a split second before he sinks his teeth into my shoulder. I scream, arching my back.

"Shit!" Alex yells from beside me. My body shakes with each punch he lands against Sal's head. I cry out as his teeth tear at my flesh, refusing to give up his hold. "Cable, he bit her!"

"Get out of my way!"

The tent overhead shakes violently. I hear the sound of shredding fabric and a moment later Cable appears over me. A glint of silver flashes before my eyes. Sal's head rears back. My blood stains his chin. I place a trembling hand over my shoulder, wincing at the pain.

"Take care of her," Cable grunts and manhandles Sal out of the tent.

I focus on Victoria's whimpers over the scuffling sounds. Alex's face is blurry as he kneels before me. I shake my head, trying to clear my thoughts, but it's a losing battle.

"Just hold on," Alex says nearby. I hear rustling but give in to the pain and close my eyes.

When I wake the sun shines just above the horizon. Beautiful pastel blues, pinks, and yellows dot the landscape as I ease myself upright. My shoulder twinges. I press my hand to the bandage and feel blood soak through.

"Easy." I turn to see Victoria sitting beside me. She no longer rocks, no longer looks lost to her own world. There is intelligence in her eyes for the first time in weeks. "You're gonna be sore for a few days."

I grimace at the pain. She *tsks* and reaches out to place a new bandage on my shoulder. The cold morning air bites at my skin and I realize that I've been stripped down to only a tank top. "How bad is it?"

"Not as bad as it feels, I'm sure."

I inhale sharply and try to look down at the wound. Victoria places a hand on my arm. "I disinfected it the best I could but..."

I understand the deeper meaning to her words. Sal was infected. It would only make sense that his bite holds the potential to spread the disease to me.

Covering my hand over my shoulder, I offer her a smile. "Thanks."

She dips her head in acknowledgment and begins tucking the cleaning supplies back in her pack. She grabs a roll of gauze and raises my arm. I notice a quake in her hands as I grit my teeth at the pain. With my free hand, I rub my throat, sure that the pale skin is a mass of bruising now. It hurts to swallow, to breathe. "And Sal?"

Her hands paused in their work, her knuckles swollen and fingers curled. Alex had mentioned that she suffers from bouts of arthritis. The cold makes it worse. The gauze she wraps around my shoulder to hold the new bandage in place falls from her fingers and she lowers her head. The chain holding her glasses swings before her chest. "Gone."

"I'm sorry," I whisper, though I know I'm not. Not sorry that he's dead. That he's no longer a part of the group. Now all I want to know is who ended it.

"Don't be." She plasters a smile back on and continues her ministrations. "He became a danger, just like you said he would."

"You...you heard all of that?"

Victoria nods. Her glasses slide down nearly to the end of her nose. She doesn't bother to push them back. "I heard a lot more than I let on."

"You were faking it?"

She offers me a pained smile. "Some. Though there were plenty of times that I would lose myself for a while. I don't blame you for thinking I was going crazy. I would have agreed with you."

"But you're back now?"

She shoves her hair back out of her face. The deep set of wrinkles and bruising along her face speaks of how hard this life has been on her. She is far too old to keep going at this pace. "For now. It comes and goes, just like before. My daughter insisted that I be checked by a specialist. That's where I was going when our flight was detoured to St. Louis."

"You flew alone?"

She nods. "Felt like a kid with those stewardesses watching over me. Might as well have stuck a little name tag on me and handed me some cookies and milk."

I grin at the imagery.

"Anywho, maybe that knock I took to the head last night set things right again. Guess old timer's was bound to catch up with me sooner or later. I'm no spring chicken anymore."

I laugh a deep genuine laugh. "You're one tough broad, Victoria. You know that?"

"You may call me Vicky now, I think. The name has begun to grow on me after all this time."

Smiling, I reach out and place my hand over hers. Veins rise through papery thin flesh. "I never thought I'd say it, but I'm kinda glad you're back. Being the only girl sucked."

She seems genuinely pleased when she squeezes my hand. "I suppose you and I didn't start out on the proper foot, did we?"

"Not so much." She lifts the tape to her mouth and tears off the piece, tucking it under. I try lifting my arm and know that it's going to take a few days before the pain begins to fade. "I'm sorry about Eva."

At the sound of my friend's name, my breath catches and I fall silent. "I should have helped more, been kinder. I suppose I was afraid. Afraid of not being needed. Of being left behind. When you reach my age, you'll understand what it's like."

If I reach your age, I amend silently.

Clearing my throat and making the decision to shove the past right back where it belongs, I pat my bandage. For a retired science teacher, she seems fairly handy with gauze and tape. "Where are Alex and Cable?"

Vicky looks toward the woods. I follow her gaze, realizing that a massive slit has been sliced through the zippered door. "He couldn't get the zipper to work so he burst in here, knife at the ready." She turns to look at me. "That man cares for you."

"I know." And I do for him, far more than I'd like to admit.

"Well," she dusts her hands off and gingerly rises. "They should be back soon. I'd best make myself useful while I still can."

I stare after her, amazed at how easily she bounces back. Was it all just a survival technique to shut down or something else? Beginning stages of dementia? Her body's way of dealing with shock?

It could have gone the wrong way. Alex could have decided to leave her behind on the side of the road. Deemed her too big of a liability.

No. Alex may be many things, but cruel for the sake of being cruel does not seem to be one of them. He cares about his people, no matter how motley the crew may be.

Grabbing a pack nearby, I search for clothes to put on. My pack is nowhere to be seen, so I grab Cable's and dig out a long sleeve black shirt. I manage to wiggle my way inside fairly well, and with only minimal swearing, but by the time I'm done I feel exhausted.

Pushing aside my weariness, I crawl out of the tent and discover a battle scene. Boot prints disturb the dirt. Blood splatters the rocky path and trees beyond. Staring at the blood, I feel weak in the knees and sink down onto a nearby rock.

"Only a little of that belongs to Cable." I look up to find Victoria watching me. I hate that my fear is so transparent. "Sal got in a few good swings before the end."

"That sounds like him." My voice is weaker than it should be. The sight of Cable's shed blood shouldn't affect me so. Heck, it shouldn't bother me at all beyond a general concern for his well-being, but it does.

At the sound of approaching footsteps, I turn to see Cable marching a few steps ahead Alex. They are covered in blood, sweat and dirt. It covers their hands and arms, soiling their shirts and caked to their pants. There is a haggardness on Alex's face that was not there yesterday. A look that only death can bring, up close and personal.

I push down on the rock and rise. A moment of dizziness nearly topples me back to the ground, but I fight through it and manage to rise fully before Cable crushes me in his embrace. I want to resist the tears that swell in my eyes, but I don't. I cling to him, digging my fingers into his back as the tears come, uncaring of the blood that soaks through his shirt into mine.

"It's okay. You're safe now."

"Am I?" I choke out and bury my face in the crook of his arm. The scent of blood is less strong here. "Are any of us really safe?"

He doesn't answer me and I know why. The truth, no matter how grim, is still the reality that we face. Uncertainty. Death. A fight for survival. The trouble is that I fear this is only the beginning.

Heat radiates out from him like a warm blanket straight out of a dryer. I noticed that color sits high in his cheeks once more, but assume it's from the hike.

"I thought he was going to kill me. Maybe he already has," I whisper, hating how hoarse my voice sounds as I draw back and cup my shoulder. My neck is raw, my windpipe bruised from Sal's squeezing. It will take some time to recover fully, if ever. It seems like this new life isn't interested in allowing recovery time before another disaster strikes. Each morning I wake up a little more tired, a little more sore, and with a heck of a lot less hope.

Cable presses his lips to the top of my head. "I would never let that happen. You know that, right?"

I nod and pull back, releasing my death grip on him to wipe at my nose. "I know you would try, but you won't always be around."

"Sure I will."

"No." I place my hand on his chest to stop him from hugging me again. "You won't. None of us know what will happen today, or tomorrow or a week from now. We've made it this long because we hid, but how long can we keep that up? We don't have any food. After we leave this place we'll have enough water for three days. Then what?"

He remains silent. I didn't expect him to give me some bullshit, sugar-coated answer. For all the optimism Cable tries to provide, he is at the core a realist. I think you have to be in times like these.

"We both know that towns are dangerous," I continue. "We've been lucky so far, but we won't always be. Sooner or later we are going to run into trouble."

"And I...we," he amends quickly, "will be there to help."

I lower my head. "I can't do this, Cable."

He reaches down and lifts my chin. I try to resist, knowing that if I meet his gaze I will be tempted to weaken, but he persists. "I'm not asking for anything from you, Avery. You know that, right?"

I want to say yes, to say that I know he's never officially asked me for a commitment, but it's there, in his eyes, every time he looks at me. Try as I might to ignore it, I know that I crave that look.

"One night. That's what you promised."

His hand falls away from my chin and I step back. An ache grows in my chest as I watch a shifting of emotions play across his face. He's usually very good at hiding them behind his stony exterior, but not now.

"We should go." I turn my back on him and wrap my arms around my waist, knowing that I've hurt him, hurt myself, but it's the way it has to be. For us to survive. For us to say goodbye when the time comes, because I know it is. It's inevitable.

Alex cautiously meets my glance and I nod at him. Pressing back my shoulders I move to stand beside him. "What's the plan?"

"We need supplies." I've heard that sentiment so many times it makes me want to vomit. Food, water, shelter...they are all that matter now. If I focus on that maybe, just maybe, I can make it. I've done it before. I just need to find a way to put Cable in the past.

Alex points to a map at his feet and I see that if we continue on this path, within half a day's hike, perhaps a little more, we will reach a town that sits a couple miles off the main interstate heading south in Kentucky. If we can find a car we might be able to make it to the border within an hour.

Looking at the town on the map, I feel apprehension coil in my gut. It's always hard to tell just how populated that town may have once been, how many survivors may still linger. Being on the main road ups the danger. It's a risk, no matter how you look at it, but some risks I would rather leave alone.

Cable moves past me, careful not to touch me as he ducks into the tent. Alex watches me and I'm careful not to show any emotion. "You okay?"

I bite my lip and nod. "How long till tear-down?"

He cocks his head to look up at the sun. "Quarter of an hour give you enough time to get yourself cleaned up?"

I grab a faded towel Victoria holds out to me. I must look pretty bad for them to already have stuff prepped for me. "Give me five minutes. That water isn't warm enough to soak in!"

TWENTY

The winds are still for the first time in weeks. A brief storm passed through during the afternoon hours, forcing us to take refuge in a small cave. We huddled together as the temperatures plummeted and the sleet came. Cable, being the largest in our group, took the outer edge, creating a makeshift wall. I huddled in the middle with Victoria. Only the chattering of our teeth could be heard. I would trade all four layers of shirts that I wear for one decent wool coat, a pair of gloves and a hat.

We continued our hike, no longer driven by the hope of reaching safety in the light of the sun, but by the need for shelter. I glance back over my shoulder at Cable and the deep-seated fear that began earlier doubles.

His fever burns high once again. His face is flushed despite the freezing temperatures. The cold doesn't faze him.

His steps are unsteady. From time to time he raises a hand to bat away unseen things. We stop frequently to drink, but water is not enough and we can't risk giving him too much too soon. Who knows when we will find another reliable water source?

I should have known he was feverish the instant I saw he return from the woods. Thinking back to the farmhouse when he seemed unusually warm, camping in the woods or the shack when a fire wasn't enough to warm him, but he'd improved, hadn't he? Days went by with little signs of discomfort, so much so that I'd let my fears slip away. Then I think on two nights before, sleeping beside him at the cabin, snuggling up to his radiating warmth. My hands upon his flaming skin...

He should have said something. Warned us. Surely he has known he was ill for several days. Maybe he's been ill since the night he broke us out of the military base and it's just taken this long to really settle in.

I have not noticed any other symptoms yet, but maybe he is hiding those as well. It doesn't matter now. Alex and Victoria see it, but I pray that they fear only that he has fallen ill with the flu, though I doubt it. Everyone jumps to the worst conclusion these days.

Both refuse to meet my gaze, so I take the lead, marching ahead with purpose. The trek through the hills is arduous. The path is steep, the crevices slick from the recently fallen sleet.

When we finally reach the edge of the forest, I halt. Ducking low, I motion for the group to do the same. Alex kneels beside me. Cable on the other side. I can feel the heat flowing in waves off him. I want to say something, but I bite my tongue. Now is not the time.

There is a gully before us, no steeper than any that we have hiked today, but this one gleams in the broken moonlight. The storm must have been worse here. A sheet of ice lies between us and the highway below.

On the other side of the road, I spy a large building. A tall gas sign rises to the sky. Several semi-trucks sit in the parking lot. A pile up of cars betrays the panic travelers experienced in an attempt to escape a fate that was already sealed.

"I don't like this," Alex mutters. Victoria nods in agreement.

I glance toward Cable and sigh, knowing we have no choice.

"Our need hasn't changed. That building looks like an old truck stop. It probably still has food, clothes, maybe even some camping supplies that we could use. That meal we had last night will only take us so far. We need to keep up our strength if we hope to keep going."

"There are probably survivors holed up inside enjoying all of those things right now."

I glance at Alex, but he shrugs, agreeing with Victoria's assessment.

"How far is the nearest town?" I ask, tugging the map from the side pocket of Alex's backpack. I open the worn pages carefully. They have been beaten and battered over the past two weeks. I don't know how much longer it will remain intact. Another reason why we need to risk going into that truck stop. We can find maps out of this state.

I watch his finger trail down the dimly lit page and blow out a breath of frustration. "Twenty miles at best. Maybe a little more."

From the corner of my eye I see Cable close his eyes. I know he's suffering in silence, trying not to be a burden.

"I'll go," I say as I try to fold the map but finally give up when I realize it's a puzzle I'm not going to figure out in the dark.

"No!" Alex and Cable shout at the same time.

"Keep your voices down," I growl, sweeping my gaze across the road. Abandoned cars dot the highway, some heading in a northerly direction along the road, but many plunged hood-first into an embankment. Several are little more than charred remains, and I try not to wonder if the driver made it out or if they now wander this road with their flesh completely melted away.

I see movement among the cars, halting and labored. I point to where several Withered Ones walk repeatedly into car doors, slamming their torsos into the metal until the door finally gives way and they can continue on their path. I shudder at the sight.

As the clouds shift overhead, casting us in darkness, it illuminates the road in the distance and my throat feels parched as I stare out over the expanse.

"There are hundreds of them," Victoria whispers. She wraps her hand around Alex's arm as she kneels beside him. She is hurting. Her limp has become more pronounced. She blames it on bad hips, but I think all of this traveling has just been hard on her.

I've never asked her age, but I'd guess she's at least in her mid-sixties. She should be bouncing grandkids on her knee instead of trekking through the woods at night.

"We should go," Alex says and starts to rise.

"No." I grab onto him. "Wait."

He turns back, shielding his face as the wind whips globs of slush from the trees. It pelts down on us. "This is insane, Avery. We need to find shelter."

"Just watch them," I whisper.

Never has there been an opportunity as great as this to just observe their behavior. From this vantage point, we are safe. Relatively, at least. The woods are to our back and we only saw three Moaners all day.

"Can you see it?"

Alex casts a glance toward me then follows the direction I'm pointing in. In the ever-shifting clouds, our window of sight narrows and expands without warning. It makes it hard to focus on any one place for long, but it's long enough. I hear the inhalation of breath from beside me.

"They are moving together," Alex says in a hushed tone.

I nod. "A herd with one apparent goal in mind."

Victoria leans out around Alex to look at me. "What goal?"

I swallow before answering. "To head south."

"Figured you would say that," Alex mutters and glances over the top of the overpass less than an eighth of a mile from us. Though that area isn't currently lit by the moon, I can still decipher movement.

"Maybe they really don't like the cold." I glance over at Cable. The dark circles under his eyes seem more prominent than before.

"We have two choices." I turn back to look at Alex. "Ride this ridge and walk parallel to those Moaners and hope we stumble across a cave or shanty to sleep in, or we head for that truck stop and find somewhere to hole up for the night. Maybe even find something to eat."

Alex glances toward Victoria. "What do you think?"

I notice that her glasses no longer perch on her nose and she's given up trying to tame her hair, instead embracing reality. Fear pinches her wrinkled features, but as she glances down at the movement on the road below, I know which she views as the lesser danger.

"I'd rather be able to see them in the light of day," is her response. I hide my smile, knowing that Cable will side with me, if for no other reason than to rest for a few moments. The tent, with its massive slit down the middle, is useless against the elements. We left it set-up in the woods. Who knows, maybe it will save some poor soul's life one day.

Alex sighs heavily. "What's the good in being a leader when my vote never counts?"

I clap him on the back. "A good leader knows when to take counsel."

"Oh?" He rises beside me. "Is that what it is? And here I thought you guys just liked telling me what to do."

Alex and Victoria lead the way toward the overpass. It is the easier of the two paths, but also far more dangerous. Despite the six cars abandoned across the bridge, there will be far too much time when we are out in the open, exposed to the naked eye.

I'm not fool enough to think that the truck stop will be empty. And if it is, I'd bet the last drops of water in my bottle that it's being watched.

Grasping Cable's hand, I follow behind, my gaze steadily sweeping our surroundings. For once, I would welcome the wind to help conceal the sound of our passing. Even the raspy moans below bring a bit of relief.

"This is a bad idea," Cable mutters. I feel the tension in his body, his muscles taut as he searches the shadows before us.

"I know, but we didn't have a choice."

"Of course, we did." He looks down at me and I see his eyebrows pinched into a frown. "I know why you pushed for this."

"Yeah, cause I'm hungry."

He yanks on my arm. "Don't play dumb, Avery. It doesn't suit you."

Ducking down behind the first car, I crane my neck to see through the passenger side window. Alex and Victoria have reached the second car but are only twenty feet ahead.

"You should have told me." I crouch back down and search the ground, wishing I had a weapon. As if sensing my frustration, Cable hands me his knife but I push it back at him. "You know how to use it better than me."

Grabbing my wrist, he uncurls my hand and places the handle in my palm. "You need to learn."

"Trial by fire, huh?"

His gaze is intense. I don't move, even when I hear Alex and Victoria advancing, leaving us behind. He digs in his pack and pulls out a short-handled ax, one of the few remaining tools we have left from the farmhouse. "How could you stand there this morning and promise that you would be with me when you knew you were infected?"

Cable grits his teeth and looks away. "Because I'm not going out like them. I'll find a way to stop it."

His sentiment is almost laughable, or at least, it would be if I didn't have tears choking off my airway. "What else are you hiding from me?"

"Nothing."

"Cable—"

"Nothing." When he turns back to face me, his face is so near I could trace every curve and line on his face, feel his breath wash over me. "You explored my body pretty in depth two nights ago. You should know."

At the mention of our time spent in each other's arms, Cable tenses. "Oh shit."

"What?"

He hangs his head. "I was infected when we...when we..."

"Don't." I grip his arm. Between Cable and Sal's bite, I know my chances are not so hot at the moment, but I refuse to regret spending that one night with him. "It happened and I'm glad it did."

"Really?"

I laugh at his blatant surprise. "Why do I get the feeling that you always think the worst about me?"

Reaching out his hand, he rubs his thumb across my cheek. "I could spend a lifetime figuring out how to read you and I'd still have so much to learn."

I sober at his words, knowing that a lifetime is exactly what he no longer has. "Hey," he whispers, tugging my chin so that I will look at him. "I'm not going anywhere. I promise."

"You can't keep that promise."

"Have I ever let you down before?"

I turn away, knowing that with every final breath he would fight the change. But it won't be enough. It never is.

"They're leaving us behind." I wipe at my nose and wipe my hand over my cheek to hide my tears. "We need to move."

Cable follows right behind me, his hand on my lower back. I'm not sure if he does that for his own peace of mind or simply that he needs to touch me as we weave from car to car. By the time we hit the final vehicle we are over halfway across, but there is a large gap between us and the end of the road.

I can't see Alex or Victoria anywhere. I look long and hard, praying that they made it to one of the semis and are waiting for us. I turn and press back against the car, trying to prepare myself.

"No matter what happens, I want you to run and keep running," Cable says. His shoulder presses against me. I am drawn to his heat like a moth to a flame. My fingers ache from the cold. I lost feeling in my toes quite some time ago. My ears and nose may still be a part of me. I'm not really sure anymore.

"Can I trust you to do the same?"

He smiles and for a moment, I almost imagine him happy and healthy again. "I guess you'll just have to find out."

"Fine. Stay on my ass and try not to fall behind."

"It will be a pleasure." I glance back to see him grinning from ear to ear as he cocks his head to openly check out my backside.

"Wow, and I thought you were a gentleman."

I don't wait to hear his response, knowing that it will only tempt me to linger. Keeping my head low, I dash out into the open. I run full out, sliding my feet like a skater over the thin layer of ice. I listen to the moans echoing up from below the overpass and the sound of Cable's boots hitting the pavement behind me.

"Over here," a hiss comes from the shadow of a semi and I veer to the left. Alex's arm reaches out for me and I slam to a stop against the truck.

"Shh," Victoria scolds as Cable slows to a halt with far more grace than I just displayed.

I toss him a "show off" glare before ducking low and crawling beneath the rig with Alex. "See anything?"

"Not so far. No movement apart from the odd Moaner. No signs of survivors. There are patches of footprints over to the right, but there's no way to know who made them."

I search the bay of darkened windows before us. Racks of books, cheap gift items, and a cash register stand not far from the door. Beyond that, I spy several aisles of shelves. The back of the shop is awash with shadow.

My breathing sounds loud in my ears. My heart thrums in my chest and I fight to lower my pulse. It won't do me any good to run in there kamikaze and get my head blown off.

"What do you think?" Alex glances over at me.

I try to shrug, but there's little room to allow for that. "We made it this far without a problem."

"Yeah," he nods and looks back at the window. "That's what worries me."

I share his sentiment but refuse to express it. The chances of this place not being under surveillance are slim to none. This is a huge risk we are taking, but glancing back at Cable, I know I'd choose the same thing all over again if I had to.

I start to move away, but Alex latches onto my wrist. "How bad is he?"

The temptation to lie, to blow it off as nothing, is strong, but Alex deserves the truth. "He's sick, but I think it's only a fever."

"For now." His words stay with me long after I wriggle back out from under the truck. Alex leads us toward the back of the semi. He leans out around the tail end, searching the parking lot.

A middle-aged Withered One shuffles across a patch of ice, arms flailing, his tongue rolled out his mouth. It is almost comical to watch it struggle to move forward. With each step, it slides back two. Alex rises and prepares to race forward when I hear a crack of the ice. I duck low and watch the Moaner slam to the ground. Blood splatters across the ice. When it raises its head I realize its nose is smashed completely, and its tongue sticks to the ice.

"That is vile," Victoria moans, clutching her stomach as she turns away. Alex places an arm around her to shield her and looks to me.

I crawl toward him. "Cable and I will go first. We'll whistle when it's clear."

"Thank you." His voice is rich with emotion as he squeezes my arm in gratitude. I glance at Victoria, at the way he holds her and realize that in some weird way he has adopted the old woman. Maybe he has mommy issues too, and Victoria has become a surrogate mother.

Cable taps my arm and I move away. "On three?"

I nod and crouch low. "Three!"

Our dash across the parking lot is anything but graceful. We slip and slide, skidding into cars and toppling trash cans. I can only imagine the muttered swearing Alex is producing as we take on the obstacle course laid out before us.

Leaping onto the sidewalk, I brace for impact and slam into the side of the building. Pain ripples through my shoulder, still sore from using that semi as a stopping board. Cable stops me as I turn toward the door. He steps gingerly around me and presses his hand against the glass.

I had expected it to be broken, the interior looted for supplies, but there are no signs of that. The truck stop has miraculously been left untouched by the horrors outside.

Cable presses a finger to his lips and ducks inside. I catch the door before it slams shut behind him and inch my way in behind. I turn and carefully ease the door closed, holding the small bell dangling from the handle so that it doesn't make a sound.

It is warmer inside than I had expected. Not comfortable by any means, but a far cry better than being outside.

I follow Cable's lead, ducking low as we search each aisle. Evidence of looting is more prevalent here, but it seems to have been cut short. I search the ground for any signs of struggle, of blood, or other bodily fluids, but see none. When we reach the final aisle, we split up. Cable heads to the bathrooms and showers while I check behind the cash register.

Nothing.

Over there, he mouths silently. I follow him toward a hallway that leads to the rear of the store. The darkness envelops us and fear begins to trickle through me. I fight to keep it at bay, but I can feel it gaining control. Cable reaches back and takes my hand as if knowing I need him.

We search through a small waiting area. The scent of oil and rubber is prevalent in this mechanic shop. It is also completely clear of danger. Cable rises and takes a moment to shove a metal chair beneath the door handle at the back of the shop. It won't stop anyone from busting through the glass, but they won't be able to just waltz right in without us hearing it.

"Come on." He tugs on my hand and leads me back to the front. Motioning for me to stay put, he heads toward the door and pokes his head out. A long, low whistle calls out into the night before he ducks back inside. "I hope they heard that over the moans."

We wait and watch from the windows, wincing at each fall Victoria makes as Alex tries to help her across the ice. I'm worried about her hips. Her body can only take so much abuse, and today has been hard.

Less than five feet away from the Moaner, I see Victoria's feet slip. I cry out as she goes down. From within the small entryway, I hear the crack as her head hits the ice.

"Cable!" He pauses with his hand on the handle as I shove the knife he gave me into his hand. "Just in case."

The front door slams open as he rushes out. I clutch my hand over my mouth as I watch Alex trying to revive Victoria. Cable slides to his side, tucking his hatchet into his bag and his knife into the sheath at his side and ducks low, wrapping his arms around her. Together they fight to stand. Their progress back to me is slow. Much too slow.

I scan the parking lot for any signs of movement. My breath falters as I see two sets of feet shuffling on the other side of the semi behind them. I press my nose against the glass, watching the halting steps closely, and breathe easier.

Alex slips on the ice and nearly takes the three of them down. I press my palms to the door, frustrated that I can't help, but someone has to remain as look out.

Movement from my left captures my eye. Two more Moaners emerge. The men are filthy, their clothes ragged, hair gnarled with what I think is blood. They stagger forward. Another captures my attention from the right. This man is slighter in stature, his features what some might call pretty.

I stare long and hard at him, noting the absence of tears, cuts, and dangling flesh. *He must be newly turned.*

Glancing back at Cable, I'm relieved to see Alex is rising to his feet. His legs slide apart as he fights to regain his balance. Cable holds tightly to an unconscious Victoria, the solid base for while Alex grasps to.

I glance at the two Moaners approaching from behind. Something doesn't feel right, but I can't quite put my finger on it. My fingers curl inward as I press against the glass, my frustration rising parallel to my alarm.

Then I see it, but it's too late.

"Cable!" I shriek and bang against the glass. He raises up at my scream, but the men are upon them. I watch in horror as they break from their stagger and dive forward. Cable is thrust to the ground, tackled from behind.

Alex takes a blow to the ribs and crashes. Victoria slides, whirling around, her arm flapping erratically around her before she plummets to the ground. The two men emerging from behind the semi pause less than five feet away. I watch them draw weapons. The glint of silver in one man's hand sends me crashing through the door just before I hear the gunshot.

A scream fills my ears as I leap onto the back of the pretty man. He wails and beats at me as I dig my nails into his cheeks, tearing through his flesh. Blood soaks my fingers as I dig my feet into his sides, squeezing. He thrashes and falls. I hit hard and roll away. Blood slickens the ice between us.

Without thinking, I scramble to my feet and dive toward him, using the ice to my advantage. I slam into his side. He yells as the momentum shoves him against the curb of the sidewalk in front of the shop doors. I grab his head, curling my hands into his long hair and bash his head against the concrete. His hands flail at my face. I lean back, trying to stay out of his reach.

His hollering terrifies me. The crunching of bone sickens me, but I don't stop. I bash his head until his hands fall away and I'm slick with blood. It streaks down my face in thick, goopy trails, clings to my throat as I swallow repeatedly, tasting his blood in my mouth. My hands shake as I fall back away from his still form.

"Avery!" Strong hands grab me under my arm and haul me to my feet. I try to help, to rise and walk, but my legs feel as if all of the bones have vanished.

The glass doors burst open before me and Cable rushes me inside before turning and barring the door. I press back against the shelving system lining the first aisle. I stare vacantly at the blood on my hands. Warmth begins to soak through the seat of my pants and I slowly look to my right. A thick pool of blood surrounds me.

"Oh, God!" I stare at it, unblinking and only barely aware of crying nearby. The blood fills my vision, consumes my thoughts. I can't think. Can't feel. Is it mine? Am I hurt?

"Avery." A face swims before my face as hands force my head back to the front. I try to focus, to think. "Avery, are you hurt?"

I blink rapidly. The sound of loud humming fills my ears.

My head rocks back and a stinging pain races across my cheek. The pain helps to clear my thoughts. Another slap and the clarity of my vision begins to return. "Cable?"

"Thank God!" He tugs me into his arms. A wet stickiness surrounds him and I pull back. A crimson stain coats his shirt.

"You're hurt!" I paw at his chest, searching for a wound.

"I'm fine." He clasps my hands to his lips with one hand. The other he cups my cheek. "Are you back with me now?"

"I..." I blink several more times, trying to piece together the last few moments. "I think so."

"Good, cause I'm going to need your help."

"With what?" I turn and follow his gaze, trailing beyond the pool of blood to where Alex kneels over Victoria. All color has fled from her face. Her mouth hangs open, her tongue protruding from the corner of her mouth. I stare at the whites of her eyes as Alex lifts her eyelids. "She's been stabbed."

TWENTY-ONE

My arms are slick with blood. It itches as it dries, tugging at the hairs on my arms. A stack of orange car waxing cloths lies in a stained puddle at my feet. A window sun-shield lies over Victoria's body. I try not to think of her final moments, the fear I'd seen in her eyes. The way she gasped for breath as blood bubbled between her lips.

I feel numb, thinking of Alex's tears and pleading for her to hang on. Cable applied pressure to the wound, but he was wrong. She hadn't just been stabbed. She'd been gutted. When I'd arrived at her side, I had slid right into a tangle of intestines.

Alex was beside himself as he clung to Victoria, holding her head in his lap. She'd tried to speak, but words failed her. It didn't take long for the life to fade from her eyes. At least we have that to be thankful for.

I glance up at the sound of rattling and peer through the dark to see Cable working relentlessly to reinforce the doors. The chains may keep the door frame itself closed, but they will just come in through the glass. I saw it before at the hospital but say nothing now. This is what Cable needs to do so I let him.

"They're gone, for now," he says as he returns. His face bears evidence of the fight. Bloodied nose. Scratches along his face and arms. Of the three of them, he fared best. He turns his gaze on Alex. A bloodied cloth is pressed to the man's shoulder where a bullet tunneled through.

"How are you feeling?" I ask Alex.

He wipes at his nose. "Better than her."

I close my eyes at the pain in his voice as he stares at Victoria. His shoulders shake with silent sobs, of regret and guilt, I'm sure. He must be numb to the pain. "Don't do that to yourself. It wasn't your fault."

"Of course, it was," He shouts back. "I knew I wasn't good on ice. I should have asked Cable to take her. To stop trying to be the hero and do what was right."

I slide across the floor, attempting to avoid the smeared mess dragging Victoria's body away created and grab his hand from the floor beside him, where it hangs limp. "Victoria didn't die because you weren't fast enough. She died because of those men out there."

Alex yanks his arm away and turns his back on me. I know he is angry, at himself, at the world, at fate, but not at me. Not like he should be. Cable was right earlier. I did push to come here. For him.

With a heavy sigh, I push up to my feet and leave him be. He wants to be near her.

I brush my hair back out of my face, wincing at the thought of how gruesome I must look covered from head to foot in blood. Victoria's blood. Alex's. That man's.

When Cable's hand falls on my shoulder I flinch.

"Easy." I go willingly into his embrace as he wraps his arms around me. I cling to him, ignoring the scent of blood and sweat. "I've got you."

Closing my eyes, I allow him to lead me away from Alex, to a darkened corner where we can be alone. Where we are hidden from sight from those who linger outside. I know they are there. We are cornered, trapped within what so quickly became a coffin. How many more of us will go out the same way Victoria did? They have the advantage. It's only a matter of time before they know it.

"What are they waiting for?" I ask, despising the tremor in my voice, the way my hands shake as I cling to him. I sink down beside him and lean into him, resting my head on his chest. All thought of food, of gathering provisions, no longer seem important. Not in the wake of losing Victoria.

"They are probably trying to figure out how many of us are still alive. I'm betting they weren't here for the whole show. Otherwise, they wouldn't have pulled back when they did."

I stare into the dark, down the hall toward the back room. That's where Cable got the supplies to help Victoria. He blocked the door that leads to the shop and the repair center beyond. I close my eyes and try not to think about how those men could be creeping up on us right now.

Cable's chest bounces as he tries to stifle a cough. I raise my head and stare at him. He looks tired, unnaturally so. His head rests back against the wall. Perspiration dampens his hair. I watch as a bead of sweat rolls down his cheek.

Pushing back from him, I crawl away.

"Where are you going?"

"I'll be right back." I count the aisles, trying to remember where I saw the first aid section. There isn't much. A few packets of pills which I stuff into my pocket. Some temporary bandages and a first aid kit. I grab the kit and tear off the packaging, tossing it aside. I rummage through it until my fingers grasp what I'm looking for.

Tucking the thermometer between my teeth, I crawl toward a row of dark doors at the back. The scent of rotting food from the refrigerator beyond hits me as I grab a bottle and crawl back to Cable's side. "Open up."

"Does it really matter?"

"Yes." I insist and grab his chin. He relents and closes his mouth over the thermometer. A minute passes before it beeps. I glance down at the illuminated screen. "103.5"

He grunts and pushes my hand away. "I'm fine."

"You're not." I tear open two packages of pain pills and force them into his hand. "Take these."

"I don't have the flu, Avery. I doubt it will help."

I twist the cap of the bottle and the scent of soda makes my mouth water. How long has it been since I had a taste? Holding out the bottle, I grasp his hand. "I need you lucid if we are going to get out of here. Alex is messed up over Victoria, and I don't know what I'm doing."

"Yes, you do." He winces at the burn of the soda as I force the bottle between his lips and tilt his head back. He swallows and pushes my hand away. "I saw what you did to that guy."

The bottle falls from my hands. Cable reaches for me, not caring that soda spills over the floor before us. "It's hard, the first time," he says with deep, knowing compassion. Cable had his first kill too, but that had been a mission on a battlefield. Probably with a gun, from a distance. He may have seen the guy drop, but he didn't feel the man's blood splatter his face as he beat him senseless.

I swallow hard and draw my knees into my chest. "I don't want to talk about it."

"You need to."

"Why?"

His grip on my shoulder tightens. "Because you don't have time to internalize it. If we are going to make it out of here, you're going to have to kill again. Maybe more than once. You have to be prepared for it."

"Is that even possible?" I scoff and clamp my eyes shut against the memory. That man's blood still taints me. I can't be free of it, not without exposing myself to go into the bathroom to clean up. My palms feel clammy as a cold sweat breaks out. "It was awful," I whisper.

"I know." He strokes my hair. "But you did what you had to."

I bite down on my lower lip, giving a hesitant nod. "I guess I didn't think it would be so...so messy."

The feel of his calloused hands on my cheek pulls me back as he lifts my chin to look at him. In the dim light of the moon spilling through the windows overhead, I know he can see my fear. His face is dark, but the warmth of his smile shines through as he slowly lowers his head and kisses me.

It does not hold the same passion or intensity of the last time our lips met. This is soft, a gentle, unspoken promise. When he draws back he places a final kiss on my nose. "Next time will be easier."

I nuzzle into his side, for the moment content to just be. He leans his cheek against my head and after a moment his breathing slows and he leans on me for support. I hold him, allowing him a rare moment of rest. He's going to need it.

Some time later I start at the sound of crashing glass. Cable leaps to his feet, slightly wobbly but alert. "Is that them?"

"No." He shakes his head and grabs my arm. "I don't think so."

I follow his lead back through the store, keeping low to make a smaller target. I have no idea how skilled those men are with guns. Anyone can hit a target at close range and Alex just happened to be a pretty good one earlier.

"Alex," I hiss when we discover him missing from beside Victoria. I stare at her body, wondering if she will come back. I didn't express my concerns with Cable, didn't have the heart to, but it's a legitimate question. Nothing about the Withered Ones has been a textbook zombie. Not the way we thought they would be. Up until now, I haven't remained near any dead bodies to see if they will rise again.

"He's down here." I look up to see that Cable has moved to the far end of the shop. He stands upright, his hands planted on his hips. I don't have to hear the disapproval in his voice to know he's not happy.

I hurry down the final three aisles and stop short when I see Alex sprawled out on the floor. "Well, I guess that accounts for the broken glass," I mutter, staring down at the collection of empty beer bottles around him.

Alex's head rolls to the side. Chip and cookie crumbles line his shirt, some sticking to the expanding stain of blood that has soaked through his bandage.

"He's trashed."

"I am not," he slurs. "I'm wasted. Big difference."

I roll my eyes and glance back at the doors. No sign of movement outside but there will be soon enough. I'm sure of it. "Was this really the best time to do this?"

Kneeling down beside him, I grab one arm and Cable the other. We lift him into a seated position. The stench of alcohol on him turns my stomach. "Imminent death is the best time, in my honest opinion."

Alex burps and giggles. I stare at Cable in open amazement. There is an ugly twist of scorn on his lips. He releases his hold on Alex and crosses his arms, thrusting out his chest. "He's a damned fool."

I can't help but agree, but I don't say it aloud. "Everyone deals with loss in their own way."

"You're making excuses for this sorry piece of shit?"

I place a hand on his arm. "He's hurting."

Cable grinds his teeth. I can see that he's trying to rein in his anger, but it's a battle. One that I don't entirely blame him for. Alex is a fool. If he didn't have a death wish before, he's got one signed and sealed now. He'll be lucky to make it to the back door.

"What do we do?"

Uncrossing his arms, Cable slides to the floor and rubs the back of his neck. He is silent for several moments. What once caused me frustration now brings me hope. An introspective Cable is far more reassuring than a hell-bent one.

"How did you know that they were going to attack?" He shifts, tilting his body toward me. He casts a glance at Alex, but the man's snores force him to look away again. "You yelled right before they struck."

I grasp my knees, feeling comfort in their pressure against my chest. I adopted this pose first as a young child every time I feel like the world is spinning out of control. That seems to happen on a near daily basis now. "I didn't see it at first. Thought they were just Moaners, but they felt...off. I watched each of them. They were good, Cable. I nearly didn't see in time. They moved in unison. They didn't blink, hardly seemed to breathe. Even their appearance was near enough that they could pass for a Moaner."

He scoots closer, his knee brushing mine. "So what gave them away?"

There is a heaviness pressing on my chest as I pinch the bridge of my nose. "They weren't moving south."

Cable leans back, his arm resting atop his knee. The other is tucked beneath him, the laces of his boot soaking up the spilled alcohol. "But that's just a theory, completely unproven and invalidated."

"It worked, didn't it?"

"This time," he agrees with hesitation. He turns and looks toward the front door. I stiffen at the sight of a brief movement, a foot drawn out of view at the last second. They are coming.

"Did you see—" I turn to see Cable holding out the knife to me.

"Take it. You'll need it more than me." He reaches into his back and pulls out a silver pistol. It looks like something a cowboy would use in an old Western. "I've got three rounds left, but I lost the ax out there in the parking lot."

"Where'd you get that gun?"

He jerks his head toward the door. "I didn't go down without a fight."

"What about him?" I look to Alex. He breathes heavily, locked into a deep sleep. "Can we wake him?"

Cable reaches over and punches Alex in the shoulder, right over the entry wound. It takes two more hard hits before Alex rears up, eyes bloodshot and filled with pain. "What the hell did you do that for?"

I clamp my hand down on his mouth to still his shout. "They're back."

He falls still and I lower my hand. He trembles as he looks toward the door. I wrinkle my nose at the scent of urine and pull back. "Alex—"

"Don't," he waves me off. "I'll be embarrassed about it later."

Fear sobers him fast. I help him to his feet, keeping my hand on his head to keep him below the height of the windows. His steps are unsteady, his gaze still glazed over, but he's on his feet. That's an improvement.

Cable is gone, slipped out of sight while I take care of Alex. He rustles around in the back and I lead Alex down the dark hallway toward him.

"We should have buried her," Alex mutters, glancing at Victoria.

"You know we couldn't."

"I know." He sounds defeated, lost. He tugs back against my arm and I release him.

"Alex, we have to keep moving."

"Just give me a minute. Go find Cable."

Torn with indecision, I don't move until I hear a grunt from up ahead. I rush forward, leaving Alex behind. The instant I hit the start of the windows I dive to my knees and crawl forward.

I hear Cable clearly now. He has gone through the door to the repair shop. The door remains cracked open and cold air seeps through. I press on the door and rear back as he appears, his arms loaded down with two large canisters.

"What are you doing?"

"Help me with these." I grab hold of the bottom and help ease them to the floor. He groans as the weight shifts to the floor. He sinks to his knee, breathing hard. "I can't do this alone."

"I'll help." I hear sloshing inside the can. The scent of oil burns in my nose. "Alex is in the hallway. You work back here and then grab him. I'll take the front."

"No."

I grab a canister and rise. "Now's not the time to argue over who's stronger or faster. I can do this. You need to let me."

Putting distance between us, just in case he tries to reach out and stop me, I shoot him a smile and dart away.

The canister is every bit as heavy as it looked when Cable carried it. Being forced to hunch over to avoid detection makes my arms quiver and my lower back ache.

I pass Alex in the hall, nearly clocking him in the head in the dark. I call back over my shoulder that he needs to find Cable and hope like heck that he listens. Readjusting my grip, I waddle down the hall, thankful to be able to stand fully upright, even if only for a minute.

The hall has never felt so long before. By the time I reach the end, I'm forced to drag the canister behind me. The screeching sound of metal against concrete is loud, certainly loud enough to be heard outside.

Peering out the front window, I see three men approaching. They walk forward with extreme caution, their knees slightly bent, their guns raised. "Shit!"

Tugging the canister, I work my way down the back aisle, past the soda and beer fridges. I pause only a second beside Victoria, remorse weighing me down. *I'm sorry.*

"Avery." I turn at the hushed call and see Cable crouching at the entrance of the hall. His gaze sweeps back and forth between me and the window. I can see the men clearly now. They are less than twenty feet from the front door. "It's too late. Dump it and run."

"Not yet," I grunt and remove the cap. I turn my face away from the potent oil scent as I dump the contents over Victoria. *Funeral by fire. It was once good enough for kings. It's the best I can do for you.*

"Avery!" I glance up and see a man testing the front door. The chains rattle against the glass. I hold my breath as he calls back over his shoulder. More men approach, each one heavily armed. "Get your ass over here!"

The oil spreads out before me, but not nearly fast enough. It will do some damage, but I want more than that. I want revenge.

I crawl forward, ignoring Cable's desperate pleas. Two aisles up ahead, I turn and lower to my belly, inching forward. It's a straight shot to the front door from here. With one swipe of a flashlight, I'd be discovered.

Grabbing a couple small metal canisters off the shelves, I bite into the cap and spit it aside. I shove them to down the aisle, toward the door, listening to the fluid spill over the floor. I reach to grab another one and pause as my hand hits a long cylinder. I yank it off the shelf and hold it up before my eyes.

"I'll be damned." I tear into the packaging and release the long handled kitchen lighter. The scent of lighter fluid mingles with the oil in my nose, making me a bit lightheaded. Grabbing two more canisters, I back down the aisle. When I reach the end I see Cable crawling toward me.

"Get back!" I wave him off. He hesitates then notices the canisters in my hand.

"Avery, that's not a good idea."

"Trust me. It'll work."

A crash of glass sends one canister spiraling from my hand. Loud shouts are followed by another pane of glass exploding. I bite down on the canister and chuck it behind me. With trembling hands, I flick the lighter.

"Rapid start my ass!" I click it again and again.

"Avery," Cable hisses.

I hear the sound of glass crunching underfoot. Their movements are slow as then enter the room. "Luke, you smell something funny?"

The footsteps pause. I click the lighter again and it flares to life.

"What is that?" a man's voice echoes through the shop as I touch the lighter to the fluid. Blue flames race away from me, curling around the corner and heading straight for the front door.

"Run!" Cable motions for me to race toward him.

I push to my feet as gunfire slams into the glass overhead. I dive, curling my arms over my head as the shards slice my arms and cheeks. The scent of burnt hair is strong in my nose.

"Dammit." Cable beats at my hair, snuffing out the flames as I roll to my side, coughing over the rising smoke. "That fire won't last long."

"I know," I choke out. Blood trails down my face. There are lacerations in more places that I care to count. I hurt all over, but I ignore the pain. I shove the lighter into Cable's hand and point to Victoria. "Light her up."

He looks stricken for a second, but another round of gunfire gets him moving. I crawl behind him, shredding my hands and knees on the glass. My teeth burrow into my lower lip as I fight through the pain, moving as fast as I can.

The instant I move past Cable, he flicks on the lighter and tosses it onto Victoria. The blast of heat is suffocating. I kick back with my feet, scooting across the floor as fast as I can toward the hall. The instant I'm clear, Cable grabs me around the waist and hauls me to my feet.

"Don't look back."

But I do. Half a dozen faces are illuminated in the windows. Each one staring right at us.

TWENTY-TWO

Cable's pressure around my waist increases as I hesitate, lost to the terror threatening to overwhelm me as I stare into the rabid gaze of the men waiting outside for us. I sense their rage, see the crazy in their eyes. Their companions flail near the front doors, their clothes set alight.

The store before me is a blazing inferno. Blistering heat licks at the ends of my hair. The scent of burnt hair mingles with the billowing smoke, but I feel none of it.

"Avery!" I turn away from the window in a daze. Cable's face appears before me. His shouts feel like white noise as I blink, trapped in slow motion. "Avery, snap out of it!"

"We'll never make it," I mutter.

I glance down at Victoria's body, at the sizzling flesh that was once a person. A person I knew. Maybe we didn't always get along, maybe we would have continued to butt heads in the days to come, but I will never know. I pushed to come here, to ignore the danger, to keep Cable safe and look what has happened.

I killed them.

Cable's grip on my arms becomes painful and I tear my gaze away from Victoria's funeral pyre. "I'm not going to die tonight and neither are you."

With every fiber of my being, I want to believe him, to have faith in some entity that maybe, just maybe, watches over me. Heck, at this point I'd even settle for dumb luck.

"Do you trust me?" Adrenaline sends a spike of energy through my body as I nod. I've already entrusted him with far more than just my life. "Then come with me."

I follow after him, knowing that I would go to the ends of the earth if he asked me to, simply because he asked, because he would be with me. I know letting myself fall for him is wrong, is setting myself up for loss. Cable is sick and I have no idea how much longer he has, but as I twine my fingers through his and run behind him, I vow to make every second count.

He pulls me to a stop at the far end of the hallway and tucks me behind him. With a flick of his thumb, he ignites a lighter and chucks it onto the oil slick. "Run!"

Strong hands yank me from Cable's grasp and I crash into Alex's side. He wraps his good arm around me and pulls me toward the back door that leads to the mechanical shop. The room ignites around us. The floor warms with a searing heat that rises through the soles of my shoes, making each step painful. Covering my mouth with my shirt, I stumble forward with Alex beside me and Cable pushing from behind through the smoke.

A terrible crash comes from the front of the shop. Glass shatters and shouts rise around the crackling roar of the flames. We burst through the door and into the blissful cool of the night. My arms and cheeks feel burned. My eyebrows singed.

Alex releases me and I drop to my knees as a racking cough seizes me. "No... time," Cable chokes beside me. He wraps his arm under mine and hauls me to my feet.

Grabbing my knife from my pocket, he places it in my palm, his hand trembling as he covers my fingers over it. "Don't think. Just do."

I try to nod, to act tough, but inside I'm terrified. I don't want to fight my way out of here, to possibly suffer the same fate as Victoria. The men I saw at that window may have looked crazed, but there was also intelligence still lingering in their eyes. That makes them deadly.

Cable grabs a wrench off the top of a tall red tool chest and Alex tightens his grip on a couple of flares. It is dark and cool in the shop. The concrete block walls keep most of the destruction out. Flames flicker along the seam that runs at the base of the door. I step away, drawn to the cold rather than the heat.

"They will be waiting for us," I say, turning toward my two final companions. Along the way, we collected and lost more people than I want to count. Staring at the men before me, I realize not all of us will make it, not to the end. To a time when maybe someone can create a cure, to reverse this mess. The odds are stacked heavily against us.

Cable reaches out and grabs my hand, squeezing it tight. Alex looks down at our embrace. "It has been an honor knowing you two."

"Cut the sentimental crap." I yank Alex into a half hug. He cries out in pain and I release him, realizing I've just grabbed his bad arm. He presses against his bullet wound, but a broad smile chases away the pain.

"Isn't this how they do it in movies? The hero pauses to say a heartfelt thank you before rushing headfirst into a battle, which he has no earthly chance of winning but somehow lives to have the final word?"

"Yeah." Cable wipes at his face. It drips with sweat. I frown, remembering the fever raging within. "I've got nothing."

"Me either." I glance toward the two metal garage doors. I see movement beyond. Our escape path wasn't exactly a secret after we set the front on fire. "But then again...that's not really our style, is it?"

Alex grins and lifts the flares. "Cover me until I reach that semi, then I'll create a diversion and meet you in the woods."

Leaning up onto my toes, I look through the garage door window to where he points. Sitting parked beneath an awning that houses six diesel pumps are three semis. I glance back at the flares in his hands. "You won't make it that far. Not in your condition."

He puffs up his chest. "I know how to hold my liquor well enough."

"I meant your arm." I jerk my head toward the blood staining through the shoulder and chest of his shirt. "You've lost blood."

Cable stares hard at Alex. The two men lock gazes and for a moment I feel forgotten, cast aside. Cable nods and pulls me toward the door. "We'll try to keep them off you."

"What? No. You know he will never make it and even if he does if he gets one of those flares near that fuel it will blow sky high."

"He knows."

I look up at Cable and see the sorrowful resignation in his gaze. Glancing back at Alex, I see only determination, not fear. "You're both crazy."

"You're darn right," Alex grins, winking at me as he grabs the bottom of the garage door. "On three."

"Three," Cable shouts and throws up the door. I only make it half a dozen steps before Cable shoves me aside. I hear the whizz of a bullet passing far too close to my ear before I hit the ground and slide. My back slams into a stack of tires. They teeter overhead. I wrap my arms around my head and prepare to be pummeled.

"Get up." Cable yanks my arm and drags me out of the way. I kick at the tires as they spiral around me. He points to the dark, away from the mechanic shop, away from Alex. "I want you to run that way and keep going. No matter what you hear."

"No. I'm not leaving you!"

"I'll take care of Alex. Just go!" He shoves me away. My arms flap wildly as my legs begin to slip apart on the ice. My footing is precarious as I attempt to remain upright. A bullet tears through my sleeve, nicking my skin as I fall on my ass. My tailbone screams as I roll to the side and pull myself behind a dumpster. Bullets ricochet off the metal and slam into the concrete wall beside me.

I suck in shallow breaths as I look around me. I can't see Cable or Alex. There is shouting all around. It's impossible to tell who is who. Glancing overhead, I spy a brilliant glow near the roof. It won't be long before this whole place goes up in flames. The scent of burning oil stings my eyes and I'm forced to wipe them several times to clear my vision.

Ducking my head out, I try to get my bearings. The open garage door is about fifteen feet behind me. Just beyond that a long low ledge of concrete stands, its purpose to funnel cars into the bays. I see a shadow of a man leap over and crouch behind that and pray that it is Cable making his way toward Alex. I peer out again, pressing my cheek close to the dumpster. Where is Alex? I never saw him after Cable and I ran out.

Three men approach from beyond the wall. They slide more than step. Their guns are poised. My fingers ache as I grip the edge of the dumpster. I try not to breathe in the foul stench within.

In less than a minute, they will converge on Cable's last known spot.

He's a soldier. He's been trained for this sort of combat, I try to remind myself as I back up to follow his last order: to run.

Fingers dig through my tangled curls from behind. I scream as I'm hauled to my feet by my hair and dragged out from behind the dumpster. "Got you."

I kick and fight against the man's grip, tossing my elbows back and wide in an attempt to wound my captor, but he remains just out of reach. Blood trickles from my scalp as the fistful of hair begins to release from my scalp. Pain darkens my vision.

His thick soled boots punch through the thin layer of ice as he leads me toward the side of the building where darkness gives way to the flickering of flames. An abandoned car sits with its doors open wide. It has been stripped of parts. The tires are missing. The cloth seats ripped away. The headlights busted out and the bulbs were stolen.

"Ain't you a pretty little thing?" The man whispers in my ear, leaning in close as he pushes me toward the car. His free hand winds around my waist and tugs me close to him. He presses his length against my back. "I always did have a thing for redheads."

His breath grows ragged as his hand slides down my hip and dips between my legs as we stop in front of the car. "Seems wrong to waste something so fine."

Pulling me to the side, he keeps a firm grip on my hair as he passes the driver's side door and hauls me toward the trunk. At first, I think he's going to shove me inside, but he angles me away and rummages around. I hear metal clanking as he tosses things out of the trunk, items useless to his pursuit. I glance around me, forced to look from the corner of my eye. I can't see anyone. Can't hear anything beyond intermittent gunfire. Are Cable and Alex still alive?

The scent of burning rubber burns in my nose as I try to look back the way I came but the man's grip on my hair is too firm. I cry out as he grabs my arm and yanks it behind me, pinning my hand with his knee. He releases his grasp on my hair and fights to gain control of my other hand. I stretch it out before me, flapping it in an attempt to resist, but he digs his teeth into the meat of my arm and latches onto my hand when I flinch back.

"Good girl," he croons in my ear. Tears burn in my eyes as he binds my hand with what feels like a bit of rope. His fumbling fingers lash the binding.

With a hard shove, he forces me toward the front of the car and presses against my back. I'm forced to bend over the side of the hood. His hips rock against me, his hands holding me in place. His breath is rank as he bites at my ear over my back and I try to turn away.

"I like it when they struggle." He yanks on another clump of hair and I cry out. The muscles in my neck twang as I fight against the pain. "Like it when they scream a little."

Using his hips to keep me in place, wedged against the car, he fumbles with his pants. Terror seizes me as I twist and turn. "Get the hell off of me!"

My head rocks forward and slams into the hood with a blow from behind. My cheek burns as it sticks to the ice coating the hood. I taste blood in my mouth from a split lip.

The man releases my hair and grips my waist with both hands. He tugs at my pants, grunting as they slowly begin to fall. "Stop!"

"Oh, no," he chuckles as his hand slides down my waistband. I clench as rough calloused hands glide over my backside. "There will be no stopping."

"Cable!" I shriek. "Help me!"

A filthy hand covers my mouth. My eyes clamp shut as I feel him press against me. The sound of my heartbeat thrashes in my ears. My legs feel weak, my nostrils flare as terror and rage mingle.

"Don't you fucking touch me!" My shout is muffled by his hand. I try to bite him, to shift or twist out of his grasp, but he has me subdued.

"Hey!" My head rears back at the sound of a voice. My cheek burns as it peels away from the ice. "Whatcha got there?"

"I call dibs. You can have her next, Gentry." He runs his hand down my side, dipping around to pinch my breast. I buck and knock his hand away. "She's a real fighter. You'll like her."

The approaching heavy footfalls sound hollow in my ears against the rushing of my pulse. I can feel the onset of a panic attack nearing as I try to see the second man. His voice is low and gruff. When a second hand, larger than the first, wraps around my hip I thrash.

The man behind me hollers and shouts in approval. "She's a wild thing," he crows as he slaps the side of my hip.

I fall still, terrified of assisting him in his plunder. The new hand tightens on my hip. "Brian will shit bricks if he hears you took her."

"We," the man says with voice slick as oil. "You and me, Gentry. Boss man don't gotta know about it. We can do away with her after. No harm done. Just a bit of sport while they wrap up that mess back there. What do you say?"

The tension in the fingers at my hip increases. Tears spill from my chin, pattering against the hood of the car as the man named Gentry brushes his thumb along the rise of my hip. He's considering it.

"You got two minutes." The hand pulls away and I yank against the rope, knowing that I'm out of time. The fibers eat into my flesh as my captor tries to force my legs apart.

A sudden blaring of a car alarm startles my attacker. I grunt and shove back, thrusting my head. It slams into something solid and I celebrate at the sickening crunch from behind.

"Bitch!" I try to duck the swinging blow but move a hair too slow. His fist grazes off my side and slams into the hood. He hops back, howling. I turn and kick wildly, aiming for anything I can reach.

The man buckles before me. The sound of running reaches me and I know Gentry didn't go far. Probably waiting for his turn.

I wiggle against the car, desperately trying to shove my pants up. About five inches of my skin is still bare when I'm tackled to the ground. I hit the pavement hard. There is no slide this time. Glancing up, I realize the flames have come around the side of the building and are heading straight for us.

"If you don't let me go we're going to die," I rasp. My lungs feel bruised. My entire left side splintering with pain.

"Shut up." A fist slams into my side and I inhale sharply, realizing for the first time how potent the scent of gasoline is. I press my nose to the ground and sniff. The car must have had a gas leak. That's why they left it behind.

"The flames," I try again. "Look at the fire!"

For a second the man does. He falls still overhead and I allow myself a second to hope. "We are lying in a pool of gasoline. I know you can smell it."

He shifts on top of me, glancing around. He tugs at my rope bindings. "When that fire reaches that car we all burn. Am I really worth dying for?"

"Shit, no." He shoves me into the ground and rises. "I'm outta here."

"Gentry!" I turn to see my initial attacker for the first time. A thick beard covers his face, dark and overgrown. It's obvious by the length of it that his beard was already well in place before the world sank into hell. His cheeks are sunken with patches of angry red, flaking rash cover his cheeks.

"You son of a bitch! You're infected!" I hurl myself at him, yanking with all my might against the ropes as I head-butt him in the stomach. The ropes give slightly. I yank again, rearing my head back and slam my forehead down onto his chest.

My vision blurs under the impact and for a second, I nearly pass out. The feel of the rope slipping over my hand brings me back. I slam my fist into the man's arms, raised to protect his face. I tremble as I beat against him, the rope dangling from my left hand with each blow.

"Never. Fucking. Touch. Me. Again." An odd numbing sensation falls over me as I land punches, hitting ribs, stomach and the side of his head, wherever he lowers his defenses. I don't feel the skin over my knuckles split. Don't react when an enormous explosion from behind me rocks the ground and sends a fireball high into the night sky, casting its orange light across the ground.

I stare into the terrified eyes of my attacker and feel something snap. I beat him till I'm panting and drenched with sweat. His pleas fuel my rage. There is no mercy, no pity to be found within me. Only a thirst for revenge that has yet to be quenched.

Smoke hangs thick in the air. I can feel its scorching heat and know I'm running out of time, but it doesn't matter anymore. All that matters is that I hurt this man.

An unseen blow rocks me backward as the man retaliates. My head spins and I fall to my side. The rough concrete tears at my palms. My fingers land on something cold and I retract them, before falling still. There, lying partially hidden beneath the car, is a tire iron.

Without thought, I grasp the iron and swing. My captor screams as I hit his raised hand. He curls in on himself as I stagger to my feet. With his feet, he pushes away, slowly inching his way up the wall. Flames lick the wooden siding not far from us. The ground less than twenty feet away begins to ignite.

There is terror in the man's eyes as he watches me approach. I grip the tire iron, my hands feeling steady for the first time. "Please," he raises a hand.

Cocking my head to the side, I smile. "I like it when they scream...just a little."

I swing the tire iron with all my might. Blood splatters my face and arms. His screams rise above the crackling flames. His attempts to protect himself diminish. I swing until my shoulders grow weary and the fire nips at my heels.

The tire iron hooks on the remnants of the man's skull. I place my foot on his chest and yank it free. Thick globs of slick matter cling to my skin as I raise my arms overhead for another blow.

Something solid tackles me from the side. I scream as I slam to the ground, bucking wildly. "Shh," Cable soothes, his firm grip stilling my fight. "It's me."

"Cable?" The tire iron slips from my hands. My fingers are sticky as I reach out for his face, unable to comprehend that he is here. That he came for me.

I try to blink away the smoke stinging my eyes. Blood mats my eyelashes together. My stomach heaves as I glance down at my attacker. "Oh, God."

"Don't look." Cable shields me, but I know the horror that lies at my feet. I did this.

"We have to get out of here," He grunts as he hauls me to my feet. I try to skirt the edge of the flames, but my legs give way beneath me. Cable scoops me into his arms and runs full out toward the overpass. He doesn't slow to duck behind the cars or weave among them. He follows the railing and flees.

Wrapping my arms around his neck, I look behind us. What was once a single fire has become a raging inferno. Flames engulf the last section of the truck stop before we reach the other side. Cable's footing is sure on the newly melted road. The scorching heat races after us as we escape into the woods.

I cling to him as the trembling finally comes. As the realization of what I did sinks in. He carries me deep into the forest, but he doesn't stop, doesn't look back. I lay my head on his shoulder and know in my heart that Alex is lost to us forever. Cable would never leave a man behind.

TWENTY-THREE

I shiver at the edge of the cave, my teeth chattering and my fingers clenched into fists in my armpits. A rain has fallen steadily for several days. The bite of the wind has shifted slightly, just enough for me to hope that spring might be on the not too distant horizon. The damp is a welcome change to the ice though it keeps us trapped. Not that we have anywhere else to be.

Cable says I'm in shock, that it will pass. I don't feel in shock, not like the first time I killed a man. This time was different. Yes, my life was in danger. Yes, he had hurt me, but I could have walked away. Could have left him for the fire to consume, but I didn't.

I wanted to finish that monster off myself.

At Cable's cough, I turn away from the outside world and hurry back to his side. He lies near the back of the small cave we discovered not an hour's hike from the burning truck stop. Too close for comfort, but he couldn't go any farther. He was spent and I welcomed the small shelter.

The dim light escaping through the thick blanket of cloud overhead is not nearly bright enough to allow me to see well, but I don't need to. I can feel the heat pouring from him, hear the moist wheezing in his chest. Cable took a turn for the worse shortly after we arrived in the cave.

For the first two days after Cable brought us here, I held on to the delusion that maybe he really did just have the flu. I was sick when he first found me and look at me now. Healthy, albeit a bit worse for wear, but I didn't turn. I survived.

He hasn't slept in nearly three nights. At first, I thought he was just wanting to keep a watchful eye in case there were any survivors from the fire. Then I began to realize it was because he couldn't sleep. The light began to hurt his eyes yesterday. Now he spends most of his time curled up into a ball, shivering and moaning from random body aches, his face turned away from the light. I try to talk to him, to give him something to think about, but we both know it's a wasted effort, but we are too stubborn to admit it.

Cable's symptoms progressed fast. Maybe it's because this is the first time he's slowed down long enough to allow it to take him. Maybe he pushed himself too close to the limit. Maybe it is just his time. Either way, as I reach out and grasp his hand in mine, I know that I'm not ready to say goodbye.

He stirs, inching his way onto his side to look at me. I shift to block the light from his eyes. They are more sunken than before. His face is pale. His lips nearly colorless.

"You're freezing." He slowly lifts his hand and presses it to my cheek. I close my eyes at his chilled touch. His fever didn't break overnight. It vanished only to be replaced by an unnatural chill that he can't shake. Natalia experienced the same thing while Eric watched her slip away. I don't know if I can do that.

"I'm fine." I smile down at him with as much sincerity as I can muster.

His eyebrows rise so swiftly that I can't help but laugh. "Okay, I'm not, but you know...I'm trying to be."

"Always the martyr," he whispers. His fingers curl around my cheek. I lean into his touch, knowing soon this will be lost to me.

"That blow to your head must have knocked something loose. You're the fool who always rushes in." I brush my finger along the fading bruise that spans from his hairline down to his chin. Cable says he got that when the blast blew him backward. I can't imagine how he managed to find his feet in time to save me, but he did. Just like he promised.

It hurts to think about Alex, about all of the people we've lost along the way. Laying my hand across his forehead, I can't begin to think of what losing Cable will be like. "How are you feeling?"

Gripping his side, Cable allows me to help him into a seated position. He presses back against the wall, his chest heaving. His cheeks are rosy, his fingertips a matching hue. There is a bit of swelling to his skin as if he's begun to retain water. Considering we've had little but handfuls of rainwater for the past few days I don't see how that's possible.

He gives me a pointed look and grins. "I'm fine."

Chuckling to myself, I sink down beside him. He slides along the wall toward me and I take the brunt of his weight as he rests his head against mine. We stare out at the darkening day. Though it is not nearly time for the sun to set, the thick layer of rain clouds overhead sucks the light from the woods early.

"Are you ever going to tell me about Alex?" I hold my breath, wondering how he will take my question. I've waited for days for him to bring it up, but he hasn't. He swallows hard and reaches down for my hand.

"You might as well know." I tuck my fingers between his as Cable finally begins to spill the details of Alex's final moment. There is pride in his voice as he speaks of Alex's brave attempt to make his way to one of the semis.

"He took several bullets along the way. One to the leg and two to the arm and shoulder. Nearly dropped him right in front of me. I managed to get him hidden in one of the cars left on the side of the shop, probably waiting for an oil change or something completely random and normal."

A ghost of a smile touches his lips as he looks at the ceiling of the cave. "I knew he wasn't going to make it, but he had a good plan. All he had to do was shove a flare into a gas tank of a semi and run like hell. I figured if I was going down I was going to take them with me, so I grabbed the flares and left Alex behind."

"I took down two men before being surrounded. They had guns pointed at my chest, back and head. I knew I wasn't going anywhere." His grip tightens against my fingers as he coughs. I hold on to him, waiting for the fit to pass. "Thought that was it until I heard the craziest thing. None of them could figure out where the heck the car horn was coming from."

I grin, imagining Alex beating the horn. "When those guys turned to search for that car, I grabbed the shotgun from the first guy and rammed it straight up under his throat. He went down hard. After that it was easy. They were standing so close together it only took one shot to take them out."

Cable's tale of Alex steering the hotwired car, its back end fishtailing wildly as he rammed into the gas tank, sounds like nothing more than a fable. One a father would try to pass on to his wide-eyed child as a bedtime story of amazing heroics. I never thought of Alex as a hero, but he saved my life. I know that I owe him a lot. We both do.

I turn my head and place a kiss against Cable's chin. "You saved my life, just like you promised."

Staring down at his feet, Cable doesn't react. I wait, waving my hand before his face. He doesn't blink, doesn't speak. Though his chest rises and falls, his face hangs without expression.

"Cable?" I shake him by the arm.

"Yeah." His gaze shifts slowly toward me. "Sorry. I guess I got lost for a moment..."

Lost. Is that what it feels like near the end? Confusion? A wiping of memory? Like a fog settling over your mind that you can't escape?

"It's okay." I feel shaky as I slowly release the breath I'd been holding, sure that I'd lost him completely. That is the first time I've seen him fade. How many more times will come before the end?

"What were you saying?" He rubs his forehead, as if trying to massage the memory back into place.

"It doesn't matter."

We sit in silence as the forest darkens. I listen to the pattering of rain beyond the walls of the cave. I used to like the rain. Now it makes me sad.

Exhaustion tugs at my eyelids. I try to fight back, to remain alert for Cable, but it's a losing battle. Some time later he shifts beside me and I rouse. A cold damp has settled over our clothes, making my hair and pants feel moist to the touch. I should build a fire, but there is nothing dry to use.

"I'm sorry," he whispers beside me.

My hands still as I rub my palms against my jeans to warm them. I turn toward him. His face is lost to the all-consuming shadow of night. "Sorry for what?"

"For cutting out on you early."

"Don't." My throat clenches. "Don't do this, Cable. Not now."

His hands quake as he reaches out for me. Tears slip between my eyes as I feel how cold he has become. I clasp his hands between mine and blow on them.

"You're a tough girl. I've always admired that about you. I know you'll make it."

A moan of despair escapes my lips as I turn toward him, propping my knee against his side. "I don't want to hear your goodbyes. I won't accept them."

The wheezing sounds rise and fall with his chest, a fight for each breath. "Tough."

Tears leak from the corners of my eyes as I cling to him. I don't want to lose him, to be all alone. Haven't I lost enough? Does the world really need to take this good soul from me?

"I knew from the moment I first met you that you were special," he whispers. His head lolls back against the stone. I reach out and press my palm to his cheek, easing the strain off his neck. "I could see the fire in your eyes."

"Most guys hated that about me."

His laughter turns to a cough. He doubles over. I beat on his back as he gasps for breath. Biting my lip doesn't help take away the gaping hole burrowing into my chest. Why him? Why now?

I help press him back against the wall. His shoulders slump. It breaks me to see a man of such strength reduced to this. Anger churns deep within my soul as I think of how many other good people have been stolen away.

"I'm not most guys." He spits to the side and wipes his mouth.

"No." I scoot as close as I can to hold him. "You're better. A thousand times better, Cable."

He leans his head forward, cradling it in the crook of my neck. I wrap my arms around him and clench my eyes as I feel the rattling in his lungs as my hands splay across his back. He is suffering.

I feel him rustling in his jacket and sit up. "Do you need help?"

"No." His arm moves against me. I stare into the dark, cursing it for not being able to see. "Let me have your hand."

I hold it out for him, moving it in the dark until he finds me. Something cold and heavy comes to rest on my palm. My fingers curl around it and I fall still. "A gun?"

"Your gun," he corrects and leans back.

"You're out of ammunition."

"No," he rasps. "I saved one final round."

The weight of his words falls heavily on me. "You could have used that bullet back at the truck stop, could have saved yourself."

"I was saving it..."

I bring the gun up to my chest, holding it close. "Saving it for me?"

Though I can't see his nod, I sense it. "Just in case."

I set the gun aside and push it away. "I don't want it."

Cable reaches out for me, his hand falling on my upper arm. He squeezes but there is little strength left in him. "I know, but I need it now."

"Cable, don't! Please don't do this to me. I can't—"

He tugs on my arm, shushing me. "I know that I promised you that I'd always take care of you. I tried to fight it, to survive for you and I'm sorry. I tried to hold on—"

"Shh," I whisper, pulling him toward me. "It's okay. We'll get through this."

"I'm dying, Avery, but I don't want to be like *them*. Promise me you'll take care of it before the end."

"Oh, God." A whimper rises from my throat. My hands shake as I clasp them over my lips. I can't lose him. I just can't.

"There's something else. I need you to know that I've never loved anyone like I—"

I pull back and press my fingers to his lips. I know he can feel how badly they shake as I try to silence him. My shoulders quake as tears fall unheeded. My chest hitches as I begin to sob, sinking into his weakened embrace. He holds me as I cry, slowly petting my hair. He murmurs to me through my hair, pressing his lips against the crown of my head from time to time.

The moon doesn't rise this night. The dark is absolute as I cling to him, desperate for the morning's return so that I can see him again. Everything seems better in the light.

He holds me for hours, sometimes humming as we rock, other times he falls completely still and I'm forced to shake him so hard I'm terrified that I might crack his head against the wall. He always comes back to me, but it's getting harder with each slip.

I ignore the cold, the numbness in my toes and nose. I ignore the growling in my stomach or the dizziness from going too long without a drink. I refuse to leave him, even for a moment.

Finally, the east begins to brighten. "The sun is coming," I whisper.

Cable doesn't move. I bump his arm and he slides sideways across the wall. The sound of his head hitting the stone floor makes me sick. "Cable!"

I crawl to my knees, rushing to pull his head into my lap. I feel for a bump or a cut but feel nothing. Sweat no longer moistens his brow. His forehead is free of worry lines. I trace my fingers down to his lips, feeling for his slow breath.

"Cable," I pat his cheeks, using my free hand to shake his shoulders. "Dammit, Cable don't do this to me! I need you!"

I look up at the sky, willing the sun to rise faster. The curve of his shoes appears first since they lie nearest to the cave entrance. I continue to call out to him as the new day arrives. The clouds have begun to dissipate to the east. Sunlight glistens off the puddles of water all around.

The outline of his legs and hands begins to take shape. I never really stopped to notice how beautiful his hands are, how powerful the muscles that line his legs. His lean torso appears, followed by his chest. I watch as the light slowly creeps up his neck and then reveals his chin.

"Can you feel the warmth?" I ask, wiping tears from my swollen eyes. I use my sleeve to wipe at my nose, snuffing back so that I can breathe. My voice is hoarse, a croaking that sounds foreign in my ears.

I wipe my fallen tears away from his cheeks. "We never did watch a sunrise together. You always complained about me being too lazy and you were right. If only I had gone with you." I hang my head. "Just once."

Stretching my leg out, I take his weight on me, cradling him beneath my chin. "I should not have been so stubborn, admitted you were right about me all along. I should have let you hold my hand or kiss me whenever you wanted to. Held you through the night and never let you go. I should have let you in sooner, when we still had time."

I clench my eyes shut as a burning in my throat chokes off my words. I press my hand to my mouth as I sob, a deep gut wrenching cry of remorse. I taste the salt of my tears as they pool in the corner of my lip. Feel them trail down to my cheek and fall away.

My mother once told me that tears are the window to a soul. That they are only for the things you hold dearest. For once, I think she was right.

I bite back a sob and embrace the pain, for it is the pain that brings truth. No more barriers. No more lies or excuses.

Lowering my gaze, I look down into Cable's unblinking eyes. "I should have told you that I love you. With all my heart, I do, and I waited too long."

Careful not to drop his head, I inch out from beneath him and lay him down on the floor. I use the rock wall to crouch beside him, my shoulders curved to allow for the low ceiling. In the light of the new dawn, I realize that Cable has never looked more handsome, more at peace.

Though his eyes hold no emotion, nothing more than a blank glazed stare, the corners of his lips pinch just enough that his smile is frozen in place.

I kneel beside him and place a hand over his chest. His heart still beats, his lungs still move, but the man I once knew is gone, withered away into nothingness.

"You are a man I could have loved till the end of my days. I didn't deserve you, but you still wanted me." Leaning down, my hair brushes against his face as I press my lips to his, one last time.

My fingers curl around my pistol at his side. As I lean back, I draw the gun to my chest. I press it to his forehead, pausing just long enough to burn the memory of him into my memory and realize the truth that I've fought for so long. "One night with you will never be enough," I whisper and close my eyes.

Bang.

EPILOGUE

I stare at the sunrise with a longing gaze, with my shoulders slumped and my posture limp against the tree. I ignore the rain that falls from above, trailing down my collar and soaking through all three of my layers. The warmer day encouraged me to shed one layer. Soon, I will be able to remove more.

The landscape remains the same. Barren. Vast. Trees as far as I can see spread out before me. A road winds through those trees, like a snake slithering along the hilly earth. I have followed its path for many days. Embraced the loneliness of the nights.

I have not spoken in the nearly three weeks since emerging from the cave. My hair falls unkempt about my face. Dirt tracks wash clean from my cheek as I turn my face to the rain.

Depression, the darkest I have ever felt, took me those first few weeks. I ate only when my body refused to let me walk any farther. Slept when I was forced to. I gathered supplies when the skies withheld rain. Gathered ammunition and weapons for survival.

The trees were my friends, resolute and silent though it felt as if they still managed to accuse me. At times I feel as if Cable is still with me, keeping his promise to watch over me. I hear his voice on the wind. Feel his palm against my cheek in those few seconds just before I wake. I know it is not real, but even in those briefest of moments, I feel alive again.

The clouds before me are broken. Shafts of light penetrate the dark rain clouds. Wide swatches of land are illuminated, basking in the radiant light. The ache in my chest has not lessened, but as I stare at the light a soft smile tugs at my lips. Cable would not want me to linger. He would tell me to get up. To fight. To be the strong woman he always knew me to be.

I buried him in that cave, piled rocks high enough to seal him into a forever tomb. I couldn't bear the thought of animals getting to him. It was the best I could do.

I have watched the sunrise each morning for him. These moments I treasure. Never again will I oversleep, let creature comforts steal away the moments most precious to me. With each rise of the sun, I'm reminded of just how valuable life truly is.

Turning away from the sunrise, I stare at the land before me. From this vantage point, I see for miles. A veil of rain falls to the north in thick sheets. A rainbow blooms just to the south. Below me, the ground is a blur of movement. Countless Withered Ones shuffle along, each one rocking in step with those surrounding them.

For a while, I envied them, their lack of emotion, or ability to feel pain. Losing Cable nearly destroyed me...nearly.

I adjust the pack on my back and lean forward, pressing tightly against the tree limb as I lean over. Cable's knife presses against my thigh as I stare at the highway looming below. I keep parallel to it, watching the road signs to make sure I'm heading in the right direction. The Withered Ones move steadily south. There is no rhyme or reason to this destination that I can detect. Only single-minded determination.

I must adopt that same determination if I am to make it to my own destination.

During the final hours, while I held Cable that last night, he spoke of his family. Of his half-brother Lenny and his mother Teresa. Of how after Lenny's mother died, Teresa showed great compassion and took the boy into her care and raised her as her own. The sins of the father did not matter to her. A boy in need did. I wish I could have met Cable's mother, met the woman who raised such an amazing man.

The last time Cable spoke with his brother, he discovered that his mother had been lost, but Cable said Lenny was a smart one. He would survive.

I owe it to Cable to try to find him. A small suburb of Nashville, Tennessee was his last known location. By best guess it would be a three or four-hour drive if I managed to find a car and a passable road to use. It would take me a month or so by foot, depending on if I got into any trouble along the way.

Trouble is exactly what I'm afraid lies between me and Nashville.

Narrowing my gaze, I chamber a round and aim my gun into the air. It is time to see if my suspicions are correct. The sounds of raspy moans and shuffling feet fill my ears as the last droplets of rain patter down on my face. I close my eyes and listen. For as long as I live I will never get used to their sound, to the potent scent that clings to their bodies. They will haunt my dreams till my final breath.

I slowly open my eyes, staring one last time at the sun before I pull the trigger. The shot ricochets through the air, echoing off the concrete embankment that rises on either side of the highway, leading to the overpass less than a quarter of a mile ahead. Birds take flight, escaping the trees around me.

The tide of rotting and tattered Withered Ones come to a complete, unified halt. Their faces tilt upward toward the sky. Silence reigns as they pause to search for the source of the sound.

Numbness settles over me as I lower my shotgun and look to the road ahead. Thousands of Moaners stand motionless for the first time ever. I fight against the sense of hopelessness and despair, knowing the path before me will be dangerous. Gangs, desperate survivors, and the lack of food were bad enough. This will be far worse.

The Withered Ones are evolving.

RESURRECT

BOOK TWO

PROLOGUE

A torrent of rain falls from the low hanging black clouds above and forces me to crouch low. Mud and blood swell high over the soles of my shoes as water carves a narrow path between my feet. Briars tangle in my hair and scratch at my face when I attempt to push farther back into the bushes to minimize the risk of being spotted.

"She went this way." The man's voice sounds muffled against the downpour but I can tell that it is getting far too close for comfort.

I should have outmaneuvered the soldiers miles ago but they have a tracker with them and none of my attempts at evasion have worked. Now I am hemmed in both by the soldiers and the foul weather.

In an attempt to conceal myself further, I slip the black hiking pack off my shoulders. Though the pack holds only minimal weight, my left shoulder gives out when I try to hold the pack above my head and I am forced to resort to curling into a ball behind it. When I scavenged for the bag a few towns back, I was worried that it might be too big but now its bulk will come as an advantage.

In the fading light, I scoop handfuls of mud onto my exposed skin and try not to think about the creeping, slithering things that are sure to live in it. They are the least of my concern now.

"Do you see her yet, Gunner?"

The shout feels as if it comes from directly over my shoulder and I stop breathing for a few seconds, waiting for a hand to grab hold of me and yank me from my hiding place.

My leg muscles ache and my lips quiver from the cold as I force rising panic from my mind. The rain has a bit of ice in it as it slips into my collar and down my back but I do not risk moving. They are too close now. Any wrong move and I may betray my location.

"I think she has probably done a runner, Cap. We ain't gonna find her in this mess unless she comes waltzing out of the woods with her hands up and I don't see her being the type. She wouldn't have made it this long if she were that fool-headed."

"Agreed," a second voice responds. "Are you sure that you clipped her?"

I bite down on my lip and force myself to breathe through the steady throbbing in my left shoulder. That jackass named Gunner did more than clip me. He jammed that bullet straight through the muscle of my shoulder and now my entire left arm feels like it is on fire. My only saving grace is that I'm a righty and stubborn as a ticked off mule.

"Hell yes, I got her. I ain't never missed before. Saw me some blood a ways back but it's all washing away faster than I can find them new tracks. Hell, she coulda circled back and I'd never know it. We won't be finding her until this flood ends or we build a big ass boat to float our way out."

Less than fifteen feet away, I catch a hint of movement through the thick undergrowth and gently peel back a few branches to get a closer look at my enemy. Even through the heavy rain, I spy the long, scruffy beard of the man I assume to be Gunner as he kneels in the mud. I would bet my last can of peas that there was a time when that man wore only flannel shirts, trucker hats and drove a jacked-up four-wheel drive truck with a "proud to be a redneck" sticker on the back. Although he is wearing a proper soldier's uniform, it has been modified with torn sleeves, missing buttons and a jagged hem.

Despite his ragged appearance, Gunner has proven to be a good tracker and a decent shot. He has that look about him like he's been torturing innocent squirrels since he was old enough to carry a pellet gun and I want nothing more to do with him.

When I accidentally stumbled across their camp in the woods several miles back, I'd only seen four sleeping bag rolls, but they were paired with two covered trucks that were bound to house other soldiers. Any idea of hijacking a truck vanished when one of the soldiers returned from the woods and caught sight of me. The roar of their engines after the warning shout sent the soldiers into a flurry of panic and sent me fleeing straight into the thickest parts of the forest so the trucks couldn't follow, but it wasn't nearly far enough.

Their pursuit was methodical and well organized, while I relied solely on instinct and a desperation to survive.

"What do you think, Nox? Should we keep hunting or hole up for the night?" The man named Cap turns to speak with someone just out of my line of sight but I don't risk adjusting my position again just in case Gunner was to look my way.

"Gunner is the best tracker that we've got, sir. If he says we call it then we call it," the man standing just out of sight responds.

When he shifts closer, I can barely make out a portion of his profile along with the pistol that he taps impatiently against his thigh. "It's nearly nightfall, sir. Perhaps our best course of action is to circle up and protect the camp. She can't get too far at night and if she's smart she will find a tree and climb."

"Agreed." Cap looks to the sky. "Let's hope the rains hold out through the night."

I frown in confusion over the soldier's words as they turn their backs on me. Why would that Nox guy say that I should climb a tree when that would obviously put me at a great disadvantage? Why would the Captain want the rains to continue? His men must be as frozen as I am and sleeping on the ground is not an option with the rising mud. As I rub out the pins and needles in my calves, I decide that they were probably trying to trap me on the off chance that I was still within hearing distance.

With a loud whistle that could easily be misconstrued as a bird's final call before nightfall, Cap holds his hand high and swirls it in a large circle. A loud rustling in the woods off to my left comes less than a minute later and four more soldiers emerge. Despite the appearance of having just wallowed in a mud pit, each man holds firm to their weapons as they approach their commander.

"I want a perimeter marked out and every potential escape route noted before you bunk down. I don't want to lose this one." Cap turns slowly to look each man in the eye. "There will be no fire tonight so stay alert. I want two lookouts posted at four-hour intervals. Nox will see to the guests' safety. If there are any disturbances in the night, you are authorized to engage on a shoot to kill basis. Are we clear?"

I don't like the sound of that. For nearly fourteen hours, this group of military grunts has hunted me and I am exhausted. The opportunities for a slip up now are too great. I will have to remain in position until they are asleep and then make a run for it.

As I watch the soldiers fan out, I lower my head to my knees and try to focus on something other than the rain beating against my head. It is my fault that I had the misfortune of stumbling across this group in the first place. I was far too careless in the predawn hours as I searched for an overlook to watch the sunrise.

Even after all of this time I continue to keep my promise to never oversleep again and miss the day's dawning. Cable Blackwell, the soldier who proved to me that all life is precious and that hope can be found even in the darkest of times, tried to share this with me before he faded away. Now I will never miss the moment again.

Being alone on the road makes an early rising an easy thing to do since I sleep with one eye open at all times, but it is the memory of Cable's smile that truly keeps me devoted to my promise. It has been weeks since I walked away from the cave tomb where I sealed Cable inside. Far too long since I felt his touch or felt a hint of safety.

I have done things since then to survive that I am not proud of. Things that in another life would never have crossed my mind, but this new world and my life has transformed into something twisted and ugly. In order to survive in it, I have to become someone I wouldn't recognize in the mirror.

Cable believed that I am stronger than I ever gave myself credit for. Back then I had my doubts. Now...I know what I'm capable of and it scares me.

I should never have revealed myself so carelessly to the soldiers. That was poor judgment on my part and now I will pay the price for that slight.

No matter what happens, I refuse to be taken alive. I won't willingly walk back into the military's hands and be their lab rat. They have proven in the past to be corrupt and nothing could make me ever trust a soldier again.

"Don't take it personally," Cap says. I look up to see him grasp Gunner's hand as he rises up from the mud and steers him away. "She's a tricky one, I'll give her that, but I have yet to see anyone smart enough to hide from you. Just chalk it up to shitty luck."

Gunner turns his face up to the sky. "Ain't got anything to do with luck, sir. It's this piss poor weather that's doing it. It's almost like someone wants the girl to escape."

"You really believe that?"

"Nah." Gunner tips his head back down and rain ran off the bill of his cap. "I reckon karma is the same little bitch she was before all of this mess. I'll find her, Cap. No doubt about that."

Cap nods as Gunner moves on ahead then he pauses and turns back, sweeping his gaze over the woods.

"I know you're out there and I know that you're armed. You took down one of my best men. That takes guts and no small amount of skill," he calls in a loud voice and waits for a response that never comes. "I promise that we don't mean you any harm. Now, I know that my promises won't mean much to you, but I'm a man of my word. You come out now I can give you a dry place to sleep and take care of that bullet wound. Then we can talk like civilized people. That's all I want."

"No deal?" I watch as he swings around in a slow circle, peering into the rapidly darkening woods. "Then we can plan to have that chat tomorrow morning after we hunt you down."

I remain crouched long after he leaves watching the buzz of activity as a temporary camp is set up. As the hours pass slowly, the cramps in my legs go from annoying to severe. I fidget as minimally as I am able, softly beating on my calves to drive away the tingling. My shivering intensifies as the nighttime temperatures plummet and I'm forced to clamp my lips tightly together to keep my teeth from chattering. Never before have I spent such a miserable night on the road. As the rains continue, I know that hypothermia is quickly becoming a serious risk.

Soon I won't be able to run even if I need to.

My options are limited and Cap knows it. I won't make it through the night out here. Either I turn myself in or I make a run for it and meet whatever fate has in store for me.

Just as I'm about to give up and risk it all with a reckless dash through the woods, I hear something crashing through the forest. The hairs on the back of my neck prickle as I glimpse something pale and fast moving toward the soldier's camp through the underbrush. The first scream pierces the night before I have a chance to locate the animal again after it leaps and I realize that it has found its prey. The scream rises to a shriek before cutting off abruptly.

"We're under attack!" I recognize Cap's voice and see two men leaping down from the back of a truck as brilliant lights surge to life atop it.

Rising up from the bushes, I watch a man hurtle through the air and slam into a tree with a loud crack. He falls limply to the ground as a second scream is quickly followed by an animalistic howl that is so loud it reverberates in my chest.

"Jenkins is down!" Cap shouts. "There are two more on your ass, Nox. Take them out!"

I hear an immediate report of gunfire and another scream. In the light, I see only shadows of the pale animals and the flash of color, but they move too fast for me to truly make out what they are.

"Get back to the trucks!" Cap yells. "Form a perimeter and do not let them through!"

As the small campsite nearly fifty feet back explodes with a spray of bullets and guttural snarls, I dig myself out of the gully and run for my life.

ONE

Staring into the gaping black hole before me, I allow my imagination to run rampant. Countless horrors could lie within the tunnel that towers nearly twice my height and triple that in width. Train tracks, long since buried in packed dirt, run between my feet and race back the way I just came. The sound of dripping echoes from within the depths but nothing more.

There are no sounds of moaning or shuffling feet. There are no screams or a single hint of light.

What if something is in there? What if the path is blocked on the other end and I can't get through? What if it's a maze of tunnels and I can't feel my way to freedom?

Lost in the dark with monsters watching my every step was not on my agenda for tonight, or any night for that matter, but the soldiers I left behind took that option away. If any of them survived they will be coming for me once they care for their dead and wounded. I need a place to hide and this is the least likely place they will think that I would go.

Confined spaces are not ideal for fighting, and by entering the cave, I might be making a huge mistake, but I can't risk staying out in the open. When the soldiers do come, I imagine they will be out for revenge.

It isn't technically my fault that they were attacked. I didn't make those animals cross their path but they were out there because they were hunting for me and by proxy, I am the first thing those hot heads should want to blame. I'd rather not stick around to let that happen.

So into the creepy ass cave I go.

Holding my shoulder with my good hand, I turn and stare at the path behind me, searching for any signs of being followed. Slate walls rise high on either side, tangled with thick growth just waking from its winter slumber. A road lies nearly a quarter mile back and rises along the hilltop but it leads directly into the heart of a small town and that is an unpredictable risk.

As a child, I used to fear the dark, but now, as an adult, I know that nothing I imagined back then could compare to the real monsters that come out at night. The Withered are bad but humans have proven to be far worse.

The road behind me is a graveyard of abandoned cars and glass littering the ground. Charred teddy bears, composting food and flesh droppings from passing Withered create a morbid path. Most of the vehicles show signs of having been thoroughly ransacked. Others were set alight with bodies still inside after being drained of fuel. The scent of gasoline soaked into my clothes during my brief time passing through and I wonder if this was also a part of the military's handiwork.

I could go back and pick a car trunk to hole up in for the day but if the gasoline fumes don't get me, the scent of decay might. It would take the soldiers a while to locate me in that mess, but eventually they would find me. I have to keep moving forward, even if that means potentially doing something really stupid.

Small pebbles crunch beneath my worn boots as I take a deep breath and step into the tunnel. I inhale small breaths as I slide forward, checking for the scent of rotting flesh. The air tastes of well-established mold and I fight not to gag. There is no light ahead to guide my path, but I can't turn on my flashlight and risk being seen from a distance.

"This feels like the opening scene for just about every scary movie I've ever watched," I mutter as I step forward, hands raised out in front of me as a guide.

The cold swells to envelop me, seeping through the three layers of rain-drenched shirts that I wear: a faded gray thermal, a black turtleneck one size too big and a dingy orange and black high school hoodie that I found abandoned in a car two weeks back. It is spattered with flecks of blood and the scent of body odor remains locked in the fibers but after a while, I just stopped caring.

The cold attacks my fingers next with aching stiffness as I grip a small ax in one hand and a heavy metal flashlight in the other, the same the police used to carry before the world went to hell. With its heavy metal casing, it doubles as a bludgeoning weapon but its weight is nearly more than my wounded arm can manage as I fight to keep a firm grip on the flashlight.

A handgun is tucked into my back pocket for extreme emergencies, but I hate to think about it. I shot the same gun back in the cave after Cable became one of *them*. Even though I know he would want me to use it now to remain safe, I just can't bring myself to shoot it again. Along the way, I have collected an array of other weapons better suited to my fighting style.

A long-handled screwdriver, great for ramming through eyes or into a gut, is laced with a bit of rope tied to the side of my leg. A hammer taps against my hip as I walk, its claw head hooked through my hiking pack for easy access.

I don't like to kill, but I will if I'm left without any other options. The soldiers made the mistake of underestimating me the first time they tried to corner me and one of them died. Cap and Gunner will not make that same mistake twice.

Hugging close to the right side of the tunnel, I trail my elbow along the uneven wall for direction. When I turn back I realize that I have only traveled thirty feet but there is a new light starting to dawn at the cave entrance. The sun has begun to rise and the soldiers will be coming for me. I didn't exactly take the time to sweep away my tracks as I ran for my life. The Withered were out in force and traveling at night no longer feels safe.

"Please don't make me regret this," I whisper to the cave as I continue forward.

When the wall takes an unexpected turn a few minutes later, I stumble to the side in search of it again. My fingertips feel nothing and I realize that another cavernous room has opened up. My pulse thumps in my ears and my breathing sounds far too loud in the dark as fear begins to rush in, a familiar yet bitter taste in my mouth as I blindly search for the wall.

No matter how many times I stare fear down, I have yet to conquer it. I guess that's a good thing, though. Fear is the one thing that reminds me that I'm still alive. That and the damn bullet stuck in my arm!

A scuttling to my left makes me freeze. Every muscle locks down as I allow my other senses to kick in. The smell has not shifted and there is no hint of rot to imply a Withered might be nearby. I stretch the flashlight out before me and wave it around in the dark, gritting my teeth against the pain that shoots through my left shoulder but there is nothing there. I tighten my grip on the ax, spreading my legs in preparation and wait.

The scurrying sound comes a little closer this time. I breathe a sigh of relief when I hear the tiny scratching of nails on the ground. It is a rat.

My first thought is to scrunch up my nose in disgust like the girl I used to be. The second thought, this one far more prevalent than the first, is to smile.

Dinner.

A few months ago I was feasting on burgers and greasy fries. Now I get excited over vermin. Oh, how low the human race has sunk!

I track the rodent farther into the darkness, flicking on my light only when I fear that I've lost it completely to conserve the battery life. Hunting blind is not my forte but the thought of having food on my stomach fuels my determination. Fresh meat, no matter what sort, is better than the scraps that I've been living on the past couple of weeks. With only a single can of peas left, I am desperate for anything that I can get, and at this point, I hate peas more than I hate rats.

The sound of skittering comes from my right this time and I veer in that direction without thought. I step lightly, willing myself to be one with the rat, all the while wondering when the moment will arrive that I walk face first into a stone wall and knock myself unconscious.

Hoisting my ax, I thumb the light switch and the rat's beady eyes glint in the light. Its whiskers flutter as it raises its nose to sniff the air then squeaks and darts in a panic.

"Shit!"

The rat's eyes burst out from its sockets under the downward force of a combat boot. Its bones snap and its fur stains with blood. Its back legs twitch as the boot shifts from side to side, crushing the rodent into the floor.

The scent of rot might not be present now but something else is—blood.

My thumb flicks off the flashlight button a second before I dive, realizing too late why I was fooled. I couldn't smell him over my own bleeding shoulder and the scent of gasoline still stuck in my nose.

Tucking my chin, I roll back to my feet and turn straight into a blind punch that momentarily helps me to forget the stabbing in my left shoulder. The right side of my face explodes with pain, from cheekbone to jaw. Even as I fight to regain my footing I know that I'm fighting a man.

A very strong man.

A patient man.

A predator.

He waited for me in the dark and was still enough to fool the rat. That means I am at a grave disadvantage.

I feel air shift in front of me a split second before a new pain lances through my right arm and slices deep through my bicep. Gritting my teeth, I refuse to allow myself to make a sound and risk giving myself away as I step back, struggling to retain my hold on the ax, but the air moves again and another attack splits my right cheek open. Warm blood seeps down my jaw, rolling toward the hollow of my neck.

How can he see me in the pitch dark?

Even with my senses on high alert, I am completely blind. Then a wild thought strikes me as I remember seeing combat boots in the flashlight beam. I engage without considering the danger of my attack if I am wrong because I know the consequences if I am not.

Flicking my flashlight on, I aim it in the direction I think my attacker is located and drive my ax in a low, hard sweep. A throaty grunt is met with a solid vibration in my arm as my blade buries deep into flesh. Blood gushes over my hand and I fight against my body's need to panic.

Death, though necessary in the world I now live in, never gets easier. Whoever said that it does is a fucking liar.

A disconcerting gurgling erupts from the dark as I swing my flashlight to my right. I miscalculated the direction of my attacker by nearly half a foot but the length of my ax compensated for the difference, burying several inches into the man's torso.

The fact that he never cries out in pain sets me on high alert as I scan him for symptoms. In the light, I spy a camouflage shirt followed by a scruffy beard and instantly sober at the sight of crimson bubbles forming at the man's lips. His knees give way suddenly and the force tugs me off balance as I grip my ax, unwilling to lose my weapon. My flashlight crashes to the ground and rolls away.

In the angled light, I can see that the man's fatigues are caked with newly drying mud and leaves. His torn camouflage shirt is already torn and shows pit stains reaching nearly to his breastbone.

Seeing this soldier's Marine Corps symbol affiliation forces me to think about Cable at a moment when I desperately need to keep my wits about me. He shifted my entire world and taught me the true meaning of sacrificial love before I was sentenced to live alone in this hellish place. He made me keep going right until he faded in my arms.

Most days I don't want to get up, to scratch and peck for what little food there is to scavenge and convince myself that any of it matters. It doesn't. If it weren't for my promise to find his brother, I probably would have used Cable's gun on myself by now. It seems a kinder death than what this world has in store for me.

Cable Blackwell gave me a glimpse of happiness that helped me to forget all of the death and shit surrounding me. He was tireless in his patience and faith, both in me and in the world. He held onto hope when none existed, but I wasn't like that. I saw things for how they were. The way I see it, there isn't much good left now to fight for.

Gritting my teeth against the barrage of unwanted emotions, I force myself to push aside the thought of being in Cable's arms and a hundred other memories that have begun to fade with time. Instead, I watch the soldier shudder and twitch as his life drains freely through his open wound and realize that he looks familiar.

Yanking back the flap of his shirt, I see his name patch: Gunner.

"Holy shit!" I jerk back and fall to the ground, crab crawling away from him.

Bloodied and broken fingernails claw at his torn pant leg but he makes no move to staunch the flow of blood in his side. I search for his gun on the floor around him but see nothing beyond the knife that landed several feet away.

"What the hell happened to you?" I ask, hating the appearance of a quake in my voice. His presence here in the cave is startling enough but to see him in this condition...how did he begin to turn so quickly?

"Did that animal do this? Are they somehow infected now too?"

I watch as he scratches at his leg without blinking. His skin, though paler than what I saw the day before, still has a bit of a rosy hue to it. From where I sit, the wound on his upper thigh doesn't look deep enough to cause any lasting nerve damage.

"Hey, are you hearing me?" I wave my hand out in front of me but he doesn't seem to notice. I can tell by the glisten of sweat along his forehead and bloodshot eyes that he is infected. He will become one of *them* soon, maybe within the day if he had not stumbled across me in the dark, but how did it happen so fast?

There is no way that he could have digressed so fast. Usually, it takes days for the transformation to become complete and he proved to be more than capable of handling himself when he was tracking me through the forest mere hours ago.

"Gunner, do you know who I am?" I lean forward to search for a response. "I'm the girl you were tracking last night. I got away because you lost sight of me in the rain. Do you remember any of that?"

When he doesn't respond, I jerk on the handle of the ax. He should be screaming in agony but instead, he stares at me with an unusual calm. With the toe of my boot, I kick aside the blade that he used against me and it clatters as it strikes the wall.

Leaning forward to grab the flashlight, I shine the light high enough to see that a film has already begun to form in his right eye. The muscles in his neck spasm as he jerks away from the light and claws at the air. With each breath, I listen to the telltale rattle in his lungs and realize that the light is painful for him.

Lowering the beam just enough to shield his eyes but not the rest of his body I survey him with a mixture of pity and resentment. I have seen what the transformation can be like, how the change can turn a peaceful man into a creature filled with rage and how sensitivity to light can drive a sane man into the depths of this colorless hell, but this soldier has gone through days' worth of transitions in less than half a night.

That's when his agitation draws my attention back to his leg. Crouching low, I watch him carefully as I tear apart the fabric of his pants to look at the wound he continues to fuss with.

"Teeth marks?" I whisper and look up at him. The markings are distinct enough for me to see that it was not an animal that did this. It was a person. "Gunner, was it a person who attacked you back in camp? Did someone in your group go crazy and start biting people like a cannibal?"

It was terrible to think of someone actually doing such a thing but the realistic side of me knew that hunger was hunger and desperation could drive people mad. I knew it had been done before. I'd seen evidence of it along the road not long after I crossed state lines but to see it up close was terrifying.

"Oh man," I blow out a breath and shove my hair back. Pain flares in my left arm and I'm instantly reminded that he is the one who shot me and tried to filet me only moments ago. How could he go from being so aggressive to passive? It was almost as if a switch had been turned in his mind.

"Where are the others?" I call out loud enough to hopefully get a rise from him but he stares over my shoulder, unblinking. The only movement is the twitching of his fingers at the edge of the raw wound and the raspy breath of his lungs filling. "What happened to your commander and the others? Did they survive the attack?"

I didn't want to care about what happened to them, especially considering the horrible things they probably intend to do to me when they catch me, but the moment I stop being a human is the moment there is no point in living. Feeling, fearing, caring...those are all of the things that tell me that I am not like *them*.

Gunner shifts to stare up at me with unblinking eyes when I shift the light closer to his face. I doubt that he even recognizes anything beyond the brightness of my light and perhaps my scent now. That's when a new thought strikes me. Maybe he wasn't trying to hurt me after all. Maybe he was just trying to get me to turn off the light.

Lifting the flashlight to point directly at his nose, Gunner comes alive and suddenly swipes at me with fingers curled into claws. I rear back but not before seeing sheer rage light in his eyes. His lips curl into a snarl as he growls and rocks in place, his hands raised toward me as he fights to overcome the ax buried in his side to get to me.

A sinking realization falls over me as I stagger to my feet and I acknowledge that he would have killed me if given the chance. The light may have drawn him to me, but in the end, directing the beam straight into his eyes is the only thing that truly saved me. It was only after he returned to the darkness that he settled down once more.

Pressing my boot to his chest, I shove hard and dislodge my ax from his side as he collapses to the ground. Fresh blood pours from the gaping wound and his legs twitch as his inches toward me, half dragging himself across the floor. I grimace at the sound of squelching as blood is forced out of his wound, soaking through both layers of his shirt.

"You would have caught me in the end," I whisper. I know that he won't hear me but I feel like I should say something nice at the end. "You fought a good fight and I'm sorry, but it's better this way."

I pause a second to feel a flood of remorse before I bring my ax down over my head and bury it in his skull.

TWO

One week later...

Dusk sits heavily in the western sky as I pause to look back over my shoulder, searching the ground for clues that I might have missed when I spot something off to my right. Clutching my left shoulder as I bend, I touch my fingertips to a low hanging bush and come away with blood.

"I thought I'd lost you." I stare at the steep decline ahead of me. The brush is thick and the night approaches far too quickly for me to be able to see if the wounded deer is nearby. Wiping the sweat from my forehead, I bite down on my lip just hard enough to allow this new pain to help me to focus while I debate my options.

It isn't safe to be out this close to dark, especially not in my condition. With my clothes drenched from a detour through a nearby creek bed that had breached its banks from recent rains, breath puffs visibly through my trembling lips. The chill in the air bites my exposed flesh as I wring water from my pants and rub feeling back into my thighs.

Hunger drives me forward as I peer down the steep slope into a landscape too thick to see much of anything. My last can of peas went down like a disgusting, squishy rock nearly four days ago and I'm desperate for something in my stomach. The deer I clipped a few hours ago has proven to be elusive but the steady growling in my stomach can't be ignored any longer. My hunger's presence and the thought of tearing into a side of deer jerky makes me ignore the setting sun and risk exposure for the sake of a meal. With my fever on the rise, I stand too high of a chance of keeling right over if I don't get some protein in me.

The infection in my left arm began not long after I stumbled my way out of the other end of the train tunnel the morning I killed Gunner. I'd located a small puddle of rainwater and tried to clean my wounds but a leaf wrapped with a partially clean strip of torn cloth wasn't the most sanitary tourniquet but it was the best I could do while on the run.

I heard the roar of the military trucks behind me, echoing through the tunnel not long after I emerged from the dark and knew the soldiers wouldn't be far behind. Their pursuit pushed me to my limits and I struggled to remain ahead of them, terrified by their relentless pursuit. My hope that they would give up after they found Gunner's body and return to their base died when they caught my trail the following day.

While the wound on my cheek and deeper laceration in my right arm have begun to heal, the bullet wound in my shoulder has grown red and inflamed, festering after only a few days. That's when the fever and chills set in. The vomiting and nausea came not long after that. I attempted to burn out the infection, heating my blade in a small fire that I dared to build in the light of the day with the hopes that it wouldn't be seen as clearly as it would at night but I passed out long before the job was finished. I knew I wouldn't make it through a second attempt and there was no way I could cauterize the exit wound on the backside of my arm by myself.

As my rising fever led to whacked out hallucinations, desperation forced me to search a town not far from the Kentucky and Tennessee border, but it had been picked clean. There wasn't so much as a single tablet of pain medicine to be found. Though I'd stumbled from house to house, digging through medicine cabinets, bedside tables and dead ladies purses, I came up completely empty handed. Whoever cleared that town had been very thorough in their sweep.

Many of the houses had been torched and razed to the ground and the bodies stacked in plastic wrapped piles. The small town looked sanitized and I knew the only people likely to do something like that were the military but I suspected that this town had been cleansed a while back. The soldiers tracking me seemed less inclined to do cleanup work.

As I push forward through the brush, I consider for the thousandth time if the soldiers know who I am and that I played a part in the destruction of the base outside of St. Louis. Technically, it wasn't my fault that the base was blown to hell. I wasn't the one who set the bombs or fired the tank at the walls, but I highly doubt that the military will let those crimes slide on my good word alone.

They want my blood, end of story, but there is no way that I am going back to another lab to be poked and prodded like an animal in a cage. I will go down fighting before that happens.

Despite my ailing health, I have managed to stay one step ahead of the soldiers. Apparently, Cap was right about Gunner being their go-to man for tracking, but over the past two days, I have noticed headlights in the distance and know that they are still gaining. When they hunt me down this time I won't be able to outrun them.

My only option is to hide after I bag the deer.

Just this morning, I returned to the woods, skirting along a deserted road until I came to an overpass that led directly to Interstate 24 and split off toward Clarksville, Tennessee. The southern road is the one that I will need to reach Nashville, but I have a long way to go and far too little supplies to keep me on my feet.

Cinching the support straps for my pack across my chest, I ignore the incessant throbbing in my shoulder and take the hill at a staggering sideways shuffle. Tree limbs snag at my hair and tear at my neck as I close my eyes and leap the final five feet, landing awkwardly, but I pinwheel my good arm to steady myself.

"Well, if that didn't scare away the deer, I don't know what will." I thread my fingers through my hair and tug twigs from my thick, frizzy curls. My hair is far longer than it has ever been and I swear all of the time that I will cut it, but I never do. Perhaps that is a sign of insanity or maybe if I actually follow through I'll had less to talk about with myself.

When I catch the sound of running water, I perk up and am just about to turn to follow when I hear the snap of a branch. I drop hard to the ground, jarring my teeth as I search the brush in the dying light. There is no way that is the deer heading my way with the wind going against me.

It is nearly impossible to see without my flashlight, but I drained too much of the battery while escaping from the train tunnel, and now I'm not sure that I can bank on it switching on. Slightly off to my left I hear a grunt followed by minimal rustling. Lifting up just high enough to see over the bushes that I'm hiding in, I strain to hear. Goosebumps rise along my arms at the sound of a guttural cry of pain followed by a loud thud.

There is something out here with me.

Moving in the direction of the sound, I step lightly back onto the narrow dirt path that animals have packed down over time on their trips to the water. The last thing I want to do is come across a coyote or wild cat feasting on my deer and have it turn on me. The sounds of heavy breathing grow more distinct as I draw nearer, along with a low, painful cry. I vow that if I can get a clean shot I will put the poor animal out of its misery.

When the deer finally comes into view, I discover a man crouching beside it less than ten paces in front of me. His heavy jowls quiver as he chews a mouthful of raw flesh and then leans over to sink his teeth back into the hind leg of the deer. The animal screams as its hide and muscle tear away.

The man rises up to stare blankly at the darkening forest, unconcerned with the bit of ligament slapping against his chin as he chews. My grip tightens around my ax. Whoever this guy is, he must be stark raving mad to dig into a live deer like that.

Watching as the man slowly works his way through the bloody string of meat, I search for an exit strategy, but a loud crashing off to my left interrupts my thoughts. The loud wheeze that follows is all too familiar by now and I know that a Withered is approaching.

Peering around the tree that I have concealed myself behind, a cold, sickening feeling sinks into my core when a woman emerges and launches herself at the deer. The animal squeals and writhes when the woman bites off half of its ear.

Her eyes are milky white and her skin appears nearly translucent in the final drops of light. Her hair is unwashed and stringy with several large chunks missing. Her clothes are torn and soiled. When she leans forward to take another bite, I see that her feet are bare and she is missing three toes on her right foot. On her upper arm, I see a large festering wound that she scratches at intermittently between bites.

Two more people appear from across the small clearing. One is a school-age boy with short cropped, white-blond hair that fails to conceal the large gash across his forehead or the nose that has been chewed off. The other is an elderly man with his throat nearly torn completely away and a twisted right foot that forces him to walk on his ankle.

My hands feel clammy as I try to process the scene as the elderly man drops to the ground and rips through the deer's neck, silencing its cries for help. Bile rises in my throat as the sound of ripping and tearing makes my stomach roll.

I try to tell myself that this isn't real. That it's just another vivid hallucination, but the sounds...those can't be fake.

Snagging my heel on a tree root, I slam ungracefully to the ground and look up to see the Withered staring at me with garish, bloody faces. Though my mind screams to run, my body refuses to respond and the boy pushes up to his knees and starts toward me. The others rise to follow.

"Shit! That's not supposed to happen!"

Digging deep into the dirt with my heels, I crawl backward as they step over the forgotten deer. Finally regaining my footing, I turn and sprint through the trees with my hands held up as a shield to fight off the branches that slash against my palms.

Sounds of their pursuit tell me that they are moving much faster than any Withered that I have encountered before. Their wheezing breaths sound as if they are directly behind me as I look to the trees, searching for something that I can climb, but the lowest branches are still just out of reach. Even if I could jump to touch them, my shoulder would never have the strength to support my weight.

I run as fast and as hard as I can, scrambling up hills and ricocheting off trees that rise up in front of me in the dark. Still, I keep going because the Withered never slow and they never tire.

By the time I emerge from the woods and stumble across a dirt road, lined with a wooden post fence wrapped in chicken wire, I am nearly spent of energy. Cupping a hand over my mouth to muffle my panting, I listen to the growls in the forest as the group closes in on me far faster than should be possible.

Something is very wrong with those Withered.

I should have easily lost them by now. It's not that I'm exactly sprinting at the moment, but a gentle jog should have put them well behind. Instead, they have kept pace, slowing only for a few moments when I run into a low lying mud pit half a mile back to sniff out my scent.

They shouldn't be able to sniff out anything. Hell, they shouldn't be running either!

"Just keep calm, Avery," I whisper to myself as I lean against a fence post to slow my breathing. "This is all in your head. Withered don't eat deer and they sure as hell can't track you. It's just a really, really bad dream."

But the growing stitch in my side tells me that it is far from a dream.

My pants are caked with mud and soaked completely through. The three layers of shirts that I wear aren't much better. I know that I'm in no condition to outrun them so I'm going to have to outsmart them.

Using the fencerow to guide me, I try not to think about how the Withered that are tracking me look at me no differently than that poor deer they made a meal of. Never before have I seen one of them show any signs of hunger. The Withered have always been docile and slow. Yes, they have grown in awareness of sounds and lights but this...this is different.

A coughing fit doubles me over as I cling to a post and fight to stay upright. It is getting harder to catch my breath with each moment that passes and I worry that after being cold and wet for so many days that I might be developing pneumonia on top of the infection.

On the distant horizon, I see the flickering of fire in the direction of Clarksdale. They are too numerous to be funeral pyres. From this distance, it appears that the whole city is burning. From time to time, I think that I hear gunfire carrying on the wind but the distance is too great and I want to keep it that way.

My mouth feels dry as I shuffle forward, searching for a break in the fence where I can slip through. In my condition, if I try to crawl over the fence and fail, I will probably not get back up again. Normally I would never get so close to a farm that I have not previously scouted but I'm out of options.

The rusty metal of the chicken wire snags my hand as I stagger and nearly go down.

"Don't be such a pansy." I cling to the fence rail with one arm slung over the top. The wooden post feels blissfully warm against my cheek, still heated from the day's sun and I know my fever is on the rise again. Pushing to my feet, I try to focus on the ground in front of me but it swells and recedes like the tides. Closing my eyes when I feel my stomach lurch, I will myself not to be sick but lose the battle.

The Withereds' growls and grunts grow closer as I spit the foul acid from my mouth and wipe my lips clean. Their staggering run has resumed and I am running out of time. On a good day, I would be able to outmaneuver them, but I haven't had many good days recently.

When I reach the end of the fencerow, it makes a sharp ninety-degree angle away from me and straight toward the looming shape of a darkened house. I absently rub the side of my pants as I stare at the curtain less windows with growing anxiety.

So many places have been abandoned since the outbreak, but many have also become refugees for desperate people. Having a girl show up on a stranger's doorstep unannounced while sporting a raging fever isn't exactly a good thing these days. I will most likely be shot on sight, presumed to be among the Withered, well on my way to completing the transformation, and I wouldn't blame them for thinking it.

Deciding that I have no alternative but to risk it, I pull myself around the corner and struggle on. My legs feel too heavy and my left arm throbs to the point of distraction as I find myself mulling over the same question that has plagued me for several days: why do I keep fighting? Wouldn't it be easier to just let the illness ravage my body and be done with it? To let the soldiers come across my body with a message stating that I went out on my own terms?

I have done things that I am ashamed of. I've stolen things, maimed people, who may or may not have been innocent, for the sake of taking their food to survive, and I've killed. Some might call me a murderer. I might even agree with them...if there were anyone left for me to speak to.

Craning my neck to search the wrap around porch on the front of the old weathered farmhouse, I search for footprints in the mud or any signs of human life but see none. The windows are all dark and there is only silence within.

The house looks a bit worse for wear as I pull myself up the steps. Two of the first-floor shutters have busted slats and bang against the siding in the wind. The clapboard siding is faded and peeling in so many places that I'm not sure it will last the summer. One window near the far corner is shattered and glass shards stick up from the warped decking of the porch. The wooden slats creak underfoot as I peer in through the window beside the door, but see nothing inside apart from darkness.

When I place my hand on the doorknob, I feel something slick. Raising my palm, I realize it is coated with fresh blood. Instantly on alert, I grab my hammer in one hand and my ax in the other.

One way or another I will hole up in the house for the night.

My stomach clenches at the thought of having to kill again. I waiver in place, blinking rapidly to focus as I turn the knob and push the door inward. A stale scent meets my nose, but nothing more. I peer through the darkness, listening closely for the sound of a footstep or breathing, but hear nothing.

Closing the door behind me and locking it for good measure, I begin a thorough sweep of the main floor. The kitchen is in complete disarray, with broken porcelain plates smashed on the floor and overturned soda bottles on the sink. A long line of ants files in and out of the sink on its way to the bottles. Several empty cans of food are strewn about. I kick at them with the toe of my boot and then move beyond to the dining room.

Several chairs are overturned with their legs and spines broken. In the center of what was once a dining room table is a pile of charred ash. Someone lit a fire here to keep warm, most likely during the hard winter months.

As I search the remaining rooms, pausing to check the recesses of the coat closets and an empty pantry, I determine that whoever was here has likely moved on. However, as I take the stairs to begin my search again, I am cautious. Someone left the blood on the door handle after all.

The farmhouse has three bathrooms in total, each one ransacked and empty. Even the shower curtains have been removed. As I finish digging through the final bedroom, gathering blankets and pillows as I go, I stand in the empty hall and listen. Though the walls and windows dull the sound, the approach of the Withered can still be heard. They have my scent and it will lead them directly to this house.

I could sleep in the hall beside the stairs, picking them off one at a time as they come up, but that probably isn't the smartest idea. Walking the length of the house with my eyes trained on the ceiling, I hunt for an attic hatch and find one near the upper landing by the stairs. A shower of dust falls over my face when I pull the cord and a pair of rickety wooden steps unfolds in front of me.

Grasping the stairs with one hand and the blankets in the other, I mount the steps slowly, grimacing with each creak and give of the wood. Anyone weighing more than me would surely snap the thin legs in half.

I am nearly halfway up the steps when the first Withered beats against the front door. Its growls and snarls rise up the stairwell and bring shivers of fear with it. I pause to listen as others slam into the wall beside it. Their nails scratch at the glass.

Hurrying up the final steps as quickly as I can, I toss the bedding aside and pull the ladder up, making sure to pull the cord in with me. I have no way of knowing if these new Withered are intelligent enough to know how to climb through the busted window but at least they will have no way of reaching me if they do.

Once I am sure that the hatch is secure, I glance around for something heavy enough to cover the opening and stumble into a stack of old boxes that sends dust billowing into the air. The crashing sound of glass from below makes me freeze in place. I focus on silencing my breathing to listen to the frenzy building below and wonder if more Withered will follow the sounds.

Using my feet to feel my way across the decking boards, I begin to get the lay of the land and plan an escape route. Over the past couple of months, I have spent my fair share of time in attics. It seems like the most logical place to go, considering I have yet to see a monster that can climb a ladder. Humans, on the other hand, are another story, and they are the reason I usually sleep with one eye open and one hand on my hammer.

After a few minutes of feeling around in the dark, I come across a large wooden frame and smooth surface that I assume to be a mirror. Rocking it from side to side, I walk it over to the hatch and gently lay it across the opening, mirror side down. If anyone does come barreling up the stairs they will get a face full of broken glass in the process.

With my exit into the house secured, I make a small nest of bedding to curl up into near the farthest wall, just below a small round window that looks out over the farm. Wrapping a spare blanket around my elbow, I smash the glass to allow a bit of fresh air into the dank attic. In a worst case scenario, I know that I can at least climb out onto the roof and find a storm drain to scale down.

Snuggled down into my bedding, I allow myself to take an inventory of my wellbeing. My skin is clammy, my cheeks feel flushed, and my heart thunders in my chest, but for now I am safe.

Tomorrow, I will tear this place apart in search of medicine after the Withered find a new toy to chew on.

THREE

Through the long night, I manage to sleep despite the growling and the glass shattering, but just after dawn, a sudden burst of gunfire sends me scrambling to my knees. Peering out of the small window, I see the two military vehicles idling in the yard and soldiers kneeling in the dirt with their weapons trained on the porch. I count at least eight men and a single girl, but assume there may be more concealed inside the flapping canvas-covered trucks.

After a second round sprays bullets into the wood siding, one man steps forward and raises his hand. The shooting stops and silence echoes all around. When he removes his hat to wipe at his face, I recognize Cap and press against the window frame to try to see as he approaches the steps and then disappears directly beneath me.

All sounds of growling have been silenced.

Cap's boots stomp loudly on the deck boards and I hold my breath when I hear him jiggling the door handle. How that door remained standing, I will never know. I guess old places like this really are built better.

"The Flesh Bags had to be tracking something," a soldier calls out as he holsters his gun. He has a second weapon slung over his back and a swagger that makes me instantly think that this guy is probably a dick. I know his type all too well from living on the streets: all muscle and just enough brains to be dangerous. They are the ones you have to watch out for. "They wouldn't hang around here if there wasn't something worth eating."

"Jax is right, Cap." A soldier calls out from beside the dick, who I now associate with being called Jax. This man stands several inches taller and is built like an ox shooting up on heavy doses of steroids. A reddish-toned beard conceals a muscular jaw, which tapers down into a thick neck, broad shoulders, and bulging biceps. I bet it was a struggle to fit into his tight little shirt this morning.

Staring hard at his breast pocket, I try to read his name but it is illegible from this distance.

"Whoa," Jax says with a cocky smirk. "Big man Fletcher actually agrees with me. Call the press, folks. We have breaking news—"

"Pipe down," Cap commands, and I can just see the top of his hat when he moves to stand on the edge of the porch steps. "What do you think, Nox? Think they were trailing her or someone else?"

"We followed her tracks into the woods. Makes sense that if she stumbled across the Flesh Bags that she would head this way. I'd say she was probably here."

I peer down at this new soldier with curiosity when he climbs down from the driver's seat of one of the trucks, having been unable to see him clearly during the rainstorm before. He is tall and lean with dark hair tucked beneath a camouflage cap that is pulled low over his eyes. He has a strong jaw and an air of confidence about him, but it is unlike the one that Jax possess. He doesn't seem cocky but rather merely sure of himself. "Is that blood on the door handle, sir?"

"Probably from the Flesh Bags, sir," Fletcher calls out while holstering his weapon.

"Negative to that," Cap replies. "This blood is dry and definitely human. Fletcher, why don't you take Jax and Nash with you and check around the perimeter to see if you find anything. If she did come through here we need to find her before more Flesh Bags catch her scent."

Cap reappears when he descends from the porch. I watch as he wipes a bloodied dagger against his camouflage pants before placing it into a small sheath on his hip. He looks like the kind of guy who is completely at home in his military garb and was most likely a soldier long before the world went to shit.

"Ryker, Warren, and Nox will take the house. Monroe and I will check the outbuildings and clear them. Gather all supplies that you find and report in fourteen minutes. We head out in fifteen, so move your asses!"

"What about me, sir?" The grim-faced girl that up to this point has been dwarfed behind Jax steps forward as each of the men move to follow Cap's command. She looks young, probably no older than sixteen or seventeen.

Cap motions for a bald soldier to go on without him and I assume that he must be the Monroe that Cap spoke of.

"I know you want to see some action today, Kenzie, but we need you on navigation." Cap steps down into the muddy yard and moves toward her. "You know the route as well as anyone and getting back to home base with these supplies is vital to our mission, so I need you to stay with the trucks and keep an eye out. If you see a Flesh Bag heading our way, I want you to send two shots into the air and we will come running."

"What about a Flesh Bag?" She asks when he turns to follow Monroe and I realize this must be their name for the Withered that I am familiar with. They must call the new ones Flesh Bags. I guess that's as good a name as any.

"Leave them be. They aren't hurting anyone yet."

It is easy to see that Kenzie isn't happy with her orders but she instantly stands down as Cap turns and jogs around the side of the building while I struggle to understand what I've just witnessed.

None of the soldiers seems surprised by the monsters that were banging down my front door. Instead, they are cool, calm, and annoyingly collected while I, on the other hand, am still pretending not to be freaked out.

These Flesh Bags are a bit too similar to the zombies that I've grown up watching on TV, apart from the running and tracking bit. I don't remember them having a conscious thought beyond "brains."

"Don't sweat it, Doll," a dark-haired soldier calls as he saunters past Kenzie, drawing my attention back. He reaches out and touches the end of the ponytail that falls over her right shoulder and she instantly bats his hand away. "Best to let the big boys do the hard work so you don't break a nail."

"Stow it, Ryker." Nox grabs the soldier by the arm and hauls him away. "You've got a job to do so I suggest you do it and let Kenzie follow her own orders. Besides, if Fletcher sees you touching his girl I'm sure he'll have something to say about it."

"Shove off," Ryker growls and tries to shake Nox off but he holds on tight. "I ain't under your command."

"No, but Kenzie is. You've already got two strikes against you. Care to make it a third and end up in the brig for a week?"

Ryker turns his head to the side and spits. When he glances back, he looks as if he would like nothing more than to rearrange Nox's nose. Nox lowers his hand to the gun at his hip and Ryker snorts, then heads for the stairs and slams the door shut behind him with enough force to send the remaining glass shards raining down on the porch.

"You okay?" Nox asks as he comes to lean against the front of the truck beside her.

"I get that you're trying to protect me, but don't. I can handle myself, sir. I've been dealing with pricks like that my entire life."

Nox laughs. "I wasn't doing it for your sake. I've seen Fletcher angry."

A small smile disrupts the disgruntled look on her face as Kenzie chuckles. "Yeah, he does tend to get carried away."

"I'd imagine love can do that and far more to a guy when given the right motivation."

"But that would never happen to you, right?" Kenzie bumps her shoulder against him. "Mr. One Night Stand."

"Oh, that's cold!" Nox grins wide, pushes off the truck, and moves toward the house. "I'm just waiting for the right girl to walk through my door."

"Sure you'd even know which one to keep around?"

When he turns his back toward the house and flips her the bird, Kenzie laughs and then hauls herself up into the driver's seat, slamming the truck door behind.

"You just going to stand there, Warren?"

I look straight down and see a younger guy standing off to the side watching the interaction, shifting his weight from foot to foot. He seems a bit on the scrawny side compared to the other men, possessing lean muscle instead of the excessive bulges of his brutish companions. Leaning closer to the window, I can't shake the feeling that I've seen him somewhere before.

"No, sir!" Warren salutes and then grips his gun tight as he hurries past Nox and up into the house. From below, I can hear Ryker already ransacking the first floor.

Nox shakes his head and follows behind, but not before pausing to look back over his shoulder at the fields all around. They are vast and sprawling, fenced in with wooden railings that line the little dirt road that I stumbled down the night before. Many of the corn stalks left behind from the forgotten fall harvest stand rotting in the muddy ground, blocking a clean line of sight. Even from my height it would be difficult to see approaching Withered.

Unease settles over me at the thought as I consider just how dangerous my escape will be through those very fields. Growing up watching horror movies has taught me to have a healthy dose of fear for fields like this, for now the monsters are very real.

When Nox turns toward the house again, he pauses and kneels several steps back from the porch to brush his fingers over the ground. My heart thumps in my chest as I realize that he has discovered one of my footprints in the drying mud. The other soldiers are bound to find more if they look anywhere near the fence line.

I step back from the window as Nox rises and return to the shadows just before his gaze falls on my window. Although there is no way that he can see me, I get a distinct feeling that he knows exactly where I am. He is a cautious one and reminds me far too much of myself. That means I need to prepare for the worst.

Scrambling across my bedding toward my pack, I grab my ax in my right hand and the slightly less weighty hammer in the other as I listen to the commotion below me. It sounds as if a stampede of elephants is crashing through walls and overturning chairs, tables and anything else that gets in their way. The soldiers move quickly through the rooms, no doubt coming to the same conclusion that I did: this place has already been cleaned out.

Wiping the sweat from my forehead, I close my eyes and take several steadying breaths as the floor begins to feel as if it is moving beneath me. It is much too warm in the attic with the sun streaming in and I suspect my fever is on the rise again. Soon enough, the others will receive word that I'm here and they will tear this place apart to find me. There is nowhere for me to hide and I am far too unsteady on my feet to make a getaway on the roof.

So, I must wait.

Several moments later, I hear the first pair of boots take to the stairs. Tension courses through my body as I think about the three bedrooms and single bathroom on the second floor. None of them will take long to search.

"Find anything?" A voice calls out.

"Nothing but your mama's panties and I'm keeping them all for myself, Warren."

"That never gets old to you, does it, Ryker?"

"Hell no. If you could see the look on your face you'd keep at it too."

"Bastard," Warren mutters from directly beneath me, but I can't make out the rest of his mumblings as the wooden floor creaks when he moves.

Footsteps move farther away and it's only when I release a small sigh of relief that I realize I was holding my breath.

"Look at this shit," a disgruntled voice that I am starting to recognize as Ryker yells. "There is floral wallpaper, drapes, bedding, and even some lame ass matching towels in here. Tell me you think some hot chick in her twenties lived here before this place went to hell."

"It was probably just some old nice couple."

When a loud crash from the room at the other end of the house makes me flinch, I am stabbed with fever aches all along my body. Sweat drips from my brow but I remain standing at the ready. I may not be 100%, but I won't go down without a fight.

"What'd you do before all of this, anyway? You always walk around like you own the place or that you think you are better than me."

"That's because I am. The truth hurts but that doesn't make it any less true. I wasn't recruited like some of you sorry asses," Ryker says and I hear the telltale groan of bedsprings. "I enlisted a few months before all of this shit went down. I was just out of boot camp and ready to save the world, one sexy lady at a time. Too bad that plan went straight down the crapper."

"So you've never seen any real action either, have you?"

"I've seen more than you can imagine, asshat!" Ryker shoves the bed against a wall with a resounding thud. "You know what your problem is, Warren? You're nothing more than a soft-spoken, big-hearted pansy trying to play with the big boys. One of these days you're going to get into a real fight and then we'll see just how well you handle yourself."

"I reckon I'll do just fine."

Ryker snorts and I move closer to the attic hatch to press my ear against it.

"What were you before the shit hit the fan? Some ivy league big shot living off of daddy's hedge fund?"

"You would think that wouldn't you?" There is a pause of silence and I wonder what they are doing. On the first floor, I can hear boots walking about and know that Nox has yet to join the second-floor hunt. "I was a singer and I was going places. I'm surprised you've never heard of me. Must be because you're from some backwoods hole in the ground and too stupid to open a magazine."

Even I know to expect the resulting punch but apparently Warren didn't. Loud crashes and grunting echoes up to where I kneel as the two brawl. From what I saw of the two of them from my window, Warren doesn't stand a chance in hell now that he's poked the wrong bear.

Boots thunder up the steps as Ryker's cursing drowns out Warren's cries of pain.

"Enough." Another loud crash comes from directly below me and I suspect the two brawlers just spilled out into the hallway. I cup my hand over my face to keep my cry of alarm muffled. "Let him go, Ryker."

"And what are you going to do about it if I don't?"

My eyes lock onto the mirror that covers the attic hatch when I hear the click of a gun. "I've got no qualms with putting you down right here and now like the dog that you are, Ryker. It's your choice."

"You sure talk tough shit now that you're Cap's favorite. Wasn't always like that, though. You think Cap will take kindly to you putting a bullet in his best soldier?"

"Second best, and even that is debatable."

I can't help but smile at that one. Nox has balls. I like that.

The silence that follows stretches out too long and I realize that the two men are staring each other down, weighing out whether or not Nox would actually pull the trigger. If he really is anything like me, he would shoot without blinking an eye.

Not being able to see what is happening is infuriating, especially when I hear someone slam into a wall. Warren cries out and stumbles backward as the two men start beating on each other. I can hear their curses and grunts easily through the hatch. Then a single gunshot sends someone falling hard to the floor.

"You bastard! You shot me in the fucking arm!"

"Stay down, Ryker or I swear I will take out your kneecap next." Nox's voice is clipped and held in check, but I can imagine the anger surging through him. "Warren, go grab Cap so he can deal with this piece of shit."

"You going to shoot me in the back, Nox?" I hear scuffling and picture Ryker trying to get to his feet. "Are you capable of being a stone cold killer?"

"If I need to be."

"Ha," Ryker laughs through the pain. "You always are a cocky little shit. I don't see why Cap likes you so much."

"Maybe he's attracted to my winning personality."

Ryker spits. "You may have him fooled, but I've been around a lot longer than you. There are rules in these parts and you're toeing a dangerous line."

"I'm following orders. That's a thing you seem to have forgotten."

A loud bellow from below sounds a second before a thud vibrates through the rafters as the two crash into the wall again. Dropping to my knees, I grip my hammer tightly as the floor begins to grow blurry. The heat in the attic has become too stifling and the energy I've expended waiting to defend myself has left me weak.

Why can't these two take their quarrel outside and leave me in peace? I use my shoulder to wipe a bead of sweat off my cheek.

"You are nothing," Ryker grunts but this time, his voice sounds strange, almost as if he has been placed in some sort of choke hold. From what I saw of Ryker from the window, he looked to be fairly stocky and more than capable of taking care of himself, but Nox has somehow taken the upper hand. I would wager that he has done his fair share of street brawling and learned a few tricks on how to play dirty when necessary.

"Goddammit, Nox. Get off of me."

"Do you yield?"

"Yield? Are you off your goddam rocker? This ain't no wrestling match!"

"Then why are you the one pinned to the floor?"

I can't help but smile again at the loud cursing that comes from Ryker. He would have been better suited as a sailor than a Marine with that foul mouth.

"You want to explain to me what all of this is about?" I'd been so focused on imagining the scene below to notice Cap's return. Apparently I wasn't the only one.

"Ain't nothing but a misunderstanding," Ryker says. I hear a grunt of pain and then boots shuffling across the floor in an attempt to rise.

"I see." The wooden hallway boards creak under Cap's slow approach. "And that little bullet wound in your arm you've got must be part of that little misunderstanding too, huh?"

For the first time, Ryker remains silent.

"Nox?"

"The issue is between Ryker and Warren, sir. I just stepped in to diffuse the situation."

"Diffuse? Seems to me like you've shot your brother in arms and ended up in a bar brawl instead."

"Yes, sir." Nox's tight-lipped response makes me wonder if Ryker managed to get a few good shots in before Cap arrived. "It won't happen again."

"See that it doesn't. Ryker, go load up. Fletcher and Nash need help with securing our guests."

"But he shot me!"

"You're a good soldier, Ryker, but you need to learn when to shut the hell up. If Nox shot you, then it was for good reason. That is on you."

I press my ear against the back of the mirror and listen to Ryker's heavy descent.

I hear a sigh from below. "Ryker may be a hot head, Nox, but he gets the job done. Go easier on him next time. We're all on the same side and I've got orders to follow, just the same as you."

"And what job would that be, sir? To demoralize part of our team? He was using Warren as a punching bag for his own sport and you know that kid isn't tough enough to win that fight."

Cap clears his throat. "I take orders from my superiors and I follow them without question, soldier. It would be wise for you to do the same if you want a decent life back home. I know things have changed a bit over the past couple of months and the rules don't seem quite so black and white from what you're used to, but the times we live in now aren't easy. Sometimes things have to be done for the good of the many, and those things change a person."

"You talk as if you know this from personal experience, sir."

"I do."

I hear Nox clear his throat. "Is there something that I should be made aware of, sir?"

"Not at this time. You're a good man, Nox and I trust you with my life, but you and your squad are still new to the team. Some things just take time."

"Meaning what, exactly?"

I imagine Cap leaning back against the wall, looking tired and burdened by his position of authority. I can hear the weariness in his voice.

"Meaning when you are ready to be a team player then we can talk again. Until then I expect you to keep your men in line."

There was a moment of silence. "May I request a transfer, sir?"

"You want to move to another sector?"

"No. I am not making the request for myself, sir. Warren is a good kid but he's still green. Learning the ropes around the likes of Ryker won't help him. I'd like to take him under my command."

"You already have four beneath you, Nox. You know the rules."

Beads of sweat drip from the end of my nose as I strain to hear. It sounds like they are starting to move away. Although a part of me is relieved that I have yet to be discovered, another part of me wants them to stay. It feels too good to hear human voices again, even if they are spoken in anger.

Anger, rage, fear...those are all emotions that I can easily relate to.

"Cyrus is a good man, Cap. He's hard working, quick to train, and won't take crap from the likes of Jax or Ryker. He would be an adequate trade to your command for Warren."

"Cyrus has also proven to be a skilled sniper. Are you willing to weaken your own team and risk their safety during missions for the sake of one Greenie's feelings?"

"No, sir. I do not see Warren as being a liability under the right circumstances. He just needs guidance and the opportunity to prove himself. I think he has potential."

"And you feel that he is incapable of doing that under my leadership?"

"I only mean to say that Ryker will pick the flesh off his bones slowly when your head is turned. We both know what he is like. Jax is worse and Monroe is a match with a short fuse. Anyone seen as a lesser man will be crushed under those three."

Cap clears his throat. "I understand your concern, Nox, but I do not agree that coddling recruits will make them stronger. Your request is denied. Warren will man up in his own time."

"But sir—"

"Denied, soldier." Cap leaves no room to question if he is willing to be pushed on the matter any further. "Did you complete your search of this floor?"

"Not personally, sir. I was interrupted."

"Then I'd get on it. We roll out in five, with or without the girl." Cap descends the stairs. The front door opens and slams closed behind him. There is a moment of silence below before I hear something slam into the wall. Nothing breaks or falls to the floor to indicate that Nox has used a lamp or chair. Sinking back onto my heels, I realize that he has most likely used his fist.

The curiosity surrounding these soldiers grows with each passing minute as I strain to hear the activity outside while maintaining the whereabouts of Nox below. What did Cap mean by his comment about escorting guests? Was someone else hiding out here after all? Are they the ones that the blood on the door handle belongs to?

Torn between wanting to hobble to the window to look out and terrified that I will step on a board wrong and alert the soldier below to my presence, I stay kneeling in place. If I were to reveal myself now, I stand a chance of getting the medical help that I desperately need. I know that I'm getting worse and it may already be too late to reverse the infection, but can I really risk them taking a blood sample and discovering that I'm special?

It has been several minutes since I heard any movement from below. Shouting outside the window and slamming doors tells me that the five minutes Nox was given is nearly up.

"It was quite clever to pull the cord up after you." When Nox calls from below, I freeze. "I'll admit that I almost missed it. Guess I'm losing my edge today, but I'm sure you can understand why, after all that you just heard."

Clamping a hand over my mouth, I fight to still my breathing.

"Seems to me like you don't want to come out and say hello. I get that. Some of those guys down there made enough noise to send a whole herd of Flesh Bags our way and I think we both know that won't end well for you."

Silence follows his statement.

"My orders state that I have to take you in, get your processed and fed, but I'm thinking you're not planning on going without a fight. To be honest, I don't really care to force you, so let's say I give you one minute to come down before I make the decision for you."

Most people would panic in this situation, especially when you factor in my declining health, but I'm not most people. I know that there is no safe way of escape and there is no way for me to stop him from coming up from below. The only advantage I have is that he will assume that I am armed and will be forced to proceed with caution.

"Why are you pursuing me?" I call out finally.

"Well, hello to you too. You got a name?"

"I asked you a question."

I can hear Nox shift below me. "Cap seems to think you're someone worth finding and this area is swarming with Flesh Bags. I don't ask questions beyond that."

Biting my lower lip, I try to discern if he's telling the truth. So far, he seems like he's fairly loyal and willing to fight for what he thinks is right...but what if he's been told that hunting me is right?

"I don't want to go with you."

"We got that message loud and clear when we found Gunner's body."

"That wasn't my fault!"

I hear a sound and pause. I can't place the noise but it makes me uncomfortable. He's proven that he's smart and resourceful. Whatever he's doing isn't going to end well for me.

"I'm not saying that it was. In fact, you did what you had to and I don't blame you. He'd have torn you apart if you'd let him live. Got bit by one of those Flesh Bags that attacked us the night before. Rotten luck, if you ask me, but you taking him down tells me you're a fighter. I can respect that but it doesn't change anything. The truth is I'm tired of following you. I'm ready for a shower and some shut eye so it seems to me you'd be doing me a favor by coming without a fight."

"Walk away and tell them you didn't find me. They will assume I got eaten and you can go home."

"Afraid I can't do that," he grunts and I press my ear to the door again. He sounds farther away.

"You won't fair well if you try to come up. I hold the advantage right now."

"Seems that way." I tighten my grip on the hammer and wait but silence is my only response.

"Shit." Looking all around, I search for any other access point that he could use and my gaze falls on the window when I hear a scratching noise on the roof. He's found a way to me.

Diving forward to push the mirror off the hatch, I see a small black canister tossed through the window land on my bedding from the corner of my eye. I know that I don't have the reserves of energy to reach the gas grenade in time, so I shove the mirror aside and slam my foot down onto the hatch. The ladder plummets to the ground as the cloud of gas penetrates my side of the room.

My eyes begin to itch and tear up within seconds. A coughing fit doubles me over as I cling to the ladder. Cupping my face with my good hand while I struggle to remain upright, I lean heavily against the stairs and clumsily work my way down, but my body doesn't seem to want to work the way I need it to.

The hallway begins to spin with each labored breath I suck in. The pain in my eyes intensifies as I blindly feel my way down. Just before I collapse, two strong hands reach up for me and I find myself staring up into Nox's intense gaze as he holds me to his chest. Even with my blurred vision, I realize that his facial features are far sharper than I'd originally thought, handsome and rugged but held tight with a grim expression.

"When you wake up, you're really going to hate me." I hear those final words before my world goes black.

FOUR

Nox was right. The instant I come to, I am out for blood. My head is still spinning and my eyes feel as if they have been rubbed with a raw onion. What's worse is that the nerves all across my body are telling me that I'm being burned alive, but I know that's not actually possible when another bucket of a cold liquid is poured over me.

I buck and scream, yanking against the bindings that bite into the flesh of my wrists.

"Easy there, love. I'm just trying to help."

My teeth chatter so loudly that I can barely hear the man speaking as I twist, trying to locate where he is standing. A bit of cloth is tied around my head and covers my eyes, concealing him from sight. "What the hell are you doing?"

"I am dousing you with vinegar. I know it stinks right now but I promise it will make you feel better. That tear gas can be some nasty stuff so you should be thankful that you weren't standing right next to the canister when it went off."

Nox's voice comes from my right and now I know exactly where he is.

I spit in his direction. "Thankful? You did this to me!"

"I did, but if you remember correctly, I also tried to give you the chance to come willingly."

"Which you knew I wouldn't do!"

"True, but you can't blame me for not being a gentleman about it."

When I jerk to one side, the ropes holding me upright tighten painfully around my wrists and my toes come off the ground. I can barely reach as it is, but any movement left or right makes it nearly impossible to steady myself.

"Jax warned me that you'd be a little hell cat. Seems he knows your type pretty well. I told him you'd see reason once you woke up but maybe I misjudged you."

"Go to hell!"

When he chuckles in response, I discover that he has shifted to my left. I fume in silence as I try to use the tips of my toes to feel the ground beneath me, but feel only a slick surface. I am obviously not in a moving vehicle which means that I've already been transported somewhere.

"How long was I out?"

"The effects of the gas are usually temporary but I'm guessing because of the infection on top, there were some complications and you passed out before I even got you to the top of the stairs. You're a bit heavier than you look."

At the mention of my illness, I realize that despite being half-naked and soaked in vinegar, I feel better than I did before. There is definitely still pain in my shoulder, but someone has treated my wounds.

"Where am I? Why are you keeping me here? Why am I tied up like this?"

"You are safe." I hear him move farther left just before another bucket of vinegar splashes against me and a portion of it slips between my lips.

I feel exposed in front of him, despite the snug cotton bra and panties that I am wearing. They do not belong to me and the soaked white bra makes me look like a porn star in a push-up, leaving little to the imagination. I close my eyes when I realize that Nox or someone else has seen me naked at some point. Even being partially clothed he's still getting quite the show.

"That tells me squat." I spit the foul liquid from my mouth.

He sets down the bucket before approaching again. "If you promise not to attack me, I will remove your blindfold. Deal?"

I remain defiantly silent.

A soft chuckle draws my attention front and center and I realize that he's already in front of me. His ability to remain nearly silent tells me that he only made sounds when he wanted me to know where he was. He has been toying with me.

When his hands fall on either side of my face, brushing against my cheekbones to alert me before he reaches around to work on the knot, I flinch back from him. With my sight stripped away, I breathe in deep to try to get a sense of my immediate surroundings and wrinkle my nose at the sharp acrid scent of vinegar paired with the refreshing smell of soap.

Nox carefully unwraps my eyes and brushes my wild curls away from my face then steps back a few paces. I blink several times to try to clear my vision but it remains blurred. "I can't see."

"We washed your eyes with Diphoterine before we put you in the truck. It's a solution we use for chemical burns and works well with tear gas, but the bandages pressing against your eyes have probably caused slight irritation. Give it a few minutes and you should be fine."

"And the vinegar? You said the effects of the gas were temporary." I lift my head to see that my hands are tied to an oversized rain showerhead that is fixed to the ceiling instead of the wall. Looking all around, I notice the tiled shower surround and glass doors.

"The vinegar helps to remove the final traces of the chemical from your skin. You had a reaction to some of the medicines we gave you, which intensified the symptoms. The vinegar should help neutralize any remaining chemical on your skin, but all of your garments had to be incinerated when we arrived."

Just beyond Nox, who with each blink becomes slightly clearer, is a spacious bathroom with a toilet, granite countertops, shiny faucets and plush white towels. The towels are pretty much the only thing I care about at this point.

"You have gassed me, burned my clothes, probably copped a feel while I was naked and unconscious, and now you're holding me in what...a hotel room? Who the hell are you people?"

Nox looks me over. "You're not exactly in any position to be demanding answers, but I will tell you that I did not cop a feel."

"But you did undress me?"

A muscle along his jaw flinches. "It was necessary for your safety."

I snort and shake my head. "Right. So I'm a prisoner here, then?"

I stare pointedly up at my secured hands then back at him. He withdraws his handgun and taps it against his thigh as a show of power, but I am not intimidated by him. If they wanted me dead they would not have treated me.

Nox leans back against the bathroom counter and crosses one leg over the other, looking annoyingly comfortable. "Well, love, I guess that depends on you. You see, I've got a few questions of my own that need answering before I untie you. There are rules and whatnot to follow when dealing with hostile guests, but honestly, I just don't trust you not to grab my gun the instant you are free and try to shoot your way out of here."

"Well, you sure are doing a bang-up job making this place seem friendly." I glare at him, wishing that I could just have two minutes alone with him and my hammer. I lean forward and spit at his feet. "And call me 'love' again and I'll rip that sarcastic tongue out the instant I'm free."

Nox grins. "Fess up your real name and I'll consider calling you that instead."

"Screw you."

"Love it is, then." Nox taps his gun against his leg before setting it aside. "I did mean what I said earlier. You are safe here. We aren't the bad guys, though I'm betting right now you're still trying to figure out how to get free so you can drive that ax of yours through my skull."

"The first chance I get."

"I would expect nothing less."

I stare him down, wondering what thoughts are going through his head. He is analyzing me, trying to discover my weakness just as I am doing the same with him. I can feel a sense of admiration coming from him and know that he has recognized the similarities between us. We are equals despite my current state of imprisonment.

I let my head droop and close my eyes. My neck muscles ache and my shoulders are on fire. Gooseflesh runs the length of my body as the vinegar trails down my bare skin toward the drain that I'm standing over.

"How do you feel?"

"Like a stinky, drowned cat. How about you? Feeling nice and clothed over there? Enjoying the view at my expense?"

For the first time, Nox looks away. "I take no pleasure in this. I want you to know that."

"Why? So that I can feel sympathy for you? Fat chance of that happening! I'm the one being violated here."

Nox pushes up to his feet. "You have been medicated, fed, and cared for around the clock. I hardly call that being violated."

"So kidnapping with the ruse of medical care is considered a kind gesture these days?"

With a small snort, he tilts his head back toward his gun. "You're going to make me use that on you, aren't you?"

"Only if you want to cheat. I get it, though. It hurts a guy's pride to be taken down by a girl."

Nox steps up to me and then shoves his hand in his pockets. This position makes his strong, muscular physique even more pronounced. He's not what some might call a "beefcake," but he is toned in all of the right ways.

Damn him for looking hot when I want to be ticked!

"That's cute," he says, leaning in close enough for me to smell the mint on his breath. "I appreciate how eager you are to bite the hand that feeds you, but a word of warning...I'm nicer than the others."

"I'll take that into consideration."

"You do that."

Just past his shoulder, on the other side of his gun, is a small pile of brilliant white fluffy towels. Ultimately, the gun is what I should be after. This guy isn't about to go down without a fight and strangling him wouldn't be an easy task. I heard how he took down Ryker in that farm house and that guy was twice my size. I don't have the strength for that sort of fight and we both know it. Despite my reservations about shooting a gun again, I am left with little choice. If I can get free, I will aim to kill.

"How you answer this next question will determine if I can let you out of the shower," he says to draw my attention back to him. "Not because I like keeping you tied up, contrary to what you might think, but because I want to make sure that you don't have any further chemical reactions. This isn't the first time I've had to hose you down."

"Bet that was a nice time for you," I grumble and shift back as far away from him as my bindings will allow, but it isn't enough. He steps closer and stares down at me. "I'm fine. You can untie me now."

"You're sure? You were having trouble sleeping earlier so I was worried that you were still suffering a bit."

Bitter laughter bubbles up from my lips before I can stop it. "So now you're going to try to sell me on some 'I care about you' bullshit speech? News flash, asshole, I don't give a rat's ass what you think. If I say I'm fine then I am and don't watch me sleep. That's just creepy."

"It's part of the job." His tone sounds off and I can tell that he's debating if I'm lying about being okay. In truth, I am. There's still a distinct burning sensation around my face and neck but I'll never tell him that.

Nox finally shrugs and turns to grab a towel. Holding one end at chest height the rest of it trails to the ground. I have to work very hard not to show how anxious I am to feel it wrapped around me. Not just for its warmth but for the luxuriousness of something normal and not covered in filth. Life on the road has been anything but easy.

"I'm sure you're aware that I hold the upper hand here," he whispers in my ear as he leans in close enough for me to realize that the strong scent of soap that I smelled over the vinegar was him. "I don't take kindly to hitting defenseless girls, but in your case, I will make an exception if I need to."

I smile as he reaches over my head to cut the ropes and press my wet body into him, molding my curves against the hard plane of his torso. He falls still and lowers his face to look at me. "Who says I'm defenseless?"

When he chuckles, I feel the vibrations work through me. He presses right back into me, pausing long enough to let his eyes lower to take in the curve of my breast. "I knew that I was going to like you. You're a little spitfire."

"Oh, you have no idea."

"I can imagine, and for now, that will have to be good enough."

"I'd look while you can because you'll never see me like this again."

A wicked grin tugs at his lips and steals my breath away. He just went from attractive to sexy as hell in two seconds flat with that smirk. "I have a feeling you might change your mind about that."

Lifting his gaze to my ropes, I watch the muscles in his arms go rigid as he saws at the fibers with the dagger he removes from a small sheath at his hip. The instant that I'm free, my knees buckle and I find myself in his arms for the second time.

"We're really going to have to stop meeting like this," he grins down at me as he scoops me into his arms and carries me out of the bathroom with the towel draped across me for a small semblance of modesty. Not that I really need it. It's obvious that we are way past that point.

Once we enter the bedroom, I realize that it has been altered to look more like a hospital room instead of a hotel. The bedding on the queen-sized mattress is twisted and the fitted sheet tore off one corner like I was trapped in a fitful sleep earlier just as he said. A table beside the bed holds water bottles, damp rags tinted red with my blood, and a few small bowls of what looks like some sort of lotion. Hanging from a pole on the right side of the bed is an IV bag.

I look down at my arm, see several bruises where the IV has been, and then look up at him. "You took care of me?"

"Don't go getting all sweet on me now, love. It was a team effort."

"But you were part of that team?" I glance over at the book lying open on the bedside table and feel my throat catch. It is a copy of The Giver, one of the few books I loved as a child. It is obvious that he's been here watching over me for a while.

"I was."

"Why?"

Nox gently sets me down on the edge of the bed and backs away. I draw the covers around me and feel the first bit of warmth since I awoke.

"It was touch and go for a while. The doctor said you had blood poisoning setting in so we had to give you some pretty aggressive treatments." Nox rubs the back of his neck. "I guess I just didn't like to hear you scream."

My hand falls still over the blanket. "I screamed?"

He looks away and swallows. "Yeah."

Touching the wet bandage on my shoulder, I run my finger along the rise and fall of sutures and feel the tiniest twinge of guilt. "Thanks. For the shoulder, I mean."

Nox laughs and when he looks at me this time, I can see some of the hard edges in the planes of his face have softened. "I bet that was a bitch to say."

"You have no idea."

"Actually, I do. Better than most of the people here."

He turns and walks toward the blackout curtains that hang from the ceiling and drape to the floor. Pulling them back to let the light in, I shield my eyes from the brightness with my hand and he hurries to pull the outer curtain. Just beyond the gossamer fabric, I can see lush greenery from tropical trees.

"I wasn't all that different from you too long ago. Got picked up not far from here, all banged up yet still determined to take on the world. Sound familiar?" he says, before I can get the chance to ask him about the odd foliage. "Cap was the one who found me, cleaned me up and put a gun back in my hand."

"And you felt so indebted that you decided to become his lap dog?"

Nox turns away from the window and I see a hint of mischief in his eyes. "Come on. You gotta admit that I make a really cute dog."

Despite myself, I laugh. "You are either mentally deranged or—"

"Or I am brilliant. I know. It's a gift. The guys around here all know it and are jealous, but what's a guy to do?"

Tugging the sheet higher around my shoulder, I allow myself a rare smile. "You take the opportunity to be a total jackass to the new girl."

"Exactly." He begins to pace beside my IV pole. "I'm not, though. A jackass, I mean. I think you and I got off on the wrong foot. I'm actually a pretty great guy when you get to know me."

"Sure," I nod. "Any guy dubbed Mr. One Night Stand must be someone worth knowing."

Nox shakes his head. "I should have known you would be eavesdropping."

"Kinda hard to miss all of that testosterone in one little house."

"No doubt." Nox rubs the back of his neck and for the first time, I wonder if he's nervous. It seems a bit out of character for a guy like him and yet he's got the telltale signs: the pacing, rubbing his neck and even the bouncing of his knee when he finally sinks down on the edge of the bed.

"How many prisoners have you interrogated before me?"

"What?" He blinks.

"How many?"

"I'm not interrogating you—"

I shoot him a withering glance and he laughs. "Okay, fine I am but don't expect this to be like good cop versus bad cop. I don't play games."

"Neither do I."

He glances over at me. "No. I don't get the feeling that you do."

"Then tell me why I'm here."

"You are recovering."

I lean forward and lay out my wrists for him to see. The flesh has been torn and bloodied by the rope bindings. "We both know it's more than that."

"Cap advised keeping you restrained for your own safety."

"And you believe that bullshit?"

Nox swallows and turns his attention to the far wall. It is barren of picture frames or any other sort of ornament.

"I have orders and I follow them."

"Just like the dutiful robot."

"It's better than being out there." His head whips around. "Believe what you want but we saved your life. Maybe the infection would have got you before the Flesh Bags but fate had already stamped you with a seal of death. I stopped that. I saved you."

"Why?"

Nox frowns. "Because it was the right thing to do."

"And you have no other ulterior motives?"

He shifts on the bed so that one leg rests on the mattress and he can face me. "Who hurt you?"

I lean back and sink rigidly into the soft pillows. Crossing my arms over my chest puts a strain on my stitches but I don't care. "People who look an awful lot like you."

"Soldiers?" I can hear the surprise in his voice and bark out a laugh.

"What? You think just because you put on a uniform that makes a man noble? Wake up and see the world for what it really is. This place, whatever you think it is, isn't good."

"You don't even know where we are."

"I don't have to." I shove my hair back from my face as the pounding of my heart grows louder in my ears. I need him to leave, to give me time to think and decompress from everything that is going on. It's all too much. I don't trust him or anyone else here. Never before have I felt so utterly alone while sitting in the same room with someone. "The military can't be trusted."

"Now you sound paranoid, love. Don't you think it's a little unfair to lump the entire military with the ones you knew?"

I turn and level him with an icy stare. "No."

With a weighted sigh, Nox pushes up from the bed. "Well, I'm sure you would feel less violated if you were dressed so your clothes are in the closet. There's a pair of boots in there that should fit you too. Once you're dressed we can continue."

The idea of being dressed sound heavenly...right up until he doesn't make a move to leave.

"This isn't a peep show, buddy."

Nox plants his feet and places his hands on his hips. "I promise I'll close my eyes."

"And I'm supposed to trust you not to look?"

He shrugs. "I don't see that you really have any options at this point, but I am a man of my word. If I say that I won't look then I won't. Like I said, I'm not a bad guy."

"Just a creepy ass voyeur," I mutter when he makes no move to look away. Drawing the blankets around me, I use the bedside table to help me stand. My legs wobble and my knees feel weak as I make my way toward the closet. Opening the double doors, I glance back over my shoulder and stare pointedly at Nox until he closes his eyes.

Slipping inside the closet, I close the door behind me apart from a few inches to allow in a sliver of light.

"You're being ridiculous," he calls out.

"How do you know if you didn't look?"

"The door hinge squeaks."

The wooden hanger above my head swings wildly when I grab the straps of a dry white cotton bra and yank it off, narrowly missing smacking myself up the side of the head. Maneuvering it around my back takes some work in the tiny space but after a few choice words and no small amount of unladylike grunting, I manage to get my arms through the straps and the cups in place.

I don't even know what to think when I discover that this bra is my exact size but the thought of Nox rummaging through a pile of spare bras to find my size is almost payment enough for him seeing me naked. Almost.

I try to reach behind me to latch the bra but the pain in my shoulder becomes overwhelming and tears sting my eyes before I'm forced to give up.

"Everything okay in there?"

I bang my elbow against the wall at the close proximity of his voice and discover that he's blocking my sliver of light. "You know damn well it's not."

"Do you need my help?"

"Well aren't you just a knight in shining armor." No matter which way I twist or turn, there is no way for me to convince my left shoulder to reach back that far.

"I'm actually a guy who cares. Deal with it." His hand lands on the closet door and for a brief second, I seriously consider biting his fingers. No, that may not be the most badass move in my poorly stocked arsenal but I am improvising. "Let me help you before you tear your stitches."

What I want to do is tell him to go to hell and stick around for a while but one glimpse at the pair of jeans that had been left for me, with no less than six buttons down the front instead of a zipper, lets me know that I am done for.

Before I can finish my heavy sigh, the door swings open to reveal Nox with his eyes closed, as promised. I can't help but laugh at him and slowly a smile dawns on his face.

"It sounds like a caged mountain lion wrestling with a bear in here." He reaches out his hands tentatively toward me and I grab his hands to steer him out of accidental groping distance.

"At least your eyes are still closed."

"Man of my word, remember?"

"My hero." I place a hand on his chest. "Stay right there and if I see you so much as a single peek I will ram my fist right up your nose."

"I believe you."

Up close, I can't help but notice that he is kind on the eyes. Under the right circumstances, he would be downright sinful to behold, but my mind has no business even considering that. Nox is the enemy.

Watching him closely to be sure that he's keeping his promise, I tuck my arms to my sides to keep my bra in place and then slide my panties down, making the switch to the new pair with a speed that impresses even me.

"Done yet?"

"You're not very patient, are you?"

"I am when I have to be."

Dipping low again, I slide my legs into the jeans and struggle to get them up to my hips but end up with them stuck at hip height. I bang my head and glower at Nox as he laughs at my attempts.

"They say pride comes before a fall, you know? You don't have to be a martyr."

"Yeah, well I'd like to see you strip in front of a complete stranger and not feel weird about it."

He shoots me an odd look. "You're not much for impromptu hook ups are you?"

The instant his words hit me, I clam up. My throat tightens and I blame my current state of exhaustion on the tears that flood into my eyes as Cable's face suddenly appears in my thoughts and sends a stabbing pang of guilt straight into my heart. Lowering my head, I try to silence a small sniffle but I know he hears.

"Are you crying?" Nox opens his eyes and catches me wiping away a tear.

"Why do you care?" I turn away from him, feeling far more exposed than my current state of undress calls for. The feelings that rise up within me are personal and I'll be damned if I'm going to let him see them.

"Because you do."

I laugh and wipe at my nose with the back of my hand. "Right. Because you're such a great guy. You keep telling yourself that but it changes nothing. I'm still your prisoner."

"Guest," he amends.

I angrily rub the tears from my eyes as I penguin hop in the jeans riding high on my thighs and turn around to face him. "Whatever helps you sleep at night."

Nox winces. "I deserve that."

"Damn right. Now either help me or get the hell out." I turn my back on him and wait for him to take hold of my bra. When he does, he touches me with such a delicate pressure that he leaves me confused. How can a guy as tough and manly as he is be so gentle?

"I'm sorry about what I said," he whispers.

"Forget about it." I start to inch past him the instant the bra latch is hooked but he reaches out and takes hold of my elbow.

"I'm serious. I may have a job to do and strange ways of going about it sometimes, but I'm not a heartless ass. I hurt you and I'm sorry. My comment was uncalled for."

I swallow hard, peering up into his eyes to try to root out the deception that I'm sure to find there but no matter how long I look, I just can't find any. Finally, I lower my gaze and nod.

"I'll need help with the shirt too," I say and clear my throat when it comes out barely above a whisper.

Nox turns to grab the black tank top off a hanger and smacks his head into the bar overhead. I laugh when he reaches up to rub his head. "Smooth, Casanova. Real smooth."

With a disgruntled expression, he snatches the shirt and ducks to avoid a smack from the hanger.

"You really suck at this," I say when he places the shirt down over my head but then struggles to figure out how to maneuver my left arm in.

"I'm not used to dressing girls. Usually, clothes are coming off instead!"

I stare at him for a moment before bursting out with laughter. "I get it now. You're the player who isn't used to being told no."

"I prefer to call it independently available and no, I've never had any complaints."

"And so modest too! Feel free to keep your head out of the gutter while you finish dressing me because I'm not interested falling for that Stockholm syndrome crap. "

"Ouch."

"The truth hurts, doesn't it?"

Nox gives me a weird look and for a second. I wonder if I've actually hurt his feelings. In the next second, I wonder why the hell I should even care.

Gently tugging the tank top back over my head, he motions for me to put my arms out in front of me and slowly eases it over, careful not to snag my shoulder bandage. Nox slides his knuckles down my spine as he slowly draws the material down to my waist. My whole body aches but, thanks to his vinegar bath, the burning sensations in my skin have begun to dissipate and the sensation of his fingers on my bare skin dredges up feelings I thought had been buried in the past.

When he reaches my hips, his fingers flinch against the elastic band of my panties and his gaze immediately drops. "You're pants aren't on."

"How observant of you. Let me guess, you're the brainiac who selected these jeans."

"Are they not your size? I was careful to take proper measurements." I suck in a breath and watch his expression shift from confusion to amusement. "Don't worry. I can size up a girl without getting too personal."

"And yet you seemed to have missed the most obvious thing. There's no zip."

For a moment, his confusion returns but then his eyebrows hike with understanding when I tap the row of buttons. "Well, that may have been a bit of poor planning."

"You think?" I turn and step back into him so that he can button my jeans and misjudge how close he is. Nox's hands fall on my hips to steady me when I slam into him and start to fall forward.

"Easy. I've got you."

"Let's just get this over with as quickly as possible."

He presses his lips to my ear. "Trust me, that's the first time a girl has every said that to me."

There is tension in his fingers as his breath washes across my bare neckline. Even through the black tank top, I can feel the sensitivity of my skin and my body betraying me as he slowly leans in and runs his hands down over my thighs. His fingers trail so close to the inner curve of my leg that my muscles naturally clench in response.

"Nox?"

"That's the first time you've used my name," he whispers in my ear.

My brain is frantically debating whether to crush his foot with my heel or allow him to continue when he seizes my jeans and lifts them into place. With deft skill he quickly has each of the six buttons in place and steps back, releasing his hold on me, and for the briefest of moments, I wish he hadn't.

When I turn to face him, I see that his breathing has increased and there is a slight flush around his neck and face. I have gotten to him, but no more so than he did to me. I can use this attraction to my advantage, but I'm unsure if I can do it without letting myself get burned in the process.

He is obviously renowned for meaningless sex. After months of longing for Cable's touch, I have been left empty and aching for something meaningless to fill that void.

Looking Nox over with new eyes, I know that he would prove to be a good distraction, but I quickly remind myself that this desire can't happen. Not now. Not ever.

Nox is the enemy. It doesn't matter how many times I chant this reminder through my mind as he steps back. I still see the smoldering heat in his gaze and know that I will always wonder what he could have been like.

FIVE

Staring down at the plate of steaming food Nox places in front of me not long after I'm settled back in bed to rest, I feel like I've just been handed the world's juiciest bribe.

"Steak? You have actual steak here?" I blink several times and then poke at the perfectly seared meat for a third time with my plastic fork just to be sure that I'm not hallucinating.

"And potatoes, corn, and a hot roll." Nox points to each item on my untouched plate like I don't have eyes or a growling stomach ready to do him bodily harm if he so much as hints at trying to take it away from me.

"How is this possible?"

"Well, the outbreak didn't affect the animals so cows do still exist. You just have to round them up from time to time." He leans back into the chair that he has placed at the end of my bed so that no matter where he looks in the room I'm still in his peripheral vision. "There's a lot you don't know about this place. For starters, don't expect that sort of meal every day. I can promise you that this is a limited time offer. The doctor wants you back on your feet quickly, so you get the good stuff for a few days then you are back on the normal chow. Trust me, after a few days you'll be wishing you licked that plate clean!"

Ignoring the aching in my stomach, I push the plate aside and force myself to look away. "I don't want it."

"Liar."

Leaning forward, I naturally cradle my left arm into my chest. The new bandage and weird yellowish ointment that Nox applied earlier feels a million times better, but I'd never tell him that. "You don't know me. I've given up far better before."

"Maybe, but I know enough about you. Like how you're a complete idiot for turning down the best meal in town just to try to prove that you're tough and don't need our help."

I'd agree with him on that one but still I hold firm.

"I also know that you're scared. I get that. I wasn't all that friendly when I arrived here either."

Looking toward the window, I stare at the greenery again, but it is lost to the coming darkness. There is something off about how the shadows move. Almost like the plants outside are somehow inside as well with a ceiling overhead blocking the sun's descent. "Where is here exactly? You've never said."

"I'll make you a deal. For every bite of food you eat, I will give you one answer."

When I level him with a scathing glance, he merely grins back and laces his fingers behind his head. "You've been on IV fluids for a couple of days. It wouldn't kill you to eat something solid for a change and I promise to be honest. That promise ends if you ask me something that I'm forbidden to say, though, got it?"

Glancing at my plate, I debate my options then grab a small scoop of potatoes and swallow. The instant the creamy chive and garlic potatoes touch my lips I moan with delight and Nox's smile widens.

"Great, huh? I'll admit I may have snuck a few bites of your breakfast. Bacon is scarce around here. My once a week ration just doesn't cut it for a guy like me." He turns to look toward the window. "In answer to your previous question, you are currently sitting in what was once the Grand Ole Opry hotel. Now we call it Alpha Base. The civilians who reside here just call it home."

I lower my fork and lick my lips. "You're telling me that you were hunting for me up near the Tennessee border and brought me all the way back to Nashville?"

"Another bite please."

With a frown, I dig into the pile of golden corn kernels and try not to show how delicious the buttery flavor is as I chew.

"Our hunting route is not normally so far north but things are changing out there. We've had to adapt our methods, and when we received a distress call on an emergency ban radio, we went hunting. Along the way, we stumbled across you and couldn't leave you out there alone and injured."

"I was only injured because that asshat shot me!"

"True," Nox nodded, "but you were moving into hostile territory. You had no clue what you were walking into so Cap made the call to save you. Like it or not, good men died doing so."

"I never asked to be saved." Stabbing a bit of marbled steak with my fork, I raise it to my lips and then pause. "Any chance I can get some ketchup with this?"

Nox smirks. "Even if I had some I wouldn't let you ruin a perfect slab of beef like that."

With a shrug, I pop the meat into my mouth and am instantly swept away to a place far from Nashville, back to a time when the world made sense and my mom made a nice meal just like this to butter me up each time we were about to move again. It was the only time I ever really remember her firing up the grill, so I always knew what was coming. Most of the time we lived barely better than traveling gypsies, but at least I got a steak out of it.

Thinking of my mom makes the meat go rancid in my mouth and I sigh. It has been so long since I thought about her and now that I am, I can't bring up a single memory of her that doesn't somehow get covered over with the sounds of those monsters tearing her apart while I hid helplessly under her hospital bed. Had it really only been a few months?

"My turn," he says, drawing me from my thoughts. "Why are you alone?"

"Everyone I knew died, either from the outbreak or from raiders of some sort. I don't trust anyone now, so it's not that hard to figure out why I'm alone."

Nox sits forward and laces his fingers together, resting his elbows on his knees. "That sounds like a lonely life."

"And yours seems so great here. I'm starting to see the error of my ways." I lift my hands high enough for them to rise up off the covers. "Managing this fork with bound hands is like fooling around with chopsticks. Care to untie me so I can eat properly?"

"Not on your life."

"Didn't think so." I tear a bit off my bread roll and chew slowly. I had forgotten how heavenly freshly baked bread smells. "So why here? Why pick a building so large and hard to defend? Seems like you're just begging to get attacked."

"By the raiders, you mean?"

When he scratches at his jawline, I notice that dark stubble has begun to grow. I have no clue how much time had passed since I woke. After our awkward dressing session, Nox cleaned my shoulder wound, tied me up with instructions to rest, and then returned some time later with food. During that alone time, I discovered that he is a wiz with knots and I was left completely weaponless. Even my dinner had been pre-cut so I wouldn't need a knife. It's not like there's much damage that I can do with a plastic fork.

"There are some among us who have been here from the beginning," he says. "After the Arnold Air Force Base was overrun, Nashville became the fallback. Cap was among the survivors that helped to create the safe zone on the south side of the city but a lot of people lost their lives in the initial weeks. Panic has a way of creating more problems than solutions."

I knew that truth all too well myself. Thinking back to the destruction of St. Louis and the speed with which the gangs formed, pushing survivors either closer to the grave or a life of servitude, made it easy to imagine what happened here.

"When the safe zone fell to raiders, the survivors were pushed back here. They took up refuge in the hotel, gathering supplies from the mall, which hadn't already been picked clean. With enough salvaged machinery, the soldiers were able to pile up concrete bollards around the hotel and made one hell of a crushed car heap. There sure were plenty of them just sitting around."

"So this place is guarded by old rust buckets and pieced together concrete bollards?" I shove my hair back out of my face for the millionth time. Now that it's nearly dry the frizziness of my curls has begun to set in. "Can't say that I'm feeling all that safe right now."

"It's not just cars. We have other..." Nox starts to explain but falls silent when he hears footsteps outside the room. I tense and shift the plate away but palm the fork just in case.

"At ease, soldier," comes a call from out in the hallway. The door opens and in step three people. The first I recognize as Cap all decked out in his full military garb. One glance at his hip shows that he has been stripped of all weapons prior to entering. When Nox catches the direction of my gaze he stifles a laugh behind his hand, but Cap is too busy making way for the two people behind him to notice.

The selection of the welcoming party is rather surprising. I'd expect big muscled brutes like Jax or Ryker to come to knock some answers out of me. Instead, I get a balding, four-eyed computer geek type and a grandmotherly woman who looks like she should be standing in a kitchen baking cookies instead of entering a prisoner's bedroom.

"Hello, dear," the woman says with a slight tremor in her voice as she approaches the bed. She places an arthritic hand on Nox's shoulder when he starts to rise. "Please stay. This will only take a moment and then you may resume your duties."

"Of course." Nox sinks back down, but I can tell that he's slightly confused. He glances toward Cap, who gives him a curt nod.

"My name is Iris." I return my attention to the woman. "It's so lovely that you are finally well enough for us to officially meet. I see that you are being well cared for."

"If being tied to a bed and held against my will means well cared for then sure, I'm just peachy," I retort.

Cap tenses but Nox just smirks and lowers his gaze. Iris's smile broadens as she turns to look at the middle-aged man just over her shoulder. "I told you she'd be a feisty one, didn't I, Brian? God, love, she has had to be to survive out in those wretched lands all on her own. I'm so glad that our boys found you in time."

"In time for what?"

Brian steps forward. "To save you from the Flesh Bags, of course."

I stare at each of the people in turn then finally settle on Cap. "Those things that were chasing me...they were different than anything I've ever come across before. I thought I hallucinated most of it, but when Nox mentioned Flesh Bags earlier, I knew some of it had to be real."

Cap waits for permission before speaking. He steps forward, plants his feet, and clasps his hands behind his back in what appears to be the most rigid stick up your backside style of standing to attention I've ever seen. This guy is in full on soldier mode. "Afraid not, ma'am. The creatures that tracked you are among the newest mutations that we have discovered. This mutation is prevalent to our area but, like a disease, they are spreading faster than we can put them down."

I frown. "Why only here?"

Although it is the slightest of movements, I notice a tic along Brian's jaw before he smiles and steps forward to block Cap from sight. "We don't know that it is only here. Our communications have been limited as of late, but we are working to improve them as we speak. I'm sure once we are fully operational we will understand more. Sadly, the technology needed, and the brain power to run certain machines, leaves us at a disadvantage. We can only work with what little we have."

"You've got a hell of a lot more to work with than anywhere else I've seen."

Iris smiles and places her hands in her lap. "We are very blessed here at Alpha Base."

There is something off about the way she watches me and I can't help but feel like she is waiting for something. Probably for me to spit pea green soup, have my head pretend to be a merry-go-round, and prove to them that I don't belong here.

"Back on the road, I still saw normal Withered heading south, just as docile and unblinking as before. That's what we call them where I'm from. It doesn't make sense that they would digress so quickly unless something about this location triggered something new in them." I watch Brian closely as I speak and I would bet that big juicy steak sitting on my plate that he knows more than he is saying when he lowers his gaze under my explorative eyes.

"The reason for the mutations are yet unknown to us." Iris reaches up and places a hand on Brian's arm. "We have our best minds working on the problem."

"I'll bet you do."

Instead of looking at her, I focus my gaze on Cap. He remains at his ready position with his chin held high and his eyes focused on the back of Brian's balding head. There is no emotion or evidence of a unique thought bouncing through his mind. If I believed futuristic technology were real, I would think he were more robot than human. He barely seems to breathe or blink.

"Are you settling in well enough?" Iris asks.

I nearly betray myself with a laugh when I see Nox roll his eyes behind their backs. It was a stupid question to ask and I'm thankful that at least he acknowledges that.

"When can I leave?"

"Leave?" Iris's eyes go wide and several of the deep age lines around her eyes disappear. "Why on earth would you want to leave?"

"I have somewhere to be."

Brian scratches at the barren space between where his sideburns end and his patchy beard begins. "You are not fully recovered yet. We can discuss this at a time that is better suited for all of us. For now, as a courtesy for the food and medicine we have provided, we simply ask that you allow Nox to get to know you a bit. We here at Alpha Base believe that knowledge is crucial. You hold a keen insight into the world beyond our own. Anything that you can share with us will be greatly appreciated."

I notice how he easily slips in the assumption that I will bend over backward to be off assistance to them.

"And if I don't feel like sharing?"

Nox shoots me a warning glance that I ignore.

Iris tugs at Brian's arm and he helps her rise from the bed. "Let's not overwhelm the poor dear all at once. She needs rest and a chance to clear her head. Once she's on her feet, we can have this discussion and explain everything that we do know."

"No." I lean forward. "I want to know now."

"I'm afraid that is all of the information we are willing to share until you start being more forthcoming with us, dear." Her smile feels condescending this time. "From what I've been told, you have yet to even share your name with us. Perhaps you would care to do that now?"

I bite down on my lip and remain silent. I can't let them know my name and risk them putting together my involvement with the doctors near the St. Louis base.

"Nox?"

"Nothing yet, ma'am. We've only just begun to chat, but I can tell you that she's not overly fond of being called 'love.'"

"Now, I can't imagine why that would be coming from a handsome young man like yourself." Iris turns and holds out her free hand to Cap. "Well, perhaps later then. I have duties that require my attention. Zoey will be in to relieve you shortly, Nox. Be sure that she understands her place. We would hate for this poor dear to get the wrong impression of us."

"Of course, ma'am." Nox nods his head and the trio turns to exit the room, leaving me more confused than I was before. The instant their footsteps disappear from the room, I pounce.

"Why are these Flesh Bags different? Was it a slow mutation or rapid? What about those bite marks that I saw on your friend Gunner? Do they have anything to do with how it spreads?"

"Whoa," Nox holds up his hands. "Easy with the whiplash interrogation, love. You heard what Iris said. Once you are up and about, we will tell you everything."

"Fuck that. I need answers now. And stop calling me 'love!'"

"No name. No deal. I can be a stubborn ass just like you." Rising to his feet, Nox comes around to the side of my bed and holds out his hand, waiting for me to allow him to check my bindings. He is no fool. He's done this on a regular basis since sending me back to bed.

With a sigh, I raise my arms and he retrieves my hidden fork first. "It wouldn't have done you much good. Everyone here has been trained to fight, including Iris. Against the four of us, you wouldn't have stood a chance with that little fork of yours. It would have only got you hurt."

"So?" I snap back.

"So, if you really want to get out of here, you need to be smart about it," he whispers back.

I start to speak and then clam up. Nox smiles and tugs on my bindings. "You're learning and that's good. I told you earlier that you are not a prisoner. You are being restrained for your own good and are in no condition to go out there on your own. Letting you do so would be signing your death warrant, and with as much medicine and manpower that we invested in you, Brian and Iris would much rather help you see things our way so that you can be an asset."

With my hands momentarily free, I rub my wrists and wince at the biting pain there. This freedom is short lived when he takes hold of my arm and ties me to a rope dangling from the poster that stands just behind my bed.

I watch him carefully as he moves around to my left. "So you drank the Kool-Aid and said thank you, is that it?"

He laughs and tugs on the rope, securing it snugly to my wrist. "Something like that. I'm a survivor and I do what it takes to make it through the next day. If anyone understands that, it is you. Being with people and the biggest stockpile of ammunition around doesn't seem like a bad decision to me."

"And you trust those two?"

"They mean well."

I scoff and look away. "Sure. It's always the nice ones you have to look out for."

"Says the girl that I just absconded a fork from."

"I never claimed to be nice."

"No. You sure didn't." Moving away from the bed, I watch Nox as he makes a sweep of the room. He refills my water glass, checks my IV pole despite not having replaced the IV, and closes the curtains once more. Darkness has fallen over the hotel, and from down below, I can hear the steady murmur of voices.

"Who is Zoey?" I ask when he finishes his rounds and glances toward the door.

"She's a friend that is a bit younger than you and damaged, but I guess that comes with the territory these days. She's an untrusting person, just like you. I'm sure you will get along just fine."

Despite knowing it is a childish thing to do, I flip him the bird. "So you're off the clock then? Ready to go find a girl to shack up with and call it a day while I'm stuck in here?"

"No." He stands at the end of the bed. "I have rounds. The perimeter won't secure itself. We work long hours here, sleep when we can, and don't complain. It's how we stay safe. With the influx of Flesh Bags in the area, I don't sleep well anyways."

"Poor you."

Nox shakes his head. "Do you ever get tired of it?"

"Of what?" I shift position in bed to relieve some of the stress on my left shoulder. Nox tied the ropes that I have enough room to wiggle but not get comfortable.

"Of hating the world."

I frown. "It's not the world that I hate. It's the people."

"We aren't all bad."

Running my hands over the soft comforter I think about how much nicer this room is than anywhere I've stayed in the past few months. I had a bedroom once with my own clothes, my own cell phone, and a laptop. Nothing is mine anymore. It's all things that I've stolen from people long since dead or fled.

Nox calls this place home. I can't imagine that I will ever have one of those again.

"Why do you think Brian and Iris came to see me?"

Nox shifts his weight to his other foot. "I'm not sure what you're asking."

"Do they always make house calls to the new guests you bring in?"

"Well," he tugs at his ear and then shrugs. "No, I suppose they don't have the time to greet every single guest."

"Yet they go out of their way to visit me, with your commander in tow. That doesn't seem odd to you?"

I can see the gears turning over in his mind and feel a glimmer of hope but a sudden knock on the door breaks the moment. He turns and moves to the door, knocks twice, and the door is opened by a heavily armed soldier in the hall.

There is a low murmur of conversation before Nox steps back into the room.

"Try to be nice. Zoey has been through a lot and she volunteered to watch over you while I see to my rounds. I know you don't like it here, but this place gave her a family to watch over her at a time she really needed it. At least take pity on her and reign in the claws."

When he steps aside, a waif of a girl squeezes by, but not without pausing to shoot him a smile that instantly tells me that there is something between them. Not a romantic sort of look, although I have zero doubt that the girl would certainly be more than happy to entertain the idea if she were a few years older, but almost like she views him as a big brother.

"Zoey here has been taking the downshifts while I get some rest. She's good company once she warms up to you, but can be shy at first." Nox pulls her in for a quick side hug and then shoots me a warning look. "Be nice."

After the door closes, Zoey slowly turns to face me. Her slender shoulders are hunched forward as she cradles her arms against her chest. Mousy brown hair drapes over the left side of her face, concealing her from sight. She is pale in complexion and I can't help but wonder when the last time was that she stepped outside. Her gaze darts around the room rapidly and I get the distinct feeling that she is easily set on edge.

"So you're my guard, huh?" I ask. She bites her lip and nods, slowly moving closer. "How old are you?"

"Old enough."

I smile and stretch out my hand to motion to the chair. "I'm not going to bite. You might as well sit down since we are going to be here for a while."

Zoey tugs at a thick strand of hair and twirls the ends around her finger. Instead of sitting, she moves toward the bathroom and disappears. Craning my neck, I try to see her as she moves about. After the faucet turns on and off, I realize that she's cleaning.

"You don't have to do that," I call out but she ignores me.

With a heavy sigh, I lean back into my pillows, hating that I'm tied down. I've never been very good with resting or staying in one place for very long. I get antsy, especially these days.

A good half an hour later, Zoey finally emerges and I see a slight flush of heat in her pale fingers. They tremble slightly as she begins running a cloth along the chest of drawers.

"Nox seems nice."

She nods without turning to look at me and lifts a lamp to dust under it.

"You seem quite taken with him."

She glances back at me over her shoulder but says nothing. I can see distrust in her eyes, a far cry from the near worship that I saw when she peered up at Nox earlier.

"He seems to think a lot of you," I say, feeling as if I'm speaking with a brick wall instead of a young girl with ears to hear and a mouth capable of responding. "He thinks you and I might be a lot alike."

Zoey falls still. I watch as her shoulder rise and fall several times.

"He is wrong," she whispers. "We are nothing alike."

SIX

Going to sleep while tied up and with someone pacing at the foot of your bed is hardly an easy task. Doing so while being guarded by a moody teen that shoots eye daggers are you on every turn is pretty much impossible. For a couple of hours, I make an effort to try to rest, if for no other reason than to ease the awkward silence that fell between Zoey and me after her final comment.

Whatever her deal is, she is right. She and I are nothing alike.

I am not a timid mouse. I am not twitchy and I do not need a guy to keep me safe.

As the hours stretch long into the night, I notice a change in Zoey. She becomes more anxious, glancing at the door to my prison with far more repetition.

"Waiting for something to happen?" I ask, finally pushing up into a seated position. The throbbing in my shoulder is enough to remind me that I am far from healed but the instant I see my chance I am out of here. I have overstayed my welcome, and given enough time, I will recover well enough to carry on.

"I don't like the dark."

I'm surprised when she actually answers me. "Why?"

She stops pacing and stands at the edge of my bed. Her long hair falls over her face and in the dim light from a candle flickering in the bathroom, she is almost ghostlike. "Bad things happen in the dark."

Nox had implied that Zoey had a rough go of it, but I'm starting to wonder if there is something more to her behavior than just fear of the Flesh Bags. It also makes me question what sort of condition she must have been in when she was rescued to be like this when she is safe.

"Would you like to light more candles? I don't mind the extra light. I doubt I'll be sleeping anymore tonight."

Zoey looks over at the chest of drawers where a row of candles sits beside a box of matches. "Nox told me you need to rest."

"Do you always do what he says?"

She nods.

"Why?" Through the curtain of hair, I see her bite down on her lower lip. "Something bad happened to you, didn't it? And he took care of you?"

"Yes," she whispers.

"Then don't you think that he would want you to feel safe now? If he knows that you are afraid of the dark, he would want you to light those candles."

When she glances back at the candles, I can see her indecision.

"It's okay, Zoey."

The young girl slowly walks over to the chest of drawers and strikes a match. She holds it out in front of her and watches it flicker before her eyes. As small tendrils of smoke rise from the wooden stick, I realize the hold that it has over her and understand why Nox warned against lighting the candles. It was not for my sake but for hers.

"You like the fire, don't you?"

"No." With a flick of her wrist, she extinguishes the flame. Her hands shake slightly as she takes a breath and when she strikes a new match this time does not hesitate to light each candle in turn.

"I've always enjoyed watching fire," I say, looking beyond her to the candles. "The way the flames dance makes you think that the fire is almost alive."

Zoey whips around and returns to the end of my bed to resume her pacing. I watch as she takes five steps to the right and immediately turns to do the same to the left.

There is something buried in her past and I know now that it involves fire or at least her unusual fixation with it. Maybe she has pyromaniac tendencies? Is it possible that she was being treated for them before the outbreak and since then has been suddenly forced off of them with dramatic ill effects that only Nox can soothe?

The more that I think about their relationship, I realize that I may have misjudged him a bit. Sure, he's a total ass but I'm starting to suspect that he might have a heart buried under all of that bullshit too.

"Maybe you would feel less agitated if you sat down? This place seems locked down tight and I'm sure there are plenty of soldiers and guns guarding us. I'm pretty sure you don't have anything to worry about."

When Zoey rapidly shakes her head, her hair tangles in her eyelashes but she doesn't try to clear it away. As she curls in on herself, I notice that she rubs her thumbs over her inner arms as she paces in what I assume to be some sort of self-soothing movement.

I am unsure if my talking is adding to her agitation but I can't just stay quiet while she gives in to her panic.

"Zoey, is there another reason why you don't feel safe here? Has someone done something to you?"

"No. No. No." A small whimper rises from her throat. She drops to the floor and draws her knees into her chest, clutching them tightly as she begins to rock. "You don't care. They told me not to talk to you. You don't care."

"Who said not to listen to me?"

Zoey remains silent as she rocks. She grips her knees tightly enough to drain the color from her fingers.

And that is when I see the markings for the first time. Along her wrists and along her inner arm I see the scar tissue. She was a cutter.

"I'm sorry," I whisper. "It's not my place to pry. You have a life here and Nox says that you are happy. I don't want to ruin that."

"Not happy."

"But you make Nox believe that, don't you?"

A small nod of her head begins to unravel the mystery around the girl. I shouldn't care. She is nothing to me but a stranger, and yet I know pain when I see it. This girl, as young and fragile as she is, has been hurt, and recently, if I were to wager a guess. Someone here has brought the nightmares back to her reality.

"Has someone hit you?"

I search her bare arms for any sign of bruising, but I know all too well that a skilled abuser is careful not to leave a mark.

Zoey presses her forehead into her raised knees. A long, low moan rises from her throat and I feel helpless to even attempt to comfort her.

I never had a sister or even a mom who cared much, but a sickening ache grows in my chest as I watch the girl. She reminds me so much of Eva, the young girl I tried to help during her labor back in St. Louis. She was taken by soldiers, just as I was. For all I know, she could be dead by now.

Zoey may not be Eva, but I see the same hopelessness when I look into Zoey's eyes.

"You need to tell Nox. He will protect you."

Wiping her nose on her arm, she looks up at me. "He can't. He doesn't know."

"Then tell him."

"No!" She wrings her hands together as she glances back toward the door. "He can't know. Not ever."

"Why?" Leaning forward, I put a strain on my shoulder just to be able to see her better.

There are tears in her eyes when she looks up at me. "This place is not good."

"I know."

"You do?"

The suspicion in her voice makes me smile. "I'm all tied up and I've done nothing wrong. It doesn't take a genius to see that something isn't kosher around here."

Zoey slowly rises to her knees, releasing her death grip as she darts a glance back over her shoulder. Then she moves closer to the bed, this time coming around to the side instead of staying so far back.

"Some people around here call me crazy because I'm a little different, but I'm not. I see things that others don't. I think they are too busy pretending to be normal to see the truth."

"And that is why someone hurt you?"

She bites down on the corner of her lip and wraps her arms around her waist, as if needing the extra support to keep herself together.

I don't want to care about the girl. In fact, I'd rather remain completely immune to her weakness so that I can exploit it when the opportunity arises, but she seems so small and helpless. Like a fawn who has lost her mother to a hunter and is left to fend for herself, but unsure of how to do that.

"Fire makes it all okay," she whispers. "It always has."

"And the cutting?"

She looks down at her arms. "It used to. Before the voices started."

I feel myself cringe at the mention of her hearing voices. That's never a good way to convince someone that you are mentally sound. "What do they say?"

She worries on her lip for a moment before tentatively looking at me. "They plead for help."

"Are there many of them?" I pat the bed beside me and she slowly sinks onto the mattress, yet maintains her distance.

"Yes. Sometimes more than others. I hear them mostly at night when the building is quiet."

"Where do you hear them?"

She releases the hold on her waist and fiddles with a stray bit of thread that has come loose from the hem of her dress. "In the walls."

I try not to let my doubts show as I look away and reconcile her statements. It is easy to see how people might think she is crazy. She is already skittish and obviously prefers isolation, but when you throw the presence of voices on top, she sounds like someone ready to check into a psych ward.

"You don't believe me," she whispers and lowers her head, turning her body away so that she faces the wall instead of me.

"I want to. That's a start, right?"

When she doesn't respond, I realize that I may have lost what little trust she was starting to build with me. I need to find a new way to get her to open up.

"Do you want to know what makes me feel better when I am afraid?" I ask, waiting for her to look at me. When she finally does, I see fear in her eyes. Not worry or anxiety but true, genuine fear. "Books."

Zoey stares back at me like I've lost my mind.

"It's true." I shift the covers, smoothing them as far out as my rope restraints will allow. "When I was younger, my mom was a pretty crap parent. I think for a while she tried to do right by me, but things just got in the way. I spent a lot of my time outside of the house just to get away from her. I needed space but I was always searching for a place to call home."

Zoey sits up a little straighter and I know that she's listening.

"Money was always pretty tight. I never had new clothes and my shoes usually came from some second-hand thrift shop. Any toys that I got were always hand-me-downs, but I didn't care. When you don't know any better you take what you're given."

I fall silent for a moment then smile when Zoey fidgets. I'm starting to reach her.

"When I hit junior high, I realized that there was only one thing in life that could make me feel like my life didn't suck so much: books. For a couple of hours, I could sink into someone else's life and experience their adventures or fall in love. Books made me happy and gave me a sense of hope that at least someone could have a happy ending."

"But you never did?"

I shrug and wince at the stabbing pain in my shoulder. I wish that I could rub it but my bindings don't allow that much range of motion. "Did any of us?"

Zoey slowly shakes her head.

"The point is that sometimes letting yourself become someone you're not can help to fight the fear like I did when I was reading my books. Anytime you feel that fear rising up inside of you, imagine yourself to be someone brave and you will act that way."

"It's that easy?"

"Well, no. It takes practice, but the next time you hear the voices or someone tries to hurt you, imagine yourself as someone that you look up to."

"It's a nice thought, but it won't work."

"Why not"

She looks at me from the corner of her eye. "Because the zombie monsters look just like you and me now."

"Monsters? I don't understand. Zoey, what are you—" My question is cut off by the deafening scream of a siren. "What is that?

Zoey clasps her hands over her ears and screams, rocking faster. "No. No. No. They are coming!"

"Who are?"

"The zombies! We are all going to die!"

My blood runs cold as I glance toward the door. It looks to be made of solid wood but any normal battering ram could beat that down. "Are you talking about the Flesh Bags? The ones that Nox fights?"

Her rocking intensifies at the first sound of a machine gun firing in the distance. My muscles lock down as I strain to hear.

"I need you to untie me."

"Can't." She rocks faster. "Nox said not to."

"Nox isn't here right now, and if those monsters come for us, you are going to need me to keep you safe, right?"

Zoey's moans rise above the sirens as they continue to whine on. An explosion rattles the glass behind the blackout curtains and the terrified girl shrinks to the floor.

"Hiding under the bed won't help either of us. If you can't untie me then go get the guard at the door. Tell him to send for Nox. You want to see him, right?"

She nods and crawls on her hands and knees toward the door. I want to scream at her to hurry but know that one misstep and I could send her into a full tilt panic that would get us both killed.

"That's it. You're doing great. Almost there."

When Zoey reaches the door, she pulls herself to her feet and raps twice on the door but nothing happens. She glances back over her shoulder at me. "Try again but a little louder this time. He might not have heard you."

When a second and third knock brings the same result, I begin to grow very nervous. Moments later another explosion rocks the building and I can hear screams from the courtyard below.

"Zoey, they are breaking through and I need you to trust me."

The terrified girl turns, pressing her back against the door as she trembles. "Nox will come. He always does."

"Always? How many times has this happened?"

Zoey rapidly shakes her head. Her fingers twitch at her side and I know without a doubt this isn't the first time the hotel has been infiltrated. Nox said they keep this place locked up tight and there haven't been any breaches, so that means...

"You were here from the beginning, weren't you?"

The twitching in her fingers increases as she taps her leg with rising intensity. "It's okay. I'm not going to let anything hurt you but I need you to focus for me. Are there any weapons in the room? A knife? A gun? Anything we can use to protect ourselves?"

My wrists flare with pain as I tug against the bindings. The rough fibers dig deep into my skin and blood seeps through, but I can't stop to worry about a minor flesh wound when our lives are seriously compromised. The zombie monsters, or Flesh Bags, as Nox calls them, won't let a single door stand between them once they catch our scent. They are too smart for that. Eventually they will find a way in.

"No. There's nothing. Nox said we can't risk it with you being hostile."

Swearing silently to myself, I watch as Zoey drains of color when a man screams from down the hall. She stumbles away from the door and hurries straight for the bed, crawling up onto it and into my side.

"It's okay," I soothe as she clutches at my arm like a frightened child.

I have never really been the mothering type, probably because I had a shitty example to live with as a child, but I try to wrap my arm around her as we wait.

"I made you a promise and I intend to keep it. I won't let anyone hurt you. Do you believe that?"

Her entire body trembles as she nods.

"Good, then I need you to think right now, okay? Is there anything else that we can use in this room to make a weapon?"

Brushing her thin hair back from her face, Zoey looks around. When her gaze falls on the chest of drawers her eyebrows rise suddenly. "Fire!"

"Good girl." I twist in the bed, drawing my legs up so that I can face her. "How many floors up are we?"

"We are on the third. There's a small balcony outside and some trees directly below. I told Nox you might like the view when you woke up."

For a brief moment, I'm touched, knowing that she included herself in that consideration.

"I need you to untie me, then once I'm free, I will barricade the door while you tear down all of the curtains. Tie them together to make a rope ladder and I will lower you to one of the trees. You will be safe there while I set the room on fire to cover our escape."

"I can't," she whimpers, glancing toward the window. "I don't like heights."

Reigning in my frustration, I reach out and take the girl's hand in mine. I try to block out the screams and the near constant reports of gunfire as I focus only on her. "You're a survivor, Zoey, and a hell of a strong girl even though you may not feel like it. You've made it this far and that's better than probably 75% of the world. You can do this. I've got faith in you."

Zoey looks at me for a moment before a small smile crosses her face. "I can see why Nox likes you."

Without giving me a chance to react to her statement, her petite fingers works the knots free on my right hand and she crawls over me to untie the left. The instant my arms are free, I rub them gingerly then tear a strip of cloth from the sheets and wrap them around my wrists to stop the bleeding. I dug in a lot deeper than I'd thought.

"The zombies aren't here yet, so I want you to take deep breaths and focus on the curtains," I call as I throw my legs over the side of the bed and dash toward the chest of drawers and set each candle on the floor.

Pressing my right shoulder against the substantial weight of the solid wood piece of furniture, I grunt as the mirror on top wobbles but does not fall over. Slowly the chest of drawers begins to slide and I shove it in front of the door.

I have no sooner turned my back on it when a terrible thud reverberates through the wood. When the doorframe splinters, I look over my shoulder to see the door shift its hinges.

"Tie faster!" I slam my shoulder into the dresser and press it fully against the door then race across the room to shove everything off of the nightstand and then begin a Tetris stacking game with anything resembling weight.

"I need help!"

Wiping the sweat from my brow, I turn to find Zoey standing on her toes attempting to tear down the final curtain but it has torn at a jagged angle instead of releasing for its clips like all of the others.

Grabbing a fistful of the fabric I yank it to the floor. Zoey stands in the pile of drapes looking forlorn at the trembling door. "It's trying to get in."

Taking hold of her arms, I stand in front of her, forcing the young girl to focus on me instead. "The door is holding for now but it won't for very long. I need you to start working while I reinforce the door. Can you do that?"

With her lips quivering and her knees visibly shaking, I hurry past her and survey the windows. The darkness beyond is sporadically lit with gunfire but I am only able to see small flashes among the trees on the other side of the building.

"I don't see anything moving down there. The action seems focused on other areas of the building. I'm guessing that it's about a ten-foot drop down to the second-floor balcony and from there you can swing over to the tree."

Flipping the lock, I lean into the door to slide it open and it doesn't budge. "What the hell?"

"The doors were welded shut. You aren't the first person we've held in here."

"Great." I run my hands through my tangled curls to think. "Does this glass shatter?"

"How should I know?" Zoey says with a roll of her eyes. "No one has ever tried."

A small squeal escapes the girl's lips a second later when the dresser stutters a few inches after a particularly hard slam against the door.

"Focus on the knots," I yell out and race back to the bathroom. The oversized chair in the bedroom is much too heavy for me to be able to lift and swing but it at least adds a little extra weight to the barricade. I need something smaller that I can use as a weapon.

Glancing all around the tile bathroom, my gaze settles on a metal towel rack. "Bingo."

With a handful of suture ripping tugs on the rack, I realize that I'm not making any headway and give up. Leaning against the counter, I suck in deep breaths, releasing the throbbing pain in my shoulder with each one. Blood trickles down my arm and I swear. "Great. Let's add fresh blood for that thing to sniff out."

Turning to stare at myself in the mirror, I see dark circles around my eyes and an unnatural pale hue to my skin. "You've survived worse than this. Suck it up and figure it out, Avery!"

Holding onto the counter for support, I lift myself up onto the toilet and slam my foot against the towel bar. The screws shift marginally in the wall. After three more kicks I grab ahold of the loosened bar and yank it free. Bits of drywall flutter to the floor around my feet.

"Hurry!" Zoey screams after a thundering crack comes from the door. I dash back into the bedroom just in time to see a pale fleshy arm reaching through the narrow gap in the door. Just beyond that, I spy the opaque whites of its eyes staring unblinkingly at me. Its growls make me shiver as it pauses to sniff the air then thrashes at the door.

"Samantha?" Zoey takes a step forward. Slowly she turns to look at me and I see how close she is to entering full-on panic mode. "It can't be. I know her. She and I played together."

"Not anymore." When the Flesh Bag drags its bloody nails across the dresser I take hold of Zoey and shake her. "Toss that blanket over your head and get down. Don't come out until I call for you. Got it?"

When she doesn't move, I step between her and her former friend and crouch down to her level. "She's gone, Zoey. That thing out there isn't Samantha and you

AMY MILES

can't think of her like that anymore. Do you understand? I need to know that you do."

"She's one of the zombies now, isn't she?" When she finally tears her gaze away from the girl, I see a profound sadness in her eyes.

"She is but I'm not going to let her hurt you. I promise."

I can feel her trembling beneath my hands but I don't have time to coddle her further. She will either listen and hide away or stand there and watch what must be done. The choice is on her now.

Hefting the towel bar in my hand, I gauge the weight. It is heavier than it looks and I know with my waning strength I'm going to need a serious dose of adrenaline to pull this off.

As I prep for my first swing at the glass window, a sudden flashback of Cable steals away my breath. I remember standing in that abandoned farm outbuilding, speaking with him about not wanting to learn to use a gun. Though he was less than happy about discussing hand-to-hand combat, he did say one thing that might just save my life: how to properly break a pane of glass.

"You always tried to look out for me," I whisper.

With a small, sad smile I swing, hitting dead center in the glass. There was no way that he could know that this information would someday save my skin, but I like to think that somehow he knows now.

"This is for you," I whisper and strike the center again. The glass begins to spider web. "Almost through, Zoey! Stay down just a little bit longer."

A sudden crack behind me sends me whirling around to see that the door has split in two and the Samantha Flesh Bag is crawling through. Her youthful size allows her ease of access as she shoves nightstands and lamps out of her way. Her teeth are nearly black with blood. Her chin drips with it, as do the fine blonde curls that grace her cheeks.

"Now, Zoey!" When I scream the command she instantly crawls over the bed and slams into me, nearly knocking me back through the glass.

"She's coming!" she squeals and clings to my side as I reach behind me to hand her the towel bar.

"Keep swinging at the glass until it shatters and if that thing gets past me then take off its head."

Zoey suddenly looks like a deer in headlights as Samantha shoves at the dresser. It skids across the carpet floor. Another hard shove and she will be free.

I slap Zoey across the face. "You can do this. I need to grab something from the bathroom and then I will be right back. I promise."

The terrified girl's fingers turn white as she clings to the bar and I turn her toward the window. "One eye on the glass and one eye on her at all times. Got it?"

She nods rapidly and I sprint toward the bathroom. Tearing open the bottom two cabinet doors under the sink, I toss around the bottles until I find the rubbing alcohol I saw Nox using.

"Help!" Zoey shrieks. "She's through the barrier!"

Unscrewing the lid as I run, I splash the rubbing alcohol onto the Flesh Bag that has just made it over the dresser and is rising to its feet.

"Hit the window!" Grabbing a lit candle off the floor I toss it toward the Flesh Bag but it falls short. "Dammit!"

An ear-shattering crash from behind is followed by Zoey's scream. I don't hesitate to look back at her as the Samantha Flesh Bag rushes me. The monster hits like a pro linebacker and knocks me backward. The wind leaves my lungs when I go down and smack my head against the padded mattress.

Snarling and drooling above me, I grasp Samantha's neck and hold it at arm's reach as I strain to grab another candle. I cry out when it drags its nails down my side, splitting my shirt and the skin beneath.

"Son of a bitch!" I curl my free hand into a fist and slam into her chin. A sickening pop signaling the loosening of her jaw is followed by a growl of fury. The thing claws at me, striking my face, neck, and my left shoulder. The scent of blood rises in my nose as I battle to keep my nausea at bay when she slams her flailing fist into my left shoulder.

The sudden flare of pain darkens my vision as the Flesh Bag comes crashing down. My elbows give way and I instinctively roll, tossing the zombie away. With her eyes closed and half of her skull caved in, Samantha almost looks like a gruesome, broken porcelain doll.

"Is she...is she dead?" I look up to see Zoey standing over me with a bloody towel rack raised over her head, ready to swing again.

"You did it." I cough and clutch my side. My hand comes away slick with blood and I know she gouged me pretty deep. "Now let's make sure she doesn't get up again."

Crawling on all fours to where the two remaining lit candles sit, I toss it on the Flesh Bag. The scent of burning rot makes us gag and I turn away and work to tie the drapes around Zoey's waist as the fire crackles behind us.

"I don't like that fire," she whispers

"Me either."

I lead her to the window's edge and we look down together. It is only when I lean over that I realize I may have underestimated the distance to the lower balcony a bit.

"I'm scared," she whispers and reaches out to take hold of my hand. "Nox should be here by now. He always comes."

With a smile, I brush her stray hair back out of her face and tuck it behind her ears. "He will be. I'm sure he's working his way here right now. There's no way he would ever let anything get you."

"Like you?"

I tap the end of her nose with my finger. "Exactly. See, maybe he was right. We are more alike than we thought."

For a moment, I wonder if Zoey is going to burst into tears, but then she suddenly wraps her arms around my waist and I'm left to awkwardly pat her on the back. "Hey, it's okay. I'm right here with you. Besides, you just singlehandedly took out a zombie and that's worth major bragging rights. You got this."

The young girl presses deeper into my side and I wrap my good arm around her, hoping that I'm right. If I lose my balance and drop her or she swings and misses this could prove disastrous to both of us.

"Thank you..." she frowns and looks up at me. There is a six-inch height gap between us, making me feel every bit the elder of this pair. "I still don't know your name."

"Promise not to tell?" I smile and lean down a bit to whisper in her ear. "My name is Avery."

Despite her matted hair, dilated pupils, and ghost-white skin, Zoey looks radiant when she smiles. I can easily see why Nox is so taken with her. She's fragile, yet kind and big hearted. Perhaps he knew that I would need a girl just like her to soften me up. "Nox will love that name."

I laugh and wrap the drapes several times around my arm, having already tied it off to the heavy wooden table beside the window for extra support, then I plant my feet. "Are you ready?"

"No." She looks down over the dark ledge. From below I can still hear sporadic gunfire but it has lessened. I can only hope that means that the soldiers are winning the battle. "But I really can't stand the smell. You're sure that she's dead?"

"Try not to think of her as a she, Zoey. When your friend died that thing came back in her place and now it is charred and crispy."

She casts a wary glance back at her former friend and then lies down on her belly and wiggles back over the ledge, letting the heavy rug I dragged over from the center of the room prevent her from tearing her skin on the broken glass. When I take on Zoey's full weight as she slips over the edge and dangles below, I grit my teeth and try to focus on Cable's face instead of the pain digging deep into my bullet wound where the stitches have torn free and blood freely seeps down my arm.

"How are you doing down there?" I call out, inching her a bit lower. The scent of burning flesh is really starting to turn my stomach but I fight through, swallowing down the bile that keeps rising in my throat.

"Lower me down another couple of feet. I can almost reach the tree limb." Her voice echoes up to me.

"Is it strong enough to hold you?" I wish that I could see what type of tree it is but I don't dare move closer to the edge. From what I had seen the space beyond my room was filled with lush, tropical plants, but those weren't known for being overly forgiving of a thirteen-year-old's weight.

"I think so. The other balcony is next to me. I'm going to push off and swing over—"

Her piercing scream nearly makes me lose my grip on the rope. Feeling an odd sway in the rope, I turn my back on the flames behind me and try to look down over the edge. "Zoey, what's happening?"

Before I can inch my way to the window, a hand tightens around my ankle and pulls me off my feet. The tension on the fabric rope goes slack and Zoey's scream echoes as she plummets into the darkness.

SEVEN

The scorching heat behind me snatches my attention back from the drop off as I kick at the barbecued Flesh Bag hanging onto my ankle. The thing that was once called Samantha is now more bone than flesh as it reaches for me. Her hair has all but burned away and half of her face is a melted mess of skin.

"Zoey!" I scream her name several times as I bash in the zombie's cheekbone and nose with my boot but there is no response from below. The flaming monster keeps fighting, trying to claw its way up my body. "Why won't you just die?"

With a solid kick, I knock the monster away and beat my leg against the ground to put out the flames before crawling toward the towel rack Zoey left behind. The metal is warm to the touch after having fallen too near to the flames, but I grip it firmly and drive it straight down through the thing's head.

"Nicely done!" I look up to see a figure in the doorway and yank the metal bar free in the preparation for another attack. "Easy, love. It's just me."

"Nox?" I wave at the smoke around my face and try to make him out. His dark camouflage blends too well with the darkness of the hall. "Get your ass in here. I need your help."

I hear his strained chuckle as he shoves against the dresser. "Seems to me like you handled that one just fine on your own."

Stumbling toward the door, I push against the heavy piece of furniture, and with his help, we shove it back far enough for him and three others to enter. I recognize two of them: one is Warren, the whiny skinny guy who was Ryker's punching bag back at the farm, and the other is Kenzie. The third is a young black man in his mid-twenties who is currently staring straight at me through the sights of his gun.

"Easy, Cyrus. I'll check her." Nox looks me over as he steps closer. When I start to back away from his advance, he raises his hands out in front of him. "I just need to check you for bite marks. That's all."

"You honestly think that I would let that monster use me as a chew toy?" I shoot a withering glance in his direction. "There's no time for you to strip search me so you're just going to have to trust me when I say that I'm good to go. Zoey needs help."

Nox grows very still. "Where is she?"

I point to the shattered window. "I was lowering her to the tree below when that thing grabbed me and I lost my grip." My voice grows thick with emotion as the young girl's terrified screams replay in my ears and I'm forced to close my eyes to conceal the tears that begin to form. "I've been calling to her but there's no answer."

Nox whips around and motions for Cyrus and Warren to get to the window. Beams of light appear on the floor, shining from the lights mounted on their weapons as they move to begin their search. Kenzie steps forward, glaring openly at me.

"Easy, Kenzie. She's not the enemy. I can vouch for her." Nox shoos her off to put out the fire, but she hesitates long enough to make her anger known.

"Are you okay?" He steps closer to me. His handsome face pinches with concern as he places a hand gently on my arm. He rolls my forearm over and stares at the blood soaking through my temporary wrist bandages. "You're hurt."

"I'm fine. I told you that I can take care of myself, but Zoey...she's not cut out for this stuff."

"And thanks to you, she's probably dead by now," Kenzie snaps as she stomps on the final embers that escaped the wet, smothering blanket she threw over the flames.

"Kenzie!" Nox's mouth falls open.

"It's the truth and you know it. She already admitted that she dropped her. Zoey's death is on her hands."

"Enough!" Nox steps between us, turning his back on me as he faces his soldier. "She did what she could. That's all any of us can do in times like these."

"How do you know that she's telling the truth? For all we know she could have chucked Zoey to save her own skin. You know the lower level is crawling with Flesh Bags. The chances of Zoey making it is—"

"I found her!"

Our trio races toward the window to find Cyrus circling his light around the tree below. Leaning over, I catch a glimpse of white near the bottom branch of the tree. Several are snapped and broken, evidence of Zoey's fall.

"She's not moving," Cyrus says.

"But something else is." Nox turns to look at me when I speak, then follows the direction of my finger as I point to the ground below. Shouldering his weapon, he targets his light on the area and his soldiers do the same. The instant the light hits the intended target, an enraged growl rises from below Zoey and we spy no less than four Withered pacing beneath her.

"Oh, shit!" Cyrus wipes sweat from his brow and his light flashes erratically around the atrium. In its light, I spy the white shine of zombie's eyes on multiple floors.

When I turn to see if Nox noticed, I realize that he is covered in soot and a blackish type of ooze that I think might be congealing blood from one of the Flesh Bags. That tells me he got a bit too close for comfort.

Nox sees nothing beyond the still form of the girl he has sworn to protect. If she wakes and shifts just the slightest amount, she will fall the rest of the way, and in her unconscious state, will not be able to fight back.

I watch as Nox does a terrible job of hiding his dismay and his soldiers respond similarly, shifting from foot to foot beside him. Looking down at the girl, guilt swells up high enough within me to feel as if I'm suffocating in it.

"I'll get her."

All four soldiers turn to look at me like I've lost my mind.

"Hoist me down and I'll get her to safety. We've already tested the rope with Zoey. I don't weigh that much more than her, so I'm sure it will hold. Once I have her, I will swing us over to the balcony below, then you can be there to take her to whatever medical facility you have here."

"Is this girl insane?" Warren stares at me with open incredulity. "We don't even know her, and after keeping her prisoner for several days, she's willing to just risk her life for a stranger? I don't buy it."

"Your opinion is noted," Nox says through a tight-lipped grimace and then looks at each of his soldiers in turn. "Anyone else have any better ideas?"

He looks to Cyrus and Kenzie before turning his attention to me, but no one answers. "Fine. Tie her up."

"What?" Warren steps forward in protest but Nox shoves him back.

"I put my ass on the line to get you on our team, Warren. Fall in line so that I don't regret that decision." Nox turns to look at me and for the first time I see genuine fear in his eyes. That is a thing that I would never have thought to see in a guy like him. "Are you sure about this? You look pretty banged up."

I smile and gingerly cup my bleeding shoulder. "I've had worse."

"Somehow I don't doubt that." Nox shifts aside to grab the fabric rope from Kenzie and then loops it tightly around my waist. I grunt when he cinches it extra tight. "Don't go falling on me, you hear?"

"Why? You going to miss me?"

Nox chuckles but then his smile wanes as he reaches out to touch my hand. "That girl down there is special to me. Take care of her."

"I will."

When I start to step toward the window, Nox pulls back on my hand. "It might help to know your name now in case you need help. It would be a bit easier than yelling 'hey dumbass,' don't you think?"

I tilt my head to the side, stretching the muscles in my neck as I observe him. I ache far more than I want to let on and for a split second, I start to question if I really can do this. In the next second, I'm wondering what sort of psychotic idiot I must be to risk my neck for a stranger, just like Warren said. After losing Cable, I vowed not to care or let anyone else in and look at the mess I'm in now. I guess I will never learn.

"Give me a knife in exchange for my name."

A small smirk raises Nox's lips before he turns to Warren. "Hand me your blade."

Warren snorts and rests his gun against his hip, but a single warning glare from Nox straightens him right up. "You're serious?"

"Hell yes, he is," Cyrus chimes in, slapping Warren on the back. "Ain't you looking at his face, boy? That was a direct order so I recommend that you do as the man says unless you want him to knock you the fuck out."

In that moment, I decide that I like Cyrus.

With cheeks flaming in anger and his eyes firmly fixated on the floor, Warren hands over his knife to Nox. I stretch out my hand to accept it but Nox holds it just out of reach. "No heroics. Get down and get safe. Anything else and I will be coming down after you. Got it?"

"Is he always this bossy?" I look to Cyrus for an answer. The man just winks at me and I turn away without agreeing to Nox's terms.

Tugging at the lasso around my waist, I check one final time to make sure I'm secure as the four line up to be my anchor and I head to the window. The air feels much cooler in the atrium compared to the furnace that was recently snuffed out in my room. The darkness below makes me a bit jumpy when I take that first step off the ledge.

From above I hear a shuffling of feet just before I plummet a couple of feet. I snatch in a quick breath and stare up at the window until Cyrus pokes his head over.

"She's fine. Keep going." He calls to the others.

"I just shit myself, but sure, I'm great," I mutter under my breath and use my feet against the wall to slowly walk myself down. Once I reach the break in the wall where the balcony below begins, I swing freely with nothing to help balance me.

"Hey, dumbass?" Nox's voice calls out over the growling beneath me. "You never told me your name!"

"Took you a while to realize."

Despite my growing anxiety I smile, but it quickly fades when I see that Zoey is in far more danger than we thought. "I need another five feet. When I give the word, I'm going to need you to let out a few extra feet of slack."

"What's that?" Cyrus's head appears above me.

"I'm going to have to jump," I shout back.

From the opening above I hear loud swearing and know that Nox has just been relayed the message. A second later, I feel the tension increase on the rope and know that they are trying to pull me up.

"I told you not to do anything stupid," Nox yells.

"Yeah, well I kinda suck at taking orders, sir." Before they have a chance to lift me another foot, I wrap my good arm around the drapes and drag my dagger across the fabric with my left hand.

A small gasp escapes me when the security of the lasso around my waist diminishes and I jerk in midair. Clinging to the severed cloth overhead, I hold myself aloft with a single arm. Propelling my legs, I begin to swing, needing to get enough momentum to close the distance between me and the balcony.

"Son of a bitch. Nox, she is cutting the rope!" Cyrus barely gets the words out of his mouth when I sever the final pieces of fabric and drop. I scream when I slam into the balcony railing and the momentum sends me toppling right over the top. I land on my back, wheezing as I fight to catch my breath.

"Dammit, dumbass! Hang on. I'm coming for you!" Nox's voice trails off as I hear pounding feet and know that they are heading for the same path that brought them to my door. I can't wait too long before I make the leap to Zoey's side—every moment counts.

From somewhere above, I hear gunfire and hope that Nox's team will arrive in time to help me get Zoey to safety.

Pushing myself upright on the balcony, I pause to let the blood rush away from my head while the floor begins to spin a bit. The back of my head throbs from where I slammed into the ground, but when I reach up to remove the flapping bandage over my bullet wound, my hand comes away slick with a large amount of blood. Every single stitch has ripped free and I'm afraid I may have torn the opening a bit.

Yanking the severed lasso of fabric from around my waist, I place one end between my teeth and tear a jagged strip of cloth free. Gritting my teeth, I tie the tourniquet tight around the wound and grip the railing to keep from blacking out.

"Son of a bitch," I mutter as I swivel my shoulder to make sure I have maintained my range of motion.

Staring at the gap between me and the tree, I see that it's a good four or five feet leap to clear the gap and hit the main branch large enough to hold my weight. Anything less and I'll take a nasty tumble.

Hoisting myself back over the railing, I grip tightly to the wrought iron as I try to balance on my toes. The boots that I wear have a thick tread and leave little room for error on the tiny lip.

"Unlock the door!" Loud banging on the hotel room door behind me follows Nox's voice. They must have cleared the stairwell quickly.

Any doubts that I was feeling about the plan vanish when I hear something hard slam into the door. Sucking in a long, slow breath, I release it and jump. For an instant, I think that I've actually managed to get myself safely across the gap, but then I remember why I never was any good at basketball: I suck at jumping.

My fingers tangle in leaves and smaller branches as I begin to fall. I scramble to grasp onto anything solid enough to sustain me as I crash down through a few layers of branches before coming to rest on a limb that would make any tree-climbing kid salivate. The abrupt halt is all thanks to my ribs slamming against the unforgiving wood and, for what feels like an eternity, I gasp to regain my breath.

As I lay there assessing the numerous points of pain, I wonder how many more times I can take a beating before my body gives up.

"You are really starting to live up to your name, dumbass! You should have waited for us."

Digging my fingers into the rough bark, I start to drag myself up into a better position so that I can flip Nox the bird, but cry out when something wraps around my boot and yanks hard enough to nearly send me toppling right out of the tree.

"Watch out!" Nox's voice rings in my ears, but the responding shouts sound muffled against the snarls rising from just beneath me.

Looking down over the branch, I can see two zombies jostling for a grip on me, their fingers caught in the laces as they claw at the steel toe of my boot.

"Move your ass! We can't get a clear shot."

I throw my weight to the side and look up to see Nox sighting me through his scope a split second before he shifts lower and the deafening report of gunfire echoes around me. There is no cry of pain from below even though I feel the splatter of blood. Instead, the guttural snarls amplify as I stretch open my jaw, trying to pop my ears so that I can hear clearly again.

"Again," I yell and yank on my leg with all my might.

I'm prepared for the second shot when it comes. The grip on my foot loosens and I pull my foot up onto the branch, breathing hard as I try to still my panic. "You were right," I shout up to the balcony. "This was a terrible idea."

Belly scooting across the tree, I make my way to the trunk but scream out when I touch the bark.

"What happened?" Nox yells down from above.

"I need your light." My voice is tight with pain and when Nox focuses his beam of light on me, I see why. Several three-inch needle-like thorns are buried in my palm.

"What the hell is this?" I raise my palm for the others to see.

"Shit. She's in one of those spiny trees," I hear Kenzie say. "If Zoey hit those when she fell..."

I don't need her to finish that thought to know that the situation just went from terrible to deadly in two seconds flat. Taking hold of the thorns, I rip them free with a hiss of pain.

As I look up at the still girl, I force myself not to think about how close we are to becoming a Flesh Bag buffet. Shouldn't someone have cleared this level by now?

"Can you see anything?" Nox yells down. His light focuses on Zoey while two other lights are directed below. From the corner of my eye, I see the zombies moving beneath me.

"I need to get closer." Unwrapping the bandages around my wrists, I retie them to protect my palms as I work to stand. It is possible to climb the tree quickly, but not without suffering some serious damage along the way.

"Don't do anything stupid, love."

Placing my hands as delicately between the thorns as I can, I hoist myself up. "What'd I tell you about calling me 'love?'"

I hear Nox's chuckle but ignore it as I work my way higher. Each hand hold is precarious, and by the time I am halfway to the girl, the outsides of my hands have been sliced and diced. Blood drips freely from my hands, creating a frenzy beneath me.

"If you get a clean shot at one of those bastards take it," I hear Nox say and his light shifts again to illuminate my path.

"Aye, sir!" I risk a glance up to the balcony and see the other three searching for an opening but the tree is thick and there are many branches between them and the monsters below.

"Zoey?" My voice croaks when I slip and a thorn jabs into my arm. After yanking it free, I clear my throat before trying again. "Can you hear me?"

"Anything?"

I blink as a drop of blood strikes my forehead. Craning my neck back, I see that the front of her pale dress is stained red.

"Oh, no," I whisper and try to hurry. Each step I take feels like balancing on a bed of nails and one wrong move would impale me.

When I reach the final branch beneath her, I can see that it is worse than I feared. Though much of her body fell on a branch not heavily littered with the thorns, her chest presses fully against the tree trunk and her blood has already stained the bark.

Another wide streak of blood trails down from her hairline but it appears that she is breathing shallowly.

"She's breathing," I yell out. "It looks like she hit her head hard on the way down. That's probably why she's unconscious."

I don't want to tell him about the thorns until I have a chance to look her over. Maybe she got lucky. The higher up in the tree the fewer thorns seem to grow.

"What about you?"

"I banged up my ribs pretty good on the way down and my hands are sliced up, but I'll get her out of here."

Brushing my frizzy curls back from my face, I vow that the next time I find a pair of scissors, I am shearing it all off. "I'm going to try to wake her up without knocking us both out of the tree. Make sure if we fall, you start shooting."

"I was right. She is insane," I hear Warren say. A second later I hear him grunt with pain and wonder if it was Nox or Cyrus that thumped him.

"If I can get her up and moving then I will position her close to the balcony. There's no way she'll be able to make the jump in her condition."

There is a pause for conversation among the soldiers as I steadily work my way up to the unconscious girl. With each vibration or snap of a branch, my heart leaps into my throat with fear that this might be the moment that I fall to my death.

Pressing my hand to Zoey's cheek, I'm alarmed by how cool she feels. Ducking to look beneath her, more blood drips onto my forehead. Using my fingers to slowly feel along her abdomen and chest, I fall still when I feel multiple thorns buried in her.

Closing my eyes, I allow a moment of weakness as a single tear slips through. Zoey is gravely injured and that's on me. Wiping away the tear, I smear some of her blood across my cheek and then poke my head out to stare up into the light.

"Nox, we have a problem."

"How bad is it?"

I don't want to say, but I know that I have to. "She's not going to be jumping anytime soon."

"Shit." His pained groan tears at me as I hear his soldiers try to offer their condolences.

I should have held on to her. I should have made sure that zombie was really dead. Zoey was right to worry. My pride and rush to get her to safety likely just killed an innocent girl.

"Can you move her?"

With a heavy sigh, I climb out as far as I dare on the branch. Three beams of light blind me and I raise my hand to shield myself from their brilliance. "I'm not sure that I should. She needs a doctor, but even then..."

A sudden static fills the space and Nox pulls away from the balcony edge. The light lowers just enough for me to see that he has grabbed a radio just as chatter floods through the speakers.

Although some of the conversation is broken, I get the message loud and clear: the hotel is not entirely secured yet.

"First floor is still on lockdown," Nox yells down to me. "I've been told that we can't risk sending any medical personnel in here until we clear it."

"How long?" I look back at the motionless girl. She won't last much longer.

"Unclear. I've been told to hold my position until I receive further orders. Cap and his team are heading our way, but it's slow going and they are losing men."

Glancing at the restless Flesh Bags pacing beneath me, I know what I have to do. The only chance at saving Zoey is to clear a path to Cap and bring help to her.

"Nox?" I call out.

"Yeah."

Looking back up into the light, I grip my knife in hand. "How fast are these bastards?"

"Oh, hell no. She isn't thinking what I think she's thinking, is she?" Cyrus's voice carries through the dark atrium.

"Don't even think about it. You won't survive if you drop down there." Nox says. "They are fast, deadly and intelligent. The higher ups don't want to admit it but there's no sense sugar coating it. Those things can communicate somehow and I've seen what they are capable of when they hunt in packs. You need to stand down."

"Do they have any weaknesses?"

"I told you she's crazy," I hear Warren. I don't want to agree with him, but there's no denying that what I'm considering is as close to suicide as I can get without slashing my own wrists.

"Nox! Are there any weaknesses?" I stare defiantly up at the balcony where all four of the soldiers lean over the railing only a few feet away. I could make that leap to safety and wait for Cap's team to arrive but doing so pretty much seals Zoey's fate. I lost one person that I love to fate. I'll be damned if I let it steal that poor girl too.

"They hate the light. Seems to hurt their eyes," he finally says. From this close distance, I can see how much he doesn't want to give me that information.

"Then light them up and I'll draw them away. Cyrus is too heavy for this branch but Warren and Kenzie can probably make the jump. Stay with Zoey, and if I make it, I'll bring back help."

"Like hell, you will!" Nox begins to climb over the railing.

"Sir!" Kenzie tugs on his arm. "Your orders are to stand down."

"I'm aware of that but I'm not going to watch her die."

"She's not one of us."

Nox drills Kenzie with a hard glare and the girl backs up a step. "She should be. She's more than proven her worth today."

"No offense, Nox, but I work better alone," I call out, watching as he surveys the tree. Backing away so that he doesn't come crashing into me, I wait and watch. I won't deny that having someone else beside me would greatly even the odds, but that just means I might have more blood on my hands.

"Tough shit," he grunts and makes the leap. His tall, lean frame closes the gap with far more grace than I managed but his footing falters. I reach out and clasp my hand around his forearm with my left arm while I anchor us to the tree trunk with the other. The smaller thorns bury two inches into my arm and side but I hold on tight, refusing to let him fall as he regains his footing. The tension on my arm eases as he finds his balance and I breathe through the pain.

"You okay?" It surprises me when he focuses on me instead of Zoey.

"I feel like I just wrestled with a porcupine and lost," I grumble as I dig out the thorns. Nox watches each grimace of pain but doesn't offer to help and he settles for placing a hand around my waist to keep me stable on the branch while I work.

"You saved my ass. Thank you," he says after I pluck out the final thorn.

"Well, it is a pretty nice ass." I smile and wipe away the pinpricks of blood.

I see a ghost of a smile touch his lips before he finally looks up at Zoey on the branch overhead. Reaching up to take her hand, he flinches at the chill of her skin.

"She's worse than you said," he whispers.

"I was trying to keep you from doing something reckless."

"Yeah." He squeezes her hand and then slowly releases it. "I'll bring help for you. I promise."

Hearing the constriction in his voice, I look away to give him a moment to collect himself. The bond between them was stronger than I thought and to see him now makes me appreciate the softer side to him that I doubt few ever witness.

Glancing down at the Flesh Bags clawing at the tree with enough force to tear the flesh from their fingers, Nox takes a deep breath. "You ready for this?"

"Hell no," I mutter, wishing that I had my ax or hammer in hand instead of someone else's dagger. Though serrated and undeniably deadly, it doesn't feel quite right in my hand. "For Zoey?"

"For Zoey." Nox grins. "On three?"

I don't even wait for him to say one before I drop to the ground and start slashing.

EiGHT

The scent of rot leaves a profound sickening hole in my stomach as I duck the waving hands of one Withered and kick a second in the groin. If it had been any normal human male, I would have sent him crashing to his knees, but this monster takes the hit and keeps on coming.

"Behind you!"

I turn and bury my blade in the Flesh Bag sneaking up on Nox but am thrown off balance when it whirls around. Losing my grip on the knife, I slam into the wall and bounce off, rolling to my right to narrowly avoid another swiping hand. "I lost my knife!"

Nox slams the butt of his gun into the nose of a Flesh Bag and rams it straight into the floor. The blackish ooze seeps out around the gun and dangles from the bottom when he yanks it free. Taking aim at the monster that tried to attack him from behind, he fires three shots into its forehead and drops it.

I crouch on the balls of my feet and try to dash away but fingers tangle in my hair and I feel several clumps tear from my scalp as I'm yanked back. Off balance and falling to the floor, I scramble on my hands and feet as the rotting Withered behind me digs her nails into my jeans.

This woman is wearing a doctor's coat that is soiled but far cleaner than it should be. Whoever this lady was, she wasn't turned all that long ago. Her name badge reads Dr. Fuentes.

"Catch!"

I glance up in time to see Nox tossing my knife toward me. Kicking the zombie solidly in the jaw, I hear a loud crack as its mouth unhinges and dangles in a gruesome grin. Clambering for the knife, I seize it with blood-slickened fingers and slice at the leg of the Flesh Bag beside me. Though its guts are splattered all over the floor from where I disemboweled it moments before, it continues to gnash its teeth.

"How do I kill them?" I shout as the lights overhead shift in my direction and I'm left blinded for a moment too long. Slammed from behind, I hit the floor hard. I can hear the clicking of a jaw beside my ear as a rank odor washes over my face.

Then suddenly the weight is lifted from me. I hear the snarl of the Flesh Bag just before it slams into the wall and Nox empties a handful of bullets into it. The monster drops like dead weight and lies still, but I've seen that trick before and vow to make a wide arc around it when we leave just in case.

Breathing deeply, Nox holds out his hand to me and helps me up. "The kill shot is to the brain. Nothing else seems to work."

Rubbing my bleeding left shoulder as I stare at the bodies littering the ground around us, I glare at him. "Don't you think that might have been an important bit of information to share with me before we jumped down here?"

Nox lifts the hem of his shirt and wipes his face clean of the smeared gore. Glancing down, I see the well-defined abs that I suspected lay beneath before he lowers the shirt and checks his magazine for ammunition. "You jumped before I had a chance."

"We were counting to three. Not still having a conversation!"

"Are you two done acting like an old married couple?" Kenzie shouts down, drawing our attention up to the second floor. "Radio says the southern and eastern quadrant has been cleared. Cap is coming in from the north but the western section is still a hostile territory."

I glance over at Nox. "Which quadrant are we standing in?"

Nox grabs another magazine and slams it into place. "Western."

"Of course we are." I wipe my blade clean and try not to think of what I would give to have a hot shower right about now.

"You are welcome to climb back up in that tree and wait for the cavalry to arrive, love." He moves over to the edge of the building and holds up his hand. Cyrus tosses down two spare magazines from above and he easily catches them.

"Like hell, I will. This was my idea, remember?"

Nox moves closer with his hand held out and I realize that he's offering me a gun. "This isn't a pissing match, love. You did your part and saved the day, but this fight isn't yours. This is my home and I gotta do what it takes to secure it."

"You can't do this on your own. I'm coming with you."

His brow furrows. "You don't owe us anything. You know that, right?"

"Doesn't change anything. You need help and I'm here to give it." Nox looks me over with an appraising glance and then tries to press the gun into my hand but I push him away. "I don't use guns unless it's an emergency."

"And what do you call this?" He waves his arms around, making sure to point out the four dead bodies at our feet.

"I call it just another day in this shitty world we live in."

Nox laughs and shakes his head, then holsters his gun. "Amen to that. Well, if we're going to do this, we might as well do it right. You ready to move?"

I smirk and step on ahead of him and plunge into the darkness, letting my actions be the answer that he needs.

From behind me, I can hear the steady low hum of his flashlight as we move down a never ending hallway. Muffled gunfire can be heard from time to time but it never sounds like it is getting any closer.

"You know that your friends are flushing them in our direction, right?" I say, looking back over my shoulder.

"The thought did cross my mind. Keep your eyes open. The Flesh Bags could be hiding anywhere. Once they catch the scent of blood they will be on us in a second."

"Great. They are just like sharks," I mutter and tug on the tourniquet on my left shoulder. The bandaging around my palms has soaked through but there's nothing I can do about it. "I might as well be walking bait."

"Glad you volunteered?" Nox holds out his hand to stop me before he sweeps his gun and light into an open doorway, pausing to clear the room. We move slowly, rapping knuckles against each doorframe that we pass to see if we can draw anything out but we make it down the first hallway and into the second before we see anything.

Nox grabs my arm and pulls me back when his flashlight beam falls on a huddled form halfway down the hall with its back turned to us. Clicking the button to turn off the light, we allow ourselves a moment to let our eyes adjust to the dark. At regular intervals along the hallway, small red lights flash on and off. They must be part of the emergency system the military installed when they took up residence.

My stomach twists at the squelching sound as I peer around the corner to watch a female digging her hands into the opened stomach of a soldier and pulling out long lengths of intestines. She sniffs them and an approving growl rises in her throat before she takes a huge bite.

"That's disgusting," Nox whispers.

"Is that normal for them?" I rise to my toes to whisper in his ear as he comes to stand next to me. When he nods, the stubble along his jaw tickles my lips.

"These new ones are always hungry."

Lowering back down to the floor, I admit to myself that we are royally screwed. When the dead first started walking I thought maybe we'd skate by with a docile breed of zombie but turns out fate was just having one hell of a laugh at our expense. What I see down that hall is a full on mind fuck that I wish I could unsee, and that thing isn't alone.

This isn't Hollywood creating creatures worthy of nightmares. This isn't some author's sick imagination spilling off the pages or a TV producer's imagination coming to life. This is reality and it's scary as hell.

"Are we just going to stand here or are we going to take it out?" I ask in a hushed voice. Although there is a concern that I might be heard, I seriously doubt that thing down the hall could hear me over its smacking lips.

Nox swivels his head back and forth between the hallways. I watch him as he leans back to stare at the directional sign on the wall. From somewhere down the hall, beyond the Withered buffet, comes a strange gurgling sound followed by a screeching moan.

Gooseflesh rises along my arms as I instinctively cling to Nox. He glances at me out of the corner of his eye. "You okay there, dumbass?"

It takes me a second to realize that he's trying to lighten the mood and I force a smile. "Avery."

"What?"

"My name is Avery. 'Dumbass' was getting a bit old and 'love' just has to go."

I search his face for any signs of recognition when he processes my name but his expression remains clear. "Avery, huh? That's kind of sexy."

A snort escapes me and Nox instantly claps his hand over my mouth but it's too late. From down the hall, the Flesh Bag has fallen silent. The chewing sounds have vanished, only to be replaced by the sound of deep breathing, like it's trying to catch our scent. Nox presses his arm tightly across my chest, holding me against the wall just around the corner.

A loud wheezing groan suddenly erupts from beside Nox and the passage is lit momentarily with a spray of bullets. In the light, I see the horrific pasty flesh of the Withered female. Its skin is peeling off its face in large chunks. Its eyes are coated with a solid white film, eerily apparent in the darkness before it vanishes from sight. She is farther gone than the four we just put down in the atrium.

Then everything goes dark.

"Nox?"

A terrible crashing sound erupts from the other end of that hallway and suddenly I'm being yanked in the opposite direction. "Run! They know we are here now."

We do not bother trying to mask the pounding of our feet as we run full out back the way we came. Nox's newly illuminated flashlight dances over the ground as he pulls me after him, urging me to move faster than I feel capable of going, and yet it isn't enough. From behind me, I can sense a presence and know that we are being closely followed.

"How many are there?" I cry out as Nox skids to a halt and shoves me through an open door. He slams the door shut behind him and barely gets the latch in place before something slams into it.

"Use anything heavy that you can find to barricade the door!" Nox is already on the move, setting his gun down so that he can shift a waist height metal and wood table in front of the door.

Turning around, I peer through the dim red light and realize that we have ended up in some sort of kitchen. A few pots and pans are stacked on long metal tables just like the one Nox just used to brace the door. Off to my right stands an industrial gas range with multiple burners. Shelves filled with dishes, cooking utensils, and mixing bowls stand off to my left.

"Help me!"

Shaken from my temporary inspection, I rush to Nox's side and lean into the weight of a massive double door fridge that could easily fit six people standing side by side. The thing weighs a ton. My boots skid across the floor as I push, using my right side to shove as blood steadily drips down my left arm.

The metal feet of the refrigerator squeal as the bulk of it moves, but it is not nearly loud enough to drown out the howls and snarls from outside the door.

"How many did you see?"

"Enough," he responds. With a final combined grunt, we shove the fridge in place and step back, breathing hard as we glance around for additional bracing. "Help me move more of these tables."

"Do you really think they can get through that fridge?"

When Nox looks at me, I can see the fear that he's trying to hide and move to help him without a second thought. The feeling of being trapped is suffocating as we systematically build a fortress wall, emptying the room of anything with any decent amount of weight to it to the opposite side of the room, but *deja vu* of building a similar barrier in my room hits me strongly as the door suffers another jarring strike.

Grabbing his gun, Nox backs away slowly away. "There's no other way out of this room. This kitchen was just a backup. I think they may have used it more for storage than actual meal prep."

"I was afraid you were going to say that." Judging by what I have seen of the space, he is right about this room only being meant as an overflow. The main kitchens had to be somewhere more prominent in the hotel and would have at least one door leading in and another back to a dining area to allow for a good flow of traffic.

Nox grabs onto my hand when something new slams into the door and the entire tower of tables shifts slightly.

"How did they get into the hotel?" I ask, staring so hard at the fridge that my vision begins to blur.

"I don't know. The perimeter was secure. I checked it myself not half an hour before the breach."

Rubbing my free hand over my eyes, I exhale slowly. "What about a Samantha? Do you know her?"

"Sure. She is Zoey's friend. They were pretty much inseparable until..." he trails off.

"Until what?" I turn to look at him but don't break the contact between us. He might be a bit of an ass at times but right now, I'll take it.

Nox frowns and casts his gaze to the floor. "A couple weeks ago, she got sick. Nothing major. Just a nasty cough that wouldn't go away. Iris took her down to medical."

"Have you seen her since then?"

Scratching at the drying blood on his cheek, Nox shakes his head. "I can't say that I really remember. I was out on that hunting party for a while. When I got back, I was busy taking care of you. Why do you ask?"

Glancing back at the door, I take a step back when there is another loud crash against it. "And the doctor that attacked us in the atrium? Did you recognize her?"

"What's this all about?" Nox releases his hold on my hand and steps in front of me to block my view of the door.

"Just answer the question. Did you recognize her?"

"Yes, but only from seeing her around from time to time. Her name was Tiffany Fuentes but that is all that I know." He crosses his arms over his chest. Even in the dim light he looks strong, confident and utterly disgusting. He reeks of zombie gore but doesn't seem to notice.

"What if these things didn't come from outside, Nox? What if they came from right here within the hotel?"

"That's impossible. We have this place locked down tight. There's no way someone would get infected without us knowing about it. Besides, it takes days for the full transformation to happen. There's no way we could be dealing with this many Flesh Bags without earlier traces of their presence."

Gripping my knife tightly in hand, I close the space between us. He isn't going to like what I have to say but he needs to hear it. "That thing that attacked Zoey and I was Samantha and that doctor you just wasted wore a lab coat that was far too clean to have been on the outside. Something terrible is happening right here under your nose. Wake up and see what's really going on around here."

Nox shakes his head. "No. They would have told us. They checked Samantha for the outbreak virus and said she was clean. I'm sure they just wanted to keep her for observation."

"And you really believe that? After what you've seen?"

Anger pinches Nox's expression as he steps so close his chest brushes against my folded arms. "What exactly are you implying?"

I shudder when I hear nails clawing into the wooden door. I force myself to remain focused. He needs to know the truth, to look beyond the facade so that if we make it out of this alive, he can do something about it.

"I warned you that this place isn't what you think. I'm not from here, so as an outsider, I'm not biased by emotions, but rather go by the facts alone. What I saw today tells me that you need to start asking some questions. Starting with where they are keeping their Flesh Bags penned up."

He falls silent for several moments, barely reacting to the commotion outside. Without his radio, there's no way to call for help and no way to alert Cap to our exact location. I may not trust the people in this place, but a few friendly faces with guns would be a welcome sight right about now.

"You're wrong."

"And you're fucking blind. Those things out there that want to eat us might be your friends." I point to the door. "It could be Zoey."

With frightening speed, Nox slams me back into the wall. His hand tightens around my throat as a vein pulses down his forehead. "Do not speak to me about her like that."

My toes barely touch the floor as he lifts me up. I pull at his fingers, struggling to breathe. With a sudden widening of his eyes, he releases his grasp and steps back. "Oh god, Avery! I'm so sorry. I didn't mean to—"

"It's fine," I croak out and rub my neck. "What I said was uncalled for, but you needed to listen. Maybe that's why she never told you the truth. She knew you wouldn't listen."

"What are you talking about? Zoey always told me everything."

"Then you already know that someone was hurting her?"

Nox inhales sharply and takes hold of my arm but this time with only enough pressure to maintain a loose grip. "She told you that?"

I nod. "She knew something, Nox, and that something made her terrified of the dark. What happened to her?"

Nox glances back at the door. For now, it is holding, but both of us get the sense that time is running out. Maybe I'm a fool for wasting precious time discussing this, but the alternative of him surviving and not digging into this further is too terrible to consider. Many lives beyond our own are at stake.

"She wasn't well when she first arrived here. The woman who found her said that she was almost catatonic." Nox turns back to look at me. "They found her in a mental ward, Avery. She was crazy and most of the people here treated her as such."

"But not you."

"No." A small weary smile draws up his lips. "I saw beyond the mask. Hidden deep within was a scared little girl in need of love. Although she never spoke about her parents, I get the feeling that they dumped her in that place."

I knew that feeling. Even having a mother, I felt abandoned most of my life. Overlooked and in the way. At least I wasn't being force-fed pills to cover up the problems.

"She told me about the voices..."

Nox runs his hands through his hair. He flinches at a loud bang against the door and then lets out a shaky breath. "They started a few months back. She swears that she could hear people calling out to her for help in the walls. I never told anyone, though. Didn't want them to justify her mental stability on that. She was just having a hard time adjusting. That's all."

I step closer and touch his arm lightly. "So you never heard them?"

"Every night when I got off patrol, I would check her room. Once, I thought I heard a man's voice, but it was probably just someone in the hall. Zoey wasn't the sort to lie for attention. Hell, she hated attention."

"But you couldn't bring yourself to believe her, could you?"

Hanging his head, Nox looks downtrodden. "She knew, but we never spoke about it. After a while, she just stopped telling me about them."

I settle my hand more firmly on his arm. "I don't think she was lying or inventing a story just to get your attention. I saw how she reacted earlier. There was genuine fear in her eyes."

Nox leans back against the wall. "It's all my fault. I should never have left her alone."

"You didn't." I squeeze his arm. When he looks down at me, I offer him a genuine smile. "She was with me."

"Yeah."

When he falls silent, I know that he must be thinking about Zoey's critical condition. All of our efforts to save her were in vain. Now we have no way of clearing a path for Cap to get through and we have become the victims in need of saving.

"This is not exactly how I thought I would go out," he finally says, running his fingers back through his hair and ruffling it at the sides.

"Had it all planned out, did you?" I glance over at him as we move toward the back wall. The refrigerator rocks again and we realize at the same moment that there's nowhere else to escape to.

Opening a drawer near him, Nox rifles through one and then quickly moves on to the next, tossing a half empty box of matches, a couple birthday candles, one of those eight-inch long fire starter lighters, and a couple of steak knives onto the counter. "Not down to the exact detail but I've thought about it a time or two. Something when I'm old and gray would be nice. You know, like falling asleep in bed and slipping peacefully away while my family all says their farewells."

Ducking down, I join in with the search and scrounge through the lower cabinets but come up with nothing more dangerous than a wok, a pair of tongs, and an unopened bottle of cooking oil. This place is sparsely furnished in the way of weapons and with each thundering bang against the door, the more my anxiety rises.

"So this is it, huh?" I say, rising back up and staring at our pitiful armory.

"I'm afraid so. Unless you want to chuck a few plates at their heads but I imagine it will only tick them off."

Nox begins an ammunition inventory as I make one final round, double checking to make sure the gas lines running to the stove don't work. It was worth a shot.

Grabbing a spare knife, I tuck it into my back pocket and meet back up with Nox as the top table clatters off the barrier mound to the floor. Just outside the door, the angry growls continue.

"It sounds like we've attracted quite a group out there. At least we will make it easy for your guys to pick them off," I mutter and use my shoulder to rub a bit of drying blood off my chin. One whiff of me and those zombies will be driven mad with hunger.

Nox wipes the black blood off the barrel of his gun with his sleeve and looks over at me. "Is that supposed to be a joke?"

"Nope." I slowly unwind the bandaging around my palms and toss them to the floor. "I'm a realist. Those things out there are going to bust in here sooner or later and we either go down fighting or the cavalry really does arrive in time and we are saved."

"So you're a realist, huh?" Nox hops up onto the counter and sets his gun across his lap to wait for the inevitable. "Sounds more like a pessimist to me."

I shrug and wince at the stab of pain in my shoulder. Fresh blood seeps out and I cup my hand over the wound. In a few minutes, that gunshot will be the least of my worries. "I guess in the end it doesn't really matter. We are all going to die someday."

"And you're okay with today being that day?"

"Hell no!" I grab the box of matches and dump them out onto the counter. There are seventeen in total. Even if I could find some cleaning solution in this place to set alight, it wouldn't be nearly enough to keep out the horde. "I'm never okay with dying, but sometimes it does seem easier."

"Wow." Nox snorts and rubs his hands over his jaw, smearing blood and zombie gore along his cheekbone.

Without his hat, I realize that his dark hair is cropped close and suits him well. I could easily lose myself in memorizing every feature on his handsome face, from his strong jaw, straight nose, sexy as hell stubble, and depthless eyes that sometimes betray him in all of the wrong moments. I guess if a girl has to go out, she might as well have a nice view.

"Something must have really messed you up along the way," he says as he pats a bit of counter next to him.

Moving to sit next to him, I push myself up and being to swing my legs. "What can I say? Life sucks and no one is going to make it any better. I had to learn that little life lesson the hard way."

Nox glances over at me then rests his hand on top of his weapon when the door at the top splinters. He looks paler than normal, but he holds his fear intact better than I suspect most would. I guess he's seen some pretty bad stuff since he came here on his missions. Things that not even I've had to deal with.

"I lost my family too," he says without looking away from the door. "At least I think I did. There's no real way of knowing without cell phones these days."

I nod with understanding. The entire world went dark around the same time. Cell towers went down first, overrun with incoming calls and texts that went undelivered. In a technologically dependent world, most people panicked when they couldn't get through to their loved ones.

I just didn't have anyone left to try to contact.

"Did you go looking for them?" I ask as another piece of the pile wobbles and falls.

"I wanted to. Hell, I had every intention of setting out, but every time I tried, something came up. Someone in my group got sick, raiders struck, or the damned weather changed. It was like something didn't want me to go. So, after a while, I just accepted that I had to stay put. They knew where I was and I figure someday, if they can, they will make their way here."

"And if they don't?

Nox stares down at his hands. There is a slight tremble in them now. "Then I hope they live and die well."

"Now who is the cynic?" I bump my shoulder against him and he laughs, leaning into me.

Maybe the affinity between us grew naturally over our brief time together, or maybe when thrust into shitting conditions like ours, you just gravitate toward human interaction, but whatever it is that makes him seek the growing connection between us is something that I suddenly find myself accepting.

"I lost someone a few months back," I admit and glance at the door as it rocks on its hinges. Closing my eyes, I fight to draw up the calm that I always felt when I was with Cable. "He was never meant to be more than just a guy in my group, but he had this way about him that found cracks in my armor. Before I knew it, he was through my walls and it was too late to shove him back through."

"I'm sorry."

"Me too." Moisture begins to well up in the corners of my eyes and I whisk it away. "But he taught me a few things, like how to survive and how to never give up hope. I wish that I had been able to hold on to that second bit, but it's just not how I'm made."

"Hope isn't a bad thing."

The weight of Nox's shoulder against mine helps to keep me grounded in the moment as Cable's image slips away. "It is when it makes you reckless."

"And for some reason, you associate recklessness with love, is that it?"

I look over at him but can't hold his gaze for long.

"I may not be the world's leading expert in that area, but I can tell you that you're wrong, Avery. Love is meant to be a good thing, especially when you are trapped in a world like ours."

"A cynic and a hopeless romantic," I chuckle, using the tip of my knife to clean the black blood from under my nails. "Somehow those two don't seem to mix."

"What can I say? I'm a complicated guy."

I grin back at him, and for the briefest of moments, I feel a little lighter. "Maybe that's not such a bad thing."

"And maybe you aren't the ice queen that I thought you to be."

I reach out and grab hold of his hand. "What did you just say?"

"Easy, Avery. I didn't mean for that to be an—"

"Shh." I wave him off and hop down from the counter, heading straight for the wall as an idea blooms in my mind.

"What are you doing?"

"Does the generator feed into this section of the building?"

"I think it might. I've seen a few of the emergency lights flickering but most of them were dismantled to conserve energy. If it's running, it won't be at full capacity."

Sliding my hand along the wall, I search for a handle in the dark. "Shine your light over here."

Jumping down, Nox quickly joins me. "What are we searching for?"

"A freezer."

Leaving him behind to question my sanity, I steer his light around the room and crow with excitement when I spy a silver handle and rush to yank it open. The air smells stale inside but has a distinct chill to it that might not be nearly as cold as I would like, but it will have to do. Glancing overhead, I smile when I find the second thing I'm hunting for.

"Avery, stop!" Nox tugs on my arm, forcing me to obey. "What is this all about?"

I don't want to have to stop and explain myself, not when time is so slim, but I know that Nox isn't about to jump on the faith train just yet.

"While I was out there on my own, I noticed a pattern among the Withered, or Flesh Bags, as you people call them. They are attracted to darkness and cold. Heat and sunlight drive them away, right? Well...I think it's time we set a little trap for our guests."

NINE

When the barricade finally comes crashing in, the overspill of Flesh Bags is simply staggering. Nox was right not to tell me how many he saw coming after us. If he had done so, I might have given up and put a gun in my mouth so that I could control my own death.

The first few zombies that regain their footing pause to sniff the air. Their decaying nostrils flare and a strange grunting sound erupts from their throats. Nox and I watch as one steps forward from the pack, appearing to assume dominance as it surveys the room.

Nox's grip on my hand is cold and clammy but I cling back to him with the same ferociousness. I can barely breathe as I watch the Withered move forward with three more following close behind as if in some way guarding its back.

The leading male clicks its teeth, weaving its head from side to side as it steps cautiously forward. Its body moves in a fluid motion that I know from past experience can suddenly erupt into a burst of speed once its baser instincts are triggered.

Four more zombies span out behind the initial group while six scramble in through the broken door. Each one looks to be in a similar state of decay, though there is one defining similarity among all of them: a bite mark somewhere on their bodies.

None of the original Withered possessed such a mark or even a desire to sink their teeth into anything. Somehow, something has changed their form of mutation. Perhaps it is nothing more than their newfound hunger that has driven them to bite, but I have yet to see one of them eating their own kind.

My fingers turn white as I grip the metal grate beneath me, staring down through the dusty vent slats as the dominant male approaches the open freezer door. His cranes his head back and breathes deeply. A sudden bark from him sends eight zombies rushing toward the freezer.

But eight is not nearly enough.

I look to Nox, feeling my own dismay mirrored by him as only part of the group takes the bait. I knew that my bloody wrist bandages would attract them. I just didn't bank on the fact that they would be smart enough to split their forces.

"What do we do?" Nox whispers.

The air vent that we are hiding in is narrow and far too small for Nox, despite being of a lean build. His shoulders are hunched as he tries to minimize his bulk. There is no way he could manage to back his way through the vent into another room and I'm not leaving him behind.

"We stick to the plan."

"But the plan didn't work!"

I twist around and stretch my arm back until I can reach the knife at my side. "They just need a little more incentive."

Running the blade across my arm, I hiss with pain and close my eyes, willing myself not to let this added blood loss take me down. I have lost a lot but I'm determined not to pass out until it is safe to do so.

The blood drips down my forearm and splatters against the slats. Applying pressure just above the cut, I place my hand over the vent cover and squeeze. When the first drop of blood falls, a frenzy begins below.

"That's enough." Nox reaches out and tugs my fingers back from my wound. "You've got their attention now let's roast the bastards!"

As the initial Flesh Bags tear apart the freezer, sniffing at the walls and bloody handprints I left behind, the remaining that lagged behind take that crucial step over the wide pool of oil that we poured out just before climbing up into the vent.

"Now!" I shout as I set the entire box of matches on fire with the stick lighter. Nox releases his grip on the grate and it clatters to the floor just behind the back row of zombies. The sound startles them and alerts those searching the freezer.

Dropping the match box into the oil, I watch as the flames come to life and race along the arch, catching several of the zombies unaware and creating a fiery barrier.

"The heat won't hold them for long and it won't kill them," I shout and lower my legs out of the vent. "We need to herd them into the freezer!"

Gripping the edge, I swing down and land a perfect kick to the chest of the Withered closest to me. It stumbles back and takes down three with it. They roll and catch their clothing on fire as they struggle back to their feet. Nox follows directly behind me and smashes in the head of another on his way to the floor.

"Grab that cart!"

I'm already on the move and heading straight for an overturned prep cart while Nox fires his gun in rapid succession. The sound is deafening in the small room, but the zombie's growls rise to counter it with each shot.

Righting the cart, I spin and race back, swerving around Nox at the last second to ram into a couple Flesh Bags who have breached the barrier, unconcerned with the state of their melting flesh. "You shoot. I'll push them back!"

Nox nods and takes aim. Three go down within seconds while I battle to keep two more from reaching him. I hear the clatter of a magazine and know that Nox is going to run out of ammo far too soon.

Reaching over the table, I stab a steak knife through the eye of a woman and she collapses backward into the flames. Another takes her place with arms reaching for me as I battle to keep the cart upright and between their gnashing teeth and me.

"Nox!" Just when I feel the cart starting to tip, the ringing of gunfire strikes me and two more zombies collapse, their weight taking the cart down with them.

"Stay away from the fire," he shouts as he takes aim and shoots a hole right through a man's head that was bearing down on me.

"I have to get to the freezer!" Glancing all around, I realize that the flames have risen too high for me to be able to just jump over from a standing position. Slamming my foot into the knee of a middle-aged woman when she reaches for me, I rush past and hoist myself up onto the counter. Jumping over pots and pans, I reach the end of the counter and leap, using a particularly disintegrated zombie as my landing pad.

My hands bury themselves in its chest and come out slick with rotting ooze as I rise.

"Down!" Nox yells and I drop and roll without a second's hesitation. A Flesh Bag staggers backward and collapses, landing heavily across my legs. "My gun is jammed! You need to move your ass!"

"I'm trying." I wiggle and try to shove it off, but its dead weight proves too heavy for me to lift. A loud growl sends my eyes flying upward and I come face to face with the dominant male.

"Nox!"

From behind me, I hear him grunting and realize that one of the zombies must have breached the line and he's resorted to hand to hand combat. Reigning in my fear, I buck and thrash, shoving at the dead zombie weighing me down, but a pair of hands seize me and hoist me free.

I scream and fight, slashing with my knife but the Flesh Bag seems completely immune to my attacks. Its grip feels like a vice and its blackened teeth reek of death as it stares at me with unblinking eyes.

"Avery!" Nox's yell sounds like it comes from underwater as I stare into the monster's eyes. Though they are pure white, I see something in them that makes my blood run cold: awareness.

This thing is far more intelligent than I suspected. It allowed the others to sacrifice themselves so that it could get to me. It had my scent and had tasted my blood. I was its sole target.

The zombie attacks with frightening speed, tossing me into the wall hard enough to break a rib or two. After my earlier tumble through the trees, that broken bone count was on the rise.

I barely have a chance to push up to my elbows before it seizes my leg and tosses me again, like a dog playing with a rabbit that it will eventually eat, but not before it enjoys the game for a while.

My screams echo in my ear when it bends over and grabs my hair, yanking my neck back. It shudders twice when Nox puts two bullets in it, but not before I feel its teeth sink into my neck, piercing the skin. Its saliva burns when it mingles with my blood and I cry out.

I've been infected.

This realization shifts something in my mind, something buried so deeply that I thought that I might have lost it: a will to survive and avenge Cable's death. To make this thing pay for the millions of people that its disease has claimed and now I have to add myself to that number.

With a deafening shout, I slam my forehead into the zombie's face and feel its nose and cheekbones shatter, spraying my head with its filth. The thing's nails tear into the muscle of my arm as I wrench my right arm free and turn to ram my knife straight up under its chin.

Its lips part and hang open. Its wide eyes continue to stare at me even as its hands fall away and I drop back to the floor. The tile is stained black and the smell turns my stomach as I watch the alpha male fall sideways with my knife still buried to the hilt, piercing its brain. My blood stains its teeth and lips as it takes one final breath and then falls still.

The sound of pounding boots hits my ears and I turn slowly, taking in the carnage around me as I look up into the incredulous face of Cap. Behind him stands Jax, Ryker, and Monroe, all three bloodied and barely standing on their feet from exhaustion.

Using a Flesh Bag as a bridge, Nox leaps over the flames and skids to my side. Placing his hands on either side of my face, he calls out to me several times before I blink.

"I'm fine," I whisper. "It's okay. I'm fine."

"Like hell you are! You're going into shock!"

He tosses his gun aside and scoops me up into his arms as though I weigh nothing more than a small child. I can hear the murmurs of the men around us as they fan into the room, but I don't care as Nox carries me back across the fiery arch and sets me down on a table that two soldiers rush to turn over for him. He stands over me, protective and fierce, just the way I suspect he has always been with Zoey.

"Were you bit? I thought I saw..." Nox's hands tremble as he pulls my collar back to check and then falls still. "Oh, shit."

"It's okay. I'll be okay." I smile through my tears but I know that I won't be. I'm going to be one of *them* now. A thing. A monster.

Nox's legs give out on him and he sinks to the floor, resting his head on my knee. "This is all my fault. I should never have let you come with me."

"Just trying to live up to my nickname. Dumbass seems fitting, doesn't it?" I place a hand on his head and feel him shudder and wonder if he's crying. I don't want him to. He owes me nothing. Hell, he barely even knows me after all.

Yet it feels good to know that I might be missed by someone.

I look up through watery tears to see Cap staring at us from a distance. Behind him, his men move systematically through the room, putting a few extra bullets in the Flesh Bags to make sure that they stay down. It is an efficient clean up that came just a few minutes too late.

"I made my choice and I don't regret it." I wince at the burning sensation in my neck and place my hand over it. It didn't take long for my entire body to feel like one bundle of nerves set to an extreme pain level but I breathe through it.

"Nox."

He raises his head and slowly pushes up to a standing position when Cap approaches. Spreading his feet, he strikes an "at the ready" pose and takes on a distant gaze instead of looking directly at his commander.

"At ease, soldier." Cap turns his attention to me. "That was quite a show you just put on, though I imagine we only caught the last few moments of brilliance."

"I had help." Clutching my left shoulder, I try to make my collar rise up higher on the right side to hide the bite mark but Cap's eyes immediately locate the blood. With a heavy sigh, he lowers his gaze. I watch his hand sink to his hip as he unlatches the safety guard holding his weapon.

"Don't." Nox's voice sounds strangled as he reaches out to stop his commander. "Please. She deserves better than that."

"She's infected now, Nox. Putting her down is the humane thing to do."

"And I'm sitting right here, guys," I growl and flex my fingers, feeling an odd stiffness beginning to set in. New sensations race through my body and it takes all of my strength not to let on to the changes. Whatever these mutations are, they don't waste time.

"My apologies for speaking so boldly in front of you, ma'am, but I am sure you understand the reasons for it. You now pose a risk to this facility and I cannot allow that to continue."

I snort at Cap's response. "Sure, because this place is perfectly safe as it is."

Cap blinks and looks to Nox for an explanation. Nox looks less than thrilled to share my analysis.

"You've got something shady going on here," I say when I realize Nox is going to remain tight-lipped. I flex my hands again, realizing that the effort has become much harder the second time around. "That girl, Samantha, Zoey's friend, is the one who attacked us in my room. Then a doctor that works here, who can't have been dead more than a day or two at the most, attacked after that. If we'd had time to stop and pay attention to the zombies attacking us, I'd wager Nox knew one of them too."

Cap turns to give Nox a hard stare but Nox keeps his eyes fixated on the ground. A part of me didn't want to make this harder on him, but I'll be damned if I let these last few minutes go to waste.

"You have proof of this?"

"Well," I frown and wipe a long line of newly formed sweat from my brow that I fear stems from something more than the flames that the soldiers are working to smother. "Samantha is a crispy critter up in my room now and that doctor is back in the atrium with Zoey."

Nox lifts his face. "Zoey! Did she make it? She's badly wounded. I told Kenzie and Cyrus not to leave her side until help arrived."

Cap glances over at Jax and Ryker, jerks his head and the two hurry out. "They will get her. Don't you worry about that, Nox. If she's still alive, she will receive the best care available."

Nox looks as if he's dead on his feet when he waivers and reaches out to use the table to steady himself. I want to comfort him and tell him that Zoey will be okay and everything we risked was worth it, but I can't. I just don't have it in me at the moment.

"Avery risked everything to save her and me," Nox says. "She deserves to go out in the way she chooses."

Cap stares hard at me and then motions for one of his soldiers to approach. "Get me a gurney and straps."

"Thank you." Nox clasps Cap on the arm.

"You did well today, Nox. A lot of lives were saved because of what you did here. Go get some rest and then check in on Zoey. I'll see to it that this one is cared for."

Nox nods and looks to me with a weary smile. "Hang in there, dumbass."

It hurts to smile back and the instant he turns and is ushered out, I don't even bother trying. Cap stands beside me for a few minutes in silence before he turns to look at me.

"We both know that I have to put you down."

"Thought you might say that." I clear my throat when my voice cracks. I refuse to sound weak, even in the face of certain death. "He will never forgive you if he finds out."

Two soldiers appear in the doorway with a foldable stretcher between them. Thick straps dangle from their arms as they approach and lower the stretcher to the floor.

"There are a lot of things that Nox is better off not knowing." I look to Cap, trying to judge the harsh edge to his tone. "We do what we must in times like these. Sometimes those things might seem to be nothing more than an abomination but its survival."

"Spoken like a true self-righteous prick."

Cap's eyes narrow. "I wouldn't expect you to understand."

"Why should I? I'm still fighting for the good side. You're just pretending, aren't you?"

The commander frowns as he turns away from me. "There is no good or bad anymore, Avery. Just the living and the dead."

"You knew my name all along, didn't you?"

"Long enough."

And that is when I realize that of everyone here, Nox is ultimately the one who has been duped. I was set up. Hell, this entire thing was probably a set up to allow Cap and the others a reason to take me and it worked.

As the soldiers reach out to take hold of me, I don't fight them. I don't have the energy. Without a word spoken, Monroe and another man lower me to the stretcher and tighten the straps. Hefting me up into the air, my head rolls to the side and I spy the bastard that sank his teeth into me.

I can already feel the changes working their way through me. Soon, I will become one of *them*. Or at least I will if Cap doesn't put a bullet between my eyes fast enough.

When he glances over at me as I am carried past, there is no hint of remorse or guilt in his eyes and I know without a doubt that he is part of the underbelly of this place. He is guilty for the events of today and he is more than willing to do whatever it takes to clean up his mess so that no one else suspects what I do.

The only saving grace is that Nox never really believed me. Maybe he didn't want to. Maybe he just couldn't bring himself to. Either way, I have to believe that he will survive this. That he will live long enough to expose whoever it is playing God in this place and get people to safety.

Because if he doesn't...I won't be the last human to die on these grounds.

TEN

Sounds are strange to me as I become aware of the fact that I am no longer trapped in consuming darkness. I struggle to sort through the hazy memories that flit through my mind faster than I can grasp hold of them. I remember being placed on a stretcher and the odd sensations that overcame me. A recurring face drifts forward in my thoughts, it is of a woman, but I can't make out who she is or why she would be important. The harder I try to focus on her features, the faster it slips away into blurred nothingness.

My eyelids feel heavy and my body oddly slow to react when I try to move for the first time. I wiggle my fingers and discover that the stiffness that I felt before has vanished. After a quick assessment, I realize that my larger limbs are less responsive.

I am weak but alive and that gives me a reason to question if I'm really awake at all. Perhaps this is some sort of whacked out version of heaven or, more likely, that I'm trapped in Hell, since I'm hardly what most people would consider a saint.

When I lick my lips, my tongue slides roughly over the cracked skin. There is a faint taste of blood but it is subtle.

"Hello?"

My voice comes out in a hoarse whisper as I roll my head to the right and squint against the painfully bright lights. Though there are no windows in the room and the overhead lights above me are turned off, I find that it takes several minutes before I can adjust enough to the luminesce from the hall beyond to fully open my eyes.

Hanging from the ceiling is a white curtain on a half-circle track. The hem looks slightly darker from the dust that has settled on the floor over time. Despite its thick, woven texture I can see movement just on the other side.

This place is all wrong. It is too bright and far too white. It feels sterile, a hospital perhaps, but I know that's not possible. There are no more working hospitals in the world. They have either been torched or ransacked so thoroughly that there is no point even entering them.

"Is anyone there?"

"Shh," a guy's voice calls back. "Don't let them know that you are awake or they will come back."

"Why? Who are you?" I try to lift my head but realize there is a brace holding me down. The skin on the right side of my neck pulls tight and I wince at a stab of pain where the Flesh Bag bit me.

Similar leather bindings are cinched around my wrists and ankles. A long, coiled IV tube hangs down from a pole overhead, taped at regular intervals along my arm, which tugs at the hairs on my forearm. If I strain just enough to lift my head an inch or two, I can barely see evidence of multiple bruises, both new and old, lining my arms.

"It doesn't matter who I am," the boy finally responds. "I'm nobody important. Just another rat stuck in this damned maze."

"A rat? Maze? What are you talking about? Why am I strapped down?"

I listen to the steady droning hum of monitors and wonder if the guy is sick like me. From behind the curtain, I can see that he has rolled over but can't tell if it's to face me or look away.

"Because you are considered a hostile. These guys don't mess around with crap like that. This place is on total lockdown right now. Seems they brought in a couple of newbies this morning and it's got them all twisted up. Enough that they forgot to bring my meds."

"Hostile?" I whisper, trying to remember, knowing that I should be far more than just hostile. I should be dead.

Cap had been clear that he planned to put a bullet between my eyes to put me down before I could transform into a Withered, or spread the word about his hidden agenda. What changed?

"Where is Cap?"

"Who is that?"

This guy's lack of information is maddening. I wish that I could see him to get a sense of whether he really is as in the dark as he appears or if he's pulling my chain. It could be another mind fuck or just a ploy to get me to talk.

A faceless voice behind a curtain isn't sufficient enough to get a genuine read, especially when he sounds like a kid rather than a man.

"How old are you?"

"Old enough."

With a heavy sigh, I clench my fists and try to reign in my frustration. The urge to scream is mounting by the second and I'm so close to giving in.

"I get it. You want to act tough and pretend like you're not scared, but I know you are. I can hear the tremor in your voice so let's drop the bullshit, okay?" I pause to gauge his response. When he says nothing I continue, "I know that you have no reason to trust me, but I can help. Whatever this place is, I may be the only ally you've got."

"Why should I trust you? They think you're dangerous."

"Oh, I am." I tug against my restraints and feel anger simmering low in my belly. "But not to you. If you want to escape you're going to have to start talking."

There is silence from beyond the curtain and I wonder if I've lost him. Finally, he responds, "What do you want to know?"

"How about we start with your name?" I twist my wrists from side to side, testing my bindings. They prove to be secure. The straps around my legs offer slightly more room to maneuver but are tight enough that there's no way I am wiggling my way out.

"Flynn."

"Nice to meet you, Flynn." I glance up at the IV pole and see three nearly empty bags. It won't be long before someone comes back to check on me. "I'm—"

"I know who you are. You're the talk of this place."

I roll my head to the side and stare at the curtain. "That doesn't sound promising."

"Trust me, it's better to be a nobody."

"Yeah," I mutter as I inch my way to the right side of the bed. "I'm starting to get that."

Just on the other side of the raised safety rail, I spy a bedside table on wheels. Any hope that I would find something useful vanishes when I realize there isn't a single thing on it.

"Are you tied down, Flynn?"

I hear the clanking of metal. "I'm handcuffed."

"Must not be such a nobody after all, huh?" I roll my head to the left and search the wall. A sterile chrome countertop is lined with glass jars of gauze, rolls of white tape, a box of tissues, and a stack of magazines. I almost laugh at how normal it all is.

"I may have tried to do a runner or two. This place is like Fort Knox. Didn't take long for them to find me, but I got a decent look at the layout before they did."

"Good. We're going to need that."

On the wall above the counter are three boxes of varying size gloves, a blood pressure cuff, and a stack of those little black plastic cones shaped things that doctors love to stick on the end of a light and ram it into your ear to get a peek.

I hate hospitals.

When my gaze falls to rest on the hanging container with the symbol of a needle on it, I smile. "Ever pick a lock before?"

"What sort of guy do you think I am?" He calls back.

"A resourceful one, I hope."

I hear a small chuckle and another clanking of metal. "I may have learned a thing or two along the way."

"Good. See if you can get over to that container on the wall where they store the used needles. I think you'll be able to jimmy the lock if you get one."

"Are you shitting me? I've been staring at that wall for days and I never thought about that!"

With a great deal of grunting and groaning, I watch Flynn's shadow as he attempts to maneuver himself and his bed closer to the wall. I'm about to call out a reminder to be quiet when I hear footsteps in the hall.

"Flynn, get back in bed," I hiss and inch back toward the center of my bed.

I can hear him scrambling to right himself and pray that he manages to pull off an innocent face when, moments later, the footsteps bypass his curtain partition and then enter mine. This person is not alone. Not too far behind them I hear a flurry of hushed whispers that fall silent only when they pull the curtain into place behind them after they step into my room.

I can smell a faint cologne in the air as a man steps up close to me and I wonder if perhaps he's been watering it down to make it last. When he leans over the check my IV, I nearly give myself away when his tie tickles my face.

"Patient 67's vitals appear to be stable apart from a slight elevation in heart rate." The monotone voice speaks from directly above me.

I hear the soft tinkling of plastic tubing against the IV pole and realize he is unhooking me. "The final dose was administered nearly six hours ago and appears to be a success. The patient is expected to wake with minimal complications and will be monitored around the clock for signs of regression."

"What is your prognosis, sir?" A meek feminine voice asks from somewhere near my feet.

"I am unable to offer more than an educated guess at this time, but I believe that she will be the first to survive."

The silence that follows his words feels heavy as I detect a faint scratching sound and struggle to place it. Two cold hands come to rest on my forearm and I force myself not to react as each of the strips of tape are yanked off and there is a small twinge of pain when the IV is removed.

"Will she require further treatments?" a man asks.

"Her tissues show promise of successful regeneration." He reaches out and pricks my finger with the end of the needle and I flinch automatically, drawing my fingers away. "As you can see the paralysis has already faded. Her nervous system has responded well and the sedatives have worn off. If the delirium and hallucinations had remained we would know about it."

My stomach rolls with each new symptom that the man mentions. I can't remember enduring any of them. It is almost as if my mind has been wiped clean of those memories.

"And the sensitivity to light?" There are more scratching sounds near my feet.

The cold hands seize my face and the instant my eye is forced open and a penlight is shined at my pupil, I react violently. The muscles in my neck cord tightly as I strain against my bindings, trying to pull my face free of his grasp.

"Easy, Avery," the man whispers, turning off the light. For a moment, I am blinded as I blink rapidly to try to clear away the dark spots that eat away at my vision. "Welcome back to the land of the living. I wondered how long you would keep up with the charade. You are a far better actress than some of the others but vital signs never lie."

It takes all of my effort not to attempt to bite his hand when he pats my cheek. Instead, I glare up at him. When I do, I see a clean shaven face staring down at me, large golden frames with a bit of tape wrapped around one arm, and nose hairs in serious need of a trim.

"How are you feeling?"

"Like shit," I growl and try to yank my face away from him, but the strap around my neck allows only minimal movement. "I want to know where I am."

"You are safe. That is all that you need to know at the moment."

"I really wish people would stop saying that when they are purposefully avoiding the answer. I'm not an idiot."

"Of course not." The doctor steps back far enough for me to see a name stitched into his lab coat: *Wiemann*. "In fact, I rather suspect that you are quite the opposite. If I were a betting man, I would place my money on you."

There is a shuffling of paper, and when I look up, I see three people standing at the end of my bed. Each one stares at me with a blank, almost robotic expression that sets me on edge. Flynn wasn't wrong about the rat in a maze analogy. I've been in a place like this before. Though these people wear pristine white lab coats, I can smell the military on them.

Straining against the straps, I realize just how weak I have become. My muscles seem to have begun to atrophy and this knowledge terrifies me. It's not possible to have lost so much so quickly so they must have done something to me.

"How long have you kept me here?"

"Time has no meaning in this place, Avery. It is an anti-world, a place where the outside does not exist."

"How long?" I repeat, this time glaring up at the man.

"Around two months, give or take a few days."

"Two months!" My eyes fly open wide and the room begins to spin as I buck against my restraints. The leather groans and I feel a slight weakening in them but not nearly enough for me to get free. "That's not possible!"

A frantic beeping from a machine near my head sends the observers into a flurry of scribbling.

"Ignore that," the man growls as he presses his hand to my forehead and reaches into his pocket. I barely feel the pinprick of the needle but the effects of the mild sedative are almost immediate. "This reaction is not a new symptom. It is her body's natural response to shock."

Turning to look down at me, he smiles as the fight slowly eases from my body and I am forced to relax. There is no compassion in his eyes, but instead, a fervor that tells me that I am nothing more than a prize experiment instead of a person.

"I apologize for my peers. They are still flustered by your awakening today, I'm sure. It wasn't planned quite this soon, but apparently you decided to be a little rebel and defy the medications. I hear that is a rather common trait for you."

Shifting to look away from him up to the white ceiling tiles, I fight against the tears that threaten to fall. I won't cry in front of this man or his cronies but this news has crushed me. Two months is an eternity now.

A part of me feels betrayed that Nox never came looking for me, but then again, why would he? He doesn't owe me anything. He was practically a stranger when I saw him last and no amount of soul bearing while preparing to accept your coming death is enough to change that.

"I can understand how all of this might be a tad overwhelming at first. Believe me, I am just as surprised at the success of your miraculous recovery as you are."

"Recovery?" I glance back down at him. "Wait a second. Are you saying that I'm somehow cured? Am I not going to become one of those things?"

"Indeed." He pauses to push his glasses up his nose. "You are a rarity, Avery, and a thing of scientific beauty. You see, your blood has proven to be extremely special, and as such, you have somehow mutated the virus that infected you.

"We've managed to isolate the mutations and have come to realize our previous inaccuracies. It is no wonder none of our earliest attempts to slow the outbreak worked. We were, how you say, barking up the wrong tree. But that is all behind us now, and thanks to you, this is a marvelous breakthrough that can quite possibly change the world."

My head hurts and none of his high-pitched blabbering is helping any as I struggle to follow along. "You know what it is now? The source of the outbreak?"

"In theory, we know what it once was. In its simplest form, it was a highly reactive variation of the rabies virus, though it is now so much more than that."

I close my eyes, needing a break from the light and the incessant staring from the robot trio at the end of my bed. Apparently, they were never taught that it is rude to creep sick people out. "So you're saying a bat or something bit someone and it spread from there?"

"Oh, dear me, no!" Dr. Wiemann laughs and I cringe when he touches my hand. His skin feels cold and clammy. "A single bite could not possibly create such a global impact. But a perfectly designed aerosol spray released in, say, a major travel hub like London Heathrow or Chicago O'Hare would easily spread the contagion. It is actually a rather brilliant plan, if I do say so."

"Designed? You think someone engineered this shit?"

"Of course! It would take a whole team of extremely talented minds to manufacture something of this quality, but it can be done. The human brain has conceived of many terrible and beautiful creations over time. Most of which have been wrongfully kept hidden from the world."

The awe in his voice disgusts me as I pull against my restraints once more, but this time with far less agitation thanks to the sedatives. Already, I can feel a heavy weight pressing down on my body and my eyes begin to grow heavy. "People died because of this outbreak."

"It is a tragedy, to be sure, but one that evolution demands from time to time. Consider the plagues of old. Millions lost their lives, but those who survived and rose above became stronger. Their gene pool became the new standard until the next evolutionary catastrophe occurred and that, my dear, is what this is all about. Survival of the fittest doesn't just mean the guy with the biggest gun. Sometimes it is the tiniest thing that can bring a nation to its knees."

"You're insane." My words sound slurred in my head and my eyelids begin to droop.

He smiles and then takes a step back, motioning for his peers to follow suit. "I prefer to call it forward thinking."

ELEVEN

The sound of intermittent dripping rouses me slowly from sleep and I look up to see that I've been hooked back up to the IV. My vision is blurred and I battle with lingering grogginess as I try to lift my head, but it is easy to see that I am still stuck in the same room. I shift in the bed and hear the hiss of the motors beneath me to compensate for my weight change.

"Hey!" Flynn whispers to me in the dark. There is a single light shining from somewhere down the hall, but it is dim enough to allow me to see without causing any major discomfort. "Are you still breathing over there?"

"Sadly, yes." I groan as I try to bend my right knee to ease the tingling and am instantly reminded that I'm restrained. "What happened?"

"That doctor knocked you out good and proper." He pauses for a second and I know that he's trying to work up to something but seems unsure of how to spit it out. "That was some pretty scary stuff that he was talking about earlier, though, right? Do you think any of that talk about the rabies virus and someone attacking the world the purpose is really true? I mean...it can't be, can it?"

Staring up at the ceiling as I try to collect my thoughts into something resembling logic, I don't really know what to think. Doctor Wiemann is no doubt certifiable, but he didn't come across as anything more than brilliantly deranged and eager to make a name for himself in this new and twisted world. I saw the truth of it in his eyes, but to think that someone would willingly unleash such a thing on the world is unthinkable.

"Avery? Are you still awake?" He calls from the other side of the curtain.

"Yeah. I'm just thinking, Flynn."

"I did a lot of that too. Not much else to do around here, you know? That can really get you in trouble, especially when I start to think about my home."

"Where are you from?"

"Not here, that's for sure!" I hear the rattling of his handcuffs as he rolls over. "I've bounced around a lot. Started out up near Maine and slowly worked my way south with a group. We got ambushed not far from DC and I took off with a couple of friends and my parents. There were a few doctors with us, so people liked to have them around. We made it all the way down to Virginia Beach before the raiders caught up to us."

"What happened?" I try to shift so that I can get a better view of the hallway through the crack in my curtain but realize that my neck bracing is pulled one belt buckle too tight for that.

"We lost most of the group. Some were taken, but others died in the crossfire. After that, we ended up down in Charleston for a while. My mom and pops worked in the hospital there. The military grunts forced us to go through blood testing each day just to make sure we were clean. For a while, things ran smoothly. I made friends. Hell, we even went to school, not that it was legit or anything, but it was normal, you know? At least as normal as it could be.

Things went south pretty fast after that, though. There were a few of us who holed up in the school and fought it out when the soldiers were ambushed and the Dead Heads arrived. We took a stand and were finally starting to get somewhere, but the grownups screwed everything up and I got landed here."

"What about your parents?"

"They didn't make it."

"I'm sorry." I don't really know what else to say. His story isn't all that different than mine. Just a different place and a different time, but in the end we both lost everything.

In the silence that settles between us, I try to listen for any sounds that might help me to determine where we are. In the distance, I can detect the sound of voices, but they are muffled by a rattling in a vent. Glancing up, I stare at the small air vent near the far wall. It is too small to fit inside.

"You've been here for a while, right? What do you know about this place?" I ask.

There's a rustling of covers as Flynn sits up. The telltale rattling of his handcuffs reminds me that he failed in his mission to free himself. The idea of being kept prisoner here is not something that I'm willing to accept.

"I know that this place runs like clockwork. You could set a watch by the soldiers doing their rounds if we had one. I've seen the same four doctors since I arrived, so they may be the only ones here. I don't really know."

"Anything else?" The curtain near the end of my bed sways gently in the current pushing down from the overhead vent. This facility is obviously running off a large generator.

Knowing the military, this is probably some secret facility buried deep underground in a self-sustaining bunker complete with more firepower than we can stand to fight against and an air scrubbing system to keep any airborne chemicals at bay. Perhaps that's why these people have remained immune all this time. I wonder if they have even been topside to see the devastation.

"Well, I can tell you that the food tastes like dog crap."

I can't help but laugh at that one. "Yeah, I'm not much of a fan of hospital food myself. What's the word on the newbies that arrived?"

When Flynn doesn't answer, I roll my head to the side and see the curtain between us shift. There is a gentle padding of bare feet and then fingers wrap around the edge of the material and I catch my first glimpse of Flynn.

He looks to be no older than seventeen or eighteen, with large brown eyes, bushy eyebrows nearly lost to an unruly mop of hair that curls at his ears and nape of his neck. He has a thin nose with a slight kink in it that makes me wonder if he broke it at some point and a prominent Adam's apple. His cheeks look shallow like he's recently lost weight.

"Hey, neighbor," he smiles then turns back to yank on his bed. It rolls a couple of inches closer. "How come you get the fancy green gown while I'm stuck with purple?"

"Matches my hair better."

He smiles. "The pretty girls always get the good stuff."

A blush rises in my cheeks and I clear my throat to diffuse his sudden discomfort when he realizes what he's said. "So...the newbies?"

"Oh, right!" He smacks his forehead with his free hand. "I haven't heard much. A few screams that tell me they are girls, but other than that, everything is pretty tight lipped around here."

Looking down at his wrist, I see a plastic tag with the number 89 and remember that Dr. Wiemann called me patient 67. "What number are they up to?"

"Pushing 100 by now, I would think. You've been here the longest from what I can tell."

"What happened to the one before me?"

Flynn looks away and I watch as his Adam's apple bobs.

"Right, well I'm not letting that happen to us. I promise."

"You seem pretty sure of yourself for a girl strapped to a bed like someone in a psych ward."

I smile and lift my right hand a few inches off the bed to look at my restraints. "I never was too keen on jewelry. It doesn't really suit my style."

Flynn blinks a couple of times and then chuckles. It starts off small but then builds into a hearty laugh. "I like that."

"Glad I can amuse you." Lowering my arm when I begin to feel too weak to hold it upright, I glance up at the IV. Whatever it is that they are pumping into me has sedative properties and needs to go. "How'd it go with the needles?"

"Not good. I tried again after those research students finally left but I think the butterfly needles are too small for the keyhole. It kept snapping on me before I could pop the cuffs."

"I was afraid of that." Glancing around the room, I search for anything that might work but come up empty handed. There isn't a bobby pin or spare bit of wire in sight. Then an idea strikes me and I turn back to look at him. "Did one of the doctors leave your chart in your room?"

Flynn's head disappears for a second. "There's a folder on the counter over there."

"Excellent. That means they are either careless or they don't consider you to be a threat, and that will be their downfall. Can you see if there is a paperclip attached to it?" I hear the bed roll and then grunting from the other side of the curtain as he disappears again.

"Almost got it..."

I hold my breath, willing Flynn to go the distance. I know all too well the pain that metal handcuffs can place on your wrists when you pull against them, but this kid seems pretty tough and sufficiently motivated to get the hell out of this place. I only hope that I'll be able to keep up with him when we are ready to escape. I promised to help and I intend to keep that promise.

Wiggling my toes, I try to ward off the numbness that ripples through my lower half. I will need to be able to run, or at least walk quickly once people are alerted to our disappearance. Flynn might be expendable, but they won't want to risk losing me, especially not after their recent discovery.

"Got it!" He soon reappears with a paperclip in hand.

"How long will it be before the next guard comes by?" I glance to the hall and listen but can't hear anything beyond a distant beeping now. I wonder how many other rooms are spread out along this hall just like ours. How many other people have been stolen and experimented on?

Flynn scrunches up his nose as he begins to pull the paper clip into a straight line, using his teeth as a replacement for his other hand. He works the end of the clip, bending it this way and that with an expert hand before inserting it into the keyhole.

"Just learned lock picking up along the way, huh?"

He grins when the cuff clicks open and rubs at his freed wrist. The bruising I see there doesn't appear to be from his most recent escape attempts. "My friend Roan was a great teacher. You would have liked him. He was a real badass and a strong dislike of the military or authority in general."

"Sounds like my kind of guy." Lifting the cuff on my wrist, I motion him over. "Now hurry and get these off of me. We don't have much time. "

Flynn closes the gap between us in three strides and takes hold of my wrist. His fingers start to thread the belt through the metal buckle then he falls still. "You're sure that you're cured? Like, if I let you out you aren't going to all of a sudden start craving a Flynn sandwich, right?"

I laugh to try to lighten the mood but I can see the fear creeping into his young face. He has been through a lot and I need to make sure that I respect that. "Trust me, if I were hungry for anyone, I'd have bit off Dr. Wiemann's nose earlier."

He snorts and works to free my hand. "I'm not sure he would taste all that good, but I like your style."

"That guy is rotten to the core, for sure."

I groan and draw my freed arm into my chest when the final buckle goes slack. The only positive I see about having been trapped in some crazy drug-induced coma for two months is that the bullet wound in my left shoulder is no longer anything more than scar tissue and a twinge of pain. That I can work with.

While I work to free my other hand, Flynn makes swift work on the bindings around my ankles and soon enough, I'm pushing back the covers and rising unsteadily to my feet.

"How are you doing there, Avery? You look a little pale."

"Wouldn't you be if you'd been stuck on an IV diet for two months?"

"Good point." He stares down at the large pouch hanging from the side of my bed. It is half full with a clear liquid and I'm grateful to discover that the catheter was removed while I was asleep. That would have been a bitch to do by myself!

"At least you are well hydrated."

"Are you always that disgustingly observant?"

Flynn looks over at me. "I learned a while back to notice stuff, especially when it comes between me and taking another breath."

"Fair enough." I take his offered hand and slowly step forward, placing real weight on my legs for the first time. My knees feel weak, and I wobble slightly, but proudly remain standing. "Do you have any idea where our clothes are?"

"Burned, most likely. When you arrive here, you are disinfected completely. The decontamination process is very thorough."

Judging by the way he says it, I imagine it was not a pleasant experience and I'm grateful that I was not conscious for it.

"So what's the plan?"

"I'm working on it." I limp over to the curtain with his help and pull it apart just far enough to see.

A nurse's station sits nearly fifty feet down the hall and appears to be vacant now. Beyond that is another identical hall of curtained wards, but it's impossible to see if any of them are occupied. I search the wall for any sort of alarm system that can be of use. Setting off a fire alarm would at least give us a few minutes distraction, but there is nothing. The walls are vacant of anything apart from a few random pictures.

Looking back the other way, the hallway becomes increasingly darker. In that direction, there are no lighted exit signs.

"Did you scout out that way when you broke free?"

Flynn pops his head around my shoulder and shakes it. "Nope. It was a creepy ass dark hallway versus brightly lit, non-horror moviesque hall. You get the picture."

"Did you find an exit down there?"

"Nope. Not a single one."

"Well, then the creepy horror movie hallway it is then!"

"You're sure?" Flynn looks at me with raised eyebrows. "I'm not afraid of the dark or anything, but it doesn't seem all that safe either."

"That's sort of the point. If it were of value, it would be lighted as well. As it is, I'd bet that no one goes back there to patrol so that gives us time to find an exit. We need to locate a back door, vent, or something else that will lead us out of here."

"And if we can't find one?"

I pat Flynn on the shoulder and take a slow, steadying breath. "Failure is not an option."

He nods and tightens his grip on my waist as I wrap my arm around his shoulder and we push through the curtain. With each step that I take, I feel as if my body is fighting me. My feet don't want to work right. My legs want to buckle and pull us toward the floor. Somehow, Flynn manages to keep me upright as we stick to the shadows and use the wall as our guide as the light over our shoulders grows dim.

As we approach a set of double doors at the far end of the hall, well away from the nurses' station and our vacant room, I pray silently that they are not locked.

"There's a return air vent here," Flynn says and eases me against the wall. He runs his fingers along the metal frame and the top corner pops off. "I think we could fit inside after we pop out the filter."

Wiping at my forehead, I feel myself starting to weaken further. There is no way I would have the energy to drag myself along that passage without his help.

"I can't."

Flynn turns back to look at me and hurries to his feet. He wraps his arm around me. "Don't worry. I've got you. We will find another way."

Leaning heavily on him, Flynn guides us toward the double doors and pushes on the handle, wincing when the latch click echoes loudly in the hall. Glancing back over my shoulder, I breathe a small sigh of relief when no one appears to follow us.

"This feels too easy," he whispers as we step through and carefully close the door behind us.

A scent suddenly hits me and my nostrils flare as I lift my face to sniff the air. Goosebumps rise along my arms when I hear the sound of a chain dragging along the floor and I dig my nails into Flynn's arm. "That's because it was."

A garbled moan rises from the dark and is followed by a high pitch whine. "Avery? It's too dark. I can't see anything."

I look over at him, surprised to be able to make out the features of his face and the details of the room. Opening my eyes wide, I see multiple bodies moving along the wall. Their white eyes glow like flashlights in the darkness as they all turn to focus on us.

"Flynn, run!"

Staggering backward, I shove him toward the door just as the air shifts in front of my face and I rear back, narrowly missing the swipe of a hand. Other wheezing moans rise from the dark now as the Flesh Bags awaken from their state of dormancy. Our presence has riled them up and I don't want to linger long enough to see if those chains around their necks will allow them to reach us.

"Get the door open!"

I duck to miss the reaching fingers of a female zombie who yanks against her chains. For a split second, I see something in her face that makes me fall still.

From behind me, I hear the click of the door lock but it sounds distant as I stare at the snarling girl. Her hair is long and greasy. Her cheeks are sunken and her eyes look buried too deep into her face, but despite her gaunt appearance, I recognize her.

"Eva," I moan and feel my knees begin to buckle. "What have they done to you?"

The memory of seeing Eva's face for the last time as she labored to bring her baby into the world floods into my mind. I failed her. I should never have left her alone to try to get supplies. Even if there was nothing I could have done to stop the military from taking her, I could have at least been there. Maybe I could have stopped them from turning her into a monster.

"Avery!" Flynn's arms wrap around my stomach just as Eva takes a wild swing at me. Her nails dig deep into my arm and my breath catches at the sudden surge of rage building up with me.

"Flynn, something is wrong," I gasp, doubling over as a pain shreds through my mind. It feels like both halves of my brain are being torn in two.

Anger rolls through me in repetitive waves as Flynn struggles to keep me upright. I can barely see as more hands reach for us, but somehow he manages to drag me free.

Dozens of voices spill through my mind as we collapse to the floor on the other side of the closed double doors. Each one rises and falls with guttural screams that make me twitch and spasm on the floor. Flynn rolls me over but I fight to curl into a ball, clutching my head as I too begin to scream.

"You have to stop yelling, Avery. They are going to hear you and come running!"

The floor feels blissfully cold against my bare skin as I hold myself. Violent tremors work their way through me as I am consumed with the outpouring of hatred.

"I can feel them," I gasp. "They are so hungry!"

Flynn rolls me onto my back and pries my hands away from my head. "I'm really sorry about this."

Drawing his fist back, he lands a solid punch on my cheek. My head slams to the side and my vision darkens when I connect with the hard tile, but it only allows me a momentary relief from the onslaught.

Flynn jumps when an alarm sounds down the hallway and swirling red lights appear in the ceiling. "We have to go, now!"

He tugs at my arms, trying to help me to my feet, but I shove him away. "I can't."

The snarls and growls behind us are terrifying, but no more so than the ones that I hear in my mind. I am a part of them somehow. Acid burns in my throat as I roll to my side and vomit, but am left with only dry heaves, since I have nothing on my stomach to expel.

"They are coming!"

Glancing up through a veil of thick hair, I see four soldiers on fast approach from the far end of the hall.

"Run, Flynn." I push weakly on his arm. "Find somewhere to hide and don't come looking for me."

"I'm not leaving you!"

"You have to."

"No. We do this together, remember?"

"Go!" I scream and shove him back into the wall. The tile cracks around the impact point and he falls to the floor. Groaning as he lifts his head, he belly crawls toward the air vent and yanks it open. Once inside, he pauses to look back at me, and I see fear blooming in his eyes, and I realize that I'm no better than the monster in the room behind me.

The ringing in my ears grows in volume as he closes the vent cover and disappears. I curl back into a ball on the floor and clutch my knees to my chest, quaking as I fight against the hunger that fills me. Not for food but for human flesh.

When someone slides to a halt at my side and rolls me over, I hear a loud intake of breath. "Avery? I thought you were dead!"

The sound of Nox's voice is the last thing I hear before the zombie voices swell to consume every sensory input and knock me into oblivion.

TWELVE

The sound of yelling feels like an ice pick ramming repeatedly through my brain as I open my eyes and squint against the fluorescent lighting overhead. I groan and press my hands to my forehead, willing the room surrounding me to stop spinning like a merry-go-round.

"You lied to me!" an enraged voice shouts off to my right. "You told me that Avery put a gun to her temple and ended it before she could turn. How could you look me in the eye every day knowing that I blamed myself for her death?"

"I understand your reservations about recent events, Nox, but nothing has changed." This second voice sounds small, frail, and decidedly female.

"That's bullshit, Iris. I deserved to know the truth!"

Clamping my eyes tightly shut, I draw up an image of the grandmotherly woman that I met only one time. Now that I can see her face, I remember that she is the one who stayed Cap's hand from killing me. She is the one who sent me to this place, but where is here? I thought I had been transported to some offsite base, but if Nox is here that means...

"Oh, hell," I groan and press back against the floor. Nox is instantly at my side, easing me to a sitting position. "I'm still in that damn hotel, aren't I?"

"In it? No." Iris turns to look down at me but she is no longer the smiling face that I remember. "You are under it."

"How is that possible? People would know if this place existed. The hotel was practically a freakin' monument a few months ago!"

Iris taps the sole of her flats against the floor and looks down at me in the same manner that I imagine she would view a petulant child. "Come now, don't be such a ninny. This grand hotel spreads across nine acres and has been renovated multiple times. Do you really think that it would be impossible to hide a *secret* military facility beneath it?"

"But why? The money to build such a place alone would be staggering."

Iris smiles. "And yet there are locations just like this one spread across our once great nation. Bunkers were a necessary evil in the world that we lived in. It was only a matter of time before someone pulled the trigger and we had to be prepared. This location served a large portion of the Midwest and was intended to be a lifeboat of sorts."

When Nox rubs his hands down my bare arms, sliding over the gooseflesh that has risen there, I realize that it is not a chill that has attacked me, but a sickness that deepens with each layer of conspiracy that I uncover. The hunger for human flesh that I felt earlier has dissipated, and Nox's presence now does not cause me any ill effects, but as I stare up at Iris, I know that I'd like nothing more than to sink my teeth into her throat and tear it out if it ever came to that.

"Are you implying that it was us that released the rabies virus to the public?" I ask.

Nox's hand falls still against my arm and he turns to look up at Iris.

"Honestly, we do not know who attacked first. Some theorized that it was the Middle East while others were sure it was some part of Asia. Take your pick. There were plenty of crazies in the world with the capabilities of engineering the virus. All we know is that by the time things spread, it was too late to retaliate properly and we were too busy barricading the door to mount any real defense."

"What is she talking about, Avery?"

I hold up my hand to silence Nox. "Maybe we didn't start it, but we for damn sure aren't trying to reverse it, either."

"Why should we?" Iris smooths down a few stray hairs falling from her tightly woven bun. "We have you now."

"Will someone please tell me what is going on?" Nox's hands tremble as he holds on to me.

The strength that I felt when I shoved Flynn has vanished just as quickly as the voices in my head. If I were to attempt to stand now, I fear that I would face plant. The floor has yet to stop moving away from me and the stabbing pains behind me right eye linger, but at least for the moment, nothing is trying to invade my mind.

"What's she's trying to say is that I'm crucial to their plans." I look beyond him to stare at a cracked tile on the far wall and will it to remain in one place. The grout is an off white color, but everything else is the same stark, clinical quality. After a moment of silence, I manage to get the rectangular tiles to sit still, but only briefly.

"I don't understand." Nox looks to Iris for answers. "What does any of this have to do with Avery? How is she even alive right now?"

"Wake up and smell the crazy, Nox!" I pull to away from him so that I'm no longer tucked under his arm. "The truth is right in front of you. It always has been, just like when I tried to get you to see it back in that damn kitchen. Iris is a monster and everything that's happening down here is far from kosher. They are killing innocent people right under your nose."

He looks back and forth between us, but I can see how hard he is still fighting to admit the truth that is staring him down. To do so would be to admit that not only had he been completely blind to the goings on in this facility, but that he has unwittingly aided in Iris's monstrous acts too. "Why don't you ask her why she's keeping zombies in her basement, Nox?"

"Iris?" Nox fixes his gaze on the woman. "Is that true? Are there Flesh Bags down here?"

"Of course," Iris says without emotion or hint of remorse. "They are a necessary risk for the sake of expanding our research and are completely under our control."

"Under control? How can you stand there and justify keeping those killers so close to our people? What if one of them found a way to get loose?" Nox's grip on my arm tightens enough to interrupt the circulation running to my hand. It doesn't take long before the tips of my fingers start tingling. "Tell me there is some damn good explanation for all of this. Tell me that Avery was mistaken about the attack we suffered two months back."

Clasping her hands in front of her floral print dress, Iris offers Nox a smile that sends me reeling back in time to when grandmothers were the epitome of goodness. This woman has proven to be nothing more than one fruit cake short and a whole bag of feral cats on top.

"The things that we do in this wing are top secret, Nox. I am not at liberty to discuss matters of state."

"Matters of state?" He shifts to wrap his arm around me again and I let him, but only because I think that I'm the one thing keeping him grounded at the moment, and I'm going to need him to help if I have any chance of escaping this place. "There is no state. There is no government anymore."

"Well, that is where you are wrong." The silvery hair pulled tight at the top of her head draws some of the wrinkles from around her eyes, but can't help conceal any of the crazy that I know lies hidden beneath.

"We are our own government now. We are the ones who will heal this world and find a way to start over again. That is why Avery is so special to us and why we have kept her living status hidden from you."

Nox looks down at me and swallows hard when he can't find the words to say.

"Although I can appreciate your frustration with me at keeping her hidden all of this time, it was done for your own benefit. After losing Zoey, I did not think that seeing Avery would bring you any relief, since she was the direct reason for the poor girl's death."

I place a trembling hand on Nox's arm and feel my heart shatter. "Is it true? Is she really gone?"

Lowering his gaze, he nods.

My throat catches. "I'm so sorry."

"You did what you could for her in that tree and fought to get her help. Her death is not on your hands."

Even though I can tell that he wants to believe the words, the sincerity in them falls short, and my throat tightens more as grief draws his handsome features into something pinched and withdrawn. He blames me and I know that he should. I'm the reason she was dropped in the first place, but as I turn to glare up at Iris, I know that there is blame to be shared around.

"Is she here too?"

Nox goes rigid beside me when Iris lowers her gaze. "Is she?"

"Of course not. She is buried with the others." The old woman's hands flutter in front of her dress as she shakes her head, but I know a lie when I see one. I just pray that Nox never comes across her like I did with Eva.

"My friend was in that room where you keep your pets chained up. Her name was Eva and she was a good person before your military scum got their hands on her. I want to know what happened to her."

Iris's eyes narrow when she turns to look at me. "I don't succumb to idle demands."

"How about forceful threats?" Nox steps forward.

"Come now, Nox. You are a good soldier and I would never want to see you harmed. I must advise you against this course of action, for both your sake and Avery's."

"Are you threatening me?"

Iris nods. "If I must."

Nox glances back at me but his expression is unreadable. He should be ticked, ranting and raging over the veiled lie Iris told about Zoey, but instead he remains deadly calm.

"I gave an oath to protect this place and its people. I would like to believe that there is still something worth fighting for." Nox turns to look at Iris. "I did not sign up for schemes and riddles. If there is nothing to hide in regards to Avery's friend, then why do you feel the need to sidestep?"

A small tic appears under Iris's eye when she slowly turns to look at me. "Your friend did not die here. As you know, she was taken into custody back in St. Louis. She gave birth to a child at the base, but it lived only a few short hours. In that short amount of time, our team discovered a cell mutation that made us begin to wonder if all children born after the outbreak would be affected by. We had to do further research so all local bases were set on alert to begin collecting newly born children.

"Once the deceased newborn proved to no longer be of use, we planned to use the mother, but as you are well aware, the military base that she was being housed in blew up. Her body was found among the remains and we infected her to keep her alive after we lost you."

Nox glances at me but I keep my emotions tightly in check.

"Many of our top minds died during your escape. I was lucky enough to have been posted here at the time. Countless valuable resources were expended in an attempt to find you once more, but you were smart. You evaded us completely and for a time, we thought you had been lost to us. But then one of our patrols spotted you not far from the border. It was a long shot that you would be able to make it so far on foot, but we had to be sure. Your red hair was a beacon and your greatest weakness, Avery."

Pressing my hand to my hair, I realize how foolish I was never to change its color. Of course I would stand out. If I had been blonde or brunette, I would have blended in, but my fiery curls stood out among all the rest.

"So you brought Eva here to be your lab rat."

"Of course. She was the closest thing to you, though once she turned, her ability to help us diminished greatly and we sent her back to live among her kind."

Disgusted by her callousness, I spit in her direction, but Nox holds me a safe distance back.

"Avery should have turned within hours of being bitten," Nox says. "You have yet to explain how she is still alive."

"Avery is not like you or me. That is a fact that we have known that for quite some time."

"How?"

"They already had my blood samples, and when they treated me for the infection, they were able to identify me," I answer Nox before Iris can.

He frowns. "That's why you didn't want me to bring you in. You already knew all of this. Why didn't you tell me?"

"Why would I? You were the stranger who gassed me so you weren't exactly at the top of my 'let's be buddies' list when we first met. How was I to know that you weren't in on it when they kept me locked up and under your protection? For all I knew they were keeping me locked up because they were afraid that I would escape before they could brainwash me and they saw you as the best deterrent."

"Brainwash you?" Iris laughs. "No, my dear. That was never our intent. Brian knew that would not be possible. You are too strong willed and distrusting to see anything but the truth. The facade that we presented to you was nothing more than a delay tactic to allow you a chance to heal."

I stare up at the woman and realize that her eyes now hold the same deranged fervor that I saw in Dr. Wiemann. They are all in on it and all so completely blinded from the truth of the horrors that they have committed.

"I suspected before that the breach came from within, but now I understand fully. You cleared the quadrant that I was in last because you wanted me to be bitten. That way you could see firsthand if I really am immune to the virus."

My pulse pounds in my ears in sync with the throbbing pain behind my eye at the thought of all of those innocent people they allowed to be slaughtered. It would have been far easier to just haul me down to their little cage and toss me inside, but then Nox would never have molded quite so nicely to their will.

Nox jerks upright, rapidly looking between Iris and me. "No. That's not possible. They wouldn't..."

"Wouldn't we?" Iris takes a step to the side and sinks down on the edge of a hospital bed. The motor instantly kicks on to adjust for her weight.

This room is a new location to me with four solid concrete block walls and a guard's head easily seen through the small window on the door. Just beside his head, I can see the barrel of his gun.

"I was once an idealist like you, Nox, and was blinded to the horrors of this world. In the beginning, I truly believed that there would be a cure for the virus and that life could go back to normal.

"But we were losing the battle badly. It is true that the mutations were slow progressing and that came as a surprising benefit, since it gave us time to prepare for phase two. Those of us who didn't make it back to the CDC before they went into lockdown set up camp at the Arnold base down south, but someone leaked the nature of our experiments and, well, we all know how that worked out.

"Other bases were working on similar testing, searching not for a cure but for a hybridization that would allow us to evolve with the new world order. We assumed the best work would come out of the CDC, but word reached us that it was overrun. A few managed to make it out alive. Brian was among them."

"Back up a second. Hybridization? CDC?" Nox slowly releases his strong grip on my arm and I rub at my bruised flesh. "Arnold was attacked by raiders searching for ammunition. Cap told me—"

"He told you exactly what he was ordered to say. Nothing more."

Nox blinks, rapidly shaking his head. "No. None of this can be true. I have fought and bled for you, run missions, and saved people on his orders. He wouldn't lie to me."

"You brought survivors to us, but their destination was never intended for the general populace. In truth, we only allowed just a handful through to make your work seem legitimate. We have over 2,000 rooms here, and you were rarely given spare time to explore. It was easy enough to conceal the truth from you and the others until your loyalty was proven.

For a while, we worried that Zoey would tattle on us. She knew and saw far too much, but we quickly realized that despite your love for her, you never believed her fantastical tales about the voices she heard." Iris clicks her tongue. "You really should have believed the poor girl. She was far smarter than you.

"And you, Avery," the woman turns to me, "you helped us to silence her for good. Leading Nox to believe that he had lost both of you ensured that he would work hard and become exactly the man that we needed him to be."

With each damning revelation that flows like guiltless silk from her tongue, Nox's face drains of color and he staggers back against the wall. "I thought I was saving people but I was really just providing you with you test subjects, wasn't I?"

Iris nods and smooths out invisible lines on her dress. "Some of them were useless to us because their genetic makeup was not strong enough to withstand the trials and they quickly became a liability, so we tossed them over the wall and forgot about them. The trouble was that we didn't count on the fact that their newfound hunger would spread so quickly, nor did we take into consideration that their bite would further the mutations. I'll admit that was a mistake on our part."

"So you're the reason for all of the Flesh Bag violence," I say.

It makes sense that it was only once I crossed into Tennessee that I hit hostile territory. The mutated virus had not had time to spread farther, but I fear that it has had plenty of time to swell beyond the borders of this one state. The implication that the CDC has been overrun implies that other places suffered the same fate. Mostly likely because they too were meddling in things best left alone.

"The blood sample analysis from Avery that was sent to us was hardly enough to synthesize a cure. Many of us even debated whether it was a false positive and some held out hope, but I don't live my life based on fantasies or lack of vital information." Iris plows straight through my comment without an outright admission of guilt. "But then Avery showed up on our doorstep in the flesh and gave us exactly what we needed to not only discover the virus' origins but also supply us with the promise of a future."

When Nox turns to glance at me, he looks physically ill. "That's why Cap kept pushing us to follow her trail, even after we lost good men on the mission."

"We had to have her and no sacrifice was too great for the task. The last reports we had were that she and her group were heading south. One among them had an intimate knowledge of this locale so it was safe to assume that he would lead them here."

"Yeah, well he didn't make it," I spit out.

Nox hugs me closer. "That's enough, Iris."

She offers an indifferent shrug and rubs her wrinkled hand across the mattress. "Either way, fortune smiled on us. Avery has proven to possess a rare form of immunity that does not resist the alien virus but instead melds with it so completely as to create something entirely new."

The light of crazed passion returns to her eyes when Iris leans forward.

"The girl you hold in your arms is no longer fully human. She is the first of her kind that we have seen, but we have barely begun to run tests. There is a whole world of knowledge that we must still delve into with her."

A knock at the door causes Iris to rise and she steps back when Brian enters with a stack of files in his hand. This time, he does not bother to try to offer a warm welcome when he towers over me.

"The boy you helped to escape is still missing. Where is he?"

"How should I know?" I curl my knees up into my chest at the breeze of his passing as he moves toward the bed to lay out the files. Although the air feels cool and the tile is frigid against my backside, I soak it in like a man lost to a scorching desert heat would devour water. The ties of my gown are loose at the back and I adjust so that patches of bare skin press against the wall as the throbbing in my head continues.

"We know that you helped conceal his escape with your little screaming antics earlier," Brian continues. "We also know that this entire facility has been locked down with zero access to the hotel above, so he has nowhere to go."

"And yet, despite all of your guns and big brained cronies, you are still utterly incompetent enough to allow a teenage boy to best you." I snort and push my hair back from my face. Bruises line my hands from multiple IV sticks and I see Nox's jaw tighten when he notices them. "That's not saying much for your security protocols, does it?"

A muscle along Brian's jaw flinches as he swallows down his frustration. "You have two options. Either give up the boy's whereabouts and he will be returned to his room without harm to resume testing, or we will remove all of our personnel to the topside and let the Flesh Bags out to find him."

"But there are other people down here!" I protest.

"Yes." Brian nods in instant agreement but looks no less determined. "I'm sure once those monsters are done with the patients they will clean up the mess you've made."

"He ran before Nox found me. There is no way that I can possibly know where he is at this exact moment."

Brian turns his gaze away from me and slowly flips open a couple of files. "Poppy and Willow, twin sisters from the Charleston Safe Zone where Flynn is from, came in with the newest group. They've proven to be real screamers."

When he pauses to look at me over the tops of his glasses, I feel my stomach churn with revulsion. "It would be a shame for Flynn to have to listen to their shrieks while they are torn apart, limb by limb, just because you remained silent."

"Stop this!" Nox roars and pushes up to his feet. "How can you stand there and talk about this like those two girls are things that can be cast aside without thought? They are people, Brian. Little girls who are probably scared and alone. Doesn't that matter to you?"

Brian smothers over a smile and taps a file with his finger. "They showed promise in the initial testing stages, but when introduced with the virus we watched as their cells began to mutate, giving way to the stronger host. They fought the desecration better than most and for a while we wondered if they might make a new link in our chain of understanding, but this morning while Avery was foolishly trying to escape, they took a turn for the worse. It would appear that they don't have much time, either way, but I assure you a bullet to the head would be far less cruel than leaving them for the Flesh Bags to gnaw on."

"You've murdered them!" Nox starts forward but the door to the room suddenly swings open and two men enter with guns raised. Cap and Jax look deadly serious as they train their sights on Nox. "Is this how it's going to be now? You turn on your own man, your brother in arms, for the sake of insanity?"

Jax leers at Nox but Cap stares back for a moment before lowering his gaze. "What they are doing here is going to save the world, Nox. You have to understand that," Cap says.

"Bullshit!" A vein pulses down his forehead as his clenches his fists at his sides, leaving me in his shadow. "They are torturing little girls. How does that make us any better than the monsters that we kill each day?"

Cap swallows hard but his finger on the trigger doesn't waiver. "I have my orders."

"From who? Iris? Brian? They aren't your commanders! They are two sick puppets with their finger on a trigger button and every reason to push it! You can't let this happen. It's wrong and you know it."

"There is no right or wrong in this world anymore," I whisper from behind him and everyone turns to look at me. "Isn't that what you said just after you told me you were going to put me down, Cap? It's just us versus them now. I guess at least now Nox knows whose side you are really on...your own."

"I looked up to you, man! You were the one guy who I could trust to always do the right thing."

"One man's perception of what is right can vary greatly from the next," Brian responds.

Nox's eyes narrow and his chest rises and falls as he struggles to hold back his anger.

"Stand down, soldier," Cap says as he takes a step forward. "Those girls' lives are not worth losing yours over."

Before I can yell out a warning, Nox turns and slugs his commander, sending the man staggering back several steps. "You're no better than they are!"

Blood seeps from Cap's nose as Nox stands up straight only to find Jax's gun pressed to his heart. "Do it, I know you want to."

"Yeah, I really do." Jax's finger twitches over the trigger and the smirk on his face tells me that he's been itching for this moment. Whatever the beef is between them, it definitely runs deep. My guess would be Jax was overlooked for leadership, too, when Nox arrived on the scene. That means Ryker and Jax both hold a grudge that I'm not sure Nox can survive now that he knows the truth.

"Enough," Brian calls out with a bored tone. He makes a show of stacking his folders, turning them this way and that as he straightens them as Jax backs down but not without a hard jab to Nox's sternum first. "He has made his bed. Now he gets to lie in it."

"Sir?" Cap wipes at the blood that continues to pour from his nose.

"Leave him with the girl. We will deal with him after the cleansing." Brian smiles at Iris and then ushers her toward the door. I look up to see Ryker standing guard when the door opens and feel the salt in the wound deepen further when he grins at me.

"You son of a bitch," Nox lunges forward but I grab onto his arm.

"He's not worth it."

"Indeed," Brian agrees and slides past Ryker and then allows Iris to move past him. "Sound the alarm and evacuate the floor. Release the hounds once everyone is clear. We don't want any accidental deaths today, do we?

"These are your orders, soldier. Sacrifices must be made for the good of all," Brian says when Cap hesitates to follow. "Don't worry about them. This room is impenetrable. Nothing will be getting in or out until we open the door."

Cap presses back his shoulders and a blank expression falls over his face. "Aye, sir. I'll see to the evacuation."

"Oh, and Cap," Brian turns back when he reaches the door. "Everything needs to be removed from this room. Let's not take any chances with these two, shall we?"

"Of course." Cap waits for Brian to exit and then calls on his radio for assistance.

Beside me, I can feel Nox seething with anger as two soldiers that I've never seen before soon make quick work of eliminating everything from the room.

"You need to remove your clothing, sir," a young, pimply faced kid says with a slight hesitation in his voice.

"Like hell I will!"

"We both know that you are still armed, Nox. Don't make this harder than it has to be." Cap and Ryker step forward and make their presence and their guns well known.

I lower my eyes while Nox begrudgingly strips down to his tank and boxers.

I have no clue what on earth they think he is capable of doing with his socks but even those are added to the pile.

"You disgust me," Nox spits in Cap's direction as the man turns to follow the soldiers out.

But the commander pauses to look back over his shoulder. "It's nothing personal, Nox. You know that I've always liked you. I had high hopes that you would see things our way." He turns to glare at me. "I guess sometimes it's hard to think with your head when you've got a pretty little piece of ass like that standing next to you. I guess I don't blame you. I'd have taken my shot with her if I'd had the chance."

"You bastard!" Nox lunges forward but the door locks in his face and seals the room shut with a hiss. He slams his fists against the metal door when Ryker glances at him through the glass and then walks away.

"It's no use," I say, resting my head back against the wall.

"You're just giving up?"

"I'm being realistic. Didn't you hear that hiss when the door closed? Those aren't normal locks on that door and I'm guessing this room was designed like a safe room. Brian was right. Nothing is breaking in and we sure as heck aren't going to find an easy way out."

"So we are trapped." Nox turns and begins to pace. I understand his need to move but don't have the energy reserves to manage it myself.

"You didn't really think they would let anything get in here and chew on me, did you?" I laugh bitterly. "I'm too valuable to them alive."

"And me?"

"My bet is that you've become a liability that they are unsure of how to deal with. They will probably head up those stairs and spend their time discussing your fate while ignoring the screams from below."

A low rumble rises in his throat just before he turns and slams his fist into the wall. It doesn't even crack or dent. Rising unsteadily to my feet, I walk over to him and take his hand in mine, brushing my fingers over his split skin. "Hurting yourself won't help."

"It makes me feel better." He breathing hitches when I lace my fingers through his and he curls his hand around mine. "I'm sorry that I didn't come for you. If I had known—"

"You would be dead already." I look up into his face and see pain, regret, and a dozen other emotions tangling together. "There was nothing you could do for me back then, but there is something you can do for me now."

"What?" He steps closer, holding my hand now. "Name it."

"Survive, no matter what." I reach up and use my fingertips to smooth away his frown lines. "I'm going to need you when all of this is done."

"For what?"

"Iris was right about me. I did help take down the St. Louis base, and after what's just happened, I'm going to do it again."

THIRTEEN

The Flesh Bags come down the hall with a thundering of feet and howls that set the hairs on the back of my neck standing up straight. Nox moves toward the door to look out and blocks the view of the window. I know that he is itching to be out there and fighting against this injustice just as much as I am.

He slams his fist uselessly against the door as the first scream comes from somewhere down the hall. "This is murder!"

"I know."

Many more screams will follow and there isn't a damn thing that we can do about it.

Nox presses his forehead against the glass as tears slip from my eyes with each cry of terror that suddenly cuts off.

"Those poor people are being torn apart. Can you imagine what it would feel like to see something eating you while you are still alive?"

I shudder at the thought. "I pray that they die quickly."

He turns back to look at me. "How can you say that?"

"Because I know what the transition feels like," I say simply. "It begins almost the instant after their teeth pierce your skin. It is horrific feeling your humanity begin to slip away."

Nox swallows hard. "Do you...do you remember much of it?"

"Bits and pieces." I lower my head and draw my legs up, hanging my hands over my knees as I focus on the floor instead of him. "There was pain and fear. I knew Cap would turn on me after you left, so looking down the barrel of his gun wasn't something that I was afraid of."

"What were you afraid of?" His hands are still white knuckled against either side of the window as he looks back at me over his shoulder.

"I'm terrified of becoming like them." I slowly look up at him. "I can hear them, Nox, not with my ears, but with my mind as well. Somehow, I'm a part of them now. I can feel their rage and sometimes..."

"What?"

I close my eyes. "I feel their hunger too."

His sharp inhale tells me all that I need to know. "You aren't one of them, Avery. You can speak and think."

"So can they." I open my eyes. "You told me that night in the tree that they were smart, but you have no idea just how much so. They are intelligent, Nox. They can think, form plans, and they can hunt together in ways you never dreamed. It's almost as if something is drawing them together. I can't quite put my finger on it but I get a sense that something is leading them toward a purpose."

"Like an end game?"

I nod. "All I know is that those things out there haven't completely lost their memories. They blame Iris, Brian, and everyone else in this building for turning them into monsters. They want revenge and are more than eager to be given this opportunity to take it."

Nox pushes off from the door and turns to face me. "But those people are innocent. They haven't harmed anyone."

"The Flesh Bags don't care. All humans are the same now. And their hunger..." I chew on my lower lip. The instant I speak of it, I am struck with an awareness of him that I don't like. I can smell him, hear the pounding of his heart, and within seconds, my mouth has begun to water.

"What? What about their hunger?" He hurries forward and crouches in front of me.

"It is growing with each bite they take."

Nox struggles to hide his revulsion while I look away. I can't admit to him that I no longer feel it as strongly as he does. He is silent for a minute, but that silence becomes a haunting symphony of screams for help that leaves me clutching my stomach.

"Did they do this to you? The effects that you're feeling...will they be temporary?"

"I don't know," I whisper. "But I think that Iris was right. I'm more than human now, Nox. I don't know how to explain it. I'm me and yet something more as well. It's all just really confusing right now."

He places a hand on my arm. "I'm sorry."

My smile feels forced as I look up at him. "Maybe it's not all bad. It seems like I may have super strength now."

"Really?" He sinks down onto the ground beside me. "That could be cool. Anything else beyond the scary as hell two-way radio you seem to have with the Flesh Bags?"

"Well," I lean against him for support, "I think I can see in the dark too."

"Okay, now *that* is cool. I may be a tiny bit jealous of you now."

I know that he's just trying to make me feel better, but I let it work. There is no way to block out the death screams that seem to come from all corners of the facility or the truth that somewhere among them are Eva and Zoey. Not even the growling in my mind is loud enough to save me from the horrors that lie just beyond our door, but somehow, just like before, Nox makes it all seem just a little less frightening.

"I'm glad you're here with me."

He smiles and leans into me. "Just like old times, huh?"

"We really need to stop meeting like this."

My words have a sobering effect and guilt sweeps in to steal away my smile. What right do we have to be smiling when so many people are being torn limb from limb?

With a cry of surprise, Nox flinches beside me when a dull thud sounds at the door, and I look up to see the outline of a smeared handprint illuminated on the glass with each cycle of the red emergency lights. I know it is bloody, not because I can see its fresh crimson color but because of the way the curve of the palm drips slowly down the glass.

Lurking in the shadows of the hallway, I see a flash of white.

"You're sure they can't get in here?"

I nod and then realize absently that he isn't looking at me. "I am."

"Why? Because Brian and Iris need you? You're willing to stake your life on that?"

He is far paler than I have ever seen him and I wonder if he too is replaying the final moments we spent together in the kitchen before I was bitten. I know from his earlier words that he was nearly consumed with grief over losing Zoey and I. The guilt must have been suffocating, but it wasn't his fault. I made my choice and did what I had to do.

My infection and subsequent life are not on him.

He reaches out to take hold of my hand as I struggle to find my voice amidst the snarling in my mind. "I have to believe that on this one thing we can trust them."

He slowly nods as a face appears in the door's window. The brilliance of its all-white gaze is a startling contrast to the darkness of our room. Although it darts its hungry eyes toward Nox, it immediately fixates on me. Craning its neck back, it releases three short barking sounds.

"What is it doing?" he whispers.

"It knows I'm here and it's relaying the message."

"And I'm guessing that's a bad thing."

I squeeze his hand as I try to interpret the barking sounds. It is like taking baby steps into a new language and I only catch a partial meaning, but it is enough. "Let's just say we really want that door to hold."

"Will the others come? Can we somehow draw them away from the survivors?"

Using myself as bait doesn't feel like a great idea, but I would be willing if there was a way. Looking around the room, I narrow my gaze to peer through the darkness, preferring the moments when the red lights blink out so that I can refocus.

"There is a small vent overhead. It's the only access point. I guess I could smear some blood on it and hope that it's enough to draw them in."

"How do you know...never mind. I remember now. You've got a built-in night vision. But how are you going to cut yourself? We don't have anything sharp in here with us."

"We have floor tiles."

Nox turns to look at me. "They are grouted and sealed, Avery. There's no way that we can—"

I bunch my fingers into a fist and slam it into the floor. A spider web crack appears around my hand

"Holy shit!" Nox scrambles to push himself in front of me in the dark. "It's breaking in. Stay behind me!"

His eyes are wide with fear as he reaches blindly for me. I take hold of his hand with my free hand while my other sifts through the tile shards until I find one large enough to do the job.

"It was just me. Relax."

"Relax? Did you just punch a hole through the floor?"

"It's not exactly a hole." I laugh and release him. Running the tile shard across my palm, I cut just deep enough to draw blood and then use his shoulder to push up to my knees. "I'm going to need you to lift me up."

His hand fumbles along my arm until he loops under my armpit and together we stand. The Flesh Bag at the door clicks its teeth and weaves in the window, watching my every move.

I guide him toward the vent. "It's right here a few feet above my head. Grab my waist and hoist me up there."

"I'm starting to have second thoughts about this plan."

I'm glad that I'm not the only one, but it is too late for that. Those people need my help and I'll be damned if I'm going to give up now.

Nox plants his feet and wraps his arms around my waist. He lifts me easily, pressing his face against my stomach as I squeeze my hand to draw out more blood then I coat the vent.

"That's it," I call and tap him on the shoulder. Nox slowly lowers me to the ground but he doesn't let go.

My hands press against his chest, feeling the rise and fall as he breathes deeply. I stare up at him as he tries to see me in the dark. With each flicker of the red emergency light, he focuses on me.

"Nox?"

"Shh." He whispers and his fingers flinch against my hips as he holds me close. "I thought I lost you once. I won't do that a second time."

When Nox lifts a hand to cup my face the zombie at the door growls and beats against the door. I feel a sudden blast of anxiety from the Flesh Bag and start to turn away to look at it but Nox holds me still.

"I wasn't right after your death," he says, softly running his thumb across my lips. "Cap told me you went on your own terms, but that didn't ease my guilt. Even after all you did, I still lost Zoey. The only reprieve I felt was that at least you didn't know. That you were in a better place, but here you are, back in this hell hole because of me."

"No." I press my hand against his heart. "None of this is your fault."

"I could have let you stay in that attic. I should have."

Raising my hand to place it on his cheek, I lean up onto my toes. "If there is one thing that I have learned, it's that being a survivor means picking your battles and admitting defeat when there is no other option. What is happening now, your decision to bring me here, even what happened to Zoey, happened for a reason. None of those were defeats, Nox. They were simply things we could not avoid."

I can feel the turmoil seething with him as his jaw clenches. "But they were orchestrated."

"Yes, and the desire to see Brian and Iris torn apart by the very monsters they have just unleashed burns deep within me. I will see to it that justice is served for these people. I know how crippling guilt can be. I have lived with it for far too long."

Swallowing hard, I close my eyes and lower my head. "Maybe it's time that we forgive ourselves. Maybe it's time to start living again."

I love Cable still and always will, but he is gone and there is nothing that I can do to bring him back. To linger and mourn long after isn't living at all.

Standing in Nox's arms, I realize that Cable would want me to be happy. He would want me to find hope again, even if that meant finding someone new to share this fucked up life with.

"Can you sense me the same way that you do with them?" Nox asks after several moments of silence between us.

I know that each scream pierces him as deeply as it does me because of the way he clings tightly to me. As if together we form two ends of a lifeline and are terrified of letting go.

"Not in any way that you would like," I whisper, feeling a shift in my thoughts to something darker and far less hopeful. It is a stark reminder that I am no longer the Avery he once knew.

"Meaning?"

With a heavy sigh, I draw my hand back from his face. "I can smell the hormones that naturally leak from your pore and hear your heart beating as clearly as if I had pressed my ear to your chest.

"I see." Nox lifts his head and his height advantage conceals his expression from me. "So does that mean that you want to—"

"No. I do not want to eat you," I laugh. "I'm just aware of you in new ways."

"Are they good ways?"

When he increases the pressure on my hips, drawing me so close that I begin to press intimately against him, I grow rigid in his arms.

"Avery?"

"I'm fine." The new waiver in my voice tells a different story and I feel Nox's hesitation. "I just...this feels a bit too familiar."

Nox is silent for a moment as I slowly release a breath. I like Nox. He has proven to be a decent guy, but *knowing* I should move on and actually *allowing* myself to has proven to be two very different things.

My physical response to him is undeniable. My palms tingle and my heart races with each touch of his hand but there is also fear welling up within me. Caring means that have to I open myself to more pain. Can I really risk losing someone else?

And what about the changes I'm going through? Will I always be me or will I slowly lose myself to the strong urges that I feel?

"I fell in love before I came here. I didn't mean to. Hell, I fought against it with everything I had, but in the end, I lost the battle. I told you that he broke through my defenses but I never told you that he changed me too. He made me need someone for the first time in my life.

"After he became infected, I watched him slowly slip away. That was before these new mutations, but he didn't want to go out like that. So he asked me to end it."

Tears slip freely from my eyes as Nox raises his hands and draws me into his chest just to hold me.

"All along, I have blamed myself for caring when I knew that this was the only possible result." After wiping at my nose, I look up at him. "I'm afraid, Nox. Not of those things out there, but that I've allowed you to slam through a door that I was sure could never open again."

His arms tighten around me as he rests his chin on top of my head. "You don't have to do this, Avery. I would never try to change you or pressure you into anything."

"I know." I lean back and smile up at him in the temporary glow of the emergency light. "I think that's why you scare me in some ways. You let me be me. You let me make mistakes and foolishly run head first into danger because you accept me for who I am. No one has ever done that before. Not even him."

"Why not?"

I feel his tank grow moist with my tears. "Because he always saw the best in people. He was kind and generous and believed the world could fix itself. When he looked at me he saw a woman with buried strength that could overcome her past."

"No," I whisper. "I just learned to accept it."

Nox smiles. "Then isn't that the same thing?"

"I guess in some way it is." I lean back to look at him. "You helped me to see that today. Seeing your guilt and the pain that you have felt over losing Zoey and then discovering that I was alive woke me up. You freed me, Nox."

He strokes his hand along my back and this time I find the touch to be comforting once more. "I'm glad but we both know that you still love him."

Am I in love with Cable still? After three months, the ache in my chest has lessened, but it is still present. I know that I will never forget him, never fully move on, but perhaps that's the point that he was trying to tell me in the very end. Hearts have the ability to make room for new people.

"I do. He was a good man who deserved to grow old and play with grandkids, not wither away in a filthy cave. And now I can't help but wonder if my blood could have saved him."

"Avery, don't."

"Why not? Isn't that what Brian and Iris are hoping for? That by blending my blood with someone I can help them become immune too?"

The heat radiating off of him feels intense as I cling to him as tears of fear, of pain and regret, of every ounce of anger that I have held on to since I lost Cable.

"I feel like I failed him, Nox. What if history repeats itself? What if I allow myself to care for you and you disappear too?"

"Shh." Nox rocks slowly, brushing his hand gently over my hair. "You haven't failed anyone and I'm not going anywhere. I'm too stubborn to let some filthy Flesh Bag get me."

"Death comes for us all eventually." I protest. "Before he died he asked two things of me: to save him from becoming a monster and to find his brother. How am I supposed to do that while I'm stuck in a place like this?"

"Is that why you were coming south? Because you were looking for the brother?"

I nod and curl my fingers around his shirt. The dull thud of the Flesh Bag pounding against the door fades and I look up to see that the window is empty now. I stretch out my mind to find it, but feel nothing. It's almost as if a curtain has fallen between us.

"You were right to try to avoid us," he says, drawing my focus back. "I only wish that I'd walked away from that attic and left you in peace."

"I would have died if you had."

"Maybe." He places his chin on top of my head again and holds me tight. "But I have a feeling you would have found a way. You're too stubborn to die."

"Seems like I took that stubbornness to the extreme now, huh?"

Nox's chest rumbles with laughter then he pushes back from the hug and he lifts my chin so that I can look up at him.

"And for that, I'm glad," he whispers. I hold my breath as I watch him lean in. A second later, I feel the softest brush of his lips against mine. There is no hesitation in his touch. Instead, I feel a gentle respectfulness as he kisses each of my cheeks and then my forehead in return.

"I meant what I said earlier. I will never pressure you, Avery. You have my word on that. We can move as fast or as slow as you want."

I laugh and gently brush my fingers over my lips. "I bet that's what you say to all of the girls."

Nox snorts and shakes his head. "Actually, it usually goes a bit more like—"

"Just shut up before you ruin the moment." I take hold of his face and kiss him, long slow and deeply. His lips move against mine and when his tongue tentatively parts my lips, I allow him access but he soon pulls back.

"Well," he grins down at me. "I'll take that as you're willing to at least consider that whole jumping into bed on the first date sort of thing."

I punch him in the arm and he stumbles backward, laughing against the wall. "Only joking!"

It feels wrong to laugh during a time like this and yet once I start, I find that I don't want to stop, because I fear that the moment I do, I will fall apart all over again.

"At least I made you smile," he whispers and this time presses his lips to my temple.

"Being a jackass does have its advantages at times."

"Too right!"

I feel myself reacting to the slow, delicate touch of his hand as he traces it up and down my arm, but something feels different and I crane my head away to listen. "Do you hear that?"

"Hear what?"

"Exactly. There aren't any Flesh Bag snarls or screams. It's silent out there."

Nox takes hold of my hand and together we walk over to the glass window and peer out. There is a body on the floor below us. I can see that the man's intestines have been ripped out and pulled down the hall, stretching out of sight. Once the emergency light turns back on Nox will see it too.

"Can you sense them?"

"I'll try." Focusing inwardly, I try to search for any signs of a nearby Withered but there is no anger, rage or hunger. I feel nothing beyond emptiness.

"What do you think—" Nox breaks off at the sound of a hiss in front of us and the door lock clicked. "Shit! Barricade the door!"

"No, I think it's okay."

"Are you serious? There are Flesh Bags out there!"

Placing a hand on top of Nox's, I ease his fingers off of the door latch. "Trust me. I'll know if we get close to one."

I don't blame him for his hesitation or reluctance to just throw open the door and march through Hell's battleground, but I know what I feel, and right now, I feel nothing. In truth, this could be a terrible plan based off of faulty abilities that I am hardly in control of, but something has happened and I need to know what it is.

"Trust me," I whisper and slowly draw the door open.

Outside of our safe room, the siren blares at eardrum-shattering levels. Nox moves forward every few seconds in time with the pulsating light and we tread lightly around the disemboweled man to find several others strewn across the ward.

"Don't look," he advises as he steps over a body and my throat clenches shut at the sight of the small hand clinging tightly to a teddy bear.

"They will pay for this." I sink down and gently tuck the bear under what remains of the girl's arm. She will never again run or play or laugh and for that Iris and Brian will die.

Nox stumbles forward, dragging me behind as we return to the wing that I was held in. Here we find that the body count is much higher and blood is splashed across walls, ceilings, curtains and the floor, making our footing on the slick tiles precarious.

This is also where we discover our first zombie body. It lies across a man whose lifeless eyes stare accusingly up at us, but I do not focus on him but rather the foam leaking from the Flesh Bag's mouth. The whites of its eyes are ruptured and spilling with blood. The skin, though still ghostly pale, has hemorrhaged and blood seeps from its pores. Its fingers are blue and ribbons of veins are easily seen along its bare flesh in the overhead emergency light.

"Avery, don't!"

Nox tries to grab hold of me as I drop to my knees but I shake him off. I have to see. "It looks like it's been poisoned."

"Sure has!" Nox and I are instantly on alert when a shadow shifts down the hall from us, heading in our direction. "I'd like to take full credit for it but Poppy and Willow made the connection first. They may be a little off in the head but they are truly brilliant."

"Flynn!" I rise up to my feet and hurry to give the teenager a hug but stop the instant I get a whiff of him and pull back. "You stink!"

"That's what happens when you take a bath in Rotter muck. It isn't pleasant but it's effective. Let me get just a hair closer than I would have sporting my own scent."

Nox comes to stand behind me. "Is this the kid Brian was hunting for?"

Flynn grins and holds out his hand. Despite his aversion to the blood and guts coating his bare skin, Nox accepts his hand. "Old four eyes never stood a chance. I spent my fair share of time back in Charleston learning from the best and most devious minds I know. I can hide when I need to."

Tugging on Flynn's arm, I draw his attention back. "How did you kill them?"

"Easy." He doubles over to pull off the extra-large hospital gown over his head and reveals a smaller, slightly less filthy one beneath. "I shot them up with your blood."

I'm sure that as I stand there staring at him with my eyes wide and my mouth gaped that I look ridiculous, but that wasn't exactly the answer I was expecting to hear.

"So you took out all of them?" Nox asks.

"Sure. Not all on my own, mind you. I managed to rescue a few before the Dead Heads were let out of their pen. We tried to save as many as we could, but..."

"It's okay," I whisper. "We get it. You did your best."

"I know." For the first time, Flynn's smile fades into nothing. "You look better."

I reach out and take hold of his hand. "I'm really sorry about shoving you. I...I guess I didn't realize my own strength."

"Don't sweat it. Bruised me up a little but I'm tougher than that. Besides, I had time to think it over and I think it's pretty awesome to have you around."

"Why's that, kid?" Nox asks and steps a bit closer to me.

Flynn's grin instantly returns. "She's a freaking super badass now. Avery, the zombie slayer. Has a nice ring to it, right." He leans in close and points to the dead man at our feet. "Are you two as pissed as I am about all of this?"

"Hell yeah, we are," Nox instantly replies.

"Good. Then there's something I want to show you. Follow me."

Together, we follow close behind Flynn as he maneuvers his way down the hall. The closer we get to the end where the zombies were once held, the unease rises within me but Nox's hand on my lower back helps to keep my anxiety in check.

"This way."

Flynn leads us through the double doors and into a room filled with blood-slickened chains. There are no less than ten covered in the gore, but at least ten more that are still clean and waiting for a new victim to contain.

"We shot up the dying too, just in case. I didn't want any of them turning on us while we get to work clearing the facility."

I glance over at Nox and know that he's thinking about Zoey, just as I am thinking about Eva. No matter what happens I have to make sure that he isn't on that cleanup crew.

From somewhere behind us a shrill scream pierces the air and Nox shoves me ahead of him as he takes up a defensive position behind.

"Relax. That's just Poppy and Willow. We positioned a few girls around the wards to keep up the facade of the attack for the ears upstairs so we have time to regroup."

The tension in Nox's shoulders eases as he gives Flynn an appraising once over. "You seem to have this all figured out."

"Well, when you spend days just staring up at ceiling tiles, there's only so many times you can count the cracks. After a while, you start plotting."

"So you thought of all of this before the attack?"

"Well," Flynn rubs the back of his neck sheepishly. "I'd love to take all of the credit for that one too, but there are some cool guys in here you need to meet. They seem to have a good understanding of this place."

Nox and I exchange a worried glance as Flynn marches straight past a puddle of blood and chunks of flesh. He reaches a small metal door at the far end of the room and wraps his fist against it three times.

"It's me. Open up."

There is a sound of clanging and the clattering of the chain followed by a grinding of metal on metal before the door finally gives way to reveal startling white light just beyond. I am forced to shield my eyes until Flynn steps in front of the lighted doorway and stretches his hands out.

"Welcome to the Lab."

FOURTEEN

The space beyond the small metal door that Flynn refers to as the Lab is exactly as I would imagine it to be, apart from the ragged and bloodied group of people hovering in the center of the room. They stand out against the gleaming chrome and brilliant whites that leave my head pounding and my eyes at half-mast as I try to adjust to the light.

"Nox!"

I turn at the sound and see three people break off from the back of the group.

"Kenzie? What the hell are you doing here?" Nox gives both Cyrus and Fletcher firm handshakes of greeting, but his eyes are solely fixed on the girl standing between them in a hospital gown just like mine. "You were supposed to be on patrol."

Despite her obvious weakness, unsteady knees, and dark circles under her eyes, she fights to stand to attention as she salutes Nox. "I was, sir. We ran a mapping mission with Fletch just this morning. We ran into some trouble and then the next thing I knew I woke up here a couple hours ago."

"What happened to you?" I ask as I step forward, noticing the matted blood in her shoulder length wavy hair.

Kenzie gives me a cold, appraising look before dismissing me. "How is she still alive?"

"It's a long and twisted story," Nox says. "Tell us what happened to you and we'll explain everything later."

She pulls down the neck of her gown just enough to show the angry red bite mark on her shoulder.

"Damn thing came out of nowhere. I didn't see it until it was on me. Fletch took it out with a shot to the temple but the others..." She clears her throat and looks away.

"We knew something was going down when we got back to base a little while ago," Fletcher said, scratching at the ruddy beard along his jaw. He looks just as large and opposing as I remember from the first time I saw him outside of the farmhouse, but there is a softness to his gaze that makes me think there is something new between him and Kenzie.

"I ran into Cap on the way to check on Kenzie and was told they were evacuating a part of the hotel, but that Kenzie would be looked after. He refused to say anything more, and as soon as he was out of sight, I grabbed Cyrus and we hid out, watching the mass exodus of doctors coming out of a doorway we'd never seen before."

Cyrus steps forward and places a gun in Nox's hands. "We heard the doctors talking about the cleansing but we never dreamed..."

"I know." Nox places a hand on his soldier's arm. "I didn't want to either."

Fletcher jerks his head toward Flynn. "That kid right there saved our asses. Busted out of a storage room and grabbed us just before those Flesh Bags came storming down the hall. After that, he gave us a quick rundown of the layout and we realized we already knew this place. Hadn't realized it, but Cap had blueprints of this facility on his desk. Didn't mean to be snooping in his stuff but you know me, Nox. I'm like that stupid cartoon monkey that never knows when to stop being curious. I thought they were just plans they kept from Arnold but once we got down here, I realized why Cap and the others disappear sometimes."

"You did well." Nox chambers a round and I watch a physical relaxing of his posture and know that he feels better having a weapon in his hand again. "These people are alive because of you."

"We didn't save enough," Cyrus mutters.

"You never can." Nox presses a hand to Kenzie's cheek. "You're burning up. We need to get her and the others somewhere safe to rest."

"No need." I look up to see Flynn sauntering up to join our group. "One dose of Avery and they should be right as rain."

Fletcher's eyebrows disappear into the brim of his cap. "Excuse me."

"Iris and Brian have been playing mad scientists down here," Nox explains. "They think that Avery's blood can counteract the effects of the transition. She may be the only one that can save Kenzie's life."

Kenzie turns a distrusting glance my way, but all I see from Fletcher is hope. "Is he right?"

I shake my head. "No. Not entirely. Iris and Brian mentioned that there were negative results and I wouldn't advise risking an untested method—"

"Hell no, it ain't untested!" Cyrus interrupts and points back toward the door that we entered. It has been secured behind us. "What do you think took down all of those Flesh Bags out there? Whatever she's got going on in her body is powerful stuff."

"Which is why I'm leery of putting it into someone else's body," I respond. "If my blood can kill one of them, what happens if it's incompatible with her? What if she's already too far gone into the transformation and instead of saving her, my blood poisons her too?"

"It's her decision," Fletcher protests, stepping forward, but Nox eases the man back out of my space.

"I'm just saying that we have no way of knowing if it can work. Are you really willing to take that risk?" I look to each of the men standing around me in turn. She is their friend. They should be just as worried as I am.

"I'm dead either way," Kenzie mutters and we all turn to look at her. "I'm in."

"Nox, help me out here!" I look to him, pleading him to join my case but I see his indecision. "You know this could backfire."

He nods and then moves away to start rustling through several drawers before finally returning with a syringe. "She's right, Avery. If we do nothing she's dead. It's worth the risk. You said so yourself earlier that you questioned if someone could be saved. Don't you want to find out?"

"At the sake of killing her? Hell no. Flynn, you're with me on this, right?" I turn to look at the young man.

"Don't look at me. I'm just the kid in the room." He backs away with his hands in the air. That's when I realize that our small group has become the center of attention. I see a mixture of fear and hope in their eyes and realize that just as easily that hope can be replaced with fear and accusation.

"Nox, please don't make me do this. I can't...not again."

"Shh," he says and reaches out to me, slowly drawing me into his embrace. "It will be okay. I'm right here with you."

From behind his back, someone takes my arm and Nox's hold on me tightens as I try to get free.

"No! Don't do this!" I struggle and buck against him but he is far stronger than I am. Tears streak down my cheeks and when I look up into Nox's face, all I can see are Cable's blank eyes. "You bastard!"

"Got it," Fletcher says and I feel the pressure vanish from my arm.

When Nox releases me I punch him hard enough to send him slamming back into the counter. He groans and sinks to the floor but holds up his hand to command Cyrus to lower the gun he has aimed directly at my head.

"I was wrong about you, Nox. You're just a bad as the rest of them."

"Avery, please." He leans heavily on the counter to pull himself to a standing position. I've hurt him and I can't find it within me to feel guilty about that. "It's for the best."

"No!" I snap and jab my finger toward Kenzie. "If she dies that's on you, Nox. Not me. I tried to warn you."

"I know." He says and takes a step in my direction but Flynn grabs hold of his arm.

"Dude, I wouldn't do that right now. She seems pretty upset."

Nox breathes out slowly as he watched me fight to reign in my anger. I could hurt him right now. The anger mingled with the newfound strength coursing through my veins tells me that I could snap him like a twig if I wanted to. A part of me does as I take several steps back. "Stay with her."

"Of course." Flynn hurries over to my side and gently takes hold of my hand. "Why don't we see if we can get you some clothes? I saw some stuff in the back room that might fit you. I betting you're ready to be out of that medical gown, huh?"

"Yeah." Glancing back over my shoulder one last time, I stare at Kenzie but she refuses to meet my gaze.

Flynn leads me to a storage room near the rear of the lab where three cots have been set up as temporary beds. In one of the cubby holes, I find a pair of female camouflage pants and a white wife beater tank that are close enough in size to make do. Flynn waits outside while I change and I have no sooner buckled my pants and pulled the tank down over my head when Flynn opens the door and closes it quickly behind him.

"Flynn?" There is a crashing sound from behind him and I start forward but Flynn shakes his head, holding out his hands to stop me. We both know that I could move him out of my way if I really want to, but I don't.

"You don't need to see that."

With a heavy sigh, I sink down onto a cot and bury my head in my hands. "I tried to warn them. I tried to save her but no one would listen to me."

"I know." The cot creaks as he sits down beside me. "But can you blame her for wanting to at least try? She was in love, Avery, and she was scared. I know that you can relate to that."

"Of course not, but to die like that..."

"Is still a much kinder death than what waited for her. She wanted to go out in her own way instead of running the risk of forcing Fletcher to be the one to put her down. It would destroy him so she did what she had to.

I get that. My parents weren't given that choice and I was told that my mom is the one who bit my dad. She...she ate his nose and ears off before someone took her out. I saw him after that. I guess the soldiers were fools and thought that he wouldn't turn and because of that, he almost killed me." Flynn places a tentative hand on my shoulder. "Sometimes having hope is the only way to live and she did up until the very end."

I struggle to swallow as my mouth goes dry. "Poppy and Willow are going to die."

"I know." Flynn hangs his head. "I overheard everything they said to you in that room. They should have sent someone smaller into the air vents to find me. Once I realized you couldn't get out, I hurried back to the Lab and prepared."

"They were your friends, right? Do they know?"

"Nah." He brushes sweaty hair back from his face. "I didn't have the heart to tell them. They'll figure it out sooner or later."

Flynn glances over at me as I turn my head away and hear nothing from the room just outside our small storage room. There are no sounds of weeping or mourning. Just an eerie silence. "What do you think will happen now?"

"I don't know." I wish that I could say something to inspire him but I'm fresh out of hope. What is the point of having blood that can save my own ass but is deadly to others?

At least now I know that I couldn't have saved Cable. Maybe that was Nox's motivation all along, but I still can't forgive him for betraying me. Not yet.

"What was Charleston like?" I ask, needing to think about anything else. "Was it safe?"

Flynn leans back against the wall and shrugs. "For a while, it wasn't all that bad. They had fences and enough soldiers to man them. People were bused in weekly from surrounding states but within the Zone life felt oddly normal. We had food, albeit rationed supplies, but it was better than what we'd had on the road. We had houses with power once a day and even a community garden project."

"And school? Didn't you say you went to one?" I rub my temples, feeling the stabbing pain behind my eye grow in severity as my pulse pounds in my ears. I try to focus on the tone of his voice instead as he answers.

"Yep. We had a school bus that would travel to each of the neighborhood testing sites and collect us. My friend Roan even dubbed it Zombie High. He spray painted that shit all across the front of the building the first day he arrived. I'm surprised no one tried to scrub it off but maybe they agreed with him. Turns out he wasn't wrong."

"Wait. Did you say testing sites?"

"Sure." He crosses one leg over the other and ruffles his unruly hair to loosen the matter strands. Even though he removed his stained gown some of the gore has clumped in his hair. "We had our blood tested each day to make sure we were clear. Those who weren't were pulled out of line and we never saw them again."

"How did they know what to test for?"

"No clue. Before all of this, I was a gamer. Didn't really care about studying."

I smile. "I wasn't much interested in school myself. Carry on with your story. Sorry, I interrupted."

"No biggie."

I like Flynn. He's a decent kid who has been through a lot and someone managed to come out on the other side of Hell with a smile and witty banter. I can respect that.

"So things were going pretty much like normal and then everything went to shit. My friend Roan noticed the changes first. They were subtle enough that most of us just blew it off, but he knew. Somehow he saw things others dismissed. He was the one who kept us alive when the base was attacked. We never knew if the first wave hit from within or came from outside but everything imploded at the same time and it just didn't matter anymore."

"How did you manage to escape?"

"I didn't. We fought back and stood our ground but over time, we lost the school piece by piece. We didn't know what we were up against. They picked us off one by one. Some were stupid deaths. Others were down to just sheer panic. After that, I was taken."

I scratch absently at the healed bite mark on my neck. "By who?"

"Men in biohazard suits. I was trying to rescue some kids trapped in the lower grade school when they busted in and took me and a few others. I never saw them again. At least not until I found Poppy and Willow today."

"But you've been here for a while, right? And they only just recently arrived."

Flynn nods slowly with a far off look. "Something's strange about them now. They smiled when they saw me and knew who I was but they were different."

"How so?" I lean forward on the cot, resting my elbows on my knees.

"I don't really know if I can say." He pushes off of the wall and wanders a short distance before turning to head back toward me. "Maybe it was something about their eyes. They look almost dull and lifeless. Like they'd seen something terrible and didn't want to talk about it."

"Did they?"

He snorts. "Haven't we all?"

"Touché."

Flynn shakes his head. "I don't know. Maybe I'm just paranoid now. Places like this have a way of really screwing with your head, but I'm worried about my friends. What if something terrible happened in Charleston and they just don't want me to know about it?"

"So you think they are just trying to protect you? Like you are doing for them?"

"Maybe."

"Or it could be something else entirely. Maybe they were held at a different facility and were transferred here later. Something could have happened to them there that they can't or won't talk about."

"Could be." He purses his lips as he thinks it over. "That might make sense but why risk the manpower for a move like that?"

Glancing at the storage room around me, my gaze falls on several lab coats with names written on with a black permanent marker instead of stitched on. I think back to Brian's words and something bothers me.

"Brian said that they showed signs of a mutation they hadn't seen before, right? What if that was partly due to some previous form of testing? What if they were brought here because I was located and they wanted to see if the progression they had shown in their initial testing phase was accurate? They could have been the next step toward hybridization, just like what Dr. Wiemann, Iris and Brian and working toward."

When he starts to speak, there is a knock at the door and Flynn moves to answer it. He doesn't allow the door to crack open any further than he needs to stick his head out. I can hear him whispering but catch none of the details as I lie down on the cot and close my eyes.

I am tired, soul weary, and scared. The only thing keeping me going is my rage toward Iris and Brian but as I let my mind expand and search, I feel something new. An awareness that wasn't there before.

"Avery?"

I look up to see Nox standing just inside the door. Flynn is gone but I suspect that he hasn't gone far. "What the hell do you want?"

"I know that you're angry and you have every right to be, but I'm not going to make excuses for my actions. She was my soldier and I don't leave anyone behind, ever."

I snort and shove my hair back out of my face as I sit up. "Does that 'proud to be a soldier' crap actually mean anything? You just killed that girl."

"I know," he whispers and his Adam's apple bobs. "But I had to hope that it would work."

"No! No, you didn't!" I push up off the bed, wobble slightly but then regain my footing. "What you needed to do was listen to me, to trust *me* for once."

Nox lowers his gaze to the floor. "I was wrong."

"You're damn right you were." I cross my arms and stew for a moment. "Did she suffer?"

He swallows again and when he refuses to meet my gaze I know the truth. "Well, that's on you too."

"I know."

Turning away, I flex my hands, needing to punch something. Instead, I grab hold of a cabinet and yank it off the wall then chuck it against the door. The wood splinters and falls to the floor. A considerable crack in the door has appeared at the site of impact

"How did you—"

"I don't know!" I scream and turn on him. "I don't know what is happening to me and that should have been enough for you to listen to me! I'm unstable, Nox. Don't you get that?"

I hold no illusions to the fact that the people outside of this room can hear my ranting as I take hold of a cot and toss it. Nox ducks and narrowly avoids taking a metal bar to the forehead.

"Avery, you need to calm down." He steps closer with his hands raised in surrender. "I know that I messed up, but that is no reason to start destroying this place. It may be the only safe haven we have for a while and people need something to sleep on." He glances over at the twisted metal bed. "We can figure this out. We just need time."

"I can't!" I rage and tear down another cabinet. My chest rises and falls as I pant. My thoughts darken and I see red when I look back at him.

"Avery, this isn't you."

Chucking the cabinet aside, I suck in deep breaths, trying to calm down but my anger continues to rise. With a scream, I turn and slam my fist into the wall. "I just feel so angry!"

Even as the words escape my lips I fall deadly still and turn to Nox in a panic. "Oh, God, you're right. This isn't me. Something is really wrong."

"What do you mean?" He instantly closes the gap between us, placing his hands on my arms as I sway in place. I close my eyes and stretch out my mind and instantly recoil. I drop to my knees under the weight of so many voices in my head.

"Tell me what's going on."

"There's going to be another breach."

"Where?"

I lift my eyes to the ceiling. "They are heading for the walls! Oh, God. They will hit every quadrant at the same time. The soldiers will be overrun!"

He grabs hold of my hand and rushes me out into the room. Flynn glances up from where he's kneeling beside a girl not that much older than him. Her arms are a patchwork of bruising just like my own and she looks frail. Whoever she is she's been here a while.

"Nox, stop." I yank on his arm and force him to stop. Fletcher looks up from where he stands bent over a figure draped in a sheet and I feel my chest clench as I look away. "You need to think."

"Our people are about to be killed. We can't just sit down here and let that happen."

"I agree," I say, squeezing his hand. "But for once just shut up and trust me. The breach isn't internal like the last one. The Flesh Bags have come over the walls in large numbers. I'm not talking about a small scouting party. This is a war."

"That's not possible," Cyrus says, walking up behind me. "The walls are heavily manned and high. No Flesh Bag could climb it without being seen."

Closing my eyes, I feel another swell of rage and fight to keep it at bay even as the sounds of the heartbeats around me make my mouth begin to water.

"Nox, I'm telling you this is different. They are communicating with each other and they are highly organized. You can't just run out there with a single gun and hope to win."

"So what do you suggest?" Nox asks.

I see movement just behind him and realize that that other survivors have circled around us. Some look barely able to stand while others appear to be itching for a fight.

"You can't be serious," Fletcher says, pushing off from Kenzie's deathbed. "You've seen what she is capable of and now you want to take orders from her. How do we even know that she's on our side? She could be leading us right into their hands."

"You're wrong. You haven't seen what I'm capable of yet, but I'm the best shot you've got at surviving this," I say before Nox can reply as I step around him to face off with Fletcher. "I can sense them from here and I know exactly where they are. Now if you want to run through the halls and get yourself killed, by all means go ahead. But if you want to live and stand a chance of avenging Kenzie, then shut the hell up and let me tell you how to do that."

"Is she always this bossy?" Flynn asks behind his hand to Cyrus.

The soldier chuckles. "Oh, yeah, she definitely is."

"Anyone else want to bitch at me or do you want to plan out an attack instead?" I turn in a slow circle, feeling adrenaline course through my veins, giving me the strength that I need to get this job done and focus on what is happening right here inside this room.

No one says a word.

"Good. We are going to need weapons and manpower. Nox, I need you to lead our group to whatever armory this place has. Cyrus, I need you to gather men you can trust and meet up with Nox."

"What about me and the big guy?" Flynn pipes up, jerking his thumb at Fletcher.

"I need you to get to Cap's office. You said you saw blueprints. Maybe there are more that will show an underground escape route. We need to get as many people to safety as we can.

"Anything else we need?" Nox asks.

"Yes." I nod and stare straight at doors that will lead us back into my waking nightmare. "We need me."

FIFTEEN

As soon as the cleanup crew heads out to clear a path to the exit, I cross the room and aim straight for the drawer that Nox left partially open earlier to begin removing handfuls of syringes still sealed in their plastic wrappings.

"What exactly did you mean by that?" Nox asks, walking up to survey my stash.

Instead of taking the time to answer him, I begin tearing apart the wrappers with my teeth and making a new pile. Nox places a hand on my arm. "Avery, stop. Tell me what you are thinking."

"Isn't it obvious?" Fletcher says from where he and Cyrus stand at the opposite end of the room counting rounds of ammunition. At least they didn't waste any time preparing for battle. "She's finally gone crazy like I warned."

Ignoring Fletcher's remark, I press my hand to Nox's cheek and turn him so that he's looking at his soldiers instead of focused on me.

"Do you see that tiny pile of ammunition they have? It won't be nearly enough. None of you have faced Flesh Bags in these numbers. The voices in my head...they are staggering. We can't win this war until you and your group reach the armory, and even then, you might not have enough to make a dent."

Placing my arm on the countertop and rolling it over, I hand Nox a roll of IV tubing. "Flynn proved that my blood can kill them. So let's dose them up and give us a fighting chance."

"You're serious? You want me to drain you right before an attack and expect me to be okay with this?"

"No," I shake my head, "but I expect you to still do it."

"This is crazy." Nox shoves the tubing away.

"It's not." I duck my head so that I can get his attention. "Do you remember what I told you while we were trapped back in that room? The reason I let you in is because you accepted me for who I am. Do that now. Prove to me that you can trust me now, instead of forcing my hand like you did with Kenzie."

"But it will weaken you," he protests, holding onto my hand to stop me from shoving the needle in my own arm.

"Just take enough to give these people a fighting chance. That's all I'm asking."

From across the room, I hear a magazine lock into place and see Fletcher shaking his head. Everyone knows the chances of surviving this are slim but his negative attitude isn't helping.

"These people are scared," I whisper, forcing Nox to draw nearer to hear me. "Give them hope."

"Don't ask me to do this." Nox closes his eyes. "I can't risk your life. I won't."

Placing my hand gently over his, I wait until he lifts his head to look at me again. "And I refuse to risk yours, especially if there is a way for me to help. Please, Nox. Let me do this for you and them. You overruled me before but I need you to stand by me this time. Show these people that there is hope."

Nox looks around him and notices that our conversation has not gone unnoticed. Several of the survivors are staring. Others are pacing and muttering to themselves. A few have shrunk down into the corner to hide.

"We are asking them to risk their lives to save the very people who have tortured them and then left them for dead."

"I know," I squeeze his hand. "But some will help us if they think there's a chance to save lives. They were innocent. Let's show them that not all of you are evil. Let's prove to them that there are still some of you who are human."

"Us." He rolls his hand over to take mine in his. "You said you but it should have been us. You are one of us still, Avery. I won't let you think anything less."

"I am not the same person that I was before and—"

"But that doesn't have to mean dangerous," he insists. Drawing my hand up to his lips, he presses a kiss to my fingers. "I'm sorry for how I behaved earlier. It was uncalled for and you're right. I do need to trust you."

"Then let me do this," I whisper and gently place the tubing back in his hand.

Nox swallows hard as his fingers close around the tubing. "I'm only agreeing to partially filled vials."

Several minutes later, I sit on a chair applying pressure to the bandage placed in the crook of my arm. Nox kept his word and took only enough to provide three syringes per person but our group of volunteers now number in the high teens and the blood donation has left me temporarily weakened, just as Nox feared.

He paces in front of me as I rub out the ache in my head while Flynn sits on the counter beside me, banging his shoes against the cabinet.

"We can't wait any longer." Fletcher takes Nox's arm and forces his commander to stop pacing. "Cyrus and the others have cleared the path to the exit and found a small stash of guns. We need to move now if we want there to be anyone left alive up there to save."

"I agree." Slipping down off the table, I fight very hard not to show the wave of dizziness that attacks me. Flynn instantly jumps down and loops his arm through mine to lead me away before Nox can get a good eyeful of my pale face.

"Thanks," I whisper as he easily takes on a bit of my weight when I lean into him.

"You bet," Flynn grins but it quickly fades when he looks back over his shoulder, "but I think you might have to do the next part on your own. Your boyfriend doesn't seem to like me helping you."

"He is not my boyfriend."

Flynn rolls his eyes. "Well, then someone should tell him that!"

He leaves me standing at the metal door to wait while the others gear up. Cyrus' search of the facility on his trip back from patrolling the halls gained us an extra four weapons, which we distribute through the group, but it won't be enough. Working on a buddy system in these conditions is hardly ideal but it's the best chance we have of making it to the armory.

"Take this." When Nox hands me a gun I start to protest but one glare from him silences me. I've obviously pushed my limits with him for the moment.

With Willow and Poppy left in charge of those who refuse to join us, I feel a sense of urgency coursing through me and I'm unsure if it stems from within me or this newfound connection that I have with the Withered. They are here for a reason but I can't get a grasp as to why that may be. Their voices sound as one, a roaring tide that crashes time and time again in my mind and the closer I come to them the harder it becomes to separate my thoughts for theirs.

What I sensed from the Flesh Bags that tore through these halls was more chaotic and individual. The ones tearing apart the hotel over our heads are far more organized and driven.

Flynn hurries on ahead of me, eager to remain close by in case I need him after my bloodletting but he is also none too eager to antagonize Nox as we exit the Flesh Bag holding room and out into the ward. Cyrus and a few of the patients worked hard to clear the way and although we have to skirt around several puddles of blood, all of the bodies and parts have been removed from sight.

Glancing over at Nox I know that he's thinking of Zoey again. I wish that I could have spared him this pain but it was not my doing. Iris and Brian have proven to be rotten to the core and I look forward to getting my hands on them.

Flynn glances down at a broken syringe that lies pressed against the crack between the floor and wall near the nurse's station and kneels to push it over. "If I'd known we would be racing into another battle so soon I would have saved a bit more of your stored blood."

"It's good that you used it all, Flynn," I say. "Now there's nothing left for them to experiment with."

Flynn nods and rising to move on again. From time to time, he glances into the darkness behind the curtains and I can't help but wonder if he is reliving those initial moments when he was forced to fight on his own. It must have been terrifying for someone so young, and yet I suspect that he has seen far more than most living within these walls.

From what little he has told me about the Charleston Safe Zone, bad things happened there and he found a way to survive it all.

Above our heads, a battle is waging that we don't stand a chance of winning. I don't tell the others that. If I do, I fear far too many of them would happily secure the door to the topside and let everyone perish, just as they themselves had been left to a gruesome death,

But I know something that they do not. There will be no survivors if we do not act now. Nearly fifteen hundred people, innocent women, men, and children who had no knowledge of Iris and Brian's plans, will die at the hands of the horde that has swarmed the building. The Withered numbers have grown at a frightening pace and the soldiers are ill-equipped to hold the line.

I am tired of letting fate rule my destiny. I want to make my own path and it is leading me straight into the fiercest battle I have ever known. Even though I know my chances of scraping by again are slim, I feel a sense of excitement all the same.

"You really think you can do this in your condition?" Nox asks as he jogs beside me, keeping a slower pace than I know he would like so that he doesn't leave me behind.

"I will be fine. I'm feeling stronger already."

It was only a partial lie. Never before have I given in to weakness. I have pushed myself to the breaking point, beyond more times than I can count, and somehow I'm still alive and kicking. I just pray that I live to see the next sunrise so that I can prove to Nox that I'm not a girl who needs to be coddled. I'm someone to be respected.

As I jog ahead, I try not to think about how much I hate the heavy weight of the gun in my hands or the sickness growing in my chest. I understand the need to put distance between these monsters and me, but guns make me nervous. I'd rather have an ax or knife in my hand instead.

"We will get through this. I have to believe that," Nox says to no one in particular but I know that everyone heard him. He is a natural born leader and even those who have only just met him gravitate to him.

Glancing over at Nox as the group bunches up when we reach the base of the stairs that lead topside, I grab onto his arm and pull him back. Several of the stragglers push past us until we are alone.

"I need you to promise me something before we go up there."

"Anything." When Nox smiles, I can see the weariness that creeps into his face. Far too much has happened in the past 24 hours and it has taken its toll, both physically and mentally on us.

"If anything happens to me—"

"It won't. I won't let it."

I place a hand on his arm and offer him a small smile. "If something does, I need you to promise that you will search for someone for me."

"You're talking about the brother of that guy you loved?"

I nod then look away as I feel the first sting of tears. I can't let myself get emotional right now.

"I don't really know what happened to him after the world went to shit but his brother said he was in this area so I had to try. I need to tell him..." Closing my eyes, I place my hands on my hips and bend over, sucking in breaths to ease the unwelcomed pain flooding into my chest.

"I get it." Nox stands still beside me, letting me deal with my emotions in my own way. Cable would have pulled me into his arms the instant I showed any sign of weakness, but Nox doesn't. Somehow he just knows that right now I need to spit this out and then suck it up and focus. "What was his brother's name?"

"Lenny," I choke out and wipe at my eyes. I hate crying. I always have.

When I look up, I see that Nox's jaw has gone rigid and I wonder if it bothers him that I'm still so easily affected by Cable's death. I suspect that the kiss we shared earlier was not as innocent as he played it off to be and I know that a part of me wanted more. Opening myself to him felt good Terrifying but definitely good.

Nox has now been with me on two different occasions when I was sure that death was knocking at my door. I have a feeling that situations like this have a way of bonding people together, even when you don't mean for them to.

I also know that I will never allow myself to need him in the same way that I needed Cable. One heartbreak is enough for a lifetime.

"It's time," Cyrus calls down from the top of the stairwell and Nox takes hold of my arm to lead me up through the group until we are at the front. "You guys ready for this?"

"Hell no," Nox replies with a strained voice. I look over at him and see that his head is lowered and his gun is pointed at the floor instead of the door. His eyes are closed and his lips are moving. I realize just before Cyrus shoves the door open and enters the upper hall with a bellowing war cry that Nox is praying.

I also realize that he never agreed to my request to find Lenny if something were to happen to me.

The instant Cyrus disappears from sight, I hear gunfire as he clears a path for us. I hurry up the final steps behind Nox and turn right, making sure to stay directly behind him, while several others veer left and into darkness. The power to the hotel appears to be out.

"There's nothing better than fighting blind." Fletcher turns on the light over his gun as the door behind us slams shut. I listen to the hollow thud of the lock falling into place, sealing the bunker off against attack. There is no going back now.

"Feels like old times," Nox mutters to Fletcher and I wonder how many abandoned homes they have searched through or how many caves they have cleared on their missions. How many times have they been forced to fight at a disadvantage just like this one?

I hear the hum of Nox's light just before it flickers to life and pain immediately stabs at my eyes. I lift my hand to block the light out of instinct but Nox quickly moves on ahead and I'm returned to blissful darkness. It is only after I blink several times that I realize that I can see clearly, not just blurred shapes in the dark but actual details.

"This never gets old." I reach out and trace my finger along the contours of the door beside me. I can actually see the wood grain.

As I marvel at how easily it is for me to see the men around me, I realize that if the mutations in my blood have enabled me to see this clearly in pitch darkness, then the Flesh Bags are sure to possess the same abilities.

"Nox!" I rush ahead and grab onto his arm just before he rounds the corner directly behind Fletcher. "We have to turn the lights back on."

I keep an eye on his light as he lowers his gun and am relieved that he keeps it trained on the floor. "I'll admit that having light would definitely help but we have bigger issues to deal with first, like getting enough guns to kill these bastards."

When he starts to walk away, as if his words should be enough to end the debate, I yank him back with enough force to nearly take him off his feet. Realizing the strength that I've just displayed, I instantly release him and see that I've torn his sleeve completely off and left his skin exposed.

"I'm sorry but you need to listen to me. The Flesh Bags can see in the dark just like me and I'm talking with crystal clarity. That's why they hate the light. They have become night dwellers by nature and I think that turning the lights on will anger them but also slow them down. They will be forced to retreat to darkness or risk opening themselves up to danger while they shield their eyes."

"How do you know all of this?"

I hesitate. "Because I have night vision too remember?"

"Did she just say she has night vision?" I hear Flynn ask but Nox waves him off, forgetting that neither of them can see very well in the dim lights attached to two of the guns.

"You need to trust me on this, Nox. Turning on the lights is the only way to give us the advantage."

Nox thinks it over for a moment and then sighs. "Even if I wanted to agree with you, we have no way of contacting Cyrus to let him know and the generator is in the opposite direction of the armory. We can't risk heading in that direction with so little ammunition."

"I agree. That's while I'll be the one going," I say without hesitation.

"Hell no! I'm not letting you go alone."

I reach out and place my hand on his cheek in the hopes that a softer touch will help to sooth him. "I can sense them and I can see them just as easily as they can see me. I'll find a way around so that I don't have to fight."

Fletcher reappears from around the corner, looking like his usual disgruntled self. "This isn't the best place to stop and have a chat, you know? This place is crawling with those Flesh Bags."

Glancing around the corner, I shake my head. "You're fine. That hall is clear."

Fletcher shoots Nox an incredulous look as he refuses to lower his weapon or the light out of my eyes, but Nox waves him off.

"We stopped because I have an idea—" I say.

"A bad one," Nox interrupts me.

Fletcher rubs his forehead. "Look, I don't care what sort of lover's spat you two are having but I'm not going to sit around here and wait for you two to hash it out. This place gives me the creeps."

Looking beyond Nox's determined face, I see Fletcher as I saw him the very first time he arrived at the farm: large, well built, strong as an ox and motivated. Exactly the sort of man I need at a time like this.

"The Flesh Bags have developed a natural night vision and you are walking into a trap. The only way to save your asses if for me to get to the generators and turn on the lights," I say, focusing on Fletcher. "Once the lights are back on the zombies will be blind and you can take them out before they can retreat. If I do this countless lives will be spared."

Fletcher scratches at his beard. I can see flecks of blood in it and wonder if it came from Kenzie before she died. "That actually sounds reasonable to me."

"It's not." Nox turns on Fletcher. "We have a plan and we are going to stick to it. End of discussion."

"The plan will fail," I say. I see movement beyond Fletcher and realize that Flynn has moved in close to listen in.

"But you just said—"

My fist flashes out and slams into Fletcher's jaw before he can finish his statement. "What the hell was that for?"

"I was just making a point." Hitting his chin should have hurt, but it didn't. As I flex my fingers I realize that my body absorbed the brunt of that punch with hardly any physical discomfort. "You didn't see me coming until you felt the pain and a Flesh Bag won't stop with a single punch.

Now take that advantage I just used against you and amplify that by a thousand and you might be getting close to the reality of what you face if you remain in the dark. You can hear the screams and the roar of pounding feet. These things aren't slowing down. They are gaining momentum. The only way to stop this horde is an attack that they won't see coming."

Fletcher rubs at his jaw as he glances at his commander. "Sir?"

"Your orders are to stand down." Nox practically growls as he yanks me back several paces. "That is enough, Avery. I won't have you risking your life for us again. The group is going to stay together."

"And how long do you expect that to last?" Flynn asks from behind Fletcher and we both turn to look at him. "We are going to be picked off one by one. That's how it always happens. How sure are you that in the dark you will really know if it's a Dead Head that you are targeting instead of one of your own people? Mistakes happen during war and you know it. I vote for Avery's plan. Let's light the bastards up and take them out!"

From behind me, I hear several others mutter in agreement.

"I'm in command and I say it's not going to happen," Nox roars with a tone of finality that leaves zero room for misinterpretation.

I stare Fletcher down, pleading silently for him to step up and pull rank just this once. The muscles along his jaw flinch as he grinds his teeth and I see that he wants to and that he knows I'm right but then he lowers his gaze and shakes his head.

"Fine," I say, "I'll go to the armory with you but as soon as we are armed then we hit the generator."

Flynn rises up onto his toes to look at me around Fletcher's broad shoulders and the instant Nox turns and his light illuminates my face, I wink back. Flynn smiles and nods so quickly that I hope that no one saw him.

Walking in a crouched single file line, with Fletcher at the front of the group and Nox directly in front of me, I feel a shiver trickle down my spine moments later and grasp his arm. "There's a group of them up ahead of us," I whisper.

Nox whistles and Fletcher halts. "Friendly?"

"Definitely not." My finger trembles over the trigger as we spread out and drop to the floor, using it to help brace as Fletcher sends off the first shot.

Snarls and growls echo down the hall toward us and within seconds, the hall is bright with gunfire. The movements of the Flesh Bags as they scrambled over each other to reach us looks eerily like large pale spiders crawling across the floor and up against the walls.

When Nox shifts to help cover Fletcher as they press forward, I hear the dull thud of bodies dropping and pray that none of them are ours.

"You ready for this?" Flynn asks, suddenly appearing at my side. A streak of blood runs down his cheek for where a piece of plaster gashed him in the bullet spray.

"We have no other choice."

"Nox will be ticked when he finds out that you've left."

"Yeah," I nod and look at Nox one last time. He is down on one knee, scope to his eye as he shouts out commands to the men standing behind him. Their wide and unskilled spray of bullets will rapidly place a hard strain on their decreasing ammunition supply.

I look down at the gun in my hand. "Are you a good shot?"

"Nope." Flynn shakes his head. "I left that job to the others while I stuck with more hands-on stuff."

"Excellent." Taking his gun, I set it on the floor beside mine and shove it in Nox's direction. They will need the spare bullets long before they reach the armory to reload.

If all goes well Cyrus will recruit a group of trusted soldiers and they can make a stand with Nox while Fletcher makes his way to Cap's office to locate the blueprints. A lot is riding on hope and 'what-ifs' but it's all we've got.

"Let's go get that generator fixed!"

SIXTEEN

As I lead Flynn in the opposite direction of Nox's group, I can't seem to shake the feeling that we are being led this way. From time to time, I spy the telltale white sheen of eyes watching us from down the hall and caution Flynn to stay behind me, but each time the Withered disappear before we arrive. This leaves me deeply unsettled.

They seem to be toying with us.

When I glance back over my shoulder at Flynn, I can easily see his fear as he clings to the red handled ax that we busted out of a firewall unit. My own dangles from my hand and points at the floor but in an instant, I can be ready for attack. Although I have no clue just how talented Flynn may be with an ax, I have faith that he would not have survived this long without a few hidden skills. I just hope that they will come in handy when the time is right.

As we move along the carpeted corridor, Flynn is blind without any light and relies on my hand to keep him moving straight or to warn him of impending danger.

"It's going to be okay," I say over my shoulder, hoping to help him feel a bit more at ease. "I promise I won't let anything eat you."

"Oh, you're a funny one now, huh?"

I look back to see him rolling his eyes and I wonder if this is what having a younger brother feels like. I find myself enjoying the witty banter. "At least I got a smile out of you."

Flynn's fingers flinch inside of mine. "You really can see, can't you?"

"I can see clearly now that the lights are off."

I pause to peer inside an open door and move on again when I see that the room is clear. Our pace is slow and arduous but steady. I only wish that I'd had a chance to ask Nox just how far away the generator was. I had hoped by now that I would run across Cyrus' group or at least a map on the wall to guide me but so far, I'm striking out on both counts.

"What's it like?"

"Seeing in the dark?" I peer around the corner and sense that for the time being it is clear. "Well, it's kinda cool, actually. I've got skills even Batman never had."

"That's not true. He had night vision."

"A mechanical version, sure but this is the real deal."

I hear Flynn's breathing behind me, steady and under control. He's a tough kid. If we all survive the night, I'll be sure to let Nox know to give him more credit. Of course, if I do make it until the morning I may not survive seeing Nox again.

"So what's it like being the new you? Are you still changing? Can you feel it happening? Are you going to wake up tomorrow with a lizard tail and shark teeth?"

I laugh and suddenly the gloom of the eerily deserted hallway doesn't seem quite so terrifying anymore. Contrary to the upbeat tone that I'm attempting to pull off for Flynn sake, I'm not overly fond of walking into a trap and with each step I am more sure that this is exactly what is happening.

"Are you always this inquisitive?"

His shrug jostles my hand. "I guess I am now. I used to be kind of a loner. Hard to believe, right? It's true, though. Before all of this happened I would spend hours locked up in my room and be perfectly happy. But after people I knew started dying I realized that we need each other to survive so I decided it was time to change."

"Just like that?"

"It's all just a mindset anyways. Fear is nothing more than impulses firing in your brain that tell you to flee or accept what's in front of you."

I stop walking and turn around to face him. "Most people ran and hid when people started getting sick and here you are talking about standing up and fighting. I'm impressed, Kid. You're some kind of special, aren't you?"

"Don't go getting all sentimental on me." In the dark, I can see a blush rising on his cheeks. When he looks away and shuffles his feet I realize that I've embarrassed him.

I tug on his hand when I turn away and let the awkwardness settle between us. I didn't actually mean to get weird with him. There is just something about him that reminds me of myself. Flynn is a fighter and I know how hard that life can be. He's already lost so much and I find myself wishing that I could keep him for any further pain.

We walk down two more hallways in silence before we come across the first body and I'm instantly grateful that Flynn can't see the gore sprayed across the wall. The chunks of flesh alone make my stomach turn as I carefully maneuver him around the dead.

I can tell by the way Flynn's fingers tremble that he's aware of what I'm doing. While he may be lacking in sight, his sense of smell must be reeling by now.

When his right foot slips in a puddle of blood and he goes down hard, one knee slams down onto a severed leg and his hand plunges into an open cavity of a man's shredded torso as he tries to steady himself. His startled cry is cut off when I clamp my hand over his mouth and kneel beside him.

"Breathe, Flynn. It's okay."

"It's not okay. This is not okay." He is trembling when I help to pull his hands free. Blood and something stringy clings to his hand. He tries to clear it away, growing steadily more anxious and he ends of flicking a bit onto his face. After taking one sniff of the rotting flesh he starts gagging. "Oh, that is disgusting!"

"It's not a human. It's just a Flesh Bag."

"I know." His cheeks puff as he clutches his stomach and makes retching noises. I hold onto his arm, sure that he will lose his stomach but he slowly regains his control "It reeks."

"Well," I chuckle and grab hold of his hand to wipe it clean on the zombie's shirt. "Dead things usually tend to stink and I'd wager this unlucky fellow has been dead for quite some time."

He gags again and cups his mouth with his clean hand. I pat his back as he gulps in huge breaths of air but that is a mistake. The instant he is assaulted by the pungent scent he throws himself to the side and wretches.

Sinking down beside him, I swivel my head back and forth, keeping a close eye on both directions to make sure that we aren't about to be ambushed. I can feel the Flesh Bags in the distance but none is near enough for me to be alarmed yet. What does alarm me is the sheer numbers that we are approaching. It's almost like they have congregated.

"How are you doing over there?" I whisper.

From somewhere down the hall I hear a groan and instantly tense. My fingers flex around the ax handle as I peer into the dark. I can't see anything but there is something definitely alive down there but I can't sense that it's a Flesh Bag.

"I'm good now." He wipes at his face and I don't have the heart to tell him that he's actually just smeared more of the gore across his cheek.

"Good, because we've got company." Hooking my hand around his, I help hoist him to his feet. We've barely begun to move forward when I spy movement up ahead and shove Flynn back a step. He instantly drops to the floor, just as I told him to do if I alerted him to danger.

"What is it?" he whispers.

I don't answer as I squint in an attempt to make out exactly what it is that I'm seeing. There is something moving on the floor. It is hard to see clearly from this distance but it looks like a snake.

"I'm not sure. I'm going to check it out." Jiggling the door handle beside me, I open the door and peer inside. Rapping my knuckles against the door, I wait a few seconds just to be sure nothing is inside ready to charge us and then shove Flynn inside. "Stay here and stay down. If anything comes through that door without announcing their name first I want you to start swinging. Got it?"

"Wait, you can't just leave me here! You need me."

I place a hand on his shoulder, meaning the gesture to be reassuring but in my haste I slam him against the wall with a bit too much force and his head smacks into the drywall. "Shit, Flynn. I'm sorry. I guess that I'm more rattled than I thought. Just do me a favor and barricade the door so that I don't have to worry about you, okay?"

"Avery, wait!" But I don't wait. Instead, I turn and slam the door shut and hope that I haven't just smashed his nose in when he tried to follow me. Kicking at the door across the hall from me, I slam my foot into it three times before it hinges give way and it slams to the ground.

"Well, if they didn't know I was here before they sure as hell do now." I grab the damaged door and shove it against Flynn's, creating a temporary wedge brace that will not last long once the Withered catch his scent but it will maybe give me a chance to get back in time to help.

Inside the room, I can hear him pounding his fist against the door and messing with the lock.

"Stop making noise," I hiss, pressing my face to the crack in the door. "Do you want to tell the whole floor where you are?"

"No, but I want to help you. That's why I came with you, remember?"

"I know." I sigh and wipe sweat from my forehead. It is too hot in this small space and I suddenly feel confined. I want to run, to climb, to fight and to kill.

Shaking my head, I shove aside those thoughts. They are not my own.

"I like you, kid. Just let me deal with what's up ahead and once the coast is clear I'll come back for you, okay?"

There is only silence in response for a moment and I'm about to walk away when I hear a hollow, "I'm not a kid anymore. You don't have to protect me."

I don't know what to say in response since I'm not that much older than Flynn. A few years extra years is hardly enough to make seeing this shit acceptable. The horrors I have experience haunt my dreams and fill m waking thoughts. I would give anything to have someone willing to protect me from it all, but there was never anyone like that. Cable would have tried but in the end, it would have caught up with me all the same.

"I know, Flynn, but there are some things that can't be unseen. You told me earlier that you lost your family and you've been fighting to survive ever since. Well, this is me giving you that chance. You can hate me later but just stay alive long enough to do that, okay? After this is over you and Nox can both take a swing at me."

Jogging down the hall away from Flynn, I try to stretch out my senses to feel the Withered. Like a mental thermal blip, I sense several of them in rooms up ahead moving about but they are not in attack mode. They seem to be searching for something.

I can't even begin to fathom what a zombie would need from a place like this or how a mindless creature could focus on a single task, but then a thought strikes me that make shivers run through my body...what if they aren't really mindless at all?

The awareness that I sensed earlier was different from any that I had felt before. It bordered the authority that I felt from the alpha Flesh Bag that sank his teeth into my neck but this presence is something more, something both powerful and controlling. That is why the Withered are acting differently. They are being led.

An alpha on the premises is proving to be strong enough to send out a some sort of telepathic signal to coordinate the attack. I should have realized it sooner. This breach is too thought out and far too advanced for a Withered to conceive on their own. They may be intelligent but they are still ruled by their based instincts.

Someone has to be controlling them and the instant I allow myself to consider the possibilities I begin to wonder if that someone might just be like me.

As I round the corner and try to shove that disturbing thought aside, I spy the long snake wiggling on the ground and hurry to catch up, but it's only when I'm right on top of it that I realize it's not a snake at all but half eaten intestines trailing behind a dying man. The thick blood that trail he leaves behind like a slimy slug smears his pants and mingles with other puddles of blood as he weaves through fallen soldiers.

I pause only a second to check each face, praying that I don't see Cyrus among them. The relief that I feel when I don't is immense. That means Nox still has a fighting chance.

"Help me," the man calls out when he hears my approach and I hurry to his side. Rolling him gently onto his back, I stare at the horrid gaping hole that was once his cheek. His skin and muscle have been gnawed down to the bone and each time he opens his mouth to speak, I can see his teeth clicking together.

The young man is dressed in a blue onesie maintenance uniform. Chunks of long white-blond hair have been ripped clean away, leaving patches of bare skin over his skull. One hand bears signs of nails chipped and torn away from dragging himself along the tile floor. His other is soaked in blood as he fights to keep his stomach inside his body.

"What's your name?" I ask, glancing down the hall. There are four zombies less than fifty feet from me. I can hear their grunts and things being knocked over inside a room but none has taken notice of my presence yet.

"Henry," he wheezes.

"That's a nice name." I press my knee into his chest and yank at the sleeves on his jumper but they have been mended several times and the knots hold strong. Slicing the cloth with my ax blade, I tear strips of cloth away. "I'm going to have to try to cover your wound."

"No." He shakes his head. "There's no point. It's too late for me."

We both know that his fate is sealed. That first bite did him in but seeing the fear in his eyes won't allow me to just give up. Turning into a zombie is bad enough but to allow him to lie there and be eaten is something I just can't do.

"It will help with the pain until..." I can't bring myself to say the words.

Rolling his head to the side, Henry stares at the ax lying on the ground beside my knee. "Please, help me."

When he rolls his head back to look at me, I see the resignation in his eyes and know that he was never really asking for help. He was asking for a mercy kill.

"No. " I back away from him when he tries to reach out for me. When he inches his torso toward my ax, I shove it away. "Don't ask that of me."

"You have no idea how much this hurts."

Tears slip through my lashes as I close my eyes and am violently thrust back into the cave with Cable. He had asked of me the same thing—to save him from becoming an empty vessel and to give him the end that he wanted. This man might be a complete stranger but he is a life, a living breathing being. Ending him now might be merciful but it was also murder and I have buckets of spilled blood on my hands already.

"I can't." I push back from him. "I'm so sorry."

Using the wall to aid my efforts to stand, I find myself weakened by the pain leaching from my heart. *Damn you, Cable! You did this to me! You made me weak!*

"Don't leave me!"

The man's cries follow me as I step over him and run. I don't stop to think of where I am going or when I will stop. I run until a cramp pinches in my side and the man is long behind me. The Flesh Bags never try to stop me as I run past and I don't slow down long enough to tangle with them. I can only hope that someone else will stumble across poor Henry and do what I could not.

It is only when I stop to catch my breath that I remember I left Flynn behind.

"Shit!"

I turn back to go and get him and slam straight into a tall fleshy chest. The monster standing before me is nearly a foot taller than me. His shoulders are broad and the tattoo on his upper right arm nearly indistinguishable under his peeling skin. Startling milky white eyes stare down at me, both unblinking and yet oddly focused.

A breath rattles in its chest as it blocks my path but it does not attack. Instead, it stands perfectly still.

Why did I not sense it sooner? In my panic to escape Henry, I must have blinded myself to its presence. Perhaps emotion drove me to distraction? Or, as a darker thought strikes me and chills race down my spine, I realize that somehow this particular Flesh Bag may have found a way to block my thoughts entirely.

With each step that I take backward, it advances, keeping pace with me without ever drawing too near. It ushers me down the hall with nearly silent footfalls.

From somewhere behind my back, I hear approaching voices. The zombie goes still and raises its head to sniff the air. Its cracked lips peel back over crooked and bloody teeth as a growl rumbles deep in its chest.

"I'm telling you it's this way," an unfamiliar voice echoes down the hall. "Cyrus said to follow this corridor on around and we would meet up with him at the rendezvous point."

"How do we even know Cyrus is still alive? There are bodies everywhere and here we are playing tag in the dark." This voice sounds higher in pitch and squeaky. I recognize it as Warren, the punk kid with a seriously annoying personality. Why Nox ever stood up for him I'll never know.

"We stick to the plan until we hear otherwise," a female voice barks out. From just around the corner I see the first flicker of light over my shoulder. The Flesh Bag behind me begins to weave and I'm suddenly caught up in a tidal wave of rage.

"Flesh bag straight around the corner," I scream and dive for the floor.

The zombie screeches and makes a wild swing for me but it's torso jerks and sprays blood as multiple rounds of bullets slam into its chest. I try yelling out to aim higher but my voice is lost to the ricocheting sound of gunfire. Still the creature struggles forward, slowed by the bullets but driven by unsated hunger. It reaches for me, sinking its cracked nails into my arm before I can get away.

It could have attacked me at any time. Why does it now decide to try to eat me? Has its rage overruled whatever is controlling it? Is it possible that mingled in with its anger is a spike of fear that makes it disobey?

Probing it's thought to try to understand its reaction, I lick my lips and breathe in deep, smelling the small group of people behind me. When I feel my stomach clench with desire I slam my left fist into the wall and the flood of pain clears my thoughts.

Rolling against the wall, I kick my foot out and wrap it around the backside of the Flesh Bag's knee to bring it crashing to the ground. The instant the gunfire ceases I bring my ax down over my head and sink it deep into the zombie's skull. It splits with far more ease than I could have imagined and a blackish ooze seeps out onto the floor.

"It's okay," I call out, using the wall to prop myself up. "It's dead."

Several pairs of boots race around the corner toward me and I hold up my hand to shield myself from their lights.

"Holy shit, that's a big one." A man sinks down onto his haunches and pokes at the Withered with the tip of his gun then he turns to give me a hard look. "Are you with Cyrus' group?"

"Hell no, she ain't!" Warren says and pushes to the front of the group of six people. "She's that girl I told you about who got Zoey killed and messed up Nox!"

The man beside me tightens his grip on his weapon. "That true, miss?"

Clutching my arm, I push back against the wall and look at the floor. It hurts too much to look anywhere near their lights. "I tried to save her."

"I thought the girl from your story died, Warren. You said she got bit after she went nuts and jumped down into the hot zone and Cap had to put her down."

I glance up at the girl who just spoke and make out shoulder length dirty blond hair falling around her shoulders from a tight bun. Her features are severe and her expression grim. Considering the hell they've just walked through I am surprised that she's as clean as she is.

"That's what I was told too, Hadley. It seems that someone has some explaining to do." Warren stares down at me with mounting suspicion.

"Look, I'm not going to sit here and shoot the shit. Zoey died and that really sucks. I liked her and she didn't deserve to go out like that. I am still alive and saving you asses. If you want more details than that then you'll have to chat with Nox back at the armory. If you want to survive, I suggest you tell me how to get to the generator and then get out the hell of my way."

"Whoa, easy there little lady," the man beside me says, pushing back on my shoulder when I reach for my ax. The name on his camouflage shirt says Monroe and I realize that I've seen him before. He was part of the group that came to the farmhouse but I haven't seen him since that day.

The bossy girl above him narrows her eyes when she sees me looking but Monroe holds out his hands between us as if he could prevent the oncoming fight. She might look tough but there is zero doubt that I could take her even before my mutations. This girl relies far too much on that fancy gun of hers.

"I think we all just need to take a breather and we can figure this out," Monroe says.

I laugh and press my head back against the wall. "You have no fucking clue what you just walked into, do you?"

"What's that?" Warren asks.

"A trap," I smile up at him, feeling bone weary and resigned to my fate. "That Flesh Bag you just filled with lead wasn't trying to kill me. It was ushering me."

SEVENTEEN

Unease spreads through the small ground surrounding me as each of them begin to shine their lights in both directions down the hall. I know that it won't make any difference. The Withered are coming.

"She's lying," Warren says in a high pitch voice that I'm beginning to realize he uses only when he's terrified, which feels like pretty much all of the time.

"I'm not."

Monroe shifts on the balls of his feet to stare at me, still crouching close enough for me to smell the stench of sweat and body odor on him. "Care to tell us why that thing didn't just shred you where you stood?"

Pursing my lips, I shrug and spread my hands wide. "Maybe it just liked my smile."

The punch that comes from my right catches me off guard and my cheek slams into the wall, bruising my cheekbone.

"That's enough, Hadley," Monroe growls and stares up at the girl.

When I roll my head back to glare up at her, I do not see fear in her eyes. Instead, I see rage but it is nothing compared to what the Flesh Bags live with. "She thinks this is some sort of sick joke. I say we leave her behind and let the Flesh Bags have her for a snack."

"You could do that," I muse, wiping the blood from my cheek. I'm not even sure it belongs to me but the girl sure packs a hell of a punch. "Or you could help me save your friends."

"How's that?" Monroe asks. When Hadley clenches her fist again, he shakes his head and she submits with a show of reluctance. "What are you doing down here all alone?"

"We have to get the lights back on."

Warren snorts. "She's afraid of the dark!"

"No," I snarl back at him, annoyed with his attitude and persistent hatred of me. "Those things will be blinded. Why do you think they disabled the generator in the first place?"

Hadley scoffs and taps her gun against her hip. "The Flesh Bags didn't do that. They aren't capable of that kind of thinking."

"Aren't they?" I push myself to a standing position so quickly that the soldiers rear back.

"How did she—"

"Do this?" I cut Warren off by seizing him by the throat and lifting him high off the ground with his back pressed against the wall. Although he is slight in stature his weight should have still made it impossible to lift and yet I do so without straining. "You were right, Warren. I did get bitten. Funny enough, I seem to be the only person in this whole place who is immune to the virus so now I am special.

I know things that you don't and trust me when I tell you we don't have much time. Either stay and help me or get the hell out of my way because this place is swarming with Flesh Bags and without me, you don't stand a chance. You are on their ground now and they aren't here to play."

Monroe looks at each of his soldiers in turn. "Cyrus told us to trust her."

"Yeah, and Cyrus also said she's doing all kinds of freaky stuff too," Hadley says. "You heard what she did to Kenzie."

"That wasn't on me," I glare at me. "I warned them against that course of action but I was forced."

"What does it matter?" Hadley pushes up into my face. My finger clenches on the ax in my hand as I lower Warren to the floor and turn to face her. "She died horribly because of what's inside of you."

"And now because of that, you just might have a chance to live if you get out of my face, yank those panties out of your ass and follow me. It's your choice. I'm done apologizing and I'm done talking."

I send her flying through the air with a small shove. She smacks hard into the wall and groans as she doubles over. I smile as I listen to her wheezing breath as I pass by.

"Wait!" I glance back over at my shoulder at Monroe. He looks torn and confused, but desperate for a solution. "How many are coming for us?"

I offer him a sad smile. "All of them."

"Shit." He runs his hands through his hair. "This can't be happening."

"Man up, will you?" I say, turning back. "Nox, Cyrus, Fletcher and every damn person in this building are going to die if you don't help me. Now I am willing to do this on my own if I have to but the chances of us surviving increase if you join me. I know which one I'd rather pick but it's on you. These are your people."

He glances at the men around him. Each one stands rigid and the scent of fear hangs thick in the air. My nostrils flare when I realize that it is an actual scent, not just something figurative. It is tantalizing and coils in my belly as I fight against the waves of hunger that roll over me.

"You okay?" I blink and realize that Monroe is now standing in front of me. When he lifts his light, I back away, shielding myself from the brilliance. "You don't like the light so much yourself, do you?"

"I see better in the dark now."

From somewhere behind him I hear Warren mutter *freak* and know that he is right. I am a freak, but I'm also their best shot at surviving.

"I only need three men to watch my back. The others need to rendezvous with Nox and gear up, but first, I need you to get something for me."

"Now she's making demands?"

I ignore Warren's snide comment and walk over to a map laid out on the wall just a few steps away and I point to the hallway that I'm pretty sure I just came from. "Halfway down, in this general area, you will find a slaughter zone. If he's not already dead, there's a man in a maintenance uniform named Henry with his intestines dragging behind him. He is lying not far from where I left a kid locked up in a storage room.

His name is Flynn and he's probably going to be pretty ticked at me when you let him out, but he needs to get back to Nox. He knows my plan and he's handy in a fight. Send your men back to get him on their way to the armory and I promise he will prove to be an asset."

Monroe rubs his hands over the stubble on his face and looks at the hallway stretching out before us. "The generators are a good five-minute walk from here in good conditions. I don't reckon we will make it in that time."

Drying my clammy hands on my pants before reaffirming my grip on the ax, I smile over at him. "We won't have to worry about that. It will be a clear shot."

"What makes you say that?"

Looking down the deserted hall, I sense the writhing tide of anger held in check in the distance. "Because they are waiting for us. If I'm right we will be allowed to walk right up to the generator without losing a single person."

Monroe puffs outs his cheeks and then releases a long, slow breath. "I'm guessing I don't want to ask what happens when we arrive."

"No." I shake my head and turn my back on him as I lead the way. "Be thankful you will be blind once we get there. It's going to be quite a sight to see."

In the end, Monroe selects Warren and Hadley to join my rescue mission while the others rush off in the opposite direction. There is no need to warn them about the dangers that might be lurking in the dark. Whatever scouts that had been on my tail have fallen back. From all around the hotel I can feel them racing in our direction, converging on the generator room.

I should have known the instant that Flesh Bag appeared behind me that this was the final destination. The alpha has proven to be too intelligent not to foresee my plans. The lights were our only hope of winning this battle and it knew that. All it had to do was sit back and wait for us to arrive.

The sound of pounding boots behind me echoes all around as we start off at a slow job. We make no effort to hide our approach as we puff and pant, weary from tension and fighting. The terrifying snarls, growls and chattering teeth from up ahead drown out everything else as we slow to a walk. The closer I draw to the horde, the stronger the tug in my mind is toward their alpha.

"Turn off your lights," I call back over my shoulder when I hit a turn in the hallway and am blasted with a thundering roar of outrage.

"Is she nuts? Like hell I'm going dark!"

"Hadley, just do it!" Monroe reaches to shut off his light. Slowly Hadley obeys and Warren is the only one remaining with his light on. It twitches against the floor, illuminating dozens of dirty feet and bloody shoes lining the hall before us.

"Warren," Monroe says and reaches behind him for the gun but meets with air instead. "Don't do anything stupid."

"Stupid?" Warren's responding laugh is shrill and screechy. I turn and see that he has tripped over into full on panic mode as he backs away. "This is suicide. Do you really want to walk through that on her word alone? No way. I'm not dying for anyone today!"

A sharp snarl over Warren's shoulders makes him squeal like a potbelly pig.

"Don't move, asshat!" I hurry toward him with my hands raised in surrender and find myself thankful that he can't see the white eyes appearing over his shoulder. If he could, he would faint dead away right then and there. "You need to turn off your light nice and slow."

Warren shakes his head and clings to his gun but a second late he screams and is yanked to the right. The sound of the gun smashing into dozens of pieces when it strikes the wall is met with a low grunting that reminds me of an ape in a zoo just before it beats its chest. Warren's light flickers out and the hallway is thrown into darkness.

"It attacked me. I almost died!"

"If it wanted you dead, Warren your head would already be on the floor by now. It was protecting itself and for good reason. You are shit with a gun," I almost want to laugh at the terrified look on his face but I worry the reaction it might have in the Withered. "Now I want you to step slowly toward me. Do not make any sudden movements or it will strike again and it looks like it's just itching to have a reason to take a bite out of you."

That was probably a cruel thing to say at a time like this but the snickers behind me tell me that I'm not alone in seeing the humor of it all. The guy needs to be taken down a peg or two.

Tremors of fear ripple through Warren's entire body as he steps forward. When the Flesh Bag moves with him, sticking close enough that I'm sure Warren can smell death on its breath I see a spreading wetness near his groin just before the pungent scent of urine reaches me.

"Did he seriously just piss himself?" I look to my right to see Hadley's nose scrunched with disgust.

Heat rises within my heart rate increases, pounding against my chest as I fight against the irrational hunger that is mirrored by every single Withered in this hallway. How is their alpha controlling them to such an extreme extent to allow us to walk freely past them without harm?

"Is it going to eat me?" Warren shuffles forward another step. The Withered follows directly behind him.

"Not if you keep moving just like that. They aren't here to kill us." Perhaps that is stretching the truth a bit. I can feel their hunger and their desire to tear Warren limb from limb but their will is temporarily chained. If given the chance, like the Flesh Bag back in the hallway, I think that they would break rank and sink their teeth into him before the alpha even knew it had happened.

"I don't want to die," he whispers.

In the dark, I can see that his nose is running and his eyes are wide and unseeing. He is nearly as pale as the zombies behind him.

"Just do as she says," Monroe says. I can see him reaching blindly for Hadley's hand. When they find each other, they draw closer together. Using verbal cues, I lead Warren to them and soon all three are linked with their guns slung over their back. Each of them knows that their survival rests solely in my hands now.

Turning away from them, I stare down the long hall and wish that I were just as blind as the people behind me. "Monroe, take hold of my shoulder and step when I step. Do not reach out to our right or left. Trust me, you don't want to know what's there."

I hear an audible gulp from behind me and then a firm grip settles on my shoulder. I place my hand over his and lead the group forward, shuffling through only a tiny portion of the horde that I know spreads beyond this path, but their fewer numbers are no less terrifying.

As I walk, I try to think about how I will distract the alpha long enough to allow someone to reach the generator. It is a flawed plan and one with far too many windows of failure, but it is the only one that I have. None of us will survive this attack if sacrifices aren't made.

"Which way?" I ask when we reach a T in the hallway. Flesh Bags fan out in a long line in both directions, standing two bodies thick. Their arms and legs reach for us but none makes contact.

"You need to turn left and head toward the convention center. That's where the generator is being housed," Hadley responds.

"I was afraid you were going to say that." Sniffing in that direction I can smell an appealing odor that my human sides knows means this is a trap.

"Do I want to know?" Monroe asks from directly behind me as I ponder the insanity of how I have already begun to compartmentalize myself into human and not. It's true that I still maintain my human thoughts, memories, and feelings but there are animalistic urges that continue to grow stronger.

Shoving aside those thoughts for a time when I can properly process them, I reply, "Let's just say it's going to get a bit slippery. Watch your step."

I lead them through the heart of the writhing mass. Less than twenty paces in we reach our first puddle of blood and I hear Warren swear when his boot slips and he collides with a Withered. I turn just in time to see one rake its nails down his arm before he rights himself.

"I thought you said they won't attack," Hadley says.

"No. I said they wouldn't kill. There's a difference." I stare a moment too long at the blood leaking from Warren's arm before mentally shaking myself and pushing on.

With each step that I take, I feel a new tension mounting within me. I have no idea what to expect when we arrive at the generator but I fear that it will be worse than I anticipate. The alpha both terrifies and draws me to continue moving forward.

"What's the plan when we arrive?" Monroe asks. This time, his voice is shaky and I wonder if he accidentally bumped one of the hands reaching for him. For the moment, blindness is a blessing for him and his small crew.

"I'm working on it."

"What about Nox and the others?" Hadley pipes up.

"They will be heading this way soon," I respond and my pace quickens. "We need to be ready for when they arrive."

"You really think we can take all of these zombies out?"

I glance back over my shoulder at Monroe. "No. We just need to drive them back. Dawn will do the rest for us."

"Anyone know how long that will be?" Warren mutters.

"At least another half hour but it could be longer. My shift on the perimeter was due to end at dawn but being stuck in this consuming darkness makes time seem like it stretches on forever," Hadley says and I feel Monroe's hand tighten on my shoulder.

Not knowing the time means that our margin of error just amplified and there's not a damn thing we can do about it. What will happen if we manage to get the lights back on only to push them out into the night where they can easily regroup and attack from a different angle?

"Let's focus on one problem at a time." I slow to a stop when we reach a set of open double doors. Just beyond that is a wide carpeted corridor and a pile of bodies. "Oh god!"

"What?" Monroe tugs on my shoulder. "What's wrong?"

"They are piling the dead, both their own and ours," I whisper and stare at the growing mound of the dead and the line of Withered carrying them in. Some come with random arms and legs while others tote whole bodies over their shoulders with blood and entrails dripping down their backs. The mound stands at least thirty feet in diameter and rises well above my head.

"I'm so sorry," I whisper, overcome with grief over the enormous loss that was suffered tonight. Nox is right. These aren't my people, but at times like these when the world is divided between us and them, people are people.

"What is that smell?" Warren asks as he huddles in close to Hadley.

She turns and tries to shove him back but he clings tightly to her as we move through the open space. Hundreds of Withered watch as we approach, working like ants in unison but as I pass I am inundated with individual pulses of rage and hunger.

"That would be the scent of shit," Hadley says to Warren. "Your muscles go weak and you shit your pants when you die. You would know that if you ever actually did anything on missions."

My mouth feels dry as an opening is created off to the right and a path clears for us. My thoughts scatter as I try to grasp onto an idea, any idea that might get us out of this situation, but none settle long enough to form. Our only hope is that Nox will arrive in time to lay down some cover fire for someone to get that generator back on line.

With each step that I take, I feel my stomach tighten. After all, that I have been through, will I finally meet my end in the main hall of the Grand Opryland Hotel? I never even liked country music.

The Withered fan out as we enter into the vast space and I feel the rush of cool air over my skin and sigh with relief. From behind me, I hear Warren swear as I try to locate the chill's source.

"Welcome," a masculine voice echoes throughout the room and the three behind me come to an abrupt halt. There is no way to know exactly where the voice came from as I look out across the ballroom. As far as I can see, Flesh Bags stretch to the far corners of the room. Over a thousand heads stare right back at us. "We have been expecting you."

"The zombies can talk now?" Warren squeaks.

"That's no zombie," Hadley hisses and stomps on his foot when he tries to climb onto her back.

The Flesh Bags pull back from us like a tide going out to sea, with skin so white they almost glow translucent. That is when I realize that they do radiate some sort of light. I can almost see a pale blue under their skin, like thousands of tiny sparks of electricity and I'm curious. Looking down at myself I do not see the same thing and wonder why I'm different.

"Do you have anything on you other than a gun?" I whisper back over my shoulder as I keep my eyes focused on the zombies.

They move as one as I sense the alpha's approach. I can feel him in the tug within my gut as if lassoed by a rope and drawn forward, but I resist. I can't let him see my weakness, even if I suspect that he can already feel it.

I glance back over my shoulder to see the ranks of zombies fall in behind us, sealing off the exit to the corridor beyond. Although the doors remain standing open, there is no way that we would make it through that mess and to the atrium beyond. The alpha is smart. He knows that once the sun rises that entire glass domed section of the hotel will be off limits. That is where Nox needs to funnel the survivors to but I have no way of communicating that to him.

"We have a couple smoke bombs, some spent magazines, a flare gun, and a broken radio. That was Warren's doing," Hadley adds as a side note with a heavy dose of contempt.

"Get that flare gun in Monroe's hand but don't pull the trigger until I say. No matter what happens, hold for my signal." I see a stirring among the Withered and turn to watch. Something is moving up ahead of me and shifting toward my right.

Monroe eases his hand back toward Henley. Together they work to load the gun in the blinding dark and I see two spare flares but I doubt we will have time to use them.

"It is rude not to respond when welcomed, don't you think?" The alpha calls again, this time from off to my right and definitely closer. I see more Withered shift to allow him room to walk and wonder if he waited to speak because he was listening to our whispered plan.

"Is this what you call a welcoming party?" I shout out. The Withered stand side by side, swaying slowly as all eyes turn and I shift to look directly down the line of my right shoulder. A parting begins and the zombies shuffle sideways to create a long gap.

"You would not have come without proper cause."

The man's voice echoes all around and I realize a hush has fallen over the crowd. Unblinking white eyes stare as a man emerges from the masses. His clothing is simple: a black tank top and camouflage pants. He could have easily walked our halls and none of the soldiers would have known that he didn't belong.

A camouflage hat is pulled down low over his eyes and I find myself frustrated to know if his are as white as all of the others.

"You can feel them all around you now, can't you?" He calls out.

His approach is achingly slow and yet with each step, I feel as if time slows even further. I can truly feel his presence for the first time and hear the steady beating of his heart as it flutters at his neck. Breathing in deep, I inhale his scent and go ramrod stiff.

Monroe's hand slips from my shoulder when my body gives off an odd spasm. "What's wrong?"

He flounders in the dark behind me as I take two steps forward. "No. It's not possible."

"But it is," the alpha responds with a voice as smooth as silk. It washes over me as I close my eyes, fighting to remember how to breathe.

"Something is moving," I hear Hadley warn as they bunch together behind me. I barely feel Monroe's hand regain its hold on my arm as I open my eyes to discover that the alpha stands before me, less than ten feet away and I have to fight every urge within me not to faint.

"How?" I choke out.

The alpha lifts his head slowly and I am lost in familiar eyes, not encased in white but the purest, more beautiful gaze I have ever known.

"You did not take the shot like I asked you to," he whispers and I hold my breath as he closes the gap between us. Reaching out his hand, he takes mine in his, and I stare up into a face meant only for my dreams.

When he presses his hand to my cheek, tears slip from my eyes as I lean into his touch and whisper, "Cable."

EIGHTEEN

A thousand sensations ripple through me as I feel Cable's touch. The temperature of his body feels cool and natural to me in comparison to Nox. The pull of his presence in my mind has become a longing to let him envelop me in his embrace and never let go.

"For months I have been consumed with guilt, knowing that I sealed you into that cave and walked away. I couldn't end your life. I tried to do what you wanted but the thought of losing you forever..." my voice cracks as I fall silent.

"Shh. It's okay." He rubs his thumb across my cheek and I lean into him.

"I have missed you so much," I whisper. "When I closed my eyes I could see you but when I opened them you were never there. I was always alone."

"I know," he whispers. I close my eyes as he presses his lips to my forehead and I cling to him, breathing in his familiar scent as memory after memory assaults me. "But I'm here now."

"What's going on?" I hear Hadley speak behind me but I don't care about her right now. Cable is all that matters.

"How did you escape the cave? I sealed you in."

Cable smiles and runs his finger down my nose. "I am stronger now, remember? Just as you are."

"The bite..." I look at his healed wound and see that it is barely more than a faint scar. "You're like me?"

"Yes." He takes both of my hands and lifts them to his lips. "If you had killed me, that would have been the end, but I've been given a second chance. We both have."

"But I don't understand. You were bitten before the mutations began. How could you—"

"Shh." He presses a finger to my lips to silence me. "The how's and why's do not matter. We are together again. Must we look beyond that to answers that neither of us have?"

"Avery," Monroe hisses behind me and I turn in his direction. His fear chips through the veil of happiness that I felt only a moment ago and it crumbles into ruins as I look back to Cable and draw my hands away from him.

"You are the alpha that I felt calling to me. You ordered this attack."

"Yes." He nods slowly and spreads his arms out to encompass his army. "These are my brethren and they do my bidding."

"But you killed innocent people!"

Cable's loving expression hardens and all hint of the smile that he wore only seconds ago vanishes so rapidly that I wonder if it was ever really there. "They are not our people anymore, Avery. They hunt and kill our kind. That makes them our enemy."

I flinch at the venom in his words. This does not sound like the man I know and love. "How can you say that? There were children living her, Cable. Are they guilty of slaughtering anyone?"

"There are always causalities in war."

His simple yet chilling statement has a profound effect on me and I step back. "This isn't you, Cable. You used to believe in people when given every reason not to. You held out hope when there was little grasp on to. You had faith when all was lost."

"I am different now."

"Should we be worried that these two have a history together?" I hear Hadley whisper into Monroe's ear and turn to look at them.

The war of emotions waging inside of me is frightening. The pull of Cable's logic speaks strongly to my new self. I am stronger, faster and better than the humans are, but I am still among them.

"This isn't right, Cable. These people never hurt you. They never even left the safety of these walls."

"Liar!" He clenches his fists at his sides. I take another step back when I see a vein pulsing madly down his forehead. He takes several calming breaths and seems to get himself back under control. "These soldiers that you stand in front of mow down my kin every day while they go out on their little missions. Do you stand here and defend their actions? And what of their leaders who create monstrosities in their lab beneath this very building?"

"How do you—"

"Know?" Cable laughs. "Come now, Avery. Surely by now you know that we can sense our kind through walls and earth. We can sense their hunger, fears, and channel their rage. We can also sense abominations and mindless beasts that will follow no one's guidance. That is what your leaders create in their test tubes. I could not allow that to continue. Not when I knew you were here."

I take a small step toward him. "Is that what this is about? You came for me?"

Cable stops and smiles. "Of course, Avery. We are meant to be together. Don't you know that by now? Fate, providence, or whatever you wish to call it has allowed this to happen. We can create a new world together. We can right the wrongs of the past and give evolution the push that it needs to wipe out the weak."

"You mean to create more Withered?"

He tilts his head to the side. "Yes and no. There are others like us out there. I can feel them and soon you will be able to as well. They are lost and untrained but we can help guide them. We can teach the humans their place and live like Gods."

I look to the floor as I gently rub the bite scar on my neck. "No."

"No?" Cable widens his stance and crosses his arms over his chest.

"It's not right. These people deserve to live as they choose, without fear or corruption. You would take them from one tyrant to the next, placing yourself on a pedestal of fear and worship only so that they can be enslaved to you."

"It is as it should be. That are now the inferior race."

"You aren't thinking straight, Cable. This isn't you."

Cable closes the gap between us in the blink of an eye. My hair shifts back from my face and I realize that he has moved faster than any Withered I have seen before. "It is me, Avery, and it will soon be you as well. In a short time, you will want what I want and will understand that this is the way of things. It is the natural order."

All around the room, the Withered grunt in affirmation. The scent of urine reaches me a second after Hadley groans and I know Warren has pissed himself again. Cable smirks as he looks over my shoulder at the soldier.

"You see his weakness? It is literally leaking right out of him."

I step between Cable and Warren, blocking his view. "What is it that you want?"

"You." He reaches out for me but I shift back. "I have searched for you these long months. It was not until you were bitten that I felt a strong tug in this direction but then it all but vanished. I was sure that something terrible had happened to you so I began to hunt for your whereabouts."

He turns and looks back over his shoulder. "They can talk, you know? Perhaps not in a language that you or I do, but soon you will begin to recognize the mental impulses and decipher them. It just takes practice. I will teach you to understand more than just what they are feeling. I will instruct you how to command them."

"How did you learn it all?"

"It was by trial and error mostly. It gets easier after our first kill."

My blood runs cold. "You...you've killed?"

Cable's smile turns almost condescending. "It is who we are now, Avery. I know you've felt the urges. You can't tell me that the scent of blood doesn't make you tingle with desire. It's almost better than sex."

My stomach twists as I look back at Monroe. To his credit, the man stands tall and strong despite having a front row seat to the most fucked up conversation probably ever known to man. Hadley looks pissed over his shoulder but her finger does not flinch off the flare gun trigger. Warren is a sopping wet mess with his lower lip trembling and snot running from his nose. If he makes it out of this alive, Nox is going to have his work cut out for him.

The thought of Nox sends a jolt straight into my stomach. Is he still alive? Did Flynn make it back to him to relay my plan so that they can mount an attack?

"Avery," Cable whispers in my ear.

I stiffen when I feel him move around behind me, pressing his chest against my back. "I know that you are confused. I was when I first transitioned but you have no idea just how amazing all of this will be once you truly open your eyes to the world around you."

"I won't. Not like you."

"You sound disappointed in me."

I flinch at the feel of his fingers slowly sliding up my bare arm. How many times have I longed for a moment just like this, when Cable would be alive and smiling? That I would feel his touch again and know that everything would be right with the world again? But it won't ever be the same because he's not Cable anymore. He's nothing more than a madman wearing his face.

"I am disappointed," I whisper and turn my face away when he tries to kiss my cheek.

His hand pauses against my elbow and for the briefest moment I feel anger wash over me. It takes me a moment to realize that it is not my own, but his.

When I was trapped in the lab beneath the hotel he must have felt my anger and my fear. That is why he attacked in such great numbers. His purpose wasn't to wipe out the entire base, though I'm sure he was more than open to that option, but to rescue me. Somehow, in that sick and twisted mind of his, he still loves me.

I close my eyes and sway backward into him as the realization hits me. "You killed all of these people for me."

"Of course, I did," he whispers in my ear. "They were hurting you and for that, they had to pay."

"No." I turn and face him, pressing back on his chest to allow some distance between us. "Those people that your pets are piling up out there did nothing wrong. They didn't hurt me. They didn't even know I existed."

"But some did..." He trails off, brushing his fingers back down my arm toward my hand. My skin rises in gooseflesh at his unwelcome touch then he laces his fingers through mine and draws me forward to follow his lead. "I have a gift for you."

"I don't want anything from you."

He smiles and presses his lips against the back of my hand. Whatever longing that I felt for him the first time I laid eyes on him has shifted into revulsion but I force myself not to react.

"Oh, I think you will very much like this." He waves out his hand toward the crowd of Withered and they instantly begin to fold in on themselves. With a bit of tugging on my hand, Cable leads me forward.

"Monroe, walk straight ahead until I tell you to stop," I call out as Cable leads me toward the middle of the room. I have to make sure that Monroe and the others do not get too far away from me. Their lives and mine depend on it.

Blood squishes up from the plush carpet beneath my boots as we walk. With each step that we take, the farther we move away from the exit and I have yet to glimpse any sign of the generator. A sinking feeling in my stomach makes me think that we might not even be in the correct room.

Where are you, Nox?

There has been no sign of the others and although I'm grateful that all attention has shifted onto our group, I'm afraid that there might still be other Flesh Bags roaming the hotel looking for a feast.

I can't let anything happen to Nox. Not after all that he has done to try to help me.

Looking over at Cable, I realize that the best thing I can do is stall as long as I can. Even if that means finding a way to allow myself to encourage Cable's advances.

There is a snarl from directly behind me and I turn to see that Monroe has inadvertently led his group in a veer off to the right and he has just walked straight into a Flesh Bag that I wouldn't have wanted to cross paths with when he was still human. It leaps onto Monroe and takes him down, breaking the human chain that the three soldiers were clinging to.

"Hadley, don't move!" I scream and try to run to Monroe's aid but Cable's vice-like grip on my hand pulls me back.

Monroe's screams send the Withered into a flurry as the scent of his blood permeates the air. I watch as the Flesh Bag digs its fingers deep into his stomach, peeling him open like a child opening a Christmas package.

"Stop this," I cry out and yank on my hand. "You can save him."

"Why should I? You're enjoying this too much."

The blank, expressionless look on Cable's face makes me fall still. I stare at him as Monroe gurgles, drowning in his own blood. I can hear the tearing and the snapping of jaws, but I don't look away from Cable. I can't because the instant I do I will feel the hunger return and I will long to join in.

"What is happening to me?" I ask.

"You are becoming one of us. Do not fight it, Avery. Instead, embrace it as your destiny and then we can be together."

"No." I feel a trembling begin in my legs and I rapidly shake my head. "I don't want this. I won't become a monster."

"You are only a monster to them." Cable steps closer and I feel the trembling intensify as Monroe's frantically beating heart consumes my thoughts. "To me you are everything."

"It's wrong," I moan as I double over and shove a finger down my throat to induce vomiting. Any taste, even as foul as that, is better than the sweet taste of Monroe's blood on the air.

"Why do you fight it?" Cable sinks down beside me as I retch. "You did not even know the man."

"Would that make a difference?" I look up through my messy curls at him. "Could you so easily kill someone you love?"

Cable thinks for a moment and I hum silently in my mind to try to cover over the sounds of eating. I refuse to look back at Hadley and Warren but I can't imagine that they are doing well. Monroe was their friend and leader and I...I'm nothing more than a volatile beast in the making.

I lead them here. His blood stains my hands alone.

"I suppose that if I were to care about someone from my past I would give it a bit more thought," Cable finally concedes, "but in the end, food is still food."

"So it's not about the need for revenge is it?" I say, wiping my mouth clean. The acid burning in my throat helps to ease the need. "You actually hunger for human flesh?"

Cable smiles. "Yes and then again no. It's complicated."

"Bullshit," a voice yells from behind me and I force myself to look back at Hadley. She stands beside the remains of her friend with her shoulders pressed back and anger etched deeply into her face. "You like eating people. At least have the balls to admit it."

Cable releases his hold on my hand and approaches the girl. He steps over the torn ribbons of meat of Monroe's legs and I force myself to look away.

A single grunt from Cable sends the Withered back into their ranks. Strips of bloody flesh dangle from their lips as they continue to chew.

"Those are bold words for a girl whose life I hold in my hands."

"Fuck you." Her muscles clench when Cable reaches out to take hold of her chin. Over her shoulder I see Warren crouched on the floor, his back hunched as he hugs his knees and rocks. At least Hadley has the courage to go out standing.

"Cable," I call out. "You mentioned a gift."

"So I did." From his profile I can see him smile. "And this one nearly made me forget it."

With a quick twist of his hands, he snaps her neck and drops her to the floor. He turns and steps back over Monroe and holds out his hand to me but I shake my head.

"Let me go to her. It is only right for me to pay my respects since we both know she will not get a proper burial."

Cable hesitates but finally concedes with a shrug. I rush past him and fall to my knees at Monroe's feet where Hadley fell.

"Avery?" Warren's voice quakes so badly that it's hard to make out my name.

"It's going to be okay, Warren," I say, placing a hand on Hadley's. Inside her palm, I feel the bulk of the flare gun and slowly begin to pry her fingers open. "Just don't move and don't speak. I'll find a way out of this."

The instant the flare gun is free I palm it and rise. There is no way that I can search for the other two flares without bringing attention to myself. Tucking my hands behind me as I move to rejoin Cable, I shove the flare gun into the back of my pants and pull my tank free of my waistband to conceal it.

"Finish the other one," Cable calls out before I have moved five feet from Monroe's body

I close my eyes and walk away as the horde dive onto Warren. His screams will haunt me for years to come, but I accept Cable's hand and walk away. I never said that I would find a way out for him. He should have known that wasn't possible.

The human side of me feels weak with disbelief at this rationale. Three lives have been needlessly snatched away before my very eyes and I did nothing to stop it.

Could I have stopped it? I honestly don't know. All that matters is that I didn't even really try and that terrifies me.

"What is this gift?" I ask as we approach a small riser and mount the three steps. Upon the stage are two chairs and Cable motions for me to sit down.

As I take my seat, I try to block out the sounds of chewing and the clicking of jaws and now that I will never get used to that sound. I don't care what Cable says. I won't be like him.

"Shield your eyes," Cable warns just before he places a hand over my face. It takes a moment for my eyes to adjust when a dim red light appears before me but when they do, I see a sight that makes my stomach twist and my pulse race with bloodlust.

There, tied up less than fifteen feet from me, are Iris and Brian. They hang from a metal lighting pole with their feet barely touching the floor and their wrists bound above their heads.

"How did you find them?" I ask, scooting to the edge of my seat. I had not expected this.

"They were trying to escape." Cable looks over at me. "After the ruckus they caused down in the lab I suspected that you would like the chance to see them again."

He is right but not for the reasons he thinks. Do I want them dead? Oh, yes. Revenge for the needless and horrific deaths of the patients of the ward would be justice, but I ultimately want to see their end for peace of mind. I need to know that no one will ever use my blood to damage another human being in an attempt to create a superior race.

Brian strains against his bindings but Iris remains still, her eyes searching mine in the dim light and I am instantly back in the lab under her microscope. Anger flares within me, warming my belly as I think about the wrongs she did to those poor, innocent people. They were humans just like her, with lives and a future and she stole that from them.

"What do you intend to do with them?" I ask.

Cable smiles and places his hand over mine in my lap. "They are yours, Avery. Do whatever you wish with them."

The sensations that his words birth within me are both frightening and foreign. I have killed my fair share of humans and Withered, but they were scum and not fit for living in this new world with decent people. Staring at Brian and Iris now, I know that they are the same and yet these deaths are not related to an immediate need for survival.

Can I justify their death now on the basis that I will be saving lives in the future? I don't think that my conscious could live with that.

If released from here I know that they will only continue to kill, mutilate and repeat until they perfect their experiments. The trouble is, all their genetic manipulation would do is create abominations, just like the ones we saw below. Whatever it is inside of Cable and I, along with the others that he claims to feel, it is natural. Something made within us by God or Mother Nature. It is not something that can be manipulated or grown.

This much I know with certainty. .

"They deserve to die," I say loudly enough for both Brian and Iris to hear. Brian twists in his bindings again and tries to plead for his life around the gag shoved in his mouth but Iris smiles.

"And excellent choice," Cable approves.

"I'm not finished." Rising from my seat, I look beyond the two prisoners and spy the generators for the first time. I know little about machinery but they looks beyond repair, having been to a twisted heap of metal.

There is no way to get the lights back on. No way to funnel the Withered back out of the doors and into the glass atrium and no way to communicate with Nox.

I am trapped.

"The sins of these people are great. Many have suffered and died by their hands," I say. "I demand blood from each of them by my hand."

Cable's face brightens with delight. "Excellent."

Turning to face him, I release a slow breath. "I choose death by fire like the witch trials of old."

He cocks his head to the side. "Burning at the stake?"

"Yes. Let their flesh be the fuel that sends those souls piled in the hallway to the afterlife." I stretch out my hand to him and smile. "Will you allow me this, Cable?"

Rising to his feet, he pulls me close and I press into him. "I would give you the world if only you would stay by my side."

The first touch of his lips against mine sends a chill running through me. His skin feels normal to me, unlike the burning heat I felt with Nox. It is a solemn reminder of how similar we are, and how distinctly different I am from Nox.

The Cable I knew would never have allowed such a thing to happen, especially not by my hand. He would have fought against this injustice instead of organized it. He would have killed for me so that my hands would remain clean. Now he is eager to see me spill blood.

Lifting his head, he brushes his fingers across my lips and smiles. It is that genuine, open smile that makes my heart clench with doubt. Could the man that I loved have survived the mutation and has simply been lost, wandering alone searching for me for too long? Is there a chance that I could save him from himself?

"I have missed you," he whispers and presses his lips to my forehead.

Closing my eyes, I answer honestly, "I never thought I would see you again. I hoped to find a cure, to find a way to bring you back, but—"

"Shh." He wraps his arms around me tight. "I'm here now. That is all that matters."

It isn't all that matters and I remind myself of that. Although there may be a sliver of hope that I could resurrect the Cable that I once knew from the monster that he has become, I know that the man whose arms I stand in now is dangerous and should not be underestimated.

No one is coming to save me now. If I want to survive, I have to do what I've always done...rely on myself.

NINETEEN

I knew that the fire and smoke would attract attention. What I didn't plan on was that I would struggle to look straight at the flames just as much as every Flesh Bag around me. The longer I remained in the dark, the more accustomed I became to it and the more at home I feel in the dark.

I watch as Brian and Iris are dragged out of the ballroom by the ropes binding their hands and feet. Carpet burn is the least of their concern as they are tossed toward the towering mound of bodies.

The stench of feces, blood and death are potent in my nose, far more so than my first trip by the pile.

"Which one will go first?" Cable asks, pacing slowly in front of the pair.

Brian's fear is something palpable that Cable feeds off of. Like a drug long since purged from a junkie's body, I close my eyes and savor the faint whiff of pleasure that comes from Brian, as if some part of me remembers what it felt like to savor it.

Yes, I have killed in the past but there was never a euphoria surrounding the death like this. This is an adaptation that I will have to strong arm into check if I want to maintain a normal life.

"I choose the man," I call out, deciding that though is death would give me less satisfaction, the risk of him remaining alive any longer places me in a precarious emotional state. I turn away from him and inhale a short breath in an attempt to clear my senses but the space is too overwhelmed with death.

Though Iris's insanity holds a great potential threat, Brian's know how and research worries me more. He can recreate his plans that he worked here. His death minimizes the risk of reproducing what happened here.

Glancing all around me, I wonder what happened to the psychotic Dr. Wiemann. Did he survive the attack or has be too been added to the pile? Surely if he had survived, Cable would have brought him here for the execution festivities.

Brian grunts and bucks as Cable reaches down and easily picks up the middle-aged man as if he were nothing more than an unruly toddler. Cable's muscles ripple but show no sign of strain as he hoists the two hundred pound man up and onto the base of the funeral pyre.

Several body parts tumble from above and strike Brian in the head as he struggles to worm his way off of his gruesome death bed.

"Do we have anything flammable?" I ask, delaying as long as I can. I look to the halls surrounding us but see nothing beyond the masses of Withered.

Where are you, Nox? If you are going to bust in and save the day, now is the time!

Cable makes a grunting sound and two groups of Flesh Bags separate from the pack and rush down the halls in both directions.

"Where did you send them?"

"To the kitchens." Cable holds out his hand to me and I accept it with only a momentary pause to steel myself for his touch. It is confusing to long for his affection while at the same time be thoroughly repulsed by it. "It should only be a moment."

I nod and then look over to Iris. Breaking off contact with Cable, I move to crouch in front of her and pull the cloth for her mouth. She licks her lips and swallows a couple of times before smiling up at me.

"I told you that evolution finds a way."

"Yes," I nod and toss the rag aside, "but not your way."

She wiggles to free the hem of her skirt from beneath her. "I have faith that we will survive this."

"The human race or Brian?"

"Oh no," she laughs and places her bound wrists back into her lap. It is unsettling just how innocent she can look when she wants to. "Brian is as good as dead. He knows too much. We both know that, but you and I...we can change the world. You friend over there is just the beginning. With my resources, we can find a way to survive."

Glancing back over my shoulder, I smile at Cable and then look back at her. "I'm pretty sure right now he'd rather just eat you."

Iris' pupils dilate and her skin pales but that is the only physical slip that reveals her fear. Leaning in close, I sniff her neck. "Yes, you are afraid. You should be."

"You wouldn't kill me," she says when I lean back. "You need me."

"For what?"

Iris's smile grows haughty. "I know the location of every military facility on the east coast, both Safe Zone test sites and underground. If you want to save humanity you are going to need my help."

"Safe Zone test sites?"

Iris tsks. "Where do you think we get our prime subjects from? They are handpicked from our labs and then brought directly to us. We can't just keep picking up stragglers along the way and hoping for positive results. The time for reckless science has passed thanks to you. If these sites do not hear my voice in twenty-four hours' time the Safe Zones will go into full lockdown and those who are unworthy of the testing will be eradicated."

"That's genocide!"

"No, Avery," Iris leans forward. "That is progress."

I bite down on my tongue to keep from snapping her neck right here and now. I know it would be easy to do. I saw Cable do it with Hadley and feel the same strength coursing through my veins.

"Avery," Cable calls and I hear the approach of feet. "It is time."

"I will be back for you." I slam my fist down onto her right leg. The cracking of her bones and her yelp of pain helps to ease the anger seething inside of me only slightly. She will die but not before I dig that information out of her, with my bare hands if needs be.

"What was that all about?" Cable asks when I return to his side.

"It was merely the conclusion of a disagreement." I clench a fist and wait for the shaking in my fingers to cease. I wish that I knew if it was from the burning rage inside of me or fear. At this point, it's hard to tell.

When I return to the mound of bodies and Brian, I see that it has been drenched in some sort of fluid. Cable holds out a box of matches. "I'll give you the honor."

Glancing at him from the corner of my eye, I see a fervor in him that scares me. Cable is eagerly anticipating this death while I just feel sickened by it all. Does Brian deserve to die? Yes, a horrible, gruesome death, but I feel no joy or excitement from it.

"Give me the honor?" I accept the match box. As I step closer to the mound, the scent of oil grows stronger and I turn back. "Is that what this is? An honor?"

"There is always honor is justice."

Holding the matches up, I stare back at him. "I am about to murder a man in cold blood."

"A guilty man."

"True, but he is still a man. How long did it take for you to stop caring, Cable?"

He frowns and shoves his hands into his pockets. "I never stopped caring about you."

"I mean about people."

"Four days."

I blink. "That's it."

He lowers his gaze to the floor. "That is how long it took me to decide to break out of the cave."

My hand falls to my side. For the first time, I see a profound sadness come over Cable and realize how terrifying that must have been to wake up in a cave, sealed in with large stones and a bullet hole buried in the cave floor next to his head.

"I'm sorry."

"Don't be." He raises his head. "It only made me stronger."

"But this is wrong. You must see that."

"Is it?" He stares at Brian without a hint of compassion. "He hurt you. Death is the only form of justice."

Finally, I fully grasp his line of thinking, as simple and uncomplicated as it could be. Brian hurt me. Brian must die. That is all that matters to Cable. There is no outside reasoning, no soul to tell him it is wrong or moral compass to guide his path. He is completely and utterly without humanity.

My heart breaks for all that he has lost and all that I stand to lose as I walk back toward him and take his hand.

"There is another way. We can find it, together. Just walk away from this and I promise I will help you."

"Help me?" Anger flickers across his handsome face, contorting him into the monster I know now lies beneath. "There is nothing wrong with me and soon enough you will see that."

Taking the matches from me, he strikes one and tosses it at Brian's feet. As the man writhes and screams, trying to beat the flames back, Cable turns his back on him and faces me. "I will give you that one, but next time I expect you to do it."

I follow his gaze as he looks toward Iris and feel my pulse quicken. How am I supposed to save her without alerting Cable to my indecision? Too many lives are at stake if she dies today. I can't let that happen.

Looking out over the Withered, I stare across a sea of death. Even if somehow I find a way to overcome this horde, more will rise up. The mutations will spread like wildfire, sweeping across the country but will it be contained within our borders or does this conspiracy affect the world on a global capacity? Is there still a chance to come back from this?

Iris may know that answer. I suspect that she has a great deal of information that could be of use if only I can find a way to spare her life.

When Cable starts toward her, I reach out and take his hand, drawing him back. "Brian is the one who signed me up for his freak show experiments. Let me enjoy this for a moment."

I turn to stare at Brian, using my hand to shield the brightness of the fire. His mouth is locked in an open scream but no sound comes out. His body twitches as the flames melt away his flesh and muscle. I force myself to watch and not give away the revulsion that I feel, but there is an undeniable sense of satisfaction as well. He tortured and killed so many. It is only right that he suffer now.

Within minutes, he will be nothing more than blackened bone and charred remains and I will watch every second of it if that means I can buy just a little more time for Nox to arrive.

Cable smiles and places his arm around my shoulders and together we watch. The scent of burning flesh is strong in my nose but not unpleasant as I watch the Withered swaying back away from the fire, raising their shoulders just enough to hide away from the brunt of the light.

That is when I see movement in the ceiling. Just off to my right, barely within the edge of my peripheral vision, I see a ceiling tile shift. The movement goes unnoticed by Cable as he stares at the flickering orange and blue flames through the shield of his hand. The fire is immense as it climbs the oil trails higher to engulf the entire pile. The waves of heat force us to retreat several paces to stand in the cool once more.

"Did you see that?" When an odd puff of green smoke shoots up from one of the Flesh Bag it grasps Cable's captures his attention again and his face shines with morbid delight.

Making sure to keep my expression neutral, I strain to see the mop of unruly brown hair that appears upside and hanging from one of the tiles. It is Flynn.

Grasping Cable around the waist, I turn him so that he won't see Flynn. I will have to find a way to distract the Withered if Flynn has any chance of aiding Nox's team in an ambush. Although the zombies are wary of the flames and showing extreme care around the light, I know that it will not be enough to cripple them because their eyes have had time to adjust. I need to truly blind them long enough to let the Flynn and the soldiers play out whatever plan they have in place.

"It is so hot," I whisper, fanning myself.

"Yes, you will find that many things feel different now. Heat, light, sounds, and smells are all amplified. It is truly an amazing thing," Cable says and smiles as he tightens his grip around my waist. "I look forward to sharing each of these wondrous moments with you as you discover new abilities."

"Why do you think we have changed so much?" I angle my body toward him so that when he looks down at me he won't see the shuddering ceiling tiles as Flynn makes his way toward us.

"I suppose some part of us is trying to adapt to our surroundings. Do you remember how the Withered originally marched south? It was almost as if they were driven in that direction. My theory is that they were drawn to the heat."

"I don't understand. If we can't handle the heat now, why would they be attracted to it then?"

Cable smiles and rests his hand on my hip, curling his fingers around to hold me possessively. "Because they were still evolving at a much slower rate than we were. Heat is what I think drives us to evolve. That is why we suffer from the fever before the initial transformation. The additional heat creates energy and it fuels our bodies. Now that we are complete we shy away from the heat as a natural instinct to pull back from any further mutations."

I frown and look up at him. "Do you think it is possible to continue to change after all that we have been through?"

"I don't know." There is a sadness to his tone that surprises me. "Perhaps one day if it is necessary for us to survive again. The food chain is fluid and shifts with Mother Nature's demands. Who are we to say that nothing will ever been greater than we are now? Did the Dinosaurs not rule the earth as terrific tyrants at one time? There was no way that they could foresee a great rock falling from the sky that would inevitably wipe them out."

Standing here surrounded by the army he has amassed, many of which he most likely turned himself, I can't fathom there being a day when something could be stronger than him. It is a sobering thought and one that I am sure I will ponder over for some time to come. How do you defeat a man who has countless lives at his disposal and few capable of rivaling him?

As I stand there thinking of what the Dinosaurs must have felt in their final moments before fire and ash returned them to the ground from which they came, my thoughts linger on the fire. If Cable is right and excess heat can fuel a mutation, then could the application of cold hold the opposite effect?

When I look back over my shoulder, I see Iris staring at me with a keen intellect. Does she suspect that somehow an exact combination of heat and cold in alternating patterns could somehow reverse the effects permanently? Perhaps there is not a blood born cure that we should be looking for, but one involving basic biochemistry instead.

My reasoning for keeping Iris alive stands on shaky ground but if anyone has the resources to prove my theory, it is her. She has the contacts, she knows the locations of the testing sites. She alone could hold the information crucial to the human race's survival.

But if she does suspect as I do then that means terrible things are planned for her test subjects as she attempts to manually manipulate the genetic code to create her superior race. It is a great risk to consider allowing her to lie but without her alive the deaths of innocents could be far more widespread.

"Cable, I was wondering if—"

The explosion that sends the ceiling crashing down around us leaves me momentarily deafened as I am thrown from Cable's grasp. I hit the ground hard and roll several times before I slam to a stop against a wall. Sticky blood has splattered my face and glued my eyelashes shut. Wiping at my eyes to peer through the haze of smoke and debris hovering in the air, I hear howls and growls mingled with gunfire as the ringing in my ears dissipates.

Cable rises near the fire and begins yelling commands. His army immediately responds as they rise from the burning embers, unconcerned with their own damaged limbs. Many are unable to regain their footing but those that do attack with vicious intent.

I hear the static of a radio and look directly overhead to see a man in full military garb lying across the metal ceiling support beams, picking the Flesh Bags off sniper style. The nametag on his breast says Thompson but I barely have a chance to read it before a Flesh Bag leaps into the air, snatches his leg and yanks him to the floor. There is a sickening crunch of bones and I turn away.

Chaos reigns all around me as more Withered attempt to fit into the space, coming from the offshoot hallways and the ballroom. They crawl over each other like mice, eating their way through the soldiers they pick off the ceilings.

"Avery!" I turn to see Flynn dangling from the ceiling nearly twenty feet away with his hands lowered to me, beckoning for me to run to him. Cable turns at the same moment and darts straight toward him.

"Flynn, no!"

I'm still ten feet back when Cable snatches onto Flynn's arm and yanks him down. The sound of the kid's shoulder popping out of place makes my knees week as Flynn flops to the floor and his head bounces off the plush carpet. His body goes rigid with pain as Cable stomps down on his hand.

"Get off of him!" I scream and launch myself at Cable.

He takes the brunt of my attack, rolling with me end over end. The carpet eats through the flesh of my arms as I slide, hanging on to Cable's shirt until we slam into the far wall and take out the legs of half a dozen Flesh bags.

"Flynn, run!" I scream and rise onto my knees to face off with Cable.

"I will not let you hurt him."

Cable's face is pale and twisted with rage as he rises to his knees. "You would defy me for a human?"

"No," I shake my head. "I would defy you for a friend. He saved me when Brian and Iris set their abominations on us in the lab. Without his help I would have died down there. I owe him my life, Cable."

A muscle beneath his eye twitches. "You owe the humans nothing!"

"This one I do and there are others here too that have helped me." I raise one hand out to him, begging him to pause long enough to hear me out. "These soldiers saved me when I was hurt and dying. I had blood poisoning from a gunshot and would have died if they had not found me. These men that you are killing took care of me, brought me here and fixed me up. They are not all evil, Cable. Some of them are good."

"Lies!" His eyes widen enough for me to see small red veins in the whites of his eyes. The muscles in his neck cord up as he leaps to his feet. "They kidnapped you. I felt your fear."

"No," I say, stepping toward him with my hands raised. "These men were following order. They were blinded by Iris and Brian but that does not make them bad people. We can help them see the truth. We can guide them to a new way of living so that there can be peace."

"Peace has never been an option."

His chest rises and falls as he looks beyond me to where Flynn lies immobilized by the pain in his shoulder. None of the Withered have attacked him so I have to think that Cable has somehow silently called dibs on him.

"It can be an option if you allow it. This is important to me, Cable. Won't you at least consider it?" I take a step back toward Flynn. "What I want and care about still matters to you, doesn't it? You came for me because you love me. Now prove to me that you do. Let Flynn live and call back your army. Show the survivors that there is a better path for us all."

His eyes darken and his fingers curl into fists at his sides. He begins to march toward me but with each step that he takes, the faster I retreat to Flynn's side. Tripping over his legs, I slam hard to the floor beside him.

I can smell Flynn's fear and instantly have to battle with the hunger that rises up inside of me. I can see Cable's need to feed in the dilation of his eyes as he stares only at the prostrate boy.

"Get out of my way, Avery."

Pushing Flynn behind me, I throw my body across his and Cable comes up short. "If you hurt him you will have to hurt me first."

Cable swears and plants his feet. "Do not force my hand."

"It is you who is doing the forcing. Walk away, Cable. This isn't a fight that you have to win."

"You would choose him over me?"

"Why can't I choose both of you?"

Cable's growl makes the hair on my arms and neck rise and I feel Flynn shrink with fear behind me.

"I asked you earlier if you would pause to think before you killed someone that you love. Well, Flynn is someone that I love, Cable. He is like a brother to me. Are you willing to take the only decent family I've ever known away from me?"

"Dammit, Avery I am your family. I am all that you will ever need!" He paces back and forth, seething with anger. "Move aside and I promise it will be over quickly."

"No." I pat Flynn's leg and rise, standing my ground in front of a man who could end me with hardly a thought. I may be strong, but he is stronger. I may be fast, but he will always be faster. He has a full grasp on his abilities while I am still struggling to even begin to comprehend mine.

"I don't want to fight you, Cable but I will if you force me to."

Cable turns and spits to the side.

"Avery."

Cable jerks around and the bulk of his large frame blocks my view of the soldier that has dropped down from the ceiling behind him, but I know his voice. "Nox, run! Get out of here!"

"No." He shifts to the side and I watch him remove his gas mask. It is only when I see him take a hesitant breath that I taste the bitterness on the air. Near the back of the room, several gas canisters spew forth their tear gas but this time I am unaffected by its effects.

Nox tosses his mask toward Flynn and the boy rushes to put it on as his eyes swell with redness and tears stream down his cheeks. Cable is deadly still as Nox slowly shifts around to the side, drawing closer to me. Cable matches his every movement, never blinking or taking his eyes off of Nox.

"How are you doing over there, dumbass?"

I blink. "This isn't a joke, Nox. I can't let you die for me just because you've got some wild hair up your ass to be a hero."

Nox surprises me by smiling but he isn't looking at me. His gaze is focused only on Cable. "I guess saving the damsel from distress runs in the family, doesn't it?."

"Dude." I barely hear Flynn's whisper through the mask. "I did not see that one coming."

I look between the two men, confused by the mounting tension between them.

Nox never looks away from Cable as he stops halfway to my side. "Hello, Cable. Long time no see."

Cable nods in his direction. "It's good to see you again, Lenny."

TWENTY

The instant I hear Cable acknowledge his brother, I'm pretty sure that I'm going to faint. It might not be the worst idea that I've had. Sure, I might wake up maimed and covered in zombie shit but it would save me from the massive brain aneurysm that I'm suffering from at the moment.

"You're shitting me. *You're* Lenny?" I screech.

Nox nods but doesn't look my way. "Lennox is my full name but the guys all know me here as Nox. I let them use it since I wasn't too eager to give away who I really am since I technically went MIA once things starting falling apart to try to get to my mom and I was worried that it would come back to bite me. Nicknames seem safer these days but Cable always loved to call me Lenny just to tick me off."

"And it always worked." I am dumbfounded when a hint of a smile touches Cable's lips and for the first time I see a bit of a resemblance in coloring of the hair, the strength of their cheek bones and even color of their eyes.

"My mind is officially blown," Flynn mutters but I wave my hand behind my back at him. The last thing I need is giving Cable a reason to shut him up.

"How could you...why didn't you... Ah, hell." I hold my head in my hands. It hurts far too much to think.

"I don't know if this is what you're asking," Nox says. "But I swear I didn't know. At least not until you pulled me aside earlier. I put the pieces together in the stairwell but with Armageddon biting at our asses I thought it might be better to wait on that conversation until we were less distracted."

Cable breaks his gaze with Nox and turns to look at me. I see the question in his eyes followed swiftly by anger when I refuse to hold his gaze.

I raise my hand in defense. "It's not what you think, Cable. You were dead and Nox was the one who saved my life. Twice actually. Or is it three times? I'm really starting to lose count."

And apparently rambling on has become a thing for me too.

"The point is that he listened. I had no one after I left you."

"So you left me behind, alive and trapped in a fucking cave, and while I was scouring the countryside to find you, you were shaking up with my brother?"

"Listen to her, Cable. Nothing happened between us." Nox steps forward with his hands raised. "She is innocent."

"But you aren't." Cable practically spits at his brother. "I should have smell you on her sooner. You always did have a way of getting what you wanted, no matter the cost."

Nox takes a step back, looking as if he's just been slapped. "That's not true."

"Isn't it?" Cable clenches and releases his fists. "How many girls did you bring home before I left for boot camp? How many one night stands and broken hearts did you leave behind? More than I can count."

Nox swallows hard and refuses to look in my direction. "I've changed."

Cable laughs and begins to pace. "Yeah, well so have I."

"I can tell."

I glance over at Nox, wishing that I could warn him not to provoke Cable but he still doesn't look my way. "What happened to you, Cable? You used to be the good guy. Now you're just an asshole with serious abandonment issues."

My breath becomes trapped in my lungs as I wait to see what Cable will do. Like a dog with raised hackles, Cable sinks lower and prepares to fight.

"Listen to me," I plead, holding my hands out as I step away from Flynn and move closer to Cable. "Nox hasn't done anything wrong. He hasn't touched me or hurt me. You know me better than that. Do you really think I would just jump in bed with him so fast?"

Cable's jaw clenches. "I know what he is like."

"Maybe you did, but trust in me. I was crushed when I lost you. Walking away from that cave nearly destroyed me but I didn't pull that trigger because I still had hope of finding a cure and someday being able to come back for you. Does that sound like a person who is ready to accept a one night stand?"

Nox glances at me from the corner of his eye but I refuse to show any emotion. Cable is a time bomb ready to explode and I have to diffuse the situation, no matter what it costs me.

"I love you, Cable. Do you hear me? I love *you.*"

His posture eases slightly and he turns to look down his shoulder at me. "Prove it."

"How?"

A slow smile stretches along his once handsome face, but now all I see is ugliness so black I wonder if there was ever truly any light in him. "Kill my brother."

"No!" Nox holds out his hand to stop me as I step forward. "Do not put that on her, brother. This is between you and me."

"Do not tell me what to do, Lenny." A low growl rises in Cable's throat as he bends his knees and enters a pose that I know will send him speeding like a bullet straight into Nox's chest a split second after he leaps.

"Cable," I call softly and wait for him to look at me again. "What is it that you truly want?"

"You. It's always been about you."

I move closer to him, stepping between the two of them. I feel Nox reach out and place a warning hand on my arm but I ignore him. "Let Nox, Flynn and the rest of the survivors live and I will go with you."

Cable arches an eyebrow. "Willingly?"

"Avery, don't!"

"Stay out of this, Nox," I hiss and pull out of his grasp. The instant I step away from him I hear the safety switch off and know that he's got his gun raised with his finger firmly seated on the trigger.

"This is intense," Flynn mutters behind me and I realize that if he says one more one-liner I'm going to throttle him myself. The kid just doesn't know when to cover his own ass.

Hell continues to rain down around us. Men and Withered alike are wounded, fall and bleed out amongst debris and ash but somehow Cable keeps us cocooned in an invisible bubble of safety. The Withered glance at us from time to time but none seem capable of penetrating our space.

I take another step forward and Cable tenses. Nox shifts toward me at the same time Cable does and I know that he will stay that way until forced to move. "Would you really kill Nox now that you've got what you want? You are brothers and you've found each other after all this time. Isn't that enough?"

"No." They both say at the same time.

"So that's it? You are going to fight it out to the death and make me watch?"

Nox flinches as he moves around to my right side to get a clear shot but Cable shows no sign of regret. Of course, he wouldn't because his goal is to eliminate all ties to my human side. By killing his brother, Cable would accomplish that for both of us.

"I won't let this happen."

Cable glances over at me. "You can't stop it."

"Can't I?" I move closer to Cable. "If you harm the people that I have grown to care about I will never forgive you."

Cable frowns. "I will have you either way."

"Perhaps." I stretch out my hand and place it on his arm. "But wouldn't it be better if I didn't fight you? If I could be grateful to you for your mercy instead of bitter over what you stole from me?"

From off to the side, I see Nox grow agitated but I force myself to ignore him and the whacked out emotional roller coaster that I'm trapped on right now. Cable should be dead and Nox shouldn't be a complication. But neither one of them seem content to be what they should.

Cable looks down at my hand on his arm. The muscles in his forearm flex as he releases one fist. "All I want is you."

"You will concede and call your army off?"

"I will."

I nod in agreement. "Then you have me."

"No!" Nox steps forward and a red laser light appears on Cable's forehead. "I'm not going to let you turn her into a monster."

Cable smiles without concern for the laser targeting his head. "She already is. She just hasn't accepted that yet."

Flynn grunts as he pushes up into a seated position behind. When I glance over my shoulder to look at him, I'm reminded of how fragile he is and how easily Cable broke him. I'm struck with a fresh wave of fear when I shift my gaze onto Nox, but I see only fierce determination in his eyes. He will fight no matter what.

"Do we have a deal?" I ask, stepping closer to expand the distance between myself and Nox.

Cable releases a long breath then turns his head away and barks out a growl. The Flesh Bags instantly cease fighting. Several who were locked in hand-to-hand combat release the soldiers and drop them awkwardly to the ground. Those who were eating their victims stop chewing and lift their head. All turn toward Cable.

Another growl sends them racing for the exits, though not the ones I would have expected. The Withered flee through the darkened hallways instead of heading for the exterior doors. The sun must already be up.

"Where will they go?" I ask.

"There are ways into the building that even your leaders were not away of," Cable says and then takes my hand. "I will show you."

As he pulls me away, I look back over my shoulder at Nox. Anger and resentment run parallel in his body language as Flynn reaches out to hold him back with his one good arm.

"You have to let me go," I say as Cable leads me past my friends. "If you don't, everyone will die."

"I won't let you be a martyr," Nox calls back.

"I'm not. I'm just a girl trying to do the right thing."

Cable tugs tightly on my arm to hurry along and I follow his lead past countless bodies, both mutilated and smoking from the fire that has raged out of control. Much of the carpet has caught on fire and I fear that the flames will spread.

I may never know many people will be saved by my actions tonight but I have to believe that I have made a difference. Nox will live and Flynn will not watch another friend mowed down. That has to count for something.

A profound sadness wells up within me as I think about what my life will be like now, surrounded by the dead. Cable is nothing like the man I once knew and yet I have to hold onto the hope that there is still some goodness buried inside of me. Not for my own sake, but because it is what he would have done.

Now watching where I'm going, I snag my foot on a bit of fabric and fall to the ground. My hands slip on blood and when I crash to the floor I come face to face with a glassy-eyed Iris. Half of her face has been chewed away. Her right shoulder and on down to her hip is shredded. Her left thigh has been exposed down to the bone.

I feel no remorse when I look back at her body. Instead, I feel terrified. If what she said is true, tomorrow the Safe Zones will go into full lock down and more innocents will die. I can't let that happen.

"Nox?" I yank back on Cable's hand and this time, he stops short. "Iris warned me about testing being done at the Safe Zones. She was the failsafe to ensure that things ran smoothly. Do what you can for them."

He swallows hard and then slowly nods. "I will."

"And make sure you take special care of Flynn. He doesn't seem to know how to stay out of trouble."

"That hurts, but she's not wrong." He offers a sheepish shrug then winces as he reaches to cradle his dislocated shoulder. "Give 'em hell, Avery."

My vision of them grows watery as tears slip from my eyes. Cable tugs on my hand and I turn away to allow him to lead me around the funeral pyre. Countless bodies lie around me, each one lost for the sake of Cable's twisted love for me. Each of their deaths are on me.

"Where will we go?" I ask.

"Home."

Glancing over at Cable, I see him smile, but I feel none of his happiness. What will happen to me once I am away from humans and surrounded by constant feelings of hunger and anger? Will I lose myself as quickly as Cable did? Will I become nothing more than a thing with teeth?

Anxiety rises up within me at the thought and I go rigid in his hand. I can't allow that to happen. I can't become something that people will fear or try to kill.

"Do you love me?" I ask.

Cable's step falters when I refuse to take another step and he turns to face me. "Of course, I do."

"Then you need to let me go."

"No." He pulls on my arm. "You said you would come willingly."

"And I meant it, but I can't be like you, Cable. I can't be who you have become. You are not the man I loved before, the one who was a heart first and a soldier last. You used to be a man who believed in me and saw the good in everything. That man who would have paid any sacrifice just to see me smile."

"That man was weak but now...I am better."

"No." New tears slide down the curve of my cheeks as I pull my hand away from his. "You're something far worse."

Cable blinks and stares down at his empty hand. I know that I only have a split second before his anger kicks in and I am struck by the force of it. Lifting my hand, I aim the flare gun at his chest.

"I am sorry, but the man that I loved is truly dead," I whisper.

When the flare strikes his chest, it explodes in brilliant light. Nox and Flynn race to my side as Cable flails and beats at his burning shirt. The rest of his clothes quickly catch fire and soon he is consumed with the flames. I close my eyes at the scent of his burning flesh and know that his screams will be added to my waking nightmares.

"I'm so sorry, Cable."

Rage and pain darken his eyes as he mouths my name and then turns and runs. His burning chest illuminates the corridor as he races past the survivors and disappears into the darkness.

"I failed him again," I whisper as my knees buckle and I collapse into Nox's arms.

"You didn't fail anyone," he whispers and gently eases me to the floor. My body tingles as I try to push aside the wave of agony that Cable thrusts at me. I have no way of knowing if he intentionally wanted me to feel it, but I would guess that it was an involuntary sharing. He is hurting because of me, and no matter how far he may have fallen, I still care for him.

I just can't be with him.

Sinking into Nox's embrace, I feel a part of my soul wither and die. The love that I once felt for Cable is tarnished and the memories have become too painful to think about.

As Nox wraps me in his arms, resting his chin on my head, I cling to him. I was wrong in thinking that I could get close to him without needing him. That is the natural order of things. That is what caring about someone is all about. Letting down the walls means that they can see you for all of the good, the bad and the wicked and you are lucky that person will still accept you in the end.

I want to be a good person and someone that is worthy of love but I know that I am no longer bound solely by my own desires, but that of the pack. Though the Withered have fled I know that they will be back. Cable will not let this diversion last for long, and when he returns, it will be with far greater numbers.

I can't remain here just as I can't risk the safety of these people. The only thing I can do now is to run as far and a fast as I can and hope that it will be enough.

Just before I close my eyes and allow exhaustion to steal me away to a place where there is no pain, fear or regret, I hear Nox give the command to follow Cable but they will never track him down in time. He knows his escape route too well and is too smart to allow himself to be penned in.

Cable will escape and he will live to get his revenge. Of that, I have no doubt. The connection between us is strong and I fear that will be my undoing.

So, I will run and pray that it is far enough to sever that connection.

I may have betrayed him today but the love bond between us is strong. In me, Cable sees an equal. With the memories of our past fresh in his mind, he will not give up until I am his and my greatest fear is that the next time he comes looking for me, I will be ready to join him.

"Hey," Nox whispers in my ear as he gently scoops me up and places me in his lap, "I think that nickname I gave you should remain on the table."

"What nickname?"

"Dumbass," he smiles and presses his lips to my forehead. "Seems kinda fitting now, don't you think?"

"Only if you let me call you Lennox from now on."

Nox grimaces. "It's a terrible name."

"I think it's actually really sexy."

"Do you?" He arches an eyebrow and easily settles into his familiar cocky grin. "Well, maybe I'll have to reconsider using it then."

"You should." I wrap his arm around my waist and snuggle into his chest. "But don't go getting any wild ideas about talking me into a one night stand. I've still my got standards to uphold."

Nox laughs and the gentle rumble in his chest soothes me. "I wouldn't dream of it."

A hive of activity bustles around us as new soldiers flood into the area to make sure the hotel is back on lockdown. Medics move from body to body checking for survivors. Those who have been bitten are removed to be dealt with out of sight. The fires are soon put out and some semblance of normal returns as Nox and I lean against the wall.

None of it matters as I close my eyes and let Nox hold me. For the first time in ages, I feel safe. I don't know when I will have to go on the run, or if it will even make any difference but I know that I will miss this. I will miss him.

Nox is not Cable and he never will be, but I have decided that is exactly what I love most about him.

AFFLICTION

BOOK THREE

AFFLICTION

A cause of mental or bodily pain, as sickness, loss,
calamity, or persecution.

BOOK THREE

PROLOGUE

The stench of death and decay grows stronger with each step that I take down the empty stairwell. The hand railings are speckled with blood and gore, coating the palm of my hand with sticky warmth. The steps are slippery underfoot as I spiral down to the hidden depths of the Opryland hotel.

Small emergency generators have been cranked and placed in those places not lit by the rising sun as soldiers and survivors work to clear each floor above, but down here in the underbelly there is no light to be found. My eyes adjust to the darkness within seconds of entering the stairwell, and as I open the basement door the hallway brightens before me with a greenish hue.

Fresh human blood glistens in wide streaks across the wall, evidence of an arterial wound that bled out the victim that lies at my feet just out of reach of the stairwell door. He was among the lucky ones that died quickly. Beside him lies another unfortunate victim who did not fare so well. This man's face has been beaten to a bloody pulp. His features are completely unrecognizable and his torso has been caved in, crushed under the weight of a foot, by the looks of the bloody toe prints left on his shirt. His lower half is shattered from pelvis to toes.

This man was not eaten by a Withered but trampled under their swift escape after Cable sounded the retreat a short time ago. Their trail of carnage was easy to follow, even without my heightened sense of smell and ability to see in the dark. I fear that once my absence is discovered Nox will try to follow me. I can't allow that to happen.

It is only a matter of time before someone notices that I am missing. Though I was a stranger to most during my time here, my face and name have spread among the survivors, whispered in reverence. They know I am the reason they survived. What they don't know is that I'm also the reason for their suffering.

With Cap and his most loyal soldiers gone, Nox became the unanimously nominated leader of the survivors. I wish that I could stay and see him rise to the challenge. I can think of no one better to lead them because in the time that I have known him, he has proven to be both a good and honorable man. A person I would be happy to follow if fate had chosen a different path for me.

I hate that he will not understand why I am leaving without saying goodbye. Perhaps it is the coward's way out, but I can't bear to lose another person that I care about. Watching Cable's final fleeting moments nearly destroyed me. Saying goodbye to Nox now would finish the job.

"In time, he will understand," I whisper to myself as I step over the squashed man.

Chunks of torn flesh squish beneath my boots as I move down the long corridor. The air feels heavy and stale as I pause to search an open doorway and find the room empty. It has been nearly an hour since Cable and his minions fled the hotel. They will have a head start on me, but I know that I will find them.

There is nowhere that I can go that Cable will not be able to feel me. The connecting bond that I now share with him is both a blessing and a curse. Already I can feel his mounting rage and his hatred for how I turned against him at the last moment. It's beginning to fade with the distance he puts between us, but there was no other way to save the lives of Nox's people and myself. He managed to track me across state lines, but I fear that I would lose him within just a couple of miles.

I need to learn to control my abilities if I stand any chance of surviving in the days to come.

Had I gone with Cable I fear how quickly I would have lost myself to his poisonous words. He gloated that I would soon enough become like him, a thing both unmerciful and filled with hatred. A monster bent on creating a new world where humans no longer have a place. I can't fathom such a world, and yet I can feel stirrings deep within me already starting to take hold. They are distortions within my soul, altering my thoughts and tainting them with evil intent.

Some of what Cable said spoke to me...and to the monster writhing just beneath the surface.

Nox would tell me that I can fight this, that I can choose to remain myself, but I can't take the risk of him being wrong. I can't become a thing for him to fear or the enemy that might end his life.

I can't let his death or anyone else's be on my hands. There has already been enough blood spilled because of me. No more innocents will have to suffer. I will make sure of that.

Sweat stings my eyes as I wipe my forehead, feeling my pulse increase with every step that I take. There is something about this place that sets me on edge. Maybe my senses are still heightened from the attack on the hotel or maybe exhaustion has made me overly wary? I wish either one of those was the real reason, but I suspect that the truth of the matter is that I feel ill at ease because the scent of human blood surrounding me isn't nearly as repulsive as it should be.

It is yet another blatant reminder that I am no longer entirely human.

After waking from a coma less than 48 hours ago to discover that I am immune to a Withered bite, my body has adapted the human-engineered rabies virus that decimated our world and I somehow mutated it into something new. Instead of becoming one of *them*, I have become something more. Something possessing great strength, speed, night vision and an intense ability to smell. I have become a killer, capable of intelligent thought and the capacity to feel and hear the Withered whenever they are near.

I have become the next link in the evolutionary chain, but I am not alone.

Cable is like me, though his transformation occurred months before mine. He has had the time to perfect his abilities to the point of being able to bend the Withered to his will while I struggle to even comprehend the changes in myself. Cable told me that there are others like me and I can sense a couple of them now among the bitten victims in the floors above that are being systematically put down. I could have told Nox to spare them, to give them a chance to live, but I remained silent as I slipped away unnoticed.

I can't let them become like me...or worse, like Cable.

He came for me last night with the intent of making me his own, of creating a new hierarchy with me by his side, but he is no longer the man that I once knew and loved. He is now something cold, uncaring, and obsessed. His hatred for humanity and his thirst for domination has twisted him into something abominable and it is all because of the mutation.

How long will it be before I lose myself to the mutation too? How long do I have before I turn on the very people that I have tried to protect? How much time do I have before I become the enemy that must be put down?

I have only one choice—I have to leave.

Once Nox realizes that I have left, he will scour the hotel, and when he does, he will locate this path through the basement and ensure that nothing will ever be able to gain access to the hotel again. Cable can't be allowed to return so easily. We have barely survived this attack. The survivors will not survive a second.

To give them a chance I have to do whatever it takes to shift Cable's focus away from them and onto tracking me instead.

I will miss Nox far more than I fear I even know. Despite my reservations against letting him through my walls, he found a way to not only become important to me, but to prove to me that I am capable of far more than I ever thought possible. All Cable wanted to do was to protect me. Nox only sought to back me up, to let me lead and find my own strength again. He gave me what I needed most, but now I need to prove to myself that I can let him go.

As I move steadily down the hall, lifting my nose to the air to sniff out the Flesh Bags' trail, I search for a hole or grate that leads underground. I know that Cable must have come up from below, most likely using an old sewer line that was abandoned after the flood that forced parts of the hotel to be renovated a few years back. Nox has his men searching the upper levels, but one whiff of the stairwell behind me told me that this was the path they took.

Room after room passes by and the scent of the Withered grows stronger. I move along one hallway and enter another, following the exposed metal pipes overhead that show signs of rust and corrosion.

Something moist and solid squishes beneath my boot as I turn the corner and I pause to lift my foot. A chunk of tanned flesh the size of my hand is caught in the tread of my boot and I instantly know that it does not belong to a Withered by the delicious scent of it.

My stomach clenches with sudden need and I lean back against the wall, sucking in large gulps of air as I drag my boot against a door frame to clean the skin away. My heartbeat quickens and my hands begin to shake as the aroma surrounds me, invading my senses, and as I lift my eyes, I see that the hallway is piled with human corpses.

Less than three feet ahead of me, I spy the first headless torso of a slightly overweight man. One of his severed legs is propped against a woman whose face has been chewed off. The man's other leg is bent at a blunt angle toward his ears with the brilliant white of bone poking through his skin.

Dozens more lie one on top of the other, intermingled and tossed aside without care. This hall is a mass grave, littered with dismembered body parts and blood so thick it rises above the soles of my boots. From somewhere within the mass I can see movement and hear chewing. One Withered has remained to continue its feast.

"Oh, my God," I moan as the hallway begins to compress in on me and I shrink back against the wall.

The blood smells too sweet and the human flesh so fresh I can imagine that a bit of warmth still lingers in it. Saliva swells in my mouth at the thought of reaching out and taking a small taste.

"No!" I back away, clinging to the wall as I flee down the hall in the direction that I just came. It is safer there. The scents are not so strong and I force myself to stop running.

"It's all in my head," I whisper to the empty hallway as I gulp down the bile rapidly rising in my throat. My knees give way and I collapse to the floor, doubling over to press my forehead against the ground as I grip my stomach. "I'm stronger than this. I am not like that thing back there!"

Minutes pass and melt into what feels like agonizing hours. With each cleansing breath that I take in, I feel a small portion of calm return. I count each breath, forcing myself not to taste the air or risk hyperventilating again. Slowly the panic attack begins to ease and the sensations of hunger subside to a manageable level.

I wipe at my mouth, wishing that I had something close to hand that could conceal the taste of blood on the air. The hairs along my arms stand to attention as my heart continues to thrum loudly in my ears.

"That's it," I whisper again, pushing my hair back from my face. "Slow breaths. You're going to be fine."

But I don't really believe that. Upstairs, with the newly dawning sun filling the glass atrium with brilliant light, it would be easy to think that everything will be okay, but here in the dark, I feel like this is what my life is destined to become. Something meant only for the shadows, where depravity and hunger will rule. Where humanity will be lost to the vile urges of men turned monsters.

What hope do I have of maintaining my humanity in a world where death is a daily occurrence? I can't outrun it, nor can I avoid it. People will die. It is an inevitable fact, and my greatest fear is that the next time I am put into a position of life or death, I might not be able to get control of myself in time to stop myself for giving in to the hunger.

As I push up to my feet I pull my shirt up and over my arms to tie around my face. It will not seal out the scent of blood, but I pray that it will be just enough to help me escape this hellhole.

With my legs trembling and my stomach clenched tightly, I move back toward the hallway of death, determined to strangle the life out of that zombie and then get the hell out of this place. I know now that I am not strong enough to be around people, living or otherwise. My plans have to change. I have to do far more than just leave Nashville for a while.

I need to disappear and never return.

ONE

Fear and self-loathing follow me out of a cloud of concrete dust and into the filthy sewer tunnel that will give me access to the outside world. As I leave the collapsed passage behind me, the scent of explosives is still strong in my nose. No one will be entering the hotel through that hole again. Nox and his people will not have to fear another attack from that access point at least.

I slosh through knee height muck and rainwater for nearly six city blocks, stumbling from time to time before I find a manhole not covered with piles of debris. The stench lingers on my clothes as I pull myself up through the hole, but I welcome the odor. It helps to clog my senses and dull the memories of tearing the zombie's head from its shoulders as it chewed on the calf muscle of a dead woman. After that I was forced to climb over a pile of bodies to the exit. I pray that I never have to go through anything like that again.

My arms quiver under my weight as I pull myself along the ground, pushing with my feet to be free of the sewer. The sun is blinding overhead when I lay back and I am forced to roll onto my side to shield my eyes. Bits of broken glass and splintered wood from a blown out grocery shop bite into my arms and exposed stomach but I don't care. I am free.

Free of the hotel. Free of death and pools of blood. Free of people.

I yank my shirt off my face and take in deep cleansing breaths of fresh air as I kick the rest of the way out of the manhole. My heart feels heavy and my body even more so as I press my cheek to the pavement, feeling the warmth of the sun beginning to heat the blacktop. The events of the previous night have left me nearly to the point of collapse but I can't rest yet. I have something that I have to do before I skip town.

Allowing only a scant few moments to rest, I drag myself to the curb and then rise slowly. I am clothed in blood, sewage and concrete dust from my feet to my chest. I pick a few bits of glass out of my stomach and wipe away the blood, amazed that I can barely feel more than a sting. I've never been good with blood before. Feels kinda ironic now.

Looking up and down the street, I spy a clothing store half a block north of my current position and hurry toward it. Pausing outside the shattered glass door only long enough to sniff the air and determine that nothing is inside, I climb through and into blissful darkness. I had seriously underestimated how painful daylight had become. This will make traveling far more challenging.

I search through racks of clothing that have been torn free of their fixtures on the wall and left scattered across the floor. In another life I would never have been able to afford a single item in this shop. A small part of me feels bad for splattering filth onto the fine clothes as I search for something that fits but then I realize how silly that is. No one is left to care about fine things anymore. Now all that matters is food, shelter, and weapons.

I grab a black tank top and a pair of designer jeans up off the floor and then begin to rummage through the lingerie section to replace my blood-soaked underclothes. With a new wardrobe in hand, I head to the back of the store in search of a bathroom to clean up.

Draping the clothes over the side of the sink, I lean in to stare at myself in the mirror but, see a complete stranger looking back at me.

My eyes are sunken and ringed with purple. My cheeks look sallow and my lips are too thin and pale. Dried blood and streaks of God-only-knows-what line my forehead and mat my hair to my head.

"Wow. I really look like shit."

I poke at my cheeks and wonder if human food will even be enough to give me the strength I need to carry out my journey. There is so much that I just don't understand about myself. I fear that these new hunger pangs for human flesh will drive me to distraction and eventually, if denied long enough, will make me slowly wither away.

"And the one person who would know the answer to that just proved to be a psychotic bastard. Great mentor there, Avery." I turn away from the mirror with a sigh.

Lifting the lid to the toilet, I grab a handful of paper towels from the wall container and dip it into the water to clean my face. Considering that I have just crawled over a pile of bodies and then through the sewers on my hands and knees, this isn't half as bad as I would have thought, but there is no way in hell I'm drinking it. I use the remaining towels and hand soap to give myself the best wash I can manage and then kneel on the floor to dunk my hair into the toilet, ringing the blood and filth from my frizzy curls.

"If this doesn't prove how far the human race has sunk, I really don't know what has," I mutter as I squeeze excess water from my hair and then lean back against the wall.

My eyes grow heavy and I allow myself a few minutes to fall slack. A snore startles me awake sometime later and I use the sink to pull myself onto my feet. I feel no less tired, but at least I managed a few minutes of rest. It might be the last that I get for a while.

Shoving my legs into my jeans and pulling my new shirt overhead, I feel almost normal again until I reach for my boots to put them on but immediately stop. I can smell blood on them.

Closing my eyes, I push the air out of my lungs and plunge the boot soles into the toilet, scrubbing them with used towels until the paper is worn through and I can no longer smell the blood. The water is now a brackish color, but it disappears in a whirlpool when I flush the toilet.

Grabbing the half a roll of toilet paper off the back of the toilet, I tuck it under my arm and begin to search through the store for a bag. As stupid as it might seem, toilet paper has become quite the luxury item in my life and I'm not about to let this opportunity to stock up pass me by.

Near the front of the store I find an old messenger bag that couldn't possibly have been sold in this store. I dump out the contents onto the floor and rifle through a couple used notebooks, a lighter, a melted Twix bar, some tissues that I stuff back inside and a pen. There is nothing really of use, but I tear open the Twix wrapper and lap up the chocolate, moaning with delight as it goes down smooth as silk.

"I'd almost forgotten what that tastes like."

Before leaving the clothing store I make a quick sweep behind the shop's counter and turn up a handgun concealed in an old book carved out to fit the shape of the gun in a drawer beneath the cash register. The door stands wide open and all of its contents have been looted, but the robber failed to see the only valuable thing in the store.

Holding the gun in my hand, I feel the weight of it. My dislike for guns has not changed, but I know it will be a necessary evil where I am going. Especially if I don't want to have to kill with my bare hands.

Tucking the gun into my back pocket, I grab a decorative sheer black scarf off a mannequin, wrap it around my face to shield my eyes and head back out onto the street. A breeze lifts my newly washed curls off my shoulders. It comes from my left and I turn to see a wall of clouds approaching.

My mood instantly drops. A coming storm will make tracking the scent of Cable and his Flesh Bags much more difficult. I'm not sure just how well I will be able to feel Cable now that he's on the move. I need to hurry.

For several hours I hunt for their exit location, moving along the sewer lines only to come across an old trail that leads me well out of my way and I am forced to circle back along the Cumberland River until I find their scent once more. Cable feels disturbingly distant as I try to narrow down his exact location and come up empty handed. The only chance I have of locating him is to track him on foot. The only sense that I can get when I try to read his is that he is headed south, but that leaves a very large area to cover.

As the winds rise and the first droplets of rain begin to fall, I catch a break when an unmistakable odor near a storm drain leading out of town proves to be stronger than anything I have smelled all day.

I scrunch up my nose in disgust. "A large group of Withered definitely came this way."

Ignoring the lead that weighs down my legs, I follow the scent, pausing to kneel at each storm drain to sniff the gutter before returning to a slow jog. With each block that I leave behind me, the farther out of the heart of the city I travel. When I enter the suburbs on the other side, Nox and the Opryland hotel are lost in the distance.

Here and there I spy the remains of bodies along the side of the road, some rotted completely through and others torn and shredded. At first I think nothing of it as I force myself to focus on the task at hand, but slowly it begins to dawn on me that I am not feeling any hunger pangs and as the next body appears in the road, I slow down.

I realize long before I crouch beside the woman that she has been dead for quite some time. Her skin has been stripped of its color and sags on her emaciated frame. Her hair has begun to fall out, lying in clumps of rotted flesh around her head. Her cheeks are missing. Only muscle and her upper teeth can be seen when I roll her head to the side to take a closer look.

Reaching out to lift her eyelids, I jerk my hand back. Her eyes are pure white.

"What the hell?"

Pushing back from the woman, I stare in horror at what remains of her body. Her lower half is missing, torn away just below her belly button. The ground is stained black with her diseased blood. Along her arms I can see teeth marks far too large to be that of a rodent.

"The Flesh Bags are eating their own kind now."

There is no way to know if she was a mutated zombie or one of the originals, the ones who were harmless, mindless walkers. I suppose it doesn't really matter. The evidence before me proves that no one, not even a mutated hybrid, is safe now.

It is hard to shake the image of the woman as I push on ahead, stumbling more than I am able to jog. The rains quickly leave me soaked and chilled as I struggle to find my way and I begin to feel discouraged.

Here and there I spy evidence of life, though it is easy to tell that the people have not been present for quite some time. The reality of the evil that has befallen this city tells me that they have either fled or been disposed of. I try not to think about it as I run, keeping the highway within sight but not risking the exposure of being on it.

Less than half an hour later I spy the Nashville International Airport off to the side and slow to catch my breath. It stands as a mechanical graveyard of abandoned planes. Bits of broken tails and wings from crash landings still spread across the tarmac in sweeping gashes of black soot. The control tower appears to have tumbled and fallen to the ground long ago, most likely taken out by a falling aircraft. The windows of the terminal have shattered and weeds have begun to grow up the sides. There is no point in detouring in search of supplies. I'm sure it was thoroughly ransacked ages ago.

I stay the course as I continue following the intermittent scent, wringing water from my scarf which now serves as a shield from the gusting winds rather than the sun. I know by the tightening in my gut that I must be getting closer. Cable came this way for sure, but how much farther did he go?

It was my own naïveté that believed he had taken up residence in the city. Of course he would seek a position of benefit to him. Being in the suburbs would provide him access without the danger of being stumbled upon by one of the patrols that was sent out in search of survivors. Cable's base of operation is nothing if not well thought out.

The scent of death amplifies as I begin to see signs for a sewage treatment plant and it all becomes clear.

"That's how you knew how to get into the hotel. You've been using the tunnels to move around the city all along."

I hold a stitch in my side and wish for the hundredth time that I could rest before I go through with my plan. Nox would say it is foolhardy, and at this point I would agree with him, but it's the best I've got.

It makes perfect sense that Cable would hole up here now that I stop to think about it. What better way for him to maneuver his army in broad daylight than to remain underground?

I jog the remaining five miles with the hopes that I am going to turn the bend and come upon Cable's destination, but as I reach the plant, I know that he didn't stop here. The trail continues further off into the heart of a shopping center and I follow it to the front doors of a storefront. From here I can't tell how exactly far their territory lies, only that I am at the gates to hell with only a handgun, a small messenger bag and a roll of soggy toilet paper. It's not hard to understand why I'm seriously beginning to second guess my plan.

As I kneel beside a cluster of shattered glass and the remains of the mangled double door frame, I can't shake the feeling that I'm about the become some zombie's chew toy the instant that I step inside the building. I doubt it will be the last time that I have this feeling either.

Despite the ceiling of gray clouds heavily pregnant with rain overhead, I sense that the sun is beginning to set. I was so focused on finding Cable that I let the hours slip by. Standing here, toeing the line of his army's home territory, I know that there is no turning back now. They can already smell me.

The thought of Cable being so close by dredges up mixed emotions. Every gut instinct tells me that I should be running as far and as fast in the opposite direction but I can't leave yet. Not until I give Cable my message.

Nearly five hundred men, women and orphaned children reside within the hotel walls that I just left behind, still paralyzed with the fear that at any moment the Flesh Bags will scale their walls and return for them. With night quickly approaching, I know Cable will be tempted to strike again. I need to create a diversion, and fast.

TWO

As I kneel in the wet entryway of what was once a big box store filled with supplies for small business owners and the odd ragged mom with six mouths to feed, I know that this is definitely the stupidest thing that I have done to date. If Nox were here, he'd called me a dumbass, and for once I would wholeheartedly agree with him.

The thought of Nox makes my chest clench with regret. I know that he will not let me go without a fight. In another life, I might have felt all warm and squishy inside over that, but that life, that world, can't exist anymore. I don't have the luxury of falling in love again, especially when I've still got a deranged ex trailing after me. How did I get so lucky to end up with a former lover turned homicidal zombie with serious attachment issues?

The only thing I can do for Nox now is to leave and let him get on with his life. Rip off that bandage before the wound has a chance to fester. In time, he will move on and forget about me. At least that's what I tell myself as I glance over my shoulder and scold myself for my wavering nerves when I hesitate at the very door that I have been trying to reach all day.

"There is no way I'm going to pussy out now." I try to bolster what few shreds of bravery remain intact.

It is not like me to lose my nerve so easily, but then again, I've never had to struggle with inner demons quite like this before. Nor has my enemy ever worn the face of the man I once loved.

I have to finish this while I still can.

"Flynn would most likely call me a pansy right about now." I stare at my reflection in the twisted metal beside me and see myself smile. "Turns out he might be right after all."

After Nox, I will miss my teenage friend Flynn the most. When he discovers that I've left him behind to go on this harebrained mission, he will be miffed about it and probably demand to join up with Nox's rescue team. Nox will tell him that he's too young, to which Flynn will find some way to tail them in a foolish attempt to prove Nox wrong. Although I've only spent a short amount of time with Flynn in the hidden bunker hospital beneath the hotel, I learned quickly to love that kid. He's a fighter with more spunk than most of those halfwit soldiers Cap used to do his dirty work. I only hope Nox can temper Flynn enough to keep him alive.

I pause to sniff the air and wrinkle my nose at the foul stench that sours the falling rain.

"Yuck. This is definitely the place." I wipe my nose with the back of my hand as I blow out the breath that is tainted with the stench of rotting flesh, feces and soiled clothes. "I never want to smell like that!"

The hairs on my forearms rise up as I peer inside the dark depths of the building. Something definitely lurks within this vast warehouse.

Casting a glance behind me toward the city, I wonder if Nox has already formed a search party to come looking for me. There will be no way for him to track me now, not with the rains washing away all traces of my footsteps. He will scour the city in vain, but I will be long gone. My only hope is that he will not endanger the lives of his soldiers this close to nightfall for my sake.

Several shards of glass splinter under the toe of my boot as I lean through the doorway to get a better look. Just inside, I see overturned magazine racks. Most of the pages are torn and have begun to fade where the sun reaches them during the day. Beyond that waits dormant checkout lines, empty snack shelves and beverage coolers. Raiders got to this place long ago.

Normally, I would never dare enter a place like this alone. There are far too many blind spots, with multiple aisles running the length of the building and vantage points from shelving up high. It is a logistical nightmare, but I have no other choice.

From somewhere within the building, I hear the telltale sounds of footfalls and freeze. The sound comes again and I allow my eyes the chance to adjust before moving forward.

Shoving logic, and what feels like every ounce of sanity, into the recesses of my mind, I step through the doorway and into the pitch dark. My own footsteps sound exaggerated against the concrete floor as I walk around overturned shopping carts, a spilled end cap with broken light bulbs still in their packages and empty Slim Jim wrappers.

Another shuffling sound reaches me. I halt and duck low to get my bearings. It came from my left and instinctively I turn toward the outdoor section to the right. Breathing deep, my nostrils flare as I catch a scent that makes my blood run cold and my anxiety rise at alarming rates.

Lowering my hand to the back of my pants, where my 9mm pistol is tucked into my waistband, I fight to still my nerves as I silently creep along the aisle. Moving past a row of kayaks and paddleboards, I press my thumb against the gun's safety catch. There is someone moving at the end of the row.

Raising my pistol as I walk in a crouched position, I keep an eye on the shelves above me in case this is a trap. I know all too well how the Flesh Bags love to hunt in packs like wild animals, but to have a human sitting right here in the middle of their territory feels wrong.

The click of my safety disengaging startles the figure in front of me and two hands fly up into the air.

"Don't shoot," a young voice calls. "I'm unarmed."

"Who the hell are you?" I stare directly at the boy as he frantically shakes a flashlight before turning it on. The beam is high intensity and the painfully blinding light forces me to look away, but not before I see a shock of red hair, followed by a healthy dose of freckles and vivid green eyes.

"I'm Bingley Emerson, but anyone who knows me just calls me Bing. Of course, no one really knows me anymore..." He trails off as his voice cracks with fear. "I'm really sorry if this is your spot. I swear I don't mean you any harm. I can just grab my stuff and head out if you want. Just please don't shoot me."

I stare at him for a moment around the edge of the bouncing light, watching as he struggles to keep the flashlight level in his shaking hands.

"How old are you, Bing?" He seems decent enough. A bit ragged from travel. The bloodshot eyes worry me. Has he been bitten?

I look to the shelves above me again but see nothing moving.

"Sixteen, give or take a week. I lost track of the days a while back. I reckon I had a birthday at some point but don't really know when."

"Are you alone here?"

I can sense that there are Flesh Bags moving closer but none have entered the main part of the store. My skin tingles with warning. I force myself to ignore it.

Bingley shouldn't be here. Looking at him fidgeting with the buttons of his shirt, I realize that he truly has no clue the shitstorm he just walked into.

"Sure am." He looks somber as he peers into the darkness, but I know that he can't see any farther than his flashlight beam. "I've been on the road for a while now, coming up from 'Bama. It's been a long walk, but I figure if those Walkers are moving south, then I'm heading north!"

I take a step forward. "Have you been bit?"

"Bit?" He scratches his head and I see a bit of dandruff fall free and float to the floor. "I can't say that I have seen many dogs around these parts the past week. Almost like they all up and ran off. Kinda weird, if you ask me."

His flashlight flickers and dies. Bingley groans and begins beating it against his hand but it refuses to turn on again. "Darn thing keeps doing this. The package said you can charge it by shaking it but I think it was just some stupid sales gimmick. It's nothing but a piece of crap."

I ignore his muttering and step closer again. "I'm not talking about being bit by a dog. I'm talking about the zombies."

His head pops up and his eyes grow wide with surprise in the dark. "You're joking right? Those Walkers out there on the streets aren't real zombies. They're harmless unless you're trying to sleep. I swear it never fails that one of them always comes stumbling past right when I'm starting to fall asleep."

This kid rambles too much and my patience is growing thin. He may not sense the approaching Withered, but I sure can, and I don't want to be here when they arrive.

"Not the Walkers." I close the gap between us to only a couple of feet. He stares blankly into the dark. He can't see or hear me. "I'm talking about the new ones. The ones who have a taste for human flesh."

Bing's face drains of color and he swallows hard. "No, I don't reckon I've seen one of those."

"Is that so?" I kick the toe of my boot against his bag and he jumps when a crushed can of corn rolls out and hits the floor. I spy some matches, a couple flare guns and duct tape sitting near the top but no other signs of food. I'd wager by the sheer bursting of the seams near the bottom that he's tried to shove an entire sleeping bag into his pack. "Well, Bing, that's all about to change. You see, this place is just about the worst place for a guy like you to be hanging out."

"Is it?" His voice cracks with uncertainty as he starts to back away but stumbles over a folding chair and hits the ground hard. He leans to the side to rub his bruised ass.

"This place is one of theirs. I tracked them here just a little while ago."

The potent scent of his fear washes over me in delicious waves and I'm forced to close my eyes as I exhale and step back from him until I reach a neutral place once more.

"Oh crapballs," he moans and blindly reaches for his bag. When he finds it, he pulls it into his lap and cradles it. "We shouldn't be here."

"No, you shouldn't, but now that you are here I think you might be able to help me."

"Help? I'm not real good with doing stuff. My last group said I was too clumsy for my own good. Guess I'm all thumbs."

"That's okay, Bingley." I feel my mouth begin to water and I lower my head, closing my eyes as I fight against the need rising within me. He smells good, oh so good. "You are actually quite perfect for the job. Fate seems to be smiling on me for the first time in a while."

I hear him scratch at his jaw and realize that he has just a hint of stubble growing there.

"I'd like to help you and all, really I would, but I just want to leave if that's okay. If those things come back, I don't really want to be here, you know?"

"I do." I skirt along the end cap and move around him, keeping my distance. It is hard to think or remain focused on why I'm here with him so close. My thoughts grow muddy as a new plan forms in my mind, one that should send me running in the opposite direction, but logic is no longer stronger than my internal instinct. "I promise it will be quick."

"And then we can leave?" He tugs the ties of his bag tight and then places the pack on his back before rising to his feet.

My pulse thunders so loudly in my ears that I nearly miss his question. I count each of his inhales and exhales, feeling the imperceptible electrical pulses in his body.

No human can hide from me now. I stand in place, swaying slightly from side to side and I let the feelings of his presence ripple through me.

It is only now that I am here with Bing that I truly understand now how Cable can enjoy killing. The sensory output from this human is nearly euphoric.

"All I need from you is to relay a simple message," I whisper. My senses are tingling like mad as I open my eyes. I am mesmerized by the steady pulse at his neck as he looks all around in the dark. His image is lit up with a subtle green hue, allowing me to see every tiny speckle of color along his cheeks and nose.

"But there's no one else here. Who am I supposed to tell?"

"Ah," I inhale sharply and taste his fear once more. It is less sweet than blood but flavored with an appealing hint of tanginess that makes my stomach twist with desire. "That is what you are meant to believe. You haven't been alone since you entered this building, Bingley. They have been waiting and watching. If I had not arrived you would already be dead."

"Oh," he breathes out. When his knees buckle he reaches out for the shelf next to him, but I make no move to help him regain his footing. "Why are we standing here talking then? We have to go!"

I lose myself to the maddening racing of his heartbeat and relinquish control of my fear as I step closer to him, breathing in deep.

"Go?" I whisper in a hushed voice that sounds unnaturally loud against the vast emptiness of the building. "There is nowhere that you can run to that will be far enough, Bingley. Haven't you figured that out by now? You are marked for death."

My hands tremble at my sides as I feel the first of the Withered enter the building. Their approach is slow and cautious, no doubt attempting to understand my presence, but the instant they catch the potency of Bingley's scent, they become ravenous and I am inundated with their need.

"I can't just sit here and wait around to become something's dinner!"

I close my eyes as the Flesh Bags move closer. I can feel them much stronger now, hear their chorus of voices in my head chanting one thing in unison: *eat*.

I feel myself smile. "The sun has set."

He stops moving. "So?"

"Night is their playtime." I tilt my head to the side. "Can you hear them? They are coming."

A low, fearful moan gurgles in his throat and the scent of urine spilling down his leg soaks the air. Bingley jerks back at the sound of a nearby growl, stumbles over the faux grass mat and takes out an end cap. Canteens and camping utensil sets sprawl over the ground as he scrambles to get back to his feet.

"Please," he crab crawls backward until he is pressed against a display tent that has a massive tear down one side, probably damaged during the initial panic and looting. "You have got to help me. There has to be a way to escape. Please, don't let them eat me!"

"Don't worry," I say as I move around behind him. "I won't let them hurt you."

"Really?" He turns toward the sound of my voice. "Thank you—"

The flash of gunfire lights up the small outdoor section and Bingley's body collapses to the floor. From the far corners of the building I hear the growls and shrieks as Flesh Bags cower back from the piercing noise. I grimace as my own ears ring painfully but I stand my ground as Bingley's hand flops to the floor. His eyes are lifeless as he stares up at the ceiling above and the small bullet wound on his forehead leaks blood. It is a perfect kill shot.

As I stare down at the boy, I feel none of the remorse or guilt that I know I should. Instead I feel empty, like the lifeless shell of a person that I sense I am becoming.

His death was inevitable. What I told him was true; he was marked for death the instant he stepped foot in Cable's territory. Killing him now was an act of mercy, but I didn't do it for his sake. I did it for my own.

I need him to send Cable a message. His death was merely...beneficial.

Grabbing a box cutter off the floor from where it spilled out of Bingley's bag, I kneel beside him and tear open his shirt. I keep waiting to feel something, anything, as I press the blade to his chest and begin to carve with methodical precision. Blood trails down his chest where hair will never grow and stains my fingers, but I cut him without a tremor in my fingers.

I killed a boy in cold blood. The words filter through my mind as I wipe the blood off the blade onto his shirt and then rise to stare down at him.

He is nothing more than a victim of bad circumstances, an innocent whose life is forfeit by sheer dumb luck. Perhaps in the days to come, I will mourn his death as I should, but I fear that after I leave this building, I will not consider him again beyond a mere passing thought. Not as a person, anyway.

Though his heart has stopped, I can smell the blood on his forehead and am tempted to lick my hands clean. The thought alone should be revolting, but it is the opposite. It has become my ultimate temptation.

Wiping my hands on his shirt to clean away the blood, I know that I have to go before I do something I will regret. As I turn my back on the boy, I can still see the smooth planes of his chest that meet the rigid crevices of flesh when I carved three bloody words: *Let them live.*

Without looking at any of the Flesh Bags that creep my way, I walk out of the store and back into the drenching rain. Cable will get my message soon enough.

The only question is: Will he accept it?

THREE

The rain does not let up as I make my way through the deserted streets of the suburb and leave the dead boy far behind me. Forks of lightning streak across the sky in the distance, illuminating the horizon just enough for me to see billowing thunderclouds towering into the night sky. This storm looks like it might stick around for quite some time.

I need to find a place to hole up for a few hours and wait it out but I can't risk it while still being so close to Cable. His reaction to my message will be unpredictable and I need to put a good deal of distance between us, even if that means pushing myself to the limit.

As I jog ahead, I try to remember the last time I ate a real meal. My memory of the time after first waking from my coma is hazy, but I can't quite picture having any food brought to me. In fact, the scent of real food almost seems foreign to me now. Having been fed intravenously for two months, my system probably would not be able to handle food in any large quantities, not that they even exist now.

Ignoring my exhaustion and the gnawing hole in my stomach, I set a slow but steady pace heading due south and away from the city. I do not know where I am heading. Only that I need to lead Cable as far away from Nox as possible.

Within an hour, the storm reaches its full intensity, buffeting me left and right as the winds send violent gusts down the road. Rain lashes against my face while lightning draws near-constant jagged lines down to the ground. Thunder reverberates through my chest as I search for shelter, but there is none to be found on this stretch of road as fields and hills surround me on both sides.

I hold my scarf overhead to keep my eyes clear to see my path, but it is drenched and sags under the weight of the rain. As the winds howl like a pack of baying dogs, my desperation to find shelter mounts and I decide that the next house or shop that I see will have to be my target.

Small chunks of hail begin to bounce off my head as I peer through the sheets of rain. My pace slows to a labored walk as I push against the winds. Half an hour later I finally spy a two-story building off to my right. I plunge through a small gully of rushing water, flailing to mount the other side and then hurry across a broken concrete parking lot in the back. With a weak kick, I jar the lock on the single loading dock door, but it remains in place. After three more kicks the handle comes loose and I am able to slide the door open and then collapse into the darkness within.

Rolling onto my back, I stare up at a warehouse style metal roof high above and realize that I've found myself in some sort of small market-style store. The walls are lined with the odd black or brown wicker basket. Many have been tossed across the floor and trampled. There is an earthy scent on the air as I roll over to my side and push sluggishly up to my feet.

The scent grows stronger as I push through sheets of plastic strips that dangle from a double doorway and into the store beyond. More rows of wicker baskets line tables, small bins and tables line the space. Three sets of refrigerated units sit dark along the back wall. A case stocked with spoiled milk and a large cow sign on top stands beside a smashed cash register. Several of the tables still hold their composting wares in plastic wrapping.

"That must be the source of the smell."

I wander down the rows, searching for anything that might be edible, but the only things left behind are things that are of no use to anyone anymore: flours, oils and seasonings. One aisle contains baking utensils, pizza pans and aprons. I stare at them longingly, knowing that I'd pretty much give my left arm for a thick-crust pizza oozing with cheese right about now.

With my stomach growling and my energy waning, I reach the far end of the store and turn the corner to find a Withered standing still in the aisle. Every muscle in my body goes taut as I come to a complete halt.

It has its back to me and oddly doesn't seem aware of my presence. Long, baggy trousers sit low on the man's bony hips. A wide dark stain covers his back side and turns my nose up at the smell. His thin arms stick out from torn dress sleeves, stained and reeking of body odor.

He shifts slowly to this right and then back again to the left. A low wheezing sound comes from him, wet and chunky, like phlegm caught in his throat.

Indecision keeps me rooted in place. If he were a Flesh Bag he would have turned and attacked by now, but what is this Withered doing just standing in the store?

Curiosity gets the better of me and I circle around to a side aisle. I duck down low when I reach the end cap and look up at the Withered and realize why he is unaware of my presence. His ears have been cut away and his eyes have been plucked from their sockets, leaving ghastly empty holes. I can see no signs of bite marks anywhere on his exposed flesh.

"Oh, my God," I whisper, covering my mouth with horror.

This was not the work of a Flesh Bag, but of a human. The cuts are too precise.

I slowly rise and step up to the man, feeling a profound sorrow fall over me. Even though I know it feels nothing, I can't leave it to just stand here. Grabbing my gun, I flip the safety and put the barrel to his temple and pull the trigger. He collapses into a heap and I turn and walk away, leaving him to whatever peace a thing like him can find in the afterlife.

Soul weary and exhausted to the point of near collapse, I stumble back toward the loading dock and shove a stack of crates across the plastic draped doorway to put distance between me and the Withered. The sounds of hail striking the roof are much louder here, but it helps to drown out the growling of my stomach. Rain has begun to come in under the back door where parts of the lower half chipped off when I forced the door to roll on the rusted track. Water trails toward the center of the room where I stand. I look around me for anything that I can use to create a makeshift bed. I am beyond being picky at this point.

Settling on two pallets to keep me up off the floor and some old grain sacks, I stack my bed and then remove my wet clothing, hanging them to dry on a shelf before sinking down onto the hardest bed that I have ever slept on.

The storm rages for hours as I toss and turn, plagued by nightmares and stiff muscles. When the morning finally arrives, the storm proves to have only weakened slightly and I am forced to remain indoors. Stretching out my back, I rise from my bed and go in search of a toilet.

I dress in damp but decidedly drier clothes and spend the next two hours ransacking boxes in the warehouse. All of the food spoiled long ago. Discouraged and unwilling to waste any more energy, I plop down onto the floor and listen to the rain. It has been a constant sound for so many hours that it's nothing more than white noise.

I used to like the rain. Now it makes me worry.

Will Cable come looking for me despite the storm? Surely he has no reason to fear it.

Sitting up, I realize that neither do I. Wind and rain can't hurt me. I have slept, albeit fitfully, and feel stronger than I did the day before. It is time to move on.

Wrapping my scarf around my neck for when the clouds decide to finally break, I turn back one last time and out of the corner of my eye I spot a silver shine under a shelf. Hurrying over, I kneel down and stretch back toward the wall and pull out a small homemade jar of peaches.

"Oh, sweet mother of sweetness!"

The brown sugar alone should give me the extra boost of energy that I will need.

Using the edge of my box knife to break the seal, I unscrew the lid and tip the can up to my lips. Streams of juice pour over the edge of my lips and down my chin but I swallow as much as I can. Then I scoop out the peaches with my finger and eat down to the bottom.

My stomach rumbles with appreciation as I toss the jar aside and watch it shatter against the wall with a sense of apathy. I have never been someone who damages other people's property, even during my more rebellious days, but there is no one left to care.

Opening the back door, I stare out into the dismal gray. The rain falls heavily, but the sky no longer rumbles with thunder. Despite the heavy cloud cover I wrap my scarf around my face to conceal my eyes with the fabric and head back out into the storm. Deciding that no one apart from Flesh Bags would be stupid enough to be out on the road in a deluge like this, I make my way toward the highway and climb the steep embankment. Pushing up over a rusting chain link fence, I land several feet back from where a concrete bollard stands between me and the main road.

Spread out before me is a mass of abandoned cars, shattered windshields, and nothingness. Nothing moves. Nothing walks. It is as if every Withered has vanished from this place

"I bet they've all been mutilated by some sick human or eaten by those Flesh Bag bastards."

Never before have I wanted to see the moaning and rotting Walkers so badly. Surely they haven't all been turned into Flesh Bags. If that is the case, then Nox and the people who have remained behind at the hotel do not stand a chance against such a force.

My only hope is to draw Cable's attention away, but where is the safest direction to head?

Knowing that there must be a road sign somewhere in the distance, I break out into a jog in search of one so that I can consider my options. After leaving St. Louis months back, our small band of mismatched friends had a purpose: get as far away from the military as possible. Then I was handed a new destination when Cable spoke of his brother stationed near Nashville, TN, but now I have nowhere that I have to be and no one waiting for me.

A northern route could potentially lead Cable to follow me into some desolate arctic landscape where no one would get hurt, but countless would be injured along the way, not to mention Cable's army would grow along the way. If I continue south, the heat and sun will be a major deterrent for both him and me.

As I stare up at the road sign I feel utterly indecisive. I can just as easily head toward Knoxville and down through the Smoky Mountains or jump state lines and loop back up toward Kentucky. The only thing I know for certain is that I need to avoid heading west during the late spring storm season. The last thing I want is to survive a man-made apocalypse only to be taken out by one of Mother Nature's tornadoes.

"Nox would know what to do." I rub my hands along my arms to warm myself up. The rain isn't nearly as cold as it was when I first stumbled across the Flesh Bags a couple short months ago. Spring has already begun to shift into summer and with it will come an insufferable heat that will be pure misery to endure.

"Knowing Nox, he would probably already have a plan in place and soldiers field dressing their AK-47s while I stand around here like a brainless ninny! Snap out of it, Avery. Make a plan and stick to it!"

But that is easier said than done. No matter which direction I follow it will take me too close to people. At some point I am bound to run across survivors or a group of Raiders. My hands tremble at the thought of close contact and I shove them deep into my pockets as I try to push aside the almost immediate hunger that I feel.

The urges are getting stronger. I can't risk being around anyone right now. Nor can I allow Cable to find me too soon.

I wipe water from my eyes and stare at the small town landscape ahead of me. Random buildings show signs of having been charred by arson fires, probably occurring not long after the outbreak began, when people pillaged and plundered to their hearts' content. Many of the brick faces have been sprayed with ammunition rounds. That was most likely done by the National Guard as they fought to maintain control, but it was a losing battle. Panic has a way of spilling over into the best of people.

As I begin to jog, I pass by abandoned tanks, burnt out military trucks, and barricades used to create roadblocks that make much of the town center impassable.

"The military sure did a number on this place. A lot of good it did them," I mutter with bitterness in my voice. Apart from Nox, my loathing of anything wearing camouflage hasn't changed.

At the thought of the suffering that I've endured at the hands of the military, my stomach sours and my lip curls with disgust. No good has ever come from their involvement. Every terrible thing that has happened to me since the outbreak has been a direct result of their meddling.

Nox may be one of them, trained and armed by them, but he doesn't have the same mindless will to obey. Not like Cap and some of the others. Nox at least feels riddled with guilt over discovering the part he played in Iris and Brian's plan to use innocent survivors in their test trials, which ended up creating the plague of Flesh Bags that now make up Cable's army. That gives me hope that he will do whatever it takes to do what is right by his people.

At the thought of Iris, the deceased former leader of the Opryland Hotel base, my hands clench into fists at my side. Without Iris alive to check in with the other Safe Zones, at dawn every Zone went into a full scale lockdown mode. After that, human testing will begin on a mass scale and more people will suffer at the hands of doctors just like Dr. Wiemann.

As the doctor's face swims before my eyes, I know exactly what Nox would do if he were standing at this crossroads. He would locate the nearest Safe Zone and attempt to rescue anyone still left alive, no matter the cost.

"But even if I had a clue where the Zones are located, I'd never make it in time." I turn to look back toward Nashville. Nox would be the hero and save the day because that's who he is. Maybe at one time I would have tried as well, but I'm not that same girl anymore. The thought of being around so many people in one place makes me nauseous and excited at the same time in a very bad way.

I kick out at the front tire of an SUV beside me and feel the worn tread give way beneath the toe of my boot. A slow and steady hiss of air sounds as the tire deflates.

"I'm dangerous," I tell myself as I turn away. "I need to get away from people, not pretend that this is my fight anymore."

But even as I speak the words I feel how wrong they are. Who will fight for these victims when no one else even knows that they are in danger? My lot in life royally sucks, but maybe I was changed for a reason. Maybe I can still do some good.

"Right," I scoff and roll my eyes as I wrap my arms around myself. "Try and be the hero and watch how long it takes you to lose your shit and take a bite out of someone's neck."

No matter how I look at the situation, I can't see a positive end. I don't trust myself, especially after killing that boy while barely batting an eye. And the hunger I felt when I smelled his fear... What if I don't walk away next time?

There is a second thought that crosses my mind that makes my breath catch. What if by trying to save those people I bring Cable, along with his horde of hungry Flesh Bags, right to their doorstep? Even if the science experiments don't go wrong, I would be sentencing them to a certain and horrific death.

My shoulders slump as I sink down onto the hood of a car and stare blankly into the distance. Cold droplets of rain fall around my face, trailing along my cheeks, but I barely feel them.

The road seems to stretch on forever in front and behind me as I sit in silence and watch a second round of storms on approach. Lightning illuminates towering thunderheads but I feel no fear. In fact, I feel little of anything until I look back at the road that will lead me away from Nox and I am filled with a strange sense of dread and a loneliness that I haven't felt since the initial days after I left Cable trapped in the cave.

"I'm sorry, Nox. You believed in me but I just can't do it..." I trail off as the wind shifts and I lift my nose to the air.

My nostrils flare as I turn south and breathe deep. The scent is faint, almost indecipherable with the rain, but I trust the twisting in my gut to lead me right. Dr. Wiemann passed this way not too long ago, and he wasn't alone.

FOUR

Dropping to the ground in search of evidence of their passing, I know the rains will have already washed away most of the signs. Moving slowly, but steadily, in a southern direction, I follow the scent of five men, each one slightly different from the other. One odor stands out among all of the rest: gunpowder residue. Wiemann has soldiers with him and I bet I know exactly who they are.

During the attack on the hotel, it would have been easy for any of the doctor's cronies to slip out undetected. If I were to bet on it, I would guess that Cap is leading the mission and judging by what I saw back at that farm house the day Nox found me, I would wager he has Ryker, Nash, and that cocky asshat Jax with him. What I wouldn't give to get my hands on them for the pain and misery they brought to the victims locked in Dr. Wiemann's underground hospital of torture.

"Maybe I can't save the people in all of the Safe Zones, but I sure as hell can stop that sick bastard from reaching one!"

Anger and a need for vengeance pushes me off the hood of the car and I run full out, pausing from time to time only long enough to be sure that I am still on their trail. Less than thirty miles outside of Nashville, I come across an outdoor car wash with one of its doors down. Sneaking up to it, I peer inside to see that a fire had been lit over the center grate not long ago. There is still a small glow to the embers near the bottom. I hurry around to the back of the car wash and kneel down to place a hand over the fire and feel lingering warmth.

"I'm not far behind."

Dashing around the front of the car wash, I hurry back onto the highway and zigzag through the debris. There is no way the soldiers packing heavy guns and an old doctor can run faster than I can. With each minute that passes, I have to believe that I am catching up.

As I run I spy the flickering of a lighted fire in an apartment building and a second in an abandoned office complex a mile further on but I keep going. Their scent hasn't detoured off the road.

Determined to do whatever it takes to catch up with them, I do not slow or stop to rest throughout the day as the storms come and go in a near constant rumbling of thunder. After a while the damp and cold no longer affects me. I am too driven to care.

When the scent begins to grow stronger I use the cover of large semi-trailer trucks and delivery vehicles to conceal my approach so that I can keep the element of surprise. All I have to do is reach them before they hit the mountains. In the undulating terrain I will hold the advantage.

I feel no fear when I think about how the odds will be stacked against me when I arrive. The doctor will be easy enough to take down. One quick snap of the neck and the world will be a much better place. Cap and his men will be armed to the teeth, but the pace they are keeping will tire them far more than it will me.

As I run I create a plan of attack in my mind. I will wait for the cover of darkness when all of them are asleep save for one lookout. The first death will be swift and silent but I plan to take my time with the doctor if I'm allowed the chance. He needs to suffer for his crimes.

Despite the clouds that hang low overhead, I sense the coming of night. My eagerness, paired with Wiemann's growing scent, urges me to push just a little faster, but as I crest a hill, the ricochet of gunfire sends me instantly to the ground.

I drop and peer out from under a semi, trying to target where the gunfire came from. Through the steady pattering of the rain, I detect what sounds like multiple forms of weaponry.

"Shit. They are under attack and there's no way in hell I'm letting anyone steal my kill!"

Leaping to my feet, I shift to the strip of grass that runs along the roadside and sprint, pumping my arms and legs in a blur of motion. I can feel the Flesh Bags even before I see the first flicker of shots and know that it's is worse than I thought.

The road is filled with bodies, some still crawling toward the pinned-down soldiers, while others lie still. From the distant tree line, I see responding shots.

"What the hell?"

I narrow my eyes and focus on the trees. Several men duck in and out of the woods, firing off rounds at the Withered before disappearing again. Others take steady aim directly at Wiemann's group.

"Really? I have to fight on two fronts?" I groan and yank the scarf off my face and wind it around my hands. "All right, just don't get shot in the ass, Avery."

With a running dive, I slide across the hood of a car and come up directly behind a Flesh Bag. Wrapping my scarf around its neck, I hoist it up and over my shoulder, snapping its neck with a twist before I kick out at a second one, driving it to its knees.

Yanking a mirror off a car door, I slam the jagged plastic down into the back of a zombie's skull and shove him away. Three of them ahead of me turn at the sound and race toward me. I duck behind an open car door and jump inside, crawling across the bucket seats to smash the opposite window. Hands grasp at my feet as I kick, fighting to wriggle through the window. Glass tears at my back and elbows before I slam onto the pavement.

"Get up!" I shout to myself and crawl toward the front of the car.

A biker boot stomps down onto my hand and I scream in pain. As a reflex, I drive an uppercut into the man's groin, but he doesn't respond to the pain. "Shit. Forgot about that."

I drive my shoulder into his knee and throw the zombie off balance, and then scramble to my feet. When I glance around I realize that I've drawn far too much attention to myself.

"Right. Well, at least Wiemann is safe...for now."

I slam my fist into the side of one zombie's head and swing a wild elbow into another as I try to clear a path like a pro linebacker. It works for about twenty feet before I slam into an abnormally well-built Flesh Bag that sends me tumbling backward. I take out two zombies that were following me and then roll to my feet.

"I'm betting you're going to be a pain in the ass to take down, right?"

Before I can react, the Flesh Bag strikes out at me and I feel my lip split.

"Yep." I shake my head as I leap back over the downed zombies. "I was right."

Glancing behind me to see several more my hot on my tail, I back up a few paces and then leap. My feet land precisely on the big Flesh Bag's stomach and together we plummet. He smashes his head into a car fender with a sickening thud and I smack hard on my elbow and skid on the wet pavement.

"Son of a bitch!" Blood trails down my arm. I lift it to see that I've scraped a good amount of skin off.

The scent of my blood will only send the nearby Withered into a feeding frenzy. I need to get my wound wrapped and get the hell out of here.

The bloody desire to have Dr. Wiemann's neck between my hands is almost more than I can bear now that he's within sight, but I have no choice. Tearing the front of a Flesh Bags shirt, I race out toward an overturned mail truck. I skid to a stop and yank on the handle until it pops free and I dive inside, sealing myself in the darkness.

Wrapping my elbow up good and tight, I clamp down on it to apply pressure and, slowly, the bleeding stops. Over the next few minutes, multiple hands slam into the back of the mail truck, rocking it from side to side.

"Cable says that I can control them," I whisper to myself as I close my eyes. "Too bad he never told me how!"

I focus all of my attention on the minds of those closest to me, pushing out a single message: Leave. After ten minutes, I realize that it's hopeless.

"Well, that was quite the epic fail."

As the battle moves off, the gunshots in the distance draw their attention away and I hear their pounding footsteps fade away. Leaning back against the boxes of undelivered mail, I sigh.

"That was way too close."

The air in the truck becomes hot and stuffy, but I linger for nearly half an hour. When I can't take it any longer, I unlock the doors and spill out, gulping in breaths of cool, damp air. Rain patters against my face from the dark sky overhead.

Crawling to my feet, I look to the road ahead and see nothing moving, but I can hear shouts in the distance. The battle rages on. This time, I will be far more cautious when I approach.

It takes less than four minutes to make up the distance between me and Wiemann's group. I test my newfound limits to reach a speed that nearly takes my breath away. This time, there are far fewer Flesh Bags following behind and plenty with bullet holes in their heads to jump over as I pursue them.

The Raiders continue to use the cover of the trees to fight from, giving them a big advantage when the zombies try to follow. I notice when I arrive that Cap and his men have become pinned down by a large pileup of cars that spans the width of the road. There is nowhere for them to run.

I skid to a stop and search for anything that might help. "What I wouldn't give for a tank right about now," I mutter and jog toward the nearest vehicle. I yank the dead woman out of the driver's seat and reach inside to pop the trunk. Rounding the car, I rummage through the contents of her vehicle, tossing suitcases with clothes and children's toys out onto the road. My stomach clenches when I realize that I didn't see a kid in the back seat.

Grabbing a tire iron, I rush back around to the front seat and jam it between the seat and the horn. It blasts loud and clear. I duck down as Flesh Bags and humans alike turn to look in my direction.

"Well, that works. Now how do I get past them to reach Wiemann?"

Running at a low crouch, I sneak past burnt out car after burnt out car, holding my breath as the first of the zombies pass by on their way to check out the horn. I see Cap's head pop up and hear him yell something, but the wind drowns out the words before I can decipher them. A bullet grazes off the underside of a car beside his head and he disappears again.

"One problem at a time," I mutter and continue to move closer.

Taking a quick count of the tops of heads in Cap's group, I spy Wiemann and two others. I frown, knowing that there should be a fourth.

"Where are you, Jax?" It seems completely out of character for the meathead to hide from a fight.

I begin to close the gap between us but move only in the darkness between gunshots. Though many of the zombies have remained behind with the blaring car, I am forced to take down two that are sneaking up on Cap from behind. I am just about to dive for the third when the back of his head explodes and splatters me with gore.

If I allow this battle to continue, I guarantee that the scales will tilt in my favor, especially if one of Cap's men goes down. But as tempting as that may be, I can't stomach the thought of the doctor being killed by anything but by my hands.

A sudden spray of bullets from the woods illuminates a small pack of zombies that have flanked the Raiders, which makes up my mind for me. I'm about to lose the only chance I have of stopping the doctor. Screams of pain and terror rip through the air and I take the distraction as a chance to make my move. Leaping over the brainless Flesh Bag, I race toward Wiemann. He is the only thing in my vision.

I am less than two hundred feet back when I hear the sound of an engine roar to life and nearly face plant in disbelief. I realize too late what Jax was doing.

"No!" I rush forward as I hear Cap shouting at his men to run. He uses his body as a shield for the doctor and together they move toward an old pickup truck straight out of the 1950s. Cap grabs the back of the doctor's shirt and pants and practically tosses him into the open bed and then follows directly behind. Jax sits behind the driver's seat and motions for the others to get in.

I watch as Nash retreats under Ryker's cover fire. He is just about to jump into the truck when a shout of pain rises from behind him and he turns to see Ryker go down. The heavens light up with the brilliance of a bolt of lightning that forces me to look away. A thunderous crack is followed by sparks of fire erupting from the struck tree and I see several men and zombies alike set aflame.

"Nash, let's go, man!" Jax shouts over the idling engine.

"Ryker is down. I'm going back for him!"

"He knew the risks, Nash." I hear Cap say. "Leave him."

Ryker calls out to Nash for help and I watch a variation of emotions play across the soldier's face as Nash shakes his head and turns to throw himself in the truck. The tires squeal as Jax peels out and the men in the truck bed slam into the side as he fishtails and then sends the vehicle plummeting over the embankment.

"Don't leave me," Ryker screams at the top of his lungs.

The gunfire turns to follow the truck as it roars back up the other side and slams into a small two-door sports car and ricochets off. Sparks fly as they ping off the metal siding. A tail light explodes in a rain of plastic and then disappears when Jax plunges them down the other side of the hill and they are gone.

I hear Ryker's scream of outrage and turn back to look at fallen soldier. From the corner of my eye I see three men cautiously step out from behind trees with their weapons high and hot. Two Flesh Bags go down the instant they leap out from behind a tree. A group have flanked around behind me and I see that they are opening fire on the horn-blaring car.

They are smart enough to know that the sound will attract more. They are well-armed and outfitted in camouflage that allows them to blend with their surroundings. Judging by the way they cautiously approach the group of Flesh Bags, these men know a thing or two about hunting zombies.

"That means the mutations have spread farther than we thought," I whisper to myself.

There is no way for me to warn Nox of this development. No way for me to warn anyone unless I find a way to reach a Safe Zone and send out a message.

One way or another, I have to complete this mission for the sake of what little remains of the human race.

FIVE

Two of the approaching Raiders appear to be in their mid-forties. The third is no older than late teens but he carries his gun with a well-trained grip.

"What do we do with the one they left behind?" The teen asks as they pick their way across the overgrown side embankment.

"Kill him. He's trespassing on our land. It's what we do," the man flanking on the right responds with a gruff voice.

"There will be no killing here tonight," the man in the center says. He turns to look at both men in turn. "Ryan, go back and tell the others to follow that truck. We need it."

"But Dad, I can help."

"I said go, Ryan."

The boy scowls but turns away to follow his father's command. I watch as he hurries back into the woods and, minutes later, ten more people emerge. They race down the embankment and out of sight. Then I hear the telltale growl of motorcycle engines starting up. Headlight beams light the lower road and swerve away in pursuit of Cap and the others. I spot several Flesh Bags turning to follow, but they will never catch up in time.

I bite down on my lower lip to stop myself from swearing aloud when I realize the two Raiders will reach Ryker before I do. Any attempt to get to him now will draw attention to myself, but the reward outweighs the risk. With the doctor mobile and a decent head start, the only way I will be able to track them is to know exactly where they are headed, and Ryker is going to give me that information.

I suppose there is still some hope that these Raiders will catch up to Cap and cut them off, slowing them down just long enough. These men seem to know the area pretty well and have proven they are more than willing to risk everything to protect what is theirs. Maybe they will do all of the hard work for me.

"You really going to let this scum live?" The gruff voice asks again and I turn my attention back to the two men that are approaching.

"Of course not, Joe. I just didn't want my boy watching." The father motions silently for Joe to move off to the side and together they move to flank Ryker.

"Take another step and it will be your last," I call out from the darkness.

Both men duck low and raise their weapons.

"Who's there?"

"That man belongs to me," I call as I move along the side of a school bus. "I will let you live if you turn around and leave now."

Joe laughs. "We don't take orders from little girls. Why don't you come out here so we can have a chat like civilized folk?"

He shoots his partner a knowing look that makes my lips peel back into a sneer. I watch as he fingers the safety and lifts the weapon's sights to his eye.

"Who said I was civilized?" I shout back.

The father chuckles. "Look, this here man is on our land. They stole something of ours and we want it back."

"I don't see how that's any of my concern. He is wounded and of no benefit to you."

The father scratches at his beard. "Well, see now that's where you're wrong. He's leverage and I'm a man who likes to hold a few cards back when I'm making a negotiation."

I sneak out from my hiding place and begin to creep forward. Without the gunfire to light the road, they will not see me approaching, nor will I will allow them to hear me. My silence unnerves them and I smile as they begin to shift their weight from one side to the other.

"I can be a reasonable man and I don't take too kindly to hurting girls. I tell you what. I'll let you say goodbyes to your man and then we will be on our way."

"I ain't no one's man." Ryker spits at the father's shoe.

The man turns and slams his boot into Ryker's stomach.

"How about it?" Joe calls to the darkness. He turns slowly, trying to locate me. He shrugs at the father. "Maybe the little girl got spooked?"

Sprinting ahead with my arms pumping and my steps silent, I tackle Joe before he even has a chance to lift his head. We roll four times before I come to a stop on his chest and instantly slam my palm straight up under his nose. Blood leaks from his nostrils and his eyes roll back as the broken bone pierces into his brain and he falls limp beneath me.

I push off of him and spit on his face. "I am no little girl."

"Joe?" The father takes a step back at the sound of our scuffle. "You okay, man?"

I cock the gun and point it at his chest. "Joe is a little dead right now."

"Shit!" The father drops his gun and points it directly at Ryker's head. "I'll do it. I'll blow his brains out!"

"I believe that you will try, but I know that you won't." I lift the gun and shift it slightly off center of his heart and see movement over his shoulder.

"Why's that?"

"Because I think you love your boy."

The father's face goes pale. "What...what are you talking about?"

"I would guess that you have about five seconds to decide. You back away and let this soldier live and I'll save your boy from the zombie that's about to take a chunk out of his neck, or you try to call my bluff and you both die."

His finger flinches against the trigger.

"Five."

Sweat beads along the man's forehead as I reach number four. In a sudden flash of lightning behind me, I am backlit and the father rears back when he sees me standing less than five paces.

"Holy fuck!" He stumbles back as I say three. "Okay, okay!"

His gun rises high in the air a split second before I pull the trigger. A body drops less than twenty feet back and I hear the boy cry out in surprise.

"Ryan!"

A very shaken response comes from the boy, but the father makes no move to reach him.

"Toss your gun away," I order as the boy approaches.

"Don't do it, dad. She'll kill us both."

Blood gushes from around Ryker's stomach wound when he laughs, squeezing between his fingers. "She doesn't need a gun to kill you, asshole. She's a freakin' mutant. You should have shot when you first heard her speak."

The father glances back at me but I am lost to the darkness. "What's he mean by that?"

"Toss the gun aside," I command again. "I will not ask a third time."

His hesitation annoys me, so I pull the trigger and send a bullet spiraling through his son's leg. The boy stumbles and falls against a car, clinging to the mirror to keep himself upright.

I say, "The next one will be to his lower abdomen, just perfectly placed so that he is paralyzed and unable to move when the zombies return to start eating."

The father begins to tremble but this time tosses his gun without a thought.

"Wrong move, old man," Ryker coughs.

"Who are you?"

I step over Joe's limp body, grab Ryan by the arm and haul him up next to his dad. They collide and cry out but cling to each other as lightning flashes again.

A growing pool of blood swells around Ryker as I press my foot down on his stomach. He screams and swears as he tries to reach for his gun.

"We both know you won't get a shot off in time," I gloat as I drop down next to him and seize his chin.

"Bitch." A bloody wad of spit splats against my face and I wipe it away.

"You have information I need, Ryker." I smile and squeeze until I feel his jawbones begin to protest the pressure. "You're going to tell me where that bastard is heading."

"Who is she talking about, dad?" Ryan asks behind me but his dad shushes him.

"I would rather die than tell you!" Ryker coughs up blood.

I trail my hand down his chest and then plunge my finger into his bullet wound. His back arches as a scream tears from his throat. The father places his arm around his son's shoulder.

"You call me a mutant like it was my fault!" I growl in Ryker's ear. "You helped to create me. I won't let Wiemann destroy anyone else's life!"

The hairs on the back of my neck rise up and I smile. "Do you hear that, Ryker? Those are the hurried footsteps of a ravenous Flesh Bag. He will be here soon."

Ryker gurgles and fear glistens in his eyes. "Tell me what I want to know and I will give you a quick death."

"No." He grits his teeth.

I remove my finger from his stomach and slowly lick it, savoring the taste. It is far better than I could have imagined. "On second thought, maybe I will kill it and eat you myself."

Ryker flinches as the boy grasps onto his father. "Is she serious, dad?"

"You wouldn't," Ryker shouts.

I lean down and lick the blood that stains his lips, tasting his fear. "It would be my pleasure."

"Dad?"

I had almost forgotten the two shivering behind me. Already I can hear the growls of the approaching zombies. I glance back at the father and the son. "The men who escaped in the truck must be stopped."

"You're insane!" Ryan shouts. "Why would we help you?"

I rise to my feet and am at his side before he can blink. I lean in and sniff his neck. His fear is far more potent than Ryker's. It carries a deliciously sweet flavor.

"Because if they are not stopped, there will be far more like me soon enough." I press my lips to his cheek and smile when he whimpers. "Be a good boy and run, while you still can."

The father's eyes are filled with rage as I step back. "I am letting you live, old man. Do not make me regret that decision. The truck must be stopped at all costs. If it is not..." I let the threat fall off as he nods and hurries his boy away.

The instant I turn back to Ryker, they are erased from my thoughts. I drop down beside him and slowly raise his hand. "You have less than a minute. In that time I can dig your beating heart out of your chest and eat it before your very eyes. The pain would be excruciating, I'm sure, or you can tell me one simply thing and I will end your suffering."

"Go to hell."

I sigh and run my fingers through his thick locks of dark hair. "I never wanted you. I may have even let you live. Cap will die, of course for his betrayal. Jax because he's a smug bastard and I just don't like him, but you and Nash had a chance."

I yank a chunk of hair out of his head. "Tell me where the doctor is heading!"

Ryker bites down on his lip as tears leak from his eyes.

"I would say I admire your tenacity if I thought it was anything other than sheer stupidity. Your friends left you behind to die. Cap ordered Nash to leave and he did so with barely a second thought. Why remain loyal to those who obviously do not care about you?"

A stream of blood trails down from his head and coats the day's growth along his chin and down his neck.

"Soldiers never leave a man behind, isn't that right?" I take his hand in mine and begin to separate his fingers, singling out his pinky. He grits his teeth and moans in pain when I snap it to the right and release it to dangle. "Do you think they didn't know that they were leaving you behind to be eaten?"

My fingers begin to tremble as the taste of his blood on my lips sends electrical currents streaming through me and I have to fight the urge to lick his face again. I breathe in deep, closing my eyes as I allow myself to feel each labored beat of his heart and then slowly exhale as euphoria washes over me.

"You know what I am," I whisper as I open my eyes and stare down at him and see him recoil for the first time in fear and I wonder what it is that he sees different in me. "Give me a reason to drag out your death and eat you bite by bite, waking you from your stupor of pain only so that you can experience the agony all over again."

I lean down and sniff his neck, drawn to him like a drug, both intoxicating and forbidden. "Do you think your heart will give out before I finish eating you?"

A strangled cry rises within him and his entire body stiffens, but he is unable to get away. Blood oozes from several other wounds and I realize that he was hit by three other bullets. I grip the hand that covers his stomach and pull it away. Blood bubbles up from the wound and I stare at it, mesmerized by the beauty of it.

At the first sound of a footfall behind me, I turn and put a bullet through the zombie's right eye. It falls backward. Ryker tries to look in that direction but fails.

"One down. Only two more to go."

I wait. Ryker's neck muscles tense as I grip two fingers in my spare hand and snap them in half. The sudden pop makes a shiver race up my spine and I feel the undeniable hope that he will let me be the one to finish him flit through my mind.

Another shot rings out and Ryker whimpers this time. "That's two down."

"Shit," he gargles as I grab hold of his thumb. I lift the gun and take aim. "Stop!" I turn to look back at him. "Yes?"

"Atlanta," he rushes to say as the zombie drags its foot around the end of the school bus. It is missing one hand and part of it's left leg, but its teeth are very much intact. "He's going to Atlanta."

"Why?"

He coughs up blood and I roll him onto his side. Thick crimson globs spill out of his mouth and onto the ground. When his airway is clear again, I roll him onto his back once more but he seems unable to breath. I grab hold of his shirt and drag him toward the truck to prop him up, and then turn to shove back the Flesh Bag, annoyed that it is interrupting.

When it takes a swing at me, I shove the end of the Raider's gun through its shoulder and jam it through the car door. "Stay," I growl.

I ignore Ryker's cries of pain and the shivers that they induce within me as I sink back down beside him. "Why Atlanta?"

His eyes fall closed, and if it were not for the fact that I can still hear his heart beating, I would think that he had died. Then he slowly opens them again to stares at me with an unfocused gaze.

"That's where his wife is. She became infected not long after the outbreak and he placed her in a coma to slow the progression. He thinks that with blood like yours he can save her."

"He can't. My blood doesn't cure the virus, it just mutates it."

Ryker nods. "I know that. I saw your charts, but Wiemann is obsessed. He will kill every living person in that Safe Zone if it means there is still a chance of finding a cure for her. Atlanta is the largest zone with thousands in residence there. He is sure one of them will work."

I close my eyes and push aside the hunger that threatens to take over me with each inhalation of his blood. Only the horror of so many innocent lives suffering at the doctor's hands is enough to bring me back as I stand and wipe my hands across my face.

The Flesh Bag reaches for me, growling and tugging against the barrel of the gun.

"You promised a quick death" Ryker chokes out.

"I did." I stare down at him with nothing more than utter revulsion. He was more than happy to stand by and let Wiemann create mass genocide for the sake of one woman's life, a woman already lost. "I lied. Enjoy your time in Hell."

Yanking the gun free, I step back as the Flesh Bag dives for Ryker. The sounds of his screams echo around me. I walk away with the gun slung over my shoulder. I press my hand against each car that I pass, smearing my blood with Ryker's as a message for Cable to follow. If Wiemann succeeds in reaching Atlanta before I can stop him, I won't stand a chance of reaching him, but maybe, just maybe, with Cable and his army at my back, I will find a way in.

"Sometimes you need the Devil at your side to get what you want," I whisper to the night and begin to whistle as Ryker's screams drag on.

SIX

Long into the night I follow the scent of the Raiders that pursue Dr. Wiemann's group. Nearly twenty-five miles from where I left Ryker, I spot skid marks that turn off onto a frontage road and spin onto a dirt country road. I follow behind the deeply rutted tracks but lose them in the grass over the next rise, only to find them once more nearly three miles farther on where they jumped a gully and raced back up onto the main highway.

There are other muddy tire tracks, smaller and obviously from motorcycles, showing that the Raiders were still in hot pursuit when they came through here. No amount of searching during the night or into the next day turns up the pickup truck.

Nearly twenty miles after I rejoin with the highway, I find a motorcycle that has plowed head first into the rear end of a bread delivery truck. The mangled body inside is smashed. One leg dangles down near the tailpipe.

After following skid marks on an overpass another mile up the road, I peer over the dented railing to find the remains of a second motorcycle. A third is dropped beside it on the ground with a body sprawled out a few feet away. The remaining seven are nowhere to be seen.

I follow the scent of gunpowder for several more miles, but see no other signs of wreckage. Their scent carries on.

"Damn it." I hold a stitch in my side, using just about every swear word known to man and a few that I invent as I begin to jog again.

The following day, after pausing to sleep only a couple of hours, I track them through the first signs of suburban outskirts of Chattanooga and then follow their erratic trail east where they headed toward Signal Mountain. Then night returns. From the highest peak, I am able to see the valley below and in the middle of wooded lots and farming fields I spot a large fireball sending smoke high into the air.

It takes me nearly an hour to reach the crash site, and by the time I do, the metal is far too hot to comb through. It is nearly impossible to tell if there were any bodies still inside, but I know without a doubt that this was the truck Jax was driving. The heat is too intense to remain close by, and I can't bear to stare into the flames for any length of time, so I move farther off to wait for the debris to cool.

Exhausted and frustrated beyond measure, I lie down on the ground and stare up at the smoky sky. It hangs in a thick cloud, covering everything within a mile radius, and dampens my senses. A new round of dangerous storms threatens to overtake me sometime in the wee hours of the morning. I am forced to take shelter in a small lean-to half a mile from the crash site that stinks of urine and rotted food. I grow restless as I pace under the leaking roof, watching the forks of lightning that stretch toward the ground with growing agitation.

Even with the fire out and the smoke settled, I won't be able to search for clues under this deluge. It is almost as if heaven itself hates me.

Not long after dawn, the brunt of the storm passes, and I emerge to find a drenched fire pit less than a hundred yards from my shelter that I hadn't noticed the night before. I sniff the air and catch the faintest whiff of three males and the ruts of a motorcycle. Glancing in the direction they are headed, I realize that they have turned back toward their home.

My hopes plummet as I wearily walk back toward the crash. If they left, that means only one thing: they believe everyone died in that crash.

The rains slowly begin to give way to a light drizzle. The thinning clouds are a welcome sight until a pinprick of a brilliant dawn peeks through and I'm reminded of why I have grown to hate the sun.

Beautiful pastel colors splash across the sky beneath the cloud layer, but I can no longer savor the beauty of a new day and I realize just how quickly I have become a thing of the night.

I turn away and hunch my back against the sun.

I spend the next hour digging through damp ash and melted metal. I kick aside the fender and toss away the license plate to find a set of teeth buried beneath.

With a heavy sigh, I sink down to my knees and lower my head. I should be happy, grateful even, but the lost opportunity to seek revenge strikes me hard. I slam my fist into the moist ground and feel mud squish between my fingers. My cry of outrage sends birds bursting into flight as I throw back my head.

I collapse onto the ground. With my hair concealing my face and my arm wrapped under my head, I finally sleep.

Sometime late in the evening, a sound wakes me. I sit upright, ears alert as I turn left and right. I zero in on the eastern hillside when I hear the distinct echo of an AK-47.

"I only found two sets of teeth," I whisper as I look back at the pile I made of jawbones. "They could still be alive."

I sprint through the trees, leaping over fences and across wide open fields with one direction in mind, without a single shred of evidence that the one shot came from a soldier, but hope forces me to run on. A second shot sends me skidding to a stop and I lift my nose to sniff the air.

There are conflicting scents here. I turn this way and that, hunting for a familiar smell, but nothing stands out to me. All I have is the sound, and amongst the hills, the echo is impossible to pinpoint accurately.

"Think, Avery. Where will they go?"

I think back to the rest area that I came across outside of Chattanooga the day before that had a map posted on the interior wall. This entire area is surrounded by forest and rising elevations. Although their plans may have been to stick to the main roads leading into Atlanta, the Raiders have forced them off course. To backtrack now would lose time and distance.

Cap will want to deliver Wiemann to the Safe Zone as fast as possible.

I look to the mountains before me and smile. "They are going to go straight through."

For once I feel as if I might have a tiny amount of luck on my side. Cap and the survivors will be forced to move slowly and with care over the rough terrain. That is where I will hold the advantage. I can't be too far behind now.

By the time I reach the CDC, it will be heavily fortified and in total lockdown. Whatever experimental drugs that have been created in their labs will already be in route to the Safe Zone and administered to the living and unsuspecting residents. With Iris and Brian no longer alive to remain in constant communication with the Zones, these experiments are likely to have already begun.

I have no way of knowing if samples of my blood have somehow made their way to the Zones, or if others like me have already been created and then duplicated. Things in Atlanta may have escalated to the point where nothing can be done to save the people inside, but I am determined to try.

As I run I reach a two lane road, I leap over downed motorcycles emptied of gas, bicycles with blown tires and car doors left open in a rush to escape whatever force blew through this area. Shrapnel long since rusted by the elements lies beside demolished vehicles, many overturned and damaged by explosions. The grass on the roadside is blackened and dead. A battle was fought here, but I am left to wonder who won.

The feeling of vulnerability grows as I keep a wary eye in front and behind while I dart across the road and return to the trees, but I see no one as the sun moves to a position high in the sky and the terrain begins to rise and fall under my feet. The strain of near constant travel wears on me and my nerves fray as the hours stretch on.

I can feel Flesh Bags around me but none of them give me any sense of having located an immediate source of food to navigate by. Their numbers are far greater than I could have imagined. I do my best to skirt around them, giving them a wide berth to conserve my energy, but when forced to, I deal with them as quickly as possible and continue on.

I pause at the edge of a tree line to survey an old abandoned dirt road that cuts across my path. It looks as if nothing has traveled this way in quite some time, but as I look to my right, I catch a distinct scent that makes me fingers twitch: humans.

Many survivalists have probably fled to the mountains in order to ride out the outbreak when the rumors first began. If they are still alive, they will be well supplied, hunkered down and heavily armed. I must tread carefully as I pass through their lands.

The night stretches out before me, cold and damp after the storms. A dew begins to form on the leaves as I swat at the occasional fly or mosquito and move rapidly through the underbrush. The air feels close within the tree cover as I struggle to keep a steady pace but I feel my strength waning on the steep mountainside.

Winded and sorely in need of water, I slow my pace and look around. The lack of food or water and unrelenting heat of the day has sapped my energy. I need to find somewhere to rest before I move on. Plodding around through the woods without a clear sense of direction is no good to anyone.

Less than half an hour later, I stumble across a winding dirt road that appears to lead to a small homestead hidden behind a thick grove of trees. I look to where the trail rises higher up the hill and sniff the air. Someone is definitely up there and they have food that I need.

Racing across the road before plunging through the disorderly tangle of shrubbery, trees and dangling vines, I can't help but marvel at some of the changes within me. My speed has increased to nearly twice that of a human across flat land, but the mountains remain a challenge. I hope that with proper nourishment I will be able to recover quickly and press on with my mission. I will rest a single night, but tomorrow I return to the hunt.

I pause beside a tree wide enough to conceal two of me and survey the house from a distance. It sits back from the dirt road about a quarter of a mile. The wide curved logs of the cabin's face look to be in good repair and the screen door and deck on this small country home are in good standing. Flowers not long dead drape over painted window boxes.

A small wooden fence with a locked gate stands before me as I take it all in with a keen eye. It looks too clean, too untouched by the desolation of the world I left behind, and for a moment, I can almost convince myself that all is right with the world again. At any minute some sweet, apron-wearing old lady might just come out onto her porch and offer me a glass of hot tea and a rocking chair to sit in while we suffer through the unbearable mountain chill.

None of that will happen, of course, but it is a nice thought.

The decking boards creak softly beneath my feet as I cautiously step up to peer into the cabin through a bay window. It appears to be a tidy, modestly furnished home with dented hardwood floors, crocheted doilies on the side tables and a wall of mounted animal heads. A knit blanket drapes across the arm of a faded blue sofa. A stack of hunting and gardening magazines sit neatly on the handmade coffee table. There is even a small pile of mail near the door, already stamped and ready to be taken to a rural post office.

There are no other signs of life moving within the cabin. I can't hear the steady thumping of a heartbeat inside and when I sniff the air I sense that the house is empty, though obviously recently occupied.

I step up to the doorway and open the screen door, waiting for a few seconds to see if anyone will react to the loud creak of the door hinges. My eyes quickly adjust to the dim interior and I feel the tension in my forehead ease. The room is indeed empty.

The only light that flows into the living room comes through a row of windows off to my right where moonlight spills over, dappled through low hanging trees. To my left, I notice a newspaper beside the stack of mail and realize that it was printed a week after the mutations began. Splashed across the headline in bold print is this: MONE Vaccine Reported to have Potentially Adverse Effects.

"That's the understatement of a lifetime," I mutter and turn the paper over.

Judging by the numerous wrinkles in the newspaper and the leathery texture under my fingertips, it has been read many times. It seems an odd thing to obsess over something that happened months before, but perhaps that day holds special meaning for the owner.

I shiver and move into the house, careful to step lightly.

"Hello?" I call as I close the door softly behind me and set the lock in place.

I have grown far too accustomed to covering my back to allow anyone to sneak up on me from behind. I would most likely catch their scent beforehand, but I would rather not take that chance.

There is not a speck of dust to be seen on any of the surfaces the furniture as I walk into the main living area. An old tube TV stands in the corner facing a well-loved arm chair. At the foot of the chair is a pair of men's slippers.

"It could almost be passed off as homey if it wasn't so anally clean."

I walk through the sitting room and into a short hallway beyond. Trailing my fingers along the wall, I stop to look at each of the family photos. Some are in black and white with a bit of yellowing at the edges. These must be from distant relatives in years past. Others are newer and obviously printed with a digital camera quality.

I stop and stare at a large framed photo prominently positioned on the wall of an old man and woman, holding hands and standing side by side near a small pond. The woman's head is slightly turned and there is a look of adoration on her face. The man wears a small yet wicked grin. As I lower my gaze I realize that he's in the middle of pinching her backside.

"I guess men never grow out of that," I muse and push aside the discomfort the photo births within me. Thinking of Nox at a time like this will hardly help.

The dining room table is empty apart from a vase of dead flowers. The heads have wilted and fallen to the wood surface. Mold clings to the brittle stems.

A china cabinet stands in the far corner of the dining room when I enter and I feel a new pang of regret when I realize how similar it is to one that my mother had when I was a child. I have not thought of her in several months, mostly out of self-preservation, but this reminder is like a slap to the face that I can't dodge. As I place my hand on the thin pane of glass and stare at the delicate blue and white tea cups, I realize that I actually miss my mom.

It feels like a silly thing to admit considering we were never close. Perhaps, because of the horrific nature of her ending, I feel closer to her now merely out of guilt. There was nothing I could have done to stop the Raiders from killing her.

Back then I was unskilled and foolish. If I had tried to help her I would have joined her in death.

Anger burns in my stomach at the thought of how those men ripped into my mother's flesh and drained her of her blood. Stupid, ignorant ideas that blood could spare a person's life in the beginning days led to so many needless deaths, and for what? By now those men have either succumbed to the virus themselves or shot each other dead in the streets. Neither of those endings bring me any comfort. They should have died gruesomely, just as my mom did.

Turning away, I force myself not to smash the china cabinet and the memories that it drags with it. I take a moment to notice that this space is almost obsessively spotless as well.

"Whoever lives here has a seriously creepy obsessive compulsive issue."

As I turn around in place, an eerie feeling falls over me. This area is remote for sure, but not so much so that it would have remained completely untouched by the outbreak. How is it that an old man and woman would survive so well when others lost everything?

"Something is definitely not right with this picture."

When I enter the kitchen, I feel like I've been sucked into a time warp and shoved straight back into the 1800s. In one corner is an old fashioned ice box and across the room, nestled in the corner, is a black pot belly stove still radiating heat. Cast iron cooking pans line the wall on small metal hooks. Spice jars and a tub of what looks like lard sits beside the stove on a small wooden shelf. Large carving knives are fixed to a magnetic strip on the wall beside the small wash basin.

"I guess these people already knew how to rough it when the power went out."

I turn in a complete circle to take it all in and bump my hip against a two-seater wooden table and chair set, all laid out with mealtime cutlery and dishes. The plates are a simple white and chipped on one edge. They are nothing fancy, unlike the ones stored in the china cabinet in the other room.

A quick check of the two bedrooms at the rear of the cabin reveal neatly made beds adorned with homemade spreads, an old fashioned pedal-powered sewing machine and a closet filled with work clothes, many of which have been mended multiple times. Oil lanterns stand on nearly every table in the house to provide light during the nighttime hours but none of them are lit.

Turning to look around the final bedroom, I frown. "How can a place look so completely unlived in when it's obvious that someone does?"

I place my hand on the bed and push down to find that a feather mattress lies beneath the covers. It looks like a godsend and I would happily sink down into is welcoming softness if not for the hairs rising on the back of my neck reminding me that the owners are here somewhere and I have yet to locate them.

Forcing myself to complete my search, I move back through the kitchen and out onto a back deck to take a look at the property. Two rocking chairs sit on either side of a small table. An unlit pipe is cradled in a small smoking dish empty of embers.

Three steps lead down into an unkempt yard, overgrown with weeds and brambles. Beyond that I spy a small trickle of a stream that crisscrosses through the yard and leads to a hand pump. The land slopes upward with a fairly sharp angle and on the rise I catch the sight of smoke. It appears to be coming from a large fire hemmed in with a dirt ditch to keep the flames from spreading.

Just beyond that, nestled near the side of the mountain, is a barn. It's wood siding has faded to an off-red in the moonlight and the white trim has peeled in several places. The roof stands two stories high and is severely pitched at the middle in an A-frame style.

A large rectangular opening at the top appears to lead to a loft area where I can just see the tops of rounded hay bales. I turn my head to listen but fail to hear mooing or the lowing of farm animals. Those most likely became food over the past few months.

To the right of the barn I spy an old pickup that has seen better days. The hood is open and nearly rusted through. A tarp covers the cab but it is easy to see that it won't be moving anytime soon by the large hole where the engine once sat.

The barn door appears to be slightly ajar and has small holes in it scattered over its surface. I step down onto the wet ground and quickly jump over the stream to make my way up the hill, but I stop short when I see footprints in front of me. Dropping to my knees, I survey the trampled ground.

"These was not done by one man," I whisper to myself as I press my finger into the different depths of indentations.

My skin begins to tingle with apprehension as I lower my nose to the ground and breathe in deep. My nostrils flare as the potent scent of death becomes unmistakable against the moist earth and smoky fire.

"Withered."

Lifting my head to look at the barn, I narrow my eyes and focus on the door. There, beside the oversized door hand, I spy a bloody handprint. It looks dry and flaky, at least a day or two old. A further examination of the door reveals that the holes were made by a spray of bullets, most likely a shotgun judging by the pattern. As I move closer, I notice lines of red paint have been scored from the door in the exact distance of fingernails.

The Flesh Bags were definitely here and put up a fight to get into that barn, but why? Did the old man and woman get caught unaware? I crouch low and hurry to the edge of the fire and in amongst the burned down kindling and wood I spy small white teeth.

"He's burning their bodies," I look through the wisps of smoke and see the long bones of fingers.

I look back toward the house, debating if I should leave now before I mark up the area further with my own scent and bring Cable down on this poor unsuspecting man and his wife when I hear a girl scream. Whipping my head around, I narrow in on the barn once more and realize that a new aroma has been added to the air: fresh blood.

SEVEN

I am on the move before I have a chance to talk myself out of it. A second scream of terror echoes from the barn. Skirting around the rim of the fire, I realize that running toward fresh blood is the stupidest thing I've done all day, but I ignore the red warning flags waving like mad in my mind and race for the tree line to conceal my approach.

The low hanging branches of a great white oak tree are heavy with new leaves that will provide partial cover for my climb. I weave among the unevenly spaced tree trunks, keeping the barn in sight while I work to give myself a decent vantage point. When I am less than a hundred feet away, I drop to my knees and listen.

My heart thumps against my rib cage but it is not a result of the sprint that I just finished. It is from adrenaline that spiked through me at the first hint of blood.

"Keep it together," I scold under my breath as I try to clear my thoughts. When sheer willpower proves inadequate to keep my mouth from watering, I dig my fingernails into the palm of my hand until I feel the skin part and the pain helps to ground me.

Once I am directly across from the barn, I bend my knees and leap high to grasp a sizeable branch and swing myself up into an oak tree nearest the building. The speed of my swing takes my breath away and before I can blink I am crouched perfectly on the branch.

"Holy shit." I press my hand against my chest to feel the racing of my heart. Heavy doses of adrenaline pump through my body, setting my nerves alight with hyper awareness so that I am ready to act at a moment's notice.

Another cry of pain refocuses me and this time I hear a resounding smack followed by whimpering.

"I told you to shut your whiny trap," a man's gravelly voice rises from the barn's interior and I grit my teeth. "Don't think I won't gag you."

I take hold of a higher branch and begin to climb, intent on reaching a height that will allow me to look down into the barn from above and get a lay of the land before I make my move. The bark is scratchy against my hands as I climb and I feel a twinge of pain as bits of wood burrow into the half-moon cuts in my palms.

Nestling as high as I dare to trust the tree to sustain my weight, I inch my way out onto a wide branch nearest the open barn window and look in. The opening is large enough for a man to lie down across the expanse twice and affords me a view of the rolled bales of hale in the loft, empty horse stalls on the main floor and various farm equipment along the walls. A large green tractor sits in one corner, partially concealed under a dusty covering. Along the wall I spy various woodworking tools and a work bench beyond, but there is no sign of movement.

This area is not nearly as clean as the house.

"Stop!" a young man calls out in a strained voice. I search for his whereabouts but he is concealed from sight by the expanse of the loft floor that stretches out in front of me. "Please, take me instead. She's just a little girl!"

The old man does not respond. Instead I hear an odd sound, like something grating against metal and with a start I realize that I know what he is doing. It is same sound that I heard each time I used to sharpen the blade of my ax against a stone while living on the road. When I glance back at the wall of tools I see that one space is empty, but there is no way for me to know exactly what was there before.

"Listen to me. She's all skin and bones. She's no good to you," the boy yells again.

This time I spy movement along the floor and realize that it is a shadow. It is low to the ground and appears stretched. He must be sitting near a lantern and is mostly likely tied up to prevent him from interfering, but what does the girl's weight have anything to do with it? Is the man trying to force her to do some sort of heavy labor work and she's resisting?

When the girl's soft whimpering rises tenfold as I hear footsteps and her frantic cries shift into muffled screams, I realize something terrible is happening below. Shifting slightly farther out on the tree branch, I search for a landing spot inside the barn. The gap between the end of the branch and the opening is a good ten feet, easily manageable, but I have to make sure I don't miss my target and plummet to the ground below.

"I'm begging you. Please, don't do this!" The desperation in the boy's voice makes my chest ache for him as I remember similar feelings of helplessness when I lay beneath my mother's hospital bed as she was gutted and drained.

I am about to leap forward when the scent of newly spilled blood paralyzes me. The girl's shriek pierces the night and if I had not already had a death grip on the tree, I might have fallen.

The boy thrashes and kicks out his feet just far enough for me to see the tips of his toes. "No!"

I swallow hard, fighting against the wave of hunger that swells within me as the girl's blood invades my nose and sets my blood boiling. I close my eyes and push out every ounce of air that I can spare from my lungs so that I can reign myself in, but I am so weak from my journey without food and tasting Ryker's wounds has enabled me to instantly revive the memory of his warm blood on my lips and I nearly succumb to my desires.

My body burns with an internal fire, as if flames were lit beneath my feet, and I am lost to the ecstasy that I know one taste would bring me of the girl's blood. So sweet and filled with life giving nourishment. My fingers dig into the flesh of the tree as I fight to push down my hunger and it is only when Nox's face fills my vision that I feel an ounce of control return.

Seconds later, the girl's screams go supersonic. They rattle around in my brain and I am forced to release one hand on the tree to clutch my stomach as bile rises in my throat with an acidic burn that helps to stave off the hunger.

She is a little girl, I repeat over and over again.

I have heard many people die since the outbreak began. Some die well, fast and painless, but far too many are forced to suffer before their end comes. I have heard the screams of people being eaten alive and this girl could easily match them shriek for shriek.

"You bastard! I'll kill you for hurting her!"

My eyes snap open at the boy's shout and I see red, almost like a physical veil of shimmering color has fallen over my vision. The unseen girl's face takes form in my mind as the young girl I tried and failed to save back at the Opryland hotel two months before. Nox had entrusted me to keep his young friend, Chloe, safe and I let her fall to her death. Though I made every attempt afterward to save her life, I still failed and her death continues to haunt me. I could not save Chloe, but I'll be damned if I let this girl die while I sit idly by.

"No one threatens me, boy," the old man rages from below. I hear a clattering of metal and then loud stomping of boots against the wooden floorboards. Before I can make the leap through the window and onto one of the rafters, I hear a loud crunch followed by a howl of pain.

"Let that be a lesson for you," I hear the man spit and then walk away.

Taking a deep breath of the last fresh air I will be able to fill my lungs with, I make the ten foot leap through the window and land on my intended rafter. I waver slightly and am forced to distribute my weight to a second beam that crisscrosses nearby. I manage to stabilize myself at the last second. I feel a slight tremor in the wood reverberate up through my legs when I land, but my presence goes unnoticed by those below.

Craning my neck around to the right, I find the wounded girl lying on a long wooden table attached to the wall. She appears to be no more than seven or eight years old, with hair the color of wheat and skin so pale she looks as if she hasn't seen the sun in months. Her clothes are soiled, her hair is slick with oil, and her nails are caked with dirt. Her shoulders are thin and her collar bone juts out of her shirt neckline. The boy was right. She really is nothing more than skin and bones.

That same teenage boy sits on a small square hay bale less than twenty feet away from the girl with his hands bound by rope and a cloth shoved in his mouth to silence his cries of pain. His eyes are wide with hatred and his lips are deeply cracked from prolonged dehydration. His nose looks as if it has been forcibly shoved to the right side of his face. Judging by the rapid swelling and gush of blood, this is the source of his most recent injury.

His clothes are filthy just like the girl's. His dark matted hair curls around his chin and his jeans show signs of dried blood and a puncture hole about two inches wide. From this height, it is hard to judge the nature of the wound, but if I had to guess,

I would say the old man either shot the boy with a gun or drove an arrow through the top of his thigh. Either way, the man has proven to be more than willing to hurt these two kids and that makes me seethe with anger.

Killing Flesh Bags and hurting adults is one thing, but to maim and torture a child is sadistic.

The teenager looks less wasted than the girl but far from what I would imagine his normal physique could be. He probably has not been here as long. Judging by the purple shadowing along his right eye he isn't the best at following orders or keeping quiet either.

I can't help but wonder how long these two have been trapped here. Days? Weeks? Months?

Casting my gaze around the room, I spy a square crack in the floor with a pull handle where a pile of hay has been shoved aside. That must be where he's been keeping them.

So far I have yet to be able to see past the man's broad shoulders where he stands beside the girl, blocking her torso from view as she strains against the leather straps. A wide brimmed straw hat covers his head. It isn't until he tilts his head down to focus on his work that I am able to spy white curls of hair at the base of his neck. His clothes are patched and threadbare in places, just like the ones I saw in the closet. An old apron is tied at his neck and around his back.

He hums a child's nursery rhyme as he works despite the girl's pleading whimpers. That has to be the creepiest thing I've ever witnessed.

I move along the rafters, ducking low through one opening to reach another beam until I am directly above the girl. What I see below me makes me stop and stare in horror. In a shallow cast iron grilling tray sits the girl's severed hand and forearm. The bone has been sawed cleanly through with a bloody cleaver just above her elbow. Blood drips down from the wooden table and splatters on the man's work boots but he pays it no mind.

Her young face has drained of color as she stares at the remaining stump of her arm. Her mouth twists in a silent scream of horror before her eyes roll back into her head and she finally passes out from the pain. The man begins to whistle as he latches two additional straps across her chest before he moves off toward a wood burning stove. It is only when he bends to stoke it that I notice a small old fashioned iron warming on top of it.

I close my eyes as I realize that despite his earlier butchery, he must be preparing to cauterize her wound. The girl is lucky to have already passed out.

What sort of sick fuck cuts off a little girl's arm and then patches her up afterward? I watch him place the grill pan with the hand on top of the stove. He scoops a bit of lard out of a small container with his finger and then sprinkles in a couple of pinches of herbs.

All hint of my former hunger vanishes and I cling to the rafter as I realize what he's doing. He's planning on feeding off that little girl!

As horrified as I may be at my own uncontrollable hunger for human flesh, I am part zombie now. This man, this beast, is nothing more than a sick monster without feeling. The urge to grab my gun and shoot the bastard in the head is almost strong enough to follow through on, but it would be a death far too kind for the likes of him.

The boy thrashes against the floor as the scent of the little girl's cooking flesh fills the barn, toppling himself onto his side, but still he tries to work the gag out of his mouth to yell. I can only imagine how many useless hours he has screamed for help while trapped in that hole in the ground and no one came. The road leading to this house has obviously not been traveled for quite some time and anyone who could have heard the cries for help and stopped might have proven to have intentions far worse than this old guy.

The man barely glances at the teenage boy as he places his hand in an elbow length black leather glove and takes hold of the iron. The bottom of it glows orange from the heat as he turns and walks slowly toward the unconscious girl.

Every fiber in my being wants to drop down from the rafters onto the man and snap his neck before he can hurt that child again but I know this must be done. If the wound is not sealed properly, she could bleed out and die. The only reason I choose to let him live now is to allow him to give her the care that she needs. This is obviously not the first time he has severed a limb and he is smart enough not about to let his food go to waste.

He will take good care of her now that he has what he wants. I just need to bide my time before I strike. Then he will pay.

Forcing myself to ignore the boy's cries, I listen for other sounds of heartbeats in the barn and realize that apart from the three down below, no one else is here. I glance back over at my shoulder outside and hang my head as I realize my mistake. He isn't burning the Flesh Bags that attacked. He is getting rid of the evidence of his last victim.

In the far corner I spy a shovel with dried dirt still on the head. Something darker is smeared there and I would bet my life that it's blood.

This boy and girl must be the last among his prisoners. If that is the case, judging by the sad state these two are in, he will be forced to start looking for replacements soon.

"There you go, my pretty. All better." The man's crooning voice breaks off into a coughing fit. He turns his head to the side to spit a nasty wad of phlegm onto the floor and I spy a bit of blood in the mixture.

Good. I hope he chokes on it next time, I think as he sets the iron on its end and removes the glove, pausing to wipe his hands on the soiled apron that he wears. I watch as he opens the top drawer of a tool cabinet and removes a roll of gauze that is several shades darker than white. For the little girl's sake, I hope that he has at least sanitized it after the last victim he bandaged up.

My peripheral vision catches movement below and I turn to see that the teenage boy has noticed my presence from where he lies on the floor. He blows out a hard breath and his hair shifts out of his eyes to stare up at me. He falls completely still, no doubt afraid of drawing further attention to himself or to me, and pleads for help with his eyes.

I wish that I could offer him a reassuring smile but the scent of blood is still too strong and I fear that my smile will turn more into a baring of my teeth that will terrify him instead. I place a silencing finger over my lips and then move along the rafters back toward the window that I jumped through before. Tucking my gun into the back of my pants, I climb into the window sill and prepare to jump.

No matter what discomfort being near that injured girl will bring to me, or how much distance I may be losing by delaying here instead of trying to catch Wiemann's trail, I can't turn my back on them and let this monster carve them into little pieces. I will stay and fight for them, but I have to do it the right way.

If the old man is going to need a new victim, I intend to give him one.

EiGHT

The drop to the ground outside should have broken my legs or at least an ankle but I barely feel the pins and needles that sting my soles as I roll back to my feet and hurry away from the barn. I duck behind trees as I move down the hill in case the old man casts his gaze out across the overgrown meadow while he finishes binding the girl's wounds. The last thing I want is to distract him from his work. In my incapable hands that girl wouldn't stand much of a chance.

When I reach the back porch of the house, I open the door and slam it hard, then turn to appear as if I've just exited the house.

"Hello?" I call in a loud voice with my hands cupped around my mouth. "Is anyone here?"

Turning my head enough to listen for movement in the barn, I wait a few seconds before walking back down the steps into the grass, adding a pronounced limp to my gait. "I got stranded in the storm earlier and all of my supplies have washed away. Do you have any food that you can spare? Maybe a place I can sleep for the night? I can sleep just about anywhere."

In the distance, I can hear the soft rushing of water in the brook that feeds the small stream that runs across the old man's land, but there is no new sound from the barn.

"Please help me," I call again as I move farther away for the house in case the old man is hard of hearing. "I'm so hungry and I just need a place to rest for a day, maybe two at the tops. I promise that I will not be any trouble."

This time the barn door rattles. I hear wood shifting and then the creak of rusted metal rollers on a sliding track as the right door opens.

"Oh, thank goodness. I was so worried that I'd come across another abandoned place," I call, waving my arms over my head as he raises a lantern to see by. I start slowly in his direction.

The old man has removed his apron and I notice that he has taken the time to wipe away any hint of the little girl's blood from his hands before opening the door. I was right. He has done this before, perhaps many times since the world became a place filled only with death and greed. How many other unsuspecting people have stumbled across this man's home and found prolonged imprisonment before a horrific and drawn out death instead of the aid that they need?

"Are you lost, missy?"

"I'm afraid so." I step through the knee-high weeds, slowing my pace to appear distressed as I hit the slope that runs up to the barn. I haven't yet reached the glow of the firelight, but he follows the sound of my voice easily enough but to know which direction I'm coming from. "I got separated from my group and have been wandering around for a couple of days trying to locate them, but my bum leg doesn't help much. It got trampled when things went to shit in Nashville a few months back and it never has healed right."

"I'm mighty sorry to hear that. Must make traveling difficult. Sure hope there weren't any other complications."

"No," I shake my head when I reach the far edge of the firelight. "I'm fit as a fiddle apart from that."

His smile makes my skin crawl but I force myself not to show my disgust as I smile back and raise a hand to wave my welcome.

"And your friends? You think they came this way?" He asks, looking around at his darkened property.

He is a cautious one.

I shrug. "I guess my tracking skills aren't so great because I can't find any sign of them. Figures they would leave me behind. I wasn't too good at keeping up."

He wipes his hands on his pant legs and tips his straw hat as I approach but he doesn't move far from the door. "I ain't got much, mind you, but I reckon I could spare a bit. My wife, Tilly, has been helping me clean an old cow in the barn. If that leg of yours will hold out a bit longer I could sure use the extra help. After we get her drained and hung up we can grab some soup and then tomorrow, if you're not needing to be moving on I could use some help with the processing in exchange for a home cooked meal."

I offer what I hope passes as a grateful smile.

"I've never done much processing before, especially this late at night," I add innocently, "but I'm a quick learner. I really appreciate the offer, mister. It's nice to know there are still a few decent people in the world."

His upper lip twitches but I don't draw attention to it.

"The name is Sally, by the way," I offer as he turns to step aside and allow me to enter the barn. "Sally Warburton. And you are?"

When I step close to the old man he lifts his light to get a better look at me and I'm dazzled by it. Raising my hand to shield my eyes, I never see the baseball bat that slams into the side of my head the moment after I step inside the barn.

When I wake sometime later I find myself dangling from a rafter several feet above the ground with a wicked pounding headache. Thick ropes bind my wrists overhead and place a heavy strain on my shoulders.

"Well, that was about the stupidest thing that I've ever seen," a nasally voice calls from somewhere behind me.

Long shadows stretch across the barn floor in front of me and I realize that the sun is already riding high in sky. I must have been knocked out for quite some time.

The scent of cooked flesh has diminished from the air and as I crane my neck around in search of the old man I discover that he is nowhere to be found. The table where I last saw the little girl is vacant and the leather bindings drape harmlessly over the edge.

Kicking out my feet, I work to maneuver myself around enough to see the young man who spoke a second ago. He has been moved away from the hay bale and now has his hands and ankles chained to the tractor. A new trail of blood is dried over his right temple and his upper lip has been split since I last saw him. Two bits of cloth have been shoved into his broken nose. They are obviously the reason for his altered tone of voice.

"Yeah, well, I have to admit that didn't exactly go as I had planned. I'm guessing he took my gun, didn't he?"

"You think?" He winces as he raises his chained hands to gingerly touch his forehead and then pinch the bridge of his nose. With a pained since he releases it and gently tugs the cloths free. They are stained red but not with any large amount of fresh blood, thank goodness.

"I know that you saw what he does to us. Why didn't just keep right on going?"

"Is that what others have done? Saved their own skin and left you behind to suffer at the hand of that bastard?"

He grits his teeth and looks away. "They did what they had to do. I can't blame them for that."

"Maybe, but I'm not that sort of person. You needed my help so here I am."

He snorts. "A lot of good you're doing hanging up there like that. What are you going to do? Stare him to death?"

"And what about you? Do you enjoy being his personal punching bag just because you can't hold that sharp tongue of yours for five seconds? You're in the wrong position to be passing judgment, kid."

His scowl falters when his lips splits further and he's forced to lower his gaze. I'm guessing he does it so that I don't see the tears welling in the corners of his eyes at the sudden flood of pain. "You wouldn't understand."

"I understand more than you think."

Despite the stifling warmth of the day, I know all too well how the spring nights in the mountains will bring with it a chill this this boy won't be able to combat if left prey to the elements. He has nothing on besides a ratty t-shirt and threadbare jeans that hang low on his hips. The old bastard didn't even leave him a blanket for the night before and there's a lingering shivering in his muscles as he slowly warms up.

"I understand that you're a survivor, kid. I also saw how much you care about that little girl. It's obviously enough to take a few punches and keep right on going, but you need to be smart about this. Letting him beat on you isn't going to help you get out of this place alive."

The boy yanks on his metal chains. They stir up a small cloud of dust when he pulls against them so that he can shift his position. His eyes darken as he sinks into the shadows. "What do you know about it?"

"Quite a lot, actually. I know a thing or two about torture and pain. It doesn't take long before it begins to wear on you, both mentally and physically. Muscles can atrophy over just a couple of weeks without proper exercise, especially when you're forced to sit or kneel. I'm guessing he kept you down in that hole under the barn floor for quite a while judging by how skinny you are. You are weak, unarmed, and malnourished. Running isn't exactly your best option against this guy."

"I could make it."

"No, you can't, and thinking that you can will just get you and that little girl killed," I snap back at him. "Before I came out here and found you I got a good look at his house. The guy has a wall filled with trophy animal kills, a psycho obsession with cleaning and he's obviously unhinged. More than that he's also patient, cunning, and skilled. This is his playing ground, not yours. You wouldn't make it a mile on your own with him tracking you, let alone trying to take that injured girl with you."

"I won't leave without her."

I nod in agreement. "I don't expect you to. That's why you need a plan."

He mulls over my words, swallowing hard as he draws his legs up into his chest and wraps his arms around them. "Why do you even care?"

"Because I'm a decent person, or at least I like to think that I am."

He snorts. "Haven't met many of those during the past few months. Seems like most people are more animal than human these days."

"Well, I'm not."

I can feel his eyes on me as they search me, no doubt trying to decide if I'm just as crazy as the old man. Finally, he nods. He really has nothing to lose at this point. "So what is my best option of breaking out of this hellhole then?"

"Me." I say without hesitation. "I'm going to finish what I started and get you out of here. I promise."

The bitter laughter that bubbles up from between his lips makes me sad. How many other people have professed the same thing only to fail him in the end?

It is human nature, at least for those people who still possess a heart, to help those younger and in need. This boy may be fourteen or fifteen years old, but he's obviously been abandoned more times than he would care to admit, whether by choice or by death. He is alone and trying like hell to look brave, but I can see that he is scared shitless.

"I won't leave you. That's another promise." But I know that I will. Just not before I know that they are safely away from this place.

I crane my neck back to study the ropes tied over the beam. They are tightly woven and braided in a slipknot that will only tighten each time I pull against it. Already my flailing has begun to give me rope burn on the flesh inside my wrists.

I look to the walls in search of a knife that I can use to cut the rope but I am too far away from any of them and the boy is chained on the opposite side of the room. There is no chance of either of us getting our hands on one.

"Where are the keys to your chains?"

The boy doesn't raise his head. "In Flannery's pocket."

"Shit." Well, that option is out. "And the girl? Did he take her too?" I ask, following the line of the rope to where it is tied off on a support beam. The rope is looped multiple times around a shiny metal boat mooring and wound tightly. No amount of bouncing and pulling against my bindings will loosen it.

"Maybe."

I look back at him. He may think that I can't see the cautious glance that his sending my way but I see him all too well in the dark. This kid has an attitude the size of this barn and as grating on my nerves as it may be, I guess I can understand. He's been through more horrors than most that have survived this long. I can't imagine a life of always wondering if you are next in line to be on the dinner table.

"Let's assume for a second that not everyone left alive is just out for themselves. Let's also assume that I did in fact risk my own neck to try to help you, which I can guarantee you is a rare thing to find on this back road. I could have walked away, minded my own business and pretended that you weren't in trouble, but the fact is, I'm not that kind of person."

That final sentence catches in my throat. "So here I am, like it or not. Now, you can either cut me a little slack and help me figure this out or you can just sit around and wait for that scumbag to get back and start hacking off your fingers and toes for his dinner. It's your choice, kid."

"I'm not a kid."

"I call it how I see it." I twist the ropes and kick my legs so that I can see behind me. The wooden table where the little girl was laid out earlier has been methodically sanitized. The stove embers have burned out and the grilled forearm and hand have been removed.

"How about we start with something simple? What's your name?"

He presses his lips tightly together.

"If you don't want me calling you 'kid' then you're going to have to give me something to work with. Trust me, I had a guy who decided my name was Dumbass for a while because I decided to be stubborn and I never lived that one down."

His lip twitches with amusement but he remains silent.

"Okay fine. I will go first. My name is Avery and I'm from St. Louis—"

"I thought your name was Sally?" He interrupts me. "I overheard you tell Flannery before he struck a home run on the back of your melon."

I grit my teeth at his description and feel the pounding in my head amplify. "If you want to survive in this world, kid, you're going to have to learn to think on your feet. Lying when you need to get by isn't always a bad thing to do."

He snorts. "So says the person telling me to give her my real name."

"Make up one up for all I care. I just need something to call you."

He scrunches up his face for a moment and I realize that he's actually trying to think of a fake name.

"Fine, Kid it is then."

"Screw you."

I laugh. "You've got quite a mouth on you, Kid. Some people might hate that but it proves you've got spunk. I can respect that."

"I don't want your respect."

"Maybe not." I search the wall behind him and see that the cleaver the old man used before has been cleaned and hung back in its rightful place. "But you've got it all the same."

"Whatever. I can live with Kid for now."

"Good. Now how about you shut that wiseass trap of yours for a few minutes while I figure out how to get us out of here before that psycho comes back?"

He looks away to stare out at the approaching dusk. "He won't come back today."

I twist back around to look at him. "How do you know?"

"He never does. He has to make sure Hope makes it through twenty-four hours before he starts cutting again." His Adam's apple bobs and I feel a sharp and sudden stab of sympathy for the kid.

"Some don't make it that long, do they?"

"No." He kicks at the ground. "That's when the rest of us would get really worried. The meat spoils too fast once the heart stops beating."

Hearing the boy call a person meat feels far too callous considering he is next in line for the chopping block, but I know that it has become his only way of surviving. Something separating yourself from something horrible is all you can do. A dead friend has to just be dead, and nothing more.

"How many people went before you?"

"There were fourteen of us when I arrived. I don't know how many there were before that." He glances back over at me and his face drains of color as he swallows hard. "After a while you sort of get numb to it. I know that sounds terrible but it's the truth. People are taken. People scream. People die. It's just the way things are here."

"And you two are the last?"

He nods and curls his legs tighter into his chest.

"Where's the wife? I think he said her name is Tilly."

The kid turns his head and presses his cheek against his raised knees. "She's been gone for a good bit. I think losing her sent him over the edge. He talks to her sometimes. I've seen him out walking in the yard with his arm out like he's escorting her ghost. From what the others said, she died in his arms. Seems she went out to the outhouse one night while he was sleeping and started screaming the woods down. By the time he found her something had already mauled her."

I stop wrestling with the ropes. "Mauled?"

He nods. "Word has it there wasn't much left of her stomach by the time Flannery got to her. He had to put her down himself."

If this story had been told to me at any other time in my life, I would have written it off as a mountain lion or a bear attack, but the sick feeling coiling in my gut tells me there's something more to this story.

"Did he see the animal that got her?"

He shrugs. "Guess not. When he arrived she was alone. Said he saw some bloody footprints and figured she was attacked and tried to get back to him."

I want to tell him that it would be impossible to walk while holding your guts in. I know from personal experience that once a Flesh Bag starts gnawing on you, you're not getting away.

"After that, he turned on the people staying with them," he says. His voice has dropped to little more than a whisper. "Laura was the last to go from that original group. She was his cousin."

My breath hitches. "He ate his own family?"

He nods. "She said something changed in him that night. When he looked at her, he had dead eyes. Like he could no longer see her as a person. She was terrified of him. I guess she had a good reason to be."

I lower my head and close my eyes. It all makes sense now. I would bet money that he saw the Flesh Bag that ate his wife. When his mind snapped from shock it allowed him to see everyone in his home as just another among the walking dead.

He probably doesn't even realize these are real, living people he's keeping prisoner.

Then a thought strikes me.

"How long ago did you say the wife died?"

His eyebrows pull in together as he thinks. "It's hard to say. I don't exactly have a calendar anymore."

I roll my eyes. "Just give me a guess."

"I've probably been here about two months by now so I'd say a month before that. Maybe a little more."

My heart makes its final plummet into my stomach. Three months ago would have been right around the time Dr. Wiemann's victims were tossed over the wall as failed experiments. It would make sense that those that survived would span out, biting and spreading the virus as they went as they were consumed with hunger. The suffering and subsequent death of all of these people are on the doctor's hands as well. Anger swells up within me as I think of how many lives Dr. Wiemann has ruined.

"He will pay for this." But even as I say the word *he*, I know that I am actually referring to both of these evil men at the same time.

NINE

I have never been all that great at coming up with a plan of escape and executing it. I guess you could say that I'm more of a "fly by the seat of my pants" sort, but this time I know that I'm going to have to put a bit more planning into it. Not just for my sake, but for the little girl's. The only way I'm getting out of these ropes is with leverage and hopefully a heck of a lot of luck, but after several hours of tugging, pulling, swinging and general thrashing, I am no closer to finding a way out of my bindings.

"You are stubborn, I'll give you that," the kid drawls out as he lets his feet drop to the sides on the floor. His lips have begun to chatter as the sun falls behind the trees, but I am untouched by the chill. My escape antics would keep me warm enough even without the added benefits of the mutations.

"Since we are obviously stuck here we might as well talk. I spent far too many days on the road alone to like the sound of my own thoughts. How about you tell me where are you from?"

Plus I need to think of something other than the pain biting into my wrists as I begin to pump my legs and swing back and forth, trying a new tactic.

"I'm from just outside of Chicago. My dad and I were lucky. We got out of there before things got really bad." He watches me swing, gaining momentum with each pass, but seems indifferent. I don't really blame him. I'm tired of trying and failing too.

"Was he here with you?"

I stretch out my foot, straining to reach the beam in front of me but I fall short. My wrists scream in agony as the skin peels further off my wrists and blood runs in steady streams down my forearms but I grit my teeth and force my legs to pump harder.

"No. He's still out there somewhere. We got separated during an attack before I stumbled across this place."

"Raiders?" I grunt.

"No. Wouldn't you know it, it was our own heroes in camo that nabbed him." He angrily tosses aside a bit of broken hay. "A whole group of soldiers showed up out of nowhere in the middle of the night and started grabbing people from our camp. They said they were trying to help but I saw those Army guys shoot three in the head when they got jumped from behind. One of them was a lady but that didn't stop them. My dad managed to shove me into a dumpster and get me covered before he led them away. I never saw him after that, but I looked for ages. He was just gone."

At the mention of soldiers I let my legs fall still and struggle to turn to see him as I fight to stop my swaying. "Where was this? Back in Nashville?"

"Yeah." He gives me a queer look. "Why? How'd you guess that?"

I wish that I could give him something good to hold on to and reassure him that his dad is just fine, but after Cable's attack on the hotel I can't do that. Even if he were taken by some of Cap's men, I have no idea if he was ever even a resident. For all I know he could have been among those sent down to the hospital lab for testing. He could even be a Flesh Bag now.

"I was taken too."

"You were?" He sits up a bit straighter as I throw out my legs to try to counter-balance my spin.

My skin tears a little more with each swing and as the floor begins to tilt I realize that I've begun to move faster than my equilibrium can keep up with. Apparently not all of my weaknesses were overcome with the mutations. I've never been very good with spinning carnival rides.

"A couple months back I was in pretty rough shape. Everyone in my group had been turned by the virus and I was left on my own. I stuck to the woods as much as I could, scavenged when I had to and then I ran into some trouble. Those soldiers found me, patched me up and took me to a hotel in Nashville. It was supposed to be a safe place for survivors."

"Supposed to be?"

Damn, this kid doesn't miss anything.

I swallow hard and force myself to focus on his face each time I spin around. "I suppose it was for a while. They had plenty of ammunition, hands to hold guns to man the walls and food for everyone. They scoured the city for supplies and hunkered down. I reckon they would have done just fine if things hadn't changed. A few nights ago there was a massive assault on the hotel and a lot of people died."

His shoulders droop and any hope of seeing his dad that I may have seen burst to life in his eyes withers and dies out. "So that means I was right. He probably is dead."

"You can't think like that. There were also a lot of survivors."

"Yeah, well if there's one thing that I've learned over the past couple of months is that fate tends to like to take a big stinking shit on me whenever it can. If my dad was alive I'd bet money that he's a goner by now."

I close my eyes to still my stomach as I finally slow to a halt. I don't feel so good but I push myself to speak again. "So that's just it? You are just going to give up on him before you even try to find out if he's alive?"

His face twists into something dark and foreign. "Why shouldn't I? It's not like he ever came looking for me."

And then I understand the root of his bitterness. He did everything he could to find his father and now, after having been abandoned by everyone here, he feels like his own father has done the same exact thing.

"Look, I don't know your dad, and I'm not exactly an expert on loving parents, but if he got you this far south and hid you in that dumpster, then I'd say that means he cares a heck of a lot. If he's alive, then I would bet my life on the fact that he is looking for you. My guess would be he has joined up with one of the security teams back at the hotel so that he can search for you while he is out on patrol."

"Do you really think so?"

The raw pain in his voice is utterly heartbreaking and I am reminded that even though he doesn't want to be called a kid, for all intents and purposes, he is still exactly that.

"Yeah, I really do, because that is what I would do if I were him."

He turns his head and wipes at his nose. He tries to muffle a small sniffle and I allow him his privacy as I begin to swing again.

He is a tough kid. I vow that once we are out of this mess and he is on his feet again, I will do everything that I can to make sure he has the weapons and supplies he needs to get back to that hotel to find his dad.

The second round of swinging tears through new layers of my skin much faster but I press on, knowing just how far I have to reach now. With only a few hard pushes, I manage to wrap the end of my boot around the wood post.

"How exactly is that going to help?" He asks as he watches me struggle to maintain my grip.

Working my other leg around the back of the beam, I slowly walk myself up the wood. Once I begin to feel a bit of slack on my arms, I grab high on the rope and begin pull myself up. My arms tremble and blood makes my palms slippery but I hold on with everything I have got left in me.

"Holy shit, that is brilliant! I can't believe that I have never thought of that before." He rises to his knees as I use my fingers and teeth to work the slipknot, loosening it just enough to get one hand free.

Moments later, I free my other hand, release my hold on the beam, and drop to the floor. This time I feel pain when I land as blood rushes back into my toes. I pause for a moment to rub circulation back into my calves and thighs, waiting until I am certain that I will not collapse when I try to move.

"All joking aside," Kid says with a wide smile, "that was totally legit."

When I laugh and push my wild curls back out of my eyes I smear a stripe of blood across my forehead. "I think I will take that as a compliment, coming from you. Now hold still while I look around for something to bust you out of your chains."

"Flannery has the keys, remember?"

"How could I forget? But there may still be something here that we can use."

I brush my fingertips along the wall of weapons, searching for something narrow and pointed. An ice pick would work great to pop the lock, but there isn't one to be found. A pair of bolt cutters would have him out of there in no time, but Flannery is not stupid enough to leave those lying around either. With sharp knives with no serration on their blades and branding irons too large to fit the keyhole, my options are woefully limited. I can't even find a blowtorch to heat the metal enough to try to break it, and there is no way to pull him close enough to the fire to try to improvise.

"You have to leave me behind."

"No." I shake my head. "I told you that I am not leaving you here."

"Look, Hope needs you more than I do right now. Go save her and then come back for me."

I turn to look over my shoulder at him. "Hope? Is that her name?"

He nods slowly.

"It's beautiful."

"Yeah," he rubs the back of his neck, "well, she's a pretty special girl. I will definitely deny saying this later but I think she will like you."

"That is a really nice thought. I hope she does." I drop down beside him to meet him at eye level. "I *will* be back for you."

He hesitates, searching my face for any signs of fear but finds none. "Just kill the bastard for me, will you?"

I pat him on the shoulder. "With pleasure."

Leaving him behind in the growing darkness feels wrong. He is too exposed, too vulnerable if a Flesh Bag comes along while I am gone, but I have no other choice. One tug on the barn door tells me that we are sealed in tight enough that he will be safe until I return with the keys to his lock.

Climbing the beam up to the loft, I skirt along the edge and back out through the rectangular window. This time I race straight down the hill under the cover of darkness and silently step up onto the porch.

The windows are lit with the flickering of candles instead of the oil lanterns. Hot wax drips down the nearly spent candles and onto the wooden windowsills. From inside the house, I can hear whistling but little else. I search from window to window, hunting for any sign of where he is keeping Hope. I circle around the house before finally locating her in the back bedroom.

She is paler than before but at least appears to be sleeping. Her eyes are closed and she has been tucked into bed with both arms concealed by a quilt, but there is no sign of Flannery anywhere. The small tea cup on the side table makes me wonder if he has drugged her somehow to be able to rest through the pain. As I shift to the next window down and look through into the hall, I see that a chair has been propped against the door and jammed up under the handle.

I move around to the front of the house and peer in through the living room window to find Flannery seated in his lounge chair. His house slippers are on his feet and a throw blanket is spread across his lap where he sits polishing the barrel of a shotgun that has been stripped for cleaning. A dirty dinner plate sits on the coffee table. At the sight of three small finger bones pushed onto one side of the plate I am forced to look away.

My back teeth grind as heat flushes through my body. My fingers clench and flex rapidly as I allow myself to imagine how delicious his death will feel. Delusional or not, this man needs to die and I want it far more than I wanted Ryker.

But I need to do it quietly so that I do not wake Hope up and give her a new monster to fear. She has already been through enough trauma for one lifetime. If I can spare her more terror, I will do whatever it takes.

Lifting my head to do a quick inventory of the room, I search for any other signs of weapons within arms reach. There is a sawed off shotgun propped against the window beside the TV and I spy my handgun on the side table less than a foot from where he sits, not to mention the one in his lap. If I bust through the front door there is no way I will get to him before he fires off at least one round. I may be a superhuman now, but I am not willing to find out if I am bulletproof.

My best option is to enter through the back of the house and sneak up on him. Hurrying around the side, I cast one glance toward the barn and listen closely, but hear nothing out of the ordinary. Just the sounds of crickets chirping and bullfrogs croaking. The birds have already settled down in their nests for the night.

I sniff the air just to be sure that I haven't missed an unseen or unheard threat, but all seems safe. I open the back screen door with painstaking care and silently slip inside. The kitchen is dark and I pass straight through, not bothering to grab a knife from the counter. I will take pleasure in killing him with my own bare hands.

Glancing down the hall toward where Hope rests, I pause to listen for her steady breathing and am relieved to discover that she is still locked in her deep slumber. From up ahead, I can hear the intermittent swipe of a cloth and know that Flannery is still polishing his gun. Torn between needing to take him out and wanting to get Hope to safety as soon as possible, I decide take care of business first and then dispose of the body before I disturb her.

Keeping to the far right side of the hallway, I tread with a light touch as I approach the living room. The candle lights are dim with their wicks nearly spent. They flicker in the cool air that passes through an open window in the dining room.

I pause just long enough to calm my breathing before I turn the corner and leap. Flannery's wrinkled eyes widen with surprise just before I hit him and together we tumble to the floor, knocking his chair over. His bony hip digs into my side before I throw him off and then jump to a crouch. Pieces of his gun scatter across the wood floor in all directions.

He slams into the corner of the TV hard enough to pull a cry of pain from his lips before he rolls to his side and slowly pushes himself up. Despite the fact that he is along in years, a lifetime spent living off the land has afforded him far more agility than I had planned on. He will not go down without a fight.

When he turns and sends a right hook flying in my direction, I nearly miss the movement and his fist grazes my cheek. I take hold of his hand and yank it over my shoulder and then straight down, snapping his arm at the elbow. Flannery howls in pain as I release his arm and turn to shove a fist into his left shoulder hard enough to snap his collar bone.

The old man stumbles back with his broken arm swinging grotesquely.

"You bitch," he spits.

"Hurts, doesn't it?" I growl and lash out at him, raking my nails across his face. "The slow and painful mutilation of your body over time is something beyond comprehension, and yet you have forced a dozen people to slowly watch as you eat their flesh."

"They were monsters. They deserved to die!"

"No," I shake my head, "they were people. Innocent, helpless people that you once cared about."

"No one is helpless in this world." He staggers backward with his arm cradled against his chest. "They are nothing more than rabid animals."

"Just like the one that ate your wife?"

Heat darkens Flannery's cheeks and spills down his neck. "Don't you dare speak about my Tilly!"

"It ate her, didn't it?"

A strangled moan rises from the man as I step forward to match his withdrawal step for step. He needs to suffer, to realize what he has done and feel excruciating pain before he meets his end. I will not make this quick, nor will I show him an ounce of mercy.

"You saw the thing that got her, didn't you? It that tore into her stomach with its bare hands and chewed on her intestines. I know you saw it all. I can see the fear and rage in your eyes even now."

I step forward again and move to keep him out of arm's reach of my gun. It fell to the floor when I knocked the end table with my boot, but in doing so, I know that I am also driving him closer to his shotgun near the TV. He may be a skilled hunter, but that broken arm of his will make getting a shot off far more difficult. I do not fear his aim, but the sound that it will make. Hope must not know what happens in this room.

"Did her screams wake you in the night?" I ask as I kick out his legs. His head smacks into the TV on the way down and I grab his gun and toss it away. The edge of the console glistens with fresh blood as he drops to the floor, blinking rapidly to clear his vision.

"I bet you can't sleep at night without hearing her calling to you for help, but you were as useless then as you are lying there right now."

I stomp down on his leg and smile at the feeling of bones shattering beneath my boot. Flannery's gruff shout cuts off when I reach down and slam my fist into his mouth, splitting his lip and dislocating a couple teeth in the process. He spits them out and they clatter to the ground.

I bunch up my fist again. "Were you afraid of that thing when you found your wife?"

"Yes, dammit," he rasps. Blood stained spittle flies from his lips as he curls in on himself. "It was terrible."

I lean over him and smile. "And you know that there are more of those things out there, don't you? You have seen them. They tried to take your prisoners from you. I saw the claw marks and the bullet holes. They came to finish the job."

Beads of sweat form over his ashen lip as he begins to tremble.

"That's why you protected those people, isn't it? They weren't just for food. You needed to feel strong, needed to feel powerful again. That thing in the woods terrified you and you had to find a way to be in control. They weren't only food. They were bait."

I reach out and smack him across the face hard enough to leave a red handprint. His head rocks to the side and remains facing away from me as tears fall down his white-stubbled cheeks.

"I will not let you hurt those kids." Rising up, I pull my foot back and connect it with his ribs. The cracking bone echoes through me and I feel a surge of excitement and awareness that I have begun to acknowledge as my dark side, the monster within who shares my face.

"I won't touch them again. I swear it." He gurgles as blood bubbles at his lips. "Take them and go."

"Go?" I sink down onto my knees beside him. He tries to pull his shattered leg away from me but I place a hand on his thigh to hold him in place. "Oh, I am not going anywhere. At least not until I avenge that little girl for the pain you caused her."

"It was just an arm!"

"And she is an innocent child!" I lose my temper and slam a punch into his face. One hit is not enough and I hit him repeatedly, savoring the feel of his face molding beneath my fist. My vision goes red with his blood as his lips and jaw turn to pulp beneath my fist and splatter my face.

The scent of him surrounds me, swirling deliciously through my nose and entwining with my senses in a dance of desire. My mouth begins to water as I draw my hand back and watch his blood trail down between my knuckles and down the back of my wrist. It is only now that blood has become a source of temptation and life for me that I realize just how beautiful blood can truly be.

A wet gurgling rises from Flannery and I shift my gaze to look at him. He is beyond the ability to speak now.

"Well, I suppose that will be the end of your confession time. I was getting rather bored of hearing your excuses anyways."

His eyes widen and his body flinches, as if in an attempt to push himself away.

"Now," I clasp my hands together in front of my chest as I lean over him with a smile. "Where should I begin?"

TEN

Lacing my fingers together, I turn my hands over and stretch. My arms and back are sore but I feel good. Nearly every inch of my body is coated in thick smears of blood as I step back to admire my handiwork.

There are very few remaining parts of Flannery that haven't been carved, burned, flayed, or punctured. His head rests to one side and his eyes are closed, passed out for the newest round of cutting. Carving my name onto his chest might seem a bit trivial, but I can guarantee that he felt every dip and sweeping swirl of each letter.

"Wakey, wakey," I pat him on the cheek but he is unresponsive. I sit back and sigh, hearing his heart still beating in his chest. "Playthings are no fun when they are asleep."

I push up to my feet and step over the line of knives that trail down his left leg, pierced deep enough to nail him to the floor. His right has been split from knee to ankle and I have placed the shattered pieces of his tibia beside his face for when he wakes up.

Although I never really paid a whole lot of attention in biology back in high school, I did take a keen liking to dissecting and as such learned all that I needed to know about where to cut. What better prize could there be at the end of the semester than to take home an entire baby pig's spinal cord, but only if you were able to remove it completely intact?

It took steady hands and a tedious amount of care, but it was the first thing in school that I could truly take pride in. People like to say that you never use the knowledge you stuff into your brain after leaving high school, but tonight I would say that Flannery got a crash course in my knowledge. Pairing that with an intimate sense of where the main arterial flows are located, I have managed to extend his torture for far longer than I could have hoped.

Returning from the water pump with a bucket of cool mountain stream water, I turn his head, open what little remains of the hole where his mouth once was, and begin to pour. He comes to in a panic but is no longer able to flail. Flannery has been riddled completely incapacitated apart from his ability to feel.

"I suppose right about now you are wondering how a girl like me can commit such a heinous act against you." I set the bucket aside and roll his head to clear his throat of water. "A couple months ago, I would never have had the stomach for it. I was a good girl, sad and ticked at the world for sure, but I still cared."

I sink down next to him and trail the end of my knife along his fingers. Three of them have been snapped in half. Two others have been sawed off with a butter knife. When I reach his thumb, I place the tip of the knife just up under his nail.

"I am no longer that girl. She is still a part of me, sure, but I am something more now. There's a little extra evil stirring around in there that just makes this whole experience with you so much...fun." With a wide grin I begin to slowly shove the knife up under his nail.

Fresh tears streak down his cheeks, watering down the blood that fell when I scalped him an hour ago.

"You see, there are things in this world that are far worse that the monster that ate your wife. Things that live and feed in the dark are something to be feared, but those of us who can control those things..." With a flick of my wrist, his fingernail pops off and he groans with pain. "Well, we have something a little extra special added in."

I tap the bloody knife against my cheek. "I haven't actually decided how I want to kill you. Like all good things, this sadly must come to an end. I can hear your heartbeat slowing and your breathing is far too labored. If it weren't for that little girl in the other room, I'd probably eat you myself, but that would make quite a mess, and honestly, you're not worth breaking my moral streak."

I hurl the knife across the room and it buries itself three inches into the wood. "If it were up to me I would continue playing right up until that final drop of blood escapes your heart, but there's a kid out in that barn who needs his freedom, and thanks to you, I'm behind schedule."

I place my open palm onto his chest, directly over his heart, feeling the ridges of flesh rise and fall under my hand. "Such a fragile thing, a beating heart. I guess you of all people already know that. You hack too much off, you cut too deep or you allow shock to set in, and it just stops beating."

A wheezing breath makes my hand rise and fall. I watch it, tilting my head to the side.

"It was fun for you, wasn't it, Flannery? I saw the look on your face right after you carved Hope up and I heard you whistling that fucking nursery rhythm as you grilled her hand. You liked killing, didn't you?"

I smile and pat his chest. "It would seem that we have that in common."

I dig my nails into his chest where a few silver hairs are stained red, tearing back the remaining flesh and ripping the muscle. "The last thing I want you to feel is what it is to be torn apart from the inside. I can't imagine a worse way to go."

He thrashes weakly as I use both hands to tear down to the bone. Grabbing ahold of his rib cage, I shove and hear a resounding snap. Flannery's eyes fall shut and his head rolls to the side as I dig my hand into his chest cavity until I feel the mass of muscle that struggles to pump blood to his dying extremities.

"I wish that you could be awake for this moment," I whisper into his ear as I yank his heart free. Blood sprays all around me. I hold his heart up high, rotating it to look at it.

The overwhelming sense of satisfaction that I feel as I squeeze the remaining blood out of his heart is electrifying and I finally understand all too well how Cable can enjoy taking a human life. There is something almost achingly erotic about holding the power of life and death in one's hand.

I place his heart on his stomach and wipe my hands clean on my shirt. I will not stain myself with his filth by tasting him. All I wanted was for him to suffer, to understand the torment he forced on others. My job here is done.

"Your death tonight cannot make up for your sins. Nor will it save you from the hellfire that awaits for you." I rise and grab the lap blanket he wore not long ago and cover him with it then stand back to stare down at him. "If there is a God, I pray that you suffer for all of eternity for what you have done, and if there is not, then my justice will have to suffice."

Reaching down to grasp the keys that I took from his pocket before I cut him up, I turn and walk away. There is no tremor in my hands or feelings of regret as I open the back porch door and step out into the cool night air. The fires still burn deep within me as I take a deep breath to cleanse his scent from my nose.

Even the human side of me knows that this was right. There will be no remorse later to feel. Only a gratitude that there is one less monster in the world.

I head to the water pump and run my hands and arms underneath, scrubbing my fingers clean. I toss my gun aside as I pull my shirt and pants off to wash. I know that after tonight I will never need a gun again. I am the weapon now.

After wringing much of the blood and water out of my clothes, I put them back on, breathing a small sigh of relief at their blissful cool against my feverish skin. I rinse my hair, watching as blood swirls in the stream and washes away, then I tear two strips of cloth from the bottom of my shirt and bind the raw flesh around my wrists.

My stomach is a mass of scratches received before I began on Flannery's fingers. None of the wounds are deep, but they do sting a bit as I stand up and look to the barn. There is no way for me to conceal what blood remains on my clothing, but I don't think the kid will mind all that much. Hope, on the other hand, will need to wait to meet me until I have a chance to change my clothes.

Glancing back toward Flannery's house, I know now that Cable was right about me. Once you let the darkness in, it leeches through you until it takes ahold. I have no idea for how much longer I will still be me. I can only be grateful that Nox is not here to see my handiwork.

Walking back up the hill toward the barn, I flip through the keys until I find one marked BARN. It twists effortlessly in the lock and I wearily shove the door open. The intense high I felt while torturing Flannery has definitely left me aching for some shut eye.

"Avery?" The kid calls from behind the tractor. I can just barely make out the top of his head where he cranes to see. "Is that you?"

"Yeah. It's me."

"You were gone a really long time. I was starting to think..."

I kneel down beside him in the dark and take hold of the lock. "Don't tell me you were starting to worry about me."

"Nah," he shakes his head. I can feel his arms trembling beneath my hand from the cold. "I was just wondering. Everything go okay?"

I laugh and sink onto my backside when the lock clicks open and he rubs his wrists. "If by okay you mean 'is he dead,' then the answer is most definitely yes."

"Right." He gives a curt nod and then pulls on the chain that still binds his feet before glancing at me again. "Do I want to know how you did it?"

"No," I shake my head and lean back against the tractor after tossing him the keys to unlock his feet. "You really don't."

He sits for several minutes beside me in silence. I guess that he needs time to process that he's actually free.

"To be honest I didn't believe you would actually do it. I mean, I hoped that you weren't all talk, and after that wicked monkey escape you pulled off earlier I thought maybe you could, but..." He trails off and I roll my head around to look at him.

"I made you a promise, Kid. I keep my promises."

He smiles just a little and nods. He probably thinks it's hidden in the dark but I see him as clear as day. "Thanks for that. I don't know how I'll ever repay you."

I snort. "How about by telling me your name?"

His smile stretches into a full grin as he laughs. "Nice try."

"It was worth a shot."

He tosses aside his chains and then runs his hands through his tangled hair. I dread to think how much filth will come off him when he finally has a wash.

"How is Hope?"

"She's resting," I assure him. "I think she has been given some sort of herbal tea to help her sleep. I promise that she remained completely unaware of my time spent with Flannery in the living room."

"That's good. She's been through enough." He groans as he pushes up to his feet. "I should help you move the body before she wakes up."

"Don't worry about it. I'll take care of the cleanup. Why don't you go slip in with Hope so that you're there when she wakes up?"

He reaches the barn door and turns back. "Why do I get the feeling you don't want me to go in the living room?"

"It's not pretty," I say.

The kid is old enough to guess that Flannery did not end well, but the extent to which he met that end is better left to the imagination. I am sure that nothing he could concoct would ever be as terrible as the reality.

He lifts his face to look up at the moon for a moment. It is large and full, partially concealed behind a thin wisp of cloud. The sky is a black blanket filled with twinkling stars. I wonder how long it's been since he was able to get an unhindered look at it. "I want to see him."

"I would not advise doing that."

"Please." When he lowers his head I see tears in his eyes. "I need to do this."

Despite my better judgment, I nod in agreement and follow behind him in silence. If the roles were reversed and it was someone telling me that Wiemann is dead I would need the same confirmation. I decide that I will allow him to uncover Flannery's face but everything beneath it needs to remain hidden, for both his safety and mine.

He takes the steps down toward the house slowly and with exaggerated care. I keep my hand out behind him just in case he falls backward, but he makes it up the back stairs and into the house without any injury. Each step across the porch is labored. There is no way he will be strong enough to travel tomorrow.

The back door screeches when I open it and step to the side to allow him to enter. Once inside, he pauses to look around and I realize that he has never been in here before. Flannery must have picked him up in the woods or wandering around his property and taken him straight to the barn.

He runs his hand along the wash basin and then up and over the ice box. "It's really old fashioned but it feels too...normal."

"I thought the same thing when I first arrived." Stepping up next to him, I point to the hall. "He's in the living room through there. I'll go first if you want."

He swallows and looks to me with uncertainty, so I lead him down the dark passage, pausing long enough to point out the chair down the intersecting hallway that blocks Hope's room.

"When you are ready, you will find her in there."

He nods and then follows on my heel as we enter the living room. For a moment he stands utterly still, staring wide eyed at the splashes of crimson that coats the walls, furniture and floor. Then he turns to look at Flannery's covered body.

"Why is the blanket raised on that one side?"

"You don't need to know why."

I watch as he slowly sinks down to his knees beside the body. His hands begin to shake when he reaches out to take hold of the blanket and I grab hold of his hand to steady it.

"You know that you do not have to do this."

"I know." He takes a deep, calming breath as I release his hand and then take hold of the blanket myself, waiting for him to signal me. "I need to."

As I gently fold the cloth back, the kid's mouth drops open with horror at the extensive wounds on Flannery's mangled face. I'm grateful that I closed the man's eyes after he died so at least the kid doesn't have to see the streaks of burst blood vessels there.

"You really messed him up," he whispers and then glances over at me. In the candlelight, the remains of the blood stains on my clothes are clearly on display.

"Does that bother you?" I am surprised to discover that his answer matters to me, though I know that no matter what his response is, I would do the same thing again if I needed to.

He thinks about it for a minute, staring down at the man who forced him to live in constant fear and squalor for months. The muscle along his jaw flinches as he shakes his head. "No. He deserved every bit of what you did to him."

ELEVEN

For an old guy who is missing a few pieces, he sure is a heavy son of a bitch. I haul him onto my shoulder. After I hear the chair outside Hope's room slide across and then the door open and close, I wait until I hear the bed frame creak before I stumble quietly down the hall. I don't mean to eavesdrop, but before I turn into the kitchen, I can't help hearing the kid whisper to Hope that she is safe.

Warmth fills my chest as I carry on and shove open the door. Despite my growing anxiety that with each minute I spend here helping these two, Dr. Wiemann is potentially getting farther away, I can't bring myself to think my decision was wrong. They needed me and I was able to help them.

Maybe I was wrong about being dangerous around people. True, the scent of blood still drives me to distraction, but when saving the kid and Hope became my priority, I was able to focus. Perhaps there is a way that I can make peace with myself.

As I dump Flannery's body on the burn pile and stare down at the gruesome mess that I created, all feelings of goodness vanish.

"I am also more than capable of this," I mutter and turn away.

Over the next half hour I work to gather sticks and larger branches and layer them with dry hay from the barn for kindling. Returning to the house to grab one of the few remaining lit candles, I toss it on the fire and step back as it goes up in flames. With my hand up as a shield against the bright light, I prod the fire, adding more wood to keep it burning hot as Flannery's flesh bubbles. Melted fat drips onto the smoldering wood, sizzling on contact.

The scent of burning skin churns in my stomach, but I refuse to allow myself to feel anything beyond revulsion. The hairs on the back of my arms wither against the heat and I finally back away to sit down on a hay bale several feet away.

I stare up into the night sky, watching as the smoke spirals into the heavens and think about Nox. Has he given up searching for me by now? Did he ever even try? The selfish part of me needs to believe that he attempted a rescue but the logical side hopes that he accepted my decision and remained behind to take care of his people.

Lifting my hand to trace a constellation, I try to figure out just how many nights I have spent out under the open sky since the outbreak, battling the elements and rabid mosquitoes. I have long since lost count. There are far too many to think about, that's for sure.

I miss having a home and a bed to call my own. I miss knowing people, of feeling safe and relatively happy. I miss Nox.

Staring up at the big moon overhead, I wonder what he's doing right now. Is he sleeping in his room or out on patrol? Has the hotel been successfully fortified against attack? Has Cable found another way to breach their defenses to seek revenge or did he leave them alone to follow after me?

I suddenly sit upright.

There were several Flesh Bags that I passed on my way here through the woods. If Cable stretches out his mind to connect with them, he will be able to pinpoint my location within a mile or two from a far greater distance than what it would take for him to get a lock on my mind.

Come first light, I have to move on, but I can't leave the kids here for Cable to track my scent to. The boy is weak and I won't truly know where Hope's condition lies until she wakes.

"How the hell am I supposed to travel with two half-dead kids?"

I stare at the dancing fire for what feels like hours as the scent of Flannery burning comes and goes and I try to figure out a way out of this mess. Taking the kids with me to Atlanta is out of the question, but I can't just dump them in a house along the way and expect Cable to pass them by.

"Shit." I toss a long branch on the fire and feel the ache of exhaustion in my weak throw. "I've saved them from one death to set them up for something far worse."

As I look back toward the house, I feel desperate. I promised the kid that I would keep him safe. I have to find a way of fulfilling that promise, but at what cost? Am I really willing to let the lives of two kids weigh against the potential thousands that might be lost at the hands of Dr. Wiemann if he arrives safely in Atlanta?

"But I don't even know if he's alive," I rage to the night, yanking at my hair as I double over. There are too many uncertainties, too many variables.

The only certainty I have is that these kids will remain in danger, with or without me.

I shove forward onto the ground and rest my head back against the hay bale. Slowly, my eyes begin to fall closed as I allow the crackling and popping of the fire soothe me to sleep.

Sometime later, when a fine dew has formed along my arms, I wake feeling stiff and sore but far less weary. I stretch the length of my body and then stand to dust myself off. The fire has burned down and the glow has diminished, but the sun has yet to rise. The house sits behind me, dark and silent. I pause to consider the events of the previous day. Just when I think that I have seen the full extent of the evil this world has to offer, I always seem to stumble across something new. Perhaps some man really did create this worldwide epidemic or maybe it was nothing more than God's way of trying to purge the earth of all of the greed, filth, and war.

If that is true, he sure did a piss poor job of it. The only ones that seem to be left have proven to be vile, repulsive and untrustworthy, but there are a few among us who remain pure. Good, hardworking men like Nox still choose to believe that we can take what life has been left to us and make it a better place. I only hope that he, and the kids in the house behind me, can find it.

Staring out across Flannery's darkened land, I know that I have to push on to Atlanta no matter the cost. I have to finish what I started, but I can't take the kids with me. This isn't their fight and they won't survive the trip across the mountains. They need to rest and time to recover. I need to find a way of hiding them until it is safe for them to come out.

When that time comes, I need to know that I have provided everything they will require to make the journey back to Nashville. It won't be an easy or a safe road, and if there was any other way, I would go with them myself, just to see them arrive into Nox's care.

With my mind made up and no turning back from the course ahead, I am surprised to realize that I am sad at the idea of saying goodbye. It's stupid, really, but true all the same. I guess the kid's spunk reminds me a bit too much of myself.

Glancing toward the barn, I frown. I know there is something I still need to do before we leave and a couple minutes later, I find myself looping my finger through the metal pull ring on the trap door in the barn floor. A small set of five rickety steps leads down to a packed dirt floor and total darkness.

I cover my nose as the stench of urine and feces rises from below and makes my eyes water. "That is putrid!"

Taking the steps slowly down, I duck my head and hunch over to enter the space. Small shafts of light from the fire outside barely reach through the floorboards. There is no way the people that were kept down here were able to see anything beyond their own hand in the dark. Being thrust out of this dark hole and into the light of day must have been excruciatingly painful.

"I can sure relate to that."

But as I look all around me, I realize in retrospect that the pain of sudden light was far more welcome than what awaited them after.

I push forward onto my hands and knees and crawl around the support beams that burrow deep into the earth to find rotting clothes and thin moldy mattresses lying about. With each one that I count, I feel my revulsion grow further. There are twenty-two in all.

"There were eight more people trapped down here before the kid arrived."

I close my eyes and allow myself to tilt over onto the floor. Drawing my knees up to my chest I try to imagine what life must have been like for Hope and the kid. There is barely any room to sit up straight without whacking my head on a beam, no water to clean with, and an overflowed rusted pail to share among everyone for excrement.

When I lower my head onto my knees, I turn to look back toward the hatch and realize there is a pile of small bones at the bottom. The state of this prison is beyond anything I could have imagined as I crawl over and lift a skeleton between my fingers.

"They were forced to eat rats," I whisper and toss the bones aside with disgust.

Glancing around me, I understand fully the mental and physical torture these poor men, women, and children suffered. Flannery may have been psychotic, feeding on the power of completely controlling these people by holding their lives in his hands, but though his depravity was extreme, I know that it is nothing compared to what Cable and his army are capable of.

Using the wooden frame to hoist myself out of the reeking pit, I slam the door shut and vow that no one will ever see this place again. While rummaging through the tables of farm equipment I stumble across a can of turpentine and begin spraying it all over the barn, soaking the wooden floor and walls. I grab a handful of hay and then close the door behind me. Setting the dried grass alight, I toss it through the rectangular opening.

The explosion is swift and powerful, rocking me back off my feet with a blast of hot air. Flames race up the door and the paint begins to bubble as smoke billows out of the narrow gaps in the wood.

"What the hell was that?"

I turn to see the kid hopping across the yard as he works to shove his leg into his pants. He races up to me and then throws up a hand to shield himself against the heat.

"I fall asleep for a couple of hours and you decide to go all pyro on me?"

Staring at the flames rising high into the sky, I know that I shouldn't have done it. With the mixture of burning skin on the air and now dancing fire, someone will see and know that we are here. Come dawn, the sky will be a wash with a thick trail of smoke that is as close to a fucking arrow pointed at our heads as we can get.

But it needed to be done. Everything that bastard touched needs to be cleansed with fire.

"It's about time someone burned that shit to the ground." I say and then glance over at him when he stops by my shoulder. "I should have let you do it."

He shakes his head. "It took me months to get out of that hellhole. Nothing could make me go back in. Not even to burn it to the fucking ground."

I don't think I can blame him one bit after what I just witnessed. "Are you okay?"

He snorts and crosses his arms over his chest, betraying his lingering fear and insecurity. "What is 'okay' anymore? I don't think I even remember the meaning of the word."

"Yeah," I nod as I think about all of the shit I've been through to reach this point. "Most days I feel the same way."

I can feel him watching me from the corner of his eye. "I should have asked earlier...there is a lot of blood on you. Did he hurt you?"

I look down at my clothes and realize that despite my attempt to wash in the well water, I still look like a walking slaughterhouse. I will have to rummage through Tilly's clothes before Hope wakes in the morning to see if there is anything that fits.

"I'm fine. All of the blood was his."

"Really? He didn't hurt you at all?"

I lift my arms and show him my wrists. "I'm not completely unscathed."

"No. I guess none of us are."

I know that he's thinking about Hope and her lost arm. I have found my own thoughts lingering on her too. To be so young and to lose something so vital is a tragedy. My only hope is that she proves to be a strong kid and that he can be the protector that she needs in the coming days.

He has a strong jawline and broad shoulders, despite his obvious state of malnourishment. I imagine once he's cleaned up a bit, he will be a fine looking young man. Once he reaches the hotel, I have no doubt Flynn and Nox will happily take these two under their wings.

"You should grab a few more hours of sleep while you can. I'll stick around and keep watch."

He darts a wary glance toward the trees surrounding us. "Are you expecting trouble tonight?"

I jerk my head toward the fire in response. "That glow will be seen for miles. I doubt anyone will come looking at this time of night, but we will want to move on before first light, just in case someone gets an early start."

"And go where? I don't exactly have a home or a family to go back to."

"You have Hope and hopefully your father. For now we can stick to the mountains and then find somewhere off the road that's remote enough for you to avoid detection until you two are strong enough to travel."

"And what? You plan on just finding a cute little place to set up a home temporarily, is that it?"

I turn back toward the fire. "I'm not the homemaking type."

His brow furrows and his lips move rapidly before he glares up at me. "You said we will find somewhere off the road that's remote enough for *you* to avoid detection. You're not sticking around, are you?"

"Trust me, Kid, this has nothing to do with you. I've just got somewhere that I have to be."

"Yeah," he snorts and backs away. "I get it. You did your good deed and now you're out. I know how the drill works."

I grab hold of his hand before he can walk away. "I did what I did today because it was the right thing to do. You two needed me and I helped, but I'm no good for you. I'm..." I don't really know what I am anymore and there's no way I can explain it to him in terms that he would understand. "You saw what I did to Flannery—"

"Yeah, I did," he interrupts me. "You know what that tells me? It tells me that you're a badass that can keep Hope safe. How can you save our lives and then just bail like that after you told me that you're different?"

"Kid, don't make this harder than it has to be. I'm doing this for your own good."

"I get it," he spits back at me and tries to pull away but I hold on tight. He glares down at my hand. "Look, all I ask is that you help me with Hope until we find somewhere, and then you can be on your way. No hard feelings, no burdens on your life, and no questions asked. You'll be free of us, just like you want."

I close my eyes at his final remark. "It's not about being free of you. There are things in this world that you don't understand. Things that are worse than that old man burning over there."

"I doubt that," he scoffs from just behind me.

"Trust me, the sooner I leave you two, the better it will be."

"For you, you mean," he mutters and shoves me hand off.

When he turns his back on me, I feel like I've just taken a bullet to my gut. I did the one thing I swore I wouldn't do: I've abandoned him just like all of the others before me, but there's not a damn thing I can do to change it.

TWELVE

A haze settles low over the ground while dawn's first light first peeks through the trees. Birds rouse and begin their sweet morning songs as I crush the final glowing embers beneath my boot and turn away from the smoldering remains of the barn. Flannery's homestead may lie in ruins, but it will never be enough to wipe him from Hope's memory.

Glancing toward the house, I feel a growing sense of foreboding. The smoke has traveled high and far. I would not doubt that it can be seen as far as Nashville. Someone will surely come to investigate.

We have to get moving.

I pause to kneel by the stream to wash away the dredges of sleep that linger and to apply new bandages to my wrists. The skin is red and raw as I peel the dried fabric away and fresh blood begins to seep through. Wiping my hands against my clothes to dry them, I am grateful for the new shirt that the kid brought out to me just before dawn. It is a little big but a simple knot near my waist has taken care of the bagginess.

There is little that I can do to salvage my jeans. No amount of washing will be enough to remove all of the splatters of blood and I'm not about to wear some old ladies pleated skirt while trekking through the woods.

When the back door to the cabin opens again, I look up to see the kid standing there with his hands shoved deep into his pockets.

"Are you about ready to leave?"

He nods. "I have packed up a couple of things for the trip. Flannery had a stash of homemade canned jars from his garden that I nabbed and some medical supplies for Hope that we might need. I didn't touch anything else. I looked all around for your bag but couldn't find anything. He must have stashed it somewhere."

"I didn't have one." I flick the last few drops of water off of my hands and then climb the stairs to join him.

"You didn't have any supplies with you?"

I hold open the door and wait for him to walk through. "Nope. I lost it."

The skin around his eyes pinches before he looks away. "Because of the attack on the hotel?"

"Don't go reading too much into all of that. I didn't run away because I was afraid I'd be next, Kid. I left for reasons that are personal to me. I lost the bag on the road between here and there when I ran into some trouble. When you've got a choice between shooting a Raider or holding your bag, you just drop and take aim."

He steps aside once we enter the kitchen and then reaches out to grab hold of my arm. "Why do I get the feeling that you are running from something?"

"Aren't we all these days?"

I can tell that he doesn't like my answer, but it is the only one he is going to get. I was honest with him the night before when I told him that he would be safer without me. Maybe now he will start to believe that.

"How is Hope?" I ask to change the subject.

"She's weak and really groggy. I'm not sure that we should move her."

Glancing at the sunlight that is streaming in through the kitchen window, I know that we have hung around far longer than we should have. "We have no choice. I will carry her."

"No way!" He shoves the duffle bag that sits open on the table toward me. "She's small but she's not that light, and besides, she's my responsibility. I should be the one to take her."

"Look, Kid, we don't really have time to argue about who cares more about her safety. You are dead on your feet as it is and I'm much stronger than I look. I will manage far better than you will with her. You just need to worry about keeping up."

He draws himself up and presses back his shoulders. "I can take care of myself."

"Right." When I reach over and give him a shove he nearly topples over. I give him a knowing look as I walk past him and enter the hallway to see that the chair has been moved aside and the door to Hope's room now stands wide open. I turn back. "Did you tell her about me?"

"Yeah. She will probably be shy around you, though, so don't take it hard. She's got a heart of gold and dimples that will ruin you, but she's scared."

I poke my head around the door to find the little girl sitting on the edge of her bed.

"Hi, Hope. My name is Avery," I say as I step lightly into the room.

Though her eyes are deep rings of purple circles and her skin is as pale as a winter snow, there appears to be a small light of recognition in her eyes when she looks up at me.

"You're safe now," I whisper. "That man isn't going to hurt you ever again."

She stares unblinking at me before lowering her gaze again.

I swallow hard as I glance at her bowed head. Her silence is unsettling after hearing the kid talk about how full of life she once was. I sink down onto the bed beside her and feel her naturally lean toward me when the soft mattress caves under my weight, but she quickly shifts over.

"You're dress is so pretty." I don't really know what more to say that that to the mute girl. Her dress is far from pretty. In truth, it is more tatters of soiled fabric and dirt than anything and I feel inadequate when I speak to her.

"You and your friend are going to come with me for a while. Do you think that would be okay? We are going to see the mountains. Have you ever been there before?"

She shifts her tiny body away from me. When I lean forward to look at her, I realize that she is holding something tucked in the crook of her injured arm. The bandages show minor bleeding and will need to be changed before the day is out.

"How is your arm? Does it hurt much?"

Once again, I am met by only silence and I feel myself beginning to fidget. How am I supposed to help her when she won't speak to me? Hope is so frail and tiny for this dangerous world. How will she ever survive the evil that waits for her?

"I'm going to go make sure everything is ready and then we can leave. Just stay here and I'll come back for you."

Without any sign of acknowledging my presence or my words, she hugs her arm tighter into her chest and I realize that she is holding a rag doll in an old faded dress.

"Is she yours? She's very lovely. I'm sure she will enjoy the mountains just as much as you will."

Her face clouds over for a second when she casts a glance up at me before she lowers her face once more. She gently brushes the doll's wiry curls.

"Does she have a name, Hope?"

Tears threaten to fall as I stare down at the little girl sitting beside me who is so trapped within her own world to realize that one exists outside of her mind. If I had not heard her screams from the day before, I would have thought her incapable of making any sound at all.

A footstep at the door alerts me to the kid's presence and I quickly wipe at me eyes before I stand. "I'll be back for you in a minute."

Hope doesn't respond. She continues to run her fingers through the doll's hair. I grab hold of the kid and drag him back down the hall.

"I need to know what happened to that little girl." I round on him after I push him back against the sink. "And you're going to tell me where her parents are. No secrets, no hiding and no side stepping the truth this time."

He sinks heavily down into a chair. "I don't know about her father and that's the honest truth. She never talked about him. Sometimes I would hear her call out to him in her sleep but she never said anything to me. She only talked about her mom."

"Did her mother die here? Is that why she's like that?"

His gaze is fixated on the floor for so long I step forward and lift his chin. "Kid? I need to know."

He scrubs his hand over his face and sags his shoulders forward until his elbows are propped up on his knees. "It happened about a month ago, I guess. Flannery came for Hope but her mom pleaded to take her place. What mother wouldn't sacrifice herself for a daughter she loves more than life itself? We hadn't eaten in nearly five days and there were only a few of us left. I tried to stop him, to save Hope's mom, but she knew it was her time. She pushed Hope toward me and made me promise to keep her little girl safe.

"Flannery dragged her up the stairs and locked us in. As he tied her up, Hope wiggled out of my arms and ran to the hatch door, beating on the wood until her fingers bled. I held her to my chest as we listened to him begin to cut."

For the sake of the damaged little girl I just left in that bedroom, I want to weep for her loss.

My stomach churns as I sink down onto a chair. "Did the mother survive long?"

"She lasted a full six days. That was nearly double the time that the others managed. I think she held out the longest with the hopes of somehow finding a way to get back to Hope. It must have been pure torture knowing that her daughter could hear her screams all the way to the end."

His voice loses power as he shakes his head. "Hope stopped speaking after that."

I sink down into a crouch beside him. "It wasn't your fault."

He turns his head away but not before I see tear tracks on his cheeks.

"Hey, Kid," I whisper and place a hand on his leg. "It's going to be okay."

"Is it?" His head whips around and all that I can see in his eyes is anger. "You're already planning on leaving us too. Tell me how that's going to make everything okay!"

"I..." I lean back and pull my hand away. His entire body is shaking as he stares at me. "I know that it doesn't feel like it but I'm just trying to keep you safe."

"Safe?" He snorts and wipes his nose with the back of his arm. "Tell that to someone who actually believes you. Oh, wait! There's no one left alive to tell!"

"Kid, wait!" I yell as he shoves past me and races out of the house. The screen door slams shut behind him.

"Shit." I sink down onto the floor and close my eyes. Leaning my head back against the table leg, I feel the weight of my exhaustion settle over me. I desperately need food, more drinking water in me and another day's worth of clean clothes. Hell, I need a month's worth of sleep to make up for the past few days.

"How did I get myself into this mess?"

Hope is beyond help, a broken shell of a girl with no one in the world to call her own apart from the one kid who is desperately trying to do the right thing by her, but is at a loss as to how to do it. That's too much pressure on his young shoulders. It would be too much for anyone.

A terrified scream sends me scrambling to my feet and bolting for the door. I hit the ground and sprint across the yard before the screen door slams behind me, splashing through the small stream and straight up the hill. From beside the crumbled barn remains I see the kid sprawled out on the ground, rapidly crawling backwards on his hands and feet.

Narrowing my eyes against the glare of the early morning light, I stare at the tree line and see movement just before the hairs on my arm rise.

"Run, Kid!"

He rolls onto his belly and pushes up to his knees as two Flesh Bags exit the woods. Their skin is pale and flaking, their eyes pure white in deeply set sockets. The

Withered on the left is large and lumbering, his gait stunted by a twisted knee. The female on the right stretches out her arms toward the kid as he scrambles back. She looks as if she was shoved into a bag with a feral cat and lost the battle. Ribbons of flesh dangle from her arms, neck, and face.

I watch as the kid rolls onto his side and wretches just before the stench of these two hits me like a battering ram. They were turned a while back. Rot and ruin began to set in long before today making them flesh stink of putrid eggs left in the sun to bake.

"Dammit, Kid, I said run!"

Grabbing him by the collar, I shove him aside just before the female makes a dive for him. A guttural growl rises from her throat as she claws at the empty ground, digging her toes into the soil as she tries to make up the difference in distance between them.

"What the hell are they?"

"Now isn't the best time to discuss this. I need you to get back inside and lock that door!"

I grunt as I am slammed from behind and roll with the woman, tumbling back down the hill several feet. Her teeth gnash as she grapples with my arm, trying to take a chunk out of my bicep.

"Oh crap. It's trying to eat you!" He shakes his head as he backs away when two more Withered emerge from the trees. "This can't be happening!"

"Focus, Kid. They followed the smell of Flannery. They weren't here for us but they have your scent now. You have to run."

His eyes are wide with panic as he watches me fight with the female. He stumbles backward through the fire pit when the slower male turns to follow him.

"Go! I will distract them while you barricade the house." I slam my elbow into the woman's face and feel her nose cave in. Black filthy ooze coats my skin as I roll away and leap to my feet to kick out the legs of the male. He goes down hard.

"Get Hope and search for a way up onto the roof. These things are smart but I have yet to see them climb before. No matter what you see or hear do not come down. Do you understand?"

He continues to stand and stare, frozen in disbelief.

"Kid!"

He blinks and looks at me.

"Move your ass!"

I stomp down on the leg of the female and feel her thigh bone shatter. She doesn't cry out in pain but only tries to twist around to get ahold of me. I duck to miss a swing from the lumbering male once he's back in his feet and grab ahold of the girl's head, smashing it repeatedly against the ground. The back of her head caves in and a thick, sludgy black mess drips from her cracked skull.

The sound of the screen door slamming shut reaches me seconds before I'm forced to roll off the female and back to my feet. The newcomers are much faster than the first two, leaving me no time to take the lumbering male down before I duck between them just as they dive for me and sprint for the trees.

I need to lead them away from the homestead before I take them out. Gunshots will only attract more Flesh Bags to the sound. I need to do this quietly.

Weaving through the trees, I go just slowly enough to be sure that I don't lose them but fast enough to stay a few feet ahead of their grasping fingers. The sun is blinding as it streams down through the forest canopy and I am forced to keep my eyes on the ground. I race across a wider section of the stream, splashing the cold mountain water high enough to soak the bottom of my shirt and dart around rotting trees.

As I reach the hilltop rise, I jump over one of Flannery's old hunting shacks, run along its decaying wooden roof and cry out when a board gives way. A large jagged edge of the broken wood stabs through my upper thigh and wedges me in place.

From behind me, I can hear the growls and hissing of the Withered. The leader of the pack misjudges the jump and skids along the rooftop, rolling past me with a spine-chilling howl. The second jumps with more care and slams into the edge of the roof and scrambles to pull itself up when a third crashes down on its head and I hear the zombie's neck snap. It falls heavily to the ground below and tumbles past the shack, kicking up decaying leaves and twigs until it slams into a tree and comes to a stop.

A snarl from directly behind sends a jolt of adrenaline racing through me as I raise my hands in defense and wait for the attack. It comes with a sudden and brutal force that rocks me backward hard enough to dislodge me from the hole in the roof. I feel my thigh tear open and blood gush down my leg.

My scream echoes through the trees as I roll down the slanted roof and hit the forest floor hard enough to knock the air out of me. I cough, grasping my chest as I roll to my side and lash out with a hard kick that snaps several ribs.

Pain ricochets through me as hands snatch my hair and yank my head back, exposing my neck. The rank breath of the Withered washes over my face as blood trickles down from the open wound on my forehead. I reach back and jab my fingers at the zombie's face in search of its eyes.

When I grasp its nose, I hook my fingers through its nostrils and pull. The muscles in my arms tremble as I tear bone and cartilage free.

"Avery!"

The back of my head slams into the Withered's cheek at the sound of my name. My first thought is that the kid has foolishly followed me, but I look up to see a familiar face pressed to the barrel of an AK-47 assault rifle.

"Shoot!" I jab my elbow into the zombie's stomach to throw it off balance and jump to the side mere seconds before a bullet whizzes past. The weight of the downed zombie falls on my wounded leg and I cry out.

"Hang on," Cyrus calls. "I'm coming for you."

From somewhere over the hill I hear three rapid-fire shots. Birds take flight in the distance as a Cyrus lowers his gun to the ground and shoves the zombie off. He stares down at the blood that pours from my leg.

"Shit, you're bleeding really badly." He presses his hand against the wound and I reach out and grab the same area, grimacing at the pain. "We need to create a tourniquet."

"Hold still," I grunt and rip a sleeve away from his camouflage uniform then hold it out to him. "Use this."

He stares at the shredded fabric for a second in amazement but then quickly begins to tie a knot right enough to make my vision darken and my head swim.

"Good?" He asks.

"Just peachy." I gulp down big breathes as I try to think around the pain. "How did you find me?"

"Same way those dead bastards did. We followed the fire."

I bite down on my lip when I try to shift and feel my skin peel apart further. The gash is wide and rapidly soaking through the cloth. "I meant before that. How did you get this far?"

Cyrus looks away. "Nox had to find you. A couple of us volunteered to join him. I'm pretty sure Fletcher just wanted to watch his back."

I nod in understanding. "You shouldn't have come."

"Nox has always been good to me. I'd do anything for that guy, including risking my neck for his girl." He smiles at me. "Nox knew you would do the stupid thing and try to lead his brother away to keep us safe, so we spent the first couple of days trying to track Cable down. We didn't have much luck, at least not until the Flesh Bags started vanishing."

I frown, trying to figure out what he means but then it hits me. "He was calling his army to him," I whisper.

Cyrus nods. "There isn't much in this world that will make my blood run cold, but I gotta tell you that seeing an interstate filled with zombies made me nearly piss myself."

I knew Cable would come. I just never stopped to consider that Nox and his men would get between us.

"We need to move." I groan as I try to stand. Applying pressure on my leg is excruciating, but with Cyrus's help I manage to stand. "There will be other Flesh Bags in the area. Keep your eyes open."

"Ain't nothing going to sneak up on—"

Cyrus doesn't have a chance to finish his sentence when I yank his arm off from around my waist and slam my hand into his chest. He stumbles back, tripping over a tree root just as a streak of white attacks from beside us.

I absorb the brunt of the woman's impact and roll end over end farther down the hill. Leaves tangle in my hair. Rocks and roots jab at me as I tumble, picking up speed on the steep decline until a towering tree rises up in my path and I slam into it.

My breath wheezes in my lungs as I hold my head, trying to steady the forest as it spins around me. The woman lands on top of me and I claw at the zombie, tearing and scratching at her hair as she grapples with my flailing arms.

When hands wrap around my right leg and yank me out from under the woman I find myself eye to eye with a barrel chested zombie. The entire right side of his body is blackened and charred and he reeks of recent smoke. It snarls down at me before it takes a swipe at me, digging its nails into my upper arm and tearing a long strip of skin away. I howl in pain and beat against it, kicking at its kneecaps with my one good leg.

The woman anchors her hands on my head and yanks it to the side. I barely have time to roll before she comes at me with her teeth barred. The movement sends my stomach hurtling into orbit and I vomit. Acid burns in my throat as I retch. Everything hurts and I am so tired but when I feel the sharp sting of teeth sinking into my shoulder I scream in outrage.

"Son of a bitch!" I beat against the Withered on my shoulder but its grip is tight. Hands and broken nails claw at my back as I try to fight it off, carving chunks of flesh away. I scream as blood trails down my back, soaking through my sweat-drenched shirt. A strange tingling sensation ripples down from my shoulder and I realize too late that I am starting to go numb.

I twist and turn, punching and scratching anything that I can get my good hand on, but they are too strong. Their hideous faces block out the light of the sun as they kneel down above me and I realize that they may be the last thing I ever seen. With all my might I try to focus and call out to them with the same commanding mental voice that I know Cable uses to command his army of Flesh Bags.

Get off of me! The mental command goes out loud and clear, but the Flesh Bags hesitate only for a second, appearing more confused than truly commanded. They open their mouths wide and I close my eyes so that I don't have to watch.

"Avery! Where are you?"

"Nox!" My voice cracks as the woman's teeth sink deeper. I can feel her jaws beginning to work as she prepares to bite clean through.

Please don't chew. It is an insane thought to have when I am facing my end, but I don't think I can bear to hear her eating me.

Two bullets slice through the air on either side of my head and blood and brain matter spray my face. Nox drops the two Withered hovering over me. Tears leak from my eyes as my hand falls limp to the ground and I stare up at the canopy of trees, feeling the numbing cold continue to spread.

From a distance I can hear Nox approaching with a controlled slide down the hill, but it sounds muffled in my ears. I slowly blink and marvel at the way the rays of light illuminate the underside of the leaves, making them a perfect light green.

"It is so beautiful," I whisper as my eyes droop closed and the numbness takes me.

THIRTEEN

Colors swirl like little rainbow tornadoes before my eyes as I blink and try to focus on them. Each one falls at different rates, some are fast while others lazily tumble toward the blanket that covers me as I lie on something soft. I flex my fingers against the soft material and feel the odd prick of feather shafts.

The air is hot and still despite the window to my right being open. I stare through the screenless space and watch a bee flit around the edge of a flower and realize that it is moving in slow motion. I can see each of its wings as it hovers in place.

That is really trippy.

As my gaze shifts away, I stare at the rounded wooden log wall in front of me and realize that I can see every individual grain knit so tightly together that it begins to blur. A loud sound from behind me applies a steady and rhythmic pressure on my eardrums, its beat so constant that it becomes nearly maddening as I look away from the wall to search for the source.

"Hey," a voice whispers beside me. I turn my head to see that Nox is sitting in one of the rocking chairs from the back porch next to the bed. The tips of his dark hair look like bursts of white light where the sunlight filters in through the window over his shoulder. "How are you feeling?"

I rub my forehead, taking special care to run my fingers along the bridge of my nose before I open my eyes again. Everything is the same and yet so very different. I know that I am in Flannery's house by the wooden walls and crocheted blanket, but it feels different. Almost as if the air is charged with a sort of kinetic energy that wasn't there before.

"Did you give me something for the pain?"

Nox frowns and leans in closer. When he does, I realize that the thrumming beat in my ear gets louder. I am hearing his heartbeat but it sounds like a bass drum now.

"Other than some water when you woke up earlier you haven't had anything. Why?"

"You are kinda glowing."

"Come again?"

Pushing against the mattress, I ease myself into a sitting position. "Something is different. The sunlight is way more intense than it was before and I think I'm seeing things. Things that I shouldn't even care to notice, but it's right there front and center and I can't stop seeing it."

"It's going to be okay." He places a soothing hand over mine.

Another sparkle of color falls in front of his eyes and as I zero in on it I realize that what I am really seeing are tiny particles of dust on the air that catch in the light.

"Is it?" I blink rapidly as I struggle to focus. "I just watched a speck of dust land on your nose. Tell me how that is okay!"

Nox takes hold of my hand and waits for me to look at him again. "Do you have any idea how long you've been out?"

I can tell from the slant of the sun that it has to be at least mid-morning. "A couple of hours?"

Nox's lips thin out and he glances back over his shoulder toward the door where I find Fletcher and Cyrus standing guard. They have their guns lowered but their fingers close enough to the trigger for me to know that their casual stance is anything but.

Nox sighs and I feel his hand squeeze mine. "You have been unconscious for two days straight, Avery."

"What?" I bolt upright and instantly feel my stomach twist in protest. The sudden movement makes the room spin and I collapse back onto the pillows in a slouched position. "Oh, that was a terrible idea."

"Easy," Nox places a hand on my shoulder. "Don't make any sudden movements. We are safe for now. There's nothing to worry about."

"Safe? There were Flesh Bags out there before I... Before I..." I frown when I try to remember what happened to me and I place my hand over my shoulder. "I was bitten, wasn't I?"

"Yes." I can tell by the tension that Nox holds in his jaw that something isn't right. "It was touch-and-go for quite some time. I thought by the time I got you back here that you were going to bleed out, but you made it, somehow. My team had cleaned out most of the area of roaming Flesh Bags by the time I found you, but I sent a few deep into the woods to set a new fire to draw the others away.

"Fletcher and I spent several hours trying to stitch you up, but you were in bad shape and we had no way of giving you any blood to replace what you had lost. Once we were done, all we could do was wait."

The pain in his voice is still raw and I see moisture in the corner of his eye.

"I'm still here," I offer him a weak smile.

He nods but I can feel a trembling in his hand. "Other than your strange vision, do you feel anything else different?"

I frown and try to think. "I don't really know. I guess maybe I can hear better too. Why?"

Fletcher shifts in the doorway and I look up to see him wiping his hand across his face before he shakes his head but remains silent.

"Nox, what is going on?"

He leans back and clears his throat. "You seem to have acquired a few new abilities since suffering that second bite."

My eyes pop open. "What new abilities?"

"You're freaking Wolverine, but in a girl-form, of course."

I look over to see Cyrus grinning from ear to ear after his outburst, but his smile falters when Nox turns to glare at his soldier. The brilliant white of Cyrus's teeth against his warm, dark chocolate skin forces me to look away.

"Care to tell me what he means by that? I'm not going to suddenly sprout claws out of my hands, am I?"

Nox's smile is strained but at least it feels mildly genuine. "As beneficial as that would be, I think what Cyrus is referring to is a tad more practical."

Gently taking hold of my hand, Nox begins to unwind the bandaging around my wrists. I tense, waiting for the inevitable pinch of pain as the gauze tugs at my torn flesh, but it never comes. In fact, the pressure Nox applies to my hand should have already made me grit my teeth in pain.

When he draws the cloth away, I inhale sharply. The skin of my arm looks new, perfect and unblemished by the rope burns. There is not a speck of blood or even a hint of pain. I lift my hands and search for other scratch marks and the areas where skin was ripped away during my fight with the Withered but there is not a wound in sight.

"The teeth mark in your shoulder healed over within a couple hours of you being bitten as well," Nox says as he drops the cloth onto the bed. "Your other wounds have somehow vanished, though we didn't notice it until the following morning. The hole in your leg has sealed over completely. Apart from your disorientation upon waking, you appear to be in perfect health."

I look to the two men standing in the doorway and then back at Nox. "I don't understand how this is even possible."

"Neither do we," Fletcher says as he fingers the trigger on his gun once more. "We were hoping you would know what's happening."

I run my hands through my hair and then draw my knees up into my chest as I press back into the pillow. Nox is right. Although I feel tired and a bit sore, there is not a single part of my body that is hurting.

"I can only assume that the second dose of the virus that was transmitted through the bite wound has forced my body to mutate even further, creating a chain reaction that has somehow stimulated a miraculous ability to self-heal."

"That would be my guess as well," Nox agrees but looks rather uncomfortable with the assessment.

"So does this mean if she gets bit a third time she will change again?" Cyrus speaks up and I can hear a hint of intrigue in his voice at the prospect of me becoming a superhero in front of his eyes.

The only problem is that I have no doubt these additional "benefits" will prove to come with some rather strong consequences.

Nox hangs his head. "I honestly don't know. Avery is walking in uncharted areas and none of us can predict what will happen."

When Fletcher snorts and rolls his eyes, Nox and I look over at him at the same time. "You have something on your mind, soldier?"

He scratches at his slightly overgrown beard. "I'm not saying anything the guys out there aren't thinking, sir. We all saw what that front room looked like when we arrived. The men are worried and I, for one, think they have every right to be. I know you care about her, but she's unpredictable. Until we know more I would suggest that we keep her under guard at all times."

A muscle in Nox's jaw flinches but I place a hand on him to stop him from speaking. "He's right."

"Like hell he is. I know you. You had nothing to do with that freak show in the living room!"

I reach out and grasp Nox's hand but look to Cyrus and Fletcher. "Can you guys give us a minute?"

Cyrus bows out first, hefting his weapon onto his shoulder before stomping back down the hall in a heavy limp, but Fletcher lingers. He casts a suspicious gaze in my direction before assuming an at-the-ready stance. "I would like my protest for this idea to be noted, sir."

I wish that I could say that I am offended by his protest. A normal person would be, but I am no longer normal. I know the risks far better than anyone else. Fletcher is right not to trust me, especially now.

"I will be fine, Fletcher. You're dismissed."

"Of course, sir." With that he turns and closes the door behind him but not being sending me an "I'll kill you if you hurt him" glare. Nox waits until he hears Cyrus call out to him before he turns to me and laces his fingers through mine.

"I'm sorry about all of that. The men are just being overprotective."

"They have every right to be—"

"I was so worried about you," he cuts me off before I can say anything more. "I don't know what happened here, Avery, but I don't care. I'm not going to lose you again."

"I know, but you shouldn't have come." I lower my eyes, unable to look at him without seeing the pain that I caused him. "I just don't want you to think that I left because of you. It was the only way I knew how to keep you safe."

"And what about me keeping you safe? Isn't that supposed to be my job?"

"Is it?" I can feel each groove of his fingerprint as he traces his thumb across the back of my hand. It is distracting and wonderful at the same time. "I don't think we ever really decided anything about us."

"You left before we could." He leans in closer and smiles. The scent of him is deliciously overpowering and I wish that I could just close my eyes, breathe him in, and never leave this moment.

"My reasons for leaving have not changed, Nox Being near me puts your life and everyone with you in grave danger. I can't let you die because of me."

"I won't."

"Yes, you will. Before Cyrus and I got separated, he told me that Cable was on his way with a horde of Flesh Bags. We can't fight that. You have to leave while you still can."

"I'm not going anywhere without you."

"You have to. It's the only way."

When I look away his grip on my fingers tighten. "What aren't you telling me?"

The answer to that could fit so many different things. I haven't told him that I think I have fallen in love with him and that it terrifies me to admit that I need him in my life. Or that I can't sleep at night because of the nightmares of Cable tearing him limb from limb just to make me suffer. I can't tell him that seeing him again makes me question everything I believe in but at the same moment seems to confirm it.

"Avery," he whispers and draws my hand up to press it against his cheek. "Talk to me."

"It's complicated, Nox. I can't...I don't..." I sigh and slump heavily against the pillows before slowly pulling my fingers out of his grip. "I want to be with you, far more than I should, but I'm afraid."

"Of me?"

"No!" I shake my head and tug at the covers until they are tucked under my armpits. "Don't you get it? I'm afraid of me. I'm not...I'm different, Nox. Even more than you realize."

Rising from his seat, he shifts over onto the edge of the bed and sinks down beside me. He gently brushes back a stray curl that tickles the edge of my nose and tucks it behind my ear.

"There is nothing that you can say that will make me want to be with you less."

"Want to bet?"

"Yes." He plants his hands on either side of my legs and leans in close enough that I can taste the sweet hint of grass on his breath. He must have been chewing on a hay earlier.

I look long and hard into his eyes. There is no condemnation or fear. Only a yearning for the truth, but can he handle it? I guess there's only one way to find out.

"The day I left, I shot a boy in the head without blinking and carved a message into his chest so that Cable would follow me. Later, I shoved a Raider's nose up into his brain because he annoyed me and then tortured Ryker for information before leaving him to be eaten by a Flesh Bag after promising him a quick death. And all of that blood your men saw in the living room..." I point toward the door. "That was me, Nox. I spent hours carving that bastard up because he hurt that boy and girl. That is who I am now."

Though his color wanes with each sin that I confess the resolve I see in his face to believe in me never wavers. "All of us do terrible things in the face of life and death situations."

"I might agree with that if there wasn't more that I haven't told you. Ever since I woke up in that lab beneath the hotel I have been experiencing strong urges."

"What sorts of urges?"

I clench my fists against the blanket. "Hunger."

"Well, that's perfectly normal. Your metabolism must be working at an accelerated rate, especially with your new ability to heal. I'm sure that it's perfectly normal..." he trails off when I shoot him a hard look and his lips form a large O. "You weren't talking about regular food, were you?"

I wish that I could drop my head into my hands and curl in on myself, to hide from the truth, but instead I stare back at him without blinking. He deserves the entire bloody truth. "I have become a monster."

"No, you haven't." When he tries to lay a hand on my arm I pull back.

"I knew shooting that boy was the merciful thing to do, but I did it for me. And those other men? I liked killing them. There was this...this feeling of ecstasy that sent me riding on a high that I've never felt before and I finally understood that Cable was right about me all along. I tried to run from it, to save you from seeing what I have become, but I can't run for what's inside of me.

"If I was like that before, what will I be like after this new bite? When I am around human blood or become enraged it's like something takes over my body and I'm helpless to stop it. No, that's not true. I just don't want to anymore."

"I don't believe that." He leans in toward me but makes no move to touch me again. "You saved those two kids when you could have just walked away. And what you did to that man wasn't just fun for you, Avery. It was justice. I know you did it for them, not for yourself and that means there is a part of you that is still in there somewhere."

"Maybe."

"While you've been unconscious, I've spent some time getting to know Liam. He's a good kid and he sure seems to trust you. I don't blame him after what you did for him and Hope."

Despite the tightness in my chest, I smile. "So the little turd finally came clean with his name, did he? He must have decided that he likes you to spill. I couldn't pull that information out of him for anything."

"Trust me it had nothing to do with my winning personality. I just happen to know his dad."

"Really? So he is alive?"

"And kicking. Steven has been hell bent on going on every patrol mission he could get since he arrived so that he could search for Liam. What are the chances that I'd find him in this place?"

The momentary happiness that I feel for Liam locating his only remaining family is quickly soured when I realize what Nox is attempting to do. "I'm happy for him, I really am, but it changes nothing."

"Doesn't it? It proves that you did something good, Avery." Nox thinks for a moment before trying a new angle. "Did those men deserve to die? The Raider and...

and Ryker?" His voice catches when he mentions his former soldier's name but he keeps his gaze steady on me.

"The Raider wanted to kill me and Ryker had information that I needed. He wasn't exactly the sharing sort."

"Then their deaths were justified." He tentatively places a hand on my knee. When I don't pull away this time he leaves it there. "You know that I have done my fair share of killing too, and I can tell you that some of their faces haunt my dreams at night, but do you know what gets me through? Knowing that I did what I had to for the sake of the people I care about. You did the same thing.

"That boy you left for Cable saved the people at the hotel. The Raider was killed in order to save your life, and Ryker...am I right in assuming that he knows where Wiemann is?"

I nod slowly. "I was tracking him when they got pinned down by the Raiders and a group of Flesh Bags. I tried to get to them but I got overrun and had to hide. But the time I caught back up, Jax found a way to escape and they got away."

Nox rubs at the back of his neck as he rises to his feet and begins to pace beside the bed. Once he reaches the closed door, he turns back to begin walking again. I that know my killing a fellow soldier can't sit well with him, but Nox shared no love for the man or those he was traveling with. Cap's betrayal and that horrific cleansing they unleashed on the people trapped in that laboratory was inhumane.

"You did what you had to. No one would fault you for that."

"You should." I look away.

"No. I get it, Avery. I may not know exactly what you are feeling or what you are going through, but I can see how you are suffering. I know you well enough to know that you would do whatever it takes to save someone else from this fate. Let me help you."

He falls still as he searches my face. "You're not going to do this on your own. There's no way I will allow that."

"It's not your decision to make," I whisper.

"Like hell it's not. I care about you, Avery. We are in this together, for better or worse, and you need to start accepting that."

The simplicity with which he makes such a profound statement is a complete mystery to me. How can he so easily profess his feelings and desires to protect me after I've just revealed the worst possible things about myself?

"The people back at your base need you, Nox. You are their leader."

He leans in and crushes his lips against mine before I have a chance to react. It intensifies as he holds my head in place, tasting my lips as I mold against him. Finally, breathless and with his heart racing in his chest, he pulls back to whisper in my ear, "And you're my girl. I'd go to the ends of this world to be with you with. No one and nothing is going to keep me from doing that if you will have me. Please say that you will, Avery."

I close my eyes, savoring each melodic tone that resonates in his voice. Never before has it sounded so beautiful to my ears. This newfound gift has enabled me to appreciate the simplest things in life and for that I am grateful, but as I place my hand over his beating heart, I know that I would sacrifice anything to make sure that it keeps on beating, even if that means sacrificing my own heart.

"No."

Nox pulls back to look at me. "No?"

I slowly open my eyes. Just the sight of him makes my toes curl with desire and the longing to be held, to be told that everything will be okay and with it the capacity to actually believe it is severe. Why can't life ever be simple? Why couldn't the evil of the world have been wiped out with the virus and only the good remain?

"I don't want you to come with me."

Nox's jaw clenches tight and I can hear each deep inhalation of breath through his flexed nostrils. "I know what you're doing."

Tugging the covers back, I roll away from him, pausing on the edge of the bed until I'm sure that the vertigo I felt earlier will not return and then rise. My bloody pants have been removed and my shirt has been changed. I stand before him in only a baggy t-shirt and panties, feeling utterly exposed and vulnerable.

I know that if he were to take me in his arms now and lay me on that bed to make love to me, I wouldn't protest. Hell, I'd beg him for it, but Nox won't do that. If there is one thing he has proven to me since the day that I met him, it is that he goes out of his way to give me exactly what I need, even when he doesn't approve.

Just like he will have to do this time.

"Go and be with your people, Nox. They need you more than I do."

"That's not true. You need me too." He rounds the bed and comes toward me.

"Stop." He halts less than three feet from me. I can see that every muscle in his body is flexed, ready to reach for me and pull me into his arms, but I can't allow that. My resolve will weaken far too easily. I have to remain strong...for him.

"Please don't make this harder than it already is," I beg. "I can't stop Wiemann if I'm worried about your safety. Those Flesh Bags that came for us know that I'm here. It's only a matter of time before Cable arrives and you will be his main target. He knows now that I care for you. I will not let you die for me. I can't. Not again."

All of the fight goes out of Nox. His body slumps and he shoves his hands deep into his pockets. "This is what you truly want?"

"It's what I need."

"What about what I need?" His voice is raw with emotion that I can't allow myself to feel. I can see his torment as he struggles to find a way through the impossible position that I have placed him in. I have made him weak and that will only get him killed. I have to stop this before it's too late.

Pressing back my shoulders, I speak the words that I know will finally get through to him and prove just what I am capable of:

"Cable is coming for me and Wiemann has too much of a head start. By the time I arrive at the Atlanta Safe Zone, it will already be too late. Those people are already dead."

"You don't know that."

"But I do, Nox," I say without showing any hint of remorse, "because I am leading Cable's army straight to them."

Nox rears back from me. "You wanted him to follow you there, didn't you? That was your plan all along."

"It is the only way," I reply without emotion.

"The only way to do what?"

I stare up at him, knowing that I am about to land the death blow. "To make sure that no one makes it out of there alive."

FOURTEEN

When a knock sounds on the door several minutes later, I know that it isn't Nox. I drove him away just as I had planned. He will need time to process what I had to say.

"Go away."

When there is a second knock I reach over and grab the oil lantern and toss it at the door. "Can't you fucking hear? I said that I want to be left alone."

The doorknob turns and a head pops through just as I scramble to cover myself. "Can I come in?"

"Liam," I sigh and feel a small amount of guilt wiggle through me. "Yeah, might as well. I'm surprised those brutes out there will let you see me without an armed escort."

He laughs and slips inside, quietly closing the door behind him. "I should have known your boyfriend would spill the beans about my name."

"He's not my boyfriend."

"Really?" He stands awkwardly by the door, fiddling with his hands in front of him and appearing to be unsure of what to do with them. Finally, he just plants them on his hips. "Are you sure he knows that you two aren't a thing, because he seems pretty protective of you."

Having this conversation with Liam isn't exactly something I care to do at the moment. Especially not while my emotions are so unveiled after stabbing Nox straight through the chest. Besides, for all intents and purposes, Liam is still a stranger, not to mention way too young to be discussing relationship issues like this.

"Yeah, well, he's a good guy. He would do the same for anyone."

"Maybe." Liam nods absently. "He has been really great with Hope. Even got her to smile a couple of times last night when she woke up screaming from a nightmare. I haven't seen her do that in a really long time. I think she's getting a bit attached to him."

I smile for his benefit. "Nox will do a great job protecting her. It's kind of what he excels at so you have nothing to worry about there. And hey, I heard your dad is officially alive and well. That's wonderful news."

"Yeah." He shuffles his feet from side to side. "Nox says he's been looking for me all this time."

"I told you he would be. That's what good parents do for their kids." Or, at least I think that's what they would do. Hell, my mom barely even knew if I was around or not until she got sick and then needed me. "I bet he will be thrilled to see you."

"Maybe." He traces his fingers over the chest of drawers but doesn't come up with a single speck of dust. "I'm not going back with them to the hotel, though."

"What?" I sit up and throw my legs over the edge of the bed, careful to make sure that I keep the throw blanket in place to remain decent in front of the kid. "Why on earth wouldn't you go see your dad?"

"Because I'm coming with you."

"Oh, no. No way. Did Nox put you up to this?" I wish that I could stand up and storm through the house to confront Nox myself for being so underhanded, but until I find some pants to wear I'm stuck. Nox is probably banking on that very fact and it burns me.

"He didn't have to say anything, honest. I could see the look on his face when he came out of here. Looked like you were pretty rough on him, not that it's any of my business," he throws up his hands in defense before I can say anything. "I just figured that you must have pulled rank on him and told him stay behind while you go and risk your life to save the world. It seems to be your MO, from what I can tell."

I wince at his astute assumption. "I didn't exactly tell him..."

Liam smiles. "But you did find a rather painful way to convince him to stay here, didn't you?"

"Look, I appreciate the concern and all. It's a bit unexpected since you've been on my ass the whole time, but I'm grateful for the thought. This is just something I gotta do on my own and if he can't handle the truth, that's on him. I'm doing what I have to do and I won't apologize for it."

"But I don't see why? Wouldn't it be easier to succeed if you had people watching your back and to help you plan?"

"You wouldn't understand."

"Try me."

His demand stumps me. Obviously it would be a huge help to have more people on my side. Hell, if I had even a handful of Nox's soldiers, I would stand a much better chance of tracking Wiemann down once I reach the Atlanta Safe Zone, but in doing so, I know that I will be marking each of them for death once Cable arrives.

"Fine. Do you remember that I told you that you'd be safer without me?"

"Yeah."

"Well, so will he. I set some plans into motion that cannot be changed. The shit is going to royally hit the fan soon enough and all of you need to be out of the way before it does."

Liam scratches the back of his head and then turns to lean back against the dresser. "So that's it? You're just going to push everyone out of your life that actually cares about you just because you're worried they might get hurt?"

"Will get hurt, Liam. You are not listening to me. It is a given. I won't let their deaths be on my hands just because you and Nox are too stubborn to accept it."

He places his hands on the dresser and hoists himself up, making himself comfortable. Apparently he plans to be here a while.

"What makes you think it will be on your hands? If we decide to go to back you up and do the right thing, then we do it for ourselves. What gives you the right to call this your own vendetta and ignore the fact that each of us have something invested in making sure that doctor doesn't make any more of those freaks?"

I lower my gaze. "Nox told you about all of that, didn't he?"

"Yep. He sure did. At least someone isn't afraid of telling me the truth, especially since one of those things tried to eat me, in case you forgot."

"Of course I didn't forget." I rub the spot on my bite wound should still be. "And I'm not afraid. I'm just—"

"Afraid."

I smirk at his gumption. He really is a lot like me.

"Well, at least I know you've still got a mouth on you, kid. But that will only get you so far. What we are facing isn't anything like you've seen before. That little taste you saw the other day was nothing. What's coming is much bigger than all of us and far deadlier."

"You talking about the army of the dead that are following you because your ex-boyfriend-turned-zombie leader wants you back?"

If I'd been drinking something at that very moment, I would have spit every bit of it out all over myself at his matter of fact tone.

"Dammit, Nox!" I shout it loud enough so that he can hear it through the closed door and across the house. "He had no right to tell you that much."

"He has every right to tell me what I'm up against. It doesn't matter if I go back to that hotel or go with you; I'll still have to deal with those zombies at some point, right?"

"Yeah, but that's totally different. One or two is hardly the same as a whole freakin' army..." I eye him. He seems to be taking the news of walking dead people with a new taste for human flesh a bit too well. "And you just happened to start believing that those things are zombies, just like that?"

"Well, I sort of figured it out on my own when that thing tried to make a snack of me. Plus I saw the bite mark on your shoulder when they carried you in. Besides, I heard Nox talking about your ex to the others when they thought I was across the house. I may have a tiny bit of an eavesdropping problem. That happens when you are raised with three older brothers who never let you in on their secrets."

"Three brothers? You never mentioned them before."

For the first time he scrunches up his nose and looks away. That says it all. They must have been some of the original Withered. I wonder if he's now thinking that maybe they've become like the Flesh Bags.

When I first found out that those things had turned into full-fledged zombies, I did not take the news nearly so well. I hate to admit it, but I was far less easily swayed with a heck of a lot more incentive to believe, considering that when Nox found me, I had a whole pack of Flesh Bags hot on my tail, but yet again Liam proves to be one tough kid.

"So Nox told you all about Wiemann's experiments, I'm assuming?"

"Sure did. He also mentioned that you're still all hung up about all that crap you went through. I get it, you know? It must be hard to be different but it's also kinda cool too, don't you think?"

I stare back at Liam as if he's just sprouted a third head and has pulled out a banana to smoke. Did he seriously just ask me if I think that the changes I've gone through are cool?

"Or not," he inserts quickly and jumps down from the dresser. "Either way, I'm coming with. I've had a couple of days to rest up so I'm pretty much good to go. I can be scrappy when I need to be and, believe it or not, I can be good company when I want to be. Besides, you could use the company to chill you out. If you ask me, you're way too serious."

"I didn't ask you and you're not coming."

Liam smiles. "I'll let you get dressed. We've got a long hike ahead of us by the sounds of it. I've never been to Atlanta. Should be fun."

He opens the door and steps out into the hall.

"You're not coming!" I shout but he just keeps right on walking. I glare at the empty doorway and huff. "That kid is going to be the death of me."

"And what about me?"

I blink, startled to see Nox come around the corner with a stack of clothes in his hand. They smell strongly of him and I know the instant I put them on I will be transported back to a time when I was enveloped in his arms, safe and sound despite the chaos around us. Now it seems that the chaos is mostly confined within myself and everything around me is white noise in comparison. At least, it was until I let a portion of that spill out onto Nox and then watched as it worked its magic to hurt him.

"This was all your idea, wasn't it?"

"No. He came up with it all on his own, actually. He's a good kid, Avery. Give him a chance to prove himself."

"He doesn't need to prove anything to me, Nox. He needs to live. Why is that such a hard concept for you to grasp?"

He smiles ruefully and places the spare clothes on the side. "I guess I can be a bit thick-headed sometimes. I'm sure you know all about that yourself, don't you?"

I bite down on my lower lip. I want to apologize for the slap in the face I gave him, but if I do it will only soften the blow and I can't let that happen. Not until I know he's safely on his way back to Nashville on a wide curve around Cable's army.

I push up to my feet and wobble slightly. Nox instinctively reaches out to steady me, but just as quickly releases his grip on my arm. "He could be good for you."

"Why are you so willing to put his life at risk?"

"Because it's his life to live. Neither of us can make that decision for him."

"And Hope? Are you going to ship her off with me too?"

Nox rolls his eyes. "Of course not."

"Well, at least you've still got some common sense rattling around in your brain."
I grit my teeth and grab the clothes from off the dresser beside him. "Aren't you are
least going to turn around while I get dressed?"

His eyebrow arches instinctively but his face quickly settles back into a somber
expression that I hate. He turns his back on me and I feel the chill that has settled
between us expand.

I never wanted this. I never wanted to hurt him and now I seem to have done it
twice.

Feeling guilt stab at me with unrelenting accuracy, I wiggle out of my clothes and
quickly slip into the new ones. The pants are baggy around the waist but feel worn
and comfortable. The shirt fits better but I still have to roll the sleeves and knot the
hem.

"You can turn around now." When he does I can see a spark in his eyes that
wasn't there a minute before. "What?"

"You do know there is a mirror pointing right at you, right?"

"Oh, for heaven's sake." I punch him on the arm just enough to leave a bruise.
"You are such a man!"

His soft chuckle follows me as I shove past him and move out into the hall. I walk
with far more care than I would like to admit, using the wall to make sure that I don't
teeter to one side. Although the vertigo doesn't return, I still feel off. Almost like my
equilibrium is on a full tilt counterbalance and I'm struggling to keep up.

Once I reach the kitchen, I find Cyrus seated on the table with Fletcher wrapping
a new bandage around his foot.

"Hey," Cyrus calls when I enter the room and several soldiers look up. Their
gazes are a mixture of distrust, anger and interest. I know that Nox has probably
told them to stand down and that I'm not a threat, but the urge to have a weapon
close to hand is a bit too much for a couple of the men as I see their hands disappear
below the table surface.

"How's the foot?" I ask, acting like I didn't notice anything out of the ordinary.

"Healing," Cyrus shrugs. "Better than having a chunk bitten out of my ass, that's
for sure. Thanks for that. If you hadn't reacted so quickly I'd have been a goner."

"Yeah, well, I'm happy to take the bullet for you." I clap him on the shoulder and
then move toward the sink. A small jug of water sits beside a stack of glasses and I
pour myself a cup, swallowing the entire thing in a single gulp.

Silence falls over the room behind me and I turn to see that Nox is leaning against
the hallway door frame. I can't help but wonder if he's taken up that position to
ensure that I don't run from the coming topic that I can see he's about to broach.
Damn him. He knows me too well.

"We need to talk," he says to no one in particular.

A couple of the soldiers shift in their seats but none reply.

"You all know why we are here and why we have stayed. You have each been
briefed on the status of Doctor Wiemann and his intended destination. Now I know

for many of you, hunting Cap and the others is a tough pill to swallow. They were our comrades and that's not easy to forget," he pauses to look each of his soldiers in the eye. "But the fact remains that they are traitors. Many of our loved ones were cleansed needlessly. They need to be brought to justice for this act."

I stare hard at Nox. "What the hell are you doing?"

"Quiet, Avery. Let the man speak," Cyrus tugs on my hand. I frown down at him but fall into a sullen silence.

"You need to know that your involvement in continuing with this new mission is strictly on a volunteer basis. None of you are expected to go with us to Atlanta and no one will think any less of you if you turn back and return to base. In fact, I hope a few of you will. We've got a sick little girl in need of care and she will be far better off back home where we can help her recover, both mentally and physically."

I look at each of the men in the room, numbering fourteen in total including Fletcher, Cyrus, and Nox. Some of them look vaguely familiar to me. Others are complete strangers.

"I'm not asking for you to decide at this very moment. We need to strip this place down and take what supplies we can. Our intel says that Cable's forces are still a good few hours out so we need to stay ahead of them. You have one hour and then we move out. Any questions or comments?"

"Yeah, this bullshit!" I growl and pull out of Cyrus' grasp. "What part of 'you're not welcome to join me' didn't you hear earlier, Nox?"

The men around me shift uneasily but I don't care.

Nox grits his teeth and slowly turns to look at me. "I do not answer to one man's heart anymore, Avery. This is a group decision. It is out of my hands."

"Like hell it is. I trusted you to do the right thing!"

"I am."

"What's all this yelling about?" a voice calls from the living room. "I say we let bygones be bygones and get this show on the road!"

I turn to see a familiar face emerge from the hallway and shake my head. "I should have known you'd be here too. It's good to see you, Flynn."

Holding out his arms, Flynn crushes me in a bear hug, lifts me off the ground. The unnatural strength in his arms surprises me and I feel a bit light headed when he spins me around. I give him bewildered look but he raises a finger to his lips and catch Nox's warning gaze.

Setting me back down on my feet, he steps back until he's at arm's length to look me over. "Wow. You look rough. You're way too skinny."

"Gee. Thanks for that," I shove my wild mane of curls back out of my face. "I didn't realize I needed to make myself pretty for company."

He turns to glare at Nox. "You told me she was okay. Does this look okay to you?"

"She will be," he replies curtly. "Trust me. She's the most stubborn person I know."

Flynn frowns at that comment but then turns back to me. "Well, once you are a picture of health again and all of this shit is behind us, I've got a real bone to pick with you about leaving me behind back at the hotel."

"I figured you might." I glance over his shoulder and see Liam hanging out in the hall. "Let me guess, was his sudden change of heart about coming along for the death ride your doing?"

Flynn glances behind him and shrugs. "I guess I just know what it feels like to want to fight for what's right. He didn't really need much persuasion."

I lean forward and whisper in his ear. "You have a lot of explaining to do, mister, but we can settle this later. There's no way I'm letting you come with me."

Flynn chuckles and throws his arm around my shoulder. "It's cute that you still think you have a say in that."

"Are we about done with the happy reunion now?" Nox growls.

I look up and realize that all eyes, both familiar and not, are on us. My cheeks flame with heat and I grimace.

"Good. We meet back here in one hour. Get to work, men." Nox turns without looking at me and walks past Liam to disappear into the living room. I start to make a move to follow but Fletcher holds out his hand to stop me.

"What he said was true. This decision isn't on him," he says and I stop to look down at him. "Once he became the leader, he swore an oath to do what was right for our people. The men may not like you very much but they agree with what you're doing. If there's anyone who can get them out of that Safe Zone alive, it's you. They are willing to follow if you two will lead."

I struggle to stuff down my annoyance. "I am not leading shit."

"Either way, this plan is already in motion and there's nothing you can do to stop it now. Nox may have wanted to let you do your thing but he has been outvoted."

"Outvoted? He's in charge!"

Fletcher shakes his head. "It is only right for him to allow these men to make up their own minds. Many of them lost people during the attack. Some of them had loved ones down in that hospital wing with you that were slaughtered during the cleansing. You're not the only one with a score to settle with Wiemann."

"You think this is about revenge for me?"

"No," Cyrus speaks up for Fletcher, "but for them it is. You can't deny them their right to avenge those that they love. If we take that away from them we tell them that there's nothing worth fighting for anymore."

"That's bullshit," I growl. "They are fighting for the living. For kids like Hope, Liam, and Flynn who still have a life to live."

"And how much longer will the living still be living if Wiemann gets his way?" Fletcher says. "Wiemann may be too arrogant to realize that he can't control the creatures that he's creating, but there are others out there who can. Your old boyfriend taught us that lesson."

He gives me an appraising look before continuing. "We know that you're one of them, Avery. You have the ability to control them too. If things go to shit like we know they are bound to do, we believe that you hold the potential to turn the tide and help us to win. This may be our only chance to stop the Armageddon that's about to be unleashed and we want to take it."

I shake my head rapidly. "I can't do what Cable did. I tried before that zombie bit my shoulder but I failed. If it hadn't been for Nox showing up when he did..."

"Aw, girl, you just failed because you didn't have the proper motivation or the extra mojo that's running through your pretty little veins now," Cyrus says with a wink. "I've got faith that when the time comes you'll know exactly what to do."

"And if I don't?"

Fletcher and Cyrus exchange a glance. "Then I guess we'll all die fighting for what we believe in."

FIFTEEN

Within an hour, Flannery's house is completely stripped down and prepped for destruction. Nox's men work with impressive efficiency as they punch holes in the roof that will allow oxygen to feed the fires once they are lit. Liam stands off to the side with his arm around Hope. Tears stream down the little girl's face as she watches the men work.

"Do you think that she will ever be okay after this?" Flynn asks from beside me when he follows my gaze.

"I need to believe that she will be."

"You saved her, Avery. She won't forget that."

I smile and tug him under my arm. "When did you get to be so wise?"

"You're just now noticing?" He scoffs and laughs when I ruffle his hair. I can feel the bulk of him beneath me and know that soon enough we will have to have that chat about the changes I see in him. Nox may have stopped it from happening in front of his men, but I know something has shifted in Flynn and they don't want anyone to know about it.

"I guess I've been gone a while."

"Not that long," he bumps my shoulder with a smile.

Gunfire sounds in the distance and everyone stops. Flynn flinches as the sound repeats multiple times, echoing off the hills. "Raiders?"

"Could be. There's at least one group not too far from here that I bet wouldn't be too thrilled about seeing Cable headed their way." I look up to see Nox motioning for his men to move. "We need to get ready to head out."

Flynn brushes off the dirt that clings to his flannel shirt. His time spent rummaging through Flannery's attic has left him a bit worse for wear. As stupid as it sounds, it's kinda nice to know that there was some dirt somewhere to be found in that psycho's house after all.

Piles of supplies have been boxed up and are in the process of being loaded into the back of two trucks, but the soldier's efforts kick into high gear as the battle continues somewhere in the distance. One truck will haul the stuff while the other will haul those returning to the base. I just hope they don't run into trouble along the way. The route Nox settled on should give them a wide berth, but who knows what else could be out there waiting for them.

"Even though I don't want you guys coming with me, splitting up now doesn't feel right either," I whisper.

"Is that your gut talking, or your stubborn-as-a-mule mind?"

I reach out and ruffle his hair. "Both, wiseass. But that doesn't mean I'm not right. Splitting up like this, those gunshots in the area…I just feel like something is going to go wrong."

Flynn's broad shoulders rise and fall with a shrug. "We're prepared for anything."

"Are you?" I turn to look at him. Just like Liam, he's been forced to grow up far too fast. Though each of them have suffered in different ways I know that they can relate to the anger and helplessness that they have felt at the hands of a sadistic man. "Can you honestly tell me that you're not going to go into that Safe Zone half-cocked and hell bent on revenge against Wiemann for what he did to you?"

"If I did, would you blame me?"

"Hell no, but that will only get you killed, Flynn. You have to be smart about this. We all do. Breaking into that base if it comes to it will not be a walk in the park. They will be well supplied, fortified and already on alert for our arrival if Wiemann reaches them first."

"Well, then I guess we need to make sure that he doesn't reach them in time, huh?"

His cocky grin reminds me so much of Nox when he's being overconfident.

"You're hopeless," I laugh.

"And yet so utterly charming at the same time." He wiggles his eyebrows and I can't help but ease up on him. Someday, some girl is going to get her heart stolen by that kid, and she will be very lucky to have him.

"Why don't you go see if Nox needs any help? I'm going to hang back and say goodbye to Hope."

Flynn tosses a wave in the air and turns on his heel. He puts a little skip in his step that has me laughing in spite of my growing concern as I head over toward the truck parked in front. I weave around soldiers hefting the last of the large boxes and larger items into the truck bed. I am amazed that Flannery's home could provide so many necessary supplies, but I am grateful that at least some good will come from this place. Perhaps it will help give a bit of aid relief to those left behind in Nashville.

A small pickup truck rumbles in the front yard with its tailgate down, and five soldiers begin piling inside at Nox's call to begin rounding up. Amongst the heavily armed men and supplies, I spy the little girl being lifted up into the truck. She looks so tiny as she takes a seat between their legs, but a small smile stretches across her face as I approach.

"I guess it's about time for me to say goodbye. These nice men are going to watch over you until you get back to their base."

She looks at me but says nothing as I shield my eyes from the late day sun. It slants over the trees and strikes me exactly at the wrong angle and I'm forced to turn my body away.

"I think you will really like the hotel. There are trees to climb in and fish in the ponds to watch, unless the cook has nabbed them already." I wink at her before continuing. "There are also some nice beds to jump on, hot meals to fill your belly and other kids to play with. I bet you will like that, won't you?"

I wish that she would say something, anything, so that I know she's okay with this decision to leave. Her smile remains in place as she leans back against one of the soldier's legs. When the middle-aged man behind her reaches down and gently pats her on the shoulder, she surprises me by not flinching at his touch.

"I'll take good care of her," he promises and smiles down at her with a father's love. "My old lady and I have always wanted a little girl but the good Lord just didn't see fit to give us one...until now."

Hope beams up at him and I feel the worry in my chest ease just a little bit. This man, Fredricks, as his name badge says, seems like a decent sort and Hope appears to already be comfortable with him. I imagine this is the first she has truly felt safe in a long time.

"Keep that arm of yours nice and clean," I lean forward and take a hold of Hope's hand. "I'll see you soon. Maybe then we can have that little chat, hmm?"

As expected I get nothing more than a shy smile and a little head nod, but it's good enough for me. I step back away from the truck as a soldier slams the tailgate into place and hoists himself up onto the back tire and over the side, then slams his palm against the side to alert the driver.

I sense a presence over my shoulder as the engine roars and turn to see Liam standing beside me. His eyes look sad but he has a smile plastered on his face as he waves goodbye.

"Are you sure you're doing the right thing leaving her with complete strangers?" I ask, trying one last time to convince Liam to join them before the truck begins to pull away.

"Fredricks seems like a nice guy. After Nox had to leave on patrol that first night after the attack, Fredricks offered to take over with Hope. He told her all sorts of silly stories about growing up on a pig farm until she fell back to sleep. That was the first night in a long time that she didn't need to curl up with me. I think she senses that these people don't want to hurt her and that helps. Besides, she's tougher than she looks and she will have my dad to watch out for her after she arrives. I've given her a note to give to him and promised her that she would be safe."

"Is that enough?"

"It will have to be."

He lifts his hand to wave again. Hope clings tightly to her doll and offers us a tiny wave in response before the truck disappears into a cloud of dirt as the tires dig deep into the ground and rumbles away.

It would have been nice to have a working vehicle for our own trek through the mountains, but cutting across the steep terrain will require going it on foot if we want to split the distance. The likelihood of us stumbling across another working vehicle is slim to none but I know Nox will be on the lookout all the same.

We turn our backs on the trucks and look to the soldiers that have remained behind. Nox, Fletcher, and Cyrus have been joined by Kira, a presence that I was none too fond of when I discovered she was among those whom I'd yet to see while out on patrol securing the perimeter. She isn't exactly my biggest fan and that feeling is definitely mutual.

Three others have remained behind to join my mission: Phillip, Bo, and Gentry. Flynn informed me during our search of the house that each of these men are loyal to a fault and quick on the draw. I guess if anyone had to stay behind, we got a few of the good ones.

"I really wish you weren't coming," I mutter under my breath as we make our way past the back of the house and head up the hill toward the barn where Nox has brought everyone together.

"And I wish you'd get your head out of your ass long enough to say 'thank you for the help.'"

I look over at him and laugh. "You know, you and Flynn are so much alike it is almost scary."

"Yeah," he smiles and nods his head in greeting to Flynn when we arrive. "He seems cool. Reminds me of my brothers."

"Just don't let his fool-headed thinking get you killed. He may have his own vendetta to see finished but it's not yours. You hear me?"

When Liam grins I punch him lightly on the shoulder and then move over to speak with Nox as Liam collects his small bag of supplies. Each of us have acquired a blanket, small throw pillow and a mismatched change of clothes. Food will be scarce and with only one water bottle each we will have to fill up anytime we run across a stream or rainfall. With as many storms as we've had come through since I left Nashville, water is the least of my concerns.

When I arrive, I notice a visible tensing in Nox and know that we still need to clear the air.

"Can we have a moment, fellas?" I say when I stop next to him and gently place a hand on his arm. Cyrus jerks his head toward Fletcher and the two of them silently move off to allow us some privacy.

"I don't want to fight about this—" Nox starts, but I hold up my hand and he falls silent.

"I came to thank you."

His eyebrows shoot nearly into his hairline. "Come again?"

I laugh. "I know it's hard to believe considering I've a bit of a hard head, but now that I don't have a say in the matter, I thought you should know that I'm glad you're here."

"Huh." He rubs the sexy-as-hell stubble on his chin and I smile. "Well, I have to say you never stop amazing me."

"Is that a good thing?" I ask, slowly stepping toward him.

"Oh, it definitely could be." He reaches out for me and draws me close. "You're sure you are okay with this now?"

"Hell no," I respond without hesitation as I place a hand over his heart. "But you were right. These guys have just as much of a right to fight as I do."

"They do, but you weren't completely wrong." He sighs and his shoulders slump forward as he rests his chin on top of my head. For the first time, I can feel the burden of leadership falling heavily on his shoulders. "I feel like every time I turn around, I am faced with an impossible decision. I couldn't bear the thought of letting you go to Atlanta alone, especially with Cable following you, but to do so left others in danger that were depending on me. No matter what decision I made, I was leaving someone I love in harm's way."

A warmth swells in my chest as I press myself against him. "Did you just throw out the 'L' word, Nox?"

"Maybe," he presses his lips to the crown of my head. "Does that scare you?"

"Maybe."

He pulls back so that he can look down at me. "I'm glad you told me the truth earlier. I'll admit that I probably could have handled that a bit better, but I understand why you did what you did. I still believe in you and I'm not going anywhere, so whatever you need to do to figure things out with these changes you are going through, we can do it together."

I smile and lean up onto my tiptoes to place a kiss on his stubbled cheek. "Just promise me you won't get yourself killed before I can give you a proper thank you for being such a stubborn ass."

A wide, sexy grin stretches across his face and he pulls my hips into him so that there isn't an inch of space between us. "Well, hot damn! How can I refuse something like that?"

I laugh and reach out to run my hands through his hair. The texture is so soft against my fingertips. "I do need you to promise me something else, though. If I do ever become dangerous, either to you or to anyone else, I want you to—"

"No." His jawline sets beneath my hand. "It won't come to that."

I swallow back my sharp retort, understanding that his denial is as much for his own peace of mind as it is for mine. "But if it did—"

He places a finger over my lips. "I won't let it. I promise you that, no matter what happens, we will find a way to make this right. I'm not going anywhere, no matter what. You can sniff me all you want but I'm not for eating."

I laugh, feeling the pleasant sensation ripple deep into my belly. It feels good to laugh.

"How do you always know how to throw me off guard when I'm trying to have a serious conversation?"

He leans forward and places a kiss on the end of my nose. "Because I'm a survivor and you, my sweet, beautiful, hard-headed Dumbass, are my biggest challenge yet."

"Is that supposed to be a compliment?"

He tilts his head to the side to pretend to think it over. I hit him in the shoulder and he stumbles back, laughing. "Okay, okay! It was a compliment."

I nod and place a kiss quick on his lips but feel the happiness diminish almost as quickly when I let him go. I wish that I could be as positive and hopeful about our future as he is.

"Are you about ready to go?" He lowers his hand and takes ahold of mine, squeezing it once before letting go.

"I'll follow you this time."

Nox's face brightens and I know that he senses a double meaning to my words. Standing beside him now I know that I would follow him anywhere, and do anything to keep him safe, but it's time to let him guide me for a while. To let him know that I trust him above all else.

As Nox calls to his men to circle up for the final time, I know that he's all too aware of the fact that I don't actually need his protection. Sure, he is skilled with a gun, but when it comes to a physical battle, I can top him in an instant. But being in a partnership, even an unspecified relationship without official boundaries or designated borders, is about letting yourself be weak sometimes so the other person can be strong.

Nox needs to lead and so I will follow him...for now.

SIXTEEN

Flynn and Liam walk beside me two days later as the sun begins to drop below the trees and the mosquitoes hang in a thick black cloud in front of our faces. The sounds of the birds welcoming the night before they bed down to rest should be a peaceful one, but I am on edge. I have been since we broke camp this morning.

Something feels off about the woods but I can't quite explain why. Maybe it's because we haven't heard any more gunfire since we entered. The silence that followed the nearly two hour long battle felt ominous. Almost like the calm before a very big and nasty storm.

As I walked that first evening and lay staring up at the stars as the others slept, I couldn't help but wonder how many of Cable's zombies the Raiders managed to take out before they were overrun. They never stood a chance against such a force, just like we won't if we don't stay ahead of them.

The second day of walking, I noticed Liam's pace had slowed. Despite his attempts to hide his growing exhaustion I could see the journey was wearing on him. I should have found a way to force him to return to the base with Hope.

Walking from sunup to sundown has been tiring on all of us, but I know that it is easiest on Flynn and I. I watch him as he moves, his confidence in his body far more pronounced that it ever was before, but I have yet to have a chance to get him alone long enough to ask him about it. Part of me thinks that Nox is orchestrating that. Another part feels like Flynn is hiding from me.

As I walk, I keep my ears tuned to the movements in the forest. Apart from the odd random Withered that we find wandering in the woods, we have yet to come across any that are not easily dealt with. Kira has proven to be an excellent marksman, though I'd rather suck on a bag of lemons before I tell her that.

"Care to tell me what's on your mind?" Flynn asks as he makes his way over to me. The group is fanned out with Nox, Fletcher and Bo at the front and Gentry and Cyrus coming up at the rear. All of us are on guard but none are quite as jumpy as I am.

"Come on. It's never a good thing when you're this quiet," Flynn says as he maneuvers around a downed tree. Its trunk is nearly as wide as his shoulders and four times his height. He kicks at the center of it with the toe of his boot and the hollow wood crumbles into a pile of rotting flesh and termites.

"How would you know that? We haven't exactly known each other all that long, remember?"

Flynn shakes the swarm of bugs off his boots and speeds up to match my pace as I move on without him, hoping to avoid this subject. I would rather keep my fears to myself until I have a better understanding of exactly what it is that I am sensing.

"Because back in that lab under the hotel, when things got bad and I knew we were in real trouble, you still talked. Even when we were walking down that creepy ass hallway with the dude dragging his guts behind him and Flesh Bags all around us you were Chatty Kathy, but for the past couple of hours you haven't said a word. That means one of two things: either you're pissed off about something, or you're worried. I don't really see how either of those bode well for us."

"Or maybe there's a third option and I'm just tired." I tug at the bit of fabric that I've tied over my face to try to help shield the sun. Stabbing pain hides behind my eyes as I try to keep my gaze focused only on the ground, watching each step that I take instead of constantly searching the trees.

Flynn snorts and brushes his hands over the bark of a towering tree as he passes by. I wince at the grating sound and then the crack as a chunk falls off and plummets to the ground. Closing my eyes, I focus on my breathing, loud and steady in my ears. This newfound sensitivity is still hard to get used to, but with each day I feel like I may be starting to control it a little better. I just have to concentrate really hard and that in and of itself can be exhausting.

"Or maybe there's a fourth option and you're still plotting a way to get rid of all of us," Flynn winks.

"You would think that, wouldn't you?" I open my eyes once more to look a few feet over to see Liam smirking like he's in on the joke as well. "That's actually what I should be doing, but I'm not. You guys won. I threw up the white flag two days ago. If you want to serve yourself up as a shish kabob then I can't stop you."

"I wonder if zombies prefer ketchup."

I snort and shoot Liam a quizzical look. "What? I used to put that stuff on everything. I had to. My dad was a terrible cook."

"Well if they could find ketchup, I'm pretty sure it would just ruin the flavor," Flynn grins as I stare at him completely dumfounded. Are these two really joking around about being eaten? And after all of that crap Liam suffered at Flannery's homestead.

"Oh, look. We've shocked Avery." Liam laughs. "Relax. I'm fine. Flynn is helping me to see how humor can help with dealing with the bad crap that's happened to me."

"I see." I swat at a fly buzzing next to my ear. "Well, then in answer to your question, no, they don't need ketchup. You would taste fine just the way you are."

Liam stops walking and looks to Flynn. "She's joking right? Why doesn't she look like she's joking?"

Flynn claps his friend on the shoulders. "Dude, she's just pulling your leg."

Oh, how I wish that were true.

I fall silent as I rub the hairs along my arms and continue walking so that they can't see that my smile doesn't reach my eyes. The hairs on the back of my neck stand tall and alert but not in the same way that they do when a Flesh Bag is near.

I hold my breath as I attempt to stretch out my senses for the hundredth time since breakfast and sense something moving in the distance, but I can't pinpoint it. Using my abilities is not an easy thing to do, considering that I don't actually know how to do it in the first place. It's like trying to move something with your mind when you've only accidentally done it once or twice before. It's a total guessing game and I feel like no matter what I do, I am going to lose.

"Seriously," Flynn steps closer, keeping his eyes on Nox's back as Liam resumes his former position off to our left. "What is going on? You're starting to freak me out and that comment back there was a bit too 'blatant honesty' for my liking. If you don't spill the beans then I will be forced to tell Nox and we both know that you don't want to worry him."

Nox and Fletcher continue to keep a steady pace nearly one hundred feet ahead of us, a distance in close enough range to react if an emergency but not so close that I have to worry about Nox overhearing Flynn's statement. I glance back over my shoulder and see that Cyrus has pulled a bit farther away than he should. The ongoing stress on his twisted ankle hasn't been good on him but he has yet to complain about it.

"Tell me again why I like you?"

Flynn shoots me a toothy grin and loops his arm through mine. "It could be my boyish charm, or my raging sarcasm, but I like to think that you have just come to not only appreciate but also rely heavily on my stellar personality."

"Nope." I shake my head. "I'm pretty sure that it's none of those."

Flynn smothers a laugh but then pokes me in the side. "I was serious about telling Nox."

With a heavy sigh, I pull back on his arm. "I know."

Keeping my voice low, I lean in toward him and see Liam change his path to draw in closer. The kid wasn't lying when he said that he has an insatiable need to eavesdrop. "Just keep your eyes open as we walk. Something isn't right out here and it's messing with my head."

"Do you think it's the zombies?" Liam sends a worried glance back over his shoulder but I already know there's nothing behind us. Whatever it is seems to be flanking us.

"No. It's something else." I turn my head to my right and breathe in deep. "There is a scent on the air that I can't quite place and it's getting closer."

"As in, it's tracking us?" I give Flynn a hard look and he goes pale. "Right. I meant hunting us. Of course that's what it's doing. Do you think it's human?"

Flynn lowers his hand to come to rest on the weapon at his hip.

"I can't be sure."

Noticing the quivering in Liam's hand, I get the distinct feeling that he has probably never held a gun before in his life. The way he holds it limply worries me.

Grabbing a hold of it, I use my thumb and flick the safety. "You're going to need this off if you want to be able to shoot."

"Right," Liam swallows hard. "I knew that."

"I'll stick close by him," Flynn vows.

"Good." I glance back to my right again before moving on. "And I'll stick with you two."

"Don't you think I can take care of myself?" Flynn puffs up his chest.

I laugh at the not-so-subtle insult in his tone. "I locked you in a room back at the hotel for a reason, Flynn. Not because you couldn't handle yourself, but because I wanted you safe. I'm not about to let you go out all guns blazing this time either."

"In case you haven't noticed, I'm not the same kid you left behind."

"Oh, I've noticed." I turn to glare at him. "Trust me, that conversation is coming, buddy."

"What about Nox?" Liam jerks his chin toward where Nox has crested a rise ahead of us. "Are you going to try to save him too?"

My back teeth grind together as I force myself to shake my head. "No. He can take care of himself."

"But who is going to take care of you?"

I turn back to look at Liam. "What do you mean?"

"Well," he trudges on ahead with steps that are becoming increasingly labored. Soon enough, he will be walking back with Cyrus. "It just seems like you're so busy worrying about everyone else that you're not stopping to consider that you are still a bit out of it. I mean, come on, you just woke up from a freakin' coma or something two days ago. You're still not totally stable on your feet and you're obviously not completely right in the head right now, no offense. I'm just wondering, who will be watching you back while you're watching everyone else's?"

I hate to admit that the kid has me pegged, and judging by the knowing grin on Flynn's face, he knows that I'm had.

"One of you was plenty to handle before. How'd I get so lucky to be stuck with the chuckle twins on this delightful vacation?" I rub at the puckered skin between my eyebrows where a headache has taken up residence. It began not long after we left this morning. I also can't help but note that it started not long after I began to sense danger approaching in the woods too.

I hate to admit that Liam is right, but I don't feel back to my full health yet. I should be resting instead of traipsing up the side of a mountain, but my life never seems to slow down long enough for me to do the right thing. According to Nox's map and our current speed heading down into the foothills, I estimate that it will take us nearly two more days to reach Atlanta and perhaps another one on top to locate the Safe Zone. That is three days too many.

If Wiemann and Cap's group didn't run into trouble, they could already be at the Safe Zone. That not only puts us at a serious disadvantage, but also numerous more lives in harm's way.

"I was wrong before. I think you should tell Nox about these feelings you've been having," Flynn speaks up sometime later.

I blink and it dawns on me that I have been lost to my thoughts about my hate Wiemann for far longer than I realized. The sun has sunk down lower in the sky and long shadows have begun to form along the ground. I blink several more times as I feel the strain on my eyes begin to lessen and sense clarity of vision starting to return.

"Don't worry," I grin as I remove the wrap from around my face and breathe deep the cool night air. It feels soothing after so much time spent recycling my own hot breath. "I promise that I won't let anything get you in the middle of the night."

"At least you will be able to see it coming," he grumbles and swats a mosquito feasting on his arm. "I won't even know it's there until it's already chewing on my leg."

Liam sends me a questioning glance but Flynn is the one to answer, "She's got night vision, remember?"

"Oh, yeah! That is so wicked!"

The topic instantly launches the two boys into a debate over just how cool it is that I can see at night. Right about the time they begin to question if I will eventually develop an animalistic night shine or adopt the freaky all white eyes of the Withered, I push on ahead so that I do not have to listen.

Less than an hour later, Nox calls for us to set up camp for the night and I'm forced to bite my tongue against my natural instinct to protest. If I were alone, I would push through, travel hard and fast to make up for lost time, but I am not alone. Nox knows his men better than I do. I have to remember that they tire far easier than I do now, even at this painstakingly slow pace.

I watch as his soldiers respond instantly to Nox's command, each with their own pre-planned role to play out. Even Flynn and Liam seem to instinctively know to begin collecting firewood while I stand in the middle of the small clearing feeling like I've been passed over.

"Anything I can do to help?" I walk up to Nox as he kneels down to check the scope on his gun. With each day that we get closer to our destination, I notice he has begun to use this tell as his sign of growing distress.

"Nope. We've got it all under control for tonight."

"Is that so?" I cross my arms over my chest.

Nox looks up and lowers his weapon onto his knee. "Is there something wrong?"

"You tell me. Cyrus and Fletcher have gone off to try to hunt for dinner despite the fact that Cyrus is limping badly. Kira is god knows where, and if I had my way would stay there. The other three are working on setting up a security perimeter around camp and even Flynn and Liam are gathering firewood."

Nox pushes up to his feet and rests his gun against his shoulder. "I'm not sure that I'm seeing the problem."

"The problem is that I'm the only one who hasn't been given a job and you know it."

Nox blows out a breath and then offers me a wry smile. "You feel left out, is that it?"

"Don't patronize me, Nox. You know damn well I can carry more weight than anyone here. I can run faster, hunt better, and hear a cricket a mile away. I'm the one who should be hunting for food, not standing here like a freakin' useless waste of space."

"Hey," Nox places a hand on my arm and slowly tugs me toward him. "I know all of that, Avery, and I swear that I'm not trying to make you feel useless. I'm just trying to let you regain some of your strength. None of us know how that second bite has really affected you yet and I want to be sure that you are ready to be back in the game again before I start placing expectations on you."

I narrow my eyes at him. "Is that really the only reason?"

He laughs and pulls me into his chest. "Why does everything always have to be a conspiracy with you?"

Reluctantly, I allow myself to mold against him. "If you haven't noticed, I haven't had the best track record with luck recently."

"Fair enough," he presses his lips to the top of my head then tilts my chin back so that he can brush his lips against mine. "Then let's make sure that we change that together."

"Why do you have to be so damn charming?"

He shrugs and settles his hands on my hips, drawing me closer. "It runs in the family, I guess."

The instant the words slip past his lips he goes stiff. "Shit. I'm sorry, Avery. I wasn't thinking."

"It's fine." I step back away from him, sad that the moment has been tainted with a reminder of Cable. It feels like every time I have a second alone with him, something spoils it. "He is your brother. It can't be easy on you either."

Nox's face hardens and his grip on his gun tightens visibly. "I don't know what that thing is that attacked us back at that hotel, but it was definitely not my brother. The Cable I knew and loved would never have killed innocent people."

"I know." I whisper and look away. I may not have known Cable nearly as long as Nox did growing up as his half-brother, but I knew enough. Cable used to be a good man. Nox is right. It does run in the family.

Nox quickly closes the gap between us and wraps me in his arms. "I hope you don't think that I was implying that you are like him."

"But I am like him, Nox. You just don't want to believe it."

"No." His fingers grip tighter against my back. "There is still goodness in you. Cable would never have cared enough to save Liam and Hope, but you did. You risked your life for them and that proves to me that you are still you."

I bury my head into his shoulder. "But I'm something more too. I can feel it inside me, Nox. Lying in wait for that perfect moment to strike. It's like a sickness that is slowly eating away at my soul."

"You are stronger than anyone I know and you're surrounded by people who love you. Well, all except Kira," he winks at me. "The point is that you're not going through this alone. You will find a way. I believe that."

I really wish that I did, but for the moment, standing in his arms, I can almost convince myself that anything is possible.

A throat clears from directly behind us and we jump apart to see Flynn and Liam standing a few feet away with knowing grins on their faces.

"I think someone was getting a little sucky face time," Flynn coos.

I drop to the ground in a blink of an eye and grab a pine cone and hurtle it at him. Flynn's eyes pop open when it pings him in the forehead and leaves a red mark.

"Okay, that hurt!" He rubs his forehead.

Nox laughs and grabs his gun off the ground. "Maybe next time you will learn to keep your wisecracks to yourself, kid."

"Oh, come on. It was funny. Right, Liam?"

Liam drops his pile of wood to the ground and raises his hand in defense. "With an aim like that, I have got nothing to say."

I laugh when I hear Flynn mutter, "Traitor," from the corner of his mouth. Nox shakes his head and leans in to kiss my temple before he grabs his gear and hauls it onto his back. Like a true leader, he has chosen to carry the heaviest burden with the bulk of our supplies. I would offer to relieve him of it if I didn't think he would take it as an insult to his position.

"Did you tell him yet?" Flynn asks as he drops his pile on top of Liam's.

"Tell me what?" Nox turns.

I shoot Flynn a death glare and then shrug. "It's nothing."

Flynn rolls his eyes and steps around me. "Avery is apparently incapable of telling the whole truth today and since I'm rather fond of keeping all of my extremities intact while I sleep tonight, I'll tell you for her. She has been sensing some weird mojo for the past few hours out in the woods. Might be a good idea to keep an extra guard on duty tonight just in case."

Nox frowns and I can tell that he is trying his best to hold his frustration with me in check in front of the kids. "What sort of bad mojo are we talking about?"

Shoving Flynn aside with enough force to send him tumbling to the ground, I sigh. "It could be nothing."

"Or it's something and you should have spoken up about a hell of a lot sooner." Nox rests his gun against his hip. "Tell me."

As Liam helps Flynn to his feet, I give Nox a brief rundown of the only intel that I have. It's not much, but it's enough to make the vein that runs down his forehead begin to pulse with anger.

He places two fingers between his lips and whistles. Within a few minutes, each of his men reappear from the darkness.

"Looks like we might have some company tonight, folks. Let's light this fire and circle up tight. I want three-man shifts at all times. Sit back to back and keep your eyes peeled. Everyone else is to bunk down and rest while you can, and tomorrow we will try to push a bit harder to get down out of these mountains."

"What exactly are we looking for?" Kira asks.

Nox looks to me to answer so I step forward. "Whatever it is, it's not going to be friendly. It's big and fast and can remain quiet when it wants to. Keep your nose to the air. If you smell anything out of the ordinary you need to stay alert. It has a strong scent but seems intelligent enough to keep down wind, so it's hard to trace. This thing knows how to track and it has been hunting us all day."

"And you're just now telling us?" Kira spits out.

Nox steps forward and places himself between his fiery soldier and me. "We know now and that's all that matters. I want Cyrus, Bo, and Phillip on the first watch. Kira, Flynn and Fletcher can take the second. Avery, Gentry, and I will take the final round."

He pauses to look each one of us in the eye. "Avery says this thing is unlike anything we've seen before. I think it's safe to say that the mutations may have spread or been tested on other things. From what we know of the Flesh Bags, they are intelligent, fast and strong. Do not underestimate anything that comes at you. Shoot to kill. That's an order."

With his speech completed, each of his soldiers moves quickly to either take up their position getting the fire lit or working to find a vantage point for the first watch of the night.

Nox laces his fingers through mine as we watch the men settle in.

"Are you scared?" He asks me as the firelight swells and casts a warm glow on the clearing.

"I know that I should be, but it's strange." I turn to look at him, pausing to admire his handsome profile. "It's almost as if it senses me. I think it's hanging back to try to get a feel of what I'm doing with you."

"So you can read its mind like the zombies?"

"No." I shake my head. "It's different. More of an awareness, I guess. It knows I'm here, just like I know it's out there. I can feel its curiosity."

"Anything else?"

"Yes." I press my palm to his heart and count ten quick beats before I answer. "It's hungry."

SEVENTEEN

The fire crackles and spits as I lie beside it. Sleep does not come as I stare up at the smoke, which twists and twirls its way up into the sky. The cloud cover is thick tonight, blocking the moon and all of the stars.

All around me I hear life in the forest, but not the sound that I most want to hear. The thing that hunts us has fallen completely silent and I can't shake the feeling that it is waiting and watching. I can't smell it. I can only feel its curiosity battling with its hunger.

I understand all too well how the hunger pangs can drive someone like me to distraction. If the hunger grows too great, it will attack.

Rising up from my bed, I look around. Flynn sleeps with his feet near Liam's head and his gun tucked against his chest. Bo, Phillip, and Cyrus sit back to back in a small oddly shaped circle nearly twenty feet away from the fire so that the glare does not dampen their ability to peer into the darkness.

Restlessness takes me and I push up to my feet.

"Going somewhere?" a voice calls and I close my eyes.

"If I said I had to pee would you believe me?" I turn back to look at Nox where he lies propped up against a tree trunk. His legs are crossed at the ankles and his hands are tucked under his armpits to keep them warm. His eyes are slatted just enough to see me.

"Not for a second."

I rise and move over to him and sink down. "Busted."

"I had a feeling you would try to do something stupid."

I lean my head down against his shoulder. "Yeah, well, I didn't earn the name Dumbass for nothing."

"Ain't that the truth." His body quakes with laughter as he frees one hand to wrap around me. "Couldn't sleep?"

"I was thinking."

"About what?" He shifts so that he has easy access to his gun.

"Do you ever wonder if things can go back to the way they were before?" I ask after a moment. "Not to just a couple of days ago, but to life as we knew it."

"No. I think the world will forever be scarred by this mess we made, but maybe it's not all bad. I don't know about you, but there a lot of things that I'm glad to be rid of."

I press against his chest to be able to sit up and look at him. "Was life really so bad that you would choose this over that?"

"No," he laughs and shakes his head. "It definitely wasn't, but I didn't have you before, did I? That's got to count for something."

"Oh, that was smooth," I grin and lie back down against him. "Do you ever just miss the simple things, though? Like the luxury of pulling through a fast food joint for a bite to eat? Downloading music, going to see a summer block buster hit on release day or a million other things that we took for granted before?"

Nox gently traces circles across my shoulder blades as he thinks it over. "Sometimes I do, I guess. Usually when I'm stuck sleeping against a tree stump instead of being tucked up in my Egyptian cotton sheets and my contour pillow, but life feels simpler now, in a way. I don't have to hurry to work in rush hour traffic, worry about finding a damn cell phone charger that I was always seeming to lose or stress over how I am going to pay my past due credit card bills. None of that stuff matters anymore. Now we have everything we need because we have each other. The other was just superficial nonsense. For the first time in my life I feel like I'm really living. What more could I ask for?"

"How about a world without zombies trying to eat your arm off?"

"You got me there. I could definitely do without them."

"Would you go back to the way things were if you had a choice?"

Nox blows out a long, slow breath. "Honestly, no. I don't think I would."

"Really?" That surprises me.

"I don't mean for that to sound selfish. I'd give anything to have my family back, to undo all of the suffering that people have experienced, but if I did all of that, I wouldn't be the same person that I am now. I wasn't a bad guy by any means, but I was different. I mucked around, jumped from relationship to relationship for the hell of it. I hurt people without considering the consequence because I was young and had the world at my fingertips. Now, I know what's really important. I place value on that people that I love."

I press a kiss to his chest and nuzzle in close. "I'd trade you in against a hot shower, flushing toilet, frozen food, and a cheesy delivery pizza in a heartbeat."

Nox tugs me close and seals me into his arms. "You're all talk."

"Like hell I am! You should learn to never underestimate my love for a cheese pizza," I look up and kiss him. "But maybe if you were really nice I would share a slice with you."

"Just one?"

I hold up a single finger and he opens his mouth to bite the tip of it and all thought of pizza vanishes. He stares at me in the firelight and I see desire flame to life in his eyes.

"Too bad we have some vicious beast hunting us right now because I can think of a few things I'd love to do to you," he whispers in my ear.

I feel heat swell between my legs as I groan at the thought of his hands on my body. "Trust me, the instant we are out of this mess I am dragging you to the nearest plot of grass and having my way with you."

Nox plunges his hands into my hair. "You say such sweet things to me."

A rustling behind us makes us jump apart and I turn to see Flynn sitting up and staring right at us.

"Yeah, uh...sorry to interrupt whatever that was, but I got to pee. Nox would you care to be my 'let's go together so we don't get eaten' buddy?"

Nox laughs and starts to stand up but I push him back. "I'll go."

Both of them exchange a confused glance that nearly has me rolling in fits of laughter. "Get your minds out of the gutter. I'm not going to watch, for goodness sake. We all know I've got the best vision right now so I'm the logical choice as a buddy."

"Apart from the fact that you're a girl and it's kinda weird." Flynn rustles his hair and I realize that sleeping on the ground has shoved his mass of curls slightly off center.

"Afraid I'm going to listen?" I snicker and push up to my feet.

"Afraid? No. I'm certain of it. Supersonic hearing is a new trait, right?"

"Sure is, but don't worry. I'll hum to myself."

"Oh great. That's so much better."

I lean down and kiss Nox once more before I pat Flynn on the back and follow him into the woods. We don't have to travel far before the darkness is all-consuming and Flynn stumbles into a tree.

"I meant to do that," he groans.

"Need me to steer you?"

"Nope. Just turn around and don't peek."

"Gross." I turn my back on him and stare out into the woods. An owl flies overhead, swooping gracefully. I watch as it circles several times before making a sharp descent and then shoots back into the air with a small rodent in its claws.

"What was that?" Flynn calls, hopping as he tries to pull his zipper up but in his panic he gets his shirt caught.

"An owl, scaredy cat. Sheesh. It's a good thing Nox didn't come out here or he'd start to think you were afraid of your own shadow."

"He knows I'm tougher than I look."

"Oh?" I turn as he begins to head back toward me and see him walking blind with his hand waving out in front of him. "And how is that?"

"I told you. I've changed."

"So I've noticed." I shove out my hand and push Flynn to a halt. His eyes go wide with surprise. "It's time that we have that little chat."

"Damn. I knew this wasn't an innocent gesture of goodwill."

He shifts from one foot to the next and in the dark I see him begin to chew on one of his fingernails.

"Why can't I feel you in the same way that I can feel Cable?" I ask and I hear the snap of him biting through his nail.

"So we are going straight for a groin shot? Got it. Well, I guess it's because I'm not exactly like you or him."

I apply a bit of pressure against his chest when he tries to move around me and I hold him in place "You need to tell me everything.

Flynn sighs. "Okay, but promise me that you won't get mad."

"Mad? Why would I be mad? It's not like you obviously did something stupid and utterly life threatening while I was gone," I growl and tighten my grip on him but it barely fazes him.

"In my defense, none of this was actually planned ahead of time," he hedges, wincing as he waits for me to explode, but I keep myself reined in tight until I hear it all, "and I may have accidentally got myself shot."

And there is the clincher that I was waiting for.

"Accidentally shot?" I struggle to keep my tone low enough so that no one back at the camp will the growing heat in our conversation. "How do you accidentally get yourself shot, Flynn?"

He at least has the decency to look ashamed when he glances at me. "Well, I may have tried to sneak over the wall to look for you when I realized you were missing and got myself mistaken for a Flesh Bag. In all fairness, though, I didn't exactly change clothes after that bloodbath so I did look pretty rough. That soldier had every right to be jumpy."

Snagging him by the arm, I yank him with me farther into the woods where we won't be overheard. I know that we don't have much time. Nox will grow suspicious soon enough and come looking for us, but I know the smell of a rat when I cross one and Flynn is going to tell me everything.

Once we are out of earshot I push him back and cross my arms over my chest. The rush of adrenaline pumping through my ears is more than enough to compensate for my earlier weakness and I feel a charge of energy surging through me.

"Where did you get shot?"

Flynn pulls his shirt down just enough for me to see a bullet wound a fraction of an inch above the top of his heart. It was a near-instant kill shot.

"Damn it, Flynn. I have never met anyone with a bigger death wish than you!"

"Present company included?"

I reach out and thump him on the shoulder. "Now is not the time for your humor. You could have died."

"But I didn't."

I want to rant and rage at him, to yell at him until I am blue in the face, but one thought trickles through and I feel myself slowly beginning to calm. "Why aren't you dead?"

"Wow, it almost sounds like you're sad that I'm not."

"I'm not stupid, Flynn" I take a hold of him. "I know that you must have dosed yourself with one of the remaining portions of my blood you still had in your gun to keep you alive. I can smell it on you now that I know what I'm looking for but why didn't it kill you like all of the others? What was different about you?"

"Maybe I'm just special?" He suggests weakly.

"Sorry, kid, but that's the wrong answer." I lean in close and breathe deep at the curve of his neck. I don't know if it is because of my newly heightened awareness after the second blast of the virus or if I was just too preoccupied to notice before, but there is something slightly off about his blood.

"Have you been dosed with anything else? Something Wiemann may have given you before I woke up?"

"Nope. Not that I know of. They ran a heck of a lot of tests while I was stuck in that lab and I'm pretty sure someone down there took a lot of pleasure in jabbing me with all sorts of medieval medical torture devices, but they never injected me with anything."

I tap my foot against the ground, trying to puzzle it out. Something is different and it is infuriating that I don't know what it is. "What about before? You said you were at a Safe Zone down south, didn't you?"

"Yeah, I was at one down in Charleston. Me and a bunch of other kids were bussed in from all over."

"Anything weird go on there?"

Flynn shrugs. "Not really? I mean not apart from the daily visits to the vampires in hazmat suits. I still have the scar tissue to prove it."

He holds out his arms and turns them over so that I can see the inside of his elbows. Running a finger down his skin I can feel small lumps. "They took your blood daily?"

"Yeah. It was their thing. A few vials each day and then they sent us on our way. The doctors said they were testing us for the virus. If you tested positive they would bust in and take you out. My friend Roan had this theory that they were doing all kinds of wild experiments on our blood but we never were able to prove it. Someone sort of blew up the lab."

I blink. "And that didn't seem suspicious to you?"

"Well, of course it did, but there was a containment breach and we were forced to go into lockdown, so it wasn't like we could just stroll over there and take a look for ourselves. Everything kinda went nuts after that. Roan and some of us were too busy taking over the school and barricading it before things got really bad."

I have heard him tell this story before but never with so many details. I hadn't realized all that he had been through before he ended up in Nashville.

"Think, Flynn. There had to be something you heard or saw that might explain why you were able to handle my blood."

He stuffs his hands into his camouflage pants and kicks at the ground. "I don't know. I mean, Roan had this fascination with one of the girls in our group in the beginning. I didn't really put much stock in it, you know, and he did keep a lot of things close to his chest, but maybe she had something to do with it. They treated her differently."

"Why?"

"She was pregnant."

I begin to pace back and forth, trying to think of why that would make a difference. Obviously, she was young if she was at the school, but I've seen people younger than Flynn turn. Hell, I even saw a Withered baby once. That thing still gives me nightmares.

"What was the reason for his fascination? Just that she was treated differently?"

"Um," Flynn scratches the side of his nose as he thinks. "Maybe. I remember him saying something about her baby. I think they wanted it. She seemed pretty scared that they were going to steal it away from her. I think she was hoping that if she dug up enough dirt for Roan about what was going on in the lab that he would offer her some sort of protection or help her escape before the baby was born."

"And did he?" The answer to that question feels vital to my ability to understand his friend's motivation.

"I don't know. Like I said, things went to hell in a hand basket and fast. Those Dead Heads came for us and we hunkered down."

"You mean Flesh Bags?" I turn to look at him. "There were actual Flesh Bags at your Safe Zone?"

"Well, yeah." He frowns. "I told you all of this, right? That's why we had to fight. The base was completely overrun."

I stop pacing and pinch the bridge of my nose. "We're too late."

"What?"

"Don't you see?" I round on him. "It had already spread long before I got bit. If those things attacked you before you arrived in Nashville, then that means the zombies were already on the move before I was even turned. Wiemann couldn't have made them using my blood. They must have had another source."

"Huh. Yeah, I never really thought about that." His face scrunches up and then his eyes go wide and he rushes to my side. "I should have thought of this before. You know my friend, Roan? Well, his dad was the one that seemed to be leading the Dead Heads."

"I'm not following you. He was like Cable and me?"

"No." He shakes his head. "He was definitely one dead dude, but he was different too. Roan was sure that his dad came looking for him. I remember him saying that his dad must have tracked him all the way from Atlanta."

Flynn's jaw goes slack. "Oh shit. He told me that his dad worked at the CDC."

My heart plummets into my stomach and I grasp onto him to keep from falling.

"Avery? Are you okay?"

"I don't feel so good."

I push away from him and throw myself around a tree before I vomit. Flynn pats my back until there is nothing left and I wipe my mouth with the back of my hand.

"We have to find Nox and warn him."

"Warn him about what?" He starts to follow me but stumbles and nearly falls to the ground. I yank on his arm impatiently and loop my arm through his as we begin to run together.

"We are walking straight into a shitstorm and there's another one right on our tail! When it collides, all hell will break lose and we will be stuck smack dab in the middle!"

EIGHTEEN

The bone-chilling howl that tears through the night comes seconds after Flynn and I emerge from the woods. It sends goose bumps racing down my arms as I watch the soldiers leap from their beds with their guns in hand.

"What the hell was that?" Fletcher yells and backs up so close to the fire that I'm sure his backside is nice and toasty.

Cyrus and his watchmen hurry back toward the fire as a group and flank Nox. A circle forms with Flynn and I taking up our place beside Liam, just as we'd promised.

"Eyes open, men. The instant you see something, kill it." Nox turns to look at me. "Is it still curious?"

"No," I call back and search the darkness, frantically trying to locate it. "I'm pretty sure it's decided the other urge is a bit stronger now."

"What urge would that be," Kira asks.

"You really don't want to know."

"Lovely." I hear her cock her gun and I'm grateful that she is standing next to Nox. She may be moody and publicly against me, but I know she is loyal and will do whatever it takes to keep Nox safe. If she lives through the night, I might even have to swallow my pride and thank her.

"Liam, I want you to stay on my ass. Where I go, you go, got it?"

"Loud and clear. Just don't go faster than I can keep up."

Flynn watches the treetops as they sway in the nighttime breeze. "I'll be right behind you if anything goes wrong."

"Pipe down," Nox orders.

There is an odd sound on the air. I turn my head to the left and listen. It almost sounds like leaves falling...

"It's in the trees!" I scream just as a giant shape leaps overhead. The soldiers open fire, wildly spraying the treetops with bullets but the creature is gone.

"Anyone get an eyeball on it?" Nox yells.

"I saw lots of hair," Bo calls.

"And long arms," Gentry adds.

"Avery?"

When I don't respond, he turns all the way around to look at me but I'm still struggling to understand exactly what I saw. Breaking his position from the circle formation, he hurries over to me and takes hold of my arm to shake me. I blink slowly and then refocus.

"What did you see?"

"I..." I frown as I shake my head. "I saw a silver back gorilla."

"Seriously?" Flynn swears beside me. "As if it wasn't bad enough having dead people eating living people, now we've got a freaking highly aggressive giant that's six times stronger than a human on a normal day swinging through the trees. Those things live for like fifty years, so even if it wasn't a mutated freak now we'd have that fun little fact to deal with. Oh, and that gorilla doesn't seem to be the least bit interested in living up to his non nocturnal habits so there goes that theory out of the window."

I turn to look at Flynn.

"What?" He doesn't look away from the trees. "I used to be a National Geographic junkie. Sue me!"

"Is there any other bit of information that might actually be useful to us?" Nox asks as he takes up a new position at my side and the circle closes back in.

"Well they are omnivores, so they typically don't eat meat."

"I've got a really bad feeling he doesn't know that," Cyrus mutters.

"Avery, are you able to connect with it at all? Sense what it's feeling?"

I stretch out my thoughts, trying to get a lock on the gorilla. "I can't pick up anything beyond its anger, which has now mounted to full blown rage after our shooting spree."

"Did we hit it?" Fletcher calls.

"No. I don't think so."

Nox's arms are flexed and tight against mine as he grips his gun. "Keep your eyes open. He's up there somewhere."

From off to my right, I hear the cracking of a branch and instinctively turn. "There!"

Nox fires off a couple of rounds. He is soon joined by a half dozen others.

Another tree limb cracks and plummets. Before it reaches the ground, it is riddled with bullet holes. I spin around when I see the top of a tree shake and yank Nox around to fire, but Cyrus has already targeted that area and opens up.

We hear a terrible howl of pain and then silence.

"Is it dead?" Cyrus asks.

"No," I whisper back as the hairs on the back of my neck stand to attend. "You just pissed it off. Don't shoot unless you actually see him. It's clever. It's taunting us, almost like it knows we are wasting our bullets."

Nox shoots a hard glance at me. "It's wearing us down?"

I nod. "This is no ordinary gorilla. It has no thought that I can decipher like I can with the Flesh Bags, but I sense a great deal of intelligence. I think this ape has been experimented on."

"You mean like a lab rat or something?" Flynn asks. His grip on his gun is so tight his knuckles have gone pure white.

"Something like that. I think he was injected with blood similar to mine. Judging by the direction that he's been traveling all day, it wouldn't surprise me if he is from Atlanta. He's probably escaped from the CDC."

"That's sick," Kira says in a hushed but decidedly disgusted tone. "I hate animal testing."

"I didn't know they did that," Bo speaks up.

"They may not have before the outbreak, but desperate times mean animal rights go out the window. Apes are the closest thing to a human test subject. It would make sense to use them first when trying to create a cure."

I duck low as the treetops sway but no one shoots. The silverback leaps from tree to tree, working to try to draw our fire. I can feel its mounting frustration and confusion when we remain still.

"Anyone have a banana so we can draw this thing out?" Fletcher asks with impatience. I know his type. He can't stand to wait on the precipice of a battle when he is armed and ready to go.

"I don't think that will be a problem for much longer." I duck again as the ape leaps across the clearing. The entire tree quivers and leaves falls free. "It's watching us and trying to figure out our weakness."

"We're human beings fighting against a rabid mutant ape. Isn't that a good enough weakness?" Liam's voice shakes and I move closer to him and farther away from Nox.

"Steady. Steady."

The silverback bursts from the tree behind me and tackles Cyrus to the ground. Before any of us have a chance to react, it crushes its powerful jaws around his face. Cyrus' cries cut out when the beast twists its head.

"Fire!" Nox roars as everyone turns and shoots. Cyrus's body jerks as he is slammed with close range shots, but the ape has already disappeared.

"Cease fire!"

Nox holds up his hand and I crane my neck to listen. There is silence all around, eerie as it is sudden.

"Where did it go, Avery?" Nox yells.

"I'm searching for it." I turn this way and that, feeling one wave after another of rage, but also a growing hunger as the beast tastes Cyrus's blood. "There!"

The group turns and shoots as it swings down from the tree and grasps hold of Bo. With powerful arms that are longer than its legs, it lifts the soldier into the air and slams him down against the ground. I grimace at the sound of his bones shattering.

"Don't let it head for the trees," I hear Fletcher yell. Gunshots echo all around me. The firelight is blinding with intensity as I turn to look at each of the men standing beside me.

I hear Flynn yell as he takes a backhand from the gorilla and spirals through the air, and slams into a tree. Liam shouts out but Gentry holds him back, stepping in front of him as he gets a shot off, piercing the ape's arm.

Flecks of blood float through the air as the beast turns and looks at me, and for that one brief moment I connect with its pain and its fear. Suddenly, it all becomes clear to me.

"Stop shooting!" I scream but I can't be heard over the ruckus so I turn to Nox and pull on his arm. "It doesn't want to hurt us."

"Like hell it doesn't. It just killed Cyrus and Bo!"

"Trust me," I plead with him, reaching for his gun. "Tell your men to stand down."

Nox stares at me for a moment and I see the fear in his eyes. If I am wrong, I could be risking the lives of every single person in the clearing under his command.

"Please. Trust me."

Swallowing hard, Nox nods and lowers his gun. "Stand down!"

"Did he say stand down?" I hear Gentry ask Fletcher.

"Cease fire," Nox roars to be heard. Two more bullets fly and then silence falls over the woods.

The silverback emerges from the forest slowly, walking on its knuckles as it approaches. Blood seeps from multiple wounds.

As I make a move to step toward it, Nox tries to pull me back and the ape barks in anger.

"It's okay," I say in a soothing tone to both Nox and the gorilla.

"I told you she was insane," I hear Kira mutter behind me, but I do not turn to look at her. Instead, I keep direct eye contact with the ape as I step past Nox.

"Avery?"

"I understand now." I toss my gun aside and slowly raise my hands out to the side to show that I am unarmed. The gorilla grunts and its nostrils flare as it sniffs the air. "You look like the men that hurt him. That's why he attacked. That's why he was so angry. He thought you were trying to hurt me. He hasn't been hunting us. He's been trying to save me."

"That's about the stupidest thing I've ever heard."

"Quite, Fletcher," Nox growls. "No sudden movements."

I step again and the silverback rises up onto its feet and beats its chest.

"Nobody move," I warn as I take another step. "Nox, if you try to come for me he will kill you."

"You expect me to just stand here and watch that thing crush you?" His voice sounds as taut as a coil ready to snap.

"I am in no danger. He's trying to communicate with me but he doesn't have the words. All I'm getting are flashes of emotions." I shake my head, trying to sort through the jumble but it's too chaotic. "I think he is scared."

"He should be," Fletcher growls and I hear the click of a gun behind me.

"Damn it, Fletcher I will beat you with that gun myself if you make one move on that animal," Nox growls. "Stand down, soldier."

When I am within five feet of the gorilla, I stretch out my hand toward it, palm up so that it can see that my hand is empty. It lowers back down onto all fours and brushes its giant hand against the ground.

"Peace," I whisper, trying to send the message mentally as well. "I will not hurt you. I am a friend."

"This is ridiculous."

I force myself not to snap at Kira. Instead, I slowly begin to lower my head, bowing to the great animal.

"What is she doing?" I hear Bo ask.

"I think she's trying to show that she is not the dominant," Flynn whispers.

Slowly, and with extreme care, I lower my body toward the ground, exposing my neck to the ape. It shifts back and forth, agitated but curious once more. I bite my lip when it reaches out and shoves its arm into mine and I nearly topple over, but somehow hold my ground.

I don't have to be connected with Nox to know that his anxiety has just shot through the treetops, but I can't back out now or it would be a sign of aggression. As my knees buckle and I sink to the ground, I place my hands against the dirt, palms up and then press my forehead to the forest floor.

The silverback grunts and hoots before me, stomping its massive feet just inches from my eyes, and then it falls still. Slowly I raise up until I am standing before it. It sinks down lower and meets me eye to eye.

"That is the coolest thing I have ever seen," Flynn whispers.

I reach out and tentatively place a hand on its chest, feeling the thunderous beating of its heart. Its flesh is riddled with scars, some old and some very recent. I press my hand against one of the graze marks from a bullet and look into its eyes.

"It is hurting," I whisper, feeling as if for the first time I am staring into a window that reveals its very soul. "I can feel its frustration. It needs me to know something, but his thoughts and emotions are too intense."

I cry out when the ape suddenly flails its arms and raises up, knocking me off my feet. It beats its chest and draws back its head to roar.

"What is it doing?" Nox yells.

Wave after paralyzing wave of fear hits me and I can't move, can't breathe. I struggle to roll over onto my back as a single image finally connects with me and my blood runs cold.

Nox meets my gaze as I stretch out my hand to point behind him. "Run!"

The soldiers look to each other but no one moves. At least not until the sound of pounding footsteps spills over the hilltop and carries down into the valley.

"Flesh Bags!" Nox and his men turn and drop to their knees and open fire. The woods come alive with gunfire as the first line of Cable's army finally arrives.

"Avery, can you stand?" Nox calls over his shoulder. I fight to overcome the ape's mental outpouring of emotions and rise to my knees. "You need to get the kids out of here. Can you do that?"

"What about you?" I make it to my feet and focus with all of my mental power to block the silverback out completely.

"If we get separated, meet me at the Safe Zone. I will find you." I connect with his determined gaze for half a second before he turns and shoves Liam at me. "Now run!"

NINETEEN

Taking Liam by the hand, I yank him back away from Nox's line of defense and race into the darkness of the trees. He stumbles and struggles as I urge him to run faster, but his legs can't keep up with mine. As a roar that shakes the forest erupts behind me, I pause and pull Liam around to my back.

"Hop on. I'll carry you."

"Are you insane? There's no way you can run with me on your back."

"Do you want to stand here and argue this while those zombies catch up to us, or do you want to do as I say and live?"

Liam bites down on his lower lip and I look to Flynn. "Sorry, dude."

He hoists Liam up and sets him down on my back. I tuck his legs under my arms and take off before he has a chance to secure his grip.

Flynn and I run in sync with each other as gunfire drowns out screams of rage and pain from the ape. We take the hills at a near sprint, weaving, ducking and leaping over debris that rises up in our path. Liam holds on to me for dear life, with his face pressed tightly into my neck so that he doesn't have to look.

Terror squeezes my chest as I strain to hear the battle behind. There is no way Nox and his men can survive that onslaught. There were hundreds pouring into the valley with countless more on their heels.

"He will be fine," Flynn says and I look over at him, wondering if he were somehow able to hear my thoughts. "He's smart. He will make it."

I have to believe that, otherwise I would give up right now and turn back. Liam needs Flynn and me, though I am forced to restrain myself to keep from outpacing Flynn.

Hot breath puffs from his lungs as we run through the night and well into the morning. Not knowing if Nox is alive or dead terrifies me, but I remain quiet, focused on running as we zigzag through the remains of the foothills. Towns lie spread out before us over miles and miles of land, dark and still in the new dawn. To our left, I spy the expansive glistening sparkle of a huge body of water and realize that we must have crossed into Georgia sometime during the night.

I remember seeing Lake Sidney Lanier on Nox's map. It was one of our final camping destinations before we made the push into Atlanta.

"I have to stop," Flynn pants and tumbles to the ground. He rolls onto his back and gasps for breath. I let Liam down onto the ground so that he can rest his arms and he too collapses in a heap.

My own heart thuds in my chest from exertion but I feel none of Flynn's exhaustion. Instead of being wearied by the run, I am invigorated as adrenaline courses through my body and I realize that it is the natural reaction to the scent of blood on the air.

I turn and look back toward the hills.

"What is it?" Liam tenses and searches the tree line for any signs of attack, but I know we have out distanced the Flesh Bags for now.

Hanging my head, I recognize the scent but no longer feel the connection that existed only a couple short hours ago. "The gorilla."

"Is it dead?" Flynn sits up as I nod. "Is it weird that this news makes me sad even though it did attack us and nearly made me piss myself?"

"No. It's not weird at all." I sink heavily onto the ground, feeling the weight of this loss in a profound way. Liam and Flynn crawl over and sit on either side, holding me as I cry.

I cry for the damaged ape that gave its life for me so that we could escape. I cry for the unknown fate of the soldiers behind me. I cry for the people that have been lost and the countless more to come.

And I cry for me.

Large, heart breaking tears of remorse and anger finally spill free from my eyes as I allow myself to feel everything that was done to me. My life was taken from me for the sake of science, stripped and mutated for some ungodly reason, and I know that I will never know the answer as to why someone was evil enough to unleash this virus on the world.

If Nox were here, he would tell me that all of this has happened to me because I'm still meant to do great things. I wish that I could believe that, but as I stare out over the town in the distance, I wonder if there is anyone even still left alive to try to rescue.

Too many have died. Too many will never be born. How can we possibly fight against such insurmountable odds?

"This is all my fault," I whisper.

Flynn tightens his grip around my shoulders. "Now, that's the worst possible thing you could be thinking right now."

"But it's the truth. I lead Cable here, Flynn. If Nox died back there..."

"Nope," he pokes me in the stomach. "You are not going to start that crap. Nox is fine. He made you a promise and you know that man well enough to know he would defy God himself to make sure that he keeps it. Isn't that right?"

I wipe at my eyes. "Has anyone ever told you that your undying optimism is really fucking annoying?"

Liam bursts out laughing. Flynn follows right after and slowly a small smile stretches across my face.

"There's my girl," Flynn nudges me. "Now how about we go kick some ass?"

Later, as the day wears on and weariness starts to drag on all of us, I know that if Flynn had not been with me on that final hilltop, I would never have got up. The will to keep going, to keep fighting, just wasn't strong enough, but Flynn doesn't let me give up.

As the miles pass by and the road signs begin to show our approach on Atlanta, I know that we could push through and reach the city before nightfall, but we are running on fumes. Turning off on an abandoned interstate exit ramp, I lead Flynn and Liam to a small gas station and try not to think about the last time I holed up in a gas station with friends. Within only a few hours, everyone was gone and I was all alone.

We clear the building quickly and efficiently before shoving a tall freezer in front of the front door and a tool chest in front of the back. The shelves are predictably empty, but food is the last thing on my mind as I stretch out onto the floor and wrap my arm under my head as a pillow. As I lay there, feeling an exhaustion behind anything I have ever felt before, I am unable to sleep.

"Hey, Avery?"

I roll my head to the side and see Flynn with his eyes wide open. Just beyond him, soft snores rise from Liam's still form.

"Yeah?"

"Do you think anyone will still be alive when we arrive in Atlanta? At the Safe Zone I mean."

"I hope so." But I have my doubts. After hearing Flynn's story about his friend's father turning zombie while being locked up in the CDC and then trailing his kid all the way down to Charleston, my hopes for finding living people have dwindled into almost nothing.

"You know," he shifts onto his side. "I was thinking about our conversation earlier. About when I mentioned the pregnant girl."

"What about it?" I roll onto my side to face him.

"Well, what if those doctors figured it out? What if they somehow discovered that something in that baby could, I don't know, cure us or something?"

"You're not cured, Flynn. You're just different."

"So do you think if I got bit I might still die?"

I sigh and tuck both of my hands behind my head. "I honestly don't know. What I do know is that there may be some answers in Charleston."

Flynn pushes up onto his elbow. "Does that mean you are thinking about heading down that way?"

"Maybe. I guess it depends on it we live through the next day or two."

He slowly traces his finger along the crack in the square linoleum tile. "What about Nox? He will have to be getting back to the hotel, right? I mean, they will need their leader back once we take out Wiemann."

I stare up at the ceiling tiles, counting all of the yellowish water leak marks. This place is the sort of dump I would have avoided in my past life. I sure as heck wouldn't have used the toilet unless it was a dire emergency, and even then, I would have coated the seat with half a roll of toilet paper first.

"You should get some sleep. We still have another forty miles to cover tomorrow."

Flynn pushes up to a seated position. "You don't think he made it out, do you?"

"I don't want to talk about it." I roll away from him.

"Nox never gave up believing that you were still alive. Everyone told him you had to be dead. There was no way Cable would let you leave, but he had faith." He sits in silence for several minutes before he speaks again. "The girl I knew wouldn't have given up, either."

"Yeah, well that girl died when she woke up from the coma that day." I mutter.

"Did she? Because I'm pretty sure that's the only girl I've ever known."

I roll over to look at him.

"Look, I know you've got tons of doubts and some serious issues with the whole blood and eating people thing, but that doesn't give you a valid reason to become some bitter old witch. You still have a life to live, so stop being a pansy and live it."

I stare at him in disbelief. "Why don't you tell me what you really think?"

He ignores my growl. "Nox is coming for you, so you need to get your head out of your ass and decide if you want to be with him because I know he loves you. I can see it in the way he looks at you and I sure as hell saw it when he pushed us all to the breaking point to find you. That isn't puppy love, Avery. That is the real deal."

I roll back over and stare at the shelf in front of me, feeling just as empty as it is. "What if I can't accept that sort of love? What if I've been burned too bad in the past and can't let him in?"

"Then you're an idiot."

I snort and close my eyes. "You and Liam really need to find a filter and use it when you speak."

"I'm serious. The guy adores you. What more could you ask for?"

"How about not having fallen in love with his half-brother, who, by the way, is now hell bent on killing anything and everyone that I love just to get to me?"

Flynn inches his way over to me until he is leaning over my shoulder. "As far as excuses go, it's not terrible, but come on: the past is the past. Nox knows that. The only one hanging onto it is you."

"Um, hello. Psycho ex-boyfriend just attacked us last night!"

"Avery!" He hisses but goes silent when Liam stirs. He waits until Liam settles back down before shaking his finger in front of my face. "You're not a monster and you're not damaged so stop seeing yourself as that, because he doesn't. Maybe you are a little different, and, yeah, we seriously need to work on that whole snacking issue, but you're still the same girl he fell in love with. Let him love you."

"If I say I'll think about it will you shut up and go to sleep?"

He grins and hugs me tight. "You know this isn't over right? I'm just letting you off the hook because I'm about ready to pass out on your shoulder and that will be totally awkward when I wake up drooling on you."

I shove him back. "Drool is definitely a deal breaker for me."

"Noted." He yawns and then stretches out. For the next several hours I don't hear a peep out of him.

When the sun rises the next morning, I wake to find the two boys rummaging through the shop.

"Well, breakfast this morning will be a package of mint flavored gum, an old starburst that I'm pretty sure got stepped on and kicked under the counter about ten years ago, and a can of Spam that went out of date a year ago." Flynn lifts the can to read the date again. "Huh. I didn't even know this stuff could actually go bad."

"You guys split the feast. I'm not hungry."

I ignore Flynn's glare of daggers and make my way to the toilet. When I emerge I find both boys standing by the front door ready to leave.

"We found you a gift," Liam grins.

I eye them up with suspicion, but they motion for me to turn around. I do so only so that we can get this over with and hit the road. The closer I get to Atlanta, the more desperate I am to find the Safe Zone and see just what we are up against.

Three people against a whole army of Withered isn't really my idea of a successful plan, but until we arrive it's all we've got.

Something plops down onto my head and smashes my hair into my eyes. I turn around in surprise.

"It's a trucker's hat," Liam grins when I part my hair to look at him. "And don't worry, I'm pretty sure it's new. I looked for stains and stuff and sniffed it. I think it passes the test."

Tugging the hat off my head, I stare at the red and white design. There is a stinging in my eyes and I know that this thoughtful gift might just make me start crying all over again.

"It's to help with the sun," Liam adds, glancing at Flynn with some hesitation.

"It's perfect," I whisper and pull Liam into a hug, then I open my other arm to Flynn. We stand in a group hug long enough for it to become awkward.

"And that's about the extent of the mushy emotional bonding that I can handle for one day," I say and push back. "You guys ready to go?"

For the next couple of hours, we make our way toward the heart of Atlanta in a mess of traffic jams that force us to backtrack four times before we finally find a decent way through. Miles and miles of abandoned cars stretch out before us as the high rises tower overhead. For the entire jog into Atlanta, we kept our eyes open for the Safe Zone, but as the sun trails across the sky, forcing me to hide in the shade of buildings when it bounces off the glass towers, I start to lose hope of finding it before dark.

"Maybe we should try to get somewhere high so we can look out instead of running all over the place. I'm starting to get the heebie-jeebies about the sun setting." Flynn glances around at the vacant street.

"He's right. We need to hole up somewhere," Liam agrees, pressing a hand to his chest as he struggles to gasp for air.

After my run yesterday with him on my back, he protested a lot more today, claiming that I needed to reserve my strength, but I think his pride may have been a bit wounded. Flynn could have carried him a bit, and offered to do just that on multiple occasions, but that would have slowed us down.

I lift a hand and point down the street. "Pick a building. Any building."

Flynn taps his finger against his lips as he looks from building to building. Some are higher than others, but show more signs of damage, which he theorizes could mean they are unstable. Others are squat and run the chance of being dwarfed by those building father in the distance and would prove to be a waste of valuable time and energy.

"Want to do *eenie meenie miney mo* while you are at it?" I chuckle from behind him.

"There is a method to my madness," Flynn says as he continues to point. Then finally he smiles. "There. That's the one I want."

I look at the tall skinny building that seems no better or worse than any of the others. "Care to share with the class how you came by this decision?"

Flynn grins as he tugs his bag over his shoulder and starts walking backwards down the road. "It's got a coffee shop. Who doesn't love one of those?"

Too tired to try to even attempt to understand that sort of madness, I just follow behind the two boys, focusing only on keeping one foot in the front of the other. We clamber over overturned tables and chairs and do a quick sweep of the coffee shop. We scope out a handful of creamers, some sugar packets and a bottle of water to share and head for the stairs. After we climb ten flights up and the stairs continue to spiral high above us, I start to realize that I should have bucked this building choice.

By the time we hit the twentieth floor, I am carrying Liam on my back and cursing up a storm. Flynn doesn't seem to be doing much better than Liam, but at least has the decency to keep his mouth shut in the face of my foul mood since this was his choice after all.

"I think this is high enough," Flynn gasps and slams through the stairwell door. He falls onto the carpet and rolls onto his back, shifting his arms and legs out in motions that make me think of a child creating angles in the snow.

I practically drop Liam when I walk past Flynn and move into an office. I crack my hip on the edge of the desk but I keep going until I have my nose pressed against the glass, and look out across the city. The fading sunlight glistens off rooftops and miles upon miles of vehicles. In every direction I look I see concrete but no lights, tents, or any sign of a military base.

"Flynn, get over here and tell me what I should be looking for."

He groans and slowly rolls to his feet and then crawls into the office. He sinks down and presses his forehead against the glass.

"Look for tall fences. They need a way of sectioning it off. The Safe Zone in Charleston was pretty much just carved out of a neighborhood."

"So there's no good way of knowing where it is apart from the fences?"

This feels hopeless.

"Well, this is only the first side of the building. We can check the others," but even I can hear doubt starting to creep in. Atlanta is such a large city. We could spend days searching and never locate it.

"Maybe we should just sleep tonight and try again in the morning," I suggest. I can't bear to admit to them my desperation to find the Safe Zone has less and less to do with finding Wiemann now that discovering Nox's fate has everything to do with me reaching those fences.

"Um, guys," Liam calls from the hallway. "I think I found something."

Flynn and I hurry as fast as we can manage out into the hall and see Liam pointing down the hall. There, at the very end, is a meeting room filled with a long table and twelve swivel chairs that right about now look like a little slice of heaven.

But beyond that, far off into the distance, I see a tower. "What is that?"

"It's a light." All of us rush toward the end of the hall. I beat the two boys as I leap over the table and use the glass on the other side as a brake. "That is a light, right? I'm not dreaming this."

"If you are we are all sharing the same dream." Flynn tugs on my arm as Liam bounces on his toes.

There, clear as day, in the distance, I can see not just one light but multiple spot lights spread around a long rectangle.

"That's the place you two want to break into? What the heck are you thinking?" Liam blurts out next to my ear. "That place looks big enough to be a fortress. There's no way you'll be able to find that doctor guy you're looking for!"

"I would agree with you if not for the fact that I know exactly where he will be."

"Oh yeah? And where's that?"

"In the medical wing. If I find that I will be sure to find him there."

"Is that some sort of airstrip?" Flynn asks, pressing so hard against the glass that I'm sure he will leave prints.

"The airport! Of course, it makes perfect sense. They must have had so many people stranded that it was the most logical place to start setting up a base of operations."

I sink back into one of the spinning chairs and breathe out a sigh of relief. "Nox, you'd better find a way to meet me there tomorrow."

TWENTY

When I wake the next morning, stretched out between two chairs, I have a nasty ache in my back and a killer headache. I would have thought sleeping on a soft chair would make me feel good but I guess after roughing it for so long my body had adapted.

"I would kill for a cup of coffee right now," I mutter, but only silence is returned to me. I pop my head up and squint against the beams of light shooting straight into the room, bouncing off a slightly taller building across the way. "Flynn? Liam? You guys still sleeping?"

Rubbing sleep for my eyes, I hobble down the hallway and stop when I see a bathroom sign. "Oh sweet mother of Jesus. This one might actually be clean!"

I push the door open and embrace the faded scent of cleaning chemicals that lingers on the tile floor. The door doesn't feel grimy when I push on it and the lock actually latches. Moments later I push down on the handle and am rewarded with a hearty gurgling flush.

"We need to make sure we take some of this toilet paper with us," I call back through the open door. "It's the softest stuff I've felt in ages."

I wash my hands and splash my face with water then head back into the hallway, pausing to listen but I hear nothing. "Guys? Please tell me you aren't playing hide and go seek? You're a bit old for that now, don't you think?"

As I pass by each office, I pause to peer inside but find them empty. "Okay guys, this isn't funny anymore. Where are you?"

I search all of the offices and start to head back toward the stairwell when I catch a glimpse of white through a narrow door window. Pushing the door open, I see Liam and Flynn just standing and staring out of the window.

"Didn't you guys hear me calling for you? I've walked this whole office and you guys were in here the whole time."

Flynn slowly turns to face me and I feel my stomach clench with fear. His eyes are wide and his mouth is frozen in a thin line of worry. Liam doesn't even turn to look at me.

"Flynn? What's wrong?" He swallows hard and then points to the window.

"Your ex has arrived."

My gaze instantly lifts to the window and when he steps aside I feel my knees go weak. There, coming across the land at great speeds from the direction of the foothills, are thousands of moving specks. "Oh, my God. There are so many of them."

My hands begin to shake as I collapse to the floor. "They couldn't have survived that. There's no earthly way. Those Flesh Bags would have run right through them."

Flynn rushes to my side as a wail rises from me. He rocks with me as tears flood down my face. "I've lost him. Oh, God, Flynn. I've lost him, too."

"You don't know that. Nox is smart. He wouldn't have stayed to fight against odds like that."

"Yes, he would." My gaze is unfocused when I look away from the window to glimpse at Flynn. "He would for me. He would have fought to his last dying breath to give us a chance to get away. You know he would."

Flynn winces and looks away, unable to deny the truth. "We need to get moving. It will do you some good to have something to focus on."

"I did this." I stare blankly at the window again. "Cable is my fault. I could have killed him, could have stopped all of this before it even began."

"No," Flynn barks at me and shakes my shoulders. "This isn't going to happen. You are not going to start blaming yourself for things out of your control. You couldn't have known Cable would live, that he would lead this army and come for you. And you will not blame yourself if Nox does not show up at that Safe Zone."

When I don't look at him, he smacks me across the face. My head rocks back and I feel a slight sting, but it is not enough to break me out of my stupor so he hits me again. When he tries for a third I grab a hold of his hand. "I'm back, Flynn. You can stop hitting me now."

"Good, because your face is really hard." He cradles his hand in his lap.

"Liam, grab your stuff. We're leaving."

The trip back down the stairs is a far sight easier than going up. In order to keep up with our pace, Liam uses the rails to slide but we still beat him to the bottom. When we reach the street I can feel the thundering of footsteps that ripples through the ground.

"Are they almost here?" Liam asks.

"No. There are just that many of them. We should reach the airport before they hit the city but that will only give us a short window." I turn my back to Liam and hunch down. "We don't have time to argue and I can't drag you along."

"Screw my pride. I like living." He hops on and instantly hooks his legs around my arms. Flynn takes the lead, guiding us through the concrete maze. All around us glass windows vibrate from the force of the approaching army, but I try not to think about it.

One thing at a time. I need to get to the Safe Zone, find Nox and then kill Wiemann. Whatever happens after that will happen.

Although the lights we saw the night before did not seem all that far, it feels like we run for nearly twenty or thirty miles to reach the first of the airport fences. We skirt along its rusted chain link, searching for an entrance to gain access. Nearly five hundred feet inside, we spy the towering fences that have been erected to create one side of the Safe Zone.

"This place is way more secure than Charleston ever was. If we'd had massive solid walls like this I bet we wouldn't have fallen so easily. Do you think they did this before or after the CDC was overrun?"

I stare at the section of fencing before me and know that I can easily scale up and over without detection. Flynn might be able to make it as well, but Liam doesn't stand a chance. With Cable's horde on our tail, Liam can no longer run. He has to go over the wall with us and then fight.

"My guess would be that they did this before. It would take a great deal of time and manpower to make something like this. Atlanta is a big city and tons of people were sent here. I would bet that this became a main source of intel. It's probably why Wiemann kept his wife here."

"His wife?" Flynn glances over at me as he and I work together to scout out the guard patrols while Liam stays hidden. From the other side of the fence we can hear movement, but can't see anything through the solid wooden wall. There are tall support beams on this side and I would wager there are more on the other, driven deep into the ground to help prevent against a full onslaught.

"That's why he's here. He's come for her."

"Well, that's...romantic, I guess." He follows me as we hurry back to a small airplane hangar where we left Liam. "So what's the plan?"

"We need to see over that way. Feel like tossing me up onto the roof?"

"You're kidding, right?"

"Nope. Lace your hands. I'll put my foot in and you can toss me. I'll just grab on to the edge of the roof and pull myself up. When I'm done you can catch me."

"Um...sure. Because that sounds super easy."

I tap him on the arm. "Did you forget you've got super strength now?"

He grins and laces his fingers. "What are we waiting for? One sky high toss coming right now!"

Liam watches as I place my hands on Flynn's shoulders and before he reaches the count of three I feet a gust of wind and then I'm dangling from the roof.

"I thought you said that you are going to pull yourself up," he hisses.

"There's someone over there," I jerk my head toward the fence and both boys instinctively drop down low. When I see the top of a head bob away I hoist my leg up and over and then belly crawl across the hot metal roof.

"It is a good thing I can heal," I mutter as I peel my sunburned skin off the metal sheeting and wiggle toward the far edge, taking my time to move across an access hatch that proves to have some sharp edges on it.

The Atlanta Safe Zone seems to stretch on for miles when I reach the top of the slanted rise. Metal fences reaching heights of no less than twelve feet run a second perimeter inside the wooden walls with mobile guard stands lifted high at regular intervals. Large wide-beam spotlights are situated to swivel from their platforms.

"Those must be what we saw last night."

From where I lay, I can see multiple guards patrolling the grounds, each one fully armed and on alert. Tents stretch out as far as I can see, some appear to be large family sized with flapping sides not tied down, and others small and narrow like single person pup tents, but I do not see any movement at all.

The entire compound appears to have been erected around a series of long and low buildings, each one attached to the next with a breezeway made of thick white canvas stretched over steel frames that we obviously added after the outbreak. Near the center of each passage, a large red cross stands out against the dull white.

At the end of all of the long plastic corridors I spot an offshoot that leads directly into the main cargo bay. Memories of rows upon rows of testing chairs and semi unconscious patients surrounding me back in St Louis float to the surface and I shiver despite the heat beating down on me from above.

"That is where they should be performing their tests."

Lifting my nose to the air, I close my eyes and inhale deeply. My head moves to the left and then to the right as I work to narrow in on Dr. Wiemann's scent. My eyes pop open when I catch an undeniable whiff of him. He passed by this exact shed no less than a day ago.

I drop a hand of warning over the side when I spot a jeep approaching from the south. Heat ripples across the tarmac as I roll onto my back and think thin thoughts in the hopes that I won't be seen as they pass by, but I hear the engine gears downshift and then the brakes squeak as the vehicle begins to slow.

Damn it. They are coming here.

As the jeep pulls off the road, the tires kick up spare bits of gravel before parking in front. When the car door opens and closes I hold my breath, praying that Liam and Flynn have found a decent hiding place.

"What are we doing out here, Jax? I thought we were making a fuel run," a nasally voice whines from below.

As I hear the two men shuffling around, I can't decide if this is pure providence that one of the bastards that I'm most looking forward to seeing during my visit here just happens to be standing below me, or I've got just about the worst luck known to man.

"I left a pack of smokes out here the other day. I can't be expected to go on an eight hour shift without something to occupy my time."

"It's not safe out here."

"Don't be a pussy. We've got guns, shit-for-brains. What do you think could possibly happen that we can't handle."

I can't imagine a better cue than that. Rolling on my side, I plummet to the ground below and land on someone's back. He sprawls to the ground and smacks his chin so hard against the ground that it knocks him clean out.

"Stanton? What are you messing around at over there?" Jax pops his head back around a stack of boxes and freezes. "You!"

"Small world, huh?" I pick myself up off the ground and dust the soldier's blood off me. "Sorry about your friend. He did a great job at breaking my fall, though."

Jax shifts his gaze a split second before he dives for his gun, but I have already rolled out of sight before he has his finger on the trigger. The warehouse may be far smaller than the big hangar that is locked away inside of the walls, but it is tall enough and wide enough to hold a heck of a lot of junk to hide behind.

"Did Nox come with you, Avery?" He calls out as I crouch behind a stack of wooden crates. I listen as Jax's boots squeak on the slick concrete as he changes position and smile. The showboat soldier is just about as dumb as he looks.

I am just about to leap out of my hiding place to tackle him when I heard him shout, "hold right there!"

"Shit," I whisper to myself when I hear a cry of pain. Glancing around the boxes, I see Liam struggling in Jax's grasp.

"I don't recognize this scrawny little thing. Is he a new friend of yours? Oh wait," he turns, looking around the room, "maybe he's a snack. You do eat people now, don't you, Avery? The Doc said that would probably be a side effect of your mutations."

"Why don't you put the kid down and find out for yourself?"

"Now why would I go and do a thing like that?"

"Because we both know you're dying to get a piece of me. You have been ever since you first found in that old farm house. I saw the way you looked at me. You would have hated me on principal alone for shooting you down, but then I had the gall to shack up with your boss, the guy who you got passed over because he became Cap's pet. Isn't that right, Jax?"

I dash between a stack of boxes when he turns away and nearly run face first into Flynn. He grabs onto to me to keep me from teetering backwards into an open aisle that would give Jax a clear view of my position and places a finger over his lips.

"Nox was always half the man I was. I deserved to be Cap's second in command."

"Sure," I call out and motion for Flynn to maneuver around so that we can come at Jax from both sides. "Just like you were resourceful when you rigged that truck when the Raider's hit back on the road out of Nashville."

Jax falls still. "How do you know about that?"

"Oh, come now, Jax. You didn't think your buddies shot that well, did you? There were Flesh Bags all over your ass. If I hadn't been there, you'd have been in pieces in some zombie's stomach."

"I got us out of there!" He yells and Liam cries out as Jax yanks him around as if he weight normal more than a sack of rice.

"Yeah, that is true. I saw the whole thing. Like how Cap left Ryker behind so he could save his own ass."

From his profile, I see Jax's face goes red. "Ryker was dead. There's wasn't anything we could do for him.

"Is that what they told you? I guess you couldn't hear quite clearly over the rumble of that engine. Too bad. It didn't end well for your friend."

Jax turns again a split second after Flynn dives for a new position and I breathe a sigh of relief that he remains unseen.

"So that's how you found us, huh? Asked old Ryker where we were headed and he spilled his guts." Jax spits on the floor. "Pansy."

"No," I call out as I weave between a different row until I am even with Jax. He stands with his back to me as I see that he's got his gun trained on Liam. "He held out better than I thought he would. Of course, most men crack under torture. Man, could he scream. In fact, he screamed just loud enough to bring a few more of those Flesh Bags over to investigate."

"You bitch!" The back of Jax's neck goes red and he shoves Liam to the floor. "You'll pay for that."

He brings the butt of his gun down onto Liam's head and the kid collapses forward.

"Now, Flynn!"

Jax turns his head and stares into the barrel of a gun. "No one hits my friend."

I see the counterattack coming before I can react. Flynn's momentary hesitation is just enough as Jax seizes his hand and twists it up behind his back. I hear the pop of bone as his wrist dislocates and Flynn howls in pain. Rising up onto his toes as Jax continues to apply pressure, tears form in Flynn's eyes.

"Let him go, Jax," I yell and step out of my hiding place.

"Ah, there you are. You should never send a kid to do your killing, Avery. It doesn't work out well. That's a lesson I learned a long time ago with your boyfriend, actually."

My eyes narrow as his smile grows wider and he jerks his gun in my direction, motioning for me to step out. "Oh, you didn't know, did you? I am the one who let the Flesh Bags free in your sector in the hotel. You see, I know Nox is an insufferable hero and wouldn't be able to resist rushing back to save you. It was a good plan, right up until you proved incapable of being killed."

"Chloe died that night because of you."

"No," he shakes his head as he keeps his gun aimed at my heart. "She died because you dropped her. That wasn't on me."

"I was attacked!"

"Of course you were. That was the whole point." He rolls his eyes. "But at least I learned a valuable lesson that night. If you want something done, you do it yourself."

"No!" I dive as he turns the gun onto Liam and fires. I slam into Jax like a battering ram that sends Flynn, Jax, and I all skidding across the floor. I shove Flynn off and get on top of Jax, using my knees to pin his arms down.

He grunts and growls as he fights against me, but I keep him down. Clenching up my fist, I slam it into his nose, over and over again. I smash his cheek bones, demolish his nose and shatter his jaw, but still I hit until the red that I see before my eyes isn't just a vision.

"Avery, enough!" Flynn tries to pull on my arm but I shake him off and hit Jax again.

"He killed Liam," I pant and hit Jax so hard his neck snaps to the side and I hear a pop.

"He didn't. It's just a shoulder wound." Flynn pulls against my shoulder. "Liam is fine."

I blink several times, trying to process his words. I turn to see Liam holding his shoulder, grimacing as blood stains his fingers, but he is alive.

I shove back off of Jax and rise shakily to my feet.

"I'm sorry, Flynn."

"It's fine. How's your hand?"

It is impossible to tell where my blood starts and his blood ends but the ache tells me that at the least I've sprained it. "I'll live."

"But we might not."

Together Flynn and I turn to where Liam in pointing. In the distance, I see the first zombie sprinting toward us.

"You have to go, Avery." Flynn shoves me toward the door. "Go find Wiemann while you still can."

"I'm not leaving you."

"And I'm not asking. I'll get Liam and me to the roof. There's some cans of gas near the back that I found. We'll soak ourselves in that and mask our smell."

"No," I shake my head, looking between the boys. "There's no way to know if that will work."

Flynn and Liam exchange a glance and then nod. Flynn smiles and places a hand on my shoulder. "We'll be fine. Do what you came here to do. We will find you after."

Before I can stop him, Flynn shoves me out of the door and rushes forward to shove the door closed behind me. I hear a terrible crash as he knocks large crates in front of the door to block it.

There is an access hatch at the rear of the building and enough crates to climb on. I only hope there is enough time for Flynn to get them both on that roof before the zombies arrive.

I turn to look in the distance. More have followed the first. If I do nothing, Flynn will only have a few short minutes.

Stretching out my hand, I dig my nails into my arm and tear deep until blood flows freely and then press my hand against the wall and run, leaving a trail behind me in the opposite direction.

"At least maybe I can buy them a few extra minutes."

TWENTY-ONE

Skirting along the perimeter wall costs me precious few minutes of running in the wrong direction as the horde of Flesh Bags bears down on me, but the line of blood that I draw as I go should be enough to stop them from barreling straight through the wall. Their instinct to hunt mixed with the intensity of the sun overhead will force them to pause and get their bearings as they search for me. By then I will be over the wall and deep inside the base.

Grabbing a hold of the corner, I throw myself around the edge and sprint ahead. My feet barely feel as if they touch the ground as I lean forward and run full out. My hair whips back from my face and the hat Liam gave me spirals up into the air, but I don't turn back. I will need as much spare time to find Dr. Wiemann as I can get.

When the air control tower comes into view, and I can just see the top of the hangar in the distance, I leap and grab hold of the wall and then drop onto the other side, startling a guard on duty. Before he had a chance to get his gun in hand, I race up the rickety steps of his crow's nest perch and toss him over the edge. His scream ends in a sickening crunch.

I turn to look over the wall and see that the horde has picked up speed. A wide trail of dust follows behind them. Somewhere among them is Cable. He will have sensed me long before they reached the city. If he finds me before I take out Wiemann all of this will be for nothing.

Leaping over the side of the perch, I land and race along the inner chain link fence. Three more soldiers die by my hand before the first alarm is raised, but I know it is not for my sake. Someone has finally noticed the approaching Flesh Bag army.

All across the airport, sirens scream out their warning. I hoist myself over the final fence and zigzag among buried land mines that, to the naked eye, would have been nearly impossible to spot. I reach the tarmac just as the first wave of zombies slam into the perimeter wall. The vibrations ripple through the wood.

I fight to still my rising panic as soldiers flood out of the hangar and race for their vehicles. Large swivel style guns on tripods spin toward the far wall in preparation. In the distance I hear the rumble of several tanks approaching. No amount of weaponry will be enough to hold the zombies back this time.

In the barely controlled chaos that erupts all around, no one takes any notice of me as I run toward the hangar. The ground trembles under foot and shouts for commanding officers can barely be heard over the protesting creaks and groans of the perimeter wall.

I make it to a side door of the building just as the first loud crack tears through the air. From over my shoulder, I see the far wall split down the middle. Hands grope through the opening, pulling and tugging at the wood.

Fear makes me nearly rip the door off the hinges. It slams hard against the wall as I dash inside. The interior is blissfully dim and it doesn't take long for my eyesight to adjust, but when it does I skid to a halt.

A twelve-foot high rectangular metal cage spans out before me, reminiscent of a cage a circus might have once used to house their trained tigers. Crammed inside are beasts no less feral than a jungle cat as they claw at the air in an attempt to get me.

Red streaks the whites of their eyes and foam sits in thick globs at their mouths. Their skin is nearly translucent, creating a vivid roadmap of veins in their exposed skin. Their backs are hunched and their shoulders and arms are deformed, elongated much like a monkey's. Their facial bone structure has been altered with a jutting jaw and thick, bony forehead. Their fingers curl inward as they beat against one another for space, but there is none to be found. They have been shoved into the cage so tightly that if one were to fall, it would be trampled immediately.

Shrill screeching rises from those nearest me as the ones behind crush the front row against the bars without mercy. And the horror does not end with this one cage of experiments. There are no less than five similar cages standing in a row beyond this one, each one with creatures in various stages of devolution.

"Oh, my God." I press a hand to my lips.

These people have endured a forced mutation, but I can only guess that their blood was spliced with some of the CDC's test animals like the ape that came for me in the woods. Experiments gone very wrong and shoved here to keep them under containment.

From outside, I hear a loud boom of a cannon and brace for the impact. The ground trembles as deafening gunfire begins.

"They must have breached the wall."

Trying to ignore the howls and screeching beside me, I lift my nose to the air and search for Dr. Wiemann's scent, but it is impossible to track over the potent scent of the things beside me. I run down the aisle, careful to keep as close to the wall as possible, and pass by several makeshift rooms with large viewing windows. I turn to stare into one and see a man strapped to an upright table. Wide chains have been looped around his wrists, ankles, chest and neck. He thrashes as bloody foam escapes between his gritted teeth. An empty syringe has been abandoned on a metal medical cart and the door left sitting wide open.

I pass six more rooms just like this one, but when I reach the seventh, I slam to a halt. There, chained to a table, is Cap. His eyes are wide with fright as he cranes his neck back, listening to the war raging outside.

"Somebody get me the hell out of here!" He screams.

His head snaps around when I open the door, and he pales when he recognizes me "You!"

"Why does everyone say that when they see me?" I step inside but leave the door open so that Cap can hear the ruckus of the beasts just beyond. "It's not like this should be a surprise. You did leave Ryker behind for me to torture information out of, after all."

Cap presses his lips tightly together. I step closer and notice a full syringe on the counter beside him. It is filled with a strange green fluid, almost iridescent in the dim light.

When I pick it up, Cap thrashes against the chains but is helpless to escape. I turn slowly to look at him as I hold it at eye level.

"You know what this will do to you, don't you?"

He spits at me. "Go to hell."

"Oh, I went there a while back," I smile and press the syringe to push out the bits of air in it. I would hate for him to die in the wrong way. "You should have killed me when you had the chance."

"It wasn't personal."

"I know." I place a hand on his arm. He flexes and struggles but I easily hold him down. "It was just business, right? Or was it pleasure? I can't ever really tell with you people."

Cap yells as I push the needle into his arm and pause. "Was it worth it?"

Even to the very end, right before I inject him with the serum and walk away to leave him to suffer, he is defiant. I listen to his cries of pain and the breaking of bones as his body begins to alter, but I do not stay to see what sort of monster he will become.

I have nearly reached the far end of the row of cages when the door I entered through crashes open. I spin around to see soldiers running backward, firing off shots as Flesh Bags pour into the building. Screams of fear and pain echo through the lofty ceiling as I look all around me for an escape.

There is no way that I can climb onto a cage without getting bitten along the way. The beasts near this end of the hangar are the closest to apelike and no doubt possess a strength even I can't match.

I spin around, looking for a weapon to use when I spy an electrical box on the wall. It looks far too new to have been original to the building. Large, thick wires run up the wall from it and fan out toward the cages. I turn to follow the lines and realize that each of them connect to a small motor housed above the close cage doors. A generator feeds to all of them.

Glancing down the hall, I see no less than fifty soldiers in a battle for their lives. There is nowhere for them to run and nowhere that they can hide. They were dead before they even entered the building.

Flipping the cover of the electrical box, I place a finger on the glowing red button. "I'm sorry."

Pressing the button, I turn and run as the doors to the cages begin to rise. Within seconds an outpouring of monsters overtake the soldiers. I try to block out their screams, but when new screams replace them, I turn back to see that the experimental mutations have begun to attack the Flesh Bags as well.

The tear through the rotting corpses, shredding them with razor sharp claws and elongated teeth. Blood splatters every inch of the hallway. I stand in disbelief until one of the mutants sniffs the air and turns its black eyes on me.

"Shit!"

Adrenaline spikes through me as I turn and sprint for the door looming ahead of me. It is tall and metal with large hinges and a thumb print key pad. Looking back over my shoulder I see that more mutants have followed my scent.

"This day just keeps getting better and better."

I yank on the door handle, feeling its immovable weight as the door locks refuse to give. Clenching my first, I beat against the metal, denting it but doing no further damage.

From behind me, I can feel the vibrations of the growls in my chest and can taste their acrid scent on the air. I have boxed myself into a corner and let no way of escape.

I turn and do the only thing that I can do: prepare to fight.

Screams of rage echo down the hall as I watch four of the mutants running toward me, using their elongated arms to propel them forward. I can feel the Flesh Bags' anger and pain as they fight back, spilling over into the hangar in a flood of rot and ruin. The scent of their black blood stings my nostrils as I stare down the oncoming beasts, and my final thought before they strike is of Nox.

I can see his face just as clearly as if he were standing in front of me, smiling and handsome. My chest clenches with a deep ache as I think about losing him, of never truly having the chance to embrace the love that I feel for him.

The feeling of injustice swells within me as I stare down death. My lips peel back into a snarl and rage fills me. I growl low and deep and launch myself at the first beast.

Its powerful arms swing at me and I duck, narrowly missing having my head knocked off my neck. The monster screams as it connects with the door. The metal screeches as it bends and I turn to see that a hole has opened near the top.

I smile as a plan forms. "Come at me again."

Flexing its fingers, the mutant swings again and I dance out of the way only to have the breath knocked out of me a second later when it comes around and hits me from behind. I slam into the wall and ricochet off. My vision darkens when its arms wrap around me in a vice-like grip, threatening to squeeze the air from my lungs. I twist and fight, scratching and clawing at its skin, shredding through muscle as strong as iron. I kick out at its feet, crushing its toes under the tread of my boot.

It howls and loosens its grip on me. I wriggled around in its arms and work to grip my hand around its face. Three others close in from behind as I squeeze with all my might and begin to feel the bone cracking beneath my palms.

The beast grapples to pull me away but I dig my nails into its face and scream as I bring my hands together. Its head crushes and a brackish blood flows over my fingers. Breathing deeply, I jump back as it falls to the ground. The other beasts do not slow at the sight of their downed brethren.

Leaping up onto the dead mutant's back, I yank at the hole in the metal door. The metal grows slick with my blood as the door groans and the opening widens another couple of inches. The space still looks too small but I have no choice but to try for it.

Stepping onto the door handle, I thrust my hands through the opening and onto the other side. The metal tears at my clothes as I wiggle my chest through and have just begun to fit my hips when I feel hands grab onto my feet. I kick out at the beasts as my arms quiver with the effort it takes to keep myself rooted in the hole.

Claws tear into my calves as I fight to pull myself through. The scent of my blood in the airs drives the three beasts into a frenzy as metal carves into my sides. I cry out from the pain as I am jostled around but feel the grip on my leg fall free. The door rocks as they fight with each other to get to me to me again as I hold my legs aloft. Taking advantage of the spare seconds of freedom, I bend in half, lower my hands, and grab ahold of the door handle to pull with every ounce of strength remaining.

My legs fly up and hit the temporary hallway ceiling tiles just before I slide through the gap, saved by the slickness of my own blood. Holding my side, I slowly rise to my feet to see eyes filled with rage staring at me through the window. The glass fogs with each humid breath.

"I hope you bastards rip each other to shreds." I spit at the door and turn to limp away.

As I turn the corner and enter a section of the hangar that has been partitioned off as a research area, the beasts behind me scream and beat against the door. Eventually they will find a way in, but so far they have proven to have a far lower intelligence level than that of the Flesh Bags. These things are nothing more than brutish animals, reacting on instinct alone.

The lights overhead flicker as I stumble forward, leaving heavily against the wall for support. The sound of gunfire continues but is far more diminished in this section of the building. I pass by empty offices set up with microscopes, test tubes, centrifuges and other lab equipment that I wouldn't have the first clue how to use.

I can smell blood on the air, thick and strong, but it turns my stomach. It is tainted, altered and foul. Glancing into a room, I see a door to a large metal refrigerator standing open and see stacks of chilled blood bags.

"If those bastards had my nose, they would have known long before they started injecting those people that it wasn't going to work."

I grimace and pull my hand away from my side to discover that I am bleeding far worse than I realized. Reaching around the corner of the door, I grab a white lab coat off a metal hook and tie its length around my waist tightly.

This entire section of the lab has been completely abandoned. Chairs have been left toppled over. Partially eaten food trays sit beside microscopes. Security access doors are left standing open.

I walk down the hallway with my hand pressed to the wall, smearing a blood trail behind me. The blood loss makes my vision blur and my knees give out on me twice, but each time I get back up.

Spying a set of swinging double doors up ahead, I make my way toward them and push through to find myself in a pitch black room. File cabinets and bookshelves stakes two deep line the walls. A messy desk with hand scribbled notes strewn across its top sits off to my right.

My nostrils flare and I shake my head to focus. The scent of Dr. Wiemann is very strong in this room.

Glancing all around me, I look for any sign of where he may have gone. I can't bear the thought of coming all this way only to let him die by something else's hand.

Then I see it. A small rectangular crack in the bookcase reveals a room behind this one. I begin shoving the books off, searching for a latch or lever and feel a small click. The door gives way and I push it open.

Ropes of electrical cables run across the floor as I step inside. A brilliant white light in the center of the room forces me to look away, but from my peripheral vision I see Dr. Wiemann huddled over a medical bed. A steady beeping comes from a heart monitor in front of him and I see two very thin and pale legs sticking out from under a hospital gown.

"I know that you think I am an evil man," he says without turning. "Perhaps you are right. I have done terrible but great things in the name of science in my time. None of them meant anything in the end. None of them were good enough to save the only thing I ever loved more than my research."

I stumble around the side, raising a hand to shield myself from the bright spotlight that illuminates a middle-aged woman with blond hair and white pale skin.

"They told me there was no hope. That there was nothing that could be done. I went to every hospital, doctor and specialist in the beginning. That was before the outbreak really began." He turns to look at me with dead eyes. "She had been on a business trip in London and felt sick when she returned. We didn't think much of it at the time. Figured it was nothing more than your typical jet-lag and that it would pass in time. But it didn't. She was among the first reported to have contracted the disease."

He reaches out and slowly brushes her hair back from her face. Her eyes are closed and appear to be a pale shade of lavender. There is no movement in her eyes related to REM sleep. She is completely motionless apart from a slow and infrequent inhalation of breath.

"The CDC took her from me nearly three weeks before the outbreak started killing. They had time to discover a cure but instead they researched, poked and prodded her as she slowly slipped away. I had skills and knowledge that they could have used, but they claimed that I was too obsessed, too personally attached. That I couldn't see her as Patient Zero instead of my wife."

His shoulders slump as he leans over his wife. "They were right, of course. I couldn't see anything beyond the woman I vowed to spend my life with. She was my everything and they just let her Wither away. But once the virus spread and panic hit the streets I knew I had to keep her safe, so I made a deal with the government. I would help them create a weapon that could be used in the event of a global threat. Those men in their fancy suits and chests filled with medals had no honor, and I used that to my advantage. I struck a deal and she was moved here to be safely housed until I delivered on my side of the bargain, but I never gave up looking for a cure."

His chair squeals as he turns to look at me. "And then you were found just outside of St. Louis. Reports of your lab work were of course sent directly to me to study. The moment I saw your results I knew you were special. I just had to have you.

"But you proved to be far more elusive than I would have liked. I spent months searching for you. If it hadn't been for Cap's gut instinct, you might have died in that farmhouse."

A wave of nausea washes over me and I lean back against a metal table to steady myself. He glances down at the spreading stain of blood at my waist. "You had no clue how important you were. It infuriated me when I discovered that Ryker had unleashed my zombies on you back at the hotel but when Cap found you he brought you straight to me and I knew, after seeing your bite wound, that something miraculous was taking place.

"We documented everything, of course while we waited for you to wake and when you did I knew you were the answer to everything. You are special beyond understanding, Avery. Together we could have changed the world."

"I would never help you," I spit at him.

"Yes," he nods slowly, "Your opinion of me was sadly tainted far earlier than I would have liked. Circumstances changed and I had to adapt. It was a rash call, I will admit but one that was necessary none the less."

"Those people were innocent."

He laughs wearily. "Is anyone really innocent these days? Most have killed to survive. Many have stolen, raped, pillaged, and plundered in their efforts to hold on to the pieces of their lives. No, my dear, Avery. There are no innocents left in this world. We have all become monsters."

I step forward and seize him by the neck. "This base is overrun with the things that you helped to create. They are killing, eating and shredding everything that stands in their way. Nothing will survive these mutations."

He smiles. "You will."

My grip on his throat tightens. His face grows red and a vein pops out on his forehead as he struggles to breathe.

"I would tear your wife apart limb from limb while you watch if I had my way, but I see now that she is no different than all of the rest. She is just another victim."

"You can still save her. Your blood can bring her back, it can reverse the virus and save the human race."

"No, Dr. Wiemann. It's already too late for that." I dig my nails into the side of his neck as I lower my face to his ear. "The human race is already extinct."

I yank his head to the side and sink my teeth into his throat.

TWENTY-TWO

There is little doubt when I untie the lab coat from around my waist to find the gash on my side already beginning to heal over that I am grateful for the benefits that the second virus dose has given me. Wiping Dr. Wiemann's blood from my lips, I feel electrical currents of energy sparking throughout my body. I flex my fingers and breathe in deep as I turn off his wife's life support and step over his dead body.

My clothes are soaked with his blood. My face, arms and hands are slick with the warmth of it but I do not care. I feel powerful, rejuvenated in ways I had not thought possible.

I walk out of Wiemann's office and back down the hall, heading for the exit sign that hangs dark against the ceiling. It is only then that I realize the power is out.

Pushing through the door I step out into a war zone of epic proportions. Smoke hangs thick in the air, blocking out the sunlight as fires from all around the compound burn. A tank has been upended and left on its side with its wheels grinding into the dirt. Pieces of bodies litter the tarmac, both human and non.

In the distance I can hear the loud booms of land mines being set off, and see eruptions of dirt shooting into the air. From somewhere within the smoke there are still some alive to fight. Moans of the dying hover in the air as I sense a presence, and turn slowly around.

Cable emerges from around the rear of the tank. Blood coats his torn shirt, splattered against his face and smeared through his hair. His teeth are painted red and in his hand he carries the head of a man. When he tosses the head high into the air, it falls and rolls at me feet, coming to a stop against my boot. I stare down into the glazed eyes of Fletcher.

"He died fighting bravely," Cable calls when I look up. "There is no dishonor to follow him to the grave."

I force myself not to react to the soldier's death. He was with Nox when I left. Does that mean there's a chance he is still alive?

"And what about you?" I ask as I push Fletcher's head aside. "Will you die today with honor?"

A wide grin tugs at Cable's lips, but it does not reach his cold, calculating eyes. There is no life there anymore. No warmth or hint of the love that once stared back at me. The man I knew is truly gone. What stands before me in nothing more than a beast dressed in his flesh.

"Do you intend to kill me, Avery? After all that we have been through?"

I slowly begin to walk toward him. Bullets whizz past and screams cry out all around but I focus only on him. On that rage that boils up within me at the very sight of him.

"I will not go with you, Cable."

His smile tightens. "I did not come all this way to give you the option, Love. You will be with me, one way or another."

"Then let us be joined in death." I dive toward him and drive my shoulder into his chest. He wraps his arms around me as we collapse back onto the ground and slide several feet. The skin on my arms shreds and I cry out in pain but I elbow him in the face and roll back to my feet.

Cable laughs as he touches his lip. It has split and begun to bleed. "You have begun to embrace your new abilities, I see."

"As if I had any choice in the matter." I throw a punch that he easily ducks, and when he grabs hold of my arm to toss me aside, I barely have a chance to brace before I slam into the side of the tank. Pain lights in multiple locations in my body as I stumble back.

Cable rises up directly behind me and takes hold of my head, twining his fingers through my hair to slam my head against the machine. I feel the edge of my hairline split and blood trickle down my face. Reaching back over my head, I take hold of one of his ears and tear it free. Cable screams and claws at me, but I duck between his arms and run.

I race past soldiers locked in combat with Flesh Bags. I see two of the mutated beasts released from their cage leap onto a pack of zombies and begin tearing through them. The air is filled with growls and gunfire as I weave through the smoke.

Cable catches up to me and launches himself at me. He clips the heel of my foot and I tumble end of end, slamming against a crow's nest guard post. I duck under the bar as Cable advances and begin to climb.

"There is nowhere that you can run, Avery."

I rattle up the metal steps and leap up onto the railing as Cable takes to the stairs to look around. He is right. There are hundreds of Withered between me and the nearest gate. Mutants continue to shove their way out of the hangar, some creating their own doorways as they bust through the siding and engage the zombies.

Everywhere I look I see desolation.

"It's over. Give up and accept your destiny."

I jump down from the railing and turn to face Cable. "I never really put my stock in that whole destiny crap."

Rushing the other side, I throw myself against the railing and feel the crow's nest begin to tip. Cable's eyes fly open wide when I leap from the platform as it tilts sideways. It crashes with a tremendous clatter as metal poles spring into the air, impaling those unlucky enough to be close by.

Grasping one of the poles, I make my way around the edge of the debris to find one of Cable's legs are pinned. I grip the pole tightly and swing the thick metal bat.

It connects with Cable's face and his head snaps back as he collapses back to the ground.

All around me I can feel the Flesh Bags starting to take notice of our fight. They screech and howl as they work together to overrun those mutants that still remain. The hairs on my arms and neck stand straight as I shove the pole down into Cable's shoulder and bury it deep into the ground.

His cry of outrage as he tries to pull it free draw the zombies in close. I can feel their anger, feel their ill-sated hunger as they stop feasting on the dying and close in on me.

"You bitch!" Spittle flies from his lips as he wrenches the pole free. Several Withered attack the platform and lift it free. Cable climbs back to his feet but he struggles to put pressure on his wounded leg.

"Bring me one," he yells and zombies scramble to obey. Within seconds I hear a girl screaming as she is dragged forward.

"No!" I start forward when Cable seizes Kira by the throat and lifts her high. "Don't do this."

Cable's face darkens with rage as he swings Kira like a rag doll. "She is nothing to the likes of you and me. She is weak, a pathetic human incapable of defending herself."

"Want to bet?"

I look up just in time to see her drive a knife hidden in her camouflage pants down into Cable's neck. Blood squirts from the severed vein and his grip on her falters. She slams to the ground with a grunt and tries to scramble away but his foot comes down on her back.

My eyes squeeze shut at the sound of her spinal cord snapping. I do not watch as I hear him tear her apart. I flinch when her blood sprays my face.

"Even in death she is useful."

I slowly open my eyes and watch as Cable lifts the remains of her torso and sinks his teeth into her flesh. Blood flows around his mouth. His eyes never leave mine and I force myself not to look away. Shock races through me when I see the skin along his neck begin to seal over and the blood ceases to squirt.

"You did not think you are the only one who has discovered the miracle of the virus, did you?"

He tosses Kira away and grabs a hold of his shirt. As the fabric tears I feel my blood run cold. There, all along his bare arms and chest are dozens of unhealed bite marks, similar to the two that I bear.

"I will admit that the discovery came as quite a shock. I hadn't planned on being bitten, but in the beginning days I was still learning how to control my abilities. After the attack on your base I knew I would need to be stronger, to make myself someone you could be proud of."

When he turns in a slow circle I see that there are more marks on his back and sides.

"You can't possibly fathom what this feels like, Avery. The power, the knowledge and pure oneness with our people. But you will soon enough."

Raising his hands, the Flesh Bags press in, forming row after row of circles around me. I am trapped. The soldiers may be able to pick off several of the rows at the back but there are still hundreds of them standing between me and them now.

"Before we leave, there is some unfinished business we need to attend to."

Cable steps back and a wave of movement ripples through the crowd. I watch as the Withered step back to allow several to march through. When I hear the cries of protest my knees go well.

"No, oh, dear God, no!"

"God isn't listening anymore." Cable turns to grin at me as Flynn emerges from the horde first. He struggles against the arms that hold him. Close on his heel is Liam, followed by a heavily limping Cyrus. "You are looking for him, aren't you?"

I feel the thundering of my heart in my chest as Cable pulls me against him and places his arm around my waist. "Although it would have brought me great pleasure to kill him when he put up a miserable fight against us in the woods, I knew that his death would be so much more special with you by my side to witness it."

My legs go limp when I see Nox shoved through the crowd. He lands hard on his hands and knees. His face is a mass of bruises and he looks as if he were drug through a lake of blood, but he is alive.

"Nox" I start forward but Cable's hand tightens on my hip.

"Now, now. There will be no spoiling the fun until you have a chance to see your final gift."

I slowly tear my eyes away from where Nox lies breathing heavily to see a twinkle of excitement in Cable's eye. "What have you done?"

"I thought it would be nice to have the whole family back together again."

My throat clenches as I turn to stare at the hole still open in the horde. The rock and moan, staring behind them, then slowly I see a flash of straw colored gold and know that my greatest horror has been realized. A strangled moan escapes my throat as Cable holds me aloft.

"Avery!" Her voice comes out so sweet, so beautiful and perfect that I am sure that I'm imagining it. Regret that it would take this terrible event to finally force her to speak nearly takes my breath away.

"No, please don't hurt her." I cry as Hope is carried out of the masses. Her eyes are wide with terror. Her dress is stained with urine and splattered with brain matter as she is tossed to the ground. Her eyes widen with horror when she looks to her right and sees Kira's body in several pieces beside her. "She is just a child!"

"Yes," Cable nods, staring at Hope without feeling. "They taste sweeter. You will see soon enough."

Tears fall steadily down the little girl's cheeks as she looks to me with pleading eyes and I know that I have failed her. I've failed them all.

"I'll do anything," I whisper. "Just spare their lives."

"Aw," Cable nuzzles into my neck. Nox grunts and arches his back as he stares up at Cable with pure hatred. "I love it when you talk dirty to me."

Tears well up as I stare at the people that I love kneeling before me. I have never had a real family before, at least not one worth speaking about, but each of these people are special to me. In another life we would never have met, never have discovered that bond that links us together far tighter than blood or DNA.

Rage, the likes of which I have never before felt, rises up inside of me as I catch sight of something that makes my heart skip a beat. I turn to look at Cable to see if he noticed but he just smiles back, smug and confident that he is about to get every bit of what he has ever wanted. "At least allow me to say goodbye."

He rolls his eyes but releases me. "Make it quick. I'm still hungry."

Stumbling away from him, I rush to Nox and pull him into a tight embrace. I cradle him against my face, digging my hands into his back.

"I'm so sorry," I whisper.

"I'm not." I lean back to stare at him and see that he is smiling weakly at me. "I got to see you again."

I crush my lips against him, desperate not to let go but Cable seizes me by the hair and shoves me toward Liam. I embrace the boy, feeling the trembling in his body as he tries to be brave.

"It will be okay, Kid."

He nods as his lower lip quivers and I press a kiss to his cheek then move on to Flynn. Despite facing death head on, he finds a way to smile at me.

"We gave 'em hell, didn't we?"

"We sure did." I wrap him into a tight embrace, and then say my goodbyes to Cyrus before I reach Hope.

"Oh, my sweet, sweet girl." I take her into my arms and hold her tight. Her fingers claw into my back as she clings to me but she does not quake like Liam does. I pull back as I kneel in front of her and wipe her tears away. "Do you remember that I promised that I would keep you safe? Well, I always keep my promises. You are a very brave little girl, aren't you?" She wipes at her nose and nods. I lean down to whisper into her ear. "Of all of these men beside you, you are the bravest of all. I know in the end you will prove that to me."

Taking ahold of her hand, I squeeze her fingers closed and shift her dress over top then slowly rise to my feet. I walk backward slowly until I am beside Cable.

"Well that was all rather revolting," he says in a bored voice and then steps forward. He begins to walk in front of each of my friends, pausing to consider them. "I just can't decide which one I want to eat first. My brother? No. He should be last. Let him suffer for thinking that he could steal you from me. The new kid? No. I don't think you care enough for him."

He turns and seizes Flynn by his hair and yanks him to his feet. "I remember you."

"Stop!" I cry out and Cable turns. "You said the girl is sweetest and I would not wish for her to suffer. Let her go first."

"Avery, no!" Flynn thrashes in Cable's grip but is not strong enough to free himself. Nox stares hard at me and I can see hurt and confusion in Liam's eyes before I look away.

Cable purses his lips. "I'll admit I would have figured you would beg me to spare her life. I might have even considered it before the end, but this pleases me far more. All right, I'll take the girl."

Flynn cries out as he is slammed back to the ground. He tries to reach for Cable's legs but the Flesh Bags nearest him instantly reach out and restrain him. My friend's fight against their captors as Cable crouches down in front of Hope.

"Your friend thinks that your suffering will be less because you go first." He reaches out and pats her cheek but she is staring at me instead. I can hear her little heartbeat thrumming in her chest. "Too bad she is wrong."

"No!" Liam screams.

Cable shifts his smug gaze to look at the boy and then cries out when Hope slashes Kira's knife across his throat. A thin line of blood appears along his adam's apple and his eyes fly open wide with surprise.

"Very clever, Avery," he seizes Hope by her good hand and squeeze. I hear her bone pop and the knife falls to the ground. "Let the innocent little girl do your dirty work."

"She's not." He turns to look at me. "She's just the distraction."

Channeling all of my anger and hatred for the monster before me, I turn to look at the Flesh Bags surrounding us.

Kill him!

The color drains out of Cable's face when he is blasted with the message that I send out to the masses, loud, strong, and confident. The Withered closest to Cable attack without thought. His screams are drowned out by the sound of tearing and biting as other swarm to join in.

I seize Hope around the waist and shove my way out of the crowd as it surges forward, keeping a hand on Liam as I lead my friends to safety. The instant we emerge from the writhing horde of frenzied zombies, I drop Hope into Liam's arms and help Cyrus to the ground. Flynn escapes last with Nox in his arms.

"Nox!" I cry and race to him, pulling him from Flynn to hold him close.

"You did it." He smiles and presses his hand against my cheek. "I knew you could."

"I guess I just needed the proper motivation."

I kiss his cheeks, his swollen eyes, and his split eyebrows.

"Does this mean that you're going to fulfill that whole promise thing to thank me for believing in you?"

"Really?" I pull back from him and laugh. "That's what you're thinking about right now? Sex?"

"Oh, Avery," he grins and cups the back of my neck, "that's all I've been thinking about since the day I met you."

"You are completely hopeless." I laugh and ignore the last of Cable's moments on this earth as I kiss Nox and realize that for the first time since the world went to hell, I finally feel safe.

EPILOGUE

As the early morning fog begins to lift and the sun's warmth returns, the war-torn compound feels too still. The sirens that blared long into the night have fallen silent, and in its wake is an eerie calm that leaves me on edge. Though I never would have thought it possible, I would happily take the mechanical screams over this tomb-like silence.

Countless bodies lie strewn across the ground, some in pieces while others remain mostly intact with random mouth-sized holes gnawed deep enough to reveal bone. The odd pop of a pistol tells me that another victim has been put down, and when I turn in a slow circle to look around me, the death toll is staggering.

As I walk through a field of torn tents, trampled supplies and large pools of blood, I feel a sense of hopelessness fall over me. Is this what my world has become? Nothing more than death and violence as far as I can see?

The mutations have spread much farther than any of us could have imagined and there is nothing that I can do to stop them now. Though my final order to the Withered after ending Cable was to kill each other, I know others will continue to sweep across the land, devouring and changing anyone in their path. As I stare down at a blood-soaked teddy bear beside my foot, I wonder if anything I have done really matters.

Wiemann is dead but his work will live on in others. Every Safe Zone along the east coast will have been overrun with their own creations by now. How long will it be before the human race is completely wiped out by their own selfish greed?

"Hey you." I look up to see Nox wearily picking his way through the mounds of bodies still waiting to be burned. He is slick with blood, both red and black but is still standing. His clothes are torn, his body weary and beaten from the events of the past two days but he is alive and that is far more than I ever dared to hope for.

We lost far too many good people tonight. Kira and Fletcher died honorably. Bo, Gentry, and Phillip were found among the dead. I will make sure that each of them will be remembered.

I step around a cistern of drinking water, now murky with blood and floating bodies. A small three-man crew attempts to lasso a female Withered with a rope and drag her out but it is a losing battle. The water is no longer fit to drink and this base is no longer inhabitable.

Those able to walk will begin the trek North to Nashville where our two communities will blend together and begin to rebuild. Perhaps in time we will be able to get the city repaired and expand our borders. The extra man power will definitely help to keep our people safe for the time being.

"How are you holding up?" Nox asks when he stops in front of me.

I don't really know how to answer that. Too much has happened for me to ever be able to say that I am fine again. I feel numb.

"I just carried a boy to the fire over there that couldn't have been more than five, Nox. I have no clue where his mother was or even what she called him. The one thing I do know is that those damn Flesh Bags ate him alive and he...he..." My throat closes, refusing to let me speak the words. "I can't unsee any of this. How are we supposed to go on after tonight when we've lost so much?"

Nox instantly pulls me into his arms. I bury my tears into his chest and cling to him, needing his strength because I have saved little for myself.

"Shh." He presses his lips against my sweaty temple and then pulls back to run his thumb down my cheek, tracing the length of my tear tracks. "We go on because that's what we do. We fight and we survive together because we know now that we aren't alone. There are other survivors out there that need our help. We have to do whatever it takes to find them and help them."

"Is there really any point? There are others like me out there, Nox. Others like Cable who will seek to take control. In the end we will not have the numbers to fight back. We will be overrun."

"Maybe, but that doesn't mean I plan on giving up hope anytime soon. I've got a life to live for and I've got you. That's all I need, Avery."

I cling to him as tears fall freely from my eyes. The cloth wrapped around my nose does little to diminish the scent of burning flesh as I watch another body being dragged toward the funeral pyre over his shoulder, and for the first time I realize the scent is no longer appealing.

There are ten fires in total spanning this side of the Safe Zone, each no less than thirty feet in diameter and rising higher than the perimeter walls. The enormity of loss sits heavily in my stomach as I force myself to look away from the flames.

"This mission wasn't a failure. We did what we came here to do. Wiemann is dead and countless Flesh Bags were killed tonight. For every one of them that dies more people will live because of what you did here and *that* most certainly matters."

"But we lost so many people."

He tilts my chin up to look at him and gently tugs the cloth away from my face so that he can truly see me. "They died knowing they were helping to make a difference. That is all any of them could ever hope for."

I steal a small, settling breath before I lift my eyes to meet his. He may be covered in gore from the crown of his head down to his military grade boots, but he is perfect. I love the man that he is, what he stands for, and his willingness to do what is right no matter the personal cost. Cable was like that once. Perhaps that is why my feelings for Nox were confused for so long because the line between them blurred so easily, but not anymore.

Now there is only Nox.

"They lived well," I whisper in agreement. "You should be proud of them."

"They didn't fight for me." He smiles down at me. "Tonight, you were the leader they looked to and that led them to victory. You are the one who needs to be proud."

Wrapping my arms around him, I allow myself to sink into his embrace. He squeezes me tight and together we stand and watch the fires eat away flesh and bone from the people that we fought to protect with every fiber of our being. We survived when others did not. I don't know how or even why but I have to believe that it is for a reason.

There are answers out there that can give us hope and people still in need. I know that now. From here I will travel south to Charleston. If any of Flynn's friends are left alive then we will find them and bring them home.

Maybe someday there will be one among us who can understand the mystery of the mutations in my blood and find a way to undo the perversion of this world. Flynn is living proof that there is a way to survive the transformation, to become something more without being tainted by the demons that will continue to haunt me. Perhaps when that day comes we will have the resources to find a true cure so that no one has to undergo that procedure, but for now, we will live.

There is little doubt now that I will ever be truly free of the zombie mutations within me. In the end, Dr. Wiemann was right. I am special. For so long I have been chasing a ghost, trying to discover 'why me' but I realize now that was the wrong question.

What I should have been asking is, "Why not me?"

Human blood is the key. It is hunger filling and life giving, but I am no monster and I refuse to be an affliction to mankind. I will find a way to survive without feeding on humans because that is what I do.

I survive.

ABOUT THE AUTHOR

Amy Miles is the author of fifteen indie published novels, including her bestselling young adult immortals books, The Arotas Series. Unwilling to be defined by any one genre, she has written paranormal romance, science fiction/fantasy, post-apocalyptic, romance, inspirational, and plans to continue to explore new genres. She is the co-Founder of Red Coat PR, a firm helping indie authors build a marketing base for their career. Amy is also the co-Founder of Penned Con, an annual two day convention held in St. Louis, MO bringing readers and authors together with industry professionals to learn, grow and give back. She and her husband are heavily involved in charity work through Action for Autism, a St. Louis based organization aiding families with autism, and founded the Penned Con scholarship to benefit area families. She is an avid reader, urban homesteader, weekend golfer and Netflix binge addict who lives with her husband and son in South Carolina.

PERMUTED
PRESS
needs *you* to help

SPREAD (THE)
INFECTION

FOLLOW US!

f | Facebook.com/PermutedPress
🐦 | Twitter.com/PermutedPress

REVIEW US!

Wherever you buy our book, they can be
reviewed! We want to know what you like!

GET INFECTED!

Sign up for our mailing list at
PermutedPress.com

PERMUTED
PRESS

THE JOURNAL SERIES
by Deborah D. Moore

After a major crisis rocks the nation, all supply lines are shut down. In the remote Upper Peninsula of Michigan, the small town of Moose Creek and its residents are devastated when they lose power in the middle of a brutal winter, and must struggle alone with one calamity after another.

The Journal series takes the reader head first into the fury that only Mother Nature can dish out.

PERMUTED
PRESS

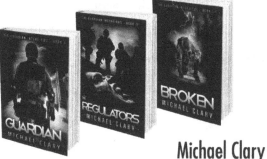

THE BREADWINNER | Stevie Kopas

The end of the world is not glamorous. In a matter of days the human race was reduced to nothing more than vicious, flesh hungry creatures. There are no heroes here. Only survivors. The trilogy continues with Book Two: *Haven* and Book Three: *All Good Things*.

THE BECOMING | Jessica Meigs

As society rapidly crumbles under the hordes of infected, three people—Ethan Bennett, a Memphis police officer; Cade Alton, his best friend and former IDF sharpshooter; and Brandt Evans, a lieutenant in the US Marines—band together against the oncoming crush of death and terror sweeping across the world. The story continues with Book Two: *Ground Zero*.

THE INFECTION WAR | Craig DiLouie

As the undead awake, a small group of survivors must accept a dangerous mission into the very heart of infection. This edition features two books: *The Infection* and *The Killing Floor*.

OBJECTS OF WRATH | Sean T. Smith

The border between good and evil has always been bloody... Is humanity doomed? After the bombs rain down, the entire world is an open wound; it is in those bleeding years that William Fox becomes a man. After The Fall, nothing is certain. *Objects of Wrath* is the first book in a saga spanning four generations.

PERMUTED PRESS